Jol

The Life of William Warburton, Lord Bishop of Gloucester

From 1760 to 1779. With remarks on his works

SALZWASSER
VERLAG

John Selby Watson

The Life of William Warburton, Lord Bishop of Gloucester

From 1760 to 1779. With remarks on his works

Reprint of the original, first published in 1863.

1st Edition 2022 | ISBN: 978-3-37500-406-4

Verlag (Publisher): Salzwasser Verlag GmbH, Zeilweg 44, 60439 Frankfurt, Deutschland
Vertretungsberechtigt (Authorized to represent): E. Roepke, Zeilweg 44, 60439 Frankfurt, Deutschland
Druck (Print): Books on Demand GmbH, In de Tarpen 42, 22848 Norderstedt, Deutschland

THE
LIFE OF BISHOP WARBURTON.

Beattie's translation is:

Encompass'd round with heaps of slaughter'd foes,
All grim in blood the pigmy champion glows,
And on th' assailing host impetuous springs,
Careless of nibbling bills and flapping wings;
And, midst the tumult, wheresoe'er he turns,
The battle with redoubled fury burns;
From every side th' avenging cranes amain
Throng, to o'erwhelm this terror of the plain;
When suddenly (for such the will of Jove),
A fowl enormous, sousing from above,
The gallant chieftain clutch'd, and, soaring high,
(Sad chance of battle!) bore him up the sky.
The cranes pursue, and, clustering in a ring,
Clatter triumphant round the captive king.
But ah! what pangs each pigmy bosom wrung,
When, now to cranes a prey, on talons hung,
High in the clouds they saw their helpless lord,
His wriggling form still lessening as he soar'd.

This is among the poetical representations which Burke remarked to be beyond the reach of painting.

When Warburton attempted to confine his matter in couplets, his energy deserted him, as a short extract will show. The commencement of Claudian's 'Panegyric on the Third Consulate of Honorius' is thus rendered:

Now in your third Trabēa you appear,
And your third fasces glad the opening year;
Bless'd shall it be, in luckier periods roll'd,
Each smiling month in quiet plenty told.
In loosen'd folds the gay Gabinian gown,
Heavy with orient gems, flows peaceful down;
Embroider'd purple to rough arms succeed,
And curule chariots to the warrior steed;
Stern victors triumph o'er the tented field,
And furling ensigns to their axes yield.
Hail, prince! who with your eastern brother *hold*,
With equal sway, a patrimonial *world*.

Warburton probably knew little of Latin prosody at any time; but he must have known very little of it indeed, when he wrote these lines, not to have learned from his original the quantity of 'trabea.' The sounds that do duty for rhymes in the last couplet are somewhat startling; but he has several couplets of an equally surprising description:

> Next, balmy Venus, that benignant breathes,
> In milder majesty, the god receives.
>
> O happy parents! here your earliest beam
> Around Arcadius' outstretch'd empire flames.
>
> Already see proud Babylon o'erthrown,
> In real flights the backward Parthian turn.
>
> Let luxury thy o'ercharg'd nature load,
> And with fantastic dainties heap thy board.

Enough of Warburton's attempts at versification. But we must not dismiss the volume without a glance at the Dedication, which, in an unlucky hour, he took a fancy to write in Latin:

EXCELLENTISSIMO

PRÆSTANTISSIMO ET HONORATISSIMO VIRO

D° ROBERTO SUTTON

EQUITI AURATO, AD GALLICUM MONARCAM, DARE MOREM CATHOLICÆ PACIS,
CUM AUTHORITATE MAXIMA PROXIME MISSO:

IN LEGATIONIBUS,

GLORIÆ BRITANNIÆ ET EUROPÆ STABILITATIS ÆQUILIBRIS, FAUTORI TENACI;

SENATU,

COMMODI PROVINCLÆ ET LIBERTATIS PATRIÆ, VINDICI EGREGIO;

DOMI,

VIRTUTUM HUMANITATIS, RELIGIONISQUE MODERATIONUM,
EXEMPLARI PERILLUSTRI;

HAS NUGAS

IN SUMMI HONORIS, ANIMIQUE DICATISSIMI TESTIMONIUM,
D. D. D.Q.

W. WARBURTON.

CIↃ IↃCC XXIII.

This specimen of Latinity provoked much animadversion from the scholars in whose way it fell. It was an unfortunate attempt; but Warburton seems to have persevered in his efforts to improve himself in writing Latin, and to have been not unwilling to exhibit his proficiency to his friends. Two Latin letters of his to Dr. Stukeley, in 1729 and 1732, preserved by Mr. Nichols, show, though not faultless, a much greater command of the Latin language than he can be supposed to have possessed when he addressed Sir Robert Sutton in it, as may be seen by the following extract from the later letter, containing some sarcastic remarks on the antiquary Peck:

'Paullo antè illustrissimus Peckius, sidus *μυώπων ἀρχαιογράφων*, inter itinera sua in domum nostram divertebat, cœnabat, discubuit. Vidula ejus de more conferta erant et cruditatibus distenta; similia bulgæ isti infernali de quâ poeta lepidus Swiftius suavissimè canit:

> His budget with corruption cramm'd,
> The contributions of the damn'd ·

id est poetarum, oratorum, historicorum, virgâ criticorum censoriâ in ærumnis atque miseriis cloacarum degere ævum damnatorum; usquedum, revolventibus fatis, hic Eques erraticus incantamentum rumpat, et illos innocentes, fœdè laceratos et spoliatos jacentes, defendat, protegat, ac in lucem revocet. Si fides sit isti primæ philosophiæ, quâ à nutrice in gynæcio nos omnes imbuti sumus, quæ docet homunciones ex Apiato oriri; jurarem per omnes Deos Deasque clarissimum hunc Antiquarium, qui à Stanfordiâ petit originem, vice Apiati, singulari fortunâ, sepulchretum istud monasticum, herbis soporificis, pro portis oppidi situm, natalitium locum habuisse; hinc amor cuculli; hinc protervitas ingenii; hinc odium in bonas literas.'

If we compare this with Swift's Latin, in his well-known criticism on Aulus Gellius, we shall, perhaps, be inclined to think the advantage on the side of Warburton.

He is said to have endeavoured, in subsequent years, to suppress this volume as far as possible, by destroying all the copies that he could by any means secure. It fell, by its own insignificance, into obscurity, till Dr. Parr, when he published 'Tracts by Warburton and a Warburtonian,' made it better known than ever.

He remained in deacon's orders for nearly four years, not being ordained priest till March 1, 1727, when Sir Robert Sutton, not offended by his imperfect Latin or his inelegant English, procured him, by a recommendation to some person of influence, the small living of Greaseley, in Nottinghamshire, which is now in the gift of Lord Palmerston, and is worth about 134*l.* a year. He was ordained in London by Bishop Gibson.

How he employed his time between his two ordinations, neither Hurd nor any other person that has written of him, has given any intimation. Perhaps it was during part of this period that he gave the assistance which has been noticed to his cousin, in Newark school.* Wherever he was, he doubtless continued his reading and study. One of the authors that engaged most of his attention was Shakspeare.

It was during the year 1726, perhaps at the time he came to London for priest's orders, that he became acquainted, by what means is not known, with several literary characters of the day, the chief of whom were Concanen and Theobald; among the others were Dennis, James Moore, Hesiod Cooke, and Roome. In his conversation with these gentlemen, he let it be known that he had by him some remarks that he had made on Shakspeare; and Theobald, who was then collecting mate-

* Nichols's Lit. Illustrations, vol. ii. p. 195.

rials, from every available source, for his notes on that author, was glad to improve his acquaintance with a gentleman from whom he might obtain supplies. But Concanen seems to have been the first of the party with whom Warburton became intimate; and through him, accordingly, Theobald made application to Warburton for such assistance as he might be willing to afford to the improvement or ornamentation of Shakspeare's pages. Warburton promised, on his return to the country, to look over his observations, of which he spoke very lightly, and to select from them such as might be of any avail for Theobald's purposes. But as Warburton, when he returned to Newark, neglected to perform what he had promised, Concanen was again employed to solicit, and addressed a letter to Warburton, reminding him of the good intentions which he had expressed towards Theobald, but had left unexecuted. Warburton replied as follows, under the date of January 2, 1727:

'Dear Sir,—Having had no more regard for those papers which I promised to Mr. Theobald than just what they deserved, I in vain sought for them through a number of loose papers that had the same kind of abortive birth. I used to make it one part of my amusement in reading the English poets—those of them, I mean, whose vein flows regularly and constantly, as well as clearly,—to trace them to their sources, and to observe what ore, as well as what slime and gravel, they brought down with them. Dryden, I observe, borrows for want of leisure, and Pope for want of genius; Milton out of pride, and Addison out of modesty.' He then makes some observations on the means of judging of imitation, which we may leave unnoticed at present, and concludes thus: 'You may now, sir, justly complain of my ill manners, in deferring till now what should have been first of all acknowledged due to you, which is my thanks for all your favours when in town, particularly for introducing me to the knowledge of those worthy and ingenious gentlemen that made up our last night's conversation. I am, sir, with all esteem, your most obliged friend and humble servant,

'W. WARBURTON.'

This letter, which was first given to the public by Akenside, in a note on his 'Ode to Edwards,' 'was found,' as Akenside states, 'by Dr. Gawin Knight, first librarian to the British Museum, about the year 1750, in fitting up a house which he had taken in Crane Court, Fleet Street; a house which had for a long time before been let in lodgings, and where, in all probability, Concanen had lodged.' Malone reprinted it in 1780, in his 'Supplement to Shakspeare,'* with the observation that, 'if it contained anything affecting the moral character of the writer, tenderness for the dead would forbid its publication;' but as such was not the case, and 'as the learned prelate was beyond the reach of criticism, there was no reason why it should be longer withheld from the public.' Malone had a manuscript copy of it, which had been given by Akenside himself to some friend.

In after days, when Warburton had written in defence of Pope, and profited by his friendship, Warburton's enemies were ready to make the most of this letter. It was very well for Warburton that it was not discovered till six years after Pope's death, or it might have had no good effect on their connexion, by giving Pope just reason to suspect the sincerity of his defender.

In the meantime, Concanen's application to Warburton led to a long correspondence, of sixty or seventy letters, written chiefly in the two following years, between Warburton and Theobald, respecting various passages in Shakspeare. Theobald's letters, with a few of Warburton's, are preserved in the 'Literary Illustrations,' by Mr.

* Vol. i. p. 222.

Nichols, to whom they were presented by Mr. Edward Roberts, of Ealing, who had them from Theobald's son, then, by the interest of the Walpole family, a clerk in the Exchequer. Of these letters we shall have occasion to take notice when we come to speak of Theobald and Warburton's editions of Shakspeare.

But in 1727, the same year in which Warburton wrote to Concanen, there appeared, from Warburton's pen, as was well understood, though his name was not affixed, a small volume entitled, 'A Critical and Philosophical Enquiry into the Causes of Prodigies and Miracles, as related by Historians; with an Essay towards restoring a Method and Purity in History; in which the characters of the most celebrated writers of every age, and of the several stages and species of history, are occasionally criticised and explained. In two Parts. *Disce, sed ira cadat naso, rugosaque sanna, Dum veteres avias tibi de pulmone revello.*' This little work, like the 'Translations,' was dedicated, but not in Latin, to Sir Robert Sutton, 'one of His Majesty's most Honourable Privy Council,' in an address containing a justification of dedications, on the ground that they are but natural tributes to exalted merit, and that whoever, by eminent virtues, attains high place, must expect to find inferiors sue to them for patronage. The virtues of Sir Robert and the Countess of Sunderland, whom he had married, are portrayed by Warburton in somewhat glaring colours.

The object of the book, which, however, is hardly apparent through its rambling and incoherent style, is to assign the causes why prodigies and miracles are more numerous in the earlier than in the later pages of history. One cause, he observes, is that the human mind, in its weakness, has a longing to hear of what is marvellous; and that historians, in primitive times, took advantage of this desire to narrate tales of wonder, deluding their readers as jugglers delude the crowd. Another cause, he says, is national pride, under the influence of which men have been eager that their histories should exhibit as many prodigies as possible, such prodigies being considered by them as Divine interpositions in their favour, indicating the country which is the scene of them to be under the special protection of Heaven; and this national pride, he adds, was flattered by both the Greek and Roman historians, and by none more than by Livy, who wrote to a people in whom national pride was strong, and who would not be satisfied unless everything was recorded that tended to prove them the favourites of the gods. Another cause is ignorance in the writer; ignorance of human nature, or of his subject, or of both; so that when he wanted sagacity or knowledge to ascertain causes of events, or motives of actions, and to discern the clue that ought to guide him through his labyrinth, he had recourse to prodigies and divine influences, by which good or evil was supernaturally promoted or retarded, introducing, like the tragic poets, a god to explain that which to himself was inexplicable.

These are the chief causes, he states, why prodigies have been so prevalent in History, and he proceeds to censure our own old English historians for having been so ready to scatter them over their pages. Raleigh and Clarendon, he says, were the only two Englishmen at the time that had produced writings worthy of the name of history. 'Almost all the rest of our histories,' he elegantly remarks, 'want life, soul, shape, and body; a mere hodge-podge of abortive embryos and rotten carcasses, kept in an unnatural ferment (which the vulgar mistake for real life), by the rank leaven of prodigies and portents, which can't but afford good diversion to the critic, while he observes how naturally one of their own fables is here mythologised and explained, "Of a church and carcass raised to set a strutting by the inflation of some hellish succubus within."'

But, as time runs on, and knowledge increases, he continues, both writers and readers become less liable to be influenced by such causes, or, as it may be expressed, less superstitious. The first historian among the Romans that appeared uninfected by superstition, he says, was Sallust, on whose works, in contrast with the Roman writers that preceded him, he then makes some laudatory remarks, and adds that he had 'a set of discourses' on Sallust's writings lying by him. He next inquires whether all prodigies and miracles, which are met with in profane history, are to be rejected as fabulous and chimerical, and replies in the negative: first, because there is universal consent in attestation of them; secondly, because, though sceptics say that any arrest or disturbance of the laws of nature would interfere with the course and harmony of the whole system of things, yet He, assuredly, who ordered and presides over all, can give new laws, for a time, to any particular portion of matter, without altering the order and constitution of the whole; thirdly, because the miracles related in sacred story countenance the belief that other deviations from the usual order of nature may have occurred.

I have been thus minute in examining the contents of this early specimen of Warburton's composition, because it shows on what kind of subjects he had at that youthful period of his life employed his thoughts; subjects which were to occupy them to a far greater extent in the chief work of his maturer years.

In regard to Sallust, he makes one very acute remark as to the question how far imaginary miracles may be admitted into history. Sallust, he says, has omitted one which he might very properly have inserted, and which is judiciously related by Plutarch and Dion Cassius. When Cicero was undecided what to do with Lentulus and his accomplices, being drawn one way by timidity and clemency, and another by justice and concern for his country, he received from his wife Terentia, who had constantly incited him against the conspirators, a message acquainting him, that while she and her women were sacrificing to the Bona Dea, there issued from the ashes on the altar a large bright flame, which the Vestal Virgins assured her portended glory and security to the Consul. This communication determined Cicero in favour of severity; and, such being the case, Sallust should not have excluded so influential an occurrence from his narrative; an occurrence which actuated Cicero's conduct, and which illustrates his character; for the historian may thus be accused of having neglected a principal law of history, by suppressing a portion of truth, and may be said to have run into one fault while he was solicitous to avoid another.

But we must not omit to notice the conclusion of the 'Enquiry,' which has subjected its author to much ridicule for copying Milton without acknowledgment. Observing that 'the late Royal Institution for the study of Modern History,' meaning the Regius Professorship of Modern History established at Cambridge by George I., had given the historical Muse hopes of regaining her old honours under 'our invincible monarch,' 'another Augustus,' who, seeing 'the abject condition of British history,' took 'this effectual method to raise and ennoble it,' 'it must,' he proceeds, 'be the office of everyone, that bears a relation to letters, to second the gracious intention of the "father of his country;" and it is my utmost ambition to have it believed that this engaged me in my present labour; for I imagined a better foundation could not be laid for the advancement of modern history than in a right intelligence of the ancient; and it is honour enough for me to be employed as an under labourer, in clearing the ground, and removing the rubbish; this noble Institution must produce the master-builders to give us that finished body of English history so long wanted, and till now despaired of. At least,' he adds, 'I have reason to expect that as the successes of the British arms, if we be provoked to employ them, will, without doubt, raise up amongst us a plentiful harvest of journalists and historians, the foregoing remarks may, perhaps, be of seasonable use to direct them in the most nice detours of the story; *the true causes of things*. . . . Such a work alone would be worth a *royal foundation*; but this has already procured far more important advantages; the *University*, conquered by repeated acts of sovereign favour, is become *ambitious* of receiving, and with unfeigned love and gratitude repeats her numerous obligations.'

Then follow the last words:

'Methinks I see her, like the mighty eagle, renewing her immortal youth, and purging her opening sight at the unobstructed beams of our benign meridian SUN, which some pretend to say had been dazzled and abused by an inglorious pestilential METEOR; while the ill-affected birds of night would, with their envious hootings, prognosticate a length of darkness and decay.'

This is copied from a passage towards the conclusion of Milton's 'Areopagitica.' Lowth caught at it, when Warburton and he became enemies, and told him that his '*musa pedestris*, in a spirit of prophetic enthusiasm, had here got on horseback in high prancing style,' and printed the passage, without changing a word, as blank verse:

> Methinks I see her, like the mighty eagle,
> Renewing her immortal youth, and purging
> Her opening sight at th' unobstructed beams
> Of our benign meridian sun; which some
> Pretend to say had been dazzled and abus'd
> By an inglorious pestilential meteor;
> While th' ill-affected birds of night would with
> Their envious hootings
> Prognosticate a length of darkness and decay.*

---

* Lowth's First Letter to Warburton, p. 56.

'Warburton was conversant with our great vernacular writers,' observes Disraeli, 'at a time when their names generally were better known than their works, and when it was considered safe to pillage their most glorious passages. The passage from Milton's 'Areopagitica' in full is this: Milton, speaking of a people having spirit and energy, not only to maintain and defend their safety and freedom, but to engage in 'the solidest and sublimest points of controversy and new invention,' observes that such a condition of things denotes the greatest glory to come. Then he adds: 'Methinks I see in my mind a noble and puissant nation rousing herself like a strong man after sleep, and shaking her invincible locks; methinks I see her as an eagle muing her mighty youth, and kindling her undazzled eyes at the full mid-day beam; purging and unscaling her long-abused sight at the fountain itself of heavenly radiance; while the whole noise of timorous and flocking birds, with those, also, that love the twilight, flutter about, amazed at what she means, and in their envious gabble would prognosticate a year of sects and schisms.'

As Warburton, long afterwards, said that the manuscript did not pass directly from his own hands to the press, it might be supposed that some meddler had mischievously tacked this quotation from Milton to the end of it, to make a sublime or ridiculous conclusion. But Warburton himself never alleged that any such trick had been played him. From a statement which he made to Hurd, indeed, many readers might conclude that he hardly knew what was in the book, and that the existence in it of the passage from Milton might never have come under his cognizance. But such could hardly have been the case. Let us consider the matter, and what he says about it.

Hurd, writing to Warburton about thirty years after the publication of the volume, states that, after reading the Bishop's other works, he 'met with the "Essay on Portents and Prodigies," which,' says he, 'I liked the better, and still like it, because I understood it was most abused by those who owed you no good will.' To this Warburton rejoined that Hurd's commendation was 'very dear' to him, 'though it calls,' said he, 'the sins of my youth to my remembrance. I was very much a boy when I wrote that thing about "Prodigies," and I had never the courage to look into it since; so I have quite forgot all the nonsense that it contains. But, since you mention it, I will tell you how it came to see the light. I met, many years ago, with an ingenious Irishman, at a coffee-house, near Gray's Inn, where I lodged. He studied the law, and was very poor. I had given him money for many a dinner; and at last I gave him those papers, which he sold to the booksellers for more money than you would think; much more than they were worth.' But are we to believe that Warburton left a book which he had elaborately dedicated, in several pages, to his patron, wholly uninspected after its publication? Are we to credit that he did not care to see that the passages in which he had flattered the University of Cambridge and King George I. were correctly printed? If we think that he never looked into the volume, we must surely be very easy of belief. If we think that he did look into it, we must feel assured that he was aware of the passage from Milton, which he knew to be a plagiarism, being attached to it.

The truth is, that the 'Enquiry' did Warburton very little honour, either as to matter or style; and, had it not been thoroughly eclipsed by his subsequent performances, the world would have heard very little of his name. Warburton himself was quite sensible of its demerits, and desirous that it should, like the 'Miscellaneous Translations,' be suppressed; and when he heard that Curll meditated a reprint of it, he was frightened at the thought. 'A few years before Curll's death,' he said to Hurd, 'he wrote me a letter to acquaint me that he had bought the property of *my excellent discourse*, and that, as it had been long out of print, he was going to reprint it; only he desired to know if I had any additions or alterations to make;—he should be glad of the honour of receiving them. The writer and the contents of his letter very much alarmed me; so I wrote to Mr. Knapton to go to the fellow, and buy my own book of him again, which he did; and so ended this ridiculous affair, which may be a warning to young scribblers.'

But Hurd, resolute to commend, persisted in speaking of it to Warburton in such terms as these, and calling Mr. Balguy to his support: 'You have a right to undervalue your first attempt in literature as much as you please. The so much greater things you have done since are your warrant for so doing. But I should not be very patient of this language from any other. The truth is—and I am not afraid to say it roundly to any man—not *one* of all the wretches that have written or rail against you was ever able, in the acmé of his parts and judgment, to produce anything half so good. Mr. Balguy and I read it together some years ago, and we agreed that there was the same ingenuity of sentiment and vigour of expression as in your other works; in a word, that it was a fine effort of genius,—not yet formed, indeed, and matured, but, even in this juvenility, portending plainly enough what you were one day to be capable of. I have read it again very lately, and I think of it just the same; so that I almost blame your anxiety about Curll's edition. It was not worth, perhaps, your owning in form; but your reputation was not concerned to suppress it. One sees in it your early warmth in the cause of virtue and public liberty, and your original way of striking out new hints on common subjects. There are many fine observations up and down; amongst which that in the Dedication, on the characters of the three great Romans [Cæsar, Cato, and Cicero], which you have since adopted on the notes on Pope, is admirable. In running it over this last time, I find I have stolen a hint from you which I was not aware of. It is what I say of the "Apes" of Plato and Aristotle, in page 79 of the Commentary on the Epistle to Augustus, taken from what you say in page 9 on that subject. I should not have said so much on this matter (for I am as much above the thought of flattering you as you are above the want of it), but that I think this shyness in acknowledging this little prolusion of your genius gives a handle to your low malignant cavillers, which you need not have afforded them. I must further request it of you, as a favour, that, if Knapton has not destroyed the copies, you would oblige me with half a dozen or so, which you may trust me to dispose of in a proper manner. I ask it the rather because I could never get one into my own possession. I have tried several times, and now very lately this winter, out of Baker's sale; but it was bought up before I could order it. Such a curiosity have both your friends and enemies to treasure up this proscribed volume.' To the same purpose Hurd expresses himself in his 'Discourse on Poetical Imitation.' *

The remark about the three great Romans, to which Hurd alludes, is, that 'the Roman that had called Catiline's factious popularity public spirit, or Antony's beastly luxury munificence, had sinned against his country's virtues, while the candid and humane Atticus had been excused, [if,] when speaking of Cæsar, who had ambition without pride or vanity; of Cato, who had pride without vanity or ambition; of Cicero, who had vanity without ambition or pride; he had called the first's ambition the love of glory, because joined with clemency; the second's

* Comm. on Ep. ad Pis., &c., vol. iii. p. 107.

pride an honest scorn, because arising from the enmity of vice; and the third's vanity a conscious merit, because never sparing in another's praise.'

But in these observations on these eminent personages there is, in reality, very little deserving of commendation. When such numerous elements enter into the composition of human characters, how can any single term serve to designate that of any particular individual? How can it be said that in the character of Cæsar there was nothing but ambition, without any mixture of pride or vanity? or in that of Cato nothing but pride, without any portion of vanity or ambition? or in that of Cicero nothing but vanity, without either ambition or pride? What injustice would it be to Cicero to call him merely vain? or to Cato, to pronounce him remarkable for nothing but pride? or to Cæsar, to say that every other feeling in him was nullified by ambition?

The observation about the 'Apes,' from which Hurd took his hint, is, 'that of the later Sophists who affected to be thought followers of Plato and Aristotle, some could arrive at no higher a conformity than the imitation of the stammering of the one, and the round shoulders of the other.'

CHAPTER II.

LITERARY MATTERS — CONCANEN — THEOBALD.

NOTICE OF CONCANEN — HIS LITERARY PERFORMANCES — HIS PRAISE OF POPE — HIS APPOINTMENT IN JAMAICA, AND DEATH — WHETHER WARBURTON CONSPIRED WITH POPE'S ENEMIES — LISTENED WITH COMPLACENCY TO THEOBALD'S EXCLAMATIONS AGAINST POPE — HIS CONCERN IN 'THE LEGAL JUDICATURE IN CHANCERY STATED'— MADE ONE OF THE KING'S MASTERS OF ARTS AT CAMBRIDGE — PRESENTED BY SIR ROBERT SUTTON TO THE LIVING OF BRANT-BROUGHTON — HIS APPLICATION TO STUDY — HIS ACQUIREMENTS — IS IN NO HASTE TO PUBLISH — HIS ASSISTANCE TO THEOBALD IN HIS 'SHAKSPEARE'— THEOBALD'S MERITS — UNDULY DEPRECIATED — SPECIMENS OF HIS EMENDATIONS — ESTRANGEMENT BETWEEN HIM AND WARBURTON, AND RECONCILIATION — THEOBALD'S DEATH — WARBURTON'S 'APOLOGY FOR SIR ROBERT SUTTON'— HIS LETTER TO POPE ON SIR ROBERT'S CHARACTER — POPE ERASES SIR ROBERT'S NAME FROM HIS SATIRES.

MATTHEW CONCANEN, to whom Warburton says he gave money for dinners, and the manuscript of his 'Enquiry into Prodigies,' seems to have been a man of more literary ability, and of better moral character, than Warburton and Pope would lead us to believe. He was an Irish barrister, but, having deserted the law for a time, he brought on the stage at Dublin, in 1721, when he was only twenty years old, a comedy called 'Wexford Wells;' and dedicated, in the same year, to Swift's 'Lawyer Bettesworth,' a poem entitled 'A Match at Football, in three Cantos.' In the following year he inscribed a volume of 'Poems on Several Occasions' to the Duchess of Grafton, and came over to London to seek his fortune, where, in 1724, he published 'Miscellaneous Poems,' and became connected with 'The London Journal,' in which he prefaced some criticisms of Theobald on Shakspeare with a very judicious introduction. He insists, in that article, on the duty of a nation to preserve the works of its authors in good condition, and to render them, by the aid of comments, intelligible to posterity. 'Every writer,' he observes, 'is obliged to make himself understood of the age in which he lives; but, as he cannot answer for the changes of manners and language which may happen after his death, those who receive pleasure and instruction from him are obliged, as well in gratitude to him as in duty to posterity, to endeavour to perpetuate his memory by preserving his meaning. Much pains,' he adds, 'have been taken to preserve to us the picture of Chaucer, while nobody has thought proper to render that better picture of him, his writings, intelligible to future ages. Butler has had a monument erected to his memory in Westminster Abbey: how much more emphatically might it be said to be *erected to his memory* if it were a comment upon his excellent "Hudibras," which, for want of such illustration, grows every day less pleasing to his readers, who lose half his wit and pleasantry, while they are ignorant of the facts he alludes to! I own it grows daily more difficult to perform this duty to old authors; and, therefore, the Italians say that a comment ought to be made when the work does not need it, for that it will be impossible to make one when it does.' Such suggestions regarding Chaucer and Hudibras were extremely pertinent at the time that they were made. After some commendation of Theobald, he observes that 'such a critic might bring the name of commentator into the repute which it has lost by the dull and useless pedantry of some pretenders to it.' In 1728, he wrote the preface to the 'Collection of all the Verses, Essays, Letters, and Advertisements occasioned by Mr. Pope and Swift's Miscellanies,' and in the same year a pamphlet, entitled 'A Supplement to the Profund,' in which, says Dr. Warton, there are 'more shrewd remarks, and more pertinent examples, than might be expected from such a writer, and enough to make us think he had some more able assistant. Concanen was at that time an intimate friend of Warburton, and, it has been suggested, was assisted by him in writing these remarks; but of this there is no positive proof.' Concanen was well able to produce it without any aid from Warburton. In this tract on 'the Profund,' which is a satire on Pope, he is accused by Warburton of having 'dealt unfairly by Pope, in not only frequently imputing to him Broome's verses (for which he might seem in some degree accountable, having corrected what that gentleman did), but those of the Duke of Buckingham and others.' Pope took his revenge in the well-known lines,

> True to the bottom see Concanen creep,
> A cold, long-winded native of the deep;
> If perseverance gain the diver's prize,
> Not everlasting Blackmore this denies;
> No noise, no stir, no motion canst thou make;
> Th' unconscious stream sleeps o'er thee like a lake.

This satire was the more malignant, as Concanen, in his 'Miscellanies,' had, in some very fair couplets, praised Pope:

> With pleasing notes the woods and valleys ring,
> If Pope's harmonious hand but touch the string;
> His gentle numbers charm the ravish'd plains,
> While still attention holds the wond'ring swains.
> To him the classics all their art have shown,
> Yet all his wit and spirit are his own;
> He knows their methods to pursue their race,
> Yet scorns their footsteps servilely to trace.

In 1732 he had so recommended himself, by his literary abilities, to the Duke of Newcastle, that he was appointed to the Attorney-Generalship of the island of Jamaica, a post which he 'filled with the utmost integrity and honour, and to the perfect satisfaction of the inhabitants, for near seventeen years.'* According to Warburton, he married an opulent widow in Jamaica, but certain it is that he acquired a considerable fortune, on which he purposed to live in his native country, but, on landing in London in 1748, he suffered so much from the change of climate, that he died of consumption early in the following year. Warburton says, 'he was of so scoundrel a temper,' that on returning to England, 'he avoided ever coming into my sight;' but he seems, even if his temper had ever so much inclined him, to have had little time for visiting Warburton. Altogether, he appears to have been a much more respectable member of society than the incautious might infer from Warburton's revilings; and, had he continued his application to literature, he might have made a far better figure in it than Pope's lines on him would seem to indicate.

I have paid this attention to Concanen's character, because he was the only one, except Theobald, among the literary persons that Warburton met at this time in London, with whom he appears to have formed any intimacy. Warburton must have liked him at first, and no sufficient reason is apparent, unless it was a desire to take Pope's part, why he should have railed at him afterwards.

It is confidently asserted by Mr. Nichols that Warburton was a conspirator with Theobald's party in their attempts to annoy or humble Pope. 'That Mr. Warburton was an associate with Theobald and Concanen,' says he, 'in the attack made on Pope's fame and talents, is indisputable.' Johnson speaks less positively on the point, but seems to be of the same opinion. 'Warburton,' he remarks, 'had pleased himself with the notice of inferior wits, and corresponded with the enemies of Pope;' and adds that, when Theobald published Shakspeare, in opposition to Pope,

* Nichols's Lit. Illustr., vol. ii. p. 192.

Warburton was ready to assist him with notes. But, that Warburton ever leagued with the heroes of the 'Dunciad' against Pope, there seems to be no positive proof. Being, in reality, no great judge of poetry, he may have formed a lower opinion of Pope's genius than he afterwards found it merited, and may have listened with complacency to undue depreciation of it; but that he combined with cavillers and calumniators to degrade Pope, is not to be believed without testimony; nor is there anything in Warburton's own writings, or in the writings of any of his contemporaries, to indicate that he ever was a member of such combination. With Concanen, there is no evidence that he maintained any correspondence after his retirement to his clerical duties in the country; and it is not apparent that he ever formed intimate connexions with any other of Pope's censors except Theobald.

Theobald he certainly allowed to speak very freely of Pope, without manifestation of displeasure, in the letters that passed between them concerning Shakspeare. 'What a dab at collating is our editor!'* cries Theobald in one place. In another, 'So far from being *an Aristarchus*, he is *a stark ass.*'† 'Unpardonable stupidity!'‡ 'Mr. Pope has made stark nonsense.'§ Pope, in 'The Taming of the Shrew,' had printed 'Socrates' Zantippe:' 'Mr. Pope,' says Theobald, 'in the next edition, perhaps, will vouchsafe to restore Xantippe.'‖ And when Theobald had thoughts of publishing a satirical 'Essay on Mr. Pope's Judgments, extracted from his own Works,' and sent Warburton a specimen of it, Warburton certainly made no opposition to the design; for Theobald, in a following letter, says, 'It is no small satisfaction to me that you approve my design with regard to my antagonist's *Judgments.*'¶ In another letter he thanks Warburton for

* Nichols's Lit. Illustr., vol. ii. p. 279. † Ib. p. 284.
‡ Ib. p. 317. § Ib. p. 319. ‖ Ib. p. 334.
¶ Ib. pp. 551, 565.

justifying him against Pope's charge of applauding fustian.* But all this will not prove Warburton to have entered into a conspiracy, or to have been a well-wisher to Theobald against Pope any further than as he was editor of Shakspeare. Warburton assuredly was not desirous to have his name connected publicly with Pope's adversaries; for Theobald remarks, in acknowledging some communication that he had received, 'As to the three printed criticisms with which you obliged me and the public, it is *a very reasonable caution*, that what is gleaned from them should come out *anonymous*; for I should be loth to have a valued friend subjected, on my account, to the outrages of Pope, virulent though impotent.'† He had, doubtless, also begun to form higher views for himself than would have been forwarded by any schemes for lowering Pope.

Another publication, in which Warburton had a share, and which appeared, anonymously, in the same year as the 'Enquiry into Prodigies and Miracles,' must not be left unnoticed. It was entitled 'The Legal Judicature in Chancery Stated,' and was the joint composition of Warburton and Mr. Samuel Burroughs, an eminent barrister. In the preceding year, some dispute having arisen among the lawyers respecting the limits of the judicial powers of the Court of Chancery and the Rolls' Court, Mr. Burroughs took the side of the Court of Chancery, in a small publication called 'The History of the Chancery,' which was printed without his name, but was well known to be his, and which was so acceptable to Lord Chancellor King, that he at once rewarded the author of it with a Mastership in Chancery. But a treatise quickly came forth in reply to it, entitled 'A Discourse of the Judicial Authority of the Master of the Rolls,' a composition so much superior to the 'History,' that the advocates of the Court of Chancery saw their cause was likely to suffer, unless they secured some additional aid.

* Nichols's Lit. Illustr., vol. ii. p. 394.

† Ib. p. 621.

'In this exigency,' says Hurd, 'Mr. Burroughs was advised by one of his friends (I forget, or never heard, his name) to have recourse to Mr. Warburton, as a person very capable of supplying his defects. Accordingly, when he had prepared the proper materials for a reply, he obtained leave to put them into Mr. Warburton's hands, and afterwards spent some time with him in the country, where, by their joint labours, the whole was drawn out, and digested into a sizable volume, which came out in 1727. This book was so manifestly superior to the "History," that such of the profession as were not in the secret, wondered at Mr. Burroughs's proficiency in the art of writing; and the Lord Chancellor King as much as anybody. The author of the "Discourse" saw it concerned him to take notice of such an adversary, and in 1728 reprinted his work "with large additions, together with a Preface occasioned by a book entitled 'The Legal Judicature in Chancery Stated.'" And with this reply, I believe, the dispute closed.'

Warburton, some years after, having become acquainted with Mr. Charles Yorke, the son of Lord Chancellor Hardwicke, happened to mention to him, as the secret was no longer necessary to be kept, the share which he had in that dispute; when Mr. Yorke asked him if he knew who had been his antagonist. Warburton replying in the negative, Mr. Yorke told him it was his father, who, though then Attorney-General, had thought proper to support his relative, Sir Joseph Jekyll, the Master of the Rolls.

In 1728, in the month of April, the King made a visit to the University of Cambridge, and Warburton, by the interest of Sir Robert Sutton, was included in the list of Masters of Arts created on that occasion. Whether any notice was taken by the people of Cambridge of the incense which he had offered to the University in his 'Enquiry into Prodigies and Miracles,' we are not told.

In June in the same year he received a more substantial mark of Sir Robert Sutton's favour, for he was presented by him to one of the livings in his gift, that of Brant-Broughton, near Newark, of the value of 560*l.* a-year, with a population under a thousand. Here he fixed himself, with his mother and sisters, and continued to reside during eighteen years of the most vigorous portion of his life, from 1728 to 1746. Greaseley he resigned, and indeed seems never to have fixed himself there at all. But it appears that in 1730 he was presented by the Duke of Newcastle, probably through Sir Robert Sutton's influence, to the living of Frisby, in Lincolnshire, with about 250*l.* a-year, which he continued to hold, though never residing on it, till 1756.*

In the retirement of Brant-Broughton he had ample leisure for that application to reading and study to which he was always so strongly inclined. The population of his parish being so small, he was at liberty to devote his week days, with little interruption, to his books, of which his income allowed him to procure a comfortable supply; and his labour, not satisfied with the hours of the day, would often be protracted far into the night. But having a strong constitution, and observing strict temperance, he needed, like Bentley, little exercise; and occasional walks, of a few miles, kept him in excellent health.

Yet his mother and sisters were at times fearful that such continuance of study must at length bring on disease; and one of his sisters, Mrs. Frances Warburton, told Hurd that they would sometimes invite themselves to take coffee with him in his library after dinner, and contrive to make their stay with him as long as possible; but that, when they retired, they always found that he returned again to his books, and continued at them till the demands of sleep obliged him to retire.

* Nichols's Lit. Ill. vol. ii. pp. 59, 845.

His reading was at all times sufficiently miscellaneous. Such protracted application of a mind so discursive, and eager for omnifarious knowledge, could not but be divided among many subjects. He passed from grave to light, and from light to grave; and when he was weary with Eusebius or Schulteus, sought relief in Cervantes or Butler. He was fond of works of wit and humour, and had read, doubtless, many of the poets; but that he had a passionate fondness for sublime poetry, as Hurd represents, is not to be credited.

Such incessant industry, aided by strong retentiveness of memory, could not but produce much fruit. 'Condo et compono,' he might say to himself, 'quod mox depromere possim.' His acquaintance with literature in general became great, though his knowledge of particular subjects, even such as he might be expected fully to understand, was in many cases but partial and superficial, and his judgment in them erroneous. He never became a scholar in the sense in which a Toup or a Tyrwhitt understood the word, but he had penetrated into numbers of books which many professed scholars had scarcely opened. He made extensive incursions into the regions of letters, though he did not always stay long enough in the same part to secure conquests. But he brought away spoils enough to show the compass of his expeditions, and to adorn and enliven his pages with allusions to all kinds of authors and subjects. He had doubtless felt the want of more knowledge when he was writing his treatise on 'Prodigies and Miracles;' for its pages are pages of poverty compared with those of 'The Divine Legation;' and he would thus be the more stimulated to enlarge his acquirements to the utmost.

How intensely his thoughts were often engaged about his subjects of study, is shown by an anecdote communicated by a correspondent to the 'Gentleman's Magazine.'*

* Vol. lxxix. p. 519.

The correspondent's father was invited to meet Warburton at dinner, at Lord Tyrconnel's, at Bilton Hall, and, arriving before Warburton, found the company talking of a fire that was said to have happened at the house of a neighbour, Mr. Fane, of Fulbeck, but of which no one had heard the particulars. Somebody observed that as Mr. Warburton must pass the place on his road from Brant-Broughton, he would doubtless bring a full account of the matter. Mr. Warburton came, but, on being questioned, had nothing to tell; he had ridden close by the house, but had noticed neither fire nor anything extraordinary. The company began to hope that the report was not true; but it was soon confirmed by a resident at Fulbeck, who, coming in with full particulars, said that he had noticed Mr. Warburton ride by without asking a question or turning his head, and apparently absorbed in some subject of meditation. Yet Warburton did not deserve, adds the narrator, to be called an absent man, but was ready, in general, to attend to anything that came before him.

With all his ardour for literary distinction, it is much to his praise that he was in no hurry to thrust himself prominently before the public with any important work. He was resolved to be well prepared for the lists before he entered them. It was not till 1736, after eight years' study at Brant-Broughton, that he presented to the world his first publication of any weight.

In the meantime, however, and during the earlier years of his residence at his country living, was produced Theobald's edition of Shakspeare, about which we have observed that Warburton and Theobald corresponded during the years 1729 and 1730. Theobald received from Warburton considerable assistance, for which he was profuse in his acknowledgments. 'When Theobald published Shakspeare,' says Johnson, 'the best notes were supplied by Warburton;' but this is an assertion which an inspection of the edition will be very far from justifying. When Johnson was asked by Dr. Burney whether he thought Warburton a superior critic to Theobald, he replied, 'Sir, he would make two and fifty Theobalds, cut him into slices.' But this judgment, in regard to Warburton and Theobald as critics and commentators, is by no means just. Whatever superiority may be allowed to Warburton in general mental power, he is assuredly not to be preferred to Theobald, either as a corrector or an illustrator. Even Dr. Burney, at the time that he asked Johnson the question, must have been somewhat surprised at the answer, for he was then inspecting a volume of Johnson's edition, and aptly remarked that Johnson appeared to have found more occasion to be severe on Warburton than on Theobald. But, since the publication of the 'Dunciad,' it had become universally the fashion to decry Theobald, and Johnson joined his voice to that of the public, pronouncing Theobald 'a man of heavy diligence, but slender powers, who escaped with reputation from his undertaking only by the good luck of having Pope for his enemy.' This was most unfair depreciation; for the best notes in Theobald's edition, of every kind, were unquestionably Theobald's own. Theobald, as a commentator, has suffered great injustice from Pope's days almost to the present time. One of the few tributes to his merits is a slight remark of Dr. Warton's. 'This edition of Tibbald,' as Pope calls him, 'was justly esteemed the best till those of Malone and Steevens appeared.' It may, indeed, be justly esteemed the basis of all the editions that have since appeared. A recent writer in the 'Notes and Queries'* has said of Theobald, with no less justice than boldness, 'Every commentator is indebted to him, and everyone has abused him, from Warburton and Pope to Coleridge;

* First Series, vol. iv. p. 28.

and without Theobald's notes and most sagacious amendments, ordinary readers would be puzzled to *read* Shakspeare.' Theobald, in acknowledging his obligations to those who had assisted him, Styan Thirlby, Hawley Bishop, Martin Folkes, Dr. Mead, Dr. Freind, Coxeter, and others, is very justly content, in speaking of Warburton, to say that he owed him *no small part of his best criticisms*, not that he owed him the greater part, adding, 'Nor, indeed, would I any further be thought to commend a friend than, in so doing, to give a testimony of my own gratitude;' and he concludes, in very modest and gentlemanly terms, 'How great a share soever of praise I must lose from myself in confessing these assistances, and however my own poor conjectures may be weakened by the comparison with theirs, I am very well content to sacrifice my vanity to the pride of being so assisted, and the pleasure of being just to their merits.'

The character of Warburton's notes and emendations shall be considered when we come to speak of his own edition of Shakspeare; at present, we shall examine the quality of some of Theobald's. I shall take a few specimens as they stand in his Letters to Warburton.

In Mark Antony, Act v. sc. 2, where Cleopatra is praising Antony after his death, he found three lines standing thus:

> For his bounty
> There was no winter in't. An Antony it was,
> That grew the more by reaping.

And, not seeing how reaping could make Antony grow, or why Antony and winter should be contrasted, he suspected that Shakspeare wrote,

> An *Autumn* 't was
> That grew the more by reaping;

an emendation the more satisfactory when the old way of spelling the words *Automne* and *Antonie* is taken into account.

In Twelfth Night, Act i. sc. 3, Sir Andrew and Sir Toby discourse thus:

Sir And. —— O had I but follow'd the arts!
Sir Tob. Then hadst thou had an excellent head of hair.
Sir And. Why, would that have mended my hair?
Sir Tob. Past question, for thou seest it does not cool my nature.

Theobald, after expressing his wonder that Pope should let this pass for sense, happily alters the last line to

Past question, for thou seest it does not *curl by* nature.

Pope allowed a well-known passage in Measure for Measure, Act iii., sc. 4, to be read,

Say to thyself,
From their abominable and beastly touches,
I drink, I eat away myself, and live;

Theobald, inquiring how it were possible that a man should eat away himself and live, however much he might drink, quietly substituted,

I drink, I eat, *array* myself, and live.

Before Theobald's time, a line in Love's Labour Lost, Act iii. sc. 3, stood,

This *Signior Junio*, giant-dwarf, Dan Cupid;

but Theobald very properly thought that he who had been *five thousand years a boy*, might well be called *Senior-Junior*, in conformity with the term *giant-dwarf*.

To Theobald also, we may observe, is due an admirable emendation of another passage in the same play, Act iv. sc. 3, which was read,

And why indeed Naso, but for smelling out the odoriferous flowers of fancy? The jerks of invention imitary is nothing; so doth the hound his master, &c.

Theobald gave it thus:

And why indeed Naso, but for smelling out the odoriferous flowers of fancy? The jerks of invention? *imitari* is nothing; so doth the hound, &c.

In the million-times quoted passage in Othello about jealousy, the 'green-ey'd monster,'

> that doth *make*
> The meat it feeds on,

was, before Theobald applied his hand to it, a green-ey'd monster

> that doth *mock*
> The meat it feeds on.

In the same play, the lines

> She was in love, and he she lov'd prov'd *mad*
> And did forsake her,

are very happily altered by Theobald into

> She was in love, and he she lov'd prov'd *bad*,
> And did forsake her.

A passage in All's Well that Ends Well, Act i. sc. 3, presents one of his most admirable emendations. Pope gave

> Fortune, she said, was no goddess,—Love, no god,—*complain'd against the* Queen of Virgins,

the words in italics having been thrust in by Rowe, according to Theobald's opinion, who saw from the context that the passage should run,

> Fortune, she said, was no goddess,—Love, no god,—*Diana, no* Queen of Virgins.

A few verses farther on, he aptly alters *loveliness* into *loneliness*.

A similar emendation to that about Diana is made in Twelfth Night, Act iv. sc. 2. All the previous editions gave,

> Master, there are three carters, three shepherds, three neatherds, and three swineherds;

but, in the space of a few lines afterwards, these are called 'four threes of *herdsmen*,' and Theobald therefore aptly conjectured that we should read *goatherds* instead of *carters*.

I have now, perhaps, given specimens enough; but I cannot forbear giving two more. In the Merry Wives of Windsor, Mr. and Mrs. Page discourse thus:

> *Mrs. P.* My Nan shall be the Queen of all the Fairies,
> Finely attired in a robe of white.
> *Mr. P.* That silk will I go buy, and in that time
> Shall Mr. Slender steal my Nan away.

Surely, said Theobald, Shakspeare did not intend Mr. Page to say that Slender should steal his daughter while he went to buy silk; we must read 'in that *tire*,' dress, habit.

In the Midsummer Night's Dream the Fairies were thus addressed:

> Then for the third part of a minute hence,
> Some to kill cankers, &c.

'The Fairies,' said Theobald, 'are here appointed their respective tasks; but are these tasks to continue only for the third part of a minute? I have little doubt but Shakspeare wrote,

> Then, '*fore* the third part of a minute, hence,

that is, as soon as your roundel and fairy-song are dispatched, then, in a trice, before the third part of a minute, get you gone, and do so and so.'

Such are some of the excellent corrections of Theobald, which succeeding editors have been extremely happy to adopt, but for which ordinary readers, and many assuming critics, know not to whom acknowledgments are due. He should have great praise, too, for having improved the sense of many passages by changes in punctuation.

All Theobald's other literary efforts are forgotten, with the exception of a few emendations of corrupt passages in Greek, in which he seems to have been a very fair scholar; and Dr. Blomfield, in editing Æschylus, paid willing attention to 'L. T.'s' suggestions. His attempts at original composition have been doomed, by the sentence alike of his contemporaries and of posterity, to oblivion; nor does it appear that the doom is at all unjust. But as a commentator on Shakspeare he deserves to live, and to have his name held in honour among those of his brethren.

In 1731, some estrangement took place between Warburton and Theobald, of which the origin is not known; but towards the end of the year they were reconciled, and their correspondence went on as before. '*As he has given me full satisfaction for his late conduct*,' writes Warburton to Dr. Stukeley, in November, 'and appears to be willing to perform the part of a man of honour, I absolve him from all hard thoughts, and am disposed to serve him all I can. This I thought proper, for good reasons, to let you know, whom I had acquainted with my (groundless as I am glad to find it) suspicions and complaints.' Perhaps Warburton had feared that some of his comments would be appropriated by Theobald without due acknowledgment; and he afterwards laid it to his charge, when he was dead, that he 'had sequestered part of his notes for the benefit, as he supposed, of some future edition.'*

Some years afterwards, in a company where Pope and Warburton were present, some one, ready to flatter them both, remarked that he wondered Warburton should ever have assisted 'such a fellow as Theobald.' Pope, as Warburton reports, replied that 'there was no wonder at all,' for Warburton 'had taken him for an honest man, as he himself had done, and on that footing had visited him.' It does not appear what cause could be alleged why Warburton should not have continued to consider him as honest a man as either himself or Pope.

He died in 1744, three years before the publication of Warburton's Shakspeare, in no very affluent condition. 'He was of a generous spirit,' said Steele, an actor, who recorded his death, 'too generous for his circumstances,

* Pref. to Shakspeare.

and none knew how to do a handsome thing, or confer a benefit, when in his power, with a better grace than himself. He was my ancient friend, of nearly thirty years' acquaintance;' and, he adds, when he was interred at St. Pancras, '*I only attended him.*'

Such was the end of him who first taught how Shakspeare's text was to be amended and illustrated, and whom succeeding commentators have followed, if not exactly, to borrow the illustration of Holofernes, *as a hound his master*, yet assuredly, at least the best of them, with close imitation.

In the year 1732, Warburton is supposed to have written, or to have assisted in writing, a pamphlet entitled 'An Apology for Sir Robert Sutton.' Sir Robert, who still continued to patronise Warburton, had been a member and director of *The Charitable Corporation*, a society which was instituted, some years before, 'for the relief of the industrious poor, by assisting them with small sums on pledges, at legal interest,' and for which, as it laboured, says the 'Apology,' 'under a lag wind' in 1725, it was thought necessary to look out for fresh subscribers, 'persons of figure and substance,' who might give countenance to the undertaking. Sir Robert Sutton, then living at Hammersmith, was induced to become a shareholder, and afterwards sold his shares at a higher price than he had bought them; but this he did, as his apologist states, not from love of lucre, but from necessity. Sir Robert was a man of business, and, looking into the books with some little attention, he found something wrong in the conduct of one of the members of the committee, and caused him to be expelled. Soon afterwards, Thomson, the secretary, and Robinson, the assistant-secretary, both proprietors, absconded with large sums of money; and some other persons, of good standing in society, were suspected of being accomplices in their dishonesty. A committee was in consequence appointed to inquire into the affair, who published an ample Report, in which it was intimated that Sir Robert Sutton was not free from blame. He accordingly fell under the censure of the House of Commons, was deprived of his seat, and in danger, for some time, of having the whole of his fortune confiscated. That Warburton should have stood forward, at such a time, in defence of his patron, was but reasonable to expect; and the style of the pamphlet, with several scriptural allusions in it, pretty plainly indicates that it was Warburton's production. The writer says of the Report, 'Here is a story well cooked up; but we shall see by-and-by whether the cook had licked his fingers to taste his sauce.' He then intimates that the charges were invented by enemies of Sir Robert, whose 'great good character in the eye of the world was his main blemish' in their estimation ('unless they took into their aid his excellent sense'); for he 'questions much whether all their characters joined together would have had any like influence.' The sum of his argument is, that Sir Robert was a man of such nice honour as to be utterly incapable of anything disgraceful.

A letter written by Warburton to Pope, some years after, for the purpose of inducing the poet to erase Sir Robert's name from his Satires, shows the character of Warburton's patron in a similar light, and may very properly be introduced here:

'I have known this gentleman,' writes Warburton to Pope, 'about twenty years. I have been greatly, and in the most generous manner, obliged to him. So I am very capable, and, you will readily believe, very much disposed, to apologise for him. Yet, for all that, if I did not really believe him to be an honest man, I would not venture to excuse him to you. Nothing is more notorious than the great character he had acquired in the faithful and able discharge of a long embassy at Constantinople, both in the public part and in the private one of the merchants' affairs. The first reflection on his character was that unhappy affair of the Charitable Corporation. I read carefully all the Reports of the Committee concerning it; and, as I knew Sir Robert Sutton's temper and character so well, I was better able than most to judge of the nature of his conduct in it. And I, in my conscience, believe that he had no more suspicion of any fraud carrying on by some in the direction than I had. That he was guilty of neglect and negligence as a director is certain; but it is only the natural effect of his temper (when he has no suspicion), which is exceedingly indolent; and he suffered sufficiently for it, not only in his censure, but by the loss of near £20,000. And at this very juncture he lost a considerable sum of money (through his negligence) by the villany of a land-steward, who broke and ran away. Dr. Arbuthnot knew him well; and I am fully persuaded, though I never heard so, that he had the same opinion of him in this affair that I have. But parties ran high, and this became a party matter; and the violence of parties no one knows more of than yourself. And his virtue and integrity have been since fully manifested.

'Another prejudice against him, with those who did not know him personally, was the character of his brother, the general, as worthless a man, without question, as ever was created. But, you will ask, why should a man in his station be engaged in any affair with such dirty people? 'T is a reasonable question; but you, who know human nature so well, will think this a sufficient answer: he was born to no fortune, but advanced to that station in the Levant, by the interest of his cousin, Lord Lexington; besides the straitness of his circumstances, the usual and constant business of that embassy gave him, of course, a mercantile turn. He had seen, in almost every country where he had been, societies of this kind, subsisting profitably to themselves and beneficially to the public; for not to think he came amongst them with a view to his own profit principally would, indeed, be absurd; yet I am sure with a view of an honest profit, for he is very far from an avaricious man. He lives up to his fortune, without being guilty of any vice or luxury. He is an extreme good and faithful husband, and with reason, indeed, for it is to one of the finest women in England. He is a tender and indulgent father to very hopeful children; a kind master, and one of the best landlords to his tenants. I speak all this of my own knowledge. He has a good estate in this place. My parishioners are good people. The times (till very lately), for this last fifteen years, have been extreme bad for the graziers; I got of him, for them, two abatements in their rents, at two several times.

'I will only beg to give you one more instance, that relates to myself, and is not equivocal in its character. I chanced to know him, when I was very young, by means of my neighbourhood to Lord Lexington (whom I never knew), where he oft came; and, without any consideration to party or election interest, he seemed to have entertained an early esteem for me. He had two good livings, on estates he had lately bought; and, without the least intimation or solicitation, he told me I should have the first that fell. He was as good as his word. But this was not all. As soon as I became possessed of the living, he told me that (from what he had been informed by my predecessor, who at his death was going to commence a suit for his just dues) the living was much injured by a low and illegal composition; that he thought I ought to right myself, and he would join with me against the other freeholders; for his estate is something more than one-half of the parish. I replied that, as he had paid all the tithes for his tenants, the greatest loss, in my breaking the composition, would fall upon himself, who must pay one-half as much more as he then did. He said he did not regard that; I was his friend, and it was my due. I answered that, however, I could not do it yet, for that the world would never conceive it to be done with his consent, but would say that I had no sooner got his living than I had quarrelled with him. But when I came to the parish I found them so good a sort of people that I had as little an inclination to fall out with them. So (though to my great injury) I have deferred the matter to this day. Though the thing, in the opinion of Sir R. Raymond, who gave it on the case as drawn up by the parishioners themselves, is clear and indisputable, yet they won't give it up without a lawsuit. In a word, there is nothing I am more convinced of than the innocence of Sir R. S. in the case of the Charitable Corporation, as to any fraud, or connivance at fraud. You, who always follow your judgment, free from prejudice, will do so here. I have discharged my duty of friendship, both to you and him.'

Sir Robert Sutton's name had been used by Pope twice; in the third epistle* of his 'Moral Essays' and in the first Dialogue of 1738; but, on the subsequent representations of Warburton, he was induced to erase it in both places. In the first, the name of Bond, one of the iniquitous Directors, is still left standing:

> Bond damns the poor, and hates them from his heart.

And a subsequent line,

> That any man in want is knave or fool,

expresses, says Pope, the very words of some of those concerned in the Charitable Corporation. To this passage Warburton, when he edited Pope's works, appended the following note:—'The poet had named a very worthy person of condition, who for a course of many years had shined in public stations much to the advantage and honour of his country. But being at once oppressed by

* Ver. 105.

popular prejudice and a public censure, it was no wonder the poet, to whom he was personally a stranger, should think hardly of him. I had the honour to be well known to this truly illustrious person, and to be greatly obliged by him. From my intimate knowledge of his character, I was fully persuaded of his innocence, and that he was unwarily drawn in by a pack of infamous cheats, to his great loss of fortune as well as reputation. At my request, therefore, the poet, with much satisfaction, retracted and struck out, in both places, his ill-grounded censure. I have since had the pleasure to understand, from the best authority, that my favourable sentiments of him have lately been fully justified in the course of some proceedings in the High Court of Chancery, the most unerring investigator of truth and falsehood.'

CHAPTER III.

'ALLIANCE BETWEEN CHURCH AND STATE'—'VELLEIUS PATERCULUS'— SIR THOMAS HANMER.

WARBURTON'S FIRST WORK OF IMPORTANCE, 'THE ALLIANCE BETWEEN CHURCH AND STATE'—SUMMARY OF ITS CONTENTS—BISHOPS HORSLEY AND HARE PLEASED WITH THE BOOK—ITS RECEPTION BY THE PUBLIC—HARE'S DESIRE TO SERVE WARBURTON—WARBURTON'S DESIRE TO EDIT 'VELLEIUS PATERCULUS'—DISSUADED FROM THE UNDERTAKING BY HARE AND MIDDLETON—SPECIMENS OF HIS PROPOSED EMENDATIONS—VISITS SIR THOMAS HANMER ABOUT SHAKSPEARE—DISAGREEMENT BETWEEN THEM.

IN 1736, as has been already observed, eight years after his presentation to Brant-Broughton, Warburton offered to the world his first important work, 'The Alliance between Church and State.' The doctrines advocated in this work it will be our business to examine.

The Puritans had maintained that the Church and the State were two distinct independent societies, and had argued that, in consequence of this independence, the magistrate had no concern with religion. Hooker, in opposition to these notions, had asserted that the Church and the State were but portions of the same society, and had alleged that in every society the State had a natural supremacy over the Church, or a right of control in religious affairs. Hobbes had advanced, in the main, the same opinions on the subject with Hooker, advocating rigorous conformity in the Church to the requirements of the State.* Warburton, agreeing with neither of these persuasions, supposed that the Church and the State,

* Warburton's Works, vol. vii. pp. 64, 84, 218, 221, 8vo.

though, indeed, originally distinct, had voluntarily formed an alliance, on just and reasonable terms, for the sake of mutual advantage; a hypothesis suggested, perhaps, by the French notion of a social contract between governors and those governed.

The dependence of one society on another, argues Warburton, must arise either from the law of nature or the law of nations. Dependency by the law of nature is from essence, or generation; but the Church could not, from essence, or generation, be dependent on the State; for the Church, or association for religious purposes, existed, as is clear from external evidence, before the State had any being.* Whatever attachment or connexion, therefore, exists between the two, must exist under the law of nations, or by civil compact.

But as man, when he submitted to become a member of civil society, necessarily relinquished some of his individual rights, so the Church, when she entered into alliance with the State, acted in a similar manner, by giving up her right of independence, which she transferred to the civil power. But as man received an equivalent for the natural rights which he relinquished in entering into society, so should the Church receive an equivalent for that which she relinquished in entering into alliance with the State.† The equivalent, then, which the Church received, for acknowledging the civil power to be her superior,‡ was, protection in her acts, and support to her authority.

The State, at the same time, was glad to have the assistance of the Church, which, when they formed a union, it expected to exert her influence for the promotion of virtue and good order in the community, and as a support to the civil jurisdiction.

One of the modes in which the State, as the protector

* Warburton's Works, vol. vii. p. 63.

† Ib. p. 248.

‡ Ib. p. 93.

and guardian of the Church, would enable her to exercise her authority in its behalf, would be by conferring on her a portion of coercive power to enjoin the observation of such duties of imperfect obligation — the duties, for instance, of charity, gratitude, hospitality, and others of a similar nature — as civil laws cannot enforce; and such others, also, of perfect obligation, as are violated by the intemperance of the several appetites. Such coercive power a Church does not possess of herself, for though she has the power of excommunication — the only power that a religious society, considered independently, needs — yet this power is not of general influence in regard to the community, but of efficiency only to preserve the purity of her own particular worship.

A great means of bestowing this coercive power on the Church is by conferring a public endowment on its ministers, assigning a fixed share of the national property for their maintenance; thus rendering that religious society, of whose aid the State has so much need, more firm and stable, and destroying that dependency of the clergy on the people which arises from their maintenance by voluntary contribution; a dependency which, in certain conditions of affairs, may be of great injury to the community, by inducing ecclesiastics, in the hope of securing the people's favour, to excite or encourage a spirit of resistance to the civil power, and which must at all times unhappily lessen the dignity and influence of the clergy in the eyes of the whole nation.

Such public maintenance for the clergy may be provided by means of tithes. Tithes, indeed, are not to be considered as prescribed to Christians because they were paid by the Jews; yet the mode of supporting a clergy by tithes may very properly be adopted by Christians, being just as eligible for modern as it was for ancient times.

The dignity of the clergy in the estimation of the people, as well as the interest and convenience of the Church itself, will be promoted by a concession from the State of a place for her superior members in the court of legislature, such as, with us, the bishops' seat in Parliament. This place in the legislature is only what the Church may justly expect; for having, when she formed an alliance with the State, relinquished to the State her independence and individual authority, she may well think it necessary for her superior members to have a voice in the legislature, to prevent that power, which the State now possesses over her, from being perverted to her injury. Had she not such voice, she would be in the position, not of a subject, but of a slave, to the State; and no laws could justly be made in the legislature concerning her, because no free man, or free body of men, can be bound by laws to which they have not given their consent. Nor is it improper that the ecclesiastical members of the legislature, when they are present in it, should give their opinions, like the other members, in regard to civil matters, as they will thus give additional sanction to the laws in the eyes of the people, when they see that the Church has concurred with the State in enacting them.*

But at the time when a State forms its union with a Church, or religious society, of the country, there may exist, in that country, more churches, or religious societies, than one. With which of them, then, will the State form its junction? Assuredly with the strongest, or most numerous, of them, acting thus from motives of policy; for the larger a religious society is, the better able will it be to be serviceable in an alliance, as having the greater number under its influence.† But how will the State act towards the less numerous religious societies? It will allow them toleration, or the free enjoyment of their opinions and forms of worship, yet under such restrictions as will keep them from injuring the religion allied with

* Warburton's Works, vol. vii. pp. 111, 112. † Ib. p. 242.

the State; for if there were no such restrictions laid upon them, the State could not be considered as fully discharging its contract with the Church to which it allies itself.

This alliance between the State and the more numerous religious society will not be indissoluble; for it will naturally subsist only so long as the religious society, thus placed in alliance with the State, maintains its superiority in number over other religious societies. If this superiority is diminished to any perceptible extent, the alliance naturally becomes void; for the allied religious society being no longer able to perform its part in the compact, by influencing the majority of the nation to the observance of morality and good order, the State is at once disengaged from the alliance; and a new alliance may now be formed with such other religious society as has become the most numerous. Thus, formerly, the alliance between the Pagan Church and the empire of Rome was dissolved, and the Christian established in its place; and, of late, the alliance between the Popish Church and the kingdom of England was broken, and another made with the Protestant in its stead.*

One reasonable method of restricting the religious societies, or sects, not in alliance with the State, from injuring that which is allied with it, is the establishment of a test-law, by which the dissenting bodies are excluded from those offices of honour and power in which they might exert influence to the hurt of the allied society. Such a test-law was very judiciously introduced in England, in the reign of Charles II., as a security to the Established Church against the Puritans; a law of which William III., both when he was Prince of Orange, and when he was King of England, acknowledged the necessity. When the Papist James inquired of his son-in-law, with whom he was then on good terms, his opinion as to

* Warburton's Works, vol. vii. p. 244.

entire toleration and the abolition of the test, the stadtholder readily admitted the propriety of toleration, but wholly disapproved of abolishing the test. When the Protestant dissenters, after he became king, desired to know his sentiments on the same points, he manifested the same determination, expressing his willingness to allow full toleration, but concurring with his councillors in refusing to abolish the test.*

As to the maintenance of the clergy in the religious society allied with the State, or, as we call it, the Established Church, the dissenters cannot justly refuse to contribute to it, because the clergy are maintained for the benefit of the State in general, not for the support of any particular religious opinions, whether at variance with those of the dissenters or not.

Nor ought dissenters to complain that they are excluded from places of honour and profit, or to assert that such exclusion, for matters of opinion, is any violation of their civil rights; for, if they will rightly consider the subject, they will see the places of honour and profit, which are in the hands of the civil power, are not lodged there as a trust, which may be claimed by all subjects, and equally shared among them, but are of the nature of prerogative, of which the civil power may dispose at pleasure, without being further accountable to the public than that the offices be filled by efficient persons, among whose qualifications will necessarily be numbered a favourable disposition to the established religion; and also that, however objectionable dissenters may think it to exclude persons from office for opinions, it is, in this case, entirely justifiable, for when opinions affect the peace of society they necessarily come within the jurisdiction of the civil power, and the peace of society is directly and necessarily affected by those opinions which a test-law makes matter

* Warburton's Works, vol. vii. pp. 251, 296.

of disqualification.* Thus the English Papist, who owns a foreign ecclesiastical power superior to all temporal dominion, the German Anabaptist, who holds capital punishment to be sinful, and the Quaker, who believes defensive war to be unchristian, are justly debarred from civil offices, as they propagate opinions inimical to the peace of the community and the stability of the government.

Such are the doctrines which Warburton advanced in his 'Alliance between Church and State,' and which, though many of them bear but little on the state of things with us in the present day, are yet worthy of attention with regard to the connexion of religion and government in general.

Before we dismiss the book, let us notice a few observations which he throws out in the course of discussing his subject.

An established church, or religious society in alliance with the government, is necessary in a state, not only on other accounts, but also for reducing men's belief into one common formulary, and making the profession of that formulary the condition of community or entire citizenship, that so there may be a summary of belief in aid of the ignorant, and a common repository that men may consult for information; and in settling this summary of belief it is to be remembered that the wider the basis of it is made, and the more general are the conditions of communion, consistently with the well-being of the society, the more wise and just will the religious institution be. As to the necessity of some religious connexion, even the Quakers themselves, who profess aversion to everything resembling a church or church-policy, have, by the act of uniting, under Penn and Barclay's arguments, into a community or corporation, borne the strongest testimony to it.†

Courts ecclesiastical can be erected only by permission

* Warburton's Works, vol. vii. pp. 253, 254. † Ib. pp. 59, 61.

of the State, and are to take cognizance only of such matters and causes as do not properly fall under civil jurisdiction; such, for instance, as concern merely the promotion of religion and good morals. But care must be taken that the ecclesiastical courts, in those matters which are permitted to their determination, do not usurp more power than is freely granted them. A proof of the necessity of such care is shown in the mode in which the clergy acted with regard to marriage. Marriage is but a civil compact, but, in order to render it more respected, the solemnisation of it was assigned to the clergy, a regulation in which there was nothing objectionable; but, by degrees, the clergy proceeded to censurable usurpations, for they not only took occasion to draw into the jurisdiction of the Church all civil matters arising from the matrimonial compact, but, though the voice of nature and of Scripture declared that divorce was in some cases allowable, yet, on the pretence that marriage was a sacrament, they pronounced the marriage contract, when not void *ab initio*, to be indissoluble.*

The superior courts must always be the civil, and appeals must be allowable to them from the ecclesiastical, otherwise the ecclesiastical courts would form an *imperium in imperio*, and might erect themselves into tyrannies. And, though the magistrate does not confer the ecclesiastical character (for, if he were to confer it, the Church would be, not allied, but incorporated with the State), yet no ecclesiastic is to be allowed to exercise his functions without the magistrate's approbation and licence.† Nor can the Church, as a body, enter into any business, even in the convocations which they may hold, without express permission from the civil power.

The proper alliance between Church and State is shown in the greatest perfection, says Warburton, in England,

* Warburton's Works, vol. vii. p. 149. † Ib. pp. 152, 154.

which possesses the most perfect of all religious establishments;* and, with regard to what he has said in his book concerning such an alliance, he thus proudly expresses himself:—'*O magna vis veritatis, quæ contra hominum ingenia, calliditatem, solertiam, contraque fictas omnium insidias, facile se, per seipsam, defendat!* Thus breaks out the illustrious Roman, transported by a fit of philosophical enthusiasm. This force of truth never shone with greater lustre than on the present occasion; where, by the assistance of a few plain and simple principles, taken from the nature of man and the ends of political society, we have cleared up a chaos of controversy, proved the justice and necessity of an *alliance between Church and State*, deduced the mutual conditions on which it was formed, and shown them to have an amazing agreement with our own happy establishment.'†

In writing to his friend Stukeley, in 1735, when he was preparing the book for the press, he calls the subject of it 'a ticklish subject,' adding,

——— res antiquæ laudis et artis
Ingredior, sanctos *ausus* recludere fontes.‡

He, doubtless, rejoiced greatly that his daring had produced so goodly a volume. Stukeley had a copy of it with some manuscript additions, but of no particular importance.§

Bishop Horsley was delighted with the book, and said that Warburton 'had shown the general good policy of an establishment, and the necessity of a test for its security, upon principles which Republicans themselves cannot easily deny,' observing that the work, as to argument, was 'one of the finest specimens that are to be found, perhaps, in any language of scientific reasoning applied to a political subject.'‖ By scientific reasoning,

* Warburton's Works, vol. vii. p. 165. † Ib. p. 240.
‡ Nichols's Lit. Illustr., vol. ii. p. 33. § Ib. pp. 35—37.
‖ Review of the Case of the Protestant Dissenters, Pref.

Horsley meant close and cogent reasoning, such as ought to be used on any subject to which reasoning is applied, whether of a scientific character or of any other.

Hare, to whom Warburton sent a copy, replied thus:—'I had formerly been very agreeably entertained with some emendations of yours on Shakspeare, and was extremely pleased to find this work was by the same hand. Good learning, great acuteness, an ingenious working head, and depth of thought, will always please in an author, though we are not entirely in the same ways of thinking. . . You have not, sir, only my thanks for what you have done, but my sincere wishes that what was intended for the use of the public may prove also to be for your own, to which my endeavours, in any proper way, shall not be wanting.'

'This,' says Hurd, with great justice, 'was candid and generous, considering that that eminent person was not altogether in the author's sentiments on the subject of his book. But he was struck with his great abilities, and became from that moment his sincere friend.'

'The truth is,' adds the same writer, 'that no sort of men, either within or without the Church, was prepared, at that time, for an indifferent reception of this new theory, which respected none of their prejudices. It was neither calculated to please the High Church divines, nor the Low; and the Laity had taken their side with the one or other of those parties.

'However, though few at that time were convinced, all were struck by this essay of an original writer, and could not dissemble their admiration of the ability which appeared in the construction of it. There was, indeed, a reach of thought in this system of church-policy, which would prevent its making its way all at once. It required time and attention, even in the most capable of its readers, to apprehend the force of the argumentation.'

In subsequent editions Warburton continued to enlarge and improve the work, and, profiting by some attempts of his adversaries to overturn its positions and deductions, endeavoured to leave it in such a condition as to be impregnable to critical assaults.

Whitaker, reviewing Hurd's edition of Warburton in 1812, when, as he said, 'in the demand for equal and universal power, all remains of decency were lost on the one hand, and all prudential regards for the great securities of the constitution were in danger of being swallowed up in a timid and helpless acquiescence on the other,' thought that 'a republication and industrious circulation of "The Alliance" might even yet have a powerful effect on the minds of all who had not ceased either to reason for themselves or to feel for their country.'*

Bishop Hare, to his praise, did not forget his intimation that he should be ready to serve Warburton, but, when 'The Alliance' came to be talked of at court, sought to avail himself of an opportunity to introduce him to the Queen. Her Majesty chanced one day, in the autumn of the year 1737, to ask the Bishop if he could recommend her a person of learning and ability, to be about her, and to entertain her, at times, with reading and conversation; when the Bishop named the author of 'The Alliance between Church and State.' The recommendation was graciously received, and the Bishop was expecting every day to hear the favourable result of it, when the Queen was suddenly seized with an illness, which carried her off in the month of November.

Warburton was meditating, at this time, an edition of 'Velleius Paterculus,' and sent Des Maizeaux, with whom he had become intimate, a plan and specimen of the work to be inserted in the 'Bibliothèque Britannique, ou His-

* Quart. Rev., vol. vii. p. 402.

toire des Ouvrages des Savans de la Grande Bretagne,' printed at the Hague, where the communication appeared in the months of July, August, and September 1736, occupying about forty pages. It was addressed to Bishop Hare, under the designation F.E.C., Francisco Episcopo Cicestrensi, to whom, as soon as it came forth, he sent a copy. Hare returned a courteous answer, but conveying admonitory hints, at which Warburton must have winced:

'Dear Sir,—I have this day received the favour of yours of the 13th, with the kind present that attended it, for which I give you many thanks.

'You do me a great deal too much honour in inscribing your remarks on Paterculus to me in the manner you have done. As I have not the book by me, I am not so capable of judging of the truth of the emendations, but, upon a slight view, see they are, many of them, very ingenious, as all your things are, and seem to arise out of the context, which is the best evidence there can be of the truth of them. I wish your printers had done you more justice. There are a great many typographical faults, and I think some that must be imputed to the haste of the editor, who seems to have attended more to the matter than to his expression. Some of your emendations put me in mind of what I remember to have heard a very ill-natured, but a very able critic, observe of Tanaquil Faber—that he could see a fault very well, but did not always know how to mend. It will, I presume, by nobody be thought strange if that should be the case in some of your conjectures, when it is but an essay, or specimen, not an edition, you give to the world. But as that is what you have done, I think so ingenious a man, who knows how easy it is to be mistaken in these matters, should generally express himself with a seeming diffidence.

'You will forgive this liberty in one who is, with great esteem, Dear Sir,

'Your most faithful friend and humble servant,

'Fr. Cicest.*

'The Vache, near Gerrard's Cross, Bucks,
'Nov. 18, 1736.'

Under these strictures, Warburton could not rest in silence, but addressed to the Bishop, in a letter which has not been preserved, something in justification of his critical attempts, mingled with many flattering compliments to his lordship. Hare replied with much good sense, but with less of cordiality than he had shown in his former epistle:

'Vache, Dec. 4, 1736.

'Sir,—I have the favour of yours of the 26th, which I scarce know how to thank you for. You are by much an overmatch for a plain man; and, if I did not think you a very good-natured man, and of a disposition extremely obliging, I should suspect you thought me a very weak one, to think myself entitled in any degree to all the fine things you are pleased to say. In earnest, I must desire you would drop all ceremony in your correspondence with me. A man that can write so well should not employ his pen in things so unnecessary as compliments.

'You extend my hint about Tan. Faber much farther than I intended it; nothing was farther from my thoughts than to make the application general. I know you can and have made very fine emendations; but sometimes the ablest critic, who is sure he sees a fault, may, for want of proper help, not be able to mend it with any degree of certainty. He may restore the sense when he cannot restore the words; and, for that reason, all emendations, though by the same hand, are not to be put upon a level,

* Kilvert's Selections from Warburton's Papers, p. 95.

and consequently should not, in my opinion, be given with the same air of assurance. As I could not think all your emendations upon Paterculus equally true, I think the speaking of them in the same manner, instead of giving weight or credit to bad or doubtful ones, does really detract from good ones; because many a reader, who cannot make an emendation for himself, may yet be so far a tolerable judge as to find sufficient reason to dislike where he should dislike in one or two instances; and if he finds them proposed with a show of certainty, he will suspect the truth of others where he is not so able to judge; and, in truth, I have always found in fact, that nothing hurts critics, and the art of criticism, so much in the esteem of the generality of readers, next to the ill treatment of one another, as the airs of assurance they are so apt to assume to themselves. The ground of criticism is, indeed, in my opinion, nothing else but distinct attention, which every reader should endeavour to be master of. Where there is in nature this ground-work, every man will be a critic in proportion to the compass of his learning in general, and upon each author in proportion to the particular application with which he has made the book familiar to him. But I am talking to one who has joined to a naturally clear attention, and just application, a happy genius and a fine imagination, which I wish, for the good of learning, you may very long enjoy; and am,

'Sir, your very faithful friend and servant,

'FR. CICEST.'*

Whether Warburton made any reply to this letter is unknown; but the good feeling of the Bishop towards him still continued.

To Conyers Middleton, also, he sent a copy of the notes on Paterculus. Middleton replied as follows:

* Kilvert's Selections from Warburton's Papers, p. 97.

'I had before seen the force of your critical genius very successfully employed on Shakspeare, but did not know you had ever tried it on the Latin authors. I am pleased with several of your emendations, and transcribed them into the margin of my edition, though not equally with them all. It is a laudable and liberal amusement to try now and then in our reading the success of a conjecture; but, in the present state of the generality of the old writers, it can hardly be thought a study fit to employ a life upon; at least not worthy, I am sure, of your talents and industry, which, instead of trifling on words, seem calculated rather to correct the opinions and manners of the world.'

The truth doubtless was, that both Hare and Middleton saw very well that Warburton was not likely to do himself much credit by emendatory criticism. His alterations in the text of Paterculus are of a similar character with those which he made in the text of Shakspeare, and of which both Conyers and the Bishop, perhaps from civility, and unwillingness to be too severe, spoke with more favour than most other readers have thought they deserved. Two specimens of his corrections he sent, seven years before, in a letter to Dr. Stukeley.* In the fourth chapter of the first book, Paterculus says, *Cumas in Italiâ condiderunt* [Chalcidenses]. *Pars horum civium magno post intervallo Neapolim condidit. Utriusque urbis semper eximia in Romanos fides. Sed aliis diligentior ritus patrii mansit custodia. Cumanos Osca mutavit vicinia.* 'Now, I dare say,' said Warburton to Stukeley, 'the word *aliis* sticks at first sight pretty much with you, for you observe this is all the way a conjoint account of the two cities, but in this part of the sentence it is dropped, and very impertinently said *others* preserved their country rites more diligently; which, certainly, so fine a writer could

* Nichols's Lit. Illustr., vol. ii. p. 7.

not be guilty of. I read, therefore, *Sed Neapolis diligentior ritus patrii mansit;* which makes it a pertinent observation, and worthy the notice of an exact historian. And it is not difficult to conceive Neapolis being corrupted to *aliis* by a stupid copier.' It may, perhaps, be doubted whether he meant *Neapolis* for *Neapolitanis*, or for the genitive case of *Neapolis*. The first seems rather to have been his meaning; both are equally absurd. Ruhnken, more wisely than Warburton, thought of reading *illis*; but Jani and Krause, the editors of the best edition, who, by-the-bye, seem never to have heard of Warburton's attempts, for they make no mention of them in their Prolegomena, very properly consider *aliis* to be for *alteris*, an interchange easily supportable by example.

The other alteration is that of *consors* into *consocer*, which is needless.

The emendations sent to the 'Bibliothèque Britannique' are thus entitled: 'Gulielmi Warburton, A.M., in C. Velleii Paterculi Historias Emendationes. Ad amplissimum virum, Theologorum literatissimum, Criticorum scientissimum, F.E.C.;' and are prefaced with some Warburtonian remarks on the Philosophers, bearing very little relation to Paterculus:—

'Communis humanitatis scientia, quæ unica sapienti convenit, ex *historicis*, quemadmodum communis tantùm dementiæ, *philosophis* discitur ab antiquis. *Hic* enim nihil nisi materiam in rerum naturâ, *ille* ne vel hilum hujus esse contendit. *Hic* materiæ portiones quasdam facultate cogitationis dotatas esse opinatur; *ille* etiam incorporales, mente carentes, excogitat actores. *Unus* propriâ de existentiâ dubitat; *alter* vel sensuum denunciationes omni erroris admistione liberatas, puras et integras semper manere, confidit. *Hic* insanus supra Deos *sapientem* suum collocat; *ille* impurus infra bestias *felicem* deturbat. *Fatuus quidam* fabas serere reformidat; *impudens alius* homines, quâcunque ingreditur viâ, serere licitum esse clamat. Usque tamen, ut ingenuè fateamur, *Historia* ipsa cognatam sibi semper servat virilem dignitatem. Veruntamen si forte *in hac pagellâ* secans cotem novacula mentem hebetet, *proximâ* vis virtutis, dum imprimit se, et quasi signat gentis barbaræ ac ferocis in animis vel suam speciem, mirificè nos afficit voluptate. Si *in hoc loco* sanguinis infernus imber perfundat nos horrore, cœlesti priscæ eloquentiæ rore *derepente* recreamur. *Hic*, si bos obscœnè vociferet, *illic* Romæ Athenarumque Genii Oracula divino afflatu fundentes audiuntur. Fragmenta veterum historicorum quantivis igitur pretii sunt æstimanda. Sanè etiam inter hæc seculi felicioris ornamenta haud infimum locum tenet Caius Velleius Paterculus. Cujus historici vis ingenii, quæ quidem summa fuit, non fugit quenquam in literis antiquis mediocriter versatum. Ob hanc, quæ in describendis, certis signis, hominum naturis, elucet maximè, illorum Scriptorum, per quos Imperii res Romani in compendia sunt redactæ, meritò Principis nomine dignatus est.'

He then laments, that of all the manuscripts of Paterculus, one only remains; and, in proof of the faultiness of the printed text, quotes Bentley 'In Tractatu eximio contra neotericos quosdam pseudo-parrhesiastas:' 'The faults of the scribes are found so numerous, and the defects beyond all redress, that, notwithstanding the pains of the learnedest and acutest critics, for two whole centuries, the work is still, and like to continue, a mere heap of errors.' His first alteration is that of *malo suo* * to *in aulâ suâ*, and the second that of *tum regem* (or *rex*) *Syriæ*† to *iterum rediens è Syriâ*, both daring enough; for if Warburton had gained scholarship enough in his early years to become fairly a critic on the classics, he would have outdone the most audacious in audacity. The next attempt is better: *neque imitanda* (or *imitandam*)‡ into *neque emendandam*, which was approved by

* I. 6. † I. 10. ‡ I. 17.

the able Ruhnken. But the reason for the change is given in most unhappy Latin. Paterculus is speaking of the old and new comedy: 'Prisca comœdia adumbratio tantum erat, sive primum comici operis lineamentum, quod Nova perficere contendit atque absolvere. Quum igitur de quodam comœdiæ genere, ut prioris reformatione et emendatione, commemorare author instituisset, suum erat docere lectorem an Novæ Comicæ artifices ad summum adduxerant eam, an opus erat profectu ulteriori.' *Suum*, and the indicatives *adduxerant* and *erat*, are sad solecisms. The next attempt seems to show that he did not see the construction, for he alters *et init alia*, a manifest corruption, into *et enitentes alias*, sc. *urbes*, where the sense requires the nominative; the later editors read, *item ut aliæ*. The two following, *quippe — huc* * into *quæ pœnam — hunc*, and *sensibus celebrem* † into *sensibus celerem*, are two of his best. But another, the change of *pecuniæ expellebatur cupidine* ‡ into *pecuniæ* pellicebatur *cupidine*, is very unfortunate; it might be thought a misprint, if he did not add, in explanation, 'Quem — regis artes ad *pellicendum* non valebant, pecuniæ cupido *pellicebat*;' for though *pelliceo*, as the grammarians tell us, was used for *pellicio*, it was assuredly found only in writers much older than Velleius Paterculus. The other attempts at emendation are but of little importance; but let us extract one more: Paterculus speaks of Cæsar, preparing to invade Britain, as *alterum pene imperio nostro ac suo quærens orbem;* Warburton turns *ac suo* into *accisum*, which, he says, is very applicable to an island, for *ad* in composition has the same force as the Greek ἀμφί; so that *accisi* (Britanni) means *undique cæsi*, or ἀμφικοποί.

Hurd says that Warburton was prompted to undertake a commentary on Paterculus by being charmed with the

* II. 1. † II. 9. ‡ II. 33.

elegance of his style; but, to say the truth, Paterculus's style has little elegance, though it has some resemblance to Warburton's own style in a certain portion of dashing animation, with no lack of parentheses. The Bishop is more fortunate in another remark, that the high estimation in which emendatory criticism was held, at the time when Warburton began to look about him in the literary world, naturally tempted a young man of enterprise to make some effort for distinction in that department of scholarship. He was prepared to adopt the usual critical pretext of condemning whatever he wished to alter as having been corrupted by 'a stupid copier.'

In May, this year, he visited Sir Thomas Hanmer, at his seat at Mildenhall, in Suffolk, on an invitation in reference to Sir Thomas's projected edition of Shakspeare. The acquaintance between them had been sought, as Hanmer affirmed, by Warburton, but, as Warburton asserted after Hanmer's death, by Sir Thomas, who had made advances to him through Sherlock, then Bishop of Salisbury. Their intercourse, however, which was very friendly at first, soon became disturbed with the suspicions of rivalry, and ended in estrangement and a violent quarrel. Which of the two was the more to blame in the disruption, we may defer examining till a subsequent part of our narrative, when we shall have to speak of Warburton's edition of Shakspeare.

CHAPTER IV.

'THE DIVINE LEGATION.'—LOWTH.

'THE DIVINE LEGATION OF MOSES' PROJECTED — ITS OBJECT — WARBURTON'S REASONING — HIS PROPOSITION THAT THE DOCTRINE OF A FUTURE STATE WAS NOT TAUGHT BY THE JEWS — OPINIONS OF GROTIUS, EPISCOPIUS, AND BISHOP BULL — WARBURTON'S NOTIONS OF THE BOOK OF JOB; SUPPOSES THAT IT WAS WRITTEN BY EZRA — HIS ARGUMENTS IN SUPPORT OF THIS HYPOTHESIS — HIS INTERPRETATION OF THE TEXT, 'I KNOW THAT MY REDEEMER LIVETH' — LOWTH'S OPPOSITION TO WARBURTON'S ASSERTION, THAT EZRA WAS THE AUTHOR OF THE BOOK OF JOB — STYLE OF EZRA — JOB PROBABLY AN IDUMÆAN — THE AUTHOR OF THE BOOK OF JOB PROBABLY A JEW.

'THE Alliance between Church and State' was a considerable effort, but it was nothing to what Warburton designed to accomplish, and had, indeed, already begun. At the end of 'The Alliance' he announced his intention to publish a work, to be entitled 'The Divine Legation of Moses demonstrated, on the Principles of a Religious Theist, from the Omission of the Doctrine of a Future State in the Jewish Dispensation.'

It had been argued by those whom Warburton delighted to call Freethinkers, that the absence of the doctrine of a future state of rewards and punishments from the religious system of Moses was a decisive proof that he was an impostor, since it was incredible that any institution of religion coming from the *Father of Lights*, should fail to support the belief in an existence after death, such belief being absolutely necessary, as well to any scheme of efficient government, as to the maintenance of any influential religious system.

What the Freethinkers asserted as an argument against the Divine original of the Jewish religion, and, consequently, against that of the Christian religion, which is founded on it, Warburton accepted as an evidence of the Divine original of the one as well as of the other, and undertook to show, first of all, that, since the Jewish religion and polity had no sanctions of a future state to support them, they must have been under the immediate protection of Heaven, or have been upheld by means of a special and extraordinary providence.

His demonstration of this position he promised to leave very little short of mathematical certainty, requiring only the following postulatum to be granted him, which he considered that all would allow to be reasonable :

'That a skilful lawgiver, establishing a religion and civil policy, acts with certain views and for certain ends, and not capriciously, or without purpose or design.'

This being granted, his proof was to be erected on three very clear and simple propositions :

1. 'That to inculcate the doctrine of a future state of rewards and punishments is necessary to the well-being of civil society :

2. 'That all mankind, especially the most wise and learned nations of antiquity, have concurred in believing and teaching that this doctrine was of such use to civil society :

3. 'That the doctrine of a future state of rewards and punishments is not to be found in, nor did make part of, the Mosaic dispensation.'

'Propositions so clear and evident,' he says, 'that, one would think, we might directly proceed to our conclusion :

'That therefore the law of Moses is of Divine original.'

The first two of these propositions might very well, it may be thought, have been condensed into one. But the conclusion that the law of Moses was of Divine origin, was to be evinced by one or both of the two following syllogisms:

'Whatsoever religion and society have no future state for their support must be supported by an extraordinary providence:

'The Jewish religion and society had no future state for their support:

'Therefore the Jewish religion and society were supported by an extraordinary providence.'

And again:

'The ancient lawgivers universally believed that such a religion could be supported only by an extraordinary providence:

'Moses, an ancient lawgiver, versed in all the wisdom of Egypt, purposely instituted such a religion:

'Therefore, Moses believed his religion was supported by an extraordinary providence.'

One great point in this demonstration was to prove that the doctrine of a future state of rewards and punishments was certainly not to be found in anything, whether of a civil or religious nature, that Moses taught the Jews; and, though Warburton does not enter formally on the proof of this point till he reaches his sixth book, yet, in taking a review of his work, it may, perhaps, be most satisfactory to look to this particular first, and to examine how he treats those texts of Scripture which were, and by many still are, thought to show that Moses believed and taught the doctrine of an existence after death. If Warburton be right on this head, let him be acknowledged to be right; if he be in the wrong, let it be shown in what respects his argumentation is unsound. But, whether he be in the right, or whether he be in error, let us see how he orders his cause; for even those who think but little of the question as a matter of theology, may like to see how the author discusses it.

Not only Freethinkers, or unbelievers in the divinity of

the mission of Moses, but some, also, among the assertors and demonstrators of its Divine authority, had affirmed or admitted that the doctrine of a future state was not to be found in his legal or religious teaching. Among these were Grotius, Episcopius or Bisschop, the Dutch theologian, and our own Bishop Bull.

'Moses,' says Grotius, 'in his institution of the Jewish religion, promised, if we look to the express provisions of his law, nothing beyond the blessings of the present life, a fertile land, abundance of food, victory over enemies, a long and vigorous old age, and a surviving offspring of good character and promise. Certainly, if there be anything beyond these specifications, it is enveloped in obscurity, and can be discovered only by searching and laborious inquiry.'

'In the whole of the Mosaic law,' observes Episcopius, 'there is no reward of eternal life promised, nor is there even any mention or intimation of an everlasting reward, whatever the Jews may now say of a world to come, of the resurrection of the dead, and of eternal life; and however they may strive to wrest, rather than to demonstrate those doctrines, from the words of the law of Moses, lest they should be obliged to acknowledge that law to be imperfect, as did the Sadducees, who, though they were Jews, yet certainly affirmed in old times, and, as I learn from the writings of the Rabbis, continue to affirm at present, that life in a future state is neither promised nor signified in the law of Moses, declaring that the notion or belief of an existence after death had been disseminated only through the cabala, or tradition, which they altogether rejected. Indeed, the discrepancy of opinions among the Jews regarding life in a world to come proves whatever promises were made in the law to have been of such a nature that nothing certain concerning a future state can be deduced from them. This even our Saviour plainly intimates, when he signifies the resurrection of the dead, in the twenty-second chapter of St. Matthew, not from any promise attached to the law, but only from that general promise of God by which he had engaged to be the God of Abraham, Isaac, and Jacob; which inference rests, however, rather on the knowledge of the Divine intention, concealed or comprehended under that general expression (of which intention Christ was fully aware), rather than on any necessary consequence, or on any evident force or meaning of the words, such as now appears in the words of the New Testament, when eternal life and the resurrection of the dead constitute the Alpha and Omega of the Christian religion, and are promised so clearly and expressly that no one can raise a question about it.'*

Bishop Bull's words are as follow:—'It is inquired whether no promise at all of eternal life is to be found in the Old Testament; for some entertain doubts on the subject. To this question Augustine seems to me to reply very well, distinguishing the senses in which the term Old Testament is to be understood; for he observes that we may understand by it, either that covenant which was made on Mount Sinai, or everything that is contained in the books of Moses, the Hagiographa, and the Prophets. If the word Old Testament is taken in the latter sense, it may perhaps be admitted that there are in it some intimations, not altogether obscure, of a future state of existence, especially in the Books of Psalms, Daniel, and Ezekiel; although even in these we shall find it very difficult to discover a clear and express promise of eternal life. But these intimations, such as they are, were only preludes and anticipations of the grace of the Gospel, and had no bearing on the Law; for the promises of the Law had regard to things on the earth, and on the earth only. If any one declares himself of a contrary opinion, it will be

* Instit. Theol. iii. 1, 2.

his business to point out a passage in which a promise of eternal life is given; and to do this is certainly impossible.—Yet that under these words [of the law] was comprehended eternal life by the purpose of God, is manifest from the interpretation of Christ himself and his Apostles. But this will not enable us to say that eternal life was promised in the Mosaic covenant; for promises, in connexion with a covenant, ought to be clear and express, so that they may be distinctly understood by each of the contracting parties. But these typical and general promises, unattended with any extrinsic interpretation, it is almost impossible for any one to understand in that sense.' *

What believers or unbelievers had asserted or conjectured on this subject, Warburton undertook to prove to the conviction of all men. All the texts in the Old Testament that seemed to indicate a knowledge of a future state as a popular article of belief among the Jews, were to be demonstrated incapable of bearing that sense. The explanation in the Book of Job, 'I know that my Redeemer liveth, and that he shall stand in the latter day upon the earth,' a text which has been constantly quoted as evidence not only that the Jews looked forward to a future state, but had an anticipation of the resurrection of the body and of the redemption of mankind, was to be the first brought under examination; partly because of the supposed strength of the text itself, and partly because of the supposed antiquity of the book that contains it; a book which some have thought to be the work of Moses himself, and some that of a writer who lived before Moses' time.

As to the age of the book, Warburton, in opposition to all those who pronounce it as early as the days of Moses, or earlier, boldly asserted that it was written some time

* Bull's Harmon. Apostol. Dissert. ii. c. x. § 8. Op. Om. p. 474, ed. 1721.

between the return of the Jews from captivity, and their thorough settlement in their own country, at the time when the extraordinary providence, which, as he says, had supported and protected the Jews, during the legal dispensation, was beginning to fail, as is seen in the circumstances of Ezra, who, when returning with Artaxerxes' commission, was ashamed to ask the king for a guard against enemies, because he had told him that special protection would be afforded him by the Almighty; but in this expectation he was deceived; and the long persecutions which he and his followers experienced from their idolatrous neighbours taught them how different was their condition from that of their forefathers. The assertions that there are no allusions in this book to the Jews, at least to the state of the Jews under the Mosaic dispensation, Warburton sets utterly at nought; affirming that the character of Job himself is but a representation of the Jewish people, and that many things which are said of Job are but descriptive of the condition of the Jewish people at the time of Moses, and in subsequent days. Thus, when Satan says, '*Hast thou not made a hedge about him?*' this is an allusion to the state of the Israelites as a selected nation. When Job says, '*I shall sleep in the dust, and thou shalt seek me in the morning, but I shall not be,*' the ill fortunes of the Jews on their return from captivity are signified, and they are to be understood as complaining that God seemed to have left them to destruction. Job, in his prosperity, signifies the Israelites under the care of an extraordinary providence; in his affliction, the Israelites, when the extraordinary providence was withdrawing from them. When Job speaks of troops coming against him, and of his brethren being put from him, the Jews are to be conceived as exclaiming against the Ammonites and Ashdodites, and against their richer brethren, who had pusillanimously remained in Babylon. When the Lord answers Job out of the whirlwind, and says, '*Who is he that darkeneth counsel by words without knowledge?*' the prophets are to be imagined as rebuking the people of Israel, and accusing them of *wearying the Lord with words without manifesting obedience.* Job's wife, who speaks as a fool and a Pagan, is the representative of the idolatrous women with whom Ezra rebuked his followers for having formed connexions. Job's three friends, Eliphaz, Bildad, and Zophar, who come professedly to comfort, but in reality exasperate him, are Sanballat the Horonite, Tobiah the servant of the Ammonite, and Geshem the Arabian, who offered to join in building the temple with Ezra and his party, but, finding their advances ill received, became the greatest opponents of the building. Elihu, the son of Barachel the Buzite, whose *spirit constrained him to speak*, was the writer of the Book of Job himself, appearing in the character of a true prophet, refusing to *accept any man's person*, or *to give flattering titles to men;* and Job's forbearance to answer Elihu represents the repentance of the Jews on the preaching of the prophets Haggai, Zechariah, and Malachi. Satan's attempts, too, on Job, it should be observed, signify the attacks which Satan, according to the prophet Zechariah, made about this time on the Jewish people. Job's silent acquiescence, under the admonitions of the Divinity, is an admonition to the nation of obedience and submission under the ordinary dispensations of Providence; and God's giving Job *twice as much as he had before* is the fulfilment of the prophecy to the Jews in the Book of Zechariah, '*I will render double unto thee.*'

It seemed proper to notice this interpretation of the Book of Job thus at length, because it is an illustration of the mode in which Warburton could find or make resemblances to suit his purposes. The Book of Job he concludes to be a work of imagination, written to illustrate the Jewish history, though, doubtless, Job himself had a real existence. In inquiring into the authorship of it, he considers, with Locke,* that it is sufficiently proved that the writer was a Jew, by Job's saying that *idolatry was an iniquity to be punished by the judge;* a sentiment that could have proceeded from none but a Jew, and must have been expressed after the giving of the law. He conceives, also, contrary to the common opinion, that there are many allusions in the Book to the state of the Jews, and occurrences among them, under the rule of Moses and the times that succeeded it; for example, the passage, *God divideth the sea with His might, and by His understanding he smiteth through the proud*, refers to the destruction of Pharaoh and his host; the words, *He commandeth the sun, and it riseth not, and sealeth up the stars*, alludes to the Egyptian darkness and the arrest of the sun's course under Joshua; and *his flesh shall be fresher than a child's*, has regard to the recovery of Hezekiah by the *laying of a lump of figs on the boil.* And having thus settled that it was written by a Jew, and with allusions to the Jewish history, he supposes the reader will concur with him in judging that the writer could hardly have been other than Ezra, who *was a ready scribe in the Law of Moses*, who settled the canon, and made a correct edition of the Scriptures, and who 'is reasonably supposed to be the author of the Books of Chronicles and Esther.'

The inquiry about the Book and its writer is but preparatory to the decision on the true interpretation of the words, *I know that my Redeemer liveth, and that He shall stand at the latter day upon the earth; and though, after my skin, worms destroy this body, yet in my flesh shall I see God; whom I shall see for myself, and mine eyes shall behold, and not another.* That they are to be understood, not of a resurrection from the dead, but of a temporal deliverance from afflictions, Warburton of course asserts without scruple: first, because to interpret them of a resurrection

* Third Letter for Toleration.

from the dead would be repugnant to the whole tenor of the argument running through the speeches of Job and his friends, and to interpret them of a temporal deliverance is perfectly agreeable to it; secondly, because the design of the Book, on Warburton's explanation, absolutely requires a reference to a temporal deliverance; and thirdly, because a spiritual sense of the words is contrary to Job's express declarations in other places, when he says that *there is hope of a tree, if it be cast down, that it may sprout again*, but that there is *no hope of a revivification of man*, and that *he that goeth down to the grave shall come up no more.* Had the doctrine of a resurrection from death to a state of bliss been urged by Job, the question in dispute, respecting the unhappiness of good men upon the earth, would, if Job's friends deemed the doctrine true, have been decided at once; or, if they deemed it false, it would have been their business to confute it; but they do neither; they neither argue against it, nor allow it to be decisive. Zophar, who speaks after Job, takes no notice of any new matter having been introduced into the discussion, but answers, if we suppose a resurrection from the dead to be meant, wide of the purpose; nor does Elihu, as moderator in the dispute, nor the Divinity, as the great Decider of it, make the least allusion to the doctrine of a resurrection, though an enforcement of the doctrine would have dispelled all difficulties.

The true sense of the passage, therefore, according to Warburton, is such as is given in a recent English paraphrase of Job's speech: 'I believe that God lives to vindicate me, and that He will hereafter justify me to my fellow-men. And, though my flesh be wasted, yet, ere I am utterly consumed, I shall find Him become my Supporter. I shall experience His protection myself, and not merely hear of it as felt by others; and my body, though weak, shall from Him receive strength.'

Those who affirm that the text is to be understood of a

resurrection from the dead, and who, at the same time, attribute the authorship of the Book to Moses, must, it has been pertinently observed,* satisfactorily answer the question why Moses, who here speaks so plainly and literally of a resurrection, spoke so obscurely of it in the Pentateuch, where, if it is indicated at all, it is indicated only under the cloud of types and figures.

In addition, it is remarked by Warburton, that resurrection from the dead, or life after death, is noticed by the prophets and other writers in the Scriptures, only to signify what is most unlikely to come to pass. Thus, in the Psalms, it is said, '*Wilt thou show wonders to the dead? Shall the dead arise and praise thee?* And when Ezekiel was shown, in a vision, the valley of dry bones, and was asked, *Can these dry bones live?* he does not answer as one who had been brought up in the belief or knowledge of a resurrection, but speaks as one surprised at the question, and to whom the thought of a return to life was strange, uttering only the words, *O Lord God, thou knowest.*

But let it be observed, that Warburton's hypothesis concerning the time at which the Book of Job was written, and his ascription of it to Ezra, have found favour in the estimation of few. His pretended allusions in it to the condition and history of the Jews are universally regarded as forced and fanciful; and nobody has concurred in the opinion that any one of Job's friends represented Tobiah or Sanballat. In attributing the work to Ezra, he forgot to consider one particular, which, however, as he was far from being qualified to judge of it, may be thought to have escaped him not unnaturally. He forgot to attend to the style, which is quite sufficient to exclude Ezra from having had any share in the composition of it. This omission gave Lowth, when he and Warburton came to strife, opportunity for some very sarcastic remarks, indicating

* Towne's 'Argument of the Div. Legat. fairly stated,' p. 134.

that, though Warburton called himself the only commentator that had rendered the Book of Job intelligible, he had never qualified himself for comment on it by reading the work in the original. When Warburton, at length, found himself obliged to say something about the style, he brought himself into a worse condition than that in which he had placed himself by his silence. He made assertions utterly inconsistent one with another; he affirmed that there was no possibility of forming a judgment concerning the age of any one of the writers of the Old Testament from his style and manner, and treated all pretences to such judgment as silly and pedantic; yet he declared, at the same time, that the style of Ezra proved him to have written when the Hebrew language was in the same state of cultivation as that of Rome in the time of Virgil, and that the Hebrew of Job might be set in comparison with the Latin of Ennius, whom he commended for 'the beauty and weight of his elegance.'

To this Lowth retorted, that Warburton could never have read either Job or Ezra in the original; that the author of the Book of Job was a poet, and that Ezra was not even a semi-barbarous poet like Ennius, being, indeed, no poet at all; and that Le Clerc, who, like Warburton, had thought of making the Book of Job subsequent to the captivity, had too much knowledge of the original to pronounce Ezra the writer of it, being well aware that Ezra was as unsuitable an author for it as he could have chosen, his style being dry and unadorned, and savouring, as Michaelis had observed, not of the golden, but of the iron age, of Hebrew. Job, he observed, was rather the Homer than the Ennius of the Hebrew classics. 'Let anyone,' said he, 'properly qualified to judge in this matter, read the plain historical narrative in the two first chapters of Job; it is neat, concise, clear in its order and method, pure and elegant in its expression; let him turn to Ezra, and find, if he can, a single Hebrew chapter on which he can, with a safe conscience, bestow any part of this commendation. Let him, moreover, take into account this last author's barbarous terms; and then let him tell me fairly whether he does not find as much difference between these two writers as between Sallust and William of Malmsbury. Let him next look into the poetical parts of Job, and let him compare them with any part of Ezra's undoubted writings; and I would ask him whether he would not as soon pitch upon Geoffry of Monmouth for the author of the Æneid, if that were a doubtful point, as Ezra for the author of the poem of Job; and I should not much doubt of his answering in the affirmative.' That he could have been the author of the Books of Chronicles and the Book of Esther, Lowth utterly denies; for the Books of Chronicles are a mere collection from previous writers, which Ezra may have compiled, but certainly did not write; and, though the narrative of Esther is much in Ezra's style, yet the matter of it is of a better description than that of the Book of Ezra.

On the whole, most critics, since Lowth, have agreed with him in supposing that the age of Job was as early, if not earlier, than that of Moses, and that the country of Job was the land of Edom, part of Arabia Petræa. 'The country of Job,' says he, 'was upon the borders of Egypt; and the age of Job was when the empire of Egypt was arrived at a high degree of improvement in all the arts of civil society. The country of Job must have had a considerable communication with Egypt, by means of the great commerce which was carried on between all the Eastern countries and Egypt, great part of which must pass through Edom; and it was a country of great reputation for wisdom, for "authors of fables, and searchers out of understanding;" a reputation probably derived from ancient times.'*

* Lowth's Letter to Warburton, p. 74, seqq. De Sacrâ Poesi Hebr. Præl. xxxii. not. 1.

Locke's opinion, that the mention of *idolatry as punishable by the judge*, is sufficient to prove the author of the book a Jew, Lowth strenuously opposes, arguing that idolatry may have been punishable by the magistrate in other countries besides Judæa, and under the patriarchs before the time of the Mosaic dispensation. Locke, indeed, may have laid somewhat too much stress upon this expression; it may have been intended only as one of strong reprobation; and the worship of more gods than one may have been regarded as foolish or vicious in other countries besides Judæa, at least among the more intelligent and reasoning class of the community. Job uses the same form of words, in the same chapter, in condemnation of adultery.

Yet the mode in which the author of the Book of Job speaks of God, and many expressions, though fewer than Warburton represents, applicable to the Jewish religion and history throughout the book, will always leave the question, whether the writer was a Jew or not, liable to discussion.

CHAPTER V.

'THE DIVINE LEGATION.'

CONSIDERATION OF OTHER PASSAGES IN THE OLD TESTAMENT THAT SEEM TO INDICATE THAT THE JEWS LOOKED FORWARD TO A FUTURE STATE; WHETHER MERELY AS A STATE OF EXISTENCE OF THE SOUL APART FROM THE BODY, OR AS A STATE OF REWARDS AND PUNISHMENTS — TEXTS IN BOOKS OF MOSES; IN THE PSALMS; IN THE BOOK OF ECCLESIASTES — FANCIFUL INTERPRETATIONS — EXAMINATION OF THE TEXTS IN THE NEW TESTAMENT THAT SEEM TO FAVOUR THE BELIEF IN A FUTURE STATE AMONG THE JEWS — TEXTS ADDRESSED TO THE SADDUCEES — PARABLE OF THE RICH MAN AND LAZARUS — THE ANSWER TO THE LAWYER.

HAVING settled the meaning of the great passage in the Book of Job, Warburton proceeds to consider the other passages in the Old Testament which have been supposed to indicate that the Jews looked for a world to come. These passages are of two kinds: such as are thought to testify merely to the immortality of the soul, or its existence apart from the body; and such as are thought to demonstrate a resurrection of the body, and a future state of reward and punishment.

Of the first kind is the text at the beginning of Genesis, *And God said, Let us make man* in our image, *after* our likeness, and *let them have* dominion *over the beasts*, &c., *And God created man* in his own image, in the image of God *created he him*. These words are understood by many to signify that man was made like God, by being endued with an immaterial and immortal soul; but Warburton supposes that man's likeness to God consisted in being gifted with reason, which was the only qualification that could maintain him in that dominion over the brute creation, which is at the same time conferred upon him. To support this interpretation he adduces the opinion of Philo-Judæus, who, alluding to this text, says, Λόγος ἐστιν εἰκὼν Θεοῦ, 'Reason is the image of God.' Certainly it would be hard to deduce the immortality of the soul from the text.

The next passage of this sort is, *And the Lord God formed man of the dust of the ground, and* breathed *into his nostrils* the breath of life, *and man became* a living soul. This is understood to mean that man received a soul, which, as it lived then, would live for ever. 'But this,' says Warburton, 'is only building on the strength of an English expression.' Everyone knows that what the translation calls *a living soul*, signifies in the original *a living animal:* hence the same writer speaks of *a dead soul*, as well as *a living soul.* Thus in the Book of Numbers (vi. 6) it is said of the Nazarite, *He shall come at no dead body;* where the same word, *nephesh*, which is spoken of Adam as a living animal, is used, with its proper accompaniment, to denote a body that is dead; and the same word is used in the same way in the Book of Leviticus, xxi. 1 and 11. 'And indeed,' continues Warburton, 'not only the propriety of the terms, but the very sense of the context, requires us to confine the meaning of *living soul* to *living animal.* God, the great plastic Artist, is here represented as making and shaping out a figure of earth or clay, which He afterwards animates or inspires with life. He *breathed*, says the sacred historian, into this statue *the breath of life*, and the lump became a living creature. But St. Paul, I hope, may be believed, whatever becomes of my explanation, who thus comments on the very text in question:—*And so it was written, the first man Adam was made* a living soul, *the last Adam was made* a quickening spirit. Here we find the apostle is so far from understanding any *immortality* in this account of man's creation, that he opposes the mortal animal Adam to the immortal-making spirit of Christ.'

The next text is the address to the serpent: *I will put enmity between thee and the woman, and between thy seed and her seed; it shall bruise thy head, and thou shalt bruise his heel;* a promise from which the Jews would doubtless form a notion of some mysterious means by which the evil spirit, that actuated the serpent, would, though he continued his enmity to man, be at length defeated by man through Divine assistance; but they would scarcely draw from it a belief in life and immortality after death.

The last text of this nature is one on which more stress may justly appear to be laid. Jacob says, *I shall go down into the grave to my son mourning*, and *ye will bring down my grey hairs with sorrow to the grave*, where the word for the grave is *scheol*, denoting, as it is generally interpreted, the Hebrew *Orcus* or *Hades*, the place in which souls, after they are separated from their bodies, dwell. The evidence to be drawn from this passage, and from others where the same word occurs, for the belief of the Jews, as early as the days of the patriarchs, in an existence after death, Warburton does not attempt to overthrow, admitting that there must have been a notion among them, in the earliest times, of some common receptacle of souls, from which the saying of a man *being gathered to his fathers*, and *gathered to his people*, doubtless had its rise; though, that as little weight as possible may be attributed to those expressions, he suggests that they may have been derived by the Hebrews from some other people, and that they are used by Moses for no other purpose than to signify the termination of existence on earth.

But none of all these passages, certainly, will prove that the doctrine of a future life formed any part of the teaching of Moses.

There remain to be considered those other texts which

are supposed to denote that a future state of reward and punishment, together with a resurrection of the body, was taught in the Mosaic law. Some, indeed, have brought an argument for this notion from the sense and purport of the whole Jewish law, which being, they say, entirely typical or spiritual, all its promises and denunciations of temporal good and evil foreshadowed a future state of reward and punishment. But this is mere visionary and groundless conceit, as it would intimate that there was nothing in reality bearing on the land of Canaan, or on the temporal condition of the Jews, in all the Mosaic law, but that everything in it had reference to a life beyond the grave.

The particular texts, thought to favour the opinion of a resurrection and a future state of rewards and punishments, Warburton discusses in the following order. God says to Abraham, 'I will give *unto thee*, and to thy seed after thee, the land wherein thou art a stranger, all the land of Canaan, for an everlasting possession;' but, say those of the opposite opinion to Warburton, God gave Abraham no inheritance in the land of Canaan, and therefore must have given him some blessing in another life to fulfil the promise. Warburton considers the promise to have been sufficiently fulfilled by the bestowal of the land on Abraham's posterity as his representative; and adds that the gift of a heavenly Canaan to Abraham could not have been a fulfilment of the promise, because an earthly Canaan was the immediate and express subject of it.

Balaam says, in his interview with Balak, *Let me die the death of the righteous, and let my last end be like his*; an exclamation by which he is understood to wish that he might be partaker of happiness with the righteous in another life. 'Had the apostate prophet said,' remarks Warburton, '*Let me live the life of the righteous*, it would have had a much fairer claim for such a meaning; as it is, both the force of the words, and their relation to the context, restrain us to this literal meaning, "Let me die in a mature old age, after a life of health and peace, with all my posterity flourishing about me; as was the lot of the righteous observers of the law." This vain wish Moses, I suppose, recorded, that the subsequent account of his immature death in battle might make the stronger impression on the serious reader, to warn him against the impiety and folly of expecting the last reward of virtue for a life spent in the gratification of every corrupt appetite. But if any one will say the words have, besides, a sublimer meaning, I have no reason to contend with him.'

It is said in the Book of Leviticus,* *Ye shall therefore keep my statutes and judgments, which if a man do, he shall live in them.* Some have said that the life promised in this text is eternal life; but the folly of such a perversion is patent to all who know anything of the use of similar expressions in other parts of the Scripture.

In noticing another passage of Leviticus,† Warburton, in a later edition, made sport of Dr. Rutherforth, author of the 'Essay on Virtue,' who became one of his assailants; and though to quote Warburton's strictures on him here may seem too much of anticipation, yet I will venture to give them. A law in the third book of Moses is stated thus: 'Whoever he be of the children of Israel, or of the strangers that sojourn in Israel, that giveth any of his seed unto Molech, he shall surely be put to death.' 'Let me,' says Warburton, 'first explain the text, before I show how it is perverted' by Dr. Rutherforth. 'There were two cases in which the offender here described might escape punishment; either the crime could not be legally proved, or the magistrate might be remiss in punishing. The Divine lawgiver obviates both; and declares that the infanticide, in such case, shall suffer

* xviii. 5.

† xx. 2.

death by God's own hand in an extraordinary manner. . . . "And if the people of the land do any ways hide their eyes from the man, when he giveth of his seed unto Molech, and kill him not, then I will set my face against that man, and against his family, and will cut him off." So much for the sense of the text. And now for the *nonsense* of our interpreter, a professor of law and divinity, the egregious Dr. Rutherforth. This provision for the execution of the law our professor being totally unconscious of, he insists that "*cutting off from among his people* can only mean eternal damnation, the being consigned to a state of punishment in another life." He is, as I say, a dealer both in law and divinity; but not having yet learned the use of his tools, he confounds law by theology, and depraves theology by law . . . To regulate a little his law ideas, let him turn to Exodus xii. 15, and Leviticus vii. 25, and he will find that the *cutting off from Israel*, and the *cutting off from the people*, are phrases which signify only capital punishment of a civil kind; unless he will suppose that what is there threatened for eating *leavened bread* and *prohibited fat* is eternal life in torments.'

Coming to the Psalms, we find, in the sixteenth, this passage: 'Thou wilt not leave my soul in hell, neither wilt thou suffer thy holy one to see corruption. Thou wilt show me the path of life; in thy presence is fulness of joy, and at thy right hand there are pleasures for evermore.' The words, *Thou wilt not leave my soul in hell*, though they afterwards received a spiritual meaning, were used by David only with a temporal view, in the sense of 'Thou wilt not suffer me to fall immaturely,' as was the lot of the transgressors of the law; and so to find joy *in the presence of God* signified the same as to appear before the Ark (Ps. xvii. 15), and to enjoy *pleasures* there *for evermore* the same as *to dwell in the house of the Lord for ever*, that is, all his days (Ps. xxiii. 6). Similar passages occur in the forty-ninth and seventy-third Psalms. 'But the texts of texts,' adds Warburton, 'the precious ones indeed, are those where a hell is mentioned; as here, *Thou wilt not leave my soul in hell;* and of this orthodox consolation there is no scarcity in the Old Testament. Mr. Whiston assures us "it is almost five times as often mentioned there as in the New." It may be so. However, instead of examining into the justness of this nice calculation, I shall choose rather to consider what is to be understood by the word, than how often it is repeated. Now, I suppose,' no one 'can have any reasonable objection to St. John's authority in this matter, who, speaking in the Book of Revelation, of the useless old furniture of the law, says, "And *death* and *hell* were cast into the *lake of fire;* this is the second death." From hence it appears, that the *hell* of the Old Testament was a very different thing from the *hell* of the New, called *the lake of fire;* since the one is made the punishment, or at least the extinction of the other. And, to remove all doubt, the Apostle, we see, calls this *casting into the lake* a *second death.* Must not, then, the *lake* itself be a *second hell?* And if so, could the *first*, or the Old Testament *hell*, be any other than the *grave?*' On this explication Warburton's reader may set what estimation he pleases.

In another passage the Psalmist says, 'Deliver my soul from the wicked, from the men of the world, *which have their portion in this life*, and whose belly thou fillest with thy hid treasure. As for me, I will behold thy face in righteousness. *I shall be satisfied, when I awake, with thy likeness.*' But as to the term *this life*, the original is a plural word, *in vitis*, having no singular, referring only to life in this world, and not being opposed, as our translators would seem to intimate, to life in another world. The Septuagint translators render it, *in their life;* the sense of the whole being 'they have their portion, or full share, of life;' that is, they are perfectly prosperous. The other words, *I shall be satisfied, when I awake, with thy likeness,* are susceptible, according to the commentators and translators, of so many renderings, and so many explanations, that it is difficult to know to what sense of them to attach the most weight; the Seventy render them *at the appearing of thy glory;* the Syriac version, *when thy fidelity shall awake;* and Castalio, *when thy likeness shall be awaked.* But many interpreters, of the highest estimation, who refer the *awaking* to David, suppose it to allude to 'his morning adorations before the Ark, the symbolic residence of the Divine presence.'

Again, *Surely goodness and mercy shall follow me all the days of my life, and I shall dwell in the house of the Lord for ever.** But here *the house of the Lord* signifies merely *the tabernacle* or *the temple;* and *for ever*, or *to length of days*, as it is in the original, means only that mature old age which was to be expected by the righteous. Other passages in the Psalms of a similar nature may be explained in a similar manner.

Looking to the Book of Ecclesiastes, we find the Preacher saying, *Wisdom giveth life to them that have it*, but this wisdom, like the law of Moses, offers only the things of this life. But he also says, *Rejoice, O young man, in thy youth, and let thy heart cheer thee in the days of thy youth, and walk in the ways of thine heart, and in the sight of thine eyes;* but know thou that for all these things God will bring thee *to judgment.* Is not this a stronger passage, it may be asked, in favour of a future state? Does it not intimate retribution to be expected in another world? No, says Warburton, the sense is simply, 'In giving an innocent and lawful indulgence to thy youth, take heed lest thou transgress the bounds of virtue and piety. For know that God will certainly punish thy offences, either in thy own person or in thy posterity.'

* Ps. xxiii. 6.

These are all the most prominent texts of the Old Testament which are urged, whether by Jews or Christians, in support of a future state and of the resurrection of the dead. 'But, besides these,' says Warburton, 'the Jews have a set of texts peculiar to themselves, which the Christians have never yet ventured to put upon duty. As they are most of them of the nature of riddles, riddles, for me, they shall remain; only, for the curious reader's satisfaction, I shall mark out what the Rabbins bring from the Pentateuch to prove the immortality of the soul and the resurrection of the body, as they are collected by the learned Manasseh Ben-Israel, in his tract, *De Resurrectione Mortuorum*.' Warburton then enumerates seventeen texts of this enigmatical kind, though not all from the Pentateuch, of which it will be sufficient to quote one or two specimens, to show of what material a learned Rabbi may avail himself for arguments. One is, 'Then Bathsheba bowed with her face to the earth, and did reverence to the king, and said, Let my lord King David live for ever.'* Another is, 'Thou shalt not take the dam with the young, but thou shalt in any wise let the dam go, that it may be well with thee, and that thou mayest prolong thy days.'† 'But,' continues the author of The Divine Legation, 'though the reader will find many diverting things on this head in Manasseh Ben-Israel, yet they must all give place to the curious comment of Rabbi Tanchum on the following words of 1 Sam. xxv. 29:—'The soul of my lord shall be bound in the bundle of life with the Lord thy God; and the souls of thine enemies, them shall he sling out, as out of the middle of a sling.' 'It is the opinion of all the interpreters on this text,' says this profound Rabbi, 'that it is given by way of admonition, to show what will be the state of the soul, and to what it will at length come, after it is separated from the body; teaching us that there are

* 1 Kings i. 3.

† Deut. xxii. 6.

two conditions of souls — some having a high place and secure position with their Lord, and enjoying eternal life, subject neither to death nor to perdition, while others are exposed to all the fluctuations of nature, so that they find no rest or fixed abode, but suffer perpetual pains and incessant tortures, *through all eternity*, like a stone projected from a sling, which is whirled in the air in proportion to the strength of the slinger, and then falls to the earth by its own weight. But in a soul there is neither weight to sink it down, nor lightness to carry it up; and it is therefore constantly agitated and unsettled, harassed with pain and grief *for ever and ever*. Such is unquestionably the opinion of WISE MEN AND PHILOSOPHERS. How profound a doctrine! and how noble an original! But this is not the first, by a thousand, that has been raised from a metaphor out of the hot-bed of theologic WISDOM AND PHILOSOPHY.'

The principal texts in the Old Testament, which apparently advocate the belief that the doctrine of a future state was taught in the law of Moses, having been considered, it remains to notice the chief of those in the New Testament that seem to support this notion. One of the first that calls for attention is the admonition of Christ: *But as touching the resurrection of the dead, have ye not read that which was spoken unto you by God, saying, I am the God of Abraham, and the God of Isaac, and the God of Jacob? God is not the God of the dead, but of the living.* But this was addressed to the Sadducees, who denied the separate existence of the soul, affirming that it perished at the death of the body, and seems to have been intended to impress on them that, as God is not the God of the dead but of the living, the souls of Abraham, Isaac, and Jacob were still surviving; so that it would be in vain for them to build a disbelief in the resurrection of the body on their notion that the soul dies with the body, a notion confuted by the words of God to Moses. That the body might be raised again, the Sadducees are left merely to infer from the *intimation* that the soul still lives. But even if it were a direct affirmation of the resurrection of the body, it would not prove that Moses taught or indicated the doctrine, or that of a future state, either in the passage in which those words are given, or in any other part of his writings. To determine whether he did so in that particular passage, we have only to consider in what sense the words would be taken by the Jews to whom he repeated them. They would simply be received as an assurance, that as God had protected Abraham, Isaac, and Jacob, he would also protect their posterity, 'whose affliction in Egypt he had surely seen.' No spiritual sense, or reference to a future state, would be attached to them.

The next text of importance is that in the parable of the rich man and Lazarus, where the rich man, being in hell, instructs Abraham, whom he saw afar off in Paradise, to send Lazarus to warn his brethren to repent, lest they also should fall into a like condition with himself; when Abraham replies, *If they hear not Moses and the prophets, neither will they be persuaded though one rose from the dead.* But as the preceding text was addressed to the Sadducees, who denied a future state, so this is addressed to the Pharisees, who admitted it, and is, in truth, nothing more than an admonition that luxury, selfishness, and want of humanity must expect punishment. The whole force of the argument, says Warburton, is, 'If they will not hear Moses and the prophets, whose authority they acknowledge, and whose missions they believe to have been confirmed by so many well-attested miracles, neither will they regard a new miracle, that of the resurrection of a dead man;' 'nor, in fact, were the Pharisees at all softened into repentance by the return of that Lazarus, the namesake of this in the parable, whom Jesus raised from the dead.' The question of a future state is not at all concerned in the parable, except only in the intimation that God will punish here or hereafter. 'Moses and the prophets threatened the punishment here, and while it was executed here, the Jews looked no farther; but when *the extraordinary providence*, by which the punishment was administered, had ceased, the Jews began, from those very promises and denunciations, to entertain some hopes of a hereafter, where all inequalities should be set even, and God's threats and promises executed to the full.' The Pharisees, therefore, had already begun to believe in the probability, or at least in the possibility, of a future state; but that Moses taught a future state, nothing can be drawn from this parable to indicate; though, from the study of the prophets and Moses in conjunction, a future state might doubtless be inferred.

The answer given to the inquiring lawyer concerning the Commandments, *This do, and thou shalt live*, and the admonition to the Jews, *Search the Scriptures, for in them ye think ye have eternal life*, have been in vain solicited, to prove that Moses taught a life beyond the grave. But the eleventh chapter of the Epistle to the Hebrews might seem to contain stronger intimations of such a doctrine having been taught by Moses, where it is said that Abel, Enoch, Noah, Abraham, Isaac, Jacob, Joseph, Moses, and others, performed acceptable works by faith, *looking for a heavenly city, seeing the promises afar off, and being persuaded of them, and embracing them, and desiring a heavenly country, all dying in the faith; Moses esteeming the reproach of Christ greater than all the treasures of Egypt; and the very women despising death in hopes to obtain a part in the resurrection of the just.* But, to understand the chapter properly, we must, as Warburton observes, look to the whole scope and argument of it. 'Without faith,' says the author of the Epistle, 'it is impossible to please God; for he that cometh to God must believe that he is, and that he is a rewarder of them that diligently seek him;' which faith he immediately proceeds to illustrate by the conduct of Noah, Abraham, Sarah, and other eminent persons, among whom is mentioned Rahab the harlot; adding the instances of the faith of the Jews in passing the Red Sea, and in surrounding the walls of Jericho; 'but was such faith,' asks Warburton, 'a faith in Jesus the Messiah, or a belief of a future state of rewards and punishments?' It was faith merely in the God of their fathers, the God of Abraham, Isaac, and Jacob. As to what is said of Abraham, that 'he looked for a city which hath foundations, whose builder and maker is God,' or of the desire of these *believers* for 'a better country, that is, an heavenly,' Warburton admits that the patriarchs and leaders of the Jewish people had a prospect of something beyond the present state of things: thus 'Abraham rejoiced to see Christ's day, and he saw it, and was glad,' beholding the resurrection of Jesus typified in the restoration of his son Isaac.* On what is said of Moses 'esteeming the reproach of Christ greater than all the treasures of Egypt,' Warburton says nothing positive, but must be regarded as understanding that Moses was willing to submit to such reproach as the Apostles had incurred, in their day, for the sake of Christ, since neither Moses, in his day, nor others, could 'have faith in that which was never yet proposed to them for the object of faith; *for how should they believe in him of whom they had not heard?*'† As to the women and others that were tortured, 'not accepting deliverance, that they might obtain a better resurrection,' Warburton refers their sufferings, as is done in the margin of our English Bibles, to the time of the Maccabees, when

* 'Remarks on Several Occasional Reflections;' Works, vol. xi. p. 298, seqq.

† Div. Leg., book vi. § 4; Works, vol. v. p. 431, 8vo.

it is acknowledged that 'the doctrine of a future state was become national.'

This portion of his work Warburton concludes by quoting the opinions of three capital supports of the Protestant Church, Grotius, Episcopius, and Bishop Bull, the passages from whom have been given at the commencement of these remarks, and who, he says, though only three, are worth a million. 'But,' he adds, 'let the man be of what church he will, so he have a superiority of understanding, and be not defective in integrity, you shall always hear him speak the same language. The great Arnauld, that shining ornament of the Gallican Church, urges this important truth with still more frankness. 'C'EST LE COMBLE DE L'IGNORANCE,' says this accomplished divine, 'de mettre en doute cette vérité, qui est une des plus communes de la religion Chrétienne, et qui est ATTESTÉE PAR TOUS LES PÈRES, que les promesses de l'ancien Testament n'étoient que temporelles et terrestres, et que les Juifs n'adoroient Dieu que pour les biens charnels.' 'And what more,' asks Warburton, 'hath been said or done by the Author of "The Divine Legation?"'

CHAPTER VI.

BAYLE.—MORAL OBLIGATION.

WHETHER A SOCIETY OF HUMAN BEINGS CAN SUBSIST WITHOUT A BELIEF IN A FUTURE STATE — BAYLE'S CONJECTURES REGARDING A COMMUNITY OF ATHEISTS — WARBURTON'S ARGUMENTS IN OPPOSITION TO BAYLE — HIS SOPHISTRY — A REASONABLE BEING MUST ACT REASONABLY — BURLAMAQUI ON EXTERNAL AND INTERNAL OBLIGATION — WARBURTON CONTRADICTS HIMSELF — OBJECTIONS TO PALEY'S DEFINITION OF VIRTUE — BAYLE LEFT UNREFUTED.

IT is thus made apparent that Moses did not teach the doctrine of a future state of reward and punishment in his system of laws. But there was another point which also required consideration: whether any form of government could be maintained without reference to the expectation of a future state as a support to it. Bayle* had argued, at great length, that a society, or form of government, might be supported and held together, not only without any acknowledgment of a future state in it, but even without any recognition of the being of a God. An Atheist, said he, may have the same reason and moral sense, the same notions of right and wrong, as any other man. A body of Atheists, living together in society, would act in the same manner as members of other societies act. They would not be deprived, by their refusal to acknowledge a Maker and Preserver of the world, of feelings of honour and shame, of the desire of glory and praise, and of the fear of censure and contempt. We should find among them men of integrity in their dealings, men

* Thoughts on the Comet, sect. 161, seqq.

willing to relieve the poor, to oppose injustice, and to observe moderation in their pleasures, being induced to such conduct either by a view to commendation, or by the hope of gaining friends and supporters, in case they should need assistance. Women would be anxious to be distinguished for virtue, as the means of securing men's love and esteem. Crimes, doubtless, of all kinds, would happen in such a society, but not more frequently than in a society of believers in a higher Power, because all the principles that prompt to good or evil in one community, reward and punishment, honour and disgrace, opinion and custom, act with equal force in the other. Anything like the sanctifying grace, indeed, adds Bayle, which enables Christians to vanquish evil habits and propensities, would not be found among them; but they would be in no worse a condition, in this respect, than Pagans or idolaters who have maintained societies.

Even Christian societies, continues Bayle, must soon be dissolved by their vices, were they not strictly held together by human laws. Men are kept in order by men. Such a city as Paris, if deprived of all other restraints on the passions, except the exhortations of preachers and confessors, would, unless miraculously preserved, be in a most deplorable state in a fortnight. An airy notion of the existence of a God, or of a world to come, does not render a Christian or Pagan society more stabile than that of a society of Atheists would be.* Soldiers, among Christians, are not restrained from disorder by belief in the existence of a God or a future state, but by discipline and fear of punishment. They accept the notion of the being of a God without question, for they have no thought of metaphysical subtleties; and they are easily excited to religious zeal and fury against any that profess different religious tenets from themselves. The Christians who engaged in

* Sect. cxxxi.

the Crusades had abundance of religion; they quitted their country to make war with infidels; they saw, as they believed, angels and saints fighting at the head of their armies, and putting their enemies to flight; and they beheld infinite numbers of prodigies and miracles. He who suspects such men of Atheism must give up all pretensions to common sense; yet they were guilty of the most outrageous excesses, so that the Christians, whom they came to defend, dreaded them not less than the Saracens. The most of the Crusaders were men incited to join in the expedition by preaching and indulgences; but were not restrained from excesses by regard for religion.*

Thus speculative opinions are not the ruling motives of our actions. A religious persuasion is no further the director of our conduct, than as it opposes us to those of a different opinion, and leads us, especially in circumstances of affliction and apprehension, to strong professions of our faith, in the trust that they may one day avail to our benefit. In the ordinary parts of their conduct, the Atheist and the believer are swayed by the same principles; that is to say, by inclination and constitution, or the force of the habits which they have each contracted. If a believer's constitution inclines him to luxury or licentiousness, to anger or to violence, he will indulge in those propensities more than an Atheist of a colder and calmer temper.† There are men who go to mass daily, yet are neither religious, nor even decent in their conversation; and, as to their actions, they are ready to overreach and deceive their fellow-creatures on all sides. Are they at war? they rob the wretched peasant and cheat the starving soldier; are they commanding officers? they have a thousand sinister ways of enriching themselves; are they in civil employment? they have a thousand tricks to delude and take advantage of those connected with them.

* Sects. cxxxix. cxl. † Sects. cxliii. cxliv.

Examine all the notions of civil life among Christians, and you will scarcely find two derived from religion. The Jews had a sect among them, the Sadducees, who openly denied the immortality of the soul, yet it does not appear that, with this opinion, they led worse lives than the other Jews; on the contrary, it is likely that they were in reality even more righteous than the Pharisees, who boasted so much of their ceremonial observances. The few among the ancients who made open profession of Atheism, as Diagoras, Theodorus, Euhemerus, are not said to have been remarkable for vicious lives. An Atheist may even have as strong a desire to secure an honourable fame after death as the believer in a Divinity. Thus, from every consideration, it is apparent that a man may have the most exact notions of moral virtue, and be extremely correct in his conduct, without believing either in a future state of reward and punishment, or even in the existence of a Superior Power.

All this array of argument or assertion Warburton undertook to put utterly to the rout. But we shall find Warburton's reasonings much more liable to objection than Bayle's. Bayle's arguments in favour of a society of Atheists are, indeed, something like those against Quintilian's position, that a great orator must be a good man; a society of Atheists may be men of upright lives, but their lives might be still better if they believed in a higher Power, as a bad man may be an effective orator in support of virtue and goodness, but a good man will be a still more effective orator, as speaking from a sincere and heartfelt attachment to virtue and goodness. But Bayle's argumentation is straightforward and clear, and of such a nature that we at once admit its justice or plausibility; while Warburton's is such that we cannot but stop from time to time to wonder at the deficiency or unsoundness of his positions. His self-confidence is great, but his success far from equal to it. He begins by affirming that though an Atheist may have 'a moral sense,' and may 'arrive at a knowledge of the real essential differences in the qualities of human actions,' he would yet be uninfluenced by them to the practice of virtue, because his moral sense, and his knowledge of the difference in the morality of actions, will not properly oblige him to act virtuously; for obligation necessarily implies an obliger; and the obliger must be, not one and the same with the obliged, but separate and distinct from him; since 'to make a man at once the obliger and obliged is the same thing as to make him enter into compact with himself, which is the highest of absurdities; for it is an unquestionable rule in law and reason, that whoever acquires a right to anything from the obligation of another towards him, may relinquish that right; if, therefore, the obliged and obliger be one and the same person, in that case all obligation must be void of course, or rather no obligation could have commenced. Yet of this absurdity,' he proceeds, 'the Atheist is guilty, when he talks of actions being *moral* or *obligatory*; for what *being* can be found whereon to place this obligation? Will he say *right reason?* But that is the very absurdity we complain of; because reason is only an attribute of the person obliged, his assistant to judge of his obligations, if he hath any, from another being; to make *this*, then, the obliger, is to make a man oblige himself. If he say he means by *reason* not every man's particular reason, but *reason in general*, I reply that this reason is a mere abstract notion, which hath no real subsistence; and how that which hath no real subsistence should *oblige*, is still more difficult to apprehend.' He then adds that moral obligation implies a law, which enjoins and forbids; but a law is the imposition of an intelligent superior, who has power to exact conformity to it; that such a law is necessary to oblige a reasonable being endued with will, who, though he may judge by his understanding of the propriety or impropriety of an act or course of action, is under no necessity to pursue or avoid it. He, therefore, that does not believe in the existence of an intelligent or rational Superior, a Predominant Reason distinct from his own, will not feel himself obliged to act according to reason.

But all this is no refutation of Bayle's arguments, and will be found, if examined, to be little better than sophistry. An Atheist, living in a society whether of Atheists or of Theists, and desirous to act, in his intercourse with those around him, like a reasonable being, (for his want of belief in a divinity, or in a future state, however unreasonable it may appear to those who think differently from him on those subjects, will not prevent him from acting reasonably in the ordinary affairs of life,) will find himself as much obliged, by his regard to his own interest and welfare, and by his judgment in respect to what is likely to do him good or harm, honour or dishonour, in the estimation of his fellows, to act reasonably, and therefore morally, in matters in which morality is concerned, as he is, in reference to his health, to eat wholesome and avoid noxious food. He is at liberty, doubtless, to act in a contrary manner; he may conduct himself so as to destroy his reputation, or may ruin his health by noxious diet, but, by acting thus, he will be considered to exclude himself from the number of reasonable beings, and to make himself unfit for any society whatever; and, therefore, as long as he would wish to continue a reasonable being, in his own estimation or that of others, he cannot be considered to be at liberty to act thus. Every reasonable being, and every moral being, properly so called, must act reasonably and morally. Every rational agent acts with a view to a rational object, or an object which he himself thinks rational; and if, in comparing five with three, he finds that five will be more for his object than three, he is obliged or necessitated, as a rational agent keeping his object in view, to choose five. Warburton, indeed, in a subsequent passage, makes a distinction between moral and natural, and says that a man who has no conception that he received his being from the will of another, would only, in preferring the fit to the unfit, act naturally, and not morally, for he can never feel under any obligation to prefer good to evil, or even life to death, until he is sensible that he is dependent on a superior Being, and accountable to him for his actions. 'Did the good or evil produced,' he argues, 'make the action moral or immoral, brutes would have morality.' But to substantiate this position, proof might be required that brutes are destitute of a sense of morality; for it may be argued that many brutes, both in their conduct towards man and towards one another, appear to give indications of a sense of morality. However, not to dispute on this point, Warburton himself admits, at the commencement of his argumentation, that an Atheist 'is capable of being affected with the moral sense,' and it is, therefore, vain to allege afterwards that *he would not act morally*, or in conformity to the moral sense with which he is affected, but would require a knowledge of dependence on a superior Power to oblige him to act in conformity with it. If no being acts morally or wisely, as Warburton's arguments go to prove, but one who is obliged so to act by the will of another, we are necessarily led to ask who it is that obliges the Great Director of all to act morally or wisely. Warburton notices this difficulty himself, and says that having no superior will to influence Him, He is obliged only by His own wisdom; yet such obligation, in the case of man, he before asserts to be no obligation at all; and if it be no obligation in one case, it can be no obligation, with reverence be it spoken, in another. Bishop Hare, at first sight of this passage, said to Warburton, 'I doubt the adversaries will think *you have yourself helped them to an answer to what you urge from the words* "oblige" and "obligation," that it infers an "obliger," since you admit that *God is obliged by His own wisdom.'* * The truth is that man, being created with a will free, must, as far as he is a reasonable being, and whether he be Atheist, or Christian, or Mahometan, exercise his free will reasonably, and, of consequence, morally, or with a view to his own welfare, and so as to secure the good opinion of his fellow-creatures. To say that man's will is not free, and that he acts under absolute obligation from a superior Power, who compels him to a particular course of action for his own good, is to deny at once that he is a reasonable being, and to leave him only the semblance of being one, for though he may appear to himself, or to others, to exercise his reason, he, in fact, exercises it not at all, but is a mere passive machine, influenced intellectually and corporeally by the will of another.

Burlamaqui, the French writer on the Principles of Natural Law, endeavoured to reconcile the difficulties about free-will and necessity, by calling the essential difference of things good and evil, right and wrong, which is discoverable by nature, and by a regard to which man regulates his conduct, the *internal obligation*, and the will or influence of God, which has ordered that he shall act under regard to such difference of things, choosing the good and avoiding the evil, from the hope of advantage or fear of inconvenience, the *external obligation*. But this is only to say that the power of God, the external obligation, makes and orders man, a being endued with a certain portion of reason ; which portion of reason, the internal obligation, he is made to use for his own benefit and preservation ; or, in other words, that man being formed, by an external power, a reasonable being, must act, from internal persuasions, reasonably. Though man's liberty, as Lavater has said, is only that of the bird in the cage,

* Kilvert, Selections from Warburton's Papers, p. 106.

yet it assuredly is liberty, and may be exercised alike by him who believes in a superior Power, and by him who believes in none. Dr. Clarke, therefore, rightly maintains that human obligation to act thus or thus, lies in the nature of things, from which man must choose what is fitting. Warburton, indeed, accuses him of confounding natural with moral choice; but by man, as a member of society, reason must be applied to the one as well as the other.

Remarking on Bayle's observation about custom, by which most men's lives are regulated, Warburton flatly contradicts himself. He first says that 'custom is a power *which opposes the moral sense, not partially, or at certain times and places, but universally*,' and refers to the custom among the ancients of exposing children, and a great number of other customs that are carefully enumerated by Sextus Empiricus and Montaigne. But, four pages farther on, observing that 'men accommodate themselves to the opinions and rules of those with whom they converse,' he says that '*those opinions and rules*, in a good measure, *correspond, in most civilized countries, with the unchangeable rule of right*, whatever Sextus Empiricus and Montaigne have been pleased to say to the contrary.' But accommodation to opinions and rules of conduct constitutes custom. He, therefore, first says, that custom universally opposes the sense of right, and then that it in most countries corresponds, 'in a good measure,' with the sense of right.

He concludes by observing that the great question is, 'whether a clear conviction of right and wrong, abstracted from all will and command, and, consequently, from the expectation of reward and punishment, be sufficient to influence the generality of men in any tolerable degree?' To this he answers that it is not; that the majority of mankind are not moved to the practice of virtue by being told that virtue is the greatest good, but are led, by the desire of gratifying their passions, to conduct inconsistent with virtue; and that to sway men in favour of virtue, something more than virtue's own attractions is necessary, which something can be only such rewards and punishments as religion proposes. But this is true, absolutely, with regard only to the less educated and baser portion of mankind. With the better instructed classes, and even with the superior part of the uninstructed, respect for what they see to be right, and the honour to be obtained by the practice of it, are sufficient to induce them to be its adherents, without being influenced by any enjoyment to be expected from it in another state of existence. What justly-reasoning man has concurred with Paley in his definition of virtue, that it is 'the doing of good to mankind, in obedience to the will of God, and for the sake of everlasting happiness?' Who, that thinks with any degree of justness, will assert (what Paley's definition requires), that no action can be virtuous unless it be done for the sake of everlasting happiness? Would Paley himself have denied that any man can be virtuous unless he performs every act of his life for the sake of everlasting happiness? Would he have denied that a disbeliever in a future state of happiness can perform a virtuous act? Surely not; and surely, then, it is a 'wonderful wonder of wonders' that such a reasoner as Paley should have produced such a definition. But if a disbeliever in future happiness can perform one virtuous act, he may perform thousands of virtuous acts, and may live in a course of 'doing good to mankind' for years and years, and die with the gratitude and applause of nations.

Paley, indeed, might as well have put misery as happiness into his definition, and have said that virtue is the doing good to mankind from the fear of everlasting punishment. One would have been as reasonable as the other. Each would have affected only a portion of mankind; *the fear of hell's a hangman's whip, to hold in order the wretch;* but the wise and well-disposed make the *restraints of honour their border.* What would Paley or Warburton have said, if either had been asked whether, through the whole course of his life, he had been induced to act rightly only through hope of eternal happiness or fear of eternal punishment?

Warburton's allegations, assuredly, are no answer to Bayle; and, for anything that the author of 'The Divine Legation' has said, a community of unbelievers in a future state, though it is by no means desirable that such communities should be multiplied, might live in great harmony, and for a long period of time.

CHAPTER VII.

ANCIENT MYSTERIES. SIXTH BOOK OF THE ÆNEID.

VARIETY OF SUBJECTS DISCUSSED IN 'THE DIVINE LEGATION'—LOWTH'S REMARK UPON IT—'FABLE OF THE BEES'—OBSERVATIONS ON THE ANCIENT MYSTERIES—MYSTERIES HAD THEIR ORIGIN IN EGYPT—LESS AND GREATER MYSTERIES—WARBURTON'S HYPOTHESIS AS TO WHAT WAS TAUGHT IN THEM—CONCEALMENT OF WHAT WAS SUGGESTED TO HIM BY LE CLERC—HIS SUPPOSITION THAT VIRGIL'S ACCOUNT OF ÆNEAS'S DESCENT INTO HELL WAS A FIGURATIVE DESCRIPTION OF INITIATION INTO THE ELEUSINIAN MYSTERIES—HIS ARGUMENTS IN SUPPORT OF THIS HYPOTHESIS—GIBBON'S ASSAULT UPON IT—SUMMARY OF GIBBON'S ARGUMENTS AGAINST IT—JORTIN'S 'DISSERTATIONS'—WHY ÆNEAS AND THE SIBYL WERE SENT OUT AT THE IVORY GATE—SUPPOSITIONS OF JORTIN, GIBBON, AND HEYNE ON THE POINT.

BUT Bayle's disquisitions were not the only subjects, little or not all connected with the argument of 'The Divine Legation,' on which Warburton was to bestow his attention. He had announced, at the beginning of his work, his purpose 'to stretch the inquiry,' in the course of it, 'high and wide,' and he does not forget what he intended. He touches, indeed, on so many matters, that his book may very well be thought to merit the sarcasm of Lowth: 'The Divine Legation of Moses,' it seems, 'contains in it all knowledge divine and human, ancient and modern; it treats, as of its proper subject, *de omni scibili et de quolibet ente*; it is a perfect encyclopædia; it includes in itself all history, chronology, criticism, divinity, law, politics, from the Law of Moses down to the late Jew-bill, and from Egyptian hieroglyphics to modern rebus-writing; and to it we are to have recourse, as to an infallible oracle, for the resolution of every question in literature. It is like Lord Peter's brown loaf; it is mutton and it is beef; it is fish and it is flesh; it is meat and it is drink; in it are contained *inclusive* all the necessaries of life.'*

Having refuted Bayle, though, it must be confessed, with little more success than the village curate refuted Bellarmine and the great Popish doctors, sounding the note of triumph, but leaving the enemy unwounded, he bestows a slight regard on Mandeville, the author of 'The Fable of the Bees,' whose system of morals represents all men as hypocrites, apparently reverencing virtue, but in reality caring only for its semblance, and which says, universally, what, if said at all, can only be said with great limitation, that private vices are public benefits. He then proceeds to devote a large portion of attention to the Eleusinian Mysteries, which he asserts to have been the invention of some ancient legislator, caught up and enlarged by succeeding legislators, till it became the important institution which was so much admired and supported in Attica.

Maintaining his position, that all lawgivers and rulers saw the necessity of inculcating the belief in a future state of reward and punishment as a support to their systems of government, he affirms that the institution of the Mysteries was intended as a means of establishing and extending that belief, being artfully so formed and conducted as to strike forcibly on the minds and imaginations of the multitude. In support of this theory, he gives what he calls a full and distinct account of the nature of the Mysteries, observing that as the ancient authors, who wrote expressly on the subject, such as Melanthius,

* Lowth's Letter to Warburton, p. 13.

Menander, and Sotades, have not come down to us, the moderns are entirely in the dark as well about their object as their origin, not excepting even Meursius, who has given the matter so much consideration.

He has been accused of concealing his obligations to Meursius; but it should not be forgotten that, at the commencement of his remarks, he acknowledges himself 'much indebted to Meursius, though only,' he says, 'for *abridging his labour* in the search of those passages of antiquity which make mention of the Eleusinian Mysteries, and for bringing the greater part of them together under one view.' For such *abridgment of his labour* he is doubtless *greatly indebted to Meursius*, without whom the array of quotations in the margin of 'The Divine Legation' would have been much smaller than it is. 'He fortunately falls in,' observes the author of 'Confusion worse Confounded,' one of the sprightliest attacks on Warburton's writings, 'with the very same quotations that had been used by Meursius in his *Eleusinia*, and mentions the name of Meursius just as the preacher did the name of Archbishop Tillotson in the *beginning* of his sermon, and then very unsuspectedly continued the quotation to the *end* of it, and gained great credit.' Warburton certainly laid himself open, by his mode of alluding to Meursius, to such sarcasms.

Mysteries had their origin, he observes, in Egypt, the first being those of Isis and Osiris. From thence they spread, with gradual variations, into different countries, and especially into Greece and its islands, where they were assigned to various deities; but those most frequently mentioned were the Mysteries of Bacchus, celebrated in Bœotia, and those of Ceres, celebrated at Eleusis. As the origin of all the Mysteries was common, so was the end; and an investigation of what was done and taught in the Eleusinian Mysteries will inform us, as far as we can now ascertain, what was done and taught in the rest.

In each kind there were two divisions, the lesser Mysteries, which were communicated to all the initiated alike, and the greater Mysteries, which were shown only to those who underwent a second initiation four years after the first.

Of what was taught the initiated in these rites, little or nothing, from the secrecy with which they were attended, has become known. Many have formed conjectures, and Warburton has given his. He says that, to support the doctrine of a providence, which, they thought, governed the world, they enforced, by every kind of contrivance, a belief in a future state of reward and punishment; adding, to strengthen it further, the doctrine of the transmigration of souls, which would indicate the soul to be immortal, passing from state to state, but never perishing. As to the future life, it was said that the souls of the initiated would be happier than those of others, as, on leaving the body, they would soar to the regions of bliss, while those of the uninitiated would sink in mire and darkness. Yet, to secure this happiness, it was necessary for the initiated to pursue virtuous lives, for it was the object of the Mysteries to restore the soul to its original purity.

Strict secrecy was inculcated, partly to excite curiosity, and thus increase, for the benefit of the priests, the number of candidates, and partly because, as Varro said, in a fragment of his book on religion, preserved by St. Augustine,* 'there were many truths, of which a general knowledge would be unprofitable to the state, and many things which, though false, it was expedient for the people to think true.' The initiation into the lesser Mysteries, which consisted chiefly in *ceremonies and shows*, would gratify the curious to a certain extent; and, if the initiated chose to proceed to the greater Mysteries, they would have the *more secret doctrines* confided to them.

* De Civ. Dei, iv. 31.

The chief of these more secret doctrines was, that men must imitate the gods; but, as the Mysteries required nothing of a person initiated which they would not enable him to perform, they taught him that the gods who were to be their examples, but in whose lives they saw so many vices and irregularities, were in reality only dead and deified mortals, and still subject to like passions and weaknesses with themselves. Yet over *these deities made from men* they were taught to consider that there presided *one supreme and true Deity*, the Being who made all things, and who had assigned to these inferior divinities, as to all other creatures, their proper place and station, appointing over what parts of the world they were to rule. When the initiated had received this portion of instruction, they were called *epoptæ*, overseers or inspectors, having previously been called *mystæ*, or simply *the initiated.*

For support to these notions concerning the Mysteries, Warburton refers to passages in Augustine,* Cicero,† Julius Firmicus,‡ and Clemens Alexandrinus;§ and these authors, indeed, afford some confirmation to the hypothesis of the initiated being taught that the gods were originally but men. For the supposition that the truth of the divine nature was taught in the Mysteries, he finds his chief support in this passage of Galen:‖ 'The study of the use of the parts of the human body is not only of service to the mere physician, but of much greater to him who joins philosophy to the art of healing; and, in order to perfect himself in this *mystery*, labours to investigate *the universal nature.* They who initiate themselves here, whether private men or bodies, will find, in my opinion, nobler instruction than in the rites either of Eleusis or Samothrace.' A passage in Josephus against Apion,¶ which he

* De Civ. Dei, iv. 27; viii. 5.

† Tusc. Disp. i. 12, 13; De Nat. Deor. i. 42.

‡ De Err. Prof. Relig. c. vi.

§ Strom. lib. v. p. 431, ed. Sylb.

‖ De Usu Part. xvii. 1.

¶ Ib. ii. 23.

forces into his service, profits him little. His suggestion that the fragment of Sanchoniatho was used in the Mysteries, is deservedly ridiculed by Gibbon as mere fancy, since, as it attributes the formation of the world to the blind powers of matter, it could not be used to inculcate the doctrine of an intelligent Cause; and his supposition that an Orphic poem, of which a fragment is quoted by Clemens Alexandrinus, used to be sung by the hierophant, is still more unhappy, for it is condemned, by the more judicious among the critics, as a forgery.

Though Warburton acknowledged his obligation to Meursius, he very disingenuously concealed what he owed to Le Clerc, for he gave no indication that his whole hypothesis, that the gods were declared in the Mysteries to have been but mortals, had been given to the world by Le Clerc several years before; so that Gibbon took occasion sarcastically to observe that the hypothesis had been adopted by Le Clerc in 1687, and invented by Warburton in 1738.

What religious doctrines were really taught in the Mysteries, or whether any were taught in them that could fairly be called religious, is a question that has been much discussed, but with scarcely any approach to certainty. The French writer, St. Croix, in his 'Recherches sur les Mystères du Paganisme,' has expressed himself of opinion that the Mysteries were instituted by early legislators to commemorate the blessings of civilization, and to influence men to repent of any crimes that they had committed, and to resolve on leading better lives in future; while the editor of the second impression of that work, Silvestre de Sacy, has maintained that such notions are altogether groundless, and that we know nothing of the Mysteries but that certain secret rites and symbols were communicated in them, which may have been utterly unmeaning, but which it was sacrilegious to reveal. Some of the

German writers, as Schelling, Creuzer, and F. C. Baur, have supposed that what was taught in them was pure monotheism, with moral doctrines something similar to those of Christianity; but all such hypotheses are entirely fanciful, and almost the only probable notion regarding the Mysteries is that of Müller,* that they had their origin in the endeavours of some conquered race to preserve their ancient worship.

The demonstration of the true character of Jupiter and the other deities, the assurance that men, by doing services to their fellow-creatures, might attain such honour as to be ranked among divinities, were, according to 'The Divine Legation,' the great reasons why it was thought proper that princes, statesmen, lawgivers, and all persons that aspired to rule and command, should be instructed in the secrets of the greater Mysteries. But to the multitude, as Varro said, the knowledge of such truths would have been useless or pernicious; for the belief in the vulgar polytheism was so rooted in their minds, that it could not have been expelled without disturbance to society.

Warburton was then led into a disquisition, which, though it was for a while regarded with favour by some of the more imaginative, has since drawn upon him as much ridicule as any portion of his work. As Æneas, the hero of Virgil, was to be a lawgiver, Warburton considered that he must have been initiated, like other lawgivers, in the Mysteries, and proceeded to make it appear that the account of his descent into the infernal regions, related in the sixth book of the Æneid, was in reality a figurative description of his initiation into the rites of Ceres; and that what he is represented as seeing was an exact picture of the Eleusinian spectacles, 'where

* Prolegomena to a Scientific Mythology. See Encycl. Brit., Art. 'Mysteries.' Thirlwall, Hist. of Greece, vol. ii. p. 140.

everything was done in show and machinery, and where a representation of the history of Ceres afforded opportunity of bringing in the scenes of heaven, hell, elysium, purgatory, and whatever related to the future state of men and heroes.'

Virgil, according to the author of 'The Divine Legation,' was not satisfied that the epic poem should be merely what it was in the hands of Homer; he aspired to comprise in it a system of politics. With this view he wrote the Æneid, 'which is, indeed,' says Warburton, 'as complete an institute in verse, by *example*, as the Republics of Plato and Tully were in prose, by *precept*.' Numerous are the instructions, in various forms, scattered throughout it. Why are Æneas's ships changed into nymphs? To admonish the Romans of the necessity of cultivating a naval power, such as should extend their commerce, and secure their dominion over the ocean. Why is the episode of Nisus and Euryalus introduced? To show how properly a legislator may cherish such an institution as that of the association of youths in Crete, or that of the sacred band, consisting of pairs of attached friends, at Thebes. Why was Æneas chosen by Virgil for his hero, and formed into the character in which Virgil represents him? Because a system of politics, designed for the instruction of mankind, and for the gratification of Augustus in particular, and delivered in the example of a great prince, 'must show him in every public adventure of life;' and hence Æneas was, of necessity, to be found 'voyaging with Ulysses, and fighting with Achilles.' 'Such a key to the Æneid,' that it is a system of politics, 'not only clears up many passages obnoxious to the critics, but adds infinite beauty to a great number of incidents throughout the whole poem.'

As Æneas was to represent a perfect hero and lawgiver, as far as anything human can be perfect, he was to be initiated in the Mysteries of Ceres, for in these Mysteries, as Warburton believes, all the ancient heroes and lawgivers were initiated. They were an instrument in the hands of lawgivers, and no lawgiver would fail to recommend a knowledge of them by his example. Jason, Orpheus, Hercules, Castor, and even, as Macrobius thinks, Tarquinius Priscus, had been initiated in the Mysteries. Hercules, when he is supposed, in the 'Hercules Furens' of Euripides, to come from Hades, is, in fact, only come from the celebration of the Mysteries, where he has learned the true doctrine about the gods,—a doctrine which Theseus, to whom he makes some allusions on the subject, had not yet learned, because, though he also had descended into hell, or had got some insight into the Mysteries, his entrance had been clandestine, and had gained him no just instruction.

'Had an old poem,' says Warburton, 'under the name of Orpheus, entitled *A Descent into Hell*, been now extant, it would probably have shown us that no more was meant than Orpheus's initiation, and that the idea of the sixth book' of the Æneid 'was taken from thence.' No poem of the kind has come down to us; but Warburton was resolved that Virgil's descent of Æneas should not fail of exactly designating an initiation into the Eleusinian secrets. The Sibyl represents the hierophant, who conducted the initiated through the whole ceremony. The golden bough, which Æneas was ordered to seek, answers to the wreath of myrtle, which the initiated were required to wear. The words of the Sibyl, *procul ô procul este, profani*, are the very words used by the hierophant at the opening of the Mysteries. Æneas is startled at the sight of the ghosts, and the initiated used to be startled at the horrid spectacles exhibited to their view. The metempsychosis was taught in the Mysteries, and the metempsychosis is also taught in the Æneid.

It was not till 1770, thirty-two years after the first edition of 'The Divine Legation' was published, that Gibbon put forth his well-known examination of this part of 'The Divine Legation;' but, for the sake of observing what the historian had to say against the divine, it may as well be noticed here. Gibbon was then thirty-three years of age, and had, as yet, published nothing in English. He disliked the dictatorial tone of Warburton, and the violence with which he wrested Virgil's poetry to suit his own views, and grew ambitious, in emulation of Lowth, who had attacked Warburton a short time before, 'of breaking a lance against the giant's shield. My pamphlet,' says he, 'was an accidental sally of love and resentment; of my reverence for modest genius, and my aversion for insolent pedantry.' Warburton's 'hypothesis, a singular chapter in "The Divine Legation of Moses," had been admitted by many,' he states, 'as true; it was praised by all as ingenious; nor had it been exposed, in a space of thirty years, to a fair and critical discussion.'

Gibbon begins by denying that the Mysteries were the invention of the magistrate or lawgiver. Surely, if the magistrate wanted an instrument of religion, he would rather have availed himself of the Oracles, which were not less ancient nor less venerable than the Mysteries. Nothing of importance was undertaken without a consultation of the Delphic oracle, the most frequented among several hundred others. 'Here, then, we might expect to perceive the directing hand of the magistrate. Yet when we study their history with attention, instead of the *alliance between Church and State*, we can discover only the ancient alliance between the avarice of the priest and the credulity of the people.'

Had Virgil intended to compose *a political institute*, argues Gibbon, he would probably have adopted something else for the main support of it than a description of the Mysteries; he would possibly have produced something more akin to what Fenelon has given in his History of Telemachus. But if we admit 'that the Mysteries exhibited a theatrical representation of all that was believed or imagined of the lower world; that the aspirant was conducted through the mimic scenes of Erebus, Tartarus, and Elysium; and that a warm enthusiast, in describing these awful spectacles, might express himself as if he had actually visited the infernal regions,' how, by this admission, would Warburton's hypothesis be advantaged? If the Mysteries professed to give a copy of what was supposed to exist in the infernal regions, the professed copy would resemble the supposed original; but who shall say that Virgil may not have intended to describe the original rather than the copy?

But had Virgil been himself initiated in the Mysteries, so as to be able to describe the matters of which they consisted? Warburton, it is evident, assumed that he had been initiated; but for such assumption there is no ground. Initiation might very well form part of the education of a young Athenian, or it might be gone through by others, Greeks or foreigners, as by Augustus, and Pomponius, and Atticus, for the sake of pleasing the Athenian people, but no such motive was likely to have induced Virgil to submit to the ceremony; his philosophy was of the Epicurean kind, and between the Epicureans and the conductors of the Mysteries a strong antipathy subsisted, the philosophers regarding the hierophants as mere deceivers of the multitude. Virgil, too, as is probable, was never out of Italy till the last year of his life, when, after visiting Athens with Augustus, in the summer, he fell ill at Megara, and, hastening homewards, expired at Brundusium in September; and though, as the Mysteries were celebrated while he was at Athens, it is not impossible that he might have undergone initiation, yet there was not time for him to introduce into his poem the descent of Æneas into hell as a representation of the Eleusinian shows; so that that part of the Æneid must have been written previously to his visit to Greece. The passage relating to Marcellus, indeed, and probably the whole of the sixth book, he had read to Augustus and Octavia about four years before.

But even if Virgil was fully acquainted with all that passed in the Mysteries, is it likely that he would have revealed it? He tells it, indeed, as Warburton supposes, under the veil of an allegory, but the allegory is such as would be well understood by all the initiated, who would have expressed, in some way, a unanimous feeling against his treachery. Every one would have directed towards him words similar to those of his contemporary Horace:

> Vetabo qui Cereris sacrum
> Vulgârit arcanæ, sub îsdem
> Sit trabibus, fragilemque mecum
> Solvat phaselon.

Such reprobation would have been cast on Virgil by all who had heard of what the Æneid consisted; and Horace, who well knew its contents, would have been considered to have written those words with the express intention of reflecting on his friend.

Nor should it be forgotten, that if Æneas's descent into Hades be an exact revelation of what was taught in the Mysteries, the doctrine which Warburton, following Le Clerc, declares to have been the great Eleusinian secret, that 'the whole rabble of licentious deities,' as 'The Divine Legation' expresses it, 'were only dead mortals,' might have been expected to be in some way set forth in it. But there is no indication of this doctrine throughout the whole book; and Warburton carefully abstains from making any allusion to its absence.

Thus we see how little support there is for Warburton's notion, that the account of Æneas's descent is a representation of the Eleusinian Mysteries. We find it to be a pure offspring of fancy, which we may allow to be ingenious, but must acknowledge to be groundless.

Gibbon's 'Critical Observations' nobody attempted to answer. Warburton's party, as he remarks, maintained a discreet silence. But the author of the 'Decline and Fall' could not forbear expressing his delight at the approbation bestowed on his remarks by Heyne, who calls him '*doctus et elegantissimus Britannus*,' though he allows that he animadverted on Warburton '*paullo acrius quàm velis*.' Nor could he 'resist the temptation of transcribing the favourable judgment of Mr. Hayley, himself a poet and a scholar: 'An intricate hypothesis, twisted into a long and laboured chain of quotation and argument, the Dissertation on the Sixth Book of Virgil remained some time unrefuted. At length a superior, but anonymous, critic arose, who, in one of the most judicious and spirited essays that has ever been produced on a point of classical literature, completely overturned this ill-founded edifice, and exposed the arrogance and futility of its assuming architect.'

Before Gibbon's 'Observations' appeared, as early, indeed, as 1755, Jortin had published a volume containing 'Six Dissertations on Different Subjects,' the sixth of which was employed on 'The State of the Dead, as described by Homer and Virgil,' in which the author bestowed some notice on the Sixth Book of Virgil, and, alluding to Warburton's hypothesis respecting the descent of Æneas, made the following remark: 'All of us who attempt to explain and illustrate Virgil, have reason to hope that we may make some discoveries, and to fear that we may fall into some mistakes; and this should induce us to conjecture with freedom, to propose with diffidence, and to dissent with civility.' This observation, with some intimations of dissent from Warburton, drew down upon Jortin the vengeance of one of Warburton's followers, of whom we shall have occasion to speak hereafter.

I am unwilling to quit this consideration of the Sixth Book of Virgil without adverting to the difficulty which all readers and commentators have experienced respecting the ivory gate at which Anchises lets out his son and the

Sibyl from Hades, and the manner in which Warburton endeavours to turn that circumstance to the purpose of his own hypothesis. Homer, Virgil's great master, said that there were two gates to the House of Sleep; one of horn, from which true dreams or visions issued; the other of ivory, from which went forth illusive and deceitful phantoms:

> Immur'd within the silent bower of Sleep,
> Two portals firm the various phantoms keep;
> Of ivory one; whence flit, to mock the brain,
> Of winged lies a light fantastic train;
> The gate oppos'd pellucid valves adorn,
> And columns fair incas'd with polish'd horn;
> Where images of truth for passage wait,
> With visions manifest of future fate.*

Virgil's words are,

> Sunt geminæ Somni portæ; quarum altera fertur
> Cornea, quâ veris facilis datur exitus umbris:
> Altera candenti perfecta nitens elephanto;
> Sed falsa ad cœlum mittunt insomnia manes.
> His ubi tum natum Anchises unàque Sibyllam
> Prosequitur dictis, portâque emittit eburnâ.

> Two gates the silent house of Sleep adorn;
> Of polish'd ivory this, that of transparent horn;
> True visions through transparent horn arise;
> Through polish'd ivory pass deluding lies.
> Of various things discoursing as he pass'd,
> Anchises hither bends his steps at last.
> Then, through the gate of ivory, he dismiss'd
> His valiant offspring, and divining guest.
>
> DRYDEN.

The reason why Æneas and the Sibyl are sent out at the ivory gate by Virgil, says Warburton, can never be satisfactorily determined, but by supposing the descent to hell to signify an initiation into the Mysteries. 'This,' he says, 'will unriddle the enigma, and restore the poet

* Odyss. xix. 656, Pope's version.

to himself.' If Virgil intended Æneas's journey as a description of the shows of the Mysteries, he would, he thinks, give some private mark to indicate his meaning. He has, therefore, at the conclusion, by taking advantage of Homer's gate of horn for true visions, and that of ivory for false, insinuated, 'by the first, the reality of another state, and, by the second, the shadowy representations of it in the shows of the Mysteries; so that not the things themselves, but only the pictures of them objected to Æneas, were false; as the scene did not lie in hell, but in the temple of Ceres.' Such is Warburton's solution, to suit his own hypothesis.

Let us next see what view Jortin takes of the question. He is worth attention, even if he fails to give us satisfaction. 'Virgil,' says he, 'after having shone out with full splendour through the sixth book, sets in a cloud. He first represents the state of departed souls in Hades as a reality, and this he was obliged to do by the very nature of his subject; then he intimates that the whole is a lying fable;' at least, it seems scarcely possible to clear him from the charge of giving this intimation.

His friends try to acquit him of it, by observing how unreasonable it is to suppose 'that the serious and judicious poet would act so strangely as to overset an elegant system which he had put together and embellished with no small pains, and which was partly calculated to promote religion and morality, and the hopes and fears of a future state of retribution.'

This observation, Jortin admits, is one of much weight, and one by which all admirers of Virgil would doubtless willingly be convinced, but expresses his fears that no such attempts in Virgil's favour will avail to set aside the natural and obvious way of interpreting him. Servius has not the least doubt that Virgil meant to intimate that all he had described was unreal: '*Vult autem intelligi falsa esse omnia quæ dixit;*' and most other commentators have adopted Servius's view of the matter. Virgil himself was of the Epicurean school, as he had already indicated in his previous writings, the Eclogues and the Georgics. He makes Silenus, in his sixth Eclogue, inscribed to Varus, who was also an Epicurean, describe the system of the world according to Epicurus's system:

> Namque canebat uti magnum per inane coacta
> Semina terrarumque, animæque, marisque, fuissent,
> Et liquidi simul ignis; ut his exordia primis
> Omnia, et ipse tener mundi concreverit orbis.

> For first he sung of Nature's wondrous birth,
> How seeds of water, air, and flame, and earth,
> Down the vast void with casual impulse hurl'd,
> Clung into shapes, and form'd this fabric of the world.
>
> BEATTIE.

In his Georgics he gives us the sentiments of an Epicurean philosophy:

> Felix qui potuit rerum cognoscere causas,
> Quique metus omnes, et inexorabile fatum,
> Subjecit pedibus, strepitumque Acherontis avari.

> Happy! who could learn
> The causes of creation; and each fear,
> And destiny inexorable, hath bow'd
> Beneath his feet, and greedy Acheron's roar.
>
> SEWELL.

But these intimations of his philosophical opinions, says Jortin, he takes care to make 'decently and obliquely, and so as not openly to attack and insult the public religion.' However, even if we suppose, with Warburton, that Virgil, by the descent of Æneas, really intended to represent his initiation, 'still the troublesome conclusion remains as it was, and, from the manner in which the hero is dismissed after the ceremonies, we learn that, in those initiations, the machinery and the whole show was, in the poet's opinion, a representation of things which had no truth and reality.

'Virgil lets Æneas out at the *gate of Sleep*. The

consequence of this seems to be, that the hero had been asleep, and had seen all these marvellous things in a dream or vision. If the poet had said no more, I should have suspected that he alluded to the ancient and common custom of consulting the gods by sleeping in sacred places, and receiving information by dreams.'

Howsoever we consider the matter, we must feel impressed with the notion that Virgil, 'by letting Æneas out *at the gate of Sleep*, intimates that his descent was not real, and, by letting him out *at the gate of False Dreams*, intimates that all which had been related concerning the state of the dead, and the infernal regions, was fiction and falsehood.

'Virgil had studied and embraced the Epicurean philosophy, and whatever use he may have made, as a poet, of the doctrines of other sects, yet this was his favourite system, and he was willing to let the learned reader know it, and not to pass for a deserter of his own principles, which in the philosophical world was held a dishonourable thing.' He conveys to his reader the same assurance as is given in the words of Seneca:

> Post mortem nihil est; ipsaque mors nihil.
> Tænara, et aspero
> Regnum sub domino, limen et obsidens
> Custos non facili Cerberus ostio,
> Rumores vacui, verbaque inania,
> Et par *sollicito* fabula *somnio*.

'It would make one smile,' concludes Jortin, 'to see poetical divines wonderfully tender and candid in their judgments of Virgil's philosophical and theological principles, looking upon him as upon a devout and religious creature, one who was honoured with glimpses of the glad tidings of salvation, and a kind of *minor prophet*. Yet I would not willingly censure them; for, after all, a man can have no more judgment than falls to his share; and, besides, it seems to be an error on the right side—

a good-natured mistake—an innocent simplicity, which thinketh no evil.'

Such is Dr. Jortin's notion of the meaning of the ivory gate. Gibbon's is less satisfactory. He supposes that Virgil, after representing the regions of Hades as Homer had represented them, and setting them before his readers as realities, 'unwarily slid into an Epicurean idea,' and turned that into falsehood which he had before given as truth; a defect which the author, if the work had not been deprived of his last revision, might have removed; but, whatever be the case, he adds, 'I had much rather reproach my favourite poet with want of care in one line, than with want of taste throughout a whole book;'—a charge which he would have deserved, if he had devoted the whole of his sixth book to the description of an initiation into the Mysteries under the guise of a descent into hell.

With this apology for a solution, the historian takes leave of the question in the body of his pamphlet. But in a postscript he adds another suggestion:

'Whilst I am writing,' he says, 'a sudden thought occurs to me, which, rude and imperfect as it is, I shall venture to throw out to the public. It is this: After Virgil, in imitation of Homer, had described the two gates of sleep, the horn and the ivory, he again takes up the first in a different sense:

> Quâ veris facilis datur exitus umbris.

The term shades, *veræ umbræ*, were those airy forms which were continually sent to animate new bodies; such light and immaterial natures as would without difficulty pass through a thin transparent substance. In this new sense, Æneas and the Sibyl, who were still encumbered with a load of flesh, could not pretend to the prerogative of true shades. In their passage over the Styx they had almost sunk Charon's boat:

Gemuit sub pondere cymba
Sutilis, et multam accepit rimosa paludem.

Some other expedient was requisite for their return; and, since the horn gate would not afford them an easy dismission, the other passage, which was adorned with polished ivory, was the only one that remained either for them or for the poet.

'By this explanation we save Virgil's judgment and religion, though, I must own, at the expense of an uncommon harshness and ambiguity of expression. Let it only be remembered that those who, in desperate cases, conjecture with modesty, have a right to be heard with indulgence.'

Such are the suggestions offered on this point by two able writers. The one that taxes Virgil with haste and thoughtlessness seems the less eligible of them. Of the rest, the reader may either choose which he pleases, or leave the question as an explicable *crux*, like the

——— Dic quibus in terris
Tres pateat cœli spatium non amplius ulnas.

Heyne, indeed, supposes that Virgil may have had no particular intention in fixing on the ivory gate. He took the gates as he found them in Homer, and desiring, when he had brought Æneas and the Sibyl towards them, to give them an exit at one of the two, he chose the ivory gate rather by chance than from design, having no motive for preferring one to the other.

CHAPTER VIII.

ATTACKS ON WARBURTON. WEBSTER, MIDDLETON, JORTIN.

'THE DIVINE LEGATION' LIKED BY HARE AND SHERLOCK — LETTERS FROM THEM — MANY OTHERS DISAPPROVED — ATTACK ON WARBURTON BY DR. WEBSTER — NOTICE OF WEBSTER — 'LETTER FROM A COUNTRY CLERGYMAN' IN THE 'WEEKLY MISCELLANY' — LETTERS FROM HARE AND SHERLOCK, WHO ADVISE WARBURTON TO REPLY — WARBURTON THOUGHT BY MANY TO HAVE SPOKEN TOO FAVOURABLY OF MIDDLETON — SUBSTANCE OF WEBSTER'S LETTERS — WARBURTON'S 'VINDICATION' OF HIMSELF — QUOTATION FROM POPE, AND EULOGY OF HIM — HARE'S APPROBATION OF 'THE VINDICATION' — CORRESPONDENCE BETWEEN WARBURTON AND MIDDLETON — LETTERS TO DR. BIRCH AND TO BISHOP SHERLOCK—OBSERVATIONS ON JORTIN'S 'REMARKS ON SPENSER.'

WHILE 'The Divine Legation' was passing through the press, Warburton sent some sheets of it to Bishops Sherlock and Hare, asking their judgment of the work. Both expressed approbation, but Sherlock at greater length; and 'it may be thought,' says Mr. Kilvert,* 'no trifling attestation to the orthodoxy of Bishop Warburton's leading arguments in "The Divine Legation," that that work should have received the countenance and approval of so sound a divine as Bishop Sherlock.' Sherlock's first acknowledgment was as follows:

'Wallington, Herts, Oct. 18, 1737.

'Reverend Sir,—Last night I received some sheets of your book, and ran them over with great pleasure, but

* Selections from Warburton's Papers, p. 54.

not with the attention which the subject and your way of treating it demand. I can, therefore, at present only thank you for the favour you have done me, and give you my opinion upon a very small matter, which yet I apprehend will greatly prejudice many readers against you.

'In page 55, speaking of Wollaston, you take occasion to quote a passage from "Don Quixote." As Wollaston was a sober, serious writer, and a scholar, and of an exceeding good character in private life, the treating his performance with an air of ridicule will be thought very injurious to him, and very improper to come from you, and will raise a good deal of unnecessary resentment. I am so much of this opinion, that, if I was to judge for you, that leaf should be reprinted, and the passage left out. I shall be in town very soon, and shall have the pleasure of seeing the sheets as they come out.

'Your very affectionate brother and servant,

'THO. SARUM.'

Bishop Hare, in sending his thanks for the sheets, made a similar animadversion on the passage referring to the 'Religion of Nature,' urging him by all means to strike out the sarcasm, 'as it would give great offence to the admirers of that book. I have besides,' he added, '*a particular reason* for advising you to alter that passage, which you shall know at a proper time;' and he begged him, in the same letter, to alter it *immediately*, 'that it might not get into many hands.' The cause of Hare's solicitude was that he was then endeavouring to introduce Warburton to the Queen; * an endeavour frustrated by the Queen's death, as has been already observed. In another letter Hare wrote: 'I can say, without any compliment, that your papers have given me high delight. So many beautiful thoughts, such ingenious illustrations of them,

* Hurd's Life of Warburton, p. 22, 8vo. ed.

such a clear connexion, such a deduction of notions, and so much good learning upon so useful a subject, all expressed in proper and fine language, cannot but give an intelligent reader the greatest satisfaction.' *

About a month afterwards Sherlock wrote again:

'Wallington, near Baldock, Herts, Nov. 29, 1737.

'Sir,—I am very much obliged to you for the pleasure you have given me in perusing the sheets of your book as they came from the press. There are many things quite new to me, and very entertaining. Your proofs of the magistrate's influence in matters of religion are very copious and strong; stronger, perhaps, than ever were produced by the gentlemen who are willing to think all religion to be the contrivance of the civil magistrate.

'I received most of the sheets in town, at the time when the Queen's illness and death left me hardly room to think sedately of anything else. I hope to see you in town before the next summer; by that time, I shall have considered the books together, and, if anything sticks with me, I shall be glad of your assistance to clear it up.

'Mr. Wollaston was, I believe, a serious Christian. He pursued his point to open the principles of natural religion by natural reason only; but towards the conclusion of his book there is a plain indication, in so many words, that *he wanted other help;* and I am well informed that he had begun the proof and explication of the Christian religion in the same method. The unfinished work was found among his papers after his death.'

When 'The Divine Legation' came forth, Hare said, in a letter to Warburton: 'I hear nobody speak of your book who do not express themselves highly entertained with it, though they think the principal point, which remains to be proved, a paradox.' And Bishop Sherlock

* Hurd's Life of Warburton, p. 17, 8vo. ed.

told him that the first part of the work 'had raised a great desire and expectation of the second.'

But there were many others who looked on Warburton's book with much less favour than these two Bishops. Some disliked the author's haughtiness; some, whose view was not very comprehensive, could hardly discern his object; some, under the influence of prejudice, thought the book would do more harm than good; and some were ready to attack the writer to gain a little notoriety for themselves. The first assault was made on him by one Dr. William Webster, a writer now little known, even to the searchers into theological controversy; a writer who, like many others of his class, spent much of a long life in producing matter for the press, but left not a page behind him that deserves to be reprinted.

As he made some impression on Warburton, however, who found it necessary to answer him, we may bestow a little attention on his character and career. He was of Cambridge, and in 1715, when he was twenty-six years of age, and was curate of St. Dunstan-in-the-West, published 'The Life of General Monk, from a manuscript of Thomas Skinner, M.D.,' dedicated to Lord Gower, who was descended from Monk's family. In 1729 he printed 'Two Discourses, one showing that *Belief in even speculative Doctrines may be necessary to Salvation*; and the other, that the Doctrine of the Trinity is *not merely Speculative*;' treatises directed against the liberal notions of Dr. Sykes, who had published a discourse 'On the Innocency of Error.' In 1731 he was deprived, for no reason that is recorded, of his curacy at St. Dunstan's, but was presented by a relative to the rectory of Deepden, in Suffolk, worth about a hundred a-year. About the same time, apparently to please Sherlock, he published 'The Fitness of the Witnesses of the Resurrection considered;' and, to propitiate Hare, two pamphlets on his behalf against Gordon, the translator of Tacitus, who had attacked him for some passages in a sermon. But these effusions brought him only barren thanks, and, to increase his income, he started the publication by which he became most notorious, the 'Weekly Miscellany,' professedly edited by 'Richard Hooker, Esq., of the Inner Temple,' an undertaking which, he said, 'was more approved than supported, procured him nothing but great trouble, much ill will, and abuse of all sorts, great expense, and much difficulties;' and which, from being overcrowded with religious essays, obtained the nickname of 'Mother Hooker's Journal.' He was author, too, of a strong pamphlet in favour of the woollen trade, and, when the sale of it declined, of another, equally strong, in depreciation of the trade. He also published a humorous 'Defence of Eustace Budgell,' inquiring how it was possible for a man, who spoke so confidently of his own honour and honesty, to league with an infamous woman to forge Tindal's pretended will. Having then, by some means, gained the notice of Archbishop Potter, he was recommended by him to the vicarage of Ware, but found the revenues of the parish in a very unsatisfactory state; so that, having gone thither in debt, he became still more and more involved during seventeen years that he held the living, and at last, in a narrative which he published a few months before his death, petitioning the Archbishops and Bishops for charity, he represented himself as in the greatest distress, incapable either of doing his duty or of hiring assistance, among parishioners who were eager to defraud him of his rights, and to render his life as uneasy as possible. He stated that he had been forty-three years employed parochially in the diocese of London, and thirty-five years a public writer. One of those who had assisted him in his distresses was the author of 'Pamela,' to whom he owed ninety pounds when he went to Ware, and who afterwards generously forgave him the whole debt.

It was in the 'Weekly Miscellany' that this unfortunate

theologaster directed his assault upon Warburton, in the form of a 'Letter from a Country Clergyman.'

Bishop Hare, noticing Webster's onslaught in that publication, sent a copy of the paper to Warburton, with the following letter:

'February 28, 1738.

'Dear Sir,—I thank you for yours of the 25th, and should have given you no further trouble, till you should give me the pleasure of seeing you in town, had it not been to communicate to you the enclosed paper, the contents of which I did not hear of till yesterday; and, as I thought fit you should see it, I take the first opportunity to send it to you, upon a supposition that you might not otherwise come soon to the knowledge of it. You will consider, first, whether you should take any notice of it or not; and next, if you should, in what manner, whether by a short pamphlet, or by a letter in some newspaper, and whether in your own name or in the person of another. I cannot at all guess who the writer is, but I should suspect it to be Dr. Waterland sooner than anybody else I know, or Dr. Webster himself; perhaps in a little time it may be known, or guessed at at least, with more certainty. I do not wonder to find you attacked, but I hoped it would not have been so soon, nor with so much warmth. I do not know what to advise in a matter I have had no time to consider of, but think some defence is pretty necessary; but I desire you would not be too hasty in it, and that it may be with more temper than one is apt to write with under so much provocation. I am, dear sir, your most faithful friend and servant,

'FR. CICEST.' *

Bishop Sherlock wrote, a few days afterwards:

'March 2, 1738.

'Reverend Sir,—The Bishop of Chichester tells me that

* Kilvert, Selections from Warburton's Papers, p. 100.

he sent you the "Miscellany" of last week, so there is no occasion to give you any account of it. The very absurd use that paper has made of the passage relating to Hickringall, &c., requires no answer. Everybody cries shame on the author for it. The other charge is equally absurd, though not so surprising. I was aware that some parts of your book would raise jealousies, though I little imagined to see them raised so high, where there are so many passages in the book to speak the author's sense plainly.

'But one passage there is, which, I find, has, above all others, given ground to those suspicions; it is Dedication, p. 18, where you say of the author * of "A Letter to Dr. Waterland," that he is one of the most formidable adversaries to the Freethinkers. This author is reckoned to have given up the divine authority of Moses, and to consider him as a mere politician, and to defend even the Christian religion as useful only for the present circumstances of life. I do not vouch for these conclusions, but those who are assured they are just, take your declaration to be approving the method, and to be a key to your own sentiments.

'I thought it right to give you this account, which will let you into the reason of the anger expressed against you, and enable you, if it should be considerable enough ever to deserve your notice, to see it in the true light; at present, I think it is not.

'I expect to see you in town, and shall be very glad to see you and talk over these matters. The learning and ability of the author of "The Divine Legation" are not called in question, and the first part has raised a great desire and expectation of the second. I am, sir, your affectionate brother and humble servant,

'THO. SARUM.' †

* Dr. Conyers Middleton.

† Kilvert, Selections from Warburton's Papers, p. 62.

In another letter, written a week afterwards, Sherlock says that Bishop Hare and himself were unanimous in thinking that it would be proper for Warburton to say something in answer to the reproaches cast upon him; 'not so much in regard to the author of the "Miscellany" as in regard to others, who may possibly be desirous to see all ground of suspicion removed. In drawing the answer,' he remarks, 'you should consider such persons much more than your angry adversary. If you treat him as he may deserve, you enter into πολεμὸν ἀσπονδόν, and may be engaged in the most disagreeable work to a scholar and a serious man. I do not mean that you have not right, or that you should not complain of the immoral conduct of your adversary; but I wish to see it done seriously, rather than angrily. I write this, not as suspecting your want either of temper or judgment, but from my own experience, who know how hard it is to return a soft answer to a public abuse.

'. . . . The case of Dr. M., which is the *hinc illæ lacrymæ* of the whole complaint, will require your best consideration, whether to mention it at all, or how to mention it. If you had not, in the 18th page, said anything of him, I should have thought the 38th page intended for him. I remember very well that, conversing with Dr. M. at Bath, about four years ago, I said to him much the same thing which I read in the 38th page.'*

The first of these passages to which Sherlock alludes is this:—'A very candid and respectable author, speaking of the ancient restraints upon free-thinking, says: "These were the maxims, these the principles, which the light of nature suggested, which reason dictated. Nor has this fine writer any cause to be ashamed of his acknowledgment."' What the other passage was I do not know.

'The Country Clergyman's Letter' I have sought, but

* Kilvert, Selections from Warburton's Papers, p. 64.

not found, for, when the best papers of the 'Weekly Miscellany' were collected for republication in volumes, of which, I believe, only two were published, that epistle, with some others that followed it from the same hand, was not included among them.

The grounds of its attack, therefore, are now to be known only from Warburton's reply, from which we gather that the author of 'The Divine Legation,' in the Country Clergyman's opinion, 'had been very severe upon *all clergymen* who take the liberty of censuring the conduct of *any of their brethren*;' and indeed, he adds, 'if I am capable of understanding the meaning and drift of his book, he had reason to apprehend it might draw upon him the censures of *all the clergy who are sincere friends to Christianity;* therefore it might be politic to obviate the force of such animadversions beforehand.' 'If,' he proceeds, 'he really means to defend Christianity, he hath published the weakest defence of it that I have ever read. . . . . He is a warmer advocate for Dr. [Middleton], who denies the Divine inspiration of the Scriptures, than for the Scriptures themselves. . . . . He must excuse me if I suspect his faith and condemn his book. This I am sure of, the author must be a subtile enemy to Revelation, or an indiscreet friend. I must own he has left me in no doubt. . . . . Mr. Warburton modestly says, they [the English Church] have undertaken to prove Christianity without understanding it.' Mr. Warburton 'has undervalued the evidence arising from miracles;' he is one of those who 'deny the divinity of Christ, the merits of his death, the obligation and effects of the sacraments, and the doctrine of grace;' and the Country Clergyman insinuates that Mr. Warburton 'should be hindered from any further advancement in the Church,' and prays 'for the forgiveness and conversion *of all bad men*.'

In his 'Vindication,' Warburton commences by saying that, 'after having twice offered his thoughts to the public on two very important subjects, and had the honour to be favourably heard, it must needs be a sufficient mortification to him to be obliged to descend to *so low a subject as himself.*' But, since an attempt had been made to render his projected defence of religion suspected, he 'thought it his duty to vindicate himself publicly from the *horrid accusations* of a letter-writer in the "Weekly Miscellany" of the 24th of February last.' As to the charge that he had been severe on all clergymen who censured their brethren, he answers that his severity had been directed, not against clergymen who censure their brethren, but against others 'who abuse the whole body of the clergy, considered as an order instituted by Christ, and established by the State;' and in reference to the insinuation that such severity had been intended to propitiate the clergy as a body, with the view, possibly, of gaining himself promotion, he says, 'When I presumed to publish, in defence of the established clergy, a vindication of the Church of England, under the title of "The Alliance between Church and State," which surely might *deserve their pardon*, lest the world *should imagine I expected more*, I put it out without my name, and now, writing *in the common cause* of Christianity, I have publicly owned it.'

With regard to the charge, that the volume was 'a weak defence of Christianity,' he observes that if he had put it forth as *a defence of Christianity*, it might indeed have been called *a weak one*, but that he had expressly stated it was 'only preparatory to the defence of Revelation,' and that, if he had not made this statement, 'the book itself would shew that it is no more a defence of Christianity than the first proposition of the three terms,' in which his argument is declared, 'is a syllogism.'

Middleton he does not desert, but continues to speak of him as before. How true an accuser the letter-writer is of Middleton, he says, we may easily see. 'Dr. [Middleton] says *it is necessary to believe of the Scriptures in general that they are divinely inspired;* and that all which he *denies* is, that *the Scriptures are of absolute and universal inspiration.* He shows that Tillotson and Grotius were of the same opinion, who, he charitably presumes, were Christians. And as he [Middleton] tells his friends and acquaintances the same he tells the public, the letter-writer must excuse me if I believe a man whose candour, sincerity, benevolence, and charity I have experienced, before him who has not given me the pleasure of remarking in him any of those Christian qualities.'

But *however warm an advocate of Dr. Middleton* the letter-writer would make him, he observes that he is not to be made responsible for all Dr. Middleton's opinions, from whom he dissents widely, in regard not only to the partial inspiration of the Scriptures, but to some other matters. 'But we can differ from each other,' he proceeds, 'and avow and maintain our difference of opinion without violation of common humanity, friendship, or Christian charity. I will give the letter-writer an instance of difference in opinion between us, from this very book he so much condemns. The writer of the "Defence of the Letter to Dr. Waterland" says, *Is the notion of the divine origin of the law and inspiration of Moses to be resolved into fiction, or fable, or political lying? No, far be it from me to think or say so. But this perhaps one may venture to say, that the supposition of some degree of such fiction may possibly be found necessary to the solving the difficulties of the Mosaic writings, without any hurt to their authority, or advantage to infidelity.* I am, as I say, of a different opinion. The writer endeavours to support *his* by several arguments, amongst which one is, *the professions and examples of the ancient sages and legislators.* Now, in the second section of my third book I have inquired into the principles that induced the ancient sages and legislators to deem it lawful to deceive for the public good, in the discovery of which, I think, I have made it evident that *those reasons or principles could have no place among the founders and propagators of the Jewish and Christian religions.*

'But I am a warm advocate for Dr. Middleton. In what? I have called him *a very formidable adversary to the Freethinkers.* And I think I had reason; for the arguments he hath used *for the truth of Christianity* against Tindal have never yet been answered by them, nor, I think, ever can. I say *for the truth of Christianity*; for his reasonings* relate only to its truth, and can be understood in no other sense. After this, to think he would have Christianity supported only *because it is useful*, is such a way of interpreting a writer as my charity will never suffer me to follow.

'The opinion I have of Dr. Middleton's abilities, and of the sincerity of his profession, were the true reasons of that esteem I express for him; being desirous of allaying all disgust, if any hath arisen in him, from the treatment of his less candid adversaries, and of engaging him to a more complete vindication of our most holy faith, at a time when the good disposition of the meanest advocate for Revelation should not, I think, in prudence, be discouraged: nay, was I so unhappy to think of Dr. Middleton as the letter-writer is disposed to do, I should yet be inclined to behave myself very differently towards him. I should be so far from estranging him further from the faith by uncharitable anathemas, that I should do all I could *to court and allure him to Christianity, by thinking well of its professors.* Thus much, I conceive, *Christian charity* would require; and how far *Christian policy* would persuade, let the *learned* say, who know what ornament his pen would be to the Christian faith, and his *acquaintance* of what example his morals to Christian practice.'

* Letter to Dr. Waterland, pp. 59-61.

Warburton then observes that he supposes the accusation, that he is *no warm advocate for the Scriptures*, to be founded on the following passage in 'The Divine Legation:' 'The New Testament does not contain any regular or complete system or digest of moral laws; the occasional precepts there delivered, how excellent and divine soever, arising only from conjunctures and circumstances that were the subjects of those preachings or writings in which such precepts are found. For the rest, for a general knowledge of the whole body of moral duty, the great pandect of the law of nature is held open by it to be searched and studied. Finally, says the Apostle Paul, *whatsoever things are true*,' &c. I suppose, if the letter-writer had any particular meaning, this was the place that was to justify him in saying that I was *no warm advocate for the Scriptures.* But does the New Testament contain *any such complete or regular system?* Will the letter-writer say so? Will any one besides say so? How *weak and indiscreet a friend* soever he may please to think me of religion, I will assure the reader that, as I make it one point of my religion to say nothing but what I think the truth, so I do not use to throw about those truths at random.'

To the charge of having said that *the English clergy had undertaken to prove Christianity without understanding it*, he replies that the letter-writer had strangely perverted what he had said, for he had merely asked whether, in the controversy with the Deists, *that might not be applied to certain advocates of revelation which was formerly said of Arnobius and Lactantius, that they undertook the defence of Christianity before they understood it.* 'Have none but Englishmen,' he adds, 'wrote of late in defence of Christianity? Have no Englishmen but the English clergy wrote in defence of it? I solemnly declare that in the passage above quoted I meant no English clergyman whatsoever. So far from that, I expressly say in the Dedication, that *the clergy of the Established Church are they who have been principally watchful in the common cause of Christianity, and most successful in repelling the insults of its enemies.*'

In reference to the accusation that he *had undervalued the existence of miracles*, he observes that he had said *that men have proved our religion actually divine thereby*; and, as to the imputation of other false opinions, he 'had affirmed,' he states, 'more than once or twice, that the doctrine of redemption is the foundation, and of the very essence of Christianity,' and that the letter-writer 'should have known that all or most of those true Christian doctrines,' which he accuses the author of 'The Divine Legation' of neglecting, 'are contained in the doctrine of redemption.'

A passage towards the end of the 'Vindication,' in which he takes an opportunity of quoting Pope, must be given at length:

'There are, and those esteemed sincere Christians too, who would have taken the names of *Infidel* and *Heretic* for favours at the hand of the letter-writer. But I am of a different humour. These titles have no charms for me. I have lived some time in the world, and, blessed be God, *without giving or taking offence.* This time has been spent in my parish church (for I am a country clergyman, and reside constantly on my cure), in the service of my neighbour, in my study, and in the offices of filial piety:

> With lenient arts t' extend a mother's breath,
> Make languor smile, and smooth the bed of death,
> Explore the thought, explain the asking eye,
> And keep a while one parent from the sky.

Excess of zeal, in such as the letter-writer, and defect of religion, in others of better breeding, so efface these feelings of nature, that I could hardly have known how to have told them, had I not both the example and the fine words too of one of the politest men of the age to keep me in countenance. The time spent in my study has been employed in confirming my own faith against the erroneous opinions the letter-writer has raked together, and *then* in planning a work to confirm my brethren. All the reward I ever had, or ever expect to have here, is the testimony of a good conscience within doors, and a good name without. The first no man can take from me; the other this letter-writer, in the most unchristian manner, has attempted to invade.

'But I heartily forgive him; and, instead of putting uncharitable constructions on his secret intentions, will believe, though I know no more of him than by his letter, that he is sincere, and only unhappily agitated by a furious zeal for the cause of God and religion, instead of thinking *he ought to be hindered from any further advancement in the Church.* Instead of *using any warm endeavours to lessen his credit*, which he professes in so many words to be his purpose against me, I wish him all increase of reputation and honour; and, instead of insulting him with the words he seems to apply to me, *I pray for the forgiveness and conversion of all bad men*, I will assure him that I pray for *him* as a brother.'

He then concludes by saying that, though he has presumed to appeal to the public on this occasion against a false charge, the public need not apprehend that he shall trouble them a second time in the same way, for it must be 'a strange provocation indeed' that would induce him to a repetition of such a task; and that, whether he is a weak defender of Christianity or not, must be submitted to the opinion of the world, but that, he is persuaded, his readers will suspend their decision till they see the whole of his performance; assuring them that what he has offered to the public concerning 'The Divine Legation of Moses,' was not a hasty, sudden thought, such as may please at first, yet give no ultimate satisfaction, but the result of long reflection on a subject 'often laid by, and then again, at proper intervals, resumed, reviewed, and turned on all sides.'

As soon as the 'Vindication' was published, a copy of it was sent to Bishop Hare, who replied as follows:

'March 23, 1738.

'Dear Sir,—I received yesterday your "Vindication," which I read twice over with great satisfaction. You have more than kept your word in promising to write with temper. I wish you had shown a little more resentment upon the first point, the misrepresentation is so very gross; not but that you have in reality chosen the better part; too much temper is a thing few writers are guilty of, under much less provocation, and, with equitable judges, will turn greatly to your credit. But I do truly wish you had quoted the passage in your own book, instead of referring to it, which would, without saying more, have made the misrepresentation appear more flagrant; and I was pleased to find the Bishops of Sarum and Bristol, who are just gone from me, of the same opinion. But they thought, as I do, that the reason of your not doing it was, that it was quite unnecessary in so gross an instance of abuse.

'The part that relates to Dr. Middleton the bishops think extremely well done. It was the only difficult part, and it cannot but please every candid writer to see you do justice to yourself, and yet not do it at his expense, nor say a word that either he or his friends can be offended at, or that is in the least giving up a man with whom you have a friendship. Here is integrity and courage very agreeably joined. . . .

'I am, dear Sir, most faithfully yours,

'F. CICESTR.'

Much correspondence took place between Warburton and Middleton about this time in reference to this affair and matters connected with it; and Hurd, who had their letters in his hands, says that Warburton employed every kind of art to soften or remove Middleton's prejudices against revealed religion, 'by joining with him sometimes in his graver complaints of bigoted divines, and sometimes in his ridicule of their pretended orthodoxy; but in taking for granted everywhere his respect for revelation, and his real belief of it, and in seeming to think that, if other opinions were entertained of him, they had proceeded from ignorance of his true character.'

He had informed Middleton of his intention to write the 'Dedication to the Freethinkers,' and had let him know that he purposed to mention him in it with respect. Dr. Middleton replied:* 'I am pleased with the manner of your address to the Freethinkers, and obliged to you for your friendly intentions with regard to myself; and though I should be as proud to have the testimony of your judgment and good opinion as of any man, yet I would have you consider how far such a declaration of it may expose you to a share of that envy which has lain, and still lies, very heavy upon me.'

This solicitude was very honourable to Middleton, but did not make Warburton alter his resolution. He wrote to him, a short time after,† saying that his book would soon be published, and that a copy of it should be sent to him; and added, in allusion to Middleton's letter: 'I have your pardon to ask for the liberty which I have taken of designing you, by your character, in one place of the body of the book, as well as in the "Dedication to the Freethinkers;" for I would fain contribute to abate an *unjust prejudice*, that might lie in the way of those honours which wait for you, and are so much your due. *And I shall reckon it for nothing, in so honest an attempt, to run the risk of sharing that prejudice with you.*'

When he replied to the letter in the 'Weekly Miscel-

* Sept. 22, 1737.

† Dec. 23, 1737.

lany,' he wrote again to Middleton,* observing, in reference to Webster: 'I am to thank him for the agreeable necessity of vindicating you (by a quotation in one of the defences that pass for yours) from his *false accusation* of denying the inspiration of Scripture'; and from his *imagination* (which is the ground of this clamour), that you defend Revelation, not as true, but only useful; and that, as to other points, you and I can differ without breach of common humanity, friendship, and Christian charity.'

Of Middleton we need say no more at present. Of Webster, Warburton professes to take leave altogether, determining to honour him with no more animadversion. Writing to Birch, and alluding to a sermon which he was about to publish, he says: 'You might perceive I was in a passion against Webster when I wrote, but his last letter against me has cured me of it, and *I design to take no manner of notice of him in the preface of my sermon.*' But in a few weeks he changed his mind, and, acquainting Birch that his sermon was in the press, he observes: 'I think *it will be the best answer to Webster*; the title of it is, "Faith working by Charity to Christian Edification." *There is a long preface to it, in which I work Venn and Webster in a manner* (though not equal to the highest provocation that ever was given, yet) *that they will have no reason to say that I sneak to them in an unorthodox manner.* This was to be positively the last time in which Webster would be noticed. 'It is a great pleasure,' he says to Birch, on sending him a copy of his sermon, 'that such judges as you approve, and that my enemies are such as Webster. As *I am resolved for the future not only not to answer, but even not to read, what that wretch writes against me*, his putting his name to what he does will be of use to me. I wish you could contrive that this should come to his ear.' Yet, alas for the frailty of human resolution, he tells Birch, in the very same epistle, that he '*has*

* March 18, 1738. Hurd's Life of Warburton, pp. 20, 21, 8vo. ed.

not yet seen Webster's "Circular Letter," ' a pamphlet addressed to the Bishops, and adds: '*Pray, when you go by Mr. Gyles's shop, desire him to send it to me.*' And in another letter he says: 'Mr. Gyles has sent me word that Webster has published all his letters together, and he thinks it proper to do the same by those newspapers wrote in defence of me. I have returned answer, that it was a matter of the utmost indifference; but that, if he thought it worth his while, I gave my consent; so I have left it to him to do what he thinks proper. To think I will ever enter into a controversy with the weakest as well as wickedest of all mankind, is a thing impossible. *This* I shall do indeed, in a short preface to the second volume—*I shall hang him and his fellows as they do vermin in a warren, and leave them to posterity to stink and blacken in the wind*; and this will I do, was the Pope himself their protector. Other business with them, in the way of argument, I shall never have any.' *

The Venn here mentioned was the Rev. Henry Venn, a person of little note but as the colleague of Webster, and as having prevented Dr. Rundle, afterwards Bishop of Derry, from being made Bishop of Gloucester, by informing against him as a Deist, for expressions in a private conversation.

Warburton accordingly 'hung' Venn and Webster in his preface to the second volume of 'The Divine Legation,' a work with which, in spite of all clamour and opposition from ignorance or timidity, he determined vigorously to proceed. 'As to my inclination,' he tells Bishop Sherlock, 'it is not a bit abated for all the scurvy usage that I have met with; for I will tell your Lordship what it is that supports me—it is a love of truth, and a thorough conviction of the reality of the Jewish and Christian revelations. I think I am not uncharitable in suspecting that it may be a want of the latter that makes some very zealous

* Nichols's Lit. Anec., vol. v. p. 548; Lit. Illustr., vol. ii. p. 87.

people cooler and more suspicious of the former than is fitting. Hence we see them almost frighted to death at every foolish book writ against religion, and betake themselves in all haste to their old posture of defence to prop and buttress up, with any materials that come to hand, what they think a sinking fabric, because they do not see the eternal foundations on which it stands. In the mean time, if any one offers to remove the rubbish that hides its beauty, or kick down an awkward prop that discredits its strength, or lays it open to its very foundations, which is all that is wanting to make it impregnable, he is sure to be called, perhaps to be thought, a secret adversary, or an indiscreet friend.' *

In the early part of this year he was made chaplain to the Prince of Wales; and his new dignity appears in the title-page of the sermon mentioned above, which, with the projected preface turned into a postscript, he published in June. It was reprinted in 1745, under the title of 'A faithful Portrait of Popery,' and is the fourteenth among the discourses inserted in his collected works by Hurd.

He did not occupy himself, however, so constantly with his great work, as not to allow himself time for noticing lighter matters. Jortin had recently published a thin octavo of 'Remarks on Spenser,' pointing out many of his imitations of the Greek and Roman writers, and modestly proposing a few emendations. Warburton, lighting on the volume, wrote some observations on it, which he sent, to be printed anonymously, to the 'Works of the Learned' for October 1738. The editor of that work introduced the communication thus:

'I am indebted for the favour of the following lines to a gentleman who has distinguished himself very eminently in the commonwealth of letters, but who will not allow

* Kilvert's Selections from Warburton's Papers, p. 65.

me the honour of naming my correspondent. There are some people of so nice a decorum, that they will not be seen in dishabille, though the graces of their person are not to be concealed by any dress they can appear in.'

Warburton commences as follows:

'A late book, intituled "Remarks on Spenser's Poems," seems not to be so well known as so learned and judicious a performance deserves. The modest, worthy, and very learned author has here given the justest plan for a good edition of Spenser (who had the ancients always in view) in the method he has observed of marking out, as he goes along, the imitations of the classic writers, which affords him an opportunity of making many useful and well-grounded remarks. The continence he has observed, with regard to the author's text, appears to have been partly owing to the modesty of his nature, in part to a reasonable conviction that Spenser's text is very pure, and principally to his disgust at some strange liberties taken of late years with English poets, on pretence of amending and restoring them. So masterly a piece of criticism, then, will well deserve anyone's notice. And I dare say nothing can be more agreeable to the author than our endeavour to satisfy a few doubts and queries which here and there occurred to him.'

Of these criticisms, which are in better style than many of his Shakspearian attempts, some specimens, it is hoped, may not unreasonably be extracted.

'Book I. Canto VI. St. 1:

> As when a ship that flies fair under sail,
> A hidden rock escap'd hath unawares,
> That lay in wait *her wreck for to bewail*, &c.

On which the author remarks, "To bewail her wreck seems unintelligible." We must remember that Spenser was always full of the poetical mythology, which tells of Scylla and the Sirens sitting on rocks, and alluring navigators to their destruction.

'Of the first, Virgil says:

> At Scyllam cæcis cohibet spelunca latebris
> Ora exertantem et naves in saxa trahentem.

And of the latter:

> Jamque adeò scopulos Sirenum advecta subibat,
> Difficiles quondam, multorumque ossibus albos.

These traitoresses, after they had wrecked the vessels, pretended *to wail over them*. To these Spenser alludes, but applies to the rock what was said of them, and not inelegantly or unlearnedly. For the original of these fables was only the perpetual howling heard about those rocks, by the waters running to and fro in the hollows of them. The allusion, too, is very just and beautiful, for the similitude is applied to one of his heroes just broke loose from the enchantments of a vicious woman.'

This is ingenious; but Upton quashes it all by suggesting that *bewail* is the same as *wale*, that is, *choose*, equivalent to the German *walen*. *Wale* is still in use among the Scotch; as in Burns, speaking of the Cotter preparing to read the Scriptures,

> He *wales* a portion with judicious care.

Thus the rock, according to Upton, lay in wait to choose or mark out the ship for a wreck.

Warburton's next criticism is more daring:

'Book I. Canto XI. St. 46:

> There grew a goodly tree him fair beside,—
> Great God it planted in that blessed sted
> With his Almighty hand, and did it call
> The tree of life, the crime of our first father's fall.

The learned author asks, "Why does he call the tree of life the *crime* of our first father's fall?" I answer, that I apprehend Spenser did not call it by any such senseless designation, but that it is a mere blunder of the printer, and that the poet wrote

> ——— and did it call
> The tree of life, the *time* of our first father's fall,

i.e., he gave it that name at the time of our first father's fall; he then named it. The particle *at* denoting time is frequently omitted by writers of that age.'

This is tasteless enough. Jortin himself saw, when he afterwards reprinted his observations, that *crime* was equivalent to *cause*, or *fatal cause*; the meaning of Spenser being that Adam, having eaten of the forbidden tree of knowledge, was made to fall, or be expelled, from Eden, lest he should also eat of the tree of life, and live for ever; the tree of life being thus, in reality, the cause of his expulsion.

'Book II. Canto XII. St. 50:

> More sweet and wholesome than the pleasant hill
> Of Rhodope.

"Methinks," says the author, "he should not have singled out Rhodope, a mountain of Thrace, as an agreeable place. The ancients are against him." But this was done in compliment to the power of poetry, and a very fine one it is; for this was the mountain on which Orpheus sung, who not only soothed the savage beasts and bent the oaks, but likewise meliorated the soil and climate by the force of harmony. This was Spenser's thought, always profound and sublime in his ideas, as his great admirer Shakspeare confesses, who, in his poem called "The Friendly Concord," seems to apologise for this very passage against the critics, in these words:

> Dowland to thee is dear, whose heavenly touch
> Upon the lute doth ravish human sense;
> Spenser to me, whose *deep conceit* is such
> As, passing all conceit, *needs no defence.*

Nay, he seems even to have paraphrased this very thought in a song, Act III. Sc. 1 of "Henry VIII.":

> Orpheus, with his lute, made trees,
> And the mountain tops that freeze,
> Bow themselves when he did sing;
> To his music plants and flowers
> Ever rose, as sun and showers
> That had made a lasting spring.'

Upton concurs in this explanation, saying that not the real but the poetical Rhodope is meant.

'Book III. Introd. St. 2:

> But *living art* may not least part express,
> Nor life-resembling pencil it can paint;
> All were it Zeuxis or Praxiteles,
> His dædal hand would greatly fail and faint.

The learned author says, "Praxiteles was no painter." No, nor did Spenser understand him such; he supposed him, as he was, a statuary, as appears by the first line, which is differenced from the second by the discretive *nor*; and, by *living art*, he had the *spirantia mollius æra* in view.'

Upton very properly refers 'living art' to Praxiteles, and 'life-resembling pencil' to Zeuxis.

'Book III. Canto XI. St. 21:

> Great Ganges and immortal Euphrates.

"He makes," says our author, "the second syllable of *Euphrates* short, and gives him the pompous epithet *immortal*, which after all is but a botch." I imagine the reason of our poet's giving Euphrates the epithet of immortal was because it was one of the rivers of Paradise.'

This seems a mere Warburtonian fancy. Spenser probably used the word 'immortal' only for *famous* or *renowned*. Todd, and the critics to whom he has recourse, are silent.

'Book VI. Canto X. St. 24. Spenser, speaking of the Graces:

> And eke themselves so in their dance they bore,
> That two of them still *forward* seem'd to be,
> But one still *towards* showed herself afore,
> That good should from us go than come, in greater store.

The learned author says, "A friend of mine conjectures that for *forward* it should be *froward*; *froward* is opposed to *toward*." But the common reading is right, and our Spenser has painted here with great exactness after the antique. For he had doubtless in his eye those ancient gems in which we find the Graces in this attitude, namely, two of them standing facing the spectator, and extending their hands; these are forward; and the third, with her face towards the other two, with her hands on each of their shoulders, and her back to the spectator: thus she showed herself towards the other two, and was afore them; that is, on the first ground of the picture. This exactly points out Spenser's moral, *that good should go from us in greater store than come to us.*'

Church supports Jortin by advocating *froward*, which, he says, is *fromward*, in opposition to *toward.*

This is all that is of any importance in Warburton's remarks.

CHAPTER IX.

DEFENCE OF POPE AGAINST CROUSAZ.

WARBURTON DETERMINES TO DEFEND POPE'S 'ESSAY ON MAN' AGAINST THE STRICTURES OF CROUSAZ — CROUSAZ'S WORKS AND QUALIFICATIONS — JOHNSON'S PRAISE OF CROUSAZ — CROUSAZ'S CHARGES AGAINST POPE'S 'ESSAY' — WARBURTON'S PROFESSED REFUTATION OF THEM — OPTIMISM — WARBURTON'S SNEERS AT CROUSAZ, AND EPITHETS WHICH HE BESTOWS UPON HIM — BLUNDERS IN THE FRENCH TRANSLATION OF POPE'S ESSAY — HURD'S REMARK ON WARBURTON'S CRITICISM — POPE PLEASED WITH THE DEFENCE — LETTER FROM POPE TO WARBURTON — REPUBLICATION OF THE DEFENCE; SUBMITTED TO POPE FOR REVISION — REMARKS ON POPE'S 'ESSAY ON MAN.'

WE have seen how lightly Warburton, in the early part of his career, had spoken of Pope in his letter to Concanen, and how patiently he had listened to sneers at him in his correspondence with Theobald. But he had now formed a different notion of Pope's abilities, or, from a view to his own interest in literature, had conceived that it would be much better to propitiate so eminent a writer than to depreciate or be at variance with him. In his 'Vindication' against Webster he expressed his pleasure, when quoting Pope, at being able to borrow 'the fine words of one of the politest men of the age' to keep him in countenance. He now availed himself of a greater opportunity of securing Pope's favour by publishing a defence of the 'Essay on Man' against Crousaz, who had accused the author of being a disciple of Spinoza, and of having inculcated throughout his work the doctrine of fatalism.

Warburton, in his younger days, is said to have expressed very unfavourable opinions of the Essay, and to have maintained, in dissertations, which he read weekly at a literary club at Newark, that it was 'collected from the worst passages of the worst authors.'* But he was now to tell a very different story to Monsieur Crousaz.

Crousaz was at this time professor of philosophy at Lausanne, and had written several mathematical and philosophical works, among which were an Essay on Logic, treatises on the Beautiful and on the Education of Children, an Examination of Pyrrhonism Ancient and Modern, and Observations on the Human Mind against Antony Collins's Liberty of Thought and Leibnitz's Pre-established Harmony; and, having met with Pope's Essay in French, and fancying that he saw much impiety in it, he resolved on exposing what he conceived to be its noxious tendency. He accordingly published, in 1737, an *Examen de l'Essai de Mr. Pope;* and, in the following year, a more formal critique, entitled *Commentaire sur la Traduction en vers de M. l'Abbé Du Resnel de l'Essai de Mr. Pope sur l'Homme.* As Du Resnel's translation was by no means faithful, and as there was a more exact version in prose by M. de Silhouette, an attaché of the French Ambassador in England, Crousaz was justly blamed for making it the basis of his animadversions, for, though he knew no English himself, he might easily have ascertained which was the more accurate of the two. Both these works were soon published in English; the first by Cave in 1738, without the name of the translator, but under the auspices of Johnson, with the title, 'An Examination of Mr. Pope's Essay on Man; containing a succinct View of the System of the Fatalists, and Confutation of their Opinions; with an Illustration of the

* Warton's Life of Pope, p. xlv.; Prior's Life of Malone, p. 430; Disraeli's Quarrels of Authors, Art. 'Warburton.'

Doctrine of Free-will, and an Enquiry what View Mr. Pope might have in touching upon the Leibnitzian Philosophy and Fatalism;' the other was sent forth by the same publisher in 1741, translated by Mrs. Carter (who withheld, however, her name), and entitled 'A Commentary on Mr. Pope's Principles of Morality, or Essay on Man; with the Abbé du Resnel's Translation of the Essay into French Verse, and the English interlined.' The titles of the versions indicate that the authors of them had no leaning in favour of Pope.

Johnson, indeed, who was concerned with both of them, seems to have had a higher opinion of the French professor's abilities, and of the justice of his animadversions on Pope, than they fairly deserved. He spoke of Crousaz, first in the 'Gentleman's Magazine,' and afterwards in the Life of Pope, as of a man who merited the highest regard as well for his powers as his virtues. In offering a 'View of the Controversy between Crousaz and Warburton' to Mr. Urban, he extracts some specimens of Crousaz's moral sentiments, by which, he says, 'it will probably be shown that he is far from deserving either indignation or contempt; that his notions are just, though they are sometimes introduced without necessity, and defended when they are not opposed; and that his abilities and parts are such as may entitle him to reverence from those who think his criticisms superfluous.'

In his Life of Pope he commends him still more strongly. 'Crousaz,' he says, 'was a professor of Switzerland, eminent for his Treatise of Logic and his "Examen de Pyrrhonisme,' and, however little known or regarded here, was no mean antagonist. His mind was one of those in which philosophy and piety are happily united. He was accustomed to argument and disquisition, and perhaps was grown too desirous of detecting faults; but his intentions were always right, his opinions were solid, and his religion pure.

'His incessant vigilance for the promotion of piety disposed him to look with distrust upon all metaphysical systems of theology, and all schemes of virtue and happiness purely rational; and therefore it was not long before he was persuaded that the positions of Pope, as they terminated for the most part in natural religion, were intended to draw mankind away from revelation, and to represent the whole course of things as a necessary concatenation of indissoluble fatality; and it is undeniable that in many passages a religious eye may easily discover expressions not very favourable to morals or to liberty.'

Warburton's observations appeared in the form of Letters in the 'Works of the Learned,' the first being printed in December 1738, and four others in the first four months of the following year. They were not published in a volume till 1742.

The great charge that Crousaz makes against the Essay on Man is that a noxious system of fatalism pervades the whole of it. 'He cries out, Fate, fate,' observes Warburton, wherever he turns his eyes, 'as men in distraction cry out, fire, fire.' Even the Eternal Being, says Crousaz, was, according to Pope, obliged by fate to create the world, or universe, as it is, because the idea of it was the most perfect of all the ideas of worlds that presented themselves to his contemplation. The poet, therefore, exhorts us to consider that part of it which we inhabit, and of which alone we can be said to have any knowledge, as ordered in the best possible manner; for all nature, with its apparent irregularities, is but consummate art; what we think fortuitous is guided by invisible direction, and what we think discordant is harmony not understood. Yet, when we look around us, and meditate on the state of things in which we are placed, we cannot but think that it is very far from perfect; that it abounds, indeed, with imperfections and disorders, such as we must admit to be not imaginary but real; and, if we ask of Pope why it is no better, we are told that of its disorders and imperfections, God himself, influenced by fate, is the author, since he formed it, and it was not in his power to form it otherwise. But, in order that we may content ourselves in this condition, believing that we are *secure to be as blest as we can bear*, we are exhorted to compare the condition of things in the moral world with that of things in the natural world :

> If plagues or earthquakes break not Heaven's design,
> Why then a Borgia or a Catiline?

Yes, says Crousaz, the mixture and agitation, often strong and vehement, of the particles of matter, is necessary to a sound and healthy state of *material existence*, and to the fermentation required for the nurture and growth of organic bodies; but monsters of wickedness, surely, are not essential to the well-being of *moral existence*. 'A continual spring, and a heaven without clouds, would be fatal to the earth and its inhabitants, but can we regard it as a misfortune that men should be always sage, calm, and temperate?' However, to make the best of what is before us, he continues, I turn to what the poet says of happiness, to inquire how it is to be obtained, and I am answered thus :

> Where grows, where grows it not? If vain our toil,
> We ought to blame the culture, not the soil:
> Fix'd to no spot is happiness sincere;
> 'Tis nowhere to be found, or everywhere:
> 'Tis never to be bought, but always free.

Happiness must then be somewhere very near me, and easily to be found; but, when I request the author to lead me to it, he simply says, 'Take nature's path.' I am willing to do so; but what am I to understand by nature? Is it rational nature that I am to follow? No; for I am told that if I *ask the learned* the way, I shall find *the learned blind.* Shall I then resign myself to the guidance of animal nature? No; for that would soon lead me into great distresses. To end my perplexities, therefore, I must just suffer myself to be borne along by the course of events, and find that to *take nature's path* is to follow in the track of destiny, which, as I understand from the beginning, is the director of everything.

As to religion, if I consult the poet on the subject, I gain very little instruction from him. I do indeed find, in the fourth epistle, that for the simple-minded man, who has learned

> To look through Nature up to Nature's God,

and who is slave to no sect, but always wishing for an increase of virtue,

> For him alone, hope leads from goal to goal,
> And opens still, and opens on his soul;
> Till, lengthen'd on to faith, and unconfin'd,
> It pours the bliss that fills up all the mind;

but I discover that this bliss is merely the result of universal benevolence, of which every good man will wish to have as great a share as possible, and that nature

> —— connects in this
> His greatest virtue with his greatest bliss;
> At once his own bright prospect to be blest,
> And strongest motive to assist the rest;

so that 'height of bliss' is 'but height of charity.' This exhortation to universal charity has no foundation but in the hypothesis that we are all parts of a whole, of which every portion is necessary to the subsistence of the rest, and, consequently, I am required to love everything in a universe in which 'whatever is, is right,' and which, as I must infer from the poet's statements, would not have been a work sufficiently worthy of God, unless there had been in it atheists, superstitious persons, persecutors, tyrants, idolaters, assassins, and poisoners.

Such is a summary of the criticism of Crousaz. Let us take a view of Warburton's elaborate and sophistical reply.

To the assertion that God was obliged to create the world such as it is, he opposes no argument, contenting himself with declaring it 'false and calumnious,' and observing that of all possible systems, as Pope says, infinite wisdom certainly did form the best. That He who made this system rules it; that the evils and disorders which arise in the moral world come, not from God, but from man's abuse of his own free-will; and that God, counteracting man's follies and vices, brings good out of ill, as health and life are extracted from the agitations of material elements. It is the passions and desires that prevent human life from stagnation, and are the causes of action. As to Crousaz's remark about the difficulty of finding happiness by Pope's direction 'to follow nature,' he says that Pope must mean rational nature, or reason, for though 'the learned are blind,' that is, the philosophers fall into errors in their disquisitions and actions, as M. Crousaz has fallen into errors in his criticisms on Pope, we must, nevertheless, not think the worse of reason on that account. As to the 'height of bliss' being but 'height of charity,' or but the satisfaction arising from universal benevolence, he takes occasion to preach a short sermon on the text, *If a man say, I love God, and hateth his brother, he is a liar; for he that loveth not his brother whom he hath seen, how can he love God whom he hath not seen?* This, as it is incomparably the best passage in Warburton's commentary, and is intended as a comprehensive and triumphant refutation of all that Crousaz has alleged, I shall extract at length. A Freethinker, he observes, may laugh at the simplicity of the argument, but would doubtless affect to admire it, could any one find it for him in Plato.

'You say you love God, says the Apostle, though you hate your brother. Impossible! The love of any object begins originally, like all the other passions, from self-love. Thus we love ourselves, by representation, in our offspring; which love extends by degrees to our remoter relations, and so on, through our neighbourhood, to all the fellow-members of our community. And now self-love, refined by reason and religion, begins to lose its nature, and deservedly assumes another name. Our country next claims our love; we then extend it to all mankind, and never rest till we have at length fixed it on that most amiable of all objects, the great Author and Original of being. This is the course and progress of human love:

> God loves from whole to parts; but human soul
> Must rise from individual to the whole.

'Now, pursues the Apostle, I reason thus: Can you, who are not yet arrived at that inferior stage of benevolence, the love of your brother, *whom you have seen*, that is, whom the necessities of civil life, and a sense of your mutual relation might teach you to love, pretend to have reached the very height and perfection of this passion, the love of God, *whom you have not seen?* that is, whose wonderful economy in His system of creation, which makes Him so amiable, you cannot have the least conception of; you, who have not yet learned that your own private system is supported on the great principle of benevolence? *Fear* Him, *flatter* Him, *fight* for Him, as you dread His *power*, you may; but to *love* Him, as you know not His *nature*, is impossible.

'This,' he adds, 'is the Apostle's grand and sublime reasoning; and it is with the same thought on which the Apostle founds his argument, that our moral poet ends his essay, as the just and necessary conclusion of his work:

Self-love but serves the virtuous mind to *wake*,
As the small pebble stirs the peaceful lake;
The *centre* mov'd, a *circle* straight succeeds,
Another still, and still *another* spreads;
Friend, parent, neighbour, first it will embrace,
His *country* next, and next *all human race*:
Wide, and more wide, th' o'erflowings of the mind
Take every creature in, of every kind;
Earth smiles around, with boundless bounty blest,
And Heav'n beholds its image in his breast.'

With regard to the notion that the doctrine of optimism, or of *partial evil being universal good*, sets aside the belief, and renders unnecessary the expectations of a future state, 'because, if the evils which good men suffer here promote the benefit of the whole, everything in the present system is in order, and nothing requires compensation elsewhere, so that the good man has no reason to expect reparation, when the ills which he suffered had a beneficial tendency,' Warburton replies that the 'good man's hopes of retribution still remain the same, whether he believes in optimism or not, for though optimism supposes that *the evils themselves* will be fully compensated by the good they produce to the *whole*, yet this is so far from supposing that *individuals* will suffer for a *general good*, that it is *essential to the system* to conclude that, at the completion of things, *particular* and *universal* good shall coincide; which coincidence can never be without a retribution to good men for the evils suffered here below.'

Such are the general nature and tendency of Warburton's remarks, in opposition to Crousaz, on Pope's Essay. Whoever would know more of them must go to the Commentary itself, for it would be vain to attempt abridging observations on particular passages.

Of his adversary he speaks in very different terms from those of Johnson. He calls him one of 'the chief of bigots,' a 'bully-critic,' and the author of 'reflections senseless and scandalous,' and says that he maliciously followed the worse French version, 'because it gave him more opportunity to calumniate.' Crousaz unluckily stated that he had been fond of logic from his infancy; that he had run through every treatise on logic that had fallen into his hands; and that he had extracted instruction in logic even from books not designed to give it; and Warburton, in consequence, omits no opportunity of charging such 'a veteran controversialist,' a student of seventy-five years, with false reasoning, with blindness to the connexions in Pope's system, and with imputing to Pope's doctrines what a rational inquirer could never have discerned in them. In addition, he dwells on the critic's want of charity, though doubtless, he says, such critics as Crousaz, when 'they insult the fame, the fortune, or the person of their brother,' think they show 'the very height of charity, a charity for his soul;' but this, though it may be 'the height of the hangman's charity, who waits for your clothes, could never be Saint Paul's,' which was 'a charity that began in candour, and inspired good opinion.' In the French translation in verse, which Crousaz chose to follow, there were a few ridiculous blunders, for which Warburton does not fail to reproach alike the translator and the critic who trusted in him. Pope, in the illustration which he borrowed from Palingenius, represents superior beings as admiring the genius of Newton, and doubting whether he should not rather be deemed of angelic than of human nature; as men, when they see striking marks of intelligence in an ape, are almost tempted to think him one of their own species:

> Superior beings, when of late they saw
> A mortal man unfold great Nature's law,
> Admir'd such wisdom in a human shape,
> And show'd a Newton as we show an ape:

But the translator, utterly mistaking the scope of his

author, imagined that he designed to depreciate Newton, and accordingly represented the angels as regarding Newton with pity:

> Des célestes esprits la vive intelligence
> Regarde avec pitié notre foible science:
> Newton, le Grand Newton, que nous admirons tous,
> Est peut-être pour eux ce qu'un singe est pour nous.

He made a similar blunder in the sense of the passage in which Pope speaks of Nature as directing man to learn the arts of life from the inferior animals:

> Thus, then, to man the voice of Nature spake,
> Go, from the creatures thy instructions take:

which he renders,

> La Nature *indignée* alors se fit entendre,
> Va, *malheureux* mortel, va, lui dit-elle, apprendre
> Des *plus vils* animaux.

'One would wonder,' says Warburton, 'what should make him represent Nature in such a passion at Man, and calling him names, when Mr. Pope supposes her in her best of good humour.'

When Pope says,

> Nor God alone in the still calm we find,
> He mounts the storm,

the translator gives,

> Dieu lui-même, Dieu sort de *son profond repos*,

making God one of the deities of Epicurus. But Crousaz, though Silhouette might have taught him better, accepts the version as faithful, and censures the passage as 'presenting us with ideas which we ought not to dwell upon.'

These strictures on Crousaz doubtless attracted attention. 'The letters,' says Hurd, 'were much read, and gave a new lustre to Mr. Warburton's reputation. They showed the elegance of his taste in polite literature, as well as his penetration into moral subjects.' That they showed the author's acquaintance with literature, may be readily allowed, but that they manifested 'the elegance of his taste' will not so readily pass unquestioned. As for his penetration into morality, it was shown in forcing into Pope's lines senses of his own. 'You have evinced the orthodoxy of Mr. Pope's principles,' said Middleton to him, 'but, like the old commentators on his Homer, will be thought perhaps in some places to have provided a meaning for him that he himself never dreamed of. However, if you did not find him a philosopher, you will make him one, for he will be wise enough to take the benefit of your reading, and make his future essays more clear and consistent. It was certainly a generous part in you, and worthy a man of capacity and leisure, to vindicate a writer of his genius, to whom the public is so highly indebted, from the groundless cavils of a dull critic, which Mr. Pope's name, and not his own, had spread into everybody's hands.'*

Pope himself was so delighted with such vigorous efforts to argue fatalism out of his 'Essay,' that he addressed, in earnest gratitude, the following letter to Warburton, with whom he was not yet personally acquainted:

'April 11, 1739.

'Sir,—I have just received from Mr. R. [Robinson] two more of your letters. It is in the greatest hurry imaginable that I write this, but I cannot help thanking you in particular for your third letter, which is so extremely clear, short, and full, that I think Mr. Crousaz ought never to have another answerer, and deserved not so good a one. I can only say, you do him too much honour, and me too much right, so odd as the expression seems, for you have

* Letter from Middleton, Jan. 7, 1740; Middleton's Works, vol. i. p. 402.

made my system as clear as I ought to have done, and could not. It is indeed the same system as mine, but illustrated with a ray of your own, as they say our natural body is the same still when it is glorified. I am sure I like it better than I did before, and so will every man else. I know I meant just what you explain, but I did not explain my own meaning so well as you. You understand me as well as I do myself, but you express me better than I could express myself. Pray accept the sincerest acknowledgments. I cannot but wish these letters were put together in one book, and intend (with your leave) to procure a translation of part, at least, or of all of them, into French; but I shall not proceed a step without your consent and opinion.'

They were afterwards translated into French by Mons. Silhouette, the same gentleman who had so accurately translated the 'Essay on Man' into French prose.*

On collecting the letters, with some slight alterations, into a volume, Warburton submitted the proofs to Pope for revision. 'As to any correction of your letters,' says Pope, in reply, 'I could make none, but what resulted from inverting the order of them, and those expressions relating to myself which I thought exaggerated. I could not find a word to alter in the last letter, which I returned immediately to the bookseller. I must particularly thank you for the mention you have made of me in your postscript to the last edition of "The Legation of Moses."' This alludes to the quotation from Pope in the 'Vindication' against Webster, which Warburton had attached to the second edition of the first three books of 'The Divine Legation.' 'I am much more pleased,' continues Pope, 'with a compliment that links me to a virtuous man, and, by the best similitude, that of a good mind, even a better and stronger tie than the similitude of studies, than

* Warburton's 'Pope,' vol. ix. pp. 329, 331.

I could be proud of any other whatsoever. May that independence, charity, and competency attend you, which sets a good priest above a bishop, and truly makes his fortune; that is, his happiness in this life as well as in the other!'

When Pope afterwards met Warburton, he told Spence that he was the greatest general critic he had ever known, the most capable of seeing through all the possibilities of things.* Many others held Warburton's commentaries in much lower estimation than Pope. Among these was Lord Marchmont, who, 'soon after Pope's acquaintance with Warburton commenced, told Pope he was convinced that he was one of the vainest men living. How so? said Pope. Because, replied Lord Marchmont, it is manifest, from your close connexion with your new commentator, you want to show positively what an exquisite poet you are, and what a quantity of dulness you can carry down on your back without sinking under the load.† .

Of Pope's 'Essay,' as has been well observed by Johnson, the great claim to admiration consists, not in the moral instruction which it conveys, but in the splendour of ornament in which its poverty of matter is enveloped. It has furnished us with lines which we quote for their happy vigour, and point, and elegance, and which will continue to be quoted as long as the language shall last; but we feel no reason to be grateful to Pope for anything that we have learned from him. The doctrine that 'whatever is, is right,' the doctrine that runs through Pope's poem, we are willing, in humble submission to the wisdom of a higher Power, to believe, but we are not more convinced of it after reading Pope than we were before; nor do we find it more forcibly illustrated in the 'Essay on Man' than we may find it elsewhere. Indeed, the most striking illustration of it is to be seen, I believe,

* Spence's Anecdotes by Singer, p. 337.

† Prior's Life of Malone, p. 386.

in the eighty-ninth number of the 'Idler,' where it is shown that the sufferings of man from physical evil are the great producers of moral good. The truth is, that good has no exercise but in opposition to evil; the influences of the two are

> Those lights and shades whose well-accorded strife
> Gives all the strength and colour of our life;

the effect of either is seen but as in contrast with the other. The exercise of man's free will, and the indulgence of his passions, though, as human nature is not perfect, often exercised and indulged to excess, are still the elements of action in life. The mind, says Bacon, would be stagnant, if the passions, as winds, did not set it in motion.

> They say best men——
> ——become much more the better
> For being a little bad.*

To eradicate the passions, as the Stoics professed to attempt, would produce but little improvement in the state of things. What sort of a world this would be without evil, may be seen in Goldsmith's 'Tale of Asem the Hermit.' But the question why the state of things is such as it is, we must leave as Pope has left it:

> He who through vast immensity can pierce,
> See worlds on worlds compose one universe,
> What varied being peoples every star,
> May tell why heaven has made us as we are.

As to the charge of Crousaz, that Pope had adopted Leibnitz's pre-established harmony, Pope himself declared that he had never read a line of Leibnitz, nor had heard of the term *pre-established harmony* until he found it in Crousaz's book.†

* Shaksp. Meas. for Meas. act v. sc. 1.

† Ruffhead's Life of Pope, 8vo. ed. p. 244.

The question whether Pope, in writing his 'Essay on Man,' was supplied with matter for it by Bolingbroke, and was unable to see the full tendency of what was given him, is one which has excited much attention among critics and biographers.

Warburton generally denied that Bolingbroke instructed or influenced Pope, but was not always consistent with himself on the point. In a letter to Hurd, in 1753, he declares 'the insidious report,' that Pope had his philosophy from Bolingbroke, sufficiently confuted by one of Bolingbroke's letters to Pope;* yet in his 'View of Lord Bolingbroke's Philosophy,' published in 1755, he calls Pope Bolingbroke's 'pupil,' and says that he was reasoned out of his master's hands by the Commentary in reply to Crousaz.†

The common belief has been that Pope had much of the tenets of the 'Essay,' and the plan of its execution, from Bolingbroke; and in support of that belief we find much testimony. When Johnson was writing his Life of Pope, Boswell made inquiries of Dr. Hugh Blair in relation to something that he had heard on the subject from Lord Bathurst. Dr. Blair replied to Boswell, by letter, that he had once dined at Lord Bathurst's, in 1763, with Mallet, Sir James Porter, Dr. Macaulay, and some other gentlemen; and that Lord Bathurst told the company, in the course of conversation, that the 'Essay on Man' was originally composed by Lord Bolingbroke in prose, and that Pope did no more than put it into verse; that he had himself read Lord Bolingbroke's manuscript in his own hand-writing, and remembered well that he was at 'a loss whether most to admire the elegance of Lord Bolingbroke's prose, or the beauty of Pope's verse.' Mallet remarked to Blair that he might well keep this statement in mind,

* Letters from an Eminent Prelate, p. 135.

† Warburton's Works, vol. xii. p. 336.

as he would probably survive Lord Bathurst, and might be a witness of what he had said. Blair accordingly registered it in a journal which he kept, whence he copied it for his letter to Boswell.*

Dr. Joseph Warton was also told by Lord Bathurst that 'he had read the whole scheme of the "Essay on Man" in the hand-writing of Bolingbroke, drawn up in a series of propositions which Pope was to versify and illustrate.'† Bishop Law, too, in his Preface to Archbishop King's 'Origin of Evil,' says that Lord Bathurst had seen the system of the 'Essay' in Bolingbroke's hand lying before Pope when he was writing.

The author of an anonymous letter to Warburton, written subsequently to the 'Epistle to the most Impudent Man living,' and supposed to have proceeded from Mallet, offers similar evidence: 'If you were as intimate with Mr. Pope as you pretend,' says the writer, 'you must know the truth of a fact which several others, as well as I, . . . have heard. The fact was related to me by a certain senior fellow of one of our universities, who was very intimate with Mr. Pope. He started some objections one day, at Mr. Pope's house, to the doctrines contained in the Ethic Epistles; upon which Mr. Pope told him that he would soon convince him of the truth of it by laying the argument at large before him; for which purpose he gave him a large prose manuscript to peruse, telling him, at the same time, the author's name. From this perusal, whatever other conviction the Doctor might receive, he collected at least this, that Mr. Pope had from his friend, not only the doctrine, but even the finest and strongest ornaments of his ethics.‡ This is less trustworthy testimony than that of Lord Bathurst, but it helps to show that belief in Bolingbroke's furnishing matter

* Croker's 'Boswell,' sub 1779, p. 284.

† Ib. note. Warton's 'Essay on Pope,' vol. ii. p. 62.

‡ Cited in Roscoe's 'Pope,' vol. i. p. 395.

to Pope was prevalent; whether Pope meant a kind of admission of Bolingbroke's assistance in the line,

> *Together* let us beat this ample field,

may be matter for consideration. But the strongest testimony of all is that which Spence records as having been given by Pope himself in their conversations. Speaking one day in praise of Bolingbroke, Pope, says Spence, 'mentioned then, and at several other times, how much (or rather how wholly) he himself was obliged to him for the thoughts and reasonings in his moral work; and once in particular, said, that beside their frequent talking over the subject together, he had received, I think, seven or eight sheets from Lord Bolingbroke in relation to it, as I apprehended by way of letters, both to direct the plan in general, and to supply the matter for the particular epistles.'*

All supports to the opinion, however, that Bolingbroke contributed the groundwork of the 'Essay,' Roscoe, in his Life of Pope, endeavours to prove wholly baseless, chiefly on the authority of two or three passages in Bolingbroke and Pope's letters.

The first epistle of the 'Essay on Man,' we may observe, was published in 1732. But Pope and Bolingbroke had been in the habit, for many years previous, of discussing together moral and metaphysical subjects, and Bolingbroke, in a letter to Swift in 1729, speaks of the work which Pope is about; which 'is a fine one, and will be in his hands an original;' and which Pope finds so easy to execute, that Bolingbroke is happy to see his judgment, in pronouncing it eminently and peculiarly adapted to Pope's genius, fully confirmed; all which expressions are supposed to refer to the 'Essay on Man.' In another letter to Swift, in August 1731, Bolingbroke

* Spence's Anecdotes by Singer, p. 144.

says, 'Does Pope talk to you of the whole work which, at my instigation, he has begun, in such a manner that he must be convinced, by this time, I judged better of his talents than he did?' In the same letter he remarks that three of the epistles are finished, and that Pope is intent on the fourth; all of which were then meant to be preliminary to several more. From another letter of Bolingbroke's to Pope, without date, but evidently written after the first three epistles of the 'Essay on Man' were concluded, it appears that Pope had requested Bolingbroke to write something on metaphysics himself, and Bolingbroke, expressing assent, replies, 'Since *you have begun at my request* the work which I have long wished that you would undertake, it is but reasonable that I *submit to the task you impose upon me;* and Pope, in a subsequent letter to Swift, but also without date, congratulates himself that he has 'contributed to turn Lord Bolingbroke to subjects moral, useful, and worthy of his pen.' Several other remarks in Bolingbroke's letters, in 1733 and 1734, intimate that his lordship was pursuing his metaphysical studies during those years.

From these passages Roscoe argues that Bolingbroke did not begin to write on moral and metaphysical subjects till after Pope had completed, or nearly completed, his 'Essay on Man,' and that consequently he could not have supplied Pope with any moral or metaphysical matter for the 'Essay.' But this is to deduce from the passages what they are far from fairly indicating. All that can be justly concluded from them is, that Bolingbroke had not begun, when Pope was writing the earlier part of his 'Essay,' to compose metaphysical treatises for the public; not that he had never made on such subjects any memoranda or hints which might have served Pope as the groundwork of his great poem. In Bolingbroke's philosophical 'Fragments,' which form part of his published works, we find several thoughts that might have given hints to Pope. Thus in Fragment forty-third: 'We ought to consider the world we inhabit no otherwise than as a little wheel in our solar system; nor our solar system any otherwise than as a little but larger wheel in the immense machine of the universe; and both the one and the other necessary, perhaps, to the motion of the whole, and to the pre-ordained revolutions in it.' And again, in Fragment sixty-third: 'In the works of men, the most complicated schemes produce, very hardly and very uncertainly, one single effect; in the works of God, one single scheme produces a multitude of different effects, and answers an immense variety of purposes.' How similar in thought to these passages are the following lines of Pope!

> In human works, though labour'd on with pain,
> A thousand movements scarce one purpose gain;
> In God's, one single can its end produce,
> Yet serves to second, too, some other use:
> So man, who here seems principal alone,
> Perhaps acts second to some sphere unknown,
> Touches some wheel, or urges to some goal;
> 'Tis but a part we see, and not the whole.*

Many such resemblances have been noticed by Wakefield and others. It may be observed, too, that the matter of Bolingbroke's disquisitions is mostly of a different character from that of Pope's 'Essay,' treating more of religion and metaphysics, while that of the 'Essay on Man' is restricted chiefly to human life and conduct; and hence it might be imagined that Bolingbroke, after giving his earlier thoughts, and those on more practical subjects, to Pope, had then burst away into wider and more airy fields of contemplation.

On the whole, the fair conclusion seems to be, that the subject of the 'Essay' was suggested to Pope as a fit exercise for his powers, by Bolingbroke; that Bolingbroke probably gave Pope, in manuscript, some hints which he

* Essay on Man, i. 53.

had made for a composition on that subject, and perhaps the whole plan of such a composition, by which Pope may have profited; but that much less aid was furnished to the poet than Lord Bathurst or Dr. Blair supposed, or than Mallet was willing to have believed; for Pope, doubtless, far from having been merely a versifier of Lord Bolingbroke's prose, supplied from the stores and powers of his own mind all the imagery and ornament, all the force and beauty of language, which make the 'Essay on Man' one of the finest efforts of poetry.

The notion that Pope was in some measure deceived by Bolingbroke, and was not fully aware of the conclusions that might be drawn from the 'Essay on Man,' appears to be not without foundation. The object of Bolingbroke was to show that good balances evil in the present distribution of things, and that the idea of a future state of being is therefore unnecessary to vindicate God's justice; a doctrine which he *plainly declares* in one of the letters to Swift, already noticed.* 'You divines admit,' says he, 'the unequal distributions of Providence in this life, and you build on this admission the necessity of a future state of rewards and punishments. But what if you should find that this future state will not vindicate the unequal distribution of Providence in this life? Would it not have been better to defend, by arguments drawn from what we see around us, the justice of God's proceedings in this world, and have left the proof of a future world to revelation?' But this view of things he did not communicate to Pope; for he observes to Swift, in continuation, '*You will not understand, by what I have said, that Pope will go so deep into the argument, or carry it so far as I have hinted.*' Bolingbroke's revelation of his sentiments to Pope was therefore not complete.

A man with such opinions regarding the uncompen-

* Aug. 2, 1731.

satory nature of a future state, might very well refuse to acknowledge the moral attributes of the Divinity. Warburton relates that when a common acquaintance of Pope and Bolingbroke, probably Warburton himself, told Pope, in his last illness, that Bolingbroke, in the course of a recent conversation, *had taken occasion to deny God's moral attributes as they are commonly understood*, Pope was so shocked that he could not rest till he had asked Bolingbroke whether his informant was not mistaken; and that Bolingbroke assured him he was. Pope repeated Bolingbroke's reply to the 'common acquaintance,' who appears to have said no more on the subject; and Pope died in the delusion that Bolingbroke was a believer in God's moral attributes.*

Whether it was through the influence of Bolingbroke or not, Pope, in writing his 'Essay,' seems to have had no intention to direct man to expect in a future state compensation for the evils of the present, but to have confined his thoughts merely to the condition of things in this life. Pope himself said that, in the 'Epistle on Happiness,' his intention was only to treat of the state of man here.† Of an existence after death, there is no passage in the whole poem that, fairly understood, gives any intimation. Young notices the absence of all allusion to this point in the 'Essay,' at the commencement of his 'Night Thoughts:'

> Oh had he press'd his theme, pursued the track
> That opens out of darkness into day;
> Oh had he mounted on his wing of fire,
> Soar'd where I sink, and sung immortal man,
> How had he bless'd mankind and rescued me!

It was its deficiency in this particular, and its apparent advocacy of fatalism, that raised an outcry against the

* View of Lord Bolingbroke's Philosophy; Warburton's Works, vol. xii. p. 91.

† Spence's Anecdotes by Singer, p. 142.

poem as likely to produce evil effects. As the clamour increased, Pope became uneasy, and, as Richardson says, 'took terror about the clergy, and about Warburton himself, at the general alarm of its fatalism and deistical tendency.' The passages that appeared to have most of this tendency had been frequently talked over by Pope and the two Richardsons in conversation; but Pope, at the time of their publication, showed no disposition to alter them. When objections were raised, however, Pope was very glad to accept Warburton as a defender; but previously, says Jonathan Richardson, *I know that he never dreamed of the scheme he afterwards adopted*, that is, of the sense and tendency which Warburton's commentaries forced upon the 'Essay.'

CHAPTER X.

ROMAINE. HARE.

WARBURTON'S DISAGREEMENT WITH ROMAINE — ROMAINE'S SERMON — LETTER FROM ROMAINE TO WARBURTON — ROMAINE'S PRETENDED OBJECTIONS OF CLERGYMEN, IN REALITY A TRANSCRIPT FROM HIS SERMON — WARBURTON WRITES TO THE 'WORKS OF THE LEARNED' — ROMAINE REPLIES IN THE 'GENERAL EVENING POST' — HIS DISINGENUOUSNESS — WARBURTON'S ABUSE OF HIM — NEW EDITION OF THE FIRST VOLUME OF 'THE DIVINE LEGATION' — REMARKS ON THE 'DEMONIACS' IN THE NEW TESTAMENT — HARE CONTINUES TO COMMEND — WARBURTON PURSUES HIS STUDIES — HIS ILLNESS AND RECOVERY — DEATH OF BISHOP HARE — WARBURTON'S CHARACTER OF HIM.

DURING this year Warburton was engaged in an unpleasant affair with Romaine. Romaine, then about twenty-five years of age, and just ordained, preached a sermon at Oxford against Warburton's assertions in 'The Divine Legation' as to the silence of the Old Testament regarding a future state, which sermon was soon after published for him by a bookseller named Bettenham. About the same time that the sermon was preached, he wrote a letter to Warburton on the subject, commencing in a very flattering style, and representing himself as a young student in divinity, sincerely desirous of instruction. The letter began thus:

Reverend Sir,—I happened lately to meet, in company, with some clergymen, when your last excellent book, 'The Divine Legation of Moses,' was the subject of their discourse. As I had read it more than once, with a great deal of pleasure, and had ever admired your elegant style, great learning, and strength of argument, and had been used to hear the same praises from others, I was very much surprised to hear those, whom, I imagined from their character, to be men of good sense, and that ought to commend and encourage whatever tended to promote true religion, speak with great disrespect of your performance. I thought myself concerned to defend the truth; and, to my great satisfaction, I found, upon a short inquiry, that what they advanced affected nothing which you had already writ, but what you had promised. Here was large room for mirth; and one could not but laugh at the oddness of some men's tempers, who are so ridiculous as to censure what they have never seen, and to condemn what it is impossible they should yet judge of. When they saw how unjust their reflections were, that they might not (like true disputants) seem to give up the point, they attacked even the proposition which you have promised to demonstrate, and I must ingenuously confess that they put some queries to me, which I, being no great proficient in divinity, was unable to answer. This, and the opportunity of returning my grateful acknowledgments for what you have wrote, was the occasion of the trouble I now give you; and as you are the only person I have heard of who has thoroughly considered this subject; as your character is concerned in the affair, and as I would (if it was in my power) hinder the least fault from entering your finished performances, and could wish that envy itself might be dumb, I hope you will favourably interpret my sending you these (which are to me, but not to you) difficulties, and oblige me with an answer to them, if ever an idle half-hour should lie heavy on your hands.' He then enumerates, as from the conversation of the clergymen, various texts, which Warburton afterwards fully considered in his book, tending to show that a future state was made known to the Jews under the Mosaic dispensation. The letter was signed 'W. Romaine.'

Warburton, on receipt of the letter, endeavoured to ascertain who 'W. Romaine' was, but, not succeeding, returned him a short, but civil, answer, in which he gave him to understand that 'it was a necessary part of the argument of "The Divine Legation" to show that the Jewish fathers, patriarchs, and prophets, had a knowledge of a future state, and an expectation of a redemption.'

But soon afterwards, when the sermon fell into Warburton's hands, he was chagrined to find that the passages in the letter, which affected to state the clergymen's objections to his notions, were, in reality, transcribed from the sermon; and he was persuaded that Romaine's object in writing the letter was 'to avoid the imputation of being so ridiculous as to censure what he had never seen, and to condemn what it was impossible he should yet judge of;' for, by communicating these objections to Warburton, before the publication of the sermon, as having been heard in conversation, he could put them forward in the sermon, not as from himself, but as common objections to Warburton's notions, or even to his own.

Warburton, in his indignation, sent Romaine's letter, with his own comments upon it, to the 'Works of the Learned.' He remarked on Romaine's disingenuousness in representing his letter, not as a transcript from what he was going to print, but as the offspring of common conversation, and concluded by saying, 'Mr. Warburton, in justice to his reverend brethren, thinks fit to declare that he does not believe one word of what the said Mr. Romaine writes of a conversation with them on the subject of his book. He is too well acquainted with their candour and learning to think they could ever afford an opportunity to this benevolent gentleman *to laugh at the oddness of their tempers*, &c., but takes it for granted that this worthy man had no other meaning than to conceal his own kind intentions under a false accusation of his brethren.'

Such animadversions Romaine could hardly be expected to take quietly; and he accordingly signified his displeasure in a letter to the editor of the 'General Evening Post;' a letter which the editor of the 'Works of the Learned,' who copied it into his journal, designated as 'hardly to be paralleled among the productions of any other clergyman:'

'Sir,—As Mr. Warburton hath violated the rules of decency by publishing in your paper a private letter of mine without my leave, I think it necessary to say that the notes upon the letter cannot be allowed to be an answer to anything advanced either in the letter or the sermon, but were designed to take off people's attention from the points in dispute to a personal quarrel. I have no bad opinion either of Mr. Warburton's capacity or learning; but he might have made a better use of them than to think he deserved, or that I meant *in earnest*, those compliments in the letter, as he did, or at least says he did. . . Unless necessity forces me, I shall not answer him any more in that *low way* which he and his bookseller have chosen to dispute in. . . He supposes the conversation was false; if he pleases to answer the sermon, or to advance anything new upon the subject, he will find that it was not false, but that there are numbers of clergymen who understand the subject, and are ready to defend it against him. Query, Hath not Mr. Warburton recanted his whole scheme, where he says, "It was a necessary part of the argument of 'The Divine Legation' to prove that the fathers, patriarchs, and prophets of the Jewish line had a knowledge of a future state, and the redemption of mankind by the Messiah?"

'W. Romaine.'

This letter, says the editor of the 'Works of the

Learned,' in words probably furnished him by Warburton, would bear 'a very curious and entertaining comment.' An edition of it, he observes, with notes, might do an editor a great deal of credit; for 'he will find in it a noble scope for the exercise of his genius. He may leave to others grammatical niceties, and employ himself in descanting on the logic of the first period; the probity and candour that shine so conspicuously in the second; the bravery and generosity that appear so eminently in the third; the sagacity and subtlety of the rest; and the uncommon modesty, notwithstanding the elegance and graces, of the whole.'

The matter certainly did Romaine little honour. If he did not mean Warburton to take his praises as sincere, he was wrong in praising him at all; and, whatever was the case, he should have had sense and grace enough not to retract the commendation which he had bestowed. If he designed, from the first, to attack Warburton, he should have attacked him openly and boldly. Warburton does not fail to heap contemptuous remarks on him in his letters to his friends. Writing to Stukeley, he says that his 'reputation is worried by the vilest of Theologasters,' Mr. William Romaine, who, as he hears from Oxford, is *calling aloud on the secular arm to make an example of him.* Whether this was said in jest or earnest, I do not know. Mr. Romaine, he adds, 'is the scoundrel I wrote to from your house. But the poor devil has done his own business. His talents show him by nature designed for a blunderbuss in church controversy; but his attack upon me being a proof-charge, and heavy-loaded, he burst in the going off; and what will become of him, let those who made use of him consider.' In a letter to Birch, he exclaims, 'Never was there a more execrable scoundrel. Do you think I can outlive such a dead-doing fellow who calls down the secular arm upon me? If I do, it will be in mere spite, to rub another volume of "The Divine Legation" in the noses of bigots and zealots.' Shall we transcribe one more passage, of true Warburtonian vehemence, from a letter to the same correspondent? 'Romaine has most amazingly betrayed the scoundrel in his remarks on my publication of his letter. The owning himself a rogue so plainly as to confess he was *not in earnest* in the letter he wrote, is such a hardened confession of villany as one seldom meets with out of Newgate. But his complaining of my *want of decency* in publishing his letter, without his leave, is incomparable. We may expect to hear the same complaint, in a little time, from our incendiaries, when their letters are published *without their leave.* And I do him honour in the comparison; for they are honester men than this church incendiary; they generously declare their enmity, are true to their companions, and commonly better than their word; but this fellow wears the mask of friendship, *betrays* his brethren, and is kindling a faggot for you while he pretends to offer incense.'

Bettenham, who published the sermon, so much disliked Romaine's retort on Warburton, that, when he took it to be printed, he replied that 'it was a knavish business, and he would have nothing to do with it,' or words to that effect; a refusal at which Warburton, who heard of it, was highly delighted.

Sherlock and Hare, to whom he communicated the whole affair, both expressed their hopes that he would, in future, be cautious of writing to persons whom he did not know either personally or by general reputation. 'For my own part,' said Hare, 'I hate giving a single line under my hand to anybody I do not very well like, because I do not know what use may be made of it. *Litera scripta manet.*'*

Towards the end of this year Warburton published a

* Kilvert, Selections, pp. 85, 122.

new edition of the first volume of the 'Divine Legation.' 'There are,' he says, in speaking of it to Birch, 'several additions, in support of my scheme, and reasonings on it, which I hope will not displease you; as, likewise, several omissions of passages which were thought vain, insolent, and ill-natured, particularly that against the author of the "Enquiry into the Demoniacs," which, I hope, will less displease you.' The author of the 'Enquiry' was Dr. Arthur Ashley Sykes, afterwards one of Warburton's great opponents, who had intimated that the Demoniacs were persons afflicted only with natural diseases, attributed to diabolical possession by the vulgar. Warburton, on the other hand, was in favour of real possession, and in the subsequent editions of 'The Divine Legation' attacks Dr. Mead for his hostility to that doctrine.

Bishop Hare, to whom he presented a copy of the second edition, still continued to commend. 'I was extremely pleased,' he wrote to Warburton, 'to see a second edition of your book so soon, notwithstanding all the pains to damn and stifle it in its birth. . . . I believe, since the first clamours of the "Miscellany" were over, all is now very quiet, at least I heard nothing to the contrary; and people will now calmly read and judge for themselves; and they that do so with any degree of temper and candour will find a great deal of pleasure and instruction. I hope not only posterity, but the present age, will do justice to so much merit, and do assure you it shall not be my fault if it does not. I only wish my power were equal to my inclination to serve you.'

The winter of 1739--40 he spent at his living in the country, where Hurd speaks of him as being intently occupied with his books.

'He was so taken up with his studies,' he says, 'and found so much delight in them, that he rarely stirred from home, which he would often say there was no good reason for doing, except necessary business, and the satisfaction of seeing a friend. What the world calls amusement, from the change of the scene, passed for nothing with him, who was too well employed to be tired of his situation, or to have a thought of running away from himself; which, after all, they who are incessantly making the experiment, find impossible to be done.'

In March 1740, he fell ill of an intermittent fever, by which his life was endangered, but the powers of bark at length restored him to health.

In April he had the misfortune to lose his friend Bishop Hare, a man to whom similarity of thinking in matters of religion had strongly attached him. The bishop was what is called a latitudinarian in theology, and a strong advocate for the right of private judgment, as he showed in his 'Letter to a young Clergyman,' the design of which is to prove that all Christian societies are interested in encouraging the study of the Scriptures, and allowing liberty of private judgment concerning them as much as is possible; and so far were the arguments of this work carried, that it was censured by Convocation, as tending to promote scepticism. How far Warburton thought himself entitled to use the right of private judgment is apparent to every one.

Writing to Middleton, shortly afterwards, he says, 'Bishop Hare has not left his fellow behind him for the love and encouragement of learning. I have had a great loss in his death. He honoured me with his esteem and friendship. This I esteemed a great obligation. I never sought to increase it by any other dependence upon him; and, by the terms on which we kept up a correspondence, he did me the justice to believe I expected no other.'

When he published the second volume of 'The Divine Legation,' he took the opportunity of giving his opinion of the Bishop's character to the world: 'In him the public has lost one of the best patrons and supporters of letters and religion. How steadily and successfully he employed his great talents of reason and literature, in opposing the violence of each religious party in their turns, when Court favour was betraying them into hurtful extremes, the unjust reproaches of libertines and bigots will never suffer us to forget. How generously he encouraged and rewarded letters, let them tell who have largely shared in his beneficence; for his character may be trusted with his enemies, or even with his most obliged friends. In him one author'—meaning himself—'has lost what he could but ill spare, one of the most candid of his readers and ablest of his critics. What he can never lose is the honour of his esteem and friendship.'

What is said of his 'opposition to the violence of each religious party' alludes to the efforts, now forgotten, which he made to allay the bitterness of the Bangorian controversy.

Mr. William Greene, a young student in divinity, afterwards Fellow of Clare Hall, Cambridge, and author of 'translations of the Psalms and other portions of Scripture from the Hebrew,' having inquired of Warburton, about this time, what theological books he should read, Warburton sent him a long list of various authors, light and heavy, but recommended 'above all Dr. Bentley and Bishop Hare, who are the greatest men in this way that ever were;' praising Greene, at the same time, for not being ashamed to acknowledge his deficiencies, 'which,' said he, 'some have not the sense to see, and others are too proud to own, which makes them blockheads for their whole life.'*

* Nichols's Lit. An. vol. viii. p. 564; ix. p. 716; Lit. Ill. vol. iv. p. 849.

CHAPTER XI.

POPE. DODDRIDGE. 'DIVINE LEGATION.'

WARBURTON INTRODUCED TO POPE — POPE'S EXPRESSIONS OF GRATITUDE TO HIM — WARBURTON STAYS A WEEK WITH POPE AT TWICKENHAM — LETTER FROM POPE TO WARBURTON — POPE'S DESIRE TO HAVE THE 'ESSAY ON MAN' TRANSLATED INTO LATIN — HIS WISH TO SETTLE WARBURTON NEARER LONDON — SOLICITS LORD CHESTERFIELD TO PROCURE HIM A LIVING — SECOND VOLUME OF 'THE DIVINE LEGATION' PREPARED — CORRESPONDENCE WITH DR. DODDRIDGE — WARBURTON'S CHANGE OF OPINION WITH REGARD TO THE 'WORKS OF THE LEARNED' — HIS DESULTORY MODE OF WRITING — PLAGIARISM OF COVENTRY, THE AUTHOR OF 'PHILEMON TO HYDASPES' —HIS INTERCOURSE WITH WARBURTON — SECOND VOLUME OF 'THE DIVINE LEGATION' PUBLISHED, AND REVIEWED IN THE 'WORKS OF THE LEARNED' BY DODDRIDGE — ABSTRACT OF THE CONTENTS OF THE VOLUME.

THE great event of Warburton's life, in the year 1740, was his meeting with Pope, which took place on May 6. Pope had expressed his wish for a visit from Warburton, 'to whom,' he said, 'he really had more obligation than to any man;' and Warburton had signified the gratification which he should feel at calling on him as soon as he should be in the metropolis. Pope, writing again to him, from Twickenham, says, 'I received with great pleasure . . . the prospect you give me of a nearer acquaintance with you when you come to town. I shall hope what part of your time you can afford me will be passed rather in this place than in London, since it is here only I live as I ought, *mihi et amicis.* I therefore depend on your promise; and so much as my constitution suffers by the winter, I yet assure you such an acquisition will make the spring much the more welcome to me, when it is to bring you hither *cum zephyris et hirundine primâ*. . . . In earnest,' he adds, in reference to the Vindication against Crousaz, 'I am extremely obliged to you for thus espousing the cause of a stranger whom you judged to be injured; but my part in this sentiment is the least: the generosity of your conduct deserves esteem; your zeal for truth deserves affection from every candid man; and as such, were I wholly out of the case, I should esteem and love you for it. I will not, therefore, use you so ill as to write in the general style of compliment: it is below the dignity of the occasion; and I can only say (which I say with sincerity and warmth) that you have made me,' &c.

It is pleasant to read these civilities between authors; and Pope was certainly very much in earnest. 'Pray let my house,' he says, in a subsequent letter, 'have its share of you; or, if I can any way be instrumental in accommodating you in town during your stay, I have lodgings and a library or two at my disposal, which, I believe, I need not offer to a man to whom all libraries ought to be open, or to one who wants them so little, but that 't is possible you may be as much a stranger to this town as I wish with all my heart I was. I see by certain squibs in the "Miscellanies" that you have as much of the uncharitable spirit poured out upon you as the author you defended from Crousaz. I only wish you gave them no other answer than that of the sun to the frogs, shining out in your second book, and the completion of your argument.'

'Let us meet,' says another communication, 'like men who have been many years acquainted with each other, and whose friendship is not to begin, but continue. All forms should be past when people know each other's mind so well. I flatter myself you are a man after my own heart, who seeks content only from within, and says to greatness, "*Tuas habeto tibi res; egomet habebo meas.*" But as it is but just your other friends should have some part of you, I insist on my making you the first visit in London, and thence, after a few days, to carry you to Twickenham for as many as you can afford me. If the press be to take up any part of your time, the sheets may be brought you hourly thither by my waterman; and you will have more leisure to attend to anything of that sort than in town. I believe, also, I have most of the books you can want, or can easily borrow them. I earnestly desire a line may be left at Mr. Robinson's, where and when I shall call upon you, which I will daily inquire for, whether I chance to be here or in the country.'

Their first meeting, however, whatever was the reason, did not take place in London. The spot in which it occurred was Lord Radnor's garden, adjacent to Pope's residence at Twickenham; and Dodsley, who was present on the occasion, told Dr. Warton that he was astonished at the high compliments paid by Pope to Warburton as they approached, the poet declaring that he looked upon Warburton as his greatest benefactor. Warburton stayed several days at Pope's house. 'I passed about a week at Twickenham,' he wrote to Middleton, 'in a most agreeable manner. Mr. Pope is as good a companion as a poet, and, what is more, appears to be as good a man.'* The intercourse seems to have been extremely agreeable to both parties. Pope continued to address Warburton with respect, and Warburton was careful not to contradict Pope. One evening, when they were walking in the garden, Pope began to converse with Warburton, very familiarly and confidentially, on his performances and feelings as an author. He observed that he considered himself to have been surpassed in every kind of writing, and particularly

* Quoted by Hurd, Life of Warburton, p. 28.

in the faculty of invention. Warburton rejoined that he would not offend his delicacy by enlarging on his merits before his face, but that he would take the liberty of mentioning one quality in which he felt certain that he was unrivalled—the power of uniting wit with sublimity. 'Your wit,' said he, 'gives a splendour and delicacy to your sublimity, and your sublimity gives a grace and dignity to your wit.'* To this compliment, which, if correctly reported, the poet must have thought rather extravagant and obscure—'wit giving splendour to sublimity, and sublimity giving grace to wit'—no reply of Pope's is recorded. But he still continued to speak of Warburton with reverence, both in his conversation and in his letters. In his talk with Spence he was never tired of expatiating on Warburton's extent of mental view, and critical perspicacity, which had excited his admiration. Writing to Warburton about a month after their separation, having received two letters from Warburton in the interval, he says:

'Civility and compliment generally are the goods that letter-writers exchange, which, with honest men, seems a kind of illicit trade, by having been, for the most part, carried on, and carried farthest, by designing men. I am therefore reduced to plain inquiries, how my friend does, and what he does, and to repetitions, which I am afraid to tire him with, *how much I love him*. Your two kind letters gave me real satisfaction, in hearing you were safe and well, and in showing me you took kindly my unaffected endeavours to prove my esteem for you, and delight in your conversation. Indeed, my languid state of health, and frequent deficiency of spirits, together with a number of dissipations, *et aliena negotia centum*, all conspire to throw a faintness and cool appearance over my conduct to those I best love, which I perpetually feel, and grieve

* Letter from Hon. C. Yorke to Lord Hardwicke, in Warton's 'Pope,' and in Harris's 'Life of Lord Hardwicke.'

at; but, in earnest, no man is more deeply touched with merit in general, or with particular merit towards me, in any one. You ought, therefore, in both views, to hold yourself what you are to me in my opinion and affection — so high in each, that I may, perhaps, seldom attempt to tell it you. The greatest justice, and favour too, that you can do me is to take it for granted.

'Do not, therefore, commend my talents, but instruct me by your own. I am not really learned enough to be a judge in works of the nature and depth of yours; but I travel through your book as through an amazing scene of ancient Egypt or Greece, struck with veneration and wonder, but at every step wanting an instructor to tell me all I wish to know. Such you prove to me in the walks of antiquity, and such you will prove to all mankind; but with this additional character, more than any other searcher into antiquities, that of a genius equal to your pains, and of a taste equal to your learning.'

Pope had longed to have his 'Essay on Man' translated into Latin verse, and had engaged Dobson, the translator of Prior's 'Solomon,' to make a version of it; but Dobson grew tired of the work, and left it incomplete. Pope then thought of a translation into Latin prose, and requested Warburton to find him a scholar equal to that undertaking. Warburton accordingly made inquiries at Cambridge, and Pope expresses great obligation to him for the pains which he took. He hunted out somebody ready to make a commencement, said to have been Christopher Smart, then a very young man, and sent Pope a specimen, done in close imitation of the style of Cicero. 'The translation,' wrote Pope in answer, 'you are a much better judge of than I, not only because you understand my work better than I do myself, but as your continued familiarity with the learned languages makes you infinitely more a master of them. I would only recommend that the translator's attention to Tully's

Latinity may not preclude his usage of some terms which may be more precise in modern philosophy than such as he could serve himself of, especially in matters metaphysical. I think this specimen close enough, and clear also, as far as the classical phrases allow; from which yet I would rather he sometimes deviated than suffered the sense to be either dubious, or clouded too much. You know my mind perfectly as to the intent of such a version, and I would have it accompanied with your own remarks translated, such only I mean as are general, or explanatory of those passages which are concise to any degree of obscurity, or which demand, perhaps, too minute an attention in the reader.'

In this letter Pope expresses a wish that Warburton was nearer to him, and, in a subsequent communication, says, 'I am not content with those glimpses of you which a short spring visit affords, and from which you carry nothing away with you but my sighs and my wishes.' In accordance with this feeling, he looked about for the means of procuring Warburton a living in the neighbourhood of London. He tells him that he longs to 'be so fortunate, and a rare fortune,' he says, 'it would be, to be able to procure, and acquaint you of, some real benefit done you by my means. But fortune,' he adds, 'seldom suffers one disinterested man to serve another. 'Tis too much an insult upon her to let two of those who most despise her favours be happy in them at the same time, and in the same instance. I wish for nothing so much at her hands, as that she would permit some great person or other to remove you nearer the banks of the Thames; though very lately a nobleman, whom you esteem much more than you know, had destined,' &c. Thus the passage in the letter, as published by Warburton, breaks off; but from a note of Warburton's on a subsequent letter, we find that the nobleman was Lord Chesterfield, who, as he gave Pope to understand, would have served his friend if he had been able. 'It is not my friendship,' writes Pope to Warburton, 'but the discernment of that nobleman I mentioned, which you are to thank for his intention to serve you. And his judgment is so uncontroverted, that it would really be a pleasure to you to owe him anything, instead of a shame, which often is the case in the favours of men of that rank. I am sorry I can only wish you well, and not do myself honour in doing you any good. But I comfort myself when I reflect few men could make you happier, none more deserving, than you have made yourself.'

Such were the terms in which Pope corresponded with Warburton; and this friendly intercourse between them continued uninterrupted till the day of the poet's death. It is to be regretted that none of Warburton's letters to Pope have been preserved.

At the commencement of the year 1741, Warburton was preparing to send forth the second volume of 'The Divine Legation,' about which he had been engaged, more or less, during the whole of the preceding year. He had even sent a portion of it to the press before December 1739, in which month he wrote to Dr. Birch, 'I have received two sheets. Two more are coming, and they cry out for more copy.' *Inter nos*, I only write from hand to mouth, as we say here; so that an east wind, a fit of the spleen, want of books, and a thousand other accidents, will frequently make the press stand still. This will be an inconvenience to Gyles, but I told him what he was to expect; and his hands are so full of great works, that I may well be spared, among the first-rate of the fleet, and cruise at leisure in a lee-shore, safe from Webster and the rest of the *guarda-de-costas*; and, when good weather and fair traffic invite, put in or out of any little creek or habour; not but that I propose to finish this volume sooner than you imagine, if it please God to grant me health and life.'

In July 1740, he tells Dr. Doddridge, who had been much delighted with the first volume of 'The Divine Legation,' and had entered into correspondence with its author, 'the second volume goes slowly on, but I hope to have it out next winter.' In the following January, when it was about to appear, Doddridge, who seems then to have had no personal acquaintance with Warburton, addressed to him a letter, offering to make an abstract of the volume for insertion in the 'Works of the Learned.' 'I am far from being pleased,' said he, 'with the manner in which the extracts from books are generally made in the "Works of the Learned," and other monthly papers of that kind. I think it would be more for the credit of our nation abroad, and the improvement of it at home, that these accounts should be a kind of abridgment of the most material things contained in books of importance; which might give those who have never read them some idea of their contents, and revive in those who have read them an impression of their most material passages. This is what I could especially wish, where so valuable a book as yours is in question. And though, where everything is so charming as this second volume will be, if it be like the first, it is difficult to know what to omit, and consequently how to abridge it; yet, if you please to trust me, I will do my best, and, busy as I am, will, in two or three successive articles, give such an abstract of it as may do it the least wrong; and, till some translation of it can be made, give the learned world abroad the justest notion of its design which so narrow limits will permit. Now, if you think this little piece of friendship worth your acceptance, I beg you would let me know, and that you would order the second volume, in sheets, to be sent me as soon as it is printed off; at the same time letting the author of this paper [the editor of the "Works of the Learned"] know that the affair is lodged in my hands, and, consequently, that he is to wait for the first article from me, which I will despatch as soon as possible.'

To this application Warburton returned a very gracious answer. Some time before he seems to have been well disposed towards the 'Works of the Learned,' having sent to it his 'Remarks on Jortin's "Notes on Spenser,"' and, it is supposed, some other smaller communications; but now he begins to rail against it in his strongest style. 'I am to thank you, dear sir, for your friendly and obliging concern for my reputation. What you observe of that absurd account of my first volume in the "Works of the Learned" is exactly true. I believe there never was *so nonsensical a piece of stuff* put together. But the journal in general is *a most miserable* one; and, to the opprobrium of our country, we have neither any better, nor, I believe, any other. And that this will never grow better I dare be confident, but by such an accidental favour as this you design it. I altogether approve of the method you propose to take in abstracting it; and Robinson, I dare say, will not presume to alter a word. I am sure I would not, and therefore my seeing it before he prints it will be needless. I will take care you shall have a copy sent you before publication. I propose to have it out about Easter; and yet (to my shame I must tell you), though it consists of three books, the first is not yet entirely printed, and the far greater part of the other two I have not yet composed.' If this was literally true, both the author and the printers must have made extraordinary haste; for the volume was ready for the public, according to Hurd, in May 1741. As the rest of the letter shows how Warburton wrote much of his great work, and tells something of his modes of reading and study, it will be well to subjoin it:

'To let you,' he says, 'into this mystery,' the mystery of dilatoriness in writing, 'I must acquaint you with my faults and imperfections, the common occasion of all profane mysteries. I am naturally very indolent, and apt to be disgusted with what has been any time in my hands or thoughts. When I published my first volume, I intended to set about the remainder immediately; but found such a disgust to an old subject, that I deferred it from month to month, and year to year, till at length, not being able to conquer my listlessness, I was forced to have recourse to an old expedient — that is, begin to set the press on work, and so oblige myself unavoidably to keep it a-going. I began this project last year, but grew weary again before I had half got through the first book; and there it stuck, till just now, when I set it a-going again, and have actually promised the bookseller to supply him constantly with copy till the whole volume is printed, and to get it ready by Lady-day. So that now I hurry through it in a strange manner; and you may expect to find it as incorrect as the former, and for the same reason. Yet I had resolved against serving this volume so, and still my evil nature prevailed; and I find at length it is in vain to strive with it. I take no pride, I assure you, in telling you my infirmities. I confess myself as to a friend, without any manner of affectation. And, that you may see it is so, I would not have you think that natural indolence alone makes me thus play the fool. Distractions of various kinds, inseparable from human life, joined with a naturally melancholy habit, contribute greatly to increase my indolence, and force me often to seek in letters nothing but mere amusement. This makes my reading wild and desultory; and I seek refuge from the uneasiness of thought from any book, let it be what it will, that can engage my attention. There is no one whose good opinion I more value than yours; and the marks you give me of it make me so vain, that I was resolved to humble myself in making you this confession. By my manner of writing upon subjects, you would naturally imagine they afford me pleasure, and attach me thoroughly.

I will assure you, no. I have amused myself much in human learning, to wear away the tedious hours inseparable from a melancholy habit. But no earthly thing gives me pleasure but the ties of natural relation and the friendship of good men. And for all views of happiness, I have no notion of such a thing but in the prospects which revealed religion affords us. You see how I treat you, as if you were my confessor. You are in a more sacred relation to me; I regard you as my friend.'

In a letter to the same correspondent in the following April, he tells him that the volume is nearly ready, and that he has written to Robinson concerning the abstract. 'When you see the book,' he adds, 'you will find what a trick I have been played, in the most impudent piece of plagiarism that, perhaps, ever was known at any time. The story is so ungrateful to me, that I cannot think of telling it twice; you will see it in an advertisement prefixed. Pray give it in some place one stroke of your pen. The man has foolishly ruined his character; but what then? The proving him a scoundrel is putting him in the way to thrive. It is a gentleman, too, and of condition — one Coventry, author of "Philemon to Hydaspes" — to whom I showed some sheets; and he has stolen my general plan of the hieroglyphics, *&c.*, in a *fourth conversation* just published. You will wonder I should let such a sort of writer see anything of mine. But suspend your censure till I tell you the whole history when I see you.'

'Philemon to Hydaspes' was a small book, in five dialogues, on the subject of false religion, or the rise and progress of superstitious worship. It was written by Henry Coventry, a man of good family, fellow of Magdalen College, Cambridge, who was engaged in composing a sixth dialogue when death put a stop to his labour. For what we know of his 'impudent piece of plagiarism,' we are indebted to a manuscript left by the Rev. John

Jones, curate, for many years, to the author of the 'Night Thoughts' at Welwyn; which manuscript Mr. Nichols has printed at large in his 'Literary Anecdotes.' From the statement of Mr. Jones, it appears that Warburton had several times met Coventry at Cambridge, at the rooms of Dr. Middleton and elsewhere, and had fallen into conversation with him on subjects of literature and religion. At length Coventry took occasion to mention what he was writing, and told Warburton, that though he had at first intended to speak only of false religion among Christians, he was now thinking of extending his inquiries to the false theories of religion amongst the heathen, in the course of which he should discuss the origin of hero-worship and symbolic writing. Warburton perceiving that Coventry's notions on the subject were wrong, or at least did not agree with his own, put him, as he considered, right; and Coventry then asked for more particular information about the Egyptian hieroglyphics. Warburton, who was preparing to publish his opinions on that subject, desired to be excused from saying more; and the matter was then dropped. But soon after he had returned to Newark, Coventry again applied to him by letter for information, and Warburton answered that he had no time to spare for entering fully on the subject in writing, but that he would endeavour to gratify his curiosity on the first opportunity, as far as he conveniently could. Coventry, dissatisfied at being thus put off again, went to Gyles, the publisher, and asked to see Warburton's manuscript; a request which Gyles very properly refused. Happening, however, to meet Warburton in London not long after, he reminded him of his promise, and Warburton sent him some of the printed sheets relating to the hieroglyphics. Some weeks afterwards Coventry's fourth dialogue came out, when Warburton, to whom a presentation copy was sent, found that he had published what had been communicated to him confidentially. Warburton immediately wrote to him through a friend, requiring an acknowledgment of his priority in the matter; but Coventry returned an unsatisfactory answer. Warburton then threatened to expose him as a plagiary; and Coventry found himself forced to write the letter to which Warburton alludes in his letter to Doddridge, and which was prefixed to the fourth book of 'The Divine Legation,' stating that he had 'formed his general way of thinking,' as to 'the deduction of animal-worship from the hieroglyphics,' on hints received from Warburton, and that Warburton's whole discourse on the hieroglyphics was finished before Coventry had begun to write about them.

The volume, having been published in May, a copious notice of it, written by Doddridge, and sent to Warburton before publication,* appeared in the 'Works of the Learned' in the following October, commencing thus:

'The first volume of this work made its way into the world without anything to patronise or recommend it, but the general character of the writer, and its own proper merit. The latter was acknowledged by the applauses of a great number of the best judges, and by the slanders of those whose envy could not brook the author's superior genius; the lustre of that was not in the power of these malignants to obscure; they aimed, therefore, at obstructing its influence, by representing it employed in the subversion of what all good men among us esteem sacred, thereby hoping to render it obnoxious to those very people whose friendship only our author desires, and in whose interests he professedly engages. The learned, the wise, and the candid, were no otherwise influenced by this outrage than to be incited to the closest examination of a performance so bitterly opposed by men pretending religion and orthodoxy; the result of which is no other than what might be expected from persons of

* Nichols's Lit. Anecd. vol. v. p. 573.

their disposition; that is, an approbation of a scheme calculated to evince the divinity of the Jewish and Christian institutions, supported by just reasoning, and adorned with the charms of polite literature. This second part of so laudable an undertaking has been impatiently expected by men of the best taste and discernment. And may we not hope their satisfaction rises as Mr. Warburton proceeds; their admiration of his system increases in proportion to the discovery of it; and that they are the more thoroughly persuaded of its strength as they see how easily the antagonists of it are foiled?'

In these three books, which constitute the second part of the work, he assumes that the universal pretences to revelation prove the high antiquity of some revelation, and particularly of the Jewish; an assumption which he endeavours to establish, not very satisfactorily, from the generally acknowledged need of a revelation, and from the exclusive nature of the Jewish revelation, which, purporting to come from the Creator himself, declared all other revelations, as they were called, to be mere fictions. He replies to Voltaire, whom, like Akenside, he contemptuously calls *a poet*, and who had objected to the exclusive polity of the Jews as rendering them necessarily hateful or contemptible, that they were miraculously separated from the nations to preserve the true worship of the Deity. He maintains, in opposition to Sir Isaac Newton, the high antiquity of Egypt, from the skill of the Egyptians in hieroglyphics and other modes of writing, and from their great knowledge of medicine; and endeavours to show that this great antiquity, as it supports the Scripture history, supports also the divinity of the mission of Moses, which was intended to set a peculiar people free from the old Egyptian false worship. He argues that, the Jewish government being a theocracy, laws against idolatry were necessary to the support of religion under it, but, he says, if his reader would wish to know what use he intends to make of his remarks on the Jewish idolatry, he must crave his patience till he comes to the last volume.* He then shows that the theocracy continued to the coming of Christ, and must have been administered by an extraordinary providence; he dwells on the omission of a future state from the Mosaic legislation, though, not to contradict the Seventh Article of the Church, he admits that it was occasionally intimated to the leading men of the Jewish nation. He then inquires into the nature of typical rites and secondary senses in prophecy, and, animadverting on Collins, who affirmed that all secondary senses in prophecy must be chimerical and absurd, and on Dr. Sykes, who asserted that of no passage of Scripture could there be more than one true sense, he brings this second part to a conclusion with a recapitulation of the steps of his argument.

In allusion to the reception of the first part, which had met such strong opposition from many, he says: 'A man less fond of TRUTH, and equally attached to RELIGION, would have stopped short,' at the end of the third book, 'and have ventured no farther in a road where he must so frequently suffer the displeasure of forsaking those he most agrees with, and the much greater mortification of appearing to go along with those he most differs from. I have often asked myself, what had I to do to invent new arguments for religion, when the old ones had outlived so many generations of this mortal race of infidels and freethinkers? Why did I not rather choose the high road of literary honours, and pick out some poor critic or small philosopher of this school, to offer up at the shrine of violated sense and virtue; things that might be exposed to their deserved contempt on any principles, or, indeed, without any? I might then have flourished in the favour of my superiors, and the goodwill of all my brethren.

* Book v. sect. 2; Works, vol. v. p. 61.

But the love of TRUTH breaks all my measures; *imperiosa trahit veritas*; and I am once more borne away into the deep and troubled torrent of Antiquity.'* The capitals in this extract are Warburton's own. Possibly, in speaking of 'picking out some poor critic or small philosopher,' he had his thoughts on Bentley's exposure of Collins.

Bentley, as Monk observed, he is, while acknowledging his abilities, at times inclined to disparage; and in Warburton's remarks on Collins's 'Grounds of the Christian Religion,' in the sixth book of 'The Divine Legation,' the Bishop thinks he discovers a desire to outshine the answer of Phileleutherus to the 'Discourse on Freethinking.' But for this notion there seems to be but little foundation.

I might have noticed, in my remarks on the first part of 'The Divine Legation,' in specifying the authors whom Warburton quotes in proof of the absence of a future state from the legislation of Moses, that a passage which he afterwards† adduces, with some qualification of his own, from Maimonides,‡ pointing out the difference between divine and human laws, might seem, to those who do not consult the original, to indicate that Warburton took the idea of his work from the Jewish expositor. *Ea tibi explicabo*, says Maimonides to his disciple, *ut planè non ampliùs dubitare queas, et differentiam habeas quâ discernere possis inter ordinationes legum conditarum ab hominibus et inter ordinationes legis divinæ*. 'Maimonides,' adds Warburton, 'saw nothing in the law but *temporal sanctions*, and was struck with the splendour of divinity which this light reflected back upon the law.' But the truth is, that Maimonides makes no allusion to 'temporal sanctions;' the difference which he specifies between divine and human laws is, that human laws concern

* Book iv. sect. 2; Works, vol. iv. p. 79.

† Ib. sect. 6; Works, vol. iv. p. 362.

‡ More Nevoch. Part II. c. 40, Buxtorf's Transl.

themselves only with civil affairs, while divine laws, affording instruction about God and celestial concerns, seek to render men better and more heavenly-minded.

It may be observed, too, that Dr. Johnson, in his tenth sermon, expresses his concurrence in the opinion that the knowledge of a future state was but partially granted to the Jews. 'The Jews,' says he, 'enjoyed a very ample communication of the Divine will, and had a religion which an inspired legislator had prescribed. But even to this nation, the only nation free from idolatry, and acquainted with the perfections of the true God, was the doctrine of a future state so obscurely revealed, that it was not necessarily consequential to the reception, or observation, of their practical religion. . . . That any man could be a Jew, and yet deny a future state, [as was the case with the Sadducees,] is a sufficient proof that it had not yet been *clearly revealed*, and that it was reserved for the preachers of Christianity to bring life and immortality to light.'

CHAPTER XII.

VISIT TO OXFORD. ALLEN. PUBLICATIONS.

WARBURTON AGAIN VISITS POPE AT TWICKENHAM — THEIR EXCURSION TO OXFORD — PROPOSAL TO CONFER DOCTORS' DEGREES ON THEM, AND DISAPPOINTMENT — CONSEQUENT ALLUSIONS TO OXFORD IN THE 'DUNCIAD' — POPE INVITES WARBURTON, ON ALLEN'S PERMISSION, TO PRIOR PARK — NOTICE OF RALPH ALLEN — PRAISES OF HIM BY HURD, WARBURTON, FIELDING — SLIGHT ILLNESS OF WARBURTON AT PRIOR PARK — SUGGESTS TO POPE THE FOURTH BOOK OF THE 'DUNCIAD' — WRITES NOTES ON POPE'S 'ETHIC EPISTLES' — THIRD EDITION OF THE FIRST VOLUME OF 'THE DIVINE LEGATION' — ARRANGEMENTS WITH BOOKSELLERS — LETTER FROM HON. CHARLES YORKE ON 'THE DIVINE LEGATION' — DISSERTATION ON THE 'ORIGIN OF BOOKS OF CHIVALRY' FOR JARVIS'S 'DON QUIXOTE' — ANOTHER VISIT TO ALLEN WITH POPE — LETTER TO RICHARDSON.

WHEN the second volume of 'The Divine Legation' had received its last touch, Warburton proceeded to visit Pope at Twickenham, where he stayed some time, and then joined the poet in a summer ramble into the country. They terminated their excursion at Oxford, when Pope, after staying there a day, went westward, and Warburton, who remained a day after him, to call on Dr. Conybeare, the Dean of Christchurch, returned to London. On the latter day a message was sent to Warburton by Dr. Leigh, the Vice-chancellor, to know if a Doctor's degree in Divinity would be acceptable to him; and Warburton returned a courteous answer, not declining the honour. About the same time a similar communication was made to Pope, offering him a Doctor's degree in Law; and Pope gave a similar reply. Both, therefore, expected to receive their degrees; but the intrigues of two or three individuals, ill affected to Warburton, contrived to throw some impediment in the way; the party favourable to Warburton was outvoted; and, as Warburton was refused his degree, Pope would not accept his. 'I have received some chagrin,' he writes to Warburton on August 12, 'at the delay of your degree at Oxford. As for mine, I will die before I receive one, in an art I am ignorant of, at a place where there remains any scruple of bestowing one on you, in a science of which you are so great a master. In short, I will be doctored with you, or not at all. I am sure, where honour is not conferred on the deserving, there can be none given to the undeserving, no more from the hands of priests than of princes.' Warburton, however, begged him not to slight, on his account, the honour offered by the University. But Pope obstinately adhered to his determination. 'We shall take our degree together in fame,' said he, 'whatever we do at the University; and, I tell you once more, I will not have it there without you.'*

It was from resentment at this affair, as some suppose, that the sneer at the Oxford Dons, as 'Apollo's Mayor and Aldermen,' was introduced into the Fourth Book of the 'Dunciad,' and that the poet said of the sons of Dulness, receiving their titles,

> 'The last, not least, in honours or applause,
> Isis and Cam made Doctors of her Laws.' †

Concluding a letter to Warburton the following year, he says, 'Call me any title you please but a Doctor of Oxford.'

In the following November, Pope paid a visit to Allen at Prior Park, and obtained Allen's permission to invite Warburton to join them. In a letter to him from Prior Park, he says, 'I am here in more leisure than I can

* Pope's Works by Warburton, vol. ix. pp. 341, 343.

† Dunciad, iv. 116, 577.

possibly enjoy, even in my own house, *vacare literis*. . . . If it were practicable for you to pass a month or six weeks from home, it is here I could wish to be with you; and if you would attend to the continuation of your own noble work, or unbend to the idle amusement of commenting upon a poet who has no other merit than that of aiming, by his moral strokes, to merit some regard from such men as advance truth and virtue in a more effectual way; in either case, this place and this house would be an inviolable asylum to you from all you would desire to avoid in so public a scene as Bath. The worthy man, who is the master of it, invites you in the strongest terms; and is one who would treat you with love and veneration, rather than what the world calls civility and regard. He is sincerer and plainer than almost any man now in this world; *antiquis moribus*. . . . . You will want no servant here; your room will be next to mine, and one man will serve us. Here is a library and a gallery ninety feet long to walk in, and a coach whenever you would take the air with me. Mr. Allen tells me you might, on horseback, be here in three days; it is less than a hundred miles from Newark, the road through Leicester, Stow-in-the-Wold, Gloucestershire, and Cirencester, by Lord Bathurst's. I could engage to carry you to London from hence, and I would accommodate my time and journey to your conveniency.

'Is all this a dream? Or can you make it a reality? Can you give ear to me?

> *Audistin'? an me ludit amabilis*
> *Insania?*'

Ralph Allen, whom Pope, in the epilogue to his Satires, first called 'low-born,' and afterwards 'humble,' in the couplet,

> 'Let humble Allen, with an awkward shame,
> Do good by stealth, and blush to find it fame,'

and who was the original of Fielding's Squire Allworthy, was a sensible, unpretending, kind-hearted man, who, having been very much the architect of his own fortune, greatly assisted Warburton in making his. His character we may very well take from Hurd, who gives it as follows:—'Mr. Allen was a man of plain good sense, and the most benevolent temper. He rose to great consideration by farming the cross-posts, which he put into the admirable order in which we now find them, very much to the public advantage as well as his own. He was of that generous composition, that his mind enlarged with his fortune; and the wealth he so honourably acquired, he spent in a splendid hospitality and the most extensive charities. His house, in so public a scene as that of Bath, was open to all men of rank and worth, and especially to men of distinguished parts and learning, whom he honoured and encouraged, and whose respective merits he was enabled to appreciate by a natural discernment and superior good sense, rather than any acquired use and knowledge of letters. His domestic virtues were above all praise. With these qualities he drew to himself a universal respect, and possessed in a high degree the esteem of Mr. Pope.' Hurd, who was introduced at his house by Warburton, grew very intimate with him, and said, when he first saw him, 'He comes up to the notion of my favourites in Queen Elizabeth's reign; good sense in conjunction with the plainest manners; *simplex et nuda veritas.*' On publishing a new edition, too, of his 'Moral and Political Dialogues,' he prefixed to it a portrait of Allen, with the following words from Seneca beneath it: '*Si nobis animum boni viri liceret inspicere, O quàm pulchram faciem, quàm sanctam, quàm ex magnifico placidoque fulgentem videremus! Nemo illum amabilem, qui non simul venerabilem, diceret.**

* Kilvert's Life of Hurd, pp. 45, 355.

Warburton's character of him was this, given in a letter to Doddridge: 'He is, I verily believe, the greatest private character in any age of the world. You see his munificence to the Bath Hospital. This is but a small part of his charities, and charity but a small part of his virtues. I have studied his character even maliciously, to find where his weakness lies, but have studied in vain. When I know it, the world shall know it too, for the consolation of the envious. . . . In a word, I firmly believe him to have been sent by Providence into the world to teach men what blessings they might expect from heaven, would they study to deserve them.'*

Fielding describes Allworthy as walking forth on his terrace in the morning, when the sun was rising in the full blaze of his majesty, 'than which,' he says, 'one object alone in this lower creation could be more glorious, and that Mr. Allworthy himself presented; a human being replete with benevolence, meditating in what manner he might render himself most acceptable to his Creator by doing most good to his creatures.' Fielding had indeed great reason to speak well of Allen, for he experienced from him, merely on account of his merits and necessities, great pecuniary assistance. He is said to have received, on one occasion, two hundred pounds, even before Allen was personally acquainted with him. Allen also aided Fielding's brother, Sir John, in making provision for his family after his death.†

He is reported to have liked Pope chiefly for the sentiments contained in his letters, and to have been at times almost alienated from him by the severity of his satires, so much at variance with his own kindness of disposition.‡

He continued still to manage the posts at the time that Warburton became known to him, and was contemplating

* Nichols's Lit. Illustr. vol. ii. p. 833.

† Sir W. Scott's Biography of Fielding.

‡ Ruffhead's Life of Pope, p. 406, ed. 8vo.

a direct conveyance of letters between Newark and Northampton, instead of the circuit round by London.*

During Warburton's stay at Allen's, his health was not good, and the doctors at Bath desired him to drink the Bath waters, which were brought to him hot every morning to take in bed. His complaint was called 'bilious indigestion,' of which, he observed to Doddridge, the writers against me declare that I have given public proofs; 'but,' he added, 'it is well for them that I can digest their usage of me.' He derived so much benefit from the springs that Allen made him promise to return for a further trial of them.†

He had, at this time, much conversation with Pope about his poems, and, to advance the ends of virtue and religion, 'prevailed on him to alter everything in his moral writings that might be suspected of having the least glance towards *fate* or *naturalism*, and to add what was proper to convince the world that he was warmly on the side of *moral government* and a *revealed will*.' Pope complied with his wishes in this respect without difficulty.‡

He also conferred with Pope about the fourth book of the 'Dunciad,' which he had previously persuaded him to add to the other three. 'I often told him,' says Warburton, 'that it was a pity so fine a poem should remain disgraced by the meanness of its subject, the most insignificant of all dunces, bad rhymers, and malevolent cavillers; that he ought to raise and ennoble it by pointing his satire against the most pernicious of all, *minute philosophers* and *free-thinkers*. I imagined, too, it was for the interests of religion to have it known that so great a genius had a due abhorrence of these pests of virtue and society. . . . The plan of this admirable satire was artfully contrived to show that the follies and defects of a

* Nichols's Lit. Illustr. vol. ii. p. 831. † Ib. p. 830.

‡ Warburton's Pope, Pref. p. viii.

fashionable education naturally led to, and necessarily ended in, free-thinking; with design to point out the only remedy adequate to so fatal an evil.'* Whatever Warburton might fancy, the reader will probably think that the fourth book of the 'Dunciad' bears much more forcibly upon the minute philosophers than upon the free-thinkers, who, though ridiculed, will be sensible of little refutation either in the text or in the notes.

During the winter he wrote some notes on Pope's 'Ethic Epistles,' of which Pope was meditating a new edition. The notes, whether written at Pope's request or of Warburton's free will, were gladly received by the poet, and destined to be attached to his verses.

Early in 1742 a third edition of the first volume of 'The Divine Legation' was published, and, soon afterwards, a second edition of the second volume, in which it was announced that the whole would be concluded in nine books.

There was some difficulty in making arrangements about the work with the executors of Gyles, the bookseller, who died in November of the preceding year, leaving his accounts with Warburton unsettled. Warburton had not parted with the copyright, nor made any agreement with Gyles, except to pay him the 'bookseller's allowance.' But, out of regard for him, he says, 'I asked only half the clear profits of the editions sold, and two-thirds of a third edition of the first volume, and a second edition of the second volume.' He saw no reason, he observed, why 'his favours should be entailed on a rich family that wanted nothing.' With the demand of two-thirds, however, the executors were unwilling to comply, pressing Warburton to be content with half, and, rather than go to law, he at last yielded, though Murray, afterwards Lord Mansfield, would have pleaded his cause

* Warburton's Pope, Pref. p. vii.; and vol. ix. pp. 343, 348.

without a fee. He retained the entire copyright in his own hands.* Pope recommended him Knapton, a man of credit in the trade, as a successor to Gyles, and with Knapton he continued to publish till he ceased to write.

In the second edition of the second volume he made some reflections on the leaders of the rising sect of Methodists, which we may defer to notice till we come to another publication of Warburton's, the 'Doctrine of Grace.'

The tone in which he spoke of the attacks made upon 'The Divine Legation' caused the following letter to be addressed to him by the Honorable Charles Yorke:†—

'July 1, 1742.

'Dear Sir,—I was pleased, on returning home the other day, after an excursion of a few weeks, to find your first volume waiting for me, with a most agreeable letter from yourself, full of kindness and vivacity. To speak the truth, I had been meditating, before I received yours, to say something to you on the very piece you allude to; but you have prevented me in it. I thought also of congratulating you, but you seem to require condolence. And surely without reason. What signifies it that your adversaries are not worth contending with? It is a proof that men of sense are all on your side. Like the spectres whom Æneas encountered, you cannot hurt them by any weapons; but it should be remembered, on the other hand, they do not injure, but tease, and will follow you the less, the more you endure and despise them. You should forgive them too, for you began hostilities. The only provision in the constitution of things for the *dull* is the indolence of the ingenious. Therefore, when a man unites great application to great parts, throws down the fences of prejudice, and strikes out new paths in know-

* Letter to Doddridge, March 3, 1742.

† Letters from an Eminent Prelate, p. 495.

ledge, they confederate against him, as a destroyer of their merit, and a dangerous invader of their property.

'After all, it is a serious and melancholy truth, that when speculative errors are to be reformed, and received opinions either rationally opposed or defended, the matter cannot be attempted without much censure. The discreet upbraid you with imprudence; the prejudiced, with absurdity; and the dull, with affectation. It is a censure, however, which generally arises from interest; for the works of such as you contribute to bury many useless volumes in oblivion.

'I rejoice that you approve of the further remarks I sent you on a few passages of Tunstall's "Epistle;" not only on account of your candour in doing it, but because your sagacity has confirmed what I had thrown out, by two or three very elegant turns of argument. Whenever you treat a subject, you leave nothing to be said after you, and, for that reason, can always improve upon others. But this is a trifle. The new edition of your book shows that you can even improve upon yourself. Tully, I think, says of his behaviour in the offices of friendship, *cœteris satisfacio quàm maximè, mihi ipsi nunquam satisfacio.* And in writing it is one mark of a superior understanding not to be contented with its own produce.

'Your correspondence is exceedingly acceptable to me. When I am conversing with you on subjects of literature or ingenuity, I forget that I have any remote interest in what is going forward in the world, nor desire in any time of life to be an actor in parties, or, as it is called somewhere, *subire tempestates reipublicœ.* . . .

'I am, dear Sir, with the greatest affection and esteem,

'Your most obliged and faithful humble servant,

'Charles Yorke.'

The 'Epistle' of Dr. Tunstall, mentioned in this letter, was addressed to Dr. Middleton, and denied, with Markland

and Ruhnken, the genuineness of the letters between Cicero and Brutus, but, to make Cicero amends, generously attributed to him the books *Ad Herennium.*

In the summer of this year Pope published the new edition of his 'Ethic Epistles,' accompanied by Warburton's comments. The nature of these annotations is well known; they are mostly superfluous and obtrusive; but Pope seems to have been much better pleased with them than his readers have been. Some verses, which Pope had previously rejected, he allowed Warburton to insert as 'Variations' at the foot of the page, giving him the inspection of his manuscripts for that purpose.

About the same time Warburton recast, and collected into a volume, his letters against Crousaz, which he published under the title of 'A Critical and Philosophical Commentary on Mr. Pope's Essay on Man.' The book received the revisal of Pope before it was published.

Warburton's intimacy with Pope brought him acquainted with Jarvis. When Jarvis's 'Don Quixote' was ready for the press, Warburton, bold to write on any subject, sent him a prefatory 'Dissertation on the Origin of Books of Chivalry,' which Jarvis cheerfully prefixed to his version, but without the name of the writer. When the book came forth, Pope, who had not been made aware of Warburton's contribution to it, and who knew as little of the origin of romance as Warburton himself, expressed himself delighted with the contents of the Dissertation, and declared that he could not be mistaken as to the author of it. 'Before I got over two paragraphs,' he wrote to Warburton, 'I cried out, *Aut Erasmus aut Diabolus!* I knew you as certainly as the ancients did the gods, by the first pace and the very gait.' Warburton's style, indeed, was easily distinguished; his manner was animated and striking, but his matter, unhappily, was quite erroneous and absurd. His assertions and his conjectures were alike groundless and vain. He was, however, so well pleased with his work, that, when he published Shakspeare, he reprinted it, almost without abbreviation, as a note at the end of 'Love's Labour Lost;' a play with which, as Malone observes, it has no more to do than with any other of Shakspeare's. The reproduction of the rhapsody afforded the good sense of Tyrwhitt an opportunity for confuting it. He appended to Warburton's note a contradictory note. Warburton had asserted that romances of chivalry were all of Spanish origin; that the heroes of them were mostly Spaniards, and the scene generally in Spain; and that the subjects of them were chiefly crusades of European Christians against the Mahometans of Asia and Africa. Tyrwhitt showed that Spain, so far from being the birthplace of chivalric romances, had produced none older than the invention of printing; that the scene of them was rarely in Spain, except in the few which treat of the affair at Roncesvalles; and that Warburton had evidently taken his notions about wars with the Mahometans from the pseudo-Turpin's 'History of Charlemagne,' and from Geoffry of Monmouth, without a due knowledge of what was in those writers, for Geoffry of Monmouth's history ends before Mahomet was born. Of his positions, as Tyrwhitt said, he offered no proofs, expecting them, apparently, to be received as indisputable truths.

In the autumn Warburton again joined Pope at Allen's. On the twenty-fourth of October we find him preaching at the Abbey Church, at Bath, for the benefit of the Bath Infirmary. He printed his sermon, with an account of the Infirmary appended, but Hurd did not think proper to include it in his works.

He had much communication, about the 'Dunciad,' notes to the 'Essay on Criticism,' and other matters, with Pope, whom he left behind him at Allen's, and who, soon after Warburton's departure, wrote to him saying, 'A project has arisen in my head to make you, in some measure, the editor of this new edition of the "Dunciad," if you have no scruple of owning some of the graver notes, which are now added to those of Dr. Arbuthnot. I mean it as a kind of prelude, or advertisement to the public, of your commentaries on the "Essay on Man," and on "Criticism," which I propose to print next in another volume proportioned to this. I only doubt whether an avowal of those notes to so ludicrous a poem be suitable to a character so established as yours for more serious studies. It was a sudden thought since we parted; and I would have you treat it as no more; and tell me if it is not better to be suppressed, freely and friendlily. I have a particular reason to make you interest yourself in me and my writings: it will cause both them and me to make the better figure to posterity. A very mediocre poet, one Drayton, is yet taken some notice of, because Seldon wrote a few notes on one of his poems.' It was accordingly settled that Warburton should appear as editor of the 'Dunciad.'

Towards the end of the year he received from Richardson a copy of a new edition of 'Pamela,' and, in acknowledging the gift, gave him his opinion, as well as that of Pope, on the work:

'Dec. 28, 1742.

'Good Sir,—This very day, on receiving my things from London, I had the pleasure to find in the box an obliging letter from you, of the 17th past, with a very kind and valuable present of a fine edition of your excellent work, which no one can set a higher rate upon. I find they have both lain all this time at Mr. Bowyer's. I have so true an esteem for you, that you may depend on anything in my power that you think may be of any service to you. Mr. Pope and I, talking over your work, when the two last volumes came out, agreed that one excellent subject of Pamela's letters in high life would have been, to have passed her judgment, on first stepping into it, on everything she saw there, just as simple nature (and no one ever touched nature to the quick, as it were, more certainly and surely than you) dictated. The effect would have been this—that it would have produced, by good management, a most excellent and useful satire on all the follies and extravagances of high life; which, to one of Pamela's low station and good sense, would have appeared as absurd and unaccountable as European polite vices and customs to an Indian. You easily conceive the effect this must have added to the entertainment of the book; and for the use, that is incontestable. And what could be more natural than this in Pamela, going into a new world, where everything sensibly strikes a stranger? But, when I have the pleasure of seeing you in town, we will talk over this matter at large; and, I fancy, you will make something extremely good of our hints. I have a great deal to say upon this subject, that, when we are together, you will not only understand more perfectly, but I shall be able to conceive more clearly by the use of your true judgment. At least I shall be always zealous of showing how much I am, good sir,

'Your very obliged
'and most affectionate humble servant,
'W. WARBURTON.'

CHAPTER XIII.

POPE. BENTLEY. DEATH OF POPE.

'BRIEF EXAMINATION OF MR. WARBURTON'S DIVINE LEGATION' BY THE FREE-THINKERS — EXTRACTS FROM THE WORK — PAGAN THEOLOGY — ORIGIN OF IDOLATRY — TILLARD'S 'FUTURE REWARDS AND PUNISHMENTS BELIEVED BY THE PHILOSOPHERS' — WARBURTON'S 'REMARKS' ON THE BOOK AND ITS AUTHOR — WARBURTON'S 'ADVERTISEMENT' — LETTER TO BIRCH ABOUT TILLARD — POPE CONTINUES HIS ENDEAVOURS TO BRING WARBURTON NEARER TO LONDON — EFFECTS A MEETING BETWEEN WARBURTON AND BOLINGBROKE — RESULT OF IT — WARBURTON'S RELATIVES — NEW EDITION OF THE 'DUNCIAD' BY WARBURTON — BENTLEY; FEELINGS OF POPE AND WARBURTON TOWARDS HIM — WARBURTON'S SUPPOSITION THAT BENTLEY HAD BORROWED FROM VIZZANIUS — HARE'S OPINION — BENTLEY IN THE 'DUNCIAD' — CIBBER'S 'ANOTHER OCCASIONAL LETTER TO POPE' — WARBURTON CORRECTS POPE'S ESSAY ON HOMER — POPE DIES, AND LEAVES THE PROPERTY OF HIS WORKS TO WARBURTON.

WE must not take leave of the year 1742 without noticing two publications directed against Warburton about this time. One of them was a book entitled 'A Brief Examination of the Rev. Mr. Warburton's Divine Legation of Moses, by a Society of Gentlemen;' one of the strongest attacks ever made on the author of 'The Divine Legation.' As Warburton never made any direct reply to this volume, we may just notice a few of the more prominent passages in it, and dismiss it with out farther concern. He attributed it, in private, to Morgan, the author of 'The Moral Philosopher,' and called him the forwardest devil of all his assailants. But it was professedly written by some of the Free-thinkers to whom Warburton had so boldly dedicated his work three years before, and of whom many were qualified to repay his sarcasms with others equally strong, and even more keen. They begin by addressing Warburton thus:

'We, the Free-thinkers of Great Britain, beg leave to approach your learned Person, and, with the profoundest humility, to return you our most grateful acknowledgments, and sincerest thanks, for your invincible Demonstration of "The Divine Legation of Moses," and particularly for the signal honour, and unmerited favour, of addressing it to us. We could never have discharged ourselves, in honour or decency, of the obligations you have laid us under, without deputing a Select Committee of our order to draw up and present to you this our address of thanks.

'You have, Sir, with irresistible evidence, proved that Moses and the prophets knew nothing, or would own nothing, of a future state of rewards and punishments for good and bad men, and that this, whether out of ignorance or design, was kept as a deep secret under the Mosaic Dispensation, and was never intended to make any part of it; and, at the same time, you have unanswerably demonstrated that this is a principle absolutely necessary to civil government. . . .'

'If we should have mistaken your argument, we shall be always ready, with the profoundest submission, to stand corrected by your deeper judgment and abler hand. And herein we only beg the favour that you would chastise us in short, and let us know the worst of it in some reasonable time; and not keep us under discipline for three years together, or force us to read more Latin and Greek than we can either understaud or believe. It is our humble opinion, that religion, true religion, virtue, and godliness, cannot depend upon dark antiquity, verbal criticisms, and the painful laborious study of dead languages. Were this so, we cannot conceive what must become of the bulk of mankind, or how they should be able to judge between you, Sir, and all the learned Jews and Christians hitherto, whom you have ventured to cast off and recede from, for the sake of a new hypothesis of your own, in this grand point of a future state, and the Divine Legation of Moses. We hope you would indulge us a little in this case, as you need so much indulgence yourself. We are very sensible, Sir, of your superiority in language and criticism, and pretend to no competition with you in this respect. But though in such a cloud we may perhaps have lost your religion, we hope we have not yet lost our own virtue and honour, and we are so vain as to persuade ourselves that we are yet in our right senses. And therefore, from your known wisdom and goodness, we expect the favour of not sending us to Bedlam till you have heard us out. . . .'

'We sincerely wish, Sir, that all your brethren of the holy order may as much congratulate you upon it [the Demonstration of Moses' Legation], and return you as hearty thanks for it, as we do. But perhaps they may be of another mind, and imagine that you cry out against the Deists only to guard and colour over a worse principle of your own. But we should be sorry, Sir, if you should incur any *præmunire* in your own Church for doing us so much service. The bigots and enthusiasts among you may perhaps unjustly condemn you as a man of no religion at all. They may think that you regard one mode or form of worship, or one order and distinction of spiritual rulers or clergy, no more than another; and that you only think it your duty, because it is your interest, to be of the established religion, and keep up the alliance with the State everywhere, and whatever it be. For no doubt but the necessity of an alliance between Church and State, for the support of society and civil government, must make it the duty of every wise and good man to be of the State religion everywhere, so far as he is a friend and well-wisher to his country.'*

Farther on, they speak their mind as follows:

'You will give us leave, Sir, to observe, that the great use you have made of the Pagan theology and churchism, in your demonstration of revealed religion, has left it doubtful to us, and to your readers in general, for what we can find, what religion you are of yourself, or whether you think there is any difference between one State religion and another, more than *political utility*. If one might judge by the rule of public utility, one must conclude, from all that you have said, that the ancient Pagan systems and schemes of religion were much better calculated and contrived for the good of civil society than any of our Christian establishments have ever been. The Pagan churchism, polytheism, and temple-worship of the Egyptians, Greeks, and Romans, never inflamed the world, armed one church and nation against another, or occasioned so much effusion of blood on the score of religion, as the Christian dogmatism has done.†

'But we would not have you conclude that we are against an institution and order of holy learned moralists, who, by a thorough acquaintance with human nature, the original springs and movements of the appetites and passions, the true natural grounds and reasons of wrong choice and moral error, and who, by exemplifying their own doctrines in life, should make it appear that virtue is its own reward, as well as the only foundation for any future happiness, and that secular wealth and power is not their aim, but that they feel, and can impress upon others, a pleasure superior to all animal sensual enjoyments, or any of the gratifications of ambition or avarice, sense or appetite. Such an order of men as this must needs be of infinite advantage to mankind, as they would convince

* Pp. 1–5.

† P. 84.

them by their own example, as well as by the rational power and irresistible evidence of their doctrine, where the point of true happiness lies.'*

Warburton having affirmed, in speaking of the origin and progress of idolatry, that local tutelar deities were unknown in the earlier ages of superstition, when the sun, moon, and stars began to be worshipped, and that they were not introduced till the worship of heroes arose, who, having been benefactors of their countries during their lives, were adored by their countrymen after their deaths as watching over them from heaven, the authors of the 'Brief Examination' reply to his assertions thus:—'The reason you have assigned for deifying and worshipping those heroes, when that sort of worship had been received, is probable enough; but it will not follow from hence that men had no notion of tutelar local deities till this hero-worship came in, since the contrary is as evident as history can make it. The notion of tutelar gods, or governing guardian-angels, presiding over particular kingdoms, provinces, families, and even individual persons, has been, so far as we can find, as ancient as the world, or as early as any accounts of states, kingdoms, or communities of men, settled upon earth. This demonism, or angel-worship, to which no era can be fixed, must necessarily have been connected with the idea of local tutelar deities for a long succession of ages, or generations of men, before anything of hero-worship, or immortal mortals, had ever been known or thought of.

'The first idolatry of the world, if it be proper to call it so, consisted in worshipping the sun, or rather the god of the sun, in such or such constellations or configurations of stars. They considered the sun as the principal seat, throne, or habitation, of the supreme Deity. In like manner they thought the moon and stars to be the seats

* P. 142.

or abodes of the subordinate celestial and immortal gods or angels, to whom the Supreme Being, or God of Gods, had committed the government of mortals, and affairs of this lower world.

'But—men came at last to worship not only the true God, as residing in, and manifesting himself chiefly by, that glorious luminary, but they invoked and worshipped the false imaginary gods, or rulers of the moon and the erratic or fixed stars. And this was the demonism, or angel-worship, of the earlier ages, before hero-worship had been brought in; and this seems plainly to have been the idolatry of Egypt and the other heathen nations in the days of Moses. The idolatry, which the Israelites relapsed into in the wilderness, conformable to what they had seen practised in Egypt, was of this sidereal, emblematical, or symbolical kind. They had borne the tabernacle of Moloch and Chiun, their images, the star of the god, or the star-god, which they had made to themselves.* From hence it is evident that besides the Supreme Deity, as residing and manifesting his glory chiefly in the sun, they worshipped the imaginary gods of the several constellations or configurations of stars.'†

This is a sufficient specimen of a book, which, if Warburton paid it but little attention in print, must have touched him not a little in secret.

The other publication was of a weaker nature, the work of one individual, a person of such slender powers and attainments as to offer Warburton a tempting object of attack, and an easy conquest. He was named John Tillard, and was a lawyer in good circumstances, who, being offended with certain positions in 'The Divine Legation,' amused his leisure with attempting assaults upon them. His effort would be hardly worth notice but for the fifty pages of retort with which Warburton replied

* Amos, v. 26. † P. 88, 90.

to it. It was entitled 'Future Rewards and Punishments believed by the Ancients, particularly the Philosophers, wherein some objections of the Rev. Mr. Warburton in his "Divine Legation of Moses" are considered.' Warburton, in his third book, had maintained that none of the ancient philosophers believed the doctrine of a future state of rewards and punishments, though, on account of its acknowledged necessity to the support of religion and civil society, they continued to teach it. Tillard sought to prove that the philosophers did believe this doctrine which they taught; but he showed such a lamentable ignorance of exoteric and esoteric doctrines, confessing at the same time, with much simplicity, that he 'had, like Lord Chief Justice Hale, lost his Greek by long advocation to studies of quite another nature,' that Warburton had only to make sport of him, and tell him that he had forgot his logic, too, if he ever had any, and that Judge Hale, though he lost his Greek, got a good deal of good sense, but that the author of this pamphlet had lost his without getting anything but the knack of writing without sense.

He blunders out of a question, said Warburton, and makes himself amends by blundering into it again. He says that he passes over Warburton's 'nice distinctions, divisions, and subdivisions, as needless curiosities;' and Warburton asks him how, when he acts thus, he can presume to offer himself as a disputant. He says, in one place, 'if I may be allowed to argue in the same way as Mr. Warburton,' and Warburton tells him he believes 'the public will pardon him, let him begin to do so when he will.' Warburton then calls on the reader to admire how the pamphleteer, though 'grievously bemired,' still 'flounders on.' Tillard blunders about a passage of Plato, and then attributes the words of Timæus to Plato, and Warburton exclaims, 'How admirable a progress hast thou made, from Plato nothing to the purpose, to no

Plato at all!' 'The schools of philosophy,' proceeds Warburton, 'like the courts of law, make no provision for fools, but, upon my word, I am not satisfied whether Mr. Tillard's extravagances be not very honest blunders; however, he has now his choice to call them what he will, so he no longer pretends to call them arguments.' And he concludes by observing that Webster and Tillard, the doctor and the student, 'have managed things so well that the one has lost his reason in the study of the law, and the other his charity in defence of the Gospel.'

Tillard published his book at first anonymously, and afterwards reprinted it with his name. Warburton, when he republished his 'Remarks,' prefixed to them this Warburtonian 'Advertisement': 'The author of the pamphlet here examined hath lately made a public confession of his authorship, signed with his own *name*, and thereby saved himself from all further correction of this kind. For he who is so lost to shame as a *writer*, to *own* what he before wrote, and so lost to shame as a *man*, to *own* what he hath now written, must needs be past all amendment, the only reasonable view in *correction*. I shall therefore but do, what indeed (were it any more than repeating what he himself hath discovered to the public) would be justly reckoned the cruellest of all things, tell my reader the name of this Miserable; which we now find to be J. TILLARD.'

Tillard was a friend of Dr. Birch, to whom Warburton, writing about the time that the pamphlet appeared anonymously, says, 'I will not tell you my sentiments of your friend's book, because he is your friend. And as to his name and quality, I do not desire to know it, nor would I. He has given us his book, and by that alone I must measure him, if ever I do take notice of him. It was an aggravation to Job's misfortunes, that *his adversaries would not write a book.* If I should esteem it a misfortune to have such adversaries as have hitherto appeared against me, I have at least this pleasure, that they will *write*—no great pleasure indeed if I were obliged to *answer*. When a man like Webster shows neither common sense nor common honesty, he must expect no notice to his arguments. But this writer, for one single instance of honesty, methinks, should not go without his reward. It is where he owns I only extended the disbelief of a future state to the philosophers. However, this writer's espousing the cause of heathen philosophy so warmly will perhaps have this good effect, that the bigots on the other side of the question (for there are bigots on both) may be induced to think less favourably of it. For my part, nothing can induce me to think more or less favourably of things or persons but the appearance of truth; a rule, I hope, I shall never depart from, though this writer has probably taken it for granted it was not at all in my view in writing "The Divine Legation."'

In a letter to Doddridge, written shortly after the publication of the 'Remarks' on Tillard, Warburton says, 'This is a man of fortune; and it is well he is so, for I have spoiled his trade as a writer; and, as he was both very abusive, free-thinking, and anonymous, I have not spared to expose his ignorance and ill-faith.'

The author of 'Confusion worse Confounded' made merry with Warburton's inconsistent condemnations of Tillard; first, because he published anonymously, as being a stabber in the dark; and secondly, when he put his name to the book, as being lost to all shame for owning such trash.

Pope continued his efforts to serve Warburton, and gratify himself, by bringing him nearer to London. In January 1743, he writes to Warburton: 'Be assured, once for all, the more I read of you, as the more I hear from you, the better I am instructed and pleased. And this misfortune of my own dulness,' the consequence of ill health, 'and my own absence, only quicken my ardent wish that some good fortune would draw you nearer, and enable me to enjoy both, for a greater part of our lives in this neighbourhood, and in such a situation as might make more beneficial friends than I esteem and enjoy you equally. I have again heard from Lord . . . . , and another hand, that the Lord I wrote to you of declares an intention to serve you. My answer (which they related to him) was, that he would be sure of your acquaintance for life, if once he served or obliged you; but that, I was certain, you would never trouble him with your expectation, though he would never get rid of your gratitude.' The nobleman whose name is omitted is said to have been Lord Granville;* but the application was ineffectual.

It was probably to this affair that Pope alluded, in a conversation with Warburton, a short time before his death. He was complaining of the professions, which many great people would make, of their readiness to serve their friends, and of the artfulness with which, when they were solicited for proofs of their good-will, they would succeed in evading performance. 'It was but the other day,' said he, 'that a Noble Lord in my neighbourhood, whom till then I had much mistaken, told me in conversation that he had a large benefice fallen, which he did not know what to do with. 'Give it to me,' said I, 'and I will promise to bestow it on one who will do honour to your patronage.' He said I should have it. I believed him, and, after waiting some time, without hearing further of it, I reminded him of what had passed, when he said, with some confusion, that his steward had disposed of it, unknown to him or his lady.'†

Pope also exerted himself, about the same time, to bring Warburton and Bolingbroke, who had never met, together. Writing to Allen, he observes, 'Lord Bolingbroke stays a month yet [at Battersea], and I hope Mr. Warburton will come to town before he goes. They will both be pleased to meet each other; and nothing, in all

* Nichols's Lit. Anecd. vol. v. p. 584.

† Ruffhead's Life of Pope, p. 488, 8vo. ed.

my life, has been so great a pleasure to my nature as to bring deserving and knowing men together. It is the greatest favour that can be done, either to great geniuses or useful men. I wish, too, he were a while in town, if it were only to lie a little in the way of some proud and powerful persons, to see if they have any of the best sort of pride left—namely, to serve learning and merit—and by that means distinguish themselves from their predecessors.' Shortly after, also, inviting Allen to visit him, he says that he may possibly, before he comes, take a flight to Battersea with Mr. Warburton, 'whom,' he adds, 'I have promised to make known to the only great man in Europe who knows as much as he.'* The meeting in consequence took place, but not till the following year, and was productive of no such good effects as Pope had contemplated. Bolingbroke hated Warburton for his expulsion of fatalism from the 'Essay on Man,' and for the ascendancy which he had acquired over Pope's mind. The three dined together, at Lord Mansfield's, a short time before Pope's death; when Bolingbroke made a remark about the moral attributes of the Deity, to which Warburton, disliking it, replied with some asperity; and a debate ensued, which ended in making each thoroughly detestable to the other.†

In the early part of this year Warburton had some trouble on account of the ill success of the husband of one of his sisters in trade; an affair which he mentions at some length in a letter to Doddridge:‡ 'I should not have been so long in making my best acknowledgments for your last kind letter, had not your absence from home, and a late unhappy domestic affair, prevented me, and engrossed all my thoughts—the misfortunes of an excellent sister and her children, by her husband's ill success in trade, yet attended to with the utmost honesty and

* Warburton's Pope, vol. ix. pp. 321, 323.

† Ruffhead's Life of Pope, p. 220.

‡ Jan. 22, 1743.

sobriety; so that, to his own ruin, he has been a considerable benefactor to the public while in trade, and his creditors at last no losers, but himself undone. I do not know whether this be an alleviation or aggravation of the misfortune. But I can tell you, with the utmost truth, that I share with this distressed sister and her children (who all live with me) the small revenue it has pleased God to bless me with, with much greater satisfaction than others spend theirs on their pleasures. I do not know how it is, but though I am far from being a hero, yet I find Brutus expresses my exact sentiments, when he says to Cicero, *Aliter alii cum suis vivunt. Nihil ego possum in sororis meæ liberis facere, quo possit expleri voluntas mea aut officium.* But you will reprove me, I know, for this false modesty in apologising for this compassion, and say, where is the wonder that a man who pretends to be a Christian should not come behind a Pagan, how great soever, in the performance of moral duties? However this may be, I can assure you my only concern on this occasion was for an incomparable mother, whom I feared the misfortunes of a favourite daughter would have too much affected. But, I thank God, religion, that religion which you make such amiable drawings of in all your writings, was more than a support to her. But I ask pardon for talking so long of myself. This is a subject I never choose to talk of, yet I could not forbear mentioning it to a man I so much esteem, and whose heart I know to be so right.'

But Warburton was not long diverted from his literary occupations. Early in the year came forth, in accordance with Pope's proposal, the new edition of the 'Dunciad,' under the editorship of Warburton, who is said to have furnished 'Richardus Aristarchus on the Hero of the Poem,' an essay to show that for the hero of the lesser epic the requisite qualities are vanity, licentiousness, and unashamed dulness, such as were to be found in Cibber, now elevated to the throne of Theobald. But as this piece, before it was published, was doubtless left to Pope to alter as he pleased, it is impossible to tell how much of it was Pope's and how much Warburton's; and the same may be said of the ludicrous notes to which Bentley's name is attached. But that Warburton was suspected of having much to do with the notes, is evident from one of his letters to Bowyer, the printer, in which he says, 'Don't mention to any, I beg of you, your suspicion about the notes. Is it not a noble poem? I am glad the "Dunciad" has had such a run. The Greek, I know, will be well printed in *your* edition, *notwithstanding the absence of Scriblerus*,'* meaning himself.

Warburton, even before he joined Pope, appears to have been willing, at times, to lower or oppose Bentley as far as possible. In speaking, in 'The Divine Legation,'† of the ancient legislators making religion and a providence the great supports of their institutes, he mentions the Prefaces to the laws of Zaleucus and Charondas, as they are given in Diodorus and Stobæus, as examples of this fact, and steps rather out of his way to maintain their genuineness, especially that of the fragments attributed to Zaleucus, against Bentley, who, from the use of certain words in them, more modern than the time at which they professed to have been written, showed that they must necessarily be regarded either as altogether spurious, or as greatly altered from their original condition. Warburton endeavours to evade the force of the argument from the recent form of the words, by suggesting that the alterations may have been made, like alterations in many other writings, for the sake of rendering the language clearer and more intelligible; and then, after remarking on the 'deal of good learning' which 'the great critic has employed' on the subject, he concludes, to his own satisfaction, though

* Nichols's Lit. Ill. vol. ii. p. 766.

† Book ii. sect. 3.

not to that of any one else (for the words are of a kind to which his remarks are inapplicable), 'that the credit of these remains stands unshaken by anything the learned critic has advanced to the contrary, and that we may safely produce them as of the antiquity they lay claim to.'

He was also desirous to lend whatever support was in his power to the charge made by Boyle and his party against Bentley of having 'pillaged Vizzanius,' an obscure editor of Ocellus Lucanus. Bentley, seeking to prove that Ocellus Lucanus, who was a Pythagorean, and of Doric origin, must have written in Doric, though his book now appears in the Attic dialect, quoted a passage of Jamblichus's 'Life of Pythagoras,' cited also by Vizzanius, in which it is said that all the Pythagoreans, whose head-quarters were at Crotona, were required φωνῇ χρῆσθαι τῇ πατρῴᾳ, which Bentley interpreted, that each individual was required 'to use his own mother-tongue.' This is the sense in which any one might take the words, who should read them for the first time as they stand in Vizzanius, without knowing anything of their context in Jamblichus. But this is not their true meaning; they signify that the Pythagoreans ordered all who joined them at Crotona, from whencesoever they came, to use *the mother-tongue of Crotona*, which was the Doric. Either way of taking the words will serve to prove that Ocellus Lucanus used the Doric dialect, but either way will not prove that he who argued from them must have taken them from the original of Jamblichus. It was therefore maintained by Bentley's adversaries that he could have seen the words only in Vizzanius, or, as they expressed it, that he 'stole the observation' about Ocellus Lucanus from Vizzanius. This Bentley stoutly denied, observing, as the strongest argument to the contrary, that Vizzanius does not understand the words in the sense which he himself had given them; a true observation; but it was apparent that neither would Bentley himself have differed from Vizzanius, if he had taken the words from Jamblichus's own text. It was, therefore, generally considered that Boyle and his party were in this instance in the right; and Bentley himself, at the conclusion of his remarks on that point, says, with something less than his usual boldness: 'Whether Vizzanius or I have hit upon the true meaning, perhaps all competent readers will not be of a mind.' Warburton argued, from this diffidence of expression, that Bentley was conscious of being in the wrong; and supposed that the great critic, when he put forth the first edition of the 'Dissertation on Phalaris,' had seen the words of Jamblichus only in Vizzanius, where, having but hastily glanced at them, he had misunderstood their tendency, but that, when he was put on his defence, he consulted Jamblichus's own text, and became aware of their right meaning.*

So far Warburton had the learned world with him. 'There is more curious learning,' said Hare in a letter to him, 'in Bentley's answer to the Oxford Critics than I ever saw in any book of that compass; but I did not therefore believe that he did not steal from Vizzanius.'† Most other learned men were of the same opinion as Hare. But Warburton was not content with opposing Bentley on this point only. The author of 'The Dissertation on Phalaris' having remarked that Timæus, who questioned whether Zaleucus had ever existed, was, though 'of a virulent style, an inquisitive and accurate writer,' Warburton, to whose argument the existence of Zaleucus was of consequence, attacked the character of Timæus, as a writer of no authority, 'the Oldmixon of the Greeks,' malignant and calumnious, and wrests passages from different writers to support his charges. But upon this matter the learned world differed from him. Warburton,

* Div. Legation, book ii. sect. 3, note B.; Letters from an Eminent Prelate, let. v.

† Kilvert, Selections from Warburton's Papers, p. 114.

said Dr. Salter, is 'quite wrong in all he says about Timæus, . . very unfairly adding, in his pretended translations, to the railing accusations against Timæus, which he cites; no one of which calls him a calumniator, or impeaches his veracity, in any respect, much less taxes him with inventing, aggravating, &c., the faults of others, from an innate malignity of heart.'* What Bentley thought of Warburton's opposition to him we are nowhere told; but when the first volume of 'The Divine Legation' was shown him, about three years before his death, he said, 'This man has a monstrous appetite, but very bad digestion.' We do not know that this sarcasm came to Warburton's ears, but, if it did, it would not lessen any feeling of antagonism that Warburton might entertain towards Bentley. When the fourth book of the 'Dunciad' appeared, the mighty critic was dead.

Warburton, assuredly, was very well disposed to take the part of Pope against Bentley; to whom Pope had been full of hostility ever since he had said that the translation of the Iliad was 'a pretty poem, but not Homer,' a remark which 'the portentous cub,' said the critic, 'never forgave.' Pope was delighted to present Bentley to Dulness as

> Her mighty scholiast, whose unwearied pains
> Made Horace dull, and humbled Milton's strains;

and Warburton was quite prepared to add his comments to the poet's verses.

The whole conduct of Warburton towards Bentley, observes Bishop Monk,† was very peculiar. He had no cause of offence against him, unless it were the sarcasm on his literary digestion; he did not, like Pope, regard the race of critics with aversion or contempt; on the contrary, he would have been willing, had his scholarship

* Note on Diss. on Phalaris, p. 242, ed. 1817.

† Life of Bentley, pp. 655, 657.

allowed, to be numbered among them; yet he seems to have felt an uncontrollable desire, at times, to detract from Bentley's fame, and to degrade him in public estimation, in a manner far from creditable; while, at other times, he manifests great anxiety to do justice to Bentley's abilities;* he applies to him, in a note on Pope, a laudatory quotation from Cicero; and he declares himself, in a letter to Hurd, charmed with Hurd's 'generous concern for the character of a truly great and much injured man, Dr. Bentley.'† He had evidently great respect for Bentley's powers, but was jealous of seeing him placed too high; and Monk thinks that, had they been more nearly of an age, or had their learning been more similar in character, the world would have seen Warburton try his strength with Bentley in controversy.

For his share in this edition of Pope's Satire, Warburton was vigorously, and not ineffectively, attacked by Cibber, in a pamphlet entitled 'Another Occasional Letter from Mr. Cibber to Mr. Pope, with an Expostulatory Address to the Rev. Mr. W. Warburton, Author of the new Preface, and Adviser in the Curious Improvements of the Dunciad.'

'Being at first in some doubt,' says Cibber, 'whether Mr. W. W. really existed, or might be some phantom of Mr. Pope's own framing, I was told by a person of distinction that you were a clergyman of parts and great learning. No one, sure, that knows how a clergyman ought to employ his time will wonder I should be a little surprised, though not totally displeased, to hear that the very person who had so judiciously assisted Mr. Tibbald in his edition of Shakspeare (wherein the idle guesses and errors of Mr. Pope, in the same undertaking, are so justly exposed and refuted), should now, almost in the same breath, blow

* Note on Pope's Imitation of Hor. Ep. to Aug. ver. 104.

† Letters from an Em. Prelate, p. 9.

hot and cold, and enter into so unexpected an alliance with Mr. Pope, whose labours he had so unluckily disgraced. But great wits, I find, like other troublers of the world's repose, are friends or enemies just as their varying interests or passions incline them. Now, though I cannot determine which motive might more induce you to a peace with him, your willingness to redeem your old ally, Mr. Tibbald, from his dishonour in the 'Dunciad,' or the regret you felt for the shame you had inadvertently brought Mr. Pope to as an editor, yet this I find to be certain, that your happy recommendation of the laureat to be hanged up in Tibbald's place has completed the work, and brought every man out of his difficulty. No comedy ever concluded with so entire satisfaction on all sides. Pope pardons you. You forgive Pope. Tibbald is released.'

One of the severest reflections ever thrown on 'The Divine Legation' is here made by Cibber:

'To my sorrow I own it, I never heard you preach in my life; but, depend upon it, whenever I know you design to mend the world or yourself from any pulpit in London, I will most penitently pay you a religious attendance. And if afterwards I should publish some occasional notes upon your discourse, why may it not be judged as proper an employment of my time as the commentaries you promise us on so carnal a writer as Mr. Pope may be of yours? Indeed, Doctor, I should rather advise you to stick to your "Divine Legation of Moses." There you are in your element; for there you may show us — what? Not any necessary part of our belief that is not enjoined in the Scriptures, I hope. For if the Scripture, which is the Word of God, does not declare his Legation to be divine, why are we to take a mortal word for it? and of all mortals, why more immediately yours? But then again, if the Scripture *does* allow your assertion to be true, why, what have you been doing all this while? Wisely holding up the lamp of your lucubrations, to show us the sun. Prodigious! to prove that at midday it is noon! What you will say to my talking of things so much above me I know not; but think it as absurd as you please, provided you will allow me to have the same thoughts of your meddling with my squabbles.' *

Pope, who said that Cibber's pamphlet was more to him than a dose of hartshorn, and that its railing would cure him of a course of flatteries, advised Warburton not to answer, and the commentator accordingly affected a dignified silence.

It was about the same time that Warburton made some alterations, or corrections as they are termed, in Pope's 'Essay on Homer.' 'It is very unreasonable,' wrote Pope to him, 'after all the labour bestowed on the "Dunciad," to give you a second trouble in revising the "Essay on Homer." But I look upon you as one sworn to suffer no errors in me; and though the common way with a commentator be to erect them into beauties, the best office of a critic is to correct and amend them. There being a new edition coming out of Homer, I would willingly render it a little less defective, and the bookseller will not allow me time to do so myself.' † Warburton, with ready pen, assented to the proposal, and made some alterations, at the same time, in the preface, for which Pope returns his thanks in the usual terms: 'Your alterations to the Preface and Essay are just; and none more obliging to me than where you prove your concern that my notions, in my first writings, should not be repugnant to those in my last. And you will have the charity to think, when I was then in an error, it was not so much that I thought wrong or perversely, as that I had not thought sufficiently.' ‡

* Pp. 21, 27.

† Pope to Warburton, June 5, 1743.

‡ Same to same, July 18, 1743.

What alterations in these compositions are due to Warburton, it would be vain to attempt to discover; for though we might note the variations from the first edition, we should be unable to tell which of the changes were Warburton's, and which of them Pope's.

This was the last service that he performed for Pope, during his life, for the poet was now sinking into his last illness, and growing too weak to attend to any literary affairs. On May 30, 1744, he died, and left Warburton, by a will made in December of the preceding year, the property of all such of his works already printed as he has written, or shall write, commentaries or notes upon, and all the profits which shall arise from such editions as he should publish without future alterations. He also left his library to Warburton and Allen, to be shared between them. The property of Pope's works was valued by Johnson at about 4,000*l.*

CHAPTER XIV.

HANMER. BURTON. AKENSIDE.

LETTER FROM MRS. CATHERINE COCKBURN — WARBURTON'S REPLY — BROWN'S 'ESSAY ON SATIRE,' ADDRESSED TO WARBURTON — WARBURTON'S NOTES IN GREY'S 'HUDIBRAS' — EDITION OF THE 'DUNCIAD,' WITH A REFLECTION ON SIR THOMAS HANMER, AND A NOTE ON DR. JOHN BURTON — NOTICE OF BURTON AND HIS WRITINGS, AND THE SATIRE ON HIM BY DR. WILLIAM KING — ANSWERS PROVOKED BY 'THE DIVINE LEGATION' — WARBURTON ATTACKS AKENSIDE ON THE QUESTION WHETHER RIDICULE BE A TEST OF TRUTH — AKENSIDE'S REMARKS — WARBURTON'S RETORT — AKENSIDE DEFENDED BY DYSON — WARBURTON RETIRES FROM THE CONTEST — LORD KAIMES'S OPINION — SOME CONCLUDING REMARKS ON THE QUESTION CONCERNING RIDICULE.

SOON after Pope's death, Warburton received a letter from the learned Mrs. Catherine Cockburn, the defender of Locke, ostensibly to condole with him on the loss of his friend, and to inquire what works of Pope he had published, but in reality to ascertain Warburton's exact notions of moral obligation, as touched upon in the first volume of 'The Divine Legation;' notions differing from her own, which were the same as those of Clarke, that man's obligation to act in certain way lies in the nature of the things that surround him.

Warburton replied with great courtesy. After answering her inquiries regarding Pope's works, he says, 'Towards the conclusion of your letter you have sent me one of the politest cartels imaginable. I think his answer was generally commended, who told the Emperor, when he pressed him, that he never would dispute with a man who had twenty legions at his back. And do you think I will enter the lists with a lady whose writings have twenty thousand charms in them? . . . We differ in what is the true foundation of morality. I have said all I have to say on the subject. And though it be hard to guess when a writer so much the mistress of her subject has said all, yet if I believed what you have said was *all*, I might perhaps be in some measure excusable, as I see you say so much more than any writer of your side of the question had done before you.

'One thing, and one only, you will give me leave, Madam, to observe: that I am a little surprised at the consequence drawn from my position that, as without a God there would be no obligation, therefore the atheist who believes there is none (and might deduce that truth concerning obligation from the principles of right reason) would have no *tie* upon him.

'Hence I concluded, and I thought rightly, that atheism was highly injurious to society. But how any one could conclude from this (for this is the amount of what I said on the subject) that, on my principles (for as to my opinion, I believe no one would question that), *an atheist is not accountable in a future state for any enormities he may commit here*, I do not see. And my reason for saying so is this:—It is a principle, I suppose, agreed on, "That crimes committed *upon wrong principles* are equally punishable with those committed *against right*; for that the falling into this wrong principle was occasioned by some punishable fault in the conduct." Now, I have not said one single word, throughout the discourse, that leads to invalidate this principle; consequently, all I have said cannot affect the truth, *That an atheist is accountable.* I ask your pardon, Madam, for this trouble. It is what I have not given to any other; though several have made the same objection. They deserved nothing at my hands, and you deserve everything.' *

* Hurd's Life of Warburton, pp. 35, 125.

In 1747, when Mrs. Cockburn, disliking the principles advocated by Rutherforth in his 'Essay on Virtue,' determined to write a reply to it, she sent her manuscript to Warburton, who, though he did not altogether approve of her arguments, yet thinking her morality preferable to Rutherforth's, whose love of singularity, he said, had made him a bad moralist, recommended the book in a short preface, saying that it exhibited 'all the strength of reason, and attachment to truth, which make books of this nature really useful.' Rutherforth's great principle was, that if man is virtuous, it is only from the selfish persuasion that adherence to virtue will promote his welfare. Mrs. Cockburn, in opposition, advocates the doctrine of Clarke, that man is led to virtue by his regard to the relations and fitnesses of things. Warburton differed from both, in making virtue to be moral obligation under the will of God as the obliger.

Among the publications, great and small, to which Pope's death gave rise, was an 'Essay on Satire,' addressed to Warburton, by Dr. John Brown, author of the 'Estimate of the Manners and Principles of the Times,' of whom we shall have occasion to say more hereafter. This Essay, a poem of about five hundred lines, is one of the best things that its author wrote, and Warburton was well pleased to attach it to his complete edition of Pope's works. It commences thus:

> Fate gave the word; the cruel arrow sped,
> And Pope lies number'd with the mighty dead!
> Resign'd, he fell; superior to the dart
> That quench'd its rage in your and Britain's heart.
> You mourn; but Britain, lull'd in rest profound
> (Unconscious Britain!) slumbers o'er her wouud.
> Exulting Dulness ey'd the setting light,
> And flapp'd her wing, impatient for the night;
> Rous'd at the signal, Guilt collects her train,
> And counts the triumphs of her growing reign;
> With unextinguishable rage they burn,
> And snake-hung Envy hisses o'er his urn;

Th' envenom'd monsters spit their deadly foam,
To blast the laurel that surrounds his tomb.
  But you, O Warburton, whose eye refin'd
Can see the greatness of an honest mind,
Can see each virtue and each grace unite,
And taste the raptures of a pure delight;
You visit oft his awful page with care,
And view the bright assemblage treasur'd there;
You trace the chain that links his deep design,
And pour new lustre on the glowing line.

It was published anonymously, but it might have been expected that a copy would be sent to Warburton; into whose hands, however, it was suffered to come by chance. 'I saw by accident on the road,' he says, writing to Dodsley, 'a poem called an Essay on Satire, occasioned by the death of Mr. Pope; and was surprised to see so excellent a piece of poetry, and, what was more uncommon, so much good reasoning. I find it has been published some time. If it be not a secret, I should be glad to know the author. If I have leisure, I shall give some account of it for the literary news of your Museum.' This intention, I believe, was not executed.

The name of the author was readily communicated to Warburton, who, by introducing him to the master of Prior Park, added another to the objects of Allworthy's beneficence.

About the same time Warburton communicated to the very learned Dr. Zachary Grey a few notes for his edition of 'Hudibras.' The assistance was thankfully acknowledged by Dr. Grey, in his Preface, who expresses himself 'highly indebted to the Rev. and Learned Mr. William Warburton for his curious and critical observations, which were procured for me by my learned and worthy friend, the Rev. Mr. James Tunstall, B.D., Public Orator of the University of Cambridge, and Fellow of St. John's College.' * It might be thought, from the way in which Dr. Grey speaks

* Dr. Grey's Preface to Hudibras, p. 35; Nichols's Lit. Anecd. vol. ii. p. 169.

of the notes, that they are very numerous and important; but the reader who searches for them will find them but few. It may be well to give a specimen or two. Those who understand the stars, says Ralpho, can tell

> What makes men great, what fools or knaves;
> But not what wise, for only of those
> The stars (they say) cannot dispose,
> No more than can the astrologians.*

These lines are somewhat obscure. Warburton gives this explanation: 'The astrologers themselves can no more dispose of (i. e. deceive) a wise man than can the stars. What makes the obscurity is the using the word *dispose* in two senses; to signify *influence* when it relates to the stars, and *deceive* when it relates to the astrologers.' The true sense seems to be, the influence of the stars can no more make a wise man, than the astrologers can deceive him when he is made.

On the verses,

> For when a shin in fight is cropp'd,
> The knee with one of timbers propp'd
> Is deem'd more honourable than th' other,
> And takes place, though the younger brother,†

Warburton's remark seems to be very just: 'Alluding to the awkward steps a man with a wooden leg makes in walking, who always sets it first.'

What is said of the shoemaker,

> Cerdon the Great, renown'd in song,
> Like Herc'les, for repair of wrong;
> Ill has he read, that never hit
> On him, in muse's deathless writ,

has brought many a reader to a stand. How is Cerdon so famous, that we, who have never hit on him, have read ill? Warburton understands it of shoemakers in general:

* Part i. canto i. ver. 616. † Part i. canto ii. ver. 146.

'Because,' he says, 'the cobbler is a very common subject in old ballads.'

We need not seek for more specimens.

The first publication that Warburton gave to the world after Pope's death was a small edition of the 'Dunciad.' In this edition appeared the lines to which we have alluded in speaking of Pope and Warburton's visit to Oxford; lines in ridicule of Sir Thomas Hanmer and his fine edition of Shakspeare: an object of Warburton's strong detestation. Sir Thomas had intended to publish his Shakspeare at his own expense, but the University of Oxford kindly took the burden on themselves:

> But (happy for him as the times went then)
> Appear'd Apollo's may'r and aldermen,
> On whom three hundred gold-capt youths await,
> To lug the ponderous volume off in state.*

These verses, according to Warburton, had been left in print by Pope, with directions that they should be inserted where they now stand as soon as Sir Thomas Hanmer's Shakspeare should be published. The whole of the sarcasm on Hanmer may be supposed to have been written at Warburton's instigation. The three hundred gold-capt youths are three hundred gentlemen commoners, said to have been influenced by the authorities to subscribe to Hanmer's book.

In this edition, also, Dr. John Burton, best known by his 'Pentalogia,' was assigned a place in a note for offence given to Warburton, by a sarcasm on Allen, in his 'Iter Bathoniense,' a playful satire on Bath, published in the preceding year. The lines to which the note is attached stand thus: they are part of a speech of Dulness:

> The common soul, of heaven's more frugal make,
> Serves but to keep fools pert, and knaves awake;
> A drowsy watchman that just gives a knock,
> And breaks our rest to tell us what's o'clock.

* Book iv. v. 115.

Previously they had stood thus:

Of souls the greater part, heaven's common make,
Serve but to keep fools pert, and knaves awake;
And most but find that sentinel of God
A drowsy watchman in the land of *Nod.*

'But to this,' said Warburton's annotation, 'there were two objections; the pleasantry was too low for the poet, and a deal too good for the goddess. For though (as he told us before, ii. 34), *Gentle Dulness ever loves a joke*, and (as this species of mirth arises from a *mal-entendu*) we may well suppose it to be much to her taste, yet this above is not genuine, but a mere counterfeit of wit, as we shall see by placing by the side of it *one of her own jokes*, which we find in the Rev. Mr. Burton's late Satire upon Bath, in the following words:—*Virum, quem non ego sanè doctissimum, at certè omnium, quotquot fere uspiam*, literatissimum *appellare ausim.* And look, the more respectable the subject, the more grateful to our goddess is the offering.'

Burton's offence is more fully stated in a letter from Warburton to Hurd: 'This man, two or three years ago, came with his wife and family to Bath. They brought with them a letter of recommendation to Mr. Allen's notice, who received them here several times with distinguished civilities. And the first thing the puppy did afterwards was to abuse the man who received him so hospitably with a saucy stupid joke. Hayter, you know whom I mean (I owe him the ceremony of no other title), got a friend to excuse him to me, as meaning no ill, but the mere effect of dulness, which mistook it for a compliment. I thought this did not excuse him being laughed at. And I did no more. His intercessor had been a witness of the civilities he had received.' *

Hayter, to whom Warburton refuses titles, was the Bishop of Norwich of that day, and afterwards Bishop

* Letters from an Em. Prelate, let. xix.

of London. How he had incurred Warburton's displeasure I do not know. At his intercession, the note was suppressed in the subsequent editions.

Dr. John Burton, 'the puppy,' was a learned and amiable man, about two years older than Warburton himself, bred at Oxford, and elected fellow of Eton College in 1733. He was fond of amusing himself with little compositions in Greek and Latin, prose and verse, which he printed from time to time, and at last collected into a volume, wishing, he said, to improve the students by offering them specimens of better composition, *absit verbo invidia*, than some of those that had been lately put before them. His harmless conceitedness often exposed him to ridicule. One sort of writing in which he delighted was the relation of a journey; he had published an *Iter Surriense* and *Sussexiense* in Greek, and, about 1743, produced in Latin an *Iter Bathoniense*, or 'Journey to Bath,' in which he bestowed some satire, very innocent, though such as exposed him to the charge of unfeeling pedantry, on the frivolous amusements, and extravagant devotion to gambling, of the company that frequented the pump-room. He supposes that his friend, to whom he addresses his account, will wish to know what he, *urbis urbanissimæ hospes inurbanus*, thought of the fine assemblies that he saw. 'Accedo,' he says, 'e multis unus. Verum ipso in limine, pede paullulum represso, suspensus hæsi; ita mihi animum repentè percussit hoc multiforme spectaculum. Interea fortè in parietem adversum oculos conjicio. En verò ibi, in pomparum opprobrium, speculum ingens obversabatur; juvabat ibi, non sine tacito risu microcosmum hunc lepidissimum contemplari, rerumque circum undique miris modis gestarum quasì compendium prælibare. Videbar mihi videre machinas quasdam gesticulantes, frequentem popellum, mirè officiosum, circumcursitare, otiari, ridere, varioque demum lusu temere lascivire. Ibi continuò hæc mecum, "quot capita, tot ineptiæ!"'

After noticing the appearance of the gamesters, at a subsequent period of the evening, with the *rixatio importuna, et malè dissimulata indignatio, imò forsan et impiæ preces*, remarkable among them, he exclaims: 'Hæ tibi sunt artes, hæ deliciæ, hæc oblectamenta, O eleganter inepta, et damnosè ingeniosa Thermopolis! . . . O miram et planè singularem, neque verò invidendam hujusce loci felicitatem! ubi omnes quasi ex pacto et deditâ operâ, (valetudinis scilicet gratiâ), nec sine aliquâ ingenii laude, sedulò desipiunt; adeò ut homini homo non ita multum præstet, stulto intelligens! ubi plurimus sine gaudio plausus, sine facetiis risus, sine tranquillitate otium, sine fructu negotium.'

But what gave special offence to many was the way in which he spoke of Nash, the Master of the Ceremonies, as *magister ineptiarum, effœtus et edentulus senex*, crowned with a white hat, and in whose countenance was *ferrugineus ardor, et sinè verecundiâ rubor immutabilis.* At the last, however, he cries, 'I have found a man:'

'Heus εὕρηκα! tandem inveni virum; instar mille unum. Facile scias eum mihi placuisse quem acceperam testimonio commendatum tuo; virum inter Bathonienses suos facile principem; quem undequaque præsentem parietes ipsi medius fidius loquuntur; quem illustrat gloriosa natalium obscuritas, fortunæ eundem et virtutis filium, τὸν αὐτοφυῆ, τὸν αὐτοδίδακτον, καὶ αὐτοτελῆ, virum quem non ego sanè doctissimum, at certe omnium quotquot fere uspiam reperiuntur *literatissimum* appellare ausim, et ex commercio suo literario fructus pro merito suo uberrimos sine invidiâ consecutum.'

Which the author of the 'Canons of Criticism' thus translates:

'But stay—I have at last found a man, one worth a thousand. You will believe that it was natural for me to be pleased with a person whose character you recommended to me; a man, by far the chief among all his fellow-citizens; whose presence among them the walls everywhere proclaim; whom the want of high birth renders the more illustrious, and shows him to be at once the child of virtue and the favourite of fortune; self-formed, self-taught, and self-complete. A man whom one may call, if not the most learned, yet certainly, upon comparison with most, a man of letters; and one who, by his literary commerce, has deservedly acquired an ample and unenvied fortune.'

For this little satirical pun upon Allen, Warburton thought the author worthy of being thrust into a note in the 'Dunciad.' But Burton's conceit afterwards brought upon him another castigation of a different kind. At the dedication of the Radcliffe Library, in 1749, Dr. William King, Principal of St. Mary Hall, delivered a Latin oration, which was received with great applause, and was praised by Warton in his 'Triumphs of Isis.' But Burton, not liking it, published a pamphlet of 'Remarks' on it, under the name of *Phileleutherus Londinensis*, pointing out inaccuracies in the language; among which was *quamvis*, in one passage, for *quum*. King, who, like his namesake, the author of the 'Account of the Heathen Gods,' was ever ready for a sportive sally, retorted with 'Elogium Famæ inserviens Jacci Etonensis sive Gigantis, or the Praises of Jack of Eton, commonly called the Giant; collected into Latin and English Metre after the manner of Thomas Sternhold, John Hopkins, John Burton, and others. To which is added a Dissertation on the Burtonic style. By a Master of Arts;' with the motto, from Swift, 'What shall I say to a pamphlet when the malice and falsehood of every line would require an answer, and when the dulness and absurdities will not deserve one?' Burton was a very tall man, and on that account was called the Giant; but King professes to call him so 'in consideration of his great talents and the extraordinary endowments of his mind.' 'Burton,' says he, 'has been constituted by himself sole judge of all Latin compositions, and, if any person shall presume, without his license and consent, to pronounce and publish a Latin oration, our Giant must necessarily deem it an invasion of his rights, and an open contempt of his supremacy. This was the unfortunate case of Dr. King. The Doctor, at the request of the Radcliffe Trustees, and with the approbation of the present Vice-Chancellor of Oxford, made a speech in the Sheldonian Theatre without consulting the Giant (of whom, it seems, he had never heard), or paying a proper regard to his censorial dignity. This excited our hero's indignation. . . . He wrote an Epistle to the Rev. Dr. Bentham, which has lately appeared in print. In this Epistle he hath vented the whole stock of matter which he had been six months collecting with much labour and many watchings. It is therefore reckoned a finished piece, and acknowledged by all judges to be the finest panegyric on *himself*, and the severest censure on the *Man* whom he hath, unprovoked and Giant-like, thought proper to defy, that hath ever yet been published in any age or language. To do honour to this great author, I have endeavoured to give a faithful abstract of this admirable production in the following poem. I have chosen the Sternholdian metre, not only as it is best adapted to an English taste, but likewise as it is that kind of verse which the Giant chiefly delights in, and which he generally makes use of when he condescends to write in English, and attempts the sublime in his mother-tongue.' Where Burton had given specimens of this kind of metre, I do not know; I have found none in any of his writings that I have inspected.

Spirit of Sternhold, me inspire,
And hither deign to bring,[lyre,
Not David's, but thine own sweet
While Giant Jack I sing.

Tu, Sternholde, mî aspira!
Sonet, non Davidis, sed O
Dulce sonet tua lyra,
Nunc, dum Jacco laudes reddo.

To beaux he showeth, and to belles
His work in Latin lore,
Who all confess it far excels
All he had wrote before.

Jactat opus; jactat sanè
Bellos inter hos et hasce:
Hi et hæ fatentur planè
Jaccum semet superâsse.

Then unto Oxenford he came,
And walked round the town,
And told all folk that his great fame
Should pull the Doctor's down.

Tum Oxonium petit, ibi
Docet doctos omnes, quò si
Famam magnam paret sibi,
Senem istum vincat, O si!

But here, alack, and well-a-day!
He met a strange rebuff;
Some friends advis'd him to delay,
Some said he wrote poor stuff.

Eheu! audit nunc, Quò tendis?
Ne festina; novâ curâ
Opus est; nunc, ut emendes
Cuncta, una sit litura.

The Giant is in doubt for a while what to do, but at last consults the landlord of the house, an apothecary, at which he lodged:

When thrice our learned landlord Hume,
And four times eke, did cry,
O do not such fine things consume,
For I no faults can spy.

Mendum nullum qui notabat,
Jacci hospes Humus, 'Heu me!'
Ter quaterque conclamabat,
Talia, Jacce, ne consume.

However, he did consume his 'fine things,' but had no sooner done so than he was seized with his old *cacoethes scribendi*, and resolved on writing again:

So up he goes to London city,
Increased in his gall,
And now he mindeth, without pity,
Unhappy King to maul.

Ad Londinum nunc advenit,
Plenus fellis, bene potus,
Et personam eam tenet,
Ut tu, senex, pereas totus.

At length a book he doth compile,
A Latin book indeed;
And so well-fashion'd is the style,
'Tis pleasant for to read.

Gaudet quid Latinum (næ est
Liber cultus) emisisse;
Omnibusque volu-pe est
Librum huncce pellegisse.

And it is printed more correctly than Pote of Eton would have printed it:

Who that hath cunning doth not note
The print is most correct?
Unlike the print of Master Pote,
Who doth his press neglect.

'En venustas quæ typorum!'
Dicet qui non est asotus;
'Quam dissimilis eorum
Utitur queis pravus Potus!'

King then turns the Epistle to Dr. Bentham into ridicule by a kind of doggrel parody, which begins thus:

Proper eulogiums how to pen,
  O NED, to thee I'll show;
For I alone of learned men
  This curious art do know.

Quî elogium componatur,
  Cupio, NEDDY, te docere,
Quum doctorum mihi datur
  Soli artem hanc callere.

He next alludes to some disappointment of Bentham's, or attack on him, and declares that he will be his defender:

And all shall see, though now you've fallen,
  By my *bon mots* I'll raise you;
And that fine thing I spake of Allen
  I'll borrow here to praise you.

Jaces; sed sermone meo
  Jam nunc te in astra feram;
Ad laudandum Allen eo
  Quo sermone usus eram.

Thus: NEDDY, you deserve a mitre
  Much better than your betters,
For, since you are a *letter writer*,
  You are *a man of letters*.

Præstans cæteris incedis:
  Cur non quoque tu mitratus?
Nam, cum *literas tot edis*,
  Sane vir es *literatus*.

There publish'd was, in London town,
  A wretched pamphlet thing,
Which, though the author be well known,
  Some say was wrote by King.

Editum est in Londino
  Audax quid. Sic hæsit quis te?
Qui sit, nescio pol omnino,
  Nisi esset senex iste.

And I affirm it was his book,
  Or at him I can't come;
And in that book he hath mistook,
  And *quamvis* wrote for *quum*.

Ipsus est, et causa patet;
  Ipsus est et verax sum;
Liber cujus mendis scatet:
  Quamvis ponitur pro *quum*.

He is then made to praise himself, in allusion to his Satire on Bath:

And while with pleasure I report
  That I'm so nicely bred,
I could give lessons to the court,
  And serve in Coteril's stead;

Quum sim elegantiarum
  Omnium elegans spectator,
Uti essem rerum harum,
  Coteril, curas quas, curator;

That Latin writers make me smile,
  For rival me can no man,
Who am the only judge of style,
  And mine is truly Roman.

Ut Latine si quis—hili
  Ne putetur, neque sanus,
Ipse quum sim censor styli
  Solus verè ac Romanus.

He is then made to call King *senex*, *calumniator*, *comœdus*, *scurra*, and, addressing his Alma Mater, says:

O mother, tell him you do hate, And eke I hate them more, All writers who appear so late, All men who 're past threescore.	Homines sexagenarios Tu odisti, ipse odi; Et scriptores, vel primarios Viros, omnes ejus-modi.
As whilom, when I was at Bath, One Nash I there did sting, For with him I had cause of wrath, The same as with this King.	Sic, cùm me recipiebam Ad Bathoniam, Nash perstringo; Simultatem tum gerebam Quocum, qualem nunc cum Kingo.
For Nash did give me no offence, But with a right to scold We always have a just pretence, If he be waxen old.	Nullam mî injuriam fecit Ille Nash: atat senescit! Malè me dixisse decet Ei, quisquis senex esset.
Besides, that very Nash (and that My choler did excite), Though he be black, did wear a hat Which was all over white.	At, quod bilem mî commovit, Senem dum hunc nigrum quæro, Vah! quis albo eum novit Ornatissimum galero?

On this passage is the following note:

'Jack in his Iter Bathoniense is very severe on Mr. Nash, a generous, charitable, good-natured man, and well esteemed by all people. The corporation of Bath have lately decreed him a statue as a testimony of their respect. A proper reward for the many great services he has done them, and the advantages which have arisen from his prudent regulations, for forty years past, in that place! But can it be expected that our Giant should govern his judgment by the opinion of others? Mr. Nash is old, and sometimes wears a white hat. Two unpardonable crimes! And such as a censor could not possibly pass by without a public mark of his resentment.'

The pun upon Allen is said to have been borrowed from the ballad of a journeyman tailor, celebrating the Heads of the Oxford Colleges, in which was this stanza:

O rare Merton College,
O rare Dr. Holland !
Thou art a man of letters,
And so is William Poland.

William Poland was letter-carrier to the University.

But Warburton was soon to give offence to a writer of far greater eminence than Dr. Burton. The variety of opinions which he advanced in 'The Divine Legation,' and the haughtiness of assertion with which he had supported them, had raised against him swarms of opponents, disliking either his matter or his manner, some of whom attacked him in the periodicals of the day, others in pamphlets, and others, directly or indirectly, in larger works. To some of these he felt an uncontrollable desire to reply, and was not long in carrying his desire into execution. Hurd, in his 'Life of Warburton,' has some remarks on the position in which he had placed himself, and the feelings by which he was actuated to retort, so very much to the purpose, that they well deserve to be cited. 'The extensive argument, and miscellaneous nature of that work, "The Divine Legation," had led him to declare his sentiments on a multitude of questions, on which he thought differently from other writers, and, of course, to censure or confute their opinions. Whole bodies of men, as well as individuals of the highest reputation, were attacked by him; and his manner was to speak his sense of all with freedom and force. So that most writers, and even readers, had some ground of complaint against him. Not only the Freethinkers and unbelievers, against whom the tenor of his book was directed, but the heterodox of every denomination were treated without much ceremony; and of those reputed orthodox, some tenet or other, which till then they had held sacred, was discussed and reprobated by him. Straggling heresies, or embodied systems, made no difference with him; as they came in his way, no quarter was given to either. . . .'

'Such a writer (independently of the envy which ever attends superior genius) must needs have innumerable enemies. And as all could not receive, nor the greater part deserve, his notice, he determined to select a few of the more respectable, out of the great body of assailants, and to quit his hands of them at once in a general comprehensive answer. This was done by "Remarks on Several Occasional Reflections," in two parts; the former published in 1744, and the second in 1745; and both executed in such a manner as was not likely to invite any fresh attacks upon him.'

What adversaries he assailed, and in what manner, in the body of these 'Remarks,' we shall see shortly; but, making a stand at the threshold, we find, in his preface, that he directed, very unnecessarily, and in a very offensive manner, an attack on the author of the 'Pleasures of Imagination,' who had not then set his name to his recently published work. Had Warburton known what opinion Pope entertained of the poem, he would doubtless have thought the poet worthy of being treated with greater respect. When the manuscript of it was offered to Dodsley, as Johnson relates, he carried it to Pope for his judgment, who advised the bookseller not to make a niggardly offer, for 'this was no everyday writer.' But Warburton was ignorant of Pope's estimate, and adverted to the poet as one of the most ordinary of ordinary scribblers.

Shaftesbury had asserted, in his 'Essays on Enthusiasm and on Wit and Humour,' that ridicule is a test of truth; there being, indeed, no mode of ascertaining what is really serious, and what ridiculous, but by 'applying ridicule to see whether it will bear;' since 'nothing is ridiculous but what is deformed, and nothing proof against ridicule but what is handsome and just.' This position, that ridicule is a test of truth, Warburton, in his 'Dedication to the Freethinkers,' published in 1738, had denied, assuring the sceptics that all their efforts to prove anything false by ridicule were futile and contemptible.

Akenside, in his poem and its notes, published in 1744, took the side of Shaftesbury, but expressed himself with somewhat less positiveness of the efficacy of the test. He represented the propensity to ridicule as implanted in us

> to aid
> The tardy steps of reason, and at once
> By this prompt impulse urge us to depress
> The giddy aims of folly.

But in his notes he made some remarks which Warburton probably considered, and perhaps not without reason, to be directed against his 'Dedication.' 'Notwithstanding the general influence of ridicule on private and civil life,' says he, 'as well as on learning and the sciences, it has been almost constantly neglected or misrepresented, by divines especially.'* That ridicule had been neglected, it seems strange that Akenside should have asserted: that it had been misrepresented or decried by divines, as Warburton and others, he might think a matter of certainty. But he adds further observations on the subject:

'Since it is, beyond all contradiction, evident that we have a natural sense or feeling of the ridiculous, and since so good a reason may be assigned to justify the Supreme Being for bestowing it, one cannot, without astonishment, reflect on the conduct of those men who imagine it is for the service of religion to vilify and blacken it without distinction, and endeavour to persuade us that it is never applied but in a bad cause. Ridicule is not concerned with mere speculative truth or falsehood. It is not in abstract propositions or theorems, but in actions and passions, good and evil, beauty and deformity, that we find materials for it; and all these terms are relative, implying approbation or blame. To ask, then,

* Note on book iii. ver. 75.

whether ridicule be a test of truth, is, in other words, to ask whether that which is ridiculous can be morally true, can be just and becoming; or whether that which is just and becoming can be ridiculous; a question that does not deserve a serious answer; for it is evident that, as in a metaphysical proposition offered to the understanding for its assent, the faculty of reason examines the terms of the proposition, and, finding some idea which was supposed equal to another to be in fact unequal, of consequence rejects the proposition as a falsehood; so in objects offered to the mind for its esteem or applause, the faculty of ridicule, finding any incongruity in the claim, urges the mind to reject it with laughter and contempt.'*

These observations Warburton chose to consider as a personal attack on himself. But, as he was not addressed by name, and as he might have seen that the author, though anonymous, was a man of learning and ability, he might have offered such remarks as he thought fit to make in reply, in a courteous and gentlemanly tone. But he chose to use the same haughty and contemptuous style to the author of a noble poem as to the meanest of those whom he called 'answerers by profession;' to the sensitive as to the unfeeling; to Akenside as to Webster. He complains of 'having been called to account, without any ceremony, by the nameless author of a poem entitled the "Pleasures of Imagination," one of those,' he says, 'to whom I applied the words of Tully, "*non decet, non datum est, non potestis*," who affect wit and raillery on subjects not meet, and with talents unequal.' He sneeringly calls him a 'poet,' and 'a man of taste,' as if he must therefore be void of understanding. He asks, in one passage, 'What is the man dreaming of?' and, after some attempts at exposing his argumentation, adds, 'Here we see, where he aims to make an absurd proposition for

* Note on book iii. ver. 259.

the use of others, it proves a reasonable one: 't is odds but we find him, before we have done, trying to make a reasonable one, for his own use, that turns out at least an absurdity.' To Akenside's notion that ridicule was given us by the Supreme Being *to aid the tardy steps of reason*, he retorts, 'just as the efficacy of poison was given us by the Supreme Being *to aid our tardy steps in pursuit of vermin*.' He tells him that his 'common sense is all turned to taste;' and reminds him of 'a plain English proverb worth all his modish *ideas of beauty and virtue*, and that is, *to be merry and wise*, which concerns him nearer than one may think.' He carps and quibbles at small matters, and produces a string of trifling objections, instead of an array of solid refutation.

Akenside did not long want a champion to defend him. Jeremiah Dyson, his munificent friend and benefactor, came forward, in a few days, with a pamphlet entitled 'An Epistle to the Rev. Mr. Warburton, occasioned by his treatment of the Author of the "Pleasures of Imagination,"' with the motto, '*Neque solùm quid istum audire, verum etiam quid me deceat dicere, considerabo*;' a production so temperately and agreeably written, and filled with argument so closely and efficiently directed, as to form a pleasing contrast to the vague remarks and graceless style of Warburton's attack. It commences thus:

'Sir,—Notwithstanding the pains you have taken to discourage all men from entering into any controversy with you, and notwithstanding the severe example you have just been making of one who, as you fancied, had presumed *to call you to account*, you must still be content to be accountable for your writings, and must once more bear the mortification of being actually called to account for them.

''T is the Preface to your late "Remarks" that you are now called upon to justify; in which you have thought fit to treat upon a mighty *free footing* (as you style it, but, in the apprehension of most people, a very injurious one), the ingenious and worthy author of the poem entitled "The Pleasures of Imagination." The favourable reception and applause the performance has met with, render it unnecessary, and indeed impertinent, for me to enlarge in its praise; especially as you, sir, have not condescended to enter into a particular censure of the poem. However, by some general hints scattered up and down, as well as by the affectation of perpetually styling the author "our poet," you have let us see how you stand affected towards it. Whether it be indeed that dull, trivial, useless thing you seem to represent it, I shall not dispute with you, but am content to leave, as to this point, Mr. Warburton's judgment staked against the general reputation of the poem. The point I am immediately concerned with is your unbecoming treatment of the author, which, as it is so interwoven through the whole course of your Preface, as to be sufficiently evident without the allegation of particular passages, so we shall find there are not wanting repeated instances of direct and notorious ill-usage; such usage as, though the provocation had been ever so just, and the imagined attack upon you ever so real, would yet have been unwarrantable, and which, therefore, cannot admit of the least shadow of an excuse, when it shall appear that you had in reality no provocation at all.'

Mr. Dyson then proceeds to assure Warburton that his notion of the note being intended as personal was an entire mistake, but tells him that, 'whether it was personal or not would have been a matter of little moment, had his preface been written with a becoming temper.' He then adverts to his complaint that 'it is his fortune to be concerned with nameless adversaries,' and reminds him that while he is so ready to misrepresent and calumniate, his opponents will be but the more inclined to attack him anonymously. 'Write,' he adds, 'with decency; treat your antagonists with civility and candour; and then, depend upon it, you will have the same fortune in this respect with the rest of the world.'

In Akenside's poem, in allusion to ridiculous assumption, are these lines:

> Others, of graver mien, behold; adorn'd
> With holy ensigns, how sublime they move,
> And, bending oft their sanctimonious eyes,
> Take homage of the simple-minded throng,
> Ambassadors of Heav'n.

This passage Warburton called 'an insult on the whole body of the clergy.' Dyson replies that the representation was never intended for them. 'That it must be so intended, you argue, because you know of none of them to whom one part of the character,' that of being ambassadors of Heaven, 'does not belong. What you may know about it, I shall not pretend to dispute. But, for my own part, I know of many of the clergy to whom no part of it belongs, and who think they have no sufficient warrant for styling themselves ambassadors of Heaven. Thus much, at least, is certain and notorious, that among those who do use this style and title, it is used in very different senses. If, therefore, there are any who, by this appellation, mean nothing more than simple ministers or teachers of the Gospel, and who do not, in consequence of this character, take upon themselves and affect a superiority over the rest of their brethren, these men do, indeed, speak improperly, but are by no means the persons here ridiculed. But if there are any who apply to themselves this title in a more exalted and dignified sense, who would have it taken in that sense by the vulgar, and who, in consequence of this fancied dignity, behave with an affected haughtiness, and expect as much homage and submission as could be due to one truly and properly an ambassador from heaven, these are the men here exposed; these are the men who are truly ridiculous, and who, wherever they are not screened by superstition or tyranny, will always be ridiculed.'

Warburton had affected to sneer at the lines as dull. Dyson tells him that, from the resentment he expresses at them, people would have been apt to imagine he found them extremely sharp, or that his feelings were extremely sensitive. He then concludes as follows: 'If differing in opinion from Mr. Warburton proves a man to be not wise, and his ridiculing what Mr. Warburton holds sacred, to be not honest, you have then a sufficient warrant for the insinuations you have advanced. But if these foundations fail, you must assign better; and you have yet to reconcile such treatment with good manners, candour, and truth. How far you may care to undertake this, or what part you may choose to act on the occasion, is a point that chiefly concerns yourself. That you cannot justify your insinuations and your ill-usage of the author, I am sufficiently secure. Should you, therefore, think fit to retract them, I shall rejoice to see justice done to a man of merit, and to find that you are not less ready to wipe off aspersions than you were to bestow them. But if, without attempting to justify them, you should, by refusing to retract them, in effect continue to assert them, I shall at least have the satisfaction of having saved every honest man, who may hereafter offend you, the trouble of answering, or at all regarding your censures and reproaches.'

To this pamphlet Warburton never replied, nor is known to have taken the least notice of it. He left Akenside without further molestation for at least twenty-eight years, when, in 1776, having been annoyed, in the meantime, by the Ode to Edwards, he reprinted the preface to the 'Remarks on Occasional Reflections,' with some abbreviation, but with the admixture of a few strictures on Lord Kames, as a 'Postscript to the Dedication to the Freethinkers.'

Lord Kames had touched, in his 'Elements of Criticism,'* on the question 'whether ridicule be a test of truth,' which, he said, was only 'whether the sense of ridicule be the proper test for distinguishing ridiculous objects from those that are not so,' and then, after making some few remarks on the subject, came to the extraordinary conclusion that 'ridicule is not only the test, but the only test of truth.'

The fact is that Warburton, on this point, was mainly in the right; though the justness of his notions hardly appears from among the words which he uses in his 'Dedication to the Freethinkers.' It is only in a note that we find anything definite and really to the purpose. 'When *reason*, the only *test of truth* I know of, has performed its office, and unmasked *hypocrisy and formal error*, then ridicule, I think, may be fairly called in to quicken the operation.' But this dictum ends in absurdity; for, after the operation of unmasking has been despatched by reason, how can ridicule assist to quicken the operation?

Akenside was in much the same error, when he said that ridicule was given *to aid the tardy steps of reason.* Reason, we may see, if we rightly consider the matter, acts quite independently of ridicule. Reason decides on every question that comes before her; and ridicule, if reason disapproves, may follow if she pleases, consenting with her, but without affording her positive aid. Let us seek for a few exemplifications of the subject.

Suppose that a body of soldiers are waiting for the arrival of a leader, to conduct them in a difficult and dangerous expedition, a person whom none of them have ever yet seen, but who, they are well assured, is a man of solid sense, and of grave and authoritative demeanour; and suppose that, while they are in expectation, there appears before them a person of entirely opposite character,

* Vol. ii. p. 55.

a vain pretender, a fop, a buffoon, of affected airs and graces, betraying, by the absurdity of his gestures, weakness and emptiness within, but declaring, at the same time, that he is the general who will show them the way to victory; every one present would receive his declaration with ridicule. But it would not be ridicule that would judge of his pretensions, and decide on their vanity; it would be reason. Reason would decide that he could not be the leader expected; and ridicule would assail him for affecting to be what he was not.

If a person, offering to demonstrate a mathematical proposition which he pretends thoroughly to understand, makes only a vain attempt at a demonstration, proving nothing but his own ignorance, his attempt may be witnessed with ridicule, or with pity, or with any other feeling. But it is neither ridicule, nor pity, nor any other feeling, that decides against his effort. Reason or judgment discerns his failure, and ridicule or pity, or any other feeling, may then follow.

If a critic make an excellent alteration in the text of an author, as that of '*smelling* gourd' into '*swelling* gourd,' it is received with admiration. If he make an evidently bad alteration, as that of 'much bound to *him*' into 'much bound to *hymn*,' it is received with ridicule. But it is no more ridicule that pronounces upon the absurd, than it is admiration that pronounces upon the judicious alteration. It is reason or judgment that decides in either case, and admiration or ridicule waits on the decision.

Akenside, however, in remodelling his poem, thought proper to omit, as Johnson observes, the lines that had provoked Warburton's animadversions.

CHAPTER XV.

MIDDLETON. POCOCKE. MANN. RICHARD GREY.

'REMARKS ON SEVERAL OCCASIONAL REFLECTIONS' — STATE OF AUTHORSHIP A STATE OF WAR — WARBURTON'S DISAGREEMENT WITH MIDDLETON — CAUSE OF IT — LETTER ON THE SUBJECT FROM WARBURTON TO DODDRIDGE — MIDDLETON'S ENMITY TO SHERLOCK — WARBURTON AND POCOCKE ON HIEROGLYPHICS — WARBURTON'S CONTROVERSY WITH MR. NICHOLAS MANN — CONSIDERATIONS ON SIR ISAAC NEWTON'S CHRONOLOGY — WHETHER OSIRIS AND SESOSTRIS WERE THE SAME PERSON — DR. RICHARD GREY ON THE BOOK OF JOB — WARBURTON'S REMARKS IN REPLY TO HIM — HIS FLATTERY OF BISHOP SHERLOCK — HIS STORY OF BERTRAM THE OPTICIAN.

THE chief writers to whom the 'Remarks on Several Occasional Reflections' were a reply, were Dr. Middleton; Dr. Pococke, the traveller in the East; Nicholas Mann, Master of the Charterhouse; and Dr. Richard Grey. Some others received chance strokes from the warrior, as he ran his career against his principal adversaries.

'The state of authorship,' said he, 'whatever that of nature is, is certainly a state of war; in which, especially if it be a holy war, every man's hand is set, not against his *enemy*, but his *brother*.' But as to himself personally, he observes, he can hardly say that he has been attacked; 'for my answerers,' he proceeds, 'write not so properly *against* me, as *for* something that they like better than me; this, for his dear *orthodoxy*; that, for his dearer *philosophers*; a third for his *lawyers*; a fourth for his *cabalists*; a fifth for himself; and a sixth for I don't know what besides the pure *love of scribbling.*' The first two of these, the champions of orthodoxy and philosophy, are Webster and Tillard, with whom we have already made acquaintance; who the others are we shall see hereafter. 'I have given them full liberty,' he adds, 'to try what they can make of it, or it of them, and wish them better luck with their readers' intellects than I have had with theirs. For, from the first to the last of them, their constant cry has been, *They do not understand me.* Now, though I can allow this to be a better reason for their writing at me than any they have hitherto assigned, yet it would be a very bad one for my answering them; because it would keep me engaged *till they did understand me*; which I presume no gentle reader would think a reasonable task for one born when human life is at the shortest.'

As to Dr. Middleton, who stands first upon the list, we have seen how Warburton had incurred censure for the commendation that he had bestowed on him in 1738. They had still continued friends; Dr. Middleton had since published his 'Life of Cicero,' and Warburton had complimented him upon it; but, as Middleton had declared himself in favour of Cicero's belief in a future state, in opposition to Warburton, Warburton, at the end of his third book of 'The Divine Legation,' took occasion to add a note in support of the contrary opinion. Middleton had said that the passages in Cicero's writings, especially those in his letters, (where he may be thought to express himself sincerely,) in which the probability of a future state is questioned, may be supposed to have been written under dejection, when the aspect of things around him was gloomy. Warburton replied that, as 'everything has two academical handles,' we might argue, on the other side, that the more unpromising Cicero's present condition appeared, and the greater were his fears of evil from it, the more he would be inclined to indulge hopes of future good. But he adhered to the opinion which he had advanced, that Cicero, like all the ancient philosophers, was destitute of any belief in a future state;* and quoted a long passage from Towne's 'Critical Inquiry into the Opinions of the Ancient Philosophers' to that effect. Writing, however, to Middleton, April 29, 1741, he says, 'We perhaps shall neither of us be esteemed orthodox writers; but this we shall do; we shall give an example to the world, which orthodox writers rarely do, and perhaps of more use to mankind, than most of the refined subjects they engage in, that we can differ in many important points, and publicly avow our difference, without the least interruption of the declared friendship and esteem we bear to each other. And the "Life of Tully," and "The Divine Legation," will be a rule, which few have set us, and perhaps few will follow, how men, who esteem and love each other, should comport themselves when they differ in opinion. So that whichever is right or wrong in *opinion*, the honest part of the world will judge both of us to be right in *sentiment*.'†

Dr. Middleton's answer was of a similar character: 'As to the circumstance from which you draw so just and useful a lesson, of our differing from each other in some particular opinions, as I was always persuaded that it could not have any other effect upon you, so I have the comfort to assure you that I never felt the least impression from it disadvantageous to our friendship. It is the necessary consequence of that privilege of our nature on which all men of sense set the highest value, the liberty of judging for ourselves; yet since it would be a great satisfaction to me in all cases to find my judgment confirmed by yours, so, when you are at full leisure, I

* Div. Leg. book iii. sect. 3, and note v.; Works, vol. iii. p. 120, 376.
† Hurd's Life of Warburton, p. 31.

should be glad to know the particular reasons which force you to differ from me on the subject of Cicero's opinions, to which alone our difference in the present case is to be referred, that, as far as possible, we may come still nearer to each other.'

But when Middleton, a few months afterwards, published his 'Letter from Rome,' in which he dwelt on the similarity of the Papal religious ceremonies to those of the ancient heathens, estrangement ensued between him and Warburton. Warburton, at the end of the fourth book of 'The Divine Legation,' had observed that many learned writers had noticed an exact and surprising likeness, in many instances, between the superstitions of Christian and Pagan Rome, and that some had concluded from thence, erroneously, though plausibly, that the Catholic must have borrowed from the heathen; and he added, as an illustration, that much of the Jewish ritual must be acknowledged to have been composed with reference to the superstitions of Egypt, as the long abode of the Israelites in that country had made them extremely fond of Egyptian customs; but to argue, therefore, as some deists have done, that they borrowed from thence their common principles of morality, is 'such an absurdity as betrays the grossest ignorance of human nature and the history of mankind.'* This passage, though it speaks of 'many writers,' Middleton chose to consider as intended entirely against himself, laying hold, especially, on the last words; and, in reprinting his 'Letter from Rome,' added, in a postscript to it, that the question whether the Catholics borrowed from the Pagans, it appeared, was to be decided, according to the notion of the author of 'The Divine Legation,' 'not by facts, but by a principle of a different kind, *a superior knowledge of human nature.*' This was sufficient to provoke Warbur-

* Div. Leg., book iv. sect. 6 sub fin., and note HHHHH.

ton to a reply; and, in his 'Remarks on Several Occasional Reflections,' he complained of his 'very learned friend, the author of the elegant and useful 'Letter from Rome,' having taken to himself what was meant of writers on that subject in general; but, in order to say something to his learned friend's disparagement, he intimated that, in pursuit of his argument, Middleton had extended his charge from the modern to the ancient Church of Rome, as being infected with the same superstitions as that of later times; so that what his 'Letter' meant to prove would henceforth stand thus: 'The religion of the present Romans was derived from their early Christian ancestors; and theirs, from the neighbouring Pagans.' Though this was but a just character of the 'Letter from Rome,' yet Warburton's strong mode of expressing himself could not but give further offence to Middleton, who, in consequence, seems to have been entirely alienated from Warburton. 'Neither side giving way,' says Hurd, 'our two candid friends cooled insensibly towards each other, and seem, thenceforward, to have discontinued their correspondence; for I find no letters that passed between them of a later date than those of this year,' 1741, 'which touch upon the difference. A memorable instance of our common weakness! which shows how little stress is to be laid on those professions of candour with which our letters and conversations overflow; and how impossible it is for any lasting friendship to subsist between men of opposite principles and persuasions, however their feelings may for a time be dissembled or disguised, even to themselves, by a show of good breeding.'

Some further account of this matter may be found in a letter from Warburton to Dr. Doddridge, Aug. 5, 1741: 'I understand, by a common friend,' says he, 'that I have much disgusted Dr. Middleton in what I have said of Moses' fraud, the serpent, and the Papists borrowing of the Pagans.' What Warburton had said of Moses, in regard to the serpent, was that he had used a pious fraud in his account of the fall, by mentioning, not the agent of the fall himself, the devil, but only his instrument, the serpent, in order to keep a future state out of sight; as there was a natural connexion between the spiritual effects of the fall, the promised redemption from its effects in the prediction that the serpent's head should be bruised, and the doctrine of a life to come.* This had not met with Dr. Middleton's approbation. What opinion Warburton had expressed about the superstitions of Papal being borrowed from Pagan Rome, we have already seen. The observation on the latter subject, continues Warburton, 'affects him most because he is about publishing a new edition of his "Letter from Rome." I find he cannot bear contradiction, though I did it with the utmost candour. Nay, he told our common friend, Dr. Taylor, that there were some things in the "Vindication" (the little pamphlet wrote soon after the publication of the first volume) which displeased him; but he attributed them to the instigation of Bishop ———, his mortal enemy. Is not this amusing, where he had taken the same kind of liberty with me in his "Tully," when he speaks of the genius of the Academic philosophers, and the sentiments of Tully about a future state? I sent such an answer as was proper. Whether he will come to a better mind I cannot tell, but you shall know when I do. You see to what disasters we authors militant are exposed.' The 'kind of liberty' which Middleton had taken with Warburton in his 'Tully' was nothing more than that of differing in opinion from him. 'Bishop ———' is Bishop Sherlock, whom Middleton hated for having prevented him from becoming Master of the Charterhouse; for when that office was vacant, on the

* Div. Leg book v. sect. 5.

death of Dr. King, Middleton, being a candidate for it, applied to Sir Robert Walpole for his support; but Sir Robert told him fairly that he could not give it, as, on talking with Bishop Sherlock about the matter, he had learned that the majority of the bishops would be against his appointment. Middleton, therefore, attributed his want of success entirely to Sherlock, and took every opportunity of showing hostility towards him; one of his manifestations of enmity being an attack on his 'Discourses on Prophecy,' which he pretended, soon after, to have inspected for the first time, though they had been published some years, and had gone through several editions. Sherlock had argued that the prophecies were links in a chain; Middleton replied that the Evangelists had taken them separately, and sneered at the Bishop for expecting *his dressed up nonsense to go down with the public.**

Waiting on Archbishop Potter, shortly after Mann's appointment, he observed to him, very abruptly, 'I suppose your Grace knows you have chosen an Arian.' The Archbishop was startled, but soon recollecting himself replied, 'An Arian, perhaps, may be better than a Deist.'

Warburton's next object of attack was Dr. Pococke. Warburton, in 'The Divine Legation,'† had said, in speaking of the Egyptian hieroglyphics, that they 'stood for things, and not for words.' Pococke, in his 'Book of Travels,' devoting a chapter to that subject, declared that they stood, 'not for things, but for sounds.' But the truth is, that both writers meant much the same; for if the figure of a crocodile, as Pococke admits, might stand *for the sound that signified malice*, it makes little difference whether we say that the figure of a crocodile indicated *the thing malice* or *the sound malice*. Pococke

* Bishop Newton's Life by Himself, p. 23. Middleton's Works, vol. v. p. 188, 190, 8vo.

† Book iv. sect. 4.

expressed himself somewhat obscurely, and Warburton diverts himself, *saltans Cyclopa*, with his language. He then declares his resolution to stick to his first assertion, and lets off a sneer at the reputed inaccuracy of some of Pococke's plates: 'As for those significative figures properly called hieroglyphics, they never denoted other than things. If there ever were an exception, it was in a late traveller, whose significative Egyptian figures, I am told, are not so properly the representatives of the *things* themselves, as of the writer's *words*, or of his verbal descriptions to the engraver.' But this sarcasm was quite harmless; Pococke's accuracy has been fully acknowledged.

Nicholas Mann, though, as he wrote little, he is now almost forgotten, was a person of great learning and ability, well worthy of distinction in his day. Having been tutor to the Marquis of Blandford, he was, through the interest of the Marlborough family, elected Master of the Charterhouse in 1737, at the time that Dr. Middleton was disappointed of the office. He was author of 'Critical Notes on some Passages of Scripture,' and of two chronological dissertations, 'De Veris Annis D. N. Jesu Christi Natali et Emortuali;' and left some manuscript notes on Antoninus's 'Itinerary.' In his 'Chronological Dissertations' he declared himself in favour of Sir Isaac Newton's hypothesis, in regard to the chronology of Egypt, that Osiris and Sesostris were the same person, a notion which Warburton, in his 'Divine Legation,'* had opposed with great force of reasoning. 'The course of my argument,' said he, 'now brings me to examine a new hypothesis against the high antiquity of Egypt, which hath the incomparable Sir Isaac Newton for its patron; a man for whose fame science and virtue seem to be at strife. The prodigious discoveries he had made in the *natural* world, and especially that superiority of

* Book iv. sect. 5.

genius which opened the way to those discoveries, hath induced some of his countrymen to think him as intimate with the *moral*, and even to believe, with a late ingenious commentator on his "Optics," that, as everything which Midas touched turned to gold, so all that Newton handled turned to demonstration.

'But the sublimest understanding has its bounds; and, what is more to be lamented, the strongest mind has its foible. And this miracle of science, who disclosed all nature to our view, when he came to correct old time, in the chronology of Egypt, suffered himself to be seduced, by little lying Greek mythologists and story-tellers, from the *Goshen* of Moses into the thickest of the *Egyptian darkness*. So pestilent a mischief in the road of truth is a favourite hypothesis; an evil we have frequent occasion to lament, as it retards the progress of our inquiry at almost every step. For it is to be observed that Sir Isaac's Egyptian chronology was fashioned only to support his Grecian; which he erected on one of those sublime conceptions peculiar to his amazing genius.

'But it is not for the sake of any private system that I take upon me to consider the arguments of this illustrious man. The truth is, his discourse of *the empire of Egypt* contradicts everything which Moses and the Prophets have delivered concerning these ancient people. Though some, therefore, of his admirers may seem to think that no more harm can derive to religion by his contradicting the *History* than by his overturning the *Astronomy* of the Bible, yet I am of a different opinion; because, though the end of the sacred history was certainly not to instruct us in Astronomy, yet it was without question written to inform us of the various fortunes of the people of God, with whom the history of Egypt was closely connected. . . .

'His whole argument for the low antiquity of Egypt may be summed up in this syllogism: Osiris advanced Egypt from a state of barbarity to civil policy; Osiris and

Sesostris were the same; therefore Egypt was advanced from a state of barbarity to civil policy in the time of Sesostris. . . . Now the minor in this syllogism being the questionable term, he has employed his whole discourse in its support. All, then, I have to do, is to show that Osiris and Sesostris were not one, but two persons, living in very distant ages.'

Warburton then proceeds to blame Newton for placing too much dependence on fanciful and fabulous writers, such as poets and mythologists, and maintaining a system that contradicts and overthrows all that is considered certain in the more trustworthy historians and other authors of antiquity. He notices the thirteen points of resemblance which Newton finds between Sesostris and Osiris, and observes that a writer living as long after William the Conqueror as Sir Isaac lived after Sesostris, might discover as many marks of similarity between the Conqueror and King Arthur, and assert the identity of the two English monarchs as plausibly as Newton had maintained that of the two Egyptians.

As the excogitation of these marks of parallelism between William and Arthur is a striking instance of Warburton's acuteness, they may not unreasonably be given here:

'1. Arthur and William were both great warriors. 2. Both were of spurious or uncertain birth. 3. Both were in the management of public affairs in their early youth. 4. Both came from France to recover Britain from the Saxons. 5. Both proved victorious in their expedition. 6. Both got the Crown of Britain by election, and not by descent. 7. Both had other dominions besides Britain to which they succeeded by right hereditary. 8. Both went frequently on military expeditions into France. 9. Both warred there with various success. 10. Both had half-brothers by the mother, who, being made very powerful, and proving guilty of manifold extortions and acts of injustice, were punished by them in an exemplary manner.

11. Both had rebellious sons or nephews, whom they met in the field, fought with in person, and subdued. 12. Both reigned [lived] upwards of fifty years. 13. And both died in war.'*

On this argumentation, Mann made the following remarks in the Dedication to his 'Chronological Dissertations.' The translation from Mann's Latin is Warburton's own:

'We are not ignorant of what has lately happened, that the author of 'The Divine Legation,' supposing it some how or other to concern Moses' divine mission to prove that Osiris was not the same with Sesostris, hath turned all that is here said into ridicule, by a comparison made between the fabulous Arthur and William the Norman, who, he says, may be made one by as good reasons (though they have scarce anything alike or in common with one another) as those which we have brought to confound Osiris with Sesostris; and on this point he draws out a disputation through seventy pages and upwards; wherein, notwithstanding, he neither denies nor confutes, but only laughs at, what we have here said of Sesostris. It is true, indeed, that some other of Newton's assertions he does oppose, as those concerning the late invention of arts, arms, and instruments, by some certain king; and of this part of the argument he has the better; for that these things were found out by the Egyptians long before the age of Sesostris, Holy Scripture commands us to believe; but whether found out by any of their kings is not so certain. However, these were matters we never touched upon, as relating nothing to our purpose; nor do they yet induce us to recede from that conclusion of the famous Newton, That Sesac was Sesostris, Osiris, and Bacchus. But the cause being now brought before the public, let the learned determine of it.'

In reply to these animadversions, Warburton, while

* Div. Leg. book iv. sect. 5.

allowing his opponent to be a 'learned and ingenuous writer,' very justly stated that he had done much more than laugh at the hypothesis, and that, far from leaving it undenied or unconfuted, he had denied it by observing that Osiris and Sesostris, though having, like Arthur and William, many points of resemblance, might yet be two different persons; and had confuted it by showing, from the unvarying testimony of the best writers of antiquity, that Osiris and Sesostris were in reality different persons, and lived at two very distant periods. If the invention of legislation and the arts, which is admitted to have been the work of Osiris, had been as late as the days of Sesostris, then Osiris and Sesostris might have been the same person; but as the general voice of antiquity declares the inventions of Osiris to have been long antecedent to the time of Sesostris, it is quite incredible that they could have been the same. If, however, there has been any confusion between them, it may have arisen, as Warburton argues, from the custom which the Egyptians had of calling their eminent persons by the names of their gods, as Cleopatra in later times was called the New Isis, and her brother the New Bacchus; and thus Sesostris may have been styled *Osiris*, or *An Osiris*.

The next assailant upon whom Warburton directed his 'Remarks' was Dr. Richard Grey, author of the well-known 'Memoria Technica,' of 'A New Method of Learning Hebrew without Points,' and of 'A Commentary on the Book of Job,' in which he dissented from Warburton's opinion respecting the time at which the Book of Job was written. Warburton had argued, as we have already seen, that the Book of Job, a dramatical and allegorical composition, but founded on true history, was written by Ezra for the comfort of the Jews after their return from Babylon, where they were about to experience, what they had not hitherto known, an ordinary and unequal providence.

To this notion Dr. Grey declared himself adverse, but admitted that Warburton had supported his allegations 'with great sharpness of wit and many sufficiently specious arguments.' What Dr. Grey advances on his side, considerably abridged, stands thus: 'In a matter which is in itself very uncertain, and which has been rendered still more uncertain by the different opinions of learned men, hardly any hypothesis can be excogitated which will give satisfaction in every respect. But for myself, as I agree with those who think the Book of Job the oldest in the canon, so I have no doubt it was written by Moses himself, who took the subject from authentic records, and clothed it in the dress of poetry. In conformity with this opinion, I consider that a no less satisfactory explanation may be given of all such texts, if indeed there be any, as contain allusions to the Jewish law or history previous to the production of the Book, than if we should allow it to have been written by Ezra, of whom there are among the learned various opinions. As to those passages which, in the judgment of the learned author of "The Divine Legation," refer to events of later times, as the sickness and recovery of Hezekiah,* and the destruction of the Assyrian army,† it will be sufficiently manifest from my comment, to which I refer the reader, that they need not to be taken in this sense, but may be more conveniently understood otherwise. As to the assertion that the main question considered in the Book of Job is whether good happens to the good and evil to the evil, or whether good and evil happen not indiscriminately to both, and that this question could never have been the subject of dispute anywhere but in the land of Judæa, nor there at any other time than that of Ezra, the truth of it depends entirely upon the truth of Mr. Warburton's hypothesis, and is in my opinion far otherwise; for I consider that the personal integrity of

* Ch. xxxiii. ver. 25. † Ch. xxxiv. ver. 20.

Job, and not the question concerning the equal or unequal distribution of good or evil, is the subject of the Book; since it was of Job's personal integrity that his friends doubted, partly on account of the sufferings inflicted on him, and partly on account of the impatience with which he bore them, and his appeals to the justice of God. But as God did not interpose to attest his innocence, and as his friends continued to urge their unjust accusations, he then appeals, we may naturally consider, to that last judgment, in which he declares that he knew his Redeemer would be present with him, and that God would decide in his favour; and thus nothing hinders us from applying that celebrated text,* not to a temporal restitution to his former condition, but to a resurrection to eternal life. And if we add,' he concludes, 'to the arguments which I have adduced in my note on the passage, those which a writer above all praise, the present Bishop of Salisbury, has beautifully interwoven in his "Opinion of the Ancients concerning the Circumstances and Consequences of the Fall," I think we shall want nothing to confirm our belief in the antiquity of the Book, and in my interpretation of this most perplexed passage.'

In replying to this argumentation, Warburton has recourse to some quibbling and petty objections; a mode in which he was very fond of dealing with his adversaries. Dr. Grey says that in an uncertain matter scarcely any hypothesis can be conceived that will give satisfaction in every respect. 'Now,' retorts Warburton, 'though this be a common-place thought, it is nevertheless a very false one; for it is only in uncertain matters that hypotheses are invented, to be applied to account for the appearances of things; and is it not of the nature of an hypothesis to be unsatisfactory?' This is mere objection for objection's sake. A hypothesis may be satisfactory in its principal points, in the judgment of the majority of

* Ch. xix.

those who contemplate it, or unsatisfactory; it may be evidently plausible, or evidently unreasonable. If, out of many hypotheses on a subject, one has a far greater appearance of truth than the rest, it will not be *unsatisfactory in its nature*, but will give more satisfaction than any of the others.

'It is equally false,' he continues, 'that an uncertain matter is, otherwise than by accident, rendered more uncertain by diversity of opinions; for the greater the diversity is, the greater is the chance of coming to the truth; as the more roads men take in an uncertain way, the greater the likelihood of finding out the right.' This again is fallacious. The comparison is not exact. A number of persons seeking for a certain road, seek for it in the belief that a certain road is to be found, and the more numerous the seekers, the greater is the chance of discovering it; but a number of persons conjecturing about an uncertain matter, such as the authorship of the Book of Job, know that they are conjecturing about that on which no certainty is attainable, and may but perplex themselves by the variety of their hypotheses, and end in greater uncertainty than they felt when they began.

The rest of Warburton's 'Remarks' amount to little more than a reiteration of his previously declared opinions. But Dr. Grey's mention of Dr. Sherlock afforded him an opportunity of offering the Bishop a little of the incense of flattery. He first observes that Sherlock's view of the Book of Job was quite different from that of Dr. Grey, and that for Dr. Grey to appeal to him as a supporter was somewhat strange. 'To seek refuge in that excellent Prelate, whose notions of the nature and design of the Book of Job overthrow all he has been saying, and confirm all he has been opposing, looks very much like distress. However, if he will submit to the Bishop's authority for the scope of the Book in general, I shall be very willing to allow his interpretation of the nineteenth chapter.' He then starts off on another matter. 'The name of that great man is auspicious to sacred truth. One can no sooner mention him, on any occasion of literature, than one sees him pointing out some truth or other, capable, if attended to, of clearing up whatever may be in question. His fine Discourse on the Book of Job abounds with instances of this kind; one of which here falls naturally in my way. And as it seems to be the best supported of his interpretations, and, at the same time, greatly confirms what I have advanced concerning the age of the Book, I shall endeavour to set it in a just light. The truth I mean is his interpretation of these words of Job, *By his spirit the heavens are garnished, his hand formed the crooked serpent*; * by which he supposes is meant the devil, the apostate dragon, δράκων ἀποστάτης, as the Septuagint, by thus translating it, seems to have understood the place.' It cannot be imagined, says the Bishop, that the formation of the crooked serpent meant nothing more, in a passage descriptive of God's mightiest works, than that God created snakes and adders. It cannot be supposed, pursues Warburton, that the crooked serpent means the great northern constellation, for the ancient Hebrews did not represent the stars under the figure of animals, until they learned the constellations, in the later ages, from the Greeks, and even then they admitted them with some reserve; so that neither Moses nor Ezra could speak of the constellation of the crooked serpent, and the consequence is, therefore, that 'his Lordship's interpretation is to be received, there being nothing else of moment to be opposed to its truth.' Few readers, however, it may be thought, will be likely to rest satisfied with Sherlock and Warburton's interpretation; for it is utterly at variance with the whole scope of the passage, which is to describe the manifestations of God's power in

* Ch. xxvi. ver. 13.

the visible world. The voice of most expositors, as the verses relate to the heavens, has been in favour of the constellation.

The author ot 'The Divine Legation' then takes leave of those whom he calls his more learned and candid adversaries, Middleton, Pococke, Mann, and Grey, with a summary of the whole argument of his book in a new light, which, he hopes, may not only be serviceable to readers of their class, but also to those of a different character, who, however limited in their conceptions, are not to be neglected, though it is likely, he thinks, that they will part from him with as little satisfaction as a certain customer parted from Bertram the optician, of whom he proceeds to tell a story: 'A grave well-dressed man,' says he, 'coming to the shop of that ingenious inventor and reliever of the distress of all those who are too dull to know what they want, and too rich to be at ease with what they have, demanded one of his best reading glasses, which, when he had examined upon all sorts of print, he returned back with solemn assurance that he could not read at all in it. Bertrand, when he had recovered from the surprise of so strange a phenomenon, fairly asked him, "Sir, could you ever read at all?" To which the other as fairly replied, "Had I been so happy, I had not come hither for your assistance." Should I not, therefore,' he adds, 'with the same forecast, have asked these people, "Gentlemen, before I put my argument for you in a new light, pray tell me, do you understand an argument in any light at all?" But would they have answered with the same ingenuity? They are silent. They modestly let *their works* speak for them.'

CHAPTER XVI.

REMARKS ON ADVERSARIES.

WARBURTON DECLINES THE CHAPLAINCY TO LORD CHESTERFIELD AS LORD LIEUTENANT OF IRELAND — HIS DEDICATION OF THE THIRD EDITION OF THE 'ALLIANCE' TO LORD CHESTERFIELD — WARBURTON MARRIES ALLEN'S NIECE — HIS NOTIONS OF THE INFLUENCE OF THE MAN OVER THE WIFE — WARBURTON RESIDES CHIEFLY AT PRIOR PARK — ELECTED TO THE PREACHERSHIP OF LINCOLN'S INN — NOTICE OF THREE OF HIS SERMONS — PROVOKES THE HOSTILITY OF DRS. SYKES AND STEBBING — CHARACTER AND WRITINGS OF DR. SYKES; OBJECTIONS TO HIS OPINIONS BY THE BISHOP OF OXFORD — SUBJECTS ON WHICH HE DIFFERED FROM WARBURTON — THEIR OPPOSITE NOTIONS REGARDING THE THEOCRACY OF THE JEWS — SPENCER, 'DE LEGIBUS HEBRÆORUM' — WARBURTON'S ASSERTIONS OF AN EQUAL PROVIDENCE AMONG THE JEWS — DR. STEBBING; WARBURTON'S REPLY TO HIM — SECOND PART OF WARBURTON'S 'REMARKS ON SEVERAL OCCASIONAL REFLECTIONS' — RUTHERFORTH; JACKSON — 'ANSWERERS BY PROFESSION' — THE FORTUNE OF WARBURTON'S BOOK COMPARED WITH THAT OF HARVEY'S DISCOVERY OF THE CIRCULATION OF THE BLOOD — THE REV. JULIUS BATE — LETTER FROM THE HON. CHARLES YORKE ON ANSWERING — SARCASM OF EDWARDS IN HIS 'CANONS OF CRITICISM.'

WARBURTON had been introduced by Pope to Lord Chesterfield, who, in 1745, accepting the office of Lord Lieutenant in Ireland, proposed to take Warburton with him as his chaplain. But Warburton had no disposition to transport himself to Ireland, and declined the offer with due acknowledgments. The civility shown him on this occasion was the cause of a new edition of the 'Alliance between Church and State' being dedicated to Lord Chesterfield, three years afterwards. 'Being willing to leave behind me a monument of my love to my country,' says Warburton, addressing his Lordship in his Dedication, 'I have taken the privilege to appeal from the ecclesiastical to a lay tribunal, under the protection of a character which is going down to posterity in the full lustre of those amiable qualities of humanity which nature delights to throw round the names of her distinguished favourites.' He designates his Lordship as a true patriot, and, as he was just then become Secretary of State, says: 'It is an uncommon happiness when an honest man can congratulate a patriot on his becoming Minister.' But, he adds, 'Your Lordship has now a nice part to manage; the people are much more reasonable in their demands on their patriots than on their ministers. Of their patriots they readily accept the will for the deed; but of their ministers they unjustly interpret the deed for the will. Our great English poet, who honoured your virtues, as much as he loved your person, was more candid. He understood the delicate situation of a minister; and in this fine apology, as I have it under his hand, does justice to their good intentions:

> Our ministers like gladiators live;
> 'T is half their business blows to ward or give;
> The good their virtue would effect, or sense,
> Dies betwixt exigents and self-defence.

Of all the strange connexions which the revolutions of Time bring about, the rarest and most accidental is that between *merit* and *reward*. . . .

'Nor are the mistakes of expectants,' he continues, in allusion to himself and other dedicators, 'far short of the difficulties of *men in power*.

'Scholars (to speak the court sense of them) who know but little of practicable [practical] life, are apt to fancy that superior distinction in letters, or superior services in their profession, may entitle them to the honours of it. But things are not so carried. High stations, even of the more spiritual kind, require *a knowledge of affairs.* The pursuit of letters keeps men from the sight of *business*; and learned impressions make them unapt and awkward in the discharge of it. The mind must be unburthened before it will be able to move there, either with ease or grace. Nothing is more unquestioned, nor, consequently, *truer* than these court-maxims. And the most that can be said for so helpless a tribe is, *That letters never made a blockhead.* But I go no farther; for indeed it must be owned that, as they find him, so they always leave him.'

'The style of compliment,' observes Hurd, 'in which Warburton addresses Lord Chesterfield, will perhaps be censured as too high. But the truth is, that specious nobleman had the fortune to be better thought of in his lifetime than he has been since. The general opinion, therefore, which came confirmed to him by Mr. Pope, very naturally inflamed the expression of his gratitude in that panegyrical epistle.'*

But an event of great importance to Warburton's fortunes was now about to happen. Allen had a favourite niece, Miss Gertrude Tucker, who lived with him at Prior Park, and to whom, according to Hurd, he had been for some time desirous to see Warburton united. Warburton, whether ardent for the marriage bonds or not, showed at least a willingness to assume them; he speaks of the lady, in a letter to Bowyer the printer, as 'one of the finest women in England,' to whom 'to offer up his freedom was to be more than free.' His notions of the connexion between man and wife, and its influence on the wife, had been expressed about fifteen years before in a letter to Dr. Stukeley. 'You have an agreeable companion at home, capable of enhancing all the pleasures, and soothing all the cares, of human life. And from the accomplishments of such a companion the man receives peculiar

* Hurd's Life of Warburton, p. 41.

honour, as the younger Pliny says of his friend, *magnâ gloriâ dignus qui uxorem, quam virginem accepit, tam peritam politamque reddiderit.* For you must know, my good doctor, that I regard woman in her natural state as one of those odd pictures that I have formerly seen at Oxford, which they use for a very pretty experiment in optics. They produce you a board, on the plane of which is thrown together a great number of colours, *as it appears*, with the utmost confusion and disorder, the most *visible* work of chance. But by applying to it a cylindrical steel mirror, there immediately rises on its bosom a beautiful reflected form in all the justness and artifice of design. A woman is this coloured table; in whose capricious and variable fancy discordant and monstrous ideas are, by the force of the passions, whimsically daubed on at random, which present no mark of the workmanship of the great plastic nature. But if, happily, a prudent husband be applied, he does the business of the cylinder. The scattered lines are now reduced in order, an elegance of design arises, and the reflected union of colours, and harmony of light and shadow, speak the workmanship divine.' * What effect the Warburtonian cylinder had on Mrs. Warburton's 'variable fancy' we do not know. She is characterised, by Mr. Cradock and others, as an accomplished and agreeable woman, both before her marriage and after it. Dr. Cuming, of Dorchester, in a letter to Dr. Lettsom, describes her, when she had been ten years wedded, thus: 'She was elegant in her person, possessed of an excellent understanding, great politeness, and a most engaging *naïveté* in conversation.'† They were married on September 5, 1745. What was said of her in connexion with Mr. Thomas Potter, son of the Archbishop, will be afterwards noticed.

* Letter to Stukeley, Aug. 18, 1731; Nichols's Lit. Illustr. vol. ii. p. 10.

† Ib. p. 838.

They are generally supposed to have lived comfortably together, though Warburton's hasty temper, during his episcopal life, when he had many causes of annoyance, appears to have sometimes interfered with his domestic quiet; for Mrs. Warburton is said to have felt the comfort, occasionally, of a visitor's arrival, to pour oil on the bishop's vinegar. 'Your gentleness wins,' he said to Hurd, 'where my roughness, I believe, revolts.'*

'From the time of his marriage,' says Hurd, 'Mr. Warburton resided chiefly at Prior Park. In so agreeable, or rather splendid a retreat, he enjoyed health, affluence, and leisure; the best company, when he chose to partake of it; and every other accommodation which could be acceptable to a man of letters. His ambition was also gratified with the highest personal reputation; and, in due time, he succeeded to the chief honours of his profession. All this he could not but be sensible of; yet I have heard him say that the most delicious season of his life was that which he had spent at Newark and Brant-Broughton. So delightful are the springing hopes of youth, and so enchanting the scenes which open to a great genius when he comes first to know himself, and to make trial of his powers.'

Early in 1746 the preachership at Lincoln's Inn became vacant; and Murray, who was then Solicitor-General, induced the Bench to offer the appointment to Warburton. Warburton accepted the honour, which, indeed, without offending Murray, he could hardly refuse, but told his friends privately that the calls of the office would hardly be agreeable to him. Writing to Dr. Robert Taylor, an eminent physician, first at Newark and afterwards in London, and a friend to him from his youth, he says: 'I think I told you in my last that the Society of Lincoln's Inn had made me a unanimous offer

* Letters from an Em. Prelate, p. 383.

of the preachership, which, therefore, I could not refuse, though I would gladly have done it; for it will require five or six months' attendance; and the advantage of the thing you may judge of by this: Mr. Allen would have me take a house, for which I pay as much rent as the whole preachership is worth—this only to you. And don't think I speak with any affectation when I tell you in your ear that nothing can be more disagreeable to me than this way of life. But I hope and determine that it shall not continue long. Don't you pity me? I shall be forced to write sermons; and God knows what will become of the "D. L." But if I can do any good in this new station, I shall know how to bear the disagreements of it, and that's all. How capricious is the fate of mortals! Any other clergyman would think himself happy in such an honour as the Society has done me. I believe it is the first that has been done to their preacher. Yet I have no joy in it.'*

By the *first honour that has been done to their preacher* he means that he was the first to whom the appointment had been unanimously offered. He disliked the office, because it diminished his leisure for objects which he had at heart; and the demand for sermons, with which, as Hurd tells us, he was but slenderly provided, was particularly distasteful to him.

A short time before his appointment to the preachership, he had delivered three sermons on the Rebellion, one of which, especially, drew upon him an attack from Dr. Stebbing, on whom, as well as on Dr. Sykes, another of his assailants, he had already made retaliation for previous hostilities, in an appendix to his 'Remarks on Several Occasional Reflections.' The three sermons were: first, 'A Faithful Portrait of Popery,' in which he

* Hurd's Life of Warburton, p. 43; Nichols's Lit. Anecd., vol. ix. p. 622.

argued that Popery, which the Pretender's army, then in England, was intended to establish, was not, in truth, a form *of religion*, but *of mere antichristian policy*. The second, preached also while the Pretender was in England, was on the happily chosen text, 'I will remove far off from you the northern army, and will drive him into a land barren and desolate.' The third was delivered on the thanksgiving day for the suppression of the rebellion, and professed to state the true nature of national offences, such as luxury and irreligion, and the great blessings of civil liberty. It was the second of these sermons, in which he touched upon his great doctrine of an equal providence among the Jews, that called forth the animadversions of Dr. Stebbing, to whom Warburton afterwards addressed an 'Apologetical Defence' of his discourse, in which he told Stebbing that, as he seemed to mean well, but to be much embarrassed, he would help him out.

I have purposely delayed to notice his controversies with these two doctors, Stebbing and Sykes, till now, in order that all that is to be said about them may be said at once, and no further thought be bestowed upon them. Their writings, though numerous, are nearly forgotten; and neither of them would deserve much attention but for the frequent recurrence of their names in many of Warburton's pages.

Dr. Sykes, as the more prominent of the two, should be noticed first. He was a divine of the liberal school of Clarke and Hoadly; he held for many years the living of Rayleigh in Essex; obtained, by Hoadly's influence, a prebend at Winchester, in 1740; and died in 1756, at the age of seventy-three. He was author of sixty-three publications, chiefly controversial pamphlets, and on transient topics, one of which was a 'Vindication of Dr. Bentley,' into whose quarrel with Boyle he rashly thrust himself, thus provoking the wrath of Conyers Middleton;

a wrath, however, only temporary, for Middleton, after having terribly mauled him in the controversy, was subsequently on good terms with him, and called him, in the 'Vindication of his Free Inquiry,' 'a learned and judicious writer.' His other most noticeable performance was a tract 'On the Innocency of Error,' showing 'how innocent a thing it is to be mistaken in any matter where industry and honesty, diligence and sincerity, have been applied to find out truth.' In this little treatise he used some expressions of so very strong a nature as to raise an outcry among many of the clergy against them. Some were offended because he asserted that Socinianism is preferable to irreligion, 'for it is better,' said he, 'to worship one person of the Godhead than to offer no worship at all.' But there were passages that gave much stronger provocation. 'Is every man,' said he, 'obliged to have a distinct knowledge of every passage of the Scripture, or be subject to condemnation? Let him that thinks so, set about explaining the Apocalypse, or the old prophets, and try whether he can do himself what he declares to be required of others. Let it be granted that it is criminal not to believe what God has thought fit to reveal, supposing we know that God has revealed it; but we may do so without having a clear and distinct knowledge of every particular revealed. Supposing a man should not know who is meant by the white horse in the Revelations, or what is the meaning of being baptised for the dead, yet, whilst he owns that God is the author of these passages, and is ready to believe them as far as he can get an understanding of them, how is he to blame? If it is criminal to err in the meaning of a passage of Scripture, the crime will not rest where we are apt to fix it, but will ascend to a place where we dare not think of guilt, even to God himself, who has delivered his will in terms that are ambiguous.

'If simple and involuntary error be punished by God,

then it would be injustice and cruelty in God to make such creatures as cannot but err. If involuntary error be punishable, it is not a few dissenters in a nation, nor ten thousand times ten thousand, that must perish; but Tartarean flames must envelope almost, if not quite, the whole of the Christian world. How many of our *happy church* are *quite in the right?* Heaven must assuredly be made only for a part of England, and a much less part, too, than is, perhaps, imagined.'

Such language induced the Bishop of Oxford to notice the work in a charge, as one that 'undermined the great truths of Christianity,' and that 'all good men would wish to have buried in perpetual oblivion.' Sykes defended himself in another pamphlet, in which he maintained all that he had stated before, and said he thought, with the Bishop of Bangor, that unbelievers might experience favour with heaven for sincerity, as well as believers, though his remarks had been intended entirely concerning Christians in a Christian country.

His great object, in all his writings, was to advocate the propriety of laying open the Church to persons of the most liberal sentiments; and he argues, in one of his tracts, that a latitude of opinion was intended to be allowed by the framers of the articles of the Church of England to all such as should subscribe to them.

Differing, however, from Warburton in his notions regarding the state of things among the ancient Jews, he attacked 'The Divine Legation' in 'An Examination of Mr. Warburton's Account of the Conduct of the Ancient Legislators, of the Double Doctrine of the Old Philosophers, of the Theocracy of the Jews, and of Sir Isaac Newton's Chronology.' When this book appeared, Warburton sent the author, he says, a civil message, to the effect that 'he supposed he would think himself neglected if no notice were taken of his work; that he was not at leisure to go through the whole, but that, if he would signify on which of the four parts he placed most dependence, he would endeavour to give him the satisfaction about it which he seemed to require.' To this Sykes replied that 'he should not be at all concerned if Warburton were to forbear all notice of him; but that if he took any, he might choose a part for himself; he expected, however, that he would keep to the merits of his book; that the attention paid him would be paid in such a manner as every good man wishes, in the love of truth, and the spirit of one that seeks it; and that he would then find in the author a mind open to conviction.' 'All this,' observed Warburton, 'was very well; and, from the reasonableness of the demand, who would not have supposed that his book was a standard of candour, politeness, and ingenuity? at least, who would have suspected the contrary?' But 'his civil preliminary, when interpreted on the principles of the Double Doctrine, is in plain English this: that the liberties which he and old honest Mr. P. (a clergyman to whom he affects to address his Remarks) have so freely taken with my book and character, should be entirely overlooked, or received as compliments; and that I should address myself to their conviction as to the service of my two best friends, who wrote only to recommend the truths I had advanced, by putting me in a way to remove all doubts and difficulties concerning them. And, therefore, that I should "keep to the merits of his book;" that is, be tender of his bad logic, and worse criticism; overlook his ill expression, and find out his meaning if I can. And, indeed, who would not engage in any labour for the sake of finding so rare a curiosity as "a mind open to conviction" in an answerer by profession?' 'But,' proceeds Warburton, 'if I receive him with good humour, it is a mere act of good will, to which neither the Doctor's manner nor matter has the least claim, as may be seen from the preliminary conversation between him and his old friend Mr. P., who is made to "call Mr. Warburton's book a learned romance," and to say, "with some humour, that the digressions in it about the Mysteries, the Hieroglyphics, and the Book of Job, are, or may be deemed, so many ingenious novels, which serve to relieve or divert the reader." Mr. P. is then made to express a doubt whether Mr. Warburton writes for utility or truth; "for he has told so much," he observes, "about the practices of those old philosophers, and how much they were wont *to lie for the public good* (and he declares himself to have come from the schools of those heathen philosophers), that *I cannot but think he may reasonably be suspected* to have received an infection from them, and *to have learned to lie for the public good, as his masters did before him.* It is true," he continues, "that Mr. Warburton does not think those men to be altogether free from blame; and it may be said in his favour, that what he blames *a little* in them, he would not do himself; but yet his censure of them is so very soft, and he is so tender of their moral character, while he is so ready to flame out against, and to show no mercy to, others who do not think as he does, that one cannot help imagining that, in his opinion, the good end they had in view did sanctify the means they used, and that it was no great fault in them to have external and internal doctrines,"' &c. 'Now,' adds Warburton, 'a man *so apt to flame out*, would have been as apt to call this a piece of scurrilous buffoonery in another writer; but in so candid a disputant as Dr. Sykes, who writes, we see by his own words, "in the love of truth, and in the spirit of one who seeks it," I can consider it only as the effect of *a pious zeal* for the interests of Revelation, which is apt to warm itself in a conversation between two such friends; and *a charitable fear* that the author of "The Divine Legation" was, indeed, artfully undermining the foundation, while he pretended to new fortify the structure, of religion; and they, good men, as faithful sentinels, thought it their duty to give the alarm.'

Warburton then proceeds to consider which portion of the book he may choose, as the choice is left to him, for the object of his remarks. The Doctor 'has handled,' he says, 'all his subjects in so unusual a manner, that all we can collect from the first of them, *On the Conduct of the Ancient Legislators*, is that, in his opinion, Moses was but of the same species with the Pagan law-givers; for he makes Moses, in giving laws for the Jews, consider, like Zaleucus, only what was good for the State, beyond which, he says, neither Moses nor Zaleucus concerned themselves; as to the *Double Doctrine of the Old Philosophers*, he has fairly shown that he knew no more of it than of *the double sense of prophecies*, which he had denied in his "Principles and Connexion of Natural and Revealed Religion;" and, with regard to *Sir Isaac Newton's Chronology*, he mistakes the very question, imagining that I disputed the truth of his Greek, instead of his Egyptian, chronology; so that, indeed, there was nothing left that I could in conscience seize upon but his *Discourse of the Theocracy of the Jews*.

'I have reason, too,' continues Warburton, 'to believe that he may esteem this the *forte* of his new excursions. *An extraordinary providence to particulars*, though expressly promised by, and, as I have shown, a necessary consequence of, the Law of Moses, yet, partly from the nature of the thing, and partly from mistaken passages of misunderstood books of Scripture, is not entirely free from objections. Here, then, he thought he could do something, though it were but retailing the objections of others. And truly, as ill as he has managed these advantages, he was not mistaken in his choice. For the rest, it is all over such argument and such criticism! as one might well conceive should be reserved to close the scene of letters in an age like this, when every science was retiring from its professors to dictionary-makers and booksellers.'

Into the dispute between Warburton and Sykes concerning the Jewish theocracy it is not necessary to enter very far. Sykes's chief charge was that Warburton had unfairly accused Spencer of absurdity in his treatise *De Legibus Hebræorum.* Spencer had said that the theocracy was established by degrees and abrogated by degrees; Warburton observed that this was 'an absurd conceit,' for theocracy, being *a form of government*, must be established at once, and, when it ceased, must cease at once; but that Spencer, as well as Dr. Sykes his defender, had confounded the theocracy with the extraordinary providence that existed under the theocracy, and both would have been right, had they said that the extraordinary providence was abrogated or withdrawn by degrees. Yet Sykes, he says, runs along, *pushing this blunder before him from page to page.* 'Spencer,' he reiterates, 'is much misrepresented; he did not mean by *abrogation* a *ceasing*, but an *alteration* and *abatement.*' Still the same confusion of theocracy with extraordinary providence. '*Abrogation, regimen abrogatum*, does not signify ceasing! Where did he get his Latin? Cicero, Livy, and all the Roman writers, lawyers as well as philosophers, use it only in the sense of dissolution, abolition, and the entire ceasing of an office or command. What then does it signify? Why, it signifies an *alteration* or *abatement.* But now where did he get his English? What! is an alteration of government only an abatement of it? The *alteration* of a *theocracy* we understand; but what is the *abatement* of it? That indeed I cannot tell.' Warburton then repeats some of his arguments for the doctrine of an extraordinary or equal providence among the Jews, in answer to a taunt of Sykes, who reminded him of having admitted, in 'The Divine Legation,' * that the *administration of an equal providence must needs be attended with such circumstances as sometimes*

* Book v. sect. 4.

to occasion men's observations of inequality; 'that is,' said Sykes, 'in plain terms, "an equal providence *must needs* be unequal." Is not this a plain acknowledgment that an equal providence cannot be administered at all?' 'No,' says Warburton; 'you take my words to signify that *men observed an unequal providence*, whereas they mean that *men observed some inequalities in an equal providence*, which, whether Dr. Sykes understands it or not, is a very different thing.'

'In taking a formal leave' of the Doctor, 'it may perhaps be expected,' he adds, 'that I say something why I ever answered *at all*, and why I answered *in this manner*. To the first of these questions, I must needs confess that I have never yet seen anything which, in my own opinion, deserved any notice. But I was willing to submit to better judgments. *The Public*, says a friend, *by what I can perceive, thinks there is something in this pamphlet—thinks there may be something in that.* Well, I subscribe to the public judgment. I examine, I write, I confute. And what do I get by it? The mortification of being told that now, forsooth, *the public wonders why I should spend my time upon such writers.* And in this manner I have been served more than once. The Public says this, the Public says that; in short, the Public is a wag, and loves to divert itself at the expense of us poor authors.'

So much for Dr. Sykes. Dr. Stebbing receives a nearly equal portion of attention. He had opposed Warburton's notion that Abraham obtained a foresight of Christ's death from the injunction laid upon him to offer up Isaac. He had also published 'An Examination of Mr. Warburton's Second Proposition, in an Epistolary Dissertation addressed to the Author,' intended to prove that a future state was believed in among the Jews, although Moses had no commission to teach it. The series of arguments advanced on these points, by each party, we need not take the trouble to pursue; it will be sufficient to notice the nature of the remarks which Warburton throws out upon his adversary.

Dr. Stebbing 'will needs know,' he observes, 'why God acted thus mysteriously with His people' in withholding from them the knowledge of a future state. 'I will tell him,' rejoins Warburton, 'when he informs me (and perhaps before) why America was for so many ages debarred the light of the Gospel. Were not these his offspring as well as the sons of Abraham? But this is the advantage that he and his followers take with the ignorant. They cry out, What! a religion from God without a future state? No; rather than this, anything. They will go a text-hunting, lie at catch for an ambiguity, divorce the sentence from its context, strip it naked; and if, after all this violence, it does but squint their way: See here, say they, as clear a proof of it as from the preaching of Jesus.' *

'That you have given,' says Stebbing to Warburton, 'great proofs of your learning and ingenuity, I shall not dispute; and you have had a fair time allowed you to receive *the compliments of the public* on that score. It may now be seasonable to call you to something which, though perhaps less agreeable to you, may yet be more profitable; and that is, to consider how much truth you have advanced, and what real service you have done, or are likely to do, to religion by this undertaking.' † 'And why,' inquires Warburton, 'will he *not dispute the great proofs of my learning and ingenuity*? He has disputed a more incontestable thing; the *truth* which that *learning and ingenuity* were employed to illustrate; and, if these appeared with any distinction, it was solely owing to the advantage of the *subject*.

'But *I have had a fair* time allowed me to receive the *compliments of the public*. How allowed me, and by whom? Certainly not by such writers as these. For if

* Warburton's Works, vol. ix. p. 307.

† Examination of Mr. W.'s Second Proposition, p. 34.

their clamours could have prevailed, I had received the *public odium* rather than its *compliments.* And the reader may see, that those clamours began the very moment the first volume of "The Divine Legation" appeared, and have continued ever since, without interruption to the publication of our author's "Epistolary Dissertation."

'But, after all, what were these *compliments?* And where have they lain hid? Nothing from *the public* ever came to my knowledge but the *clamours of my adversaries.* In some sense, indeed, these may be called *compliments,* and substantial ones too; for, next to the old way of complimenting, *laudari à laudato viro,* I prize the new, now all in fashion, *vituperari à putidissimo quoque.* . . .

'I know of nothing for which I had more reason to expect *the compliments of the public* than for the "Alliance between Church and State," as it was a defence (and, I will presume, from its being yet unanswered, an effectual one) of the justice and equity of our present happy establishment; at a time when the enemies of all Church establishments were commonly supposed to have demonstrated it to be indefensible. Yet what *public compliment* did I ever receive for this service? unless it may be reckoned a compliment that those, in whose behalf it was particularly written, have never yet publicly disavowed the free and moderate principles on which it goes.' *

Warburton does not yet, however, leave Sykes and Stebbing at peace. He devotes to some additional matter of theirs a second part of his 'Remarks,' and throws out an observation or two, at the commencement of it, on Rutherforth, the author of the 'Essay on Virtue,' who had maintained that 'natural religion has not, which the law of Moses has, the sanctions of future rewards and punishments,' and on the Rev. John Jackson, who had published a treatise to prove that 'a future state was a fundamental

* Warburton's Works, vol. xi. pp. 322—324.

article of belief in the religion of the Hebrews.' But he is not so fond of controversy, he says, as to enter into a dispute with him who would advocate the first of these propositions, or with him who would support the second, whose 'objections, even to the very blunders, he had obviated or answered long ago.' *

The great charge which these *answerers* brought against the author of 'The Divine Legation' was, that 'instead of placing Christianity upon a surer bottom, he had only furnished out more handles to unbelievers.' 'In this manner,' says Warburton, 'has every honest man been treated before me, whenever he did, or did but endeavour, to save mankind. Harvey himself, who had more and much abler *examiners of the absurdity of his conceit* than I have had of mine, scarce got better off with one Æmilius Parisanus, a man of great name in Italy, who wrote a complete *refutation* (as he called it) of the Doctor's arguments for the circulation of the blood; a discovery which appears to have given this Italian no less disturbance than "The Divine Legation" has given our Examiner [Dr. Stebbing]. *Quamobrem nos aliter philosophati et ratiocinati, de Harveii fidentiâ*, says he, *admirati; de clarissimæ Londinensis Academiæ consensu et conspiratione obstupefacti. Verùm enimvero collecto spiritu, missâ tandem maximæ novitatis admiratione, melius nobis consulti, ad vivum Harveii allata resecantes, ut commenticia et ficta excogitata colligentes*, propriâ nostrâ sententiâ *permansimus. Semper in ore atque in animo habere debemus, ut homines nos esse meminerimus, eâ lege natos, ut exposita fortunæ telis omnibus et nostra sit vita, et nostræ actiones cunctæ sub censoribus semper extent. Proindeque* perpetuò pugnandum sit, *et nunc quàm maximè, quum pro aris et focis atque etiam Larariis* (quippe *de Corde, &c.*) *fortiter decertandum.* Seriously, this was a sad story. The poor

* Warburton's Works, vol. xi. pp. 351, 352.

gentleman was plainly frighted. But still he laments like a gentleman. Here are no insinuations that Harvey had suffered himself to be diverted *by matters less suitable to his medical function*, while he was exploring the use of the *venal valves*. Nor does he take the liberty to tell him that he *ought to make amends for the wrong he has done to physic*, though he thought he had done a great deal; or that he had *furnished out more handles for empirics*, though he thought they had already too many; but he politely lays the fault upon the restless temper of human nature itself, which will never suffer us to enjoy our old opinions in quiet. But our Examiner is of another cast; and nothing can save you harmless, when once you have incurred the danger of *offence*, but the *absurdity of your conceits*, though *offence*, that fatal enemy to truth, be, of all *conceits*, the most *absurd*, whenever it is taken before it is given. It is true the good Æmilius comes a little to himself, and nearer to our Examiner, in the language of his conclusion. He had recovered heart; his victories had elated him; and Harvey's numerous experiments upon all animal nature afforded him as happy an occasion of raillery as the *Dissertations* in "The Divine Legation" have given those who took them for *digressions*. *Jam diu*, says he, *per dumeta, vepres, syrtes, et scopulos, duxit nos Harveius; diuque in ejus vivariis et piscinis inter testudines, anguillas, cochleas, ranas, bufones, et serpentes, vagati sumus; omnia tamen evertimus, ejusque perversa vestigia cuncta deteximus; omnia cum pulvisculo everrentes quàm longissime ablegavimus. Quæ* in celebrium antiquorum recentiorumque omnium, ab Harveio immerito notatorum, defensionem *dicta sunto. Huc — redeamus, ut quæ jam reprobata et ablegata sunt, ratione, sensu, aùtopsiâ, experimentis, in veritatis gratiam fortiùs obstringantur—prædictæ opinionis omnia destruendo, et* inter sese pugnantia *ulteriùs ostendendo, &c.* And in the same strain our Examiner.' *

* Warburton's Works, vol. xi. pp. 357, 358.

This comparison of his case with that of Harvey is very happy; though it might have been turned against him by his adversaries as a proof of self-conceit.

'But though,' he adds, 'I had the caduceus of peace in my hands, yet it was only in cases of necessity that I made use of it. And therefore I chose to let pass, without any chastisement, such impotent railers as Dr. Richard Grey, and one Bate, a zany to a mountebank.' Warburton has now altered his tone, we see, with regard to Dr. Grey, whom, in the first part of his 'Remarks,' he called 'a candid and learned writer,' and 'the truly learned and worthy editor of the Book of Job.'* But Grey, in the meantime, had published a pamphlet in reply to Warburton, written 'with a good deal of resentment.' 'The pamphlet,' said Hurd, in a letter to the Rev. John Devey,† 'is thought to be well wrote, and with so much smartness as to be much admired by the enemies of Mr. Warburton.' Julius Bate was a good Hebrew scholar, author of a Hebrew Dictionary *without points*, to which he was a decided enemy; and, disliking Warburton's treatment of the third chapter of Genesis, he had published a pamphlet in reply to it, and another denying that the Jews were ignorant of a future state, or under an equal providence; provocations sufficient to call forth Warburton's hostility. But the accusation made in the Preface to 'The Divine Legation,'‡ that 'one Julius Bate, in conjunction with one Romaine, had betrayed conversation, and written fictitious letters,' had probably, though partially applicable to Romaine, little or no foundation with regard to Bate, who seems to have been a man of good principles. He wrote several other works, though none worthy of being disinterred, yet of such a character that their author is far above deserving to be called 'a zany.' 'On the other hand,' proceeds

* Warburton's Works, vol. xi. p. 347.

† Aug. 23, 1744. Kilvert's Hurd, p. 22.

‡ Edit. 1741.

Warburton, 'when I happened to be engaged with such very learned and candid writers as Dr. Middleton and the Master of the Charterhouse, I gave sufficient proof how much I preferred a different manner of carrying on a controversy, would my *answerers* but afford me the occasion. But alas! as I never *should* have such learned men long my adversaries, and never *would* have these other my friends, I found that, if I wrote at all, I must be condemned to a manner which all, who know me, know to be most abhorrent to my natural temper.' The ardour of Warburton's temper is too apparent through all his writings to leave it credible that the mode in which he answered his adversaries was abhorrent to it. 'So, on the whole,' he concludes, 'I resolved to quit my hands of them at once, and turn again to nobler game, *more suitable*, as Dr. Stebbing tells me, *to my clerical function*, that pestilent herd of libertine scribblers, with which the island is overrun: whom I would hunt down, as good King Edgar did his wolves, from the mighty author of "Christianity as Old as the Creation," to the drunken blaspheming *cobbler* who wrote *against Jesus and the Resurrection*.'

The pamphlet against 'Jesus and the Resurrection,' published about the time when Warburton was writing, was professedly the production of a cobbler, but was generally attributed to Morgan, the author of the 'Moral Philosopher.'

Hurd, writing to Devey, at the time when these replies of Warburton appeared, says: 'The attention of the learned world at present turns entirely almost on the author of "The Divine Legation of Moses," who is mowing down his adversaries with as great zeal and success as ever old Bentley did before him. Indeed, the superior genius and abilities of that writer give him a very great advantage over all the gentlemen that have appeared against him, whatever may be determined finally of his cause. A piece he has just now published in answer to

Drs. Stebbing and Sykes is very ingenious, but wrote with a severe satiric spirit peculiar to himself and his friend Mr. Pope.' *

When he was sitting one day with Allen at Prior Park, Allen said to him, in reference to 'The Divine Legation:' 'Doctor, your adversaries appear to me to advance only weak and futile arguments against you.' 'Sir,' replied Warburton, 'you have spoken more to the purpose in those few words than all the rascals, in all their volumes, have written.' †

The Honourable Charles Yorke, writing about the same time ‡ to Warburton, reminds him of a kind of promise that he had made him not to write more against his opponents, and adds some remarks on answering, in general, as well as on Warburton's in particular, so excellent as fully to deserve quotation: 'It is to be expected, where any writer has the marks of an original, and thinks for himself, producing *de suo penu* things wholly new to most understandings, that some will have their difficulties to propose; others their tenets to maintain; and few will give a ready assent to truths which contradict prevailing notions, till time and posterity have wrought a gradual change in the general state of learning and opinions. What wonder, then, that many should write against you? How natural that you should defend! It was expected from you. The zeal for knowledge is commendable; the deference to mankind becomes you. But here lies the mischief. You and your adversaries stand upon unequal ground. They engage with that best friend and second on their side, vulgar prejudice. Let their insinuations be ever so malignant, provided they write *dully*, they gain the character of writing *coolly*. How natural that you should expostulate! If your expostulations have been

* Kilvert's 'Life of Hurd,' p. 23.

† Warner's 'New Guide through Bath.'

‡ Sept. 30, 1746.

sometimes too warm, they were not the bitter overflowings of an ill-natured mind, but the unguarded sallies of a generous one. Yet even such sallies are scarce forgiven you; not because those you answer have deserved better, but because sensible and candid men are disposed to think too well and too highly of you to forgive that in you which they would overlook in others. And, therefore, could modesty permit you to reverence yourself as much as I do, you would wait with patience that period when *answers* will be forgotten, unless, according to the epigram in Martial, you choose to give flies a value and an immortality, by entombing them in amber. It is to flatter me exceedingly to intimate that I have contributed to lead you into these sentiments, in which the very tædium of controversy and the pursuit of nobler designs must necessarily confirm you.' *

Let us not omit to notice that in the titlepages of both parts of these 'Remarks,' Warburton had placed a very coarse quotation from the Epodes of Horace, on which his enemy Edwards, when he afterwards published the 'Canons of Criticism,' did not fail to animadvert. 'As there is luck in odd numbers,' says he, 'I would recommend this quotation to his use a third time before his next edition of the "Dunciad;" and here subjoin a translation of it, that he may have the reputation, and the world may see the whole force of that fine compliment he has paid to Dr. Middleton, Dr. Pococke, Dr. Richard Grey, Dr. Akenside, Dr. Sykes, Dr. Stebbing, and other gentlemen, in the application of these lines to them:

> Quid inmerentes hospites vexas, CANIS,
> Ignavus adversum lupos?
>
> . . . .
>
> Nam, qualis aut Molossus, aut fulvus Lacon,
> AMICA VIS PASTORIBUS,

---

* Letters from an Eminent Prelate, p. 503.

Agam per altas aure sublatâ nives,
Quæcunque præcedet fera.
Tu, quum timendâ voce complêsti nemus,
Projectum odoraris CIBUM.

Hor. Epod. 6.

Here are the characters of two *puppies*; one Mr. Warburton gives to the gentlemen mentioned above; the other he applies to himself; but to divide and choose is not quite fair. Let the reader judge which fits each. I proceed to the translation:

To kennel, *Looby*, yelping cur,
Teasing the harmless passenger,
While your great Master's sheep,
Those two fair flocks, unguarded stray,
To foxes and to wolves a prey,
Those flocks you 're fed to keep.

See faithful *Trueman*, honest hound,
Far from the sheep-cotes all around
Chase every rav'nous beast;
You, when the hills and vales have rung
With echo of your tattling tongue,
Turn tail, and scent the feast.

'Note, *the two flocks in this allegory* seem to mean *preferments*; perhaps a chapel in town and a living in the country; and the feast, profit in general.' *

* Edwards's Canons of Criticism, Appendix, p. 257.

CHAPTER XVII.

SHAKSPEARE. HANMER.

WARBURTON'S ATTENTION TO SHAKSPEARE — WHEN HE BEGAN TO THINK OF EDITING SHAKSPEARE — HIS ACQUAINTANCE WITH SIR THOMAS HANMER — SPECIMENS OF WARBURTON'S INTENDED EDITION INSERTED IN BIRCH'S 'GENERAL DICTIONARY' AND 'THE WORKS OF THE LEARNED' — WARBURTON'S CRITICISM ON THEOBALD AND HANMER IN HIS PREFACE — CONSIDERATIONS ON WARBURTON'S CONNEXION WITH THEOBALD — THEOBALD'S MERITS — HISTORY OF THE AFFAIR BETWEEN WARBURTON AND HANMER — PHILIP NICHOLS — LETTER FROM HANMER TO DR. JOSEPH SMITH, INSERTED IN THE 'BIOGRAPHIA BRITANNICA,' AND AFTERWARDS SUPPRESSED — WARBURTON ACCUSES HANMER OF FALSEHOOD — HANMER'S LETTER SUPPRESSED AT WARBURTON'S SOLICITATION — CHARACTER OF PHILIP NICHOLS — LETTERS FROM SHERLOCK AND HARE.

IT has been observed that one of Warburton's assailants, Dr. Stebbing, had reproached him with 'suffering himself to be diverted from his purpose,' the completion of 'The Divine Legation,' 'by matters of another kind, less suitable to his clerical function.' 'But will the good man,' asks Warburton, in reply, 'be so kind to tell us what this diversion is? As things are now carried, and left in the dark, who knows but the reader, in excess of charity, may take it to be a—horse-race, or a good job of simony, a party pamphlet, or levee-hunting, or Exchange Alley, or, in short, twenty things besides, each of them sufficient to discredit the mere unorthodox man? With this good luck, I have no doubt that he would wipe his mouth, and applaud his innocent address. Well, then, since the meanness and malignity of his heart will not suffer him to tell,

I will. The *diversion* he hints at, and yet dare not name, is a critical defence and illustration of the writings of one of the greatest geniuses of this, or indeed of any age, to convince the prejudiced and ignorant that the incomparable writer hath been always on the side of truth, virtue, and religion. And now the secret is out.' *

Warburton had begun to think of editing Shakspeare as early as 1737. In a letter to Dr. Birch, written in October of that year, he says: 'You are pleased to inquire about Shakspeare. I believe (to tell it as a secret) I shall, after I have got the whole of this work out of my hands which I am now engaged in,' meaning 'The Divine Legation,' '*give an edition of it to the world.*† Sir Thomas Hanmer,' he adds, 'has *a true critical genius, and has done great things in this author*; so you may expect to see a very extraordinary edition of its kind. I intend to draw up and prefix to it a just and complete critique on Shakspeare and his Works.' At the time when he communicated notes to Theobald, in 1729 and 1730, he does not seem to have contemplated an edition of his own.

Nor does he appear to have resolved on becoming an editor even so late as the May before he wrote to Birch, 1737, when, as we have related, he paid a visit to Sir Thomas Hanmer, at his seat at Mildenhall, near Newmarket. The acquaintance between him and Hanmer was brought about by Bishop Sherlock.‡ The visit had reference to Sir Thomas's contemplated edition of Shakspeare; and Warburton put his notes on Shakspeare into Sir Thomas's hands. Warburton stayed a week with the Baronet, but they seem to have parted in anger.§

In six months afterwards, Warburton, with altered feelings, had determined, as we see, on giving an edition

* Warburton's Works, vol. xi. pp. 320, 356.

† Nichols's Lit. Illustr. vol. ii. p. 72.

‡ Kilvert, Selections from Warburton's Papers, pp. 84, 85.

§ See *antè*, p. 67.

of his own, which should, if possible, throw Sir Thomas's into the shade. He accordingly sent to Birch, for insertion in the Life of Shakspeare in his 'General Dictionary,' a specimen of his intended annotations, which appeared in that work in the following year, introduced thus: After observing that Shakspeare's plays had recently been edited by Rowe, Pope, and Theobald, the article proceeds to say, 'But we may expect a much more correct edition of them from the Reverend and Learned Mr. William Warburton, author of "The Divine Legation of Moses Demonstrated," who, in his edition, besides a general character of Shakspeare and his writings prefixed, will give the rules which he observed in correcting his author, and a large Glossary. We shall give the reader a specimen of this intended edition in several curious remarks, which this excellent critic has communicated to us.' Then follows the specimen, occupying several pages. In 1740, also, another notice of the intended edition was inserted in the 'History of the Works of the Learned,' with these observations: 'After all that the incomparable Mr. Pope, the ingenious Mr. Rowe, and the plodding Mr. Theobald, have done to cleanse and restore Shakspeare to his native lustre, there still remain in him many faults to be amended, and a thousand graces which have never yet been displayed. In truth, both of these were so multifarious, that it required the joint endeavours of many (and those of the ablest) hands, to rectify the one, and to explicate the other; therefore we are not to wonder if men of consummate ability still think their talents very worthily employed in so laudable a task. Accordingly, the Rev. Mr. Warburton has bestowed thereon some of those leisure hours which he could spare from the duties of his sacred function. He is determined to add his labours to those of that illustrious critic and the others above-named, in removing the blemishes and exemplifying the beauties of this inestimable author, which did not fall under their consideration; so that we are like to be shortly furnished with a more complete and accurate edition of his writings than has hitherto been published.' The specimen, as given in the 'General Dictionary,' is then appended.

In January, 1743, Warburton writes to Birch from Newark, 'For my amusement, from time to time, I go on in preparing Shakspeare for the press. I am in hopes that, in a little time, Sir Thomas Hanmer's plates will be of so little use to any other purpose, that I may get them for my edition, as Mr. Pope did those of Ogilby's Homer for his. I hear the University [of Oxford] intend to open a subscription [for Sir Thomas's edition]; but sure they will not do that which has been adjudged below *my* character to do.'*

When Warburton's edition appeared, in 1747, the preface contained the following passage concerning Hanmer and Theobald. Having extolled Pope's edition, as 'the best foundation for all further improvements,' Warburton says: 'Nothing will give the common reader a better idea of the value of Mr. Pope's edition, than the two attempts which have been since made by Mr. Theobald and Sir Thomas Hanmer in opposition to it; who, although they concerned themselves only in—restoring the text, yet succeeded so very ill in it, that they left their author in ten times a worse condition than they found him. But, as it was my ill fortune to have some accidental connexion with these two gentlemen, it will be incumbent on me to be a little more particular concerning them.

'The one was recommended to me as a poor man; the other as a poor critic; and to each of them, at different times, I communicated a great number of observations, which they managed, as they saw fit, to the relief of their several distresses. As to Mr. Theobald, who wanted money, I allowed him to print what I gave him for his

* Nichols's Lit. Illustr. vol. ii. p. 129.

own advantage; and he allowed himself the liberty of taking one part for his own, and sequestering another for the benefit, as I supposed, of some future edition. But as to the Oxford editor, who wanted nothing but what he might very well be without, the reputation of a critic, I could not so easily forgive him for trafficking with my papers without my knowledge; and, when that project failed, for employing a number of my conjectures in his edition against my express desire not to have that honour done unto me.'

Warburton also adds that Hanmer, though 'absolutely ignorant of the art of criticism,' was yet 'not absolutely destitute of all *art*. For,' he says, 'having a number of my conjectures before him, he took as many of them as he saw fit, to work upon; and, by changing them to something he thought synonymous, or similar, he made them his own, and so became a critic at a cheap expense.'

These passages contain much, we fear, that is disingenuous, not to say false. Let us first consider what is said of Theobald. Warburton, from what we have seen of the commencement of his intercourse with Theobald, appears rather to have been recommended to him than he to Warburton. Warburton seems to have been quite as eager to offer him notes on Shakspeare as he was to receive them. But he was now to be depreciated; not only because Pope, Warburton's patron, had set him at nought, but in order that Warburton's own edition, or rather Warburton and Pope's joint edition, might be elevated at the expense of his. To the charges, accordingly, of 'being a poor man,' and of having 'sequestered part of what he was allowed to print,' Warburton adds the allegation that he was a weak and pernicious critic: 'Mr. Theobald was naturally turned to industry and labour—what he read he could transcribe; but, as what he thought, if he ever did think, he could but ill express, so he read on; and by that means got a character of learning, without risking, to every observer, the imputation of wanting a better talent. By a punctilious collation of the old books, he corrected what was manifestly wrong in the latter editions by what was manifestly right in the earlier. And this is his real merit, and the whole of it. For, when the phrase was very obsolete or licentious in the common books, or only slightly corrupted in the other, he wanted sufficient knowledge of the progress and various stages of the English tongue, as well as acquaintance with the peculiarities of Shakspeare's language, to understand what was right; nor had he either common judgment to see, or critical sagacity to amend, what was manifestly faulty. Hence he generally exerts his conjectural talent in the wrong place; he tampers with what is found in the common books; and, in the old ones, omits all notice of variations, the sense of which he did not understand.'

What appears to have been the real merit of Theobald has been already specified. But we may here add what is said in his praise by Thomas Warton, who, in his 'Remarks on Spencer's Fairy Queen,' observes, 'Experience has fatally proved that the commentator on Spencer, Jonson, and the rest of our elder poets, will in vain give specimens of his classical erudition, unless, at the same time, he brings to his work a mind intimately acquainted with those books which, though now forgotten, were yet in common use and high repute about the time in which his authors respectively wrote, and which they, consequently, must have read. While these are unknown, many allusions and many imitations will either remain obscure, or lose half their beauty and propriety, "as the figures vanish when the canvass is decayed."

'Pope laughs at Theobald for giving us, in his edition of Shakspeare, a sample of

— all such reading as was never read;

but these strange and ridiculous books which Theobald quoted, were unluckily the very books which Shakspeare himself had studied ; the knowledge of which enabled that useful editor to explain so many different allusions and obsolete customs in his poet, which otherwise could never have been understood. For want of this sort of literature, Pope tells us that *the dreadful sagittary* in "Troilus and Cressida" signifies Teucer, so celebrated for his skill in archery. Had he deigned to consult an old history, called the "Destruction of Troy," a book which was the delight of Shakspeare and of his age, he would have found that this formidable archer was no other than an imaginary beast which the Grecian army brought against Troy. If Shakspeare is worth reading, he is worth explaining, and the researches used for so valuable and elegant a purpose merit the thanks of genius and candour, not the satire of prejudice and ignorance. That labour, which so essentially contributes to the service of pure taste, deserves a more honourable repository than the Temple of Dulness.'

The kind of reading for which Warburton, following Pope, affected to contemn Theobald, was exactly the kind which an editor of Shakspeare required, and which Steevens and Malone pursued farther, and with greater success. Alexander Chalmers calls Zachary Grey the founder of that species of criticism which has been employed to illustrate Shakspeare, by collecting information from books contemporary with the author ; but the honour of this title seems rather to be due to Theobald. And assuredly for 'want of knowledge of the English tongue, or of common judgment or critical sagacity,' or for 'conjecturing in wrong places,' such a critic as Warburton had no right to heap condemnation on Theobald's head. As to his amendments, even Johnson, in 1745, relying on his own judgment, previously to Warburton's disparaging criticism, pronounced 'some of them so excellent that, even where he has failed, he ought to be treated with indulgence and respect.'*

But Warburton's transactions with Hanmer require further examination. As to Hanmer's merits as a critic, indeed, though Johnson praises him, in his preface to Shakspeare, as 'eminently qualified by nature for critical studies,' and as 'often learned without show,' his edition, though it manifests less ignorance in the editor than Warburton alleges, may very well be set at the value at which Warburton rates it, and at which it is estimated by Malone, who thinks it necessary to say nothing more of the Oxford editor than that 'he adopted almost all the innovations of Pope, adding to them whatever caprice dictated.' But as for *trafficking with Warburton's papers without Warburton's knowledge*, Sir Thomas, who had borne a high character as Speaker of the House of Commons, and throughout all his public and private life, must surely be thought too honourable for such clandestine proceeding; and we may find some light thrown on the affair between him and Warburton by a letter of Sir Thomas's, which was sent for publication to the 'Biographia Britannica,' but which, after being actually printed in the work, was, to gratify Warburton, excluded from it.

There was one Philip Nichols, who was for a time a writer in the 'Biographia,' and afterwards bought a small share in the publication, and who, though not, as we shall find, a man much to be trusted, gave a narrative of the matter which has never been contradicted. His account is that, when the 'Biographia Britannica' was drawing towards the close, about New Year's Day, 1761, the copies of three original letters from Sir Thomas Hanmer to Dr. Joseph Smith, Provost of Queen's College, Oxford, were sent to him to be inserted in the article 'Joseph Smith.' Nichols hastened with them to the press, but found the

* Observations on Macbeth, note iii.

article completed, and had some difficulty in persuading the printer to insert them at the end of it. But, in a post or two after, the gentleman who sent them wrote to Nichols, saying that, having shown the third of these letters, relating to Sir Thomas Hanmer's quarrel with Warburton (now Bishop of Gloucester), to some friends, they had advised him to withdraw it, as Warburton would be greatly offended at its insertion, and he himself would prefer his quiet to a broil with Warburton. Nichols replied that it was too late, as the article was now entirely printed off. The letter was, therefore, left standing; but, on reflection, Nichols thought it better to send Warburton a copy of it, and accordingly did so, with a note assuring him that it should not have passed through his hands to the press, 'had he seen anything in it derogatory to his real merit, which he revered;' adding, that he would call next day for an answer. Sir Thomas Hanmer's letter was as follows:

'To the Rev. Dr. Smith, President of All Souls' * College.

'Mildenhall, near Newmarket, Suffolk: Oct. 28, 1742.

'DEAR SIR,—I have much doubted with myself whether it were proper for me to return an answer to the favour of your letter, till after hearing again from you or Dr. Shippen. There seem to arise some difficulties with respect to the design of printing a new edition of "Shakspeare," and I beg it may be laid aside, if you are not fully satisfied that some advantage may arise from it to the University; for I have no end in view to myself to make me desire it. I am satisfied there is no edition coming, or likely to come, from Warburton; but it is a report raised to serve some little purpose or other, of which I see there are many on foot. I have reason to know that gentleman is very angry with me, for a cause of which, I think, I have no

* A mistake for 'Queen's.'

reason to be ashamed, or he to be proud. My acquaintance with him began upon an application from himself; and at his request the present Bishop of Salisbury introduced him to me for this purpose only, as was then declared, that, as he had many observations upon Shakspeare then lying by him, over and above those printed in Theobald's book, he much desired to communicate them to me, that I might judge whether any of them were worthy to be added to those emendations which he understood I had long been making upon that author. I received his offer with all the civility I could; upon which a long correspondence began by letters, in which he explained his sense upon many passages, which sometimes I thought just, but mostly wild and out of the way. Afterwards he made a journey hither on purpose to see my books. He stayed about a week with me, and had the inspection of them; and all this while I had no suspicion of any other design, in all the pains he took, but to perfect a correct taste in 'Shakspeare,' of which he seemed very fond. But, not long after, the views of interest began to show themselves; several hints were dropped of the advantage he might receive from publishing the work thus corrected; but, as I had no thoughts at all of making it public, so I was more averse to yield to it in such a manner as was likely to produce a paltry edition, by making it the means only of making a greater sum of money by it. Upon this he flew into a great rage, and there is an end of the story: with which I have thought it best to make you acquainted, that, as you mention the working of his friends, you may judge the better of what you see and hear from them, and may make what use you please of the truth of facts which I have now laid before you.

'As to my own particular, I have no aim to pursue in this affair. I propose neither honour, reward, or thanks; and should be very well pleased to have the books continue upon their shelf in my own private closet. If it is thought they may be of use or pleasure to the public, I am willing to part with them out of my hands, and to add, for the honour of Shakspeare, some decorations and embellishments at my own expense. It will be an unexpected pleasure to me, if they can be made, in any degree, profitable to the University, to which I shall always retain a gratitude, a regard, and reverence; but, that I may end as I began, I beg the favour of you, if, upon more mature consideration among yourselves, you see reason to discourage you from proceeding in this affair, that you will give it over, and not look upon yourselves to be the more obliged to prosecute it from any steps already taken with, Sir,

'Your most humble and obedient servant,

'THO. HANMER.'

When Philip Nichols called, the next day, according to notice, for a reply, he was civilly received by Warburton, who expressed himself very indignant at the 'impertinence' of Nichols's friend, in sending the letter to the press, but acknowledged his obligation for the sight of it before it was made public. Nichols offered to insert any reply to it in a subsequent part of the same volume of the 'Biographia Britannica;' and Warburton accordingly wrote a reply, which was 'put into the hands of one of his booksellers,' Mr. David Browne, one of the proprietors of the 'Biographia,' and a member of the committee for conducting it. A meeting of the committee was called, at Browne's request, at which Nichols was summoned to attend, and was blamed by the members present for his 'needless compliment in discovering the letter to the Bishop;' but when they came to deliberate on the Bishop's answer, which Browne submitted to them, they all concurred in expressing dislike of it. The answer was this, as copied from the 'St. James's Chronicle,' to which Warburton afterwards sent it:

'Sir Thomas Hanmer's letter from Mildenhall to Oxford, Oct. 28, 1742, is one continued falsehood from beginning to end. It is false that my acquaintance with him began upon an application from me to him. It began on an application from the present Bishop of London to me, in behalf of Sir Thomas Hanmer, and, as I understood, at Sir Thomas Hanmer's desire. The thing speaks for itself. It was publicly known that I had written notes on Shakspeare, because part of them were printed. Few people knew that Sir Thomas Hanmer had; I certainly did not know: nor, indeed, whether he was living or dead.

'The falsehood is still viler (because it skulks under an insinuation) that I made a journey to him to Mildenhall, without invitation, whereas it was at his earnest and repeated request, as appears by his letters, which I have still by me.

'It is false that the views of interest began to show themselves in me to this *disinterested gentleman.* My resentment at Sir Thomas Hanmer's behaviour began on the following occasion: A bookseller in London, of the best reputation, had wrote me word that Sir Thomas Hanmer had been with him, to propose his printing an edition of Shakspeare on the following conditions—of its being pompously printed with cuts (as it afterwards was at Oxford), at the expense of the said bookseller, who, besides, should pay one hundred guineas, or some such sum, to a friend of his (Sir Thomas Hanmer's), who had transcribed the Glossary for him. But the bookseller, understanding that he made use of my notes, and that I knew nothing of the project, thought fit to send me this account; on which I wrote to Sir Thomas Hanmer, upbraiding him for his behaviour, and demanding out of his hands all the letters I had written to him on the subject, which he unwillingly complied with, after cavilling about the right of property in those letters, for which he had, he said, paid the postage.

'When the bookseller would not deal with him on these terms, he applied to the University of Oxford, and was at the expense of his purse in procuring cuts for his edition; and at the expense of his reputation in employing a number of my emendations on the text, without my knowledge or consent; and this behaviour was what occasioned Mr. Pope's perpetuating the memory of the Oxford edition of Shakspeare in the "Dunciad."

'This is a true and exact account of the whole affair, which I never thought worth while afterwards to complain of, but to the Bishop of London, at whose desire I lent Sir Thomas Hanmer my assistance; nor should ever have revived it, but for the publication of this scandalous letter, *sent from Oxford to this Philip Nichols*, to be inserted in the "Biographia Britannica."

'W. GLOUCESTER.'

Nichols observed to the committee, he says, that 'the futility of the matter' in Warburton's reply, and 'the intemperance of the style,' were 'plain indications that Warburton was not able to give any good or sufficient answer.' It would, indeed, have been better for Warburton if he had substantiated his case by quotations from Hanmer's letters *which he had by him*, or by some other testimony in addition to his own word. The resolution to which the committee came was to take no notice of Warburton's reply in the 'Biographia Britannica;' and Browne carried off the reply in his pocket.

Some of the members, however, expressed dissent from Nichols, as to the notion that Sir Thomas Hanmer's letter contained 'nothing derogatory to the Bishop's real merit;' and Nichols began to suspect, soon after, that some application had been privately made to the committee to have the letter expunged. In this suspicion he was confirmed when Warburton's edition of Shakspeare came out, in the preface to which Warburton's *first occasion of his quarrel with Hanmer is kept completely out of sight.* Nevertheless, as no steps were taken for the ejection of the letter, he inserted, in the article 'Spelman,' which was then being printed off, some allusion to Warburton and Hanmer, in the supposition that Hanmer's letter would keep its place; but, after some months, he heard that it was seriously proposed to suppress it, *at Warburton's instance.* Repairing to Browne, to inquire about the matter, he was told by Browne that he could not say the suppression was contemplated *at Warburton's instance,* but admitted that, when the notion of suppression was communicated to him, he 'expressed a particular satisfaction.' Nichols had then no doubt that Warburton was making interest with the committee, who, however, were slow to determine on expunging; and one party proposed, while they retained the letter, to reprint the whole sheet so closely as to make room for Warburton's answer; but Browne, on hearing this, declared, in some confusion, that he had lost the answer. Nichols, however, observed that he had kept a memorandum of the chief points of it, which memorandum, at the direction of the committee, he enclosed to Warburton for his inspection; but Warburton took no notice of the receipt of it. At another conference with Browne about the matter, Browne showed him, what he had not seen before, the following passage in an advertisement prefixed by the booksellers to the London reprint of Sir Thomas Hanmer's Shakspeare in 1745, to which some notes were attached: 'As to the —— emendations and notes of Mr. Warburton —— we are only commissioned to say thus much, that he desires the public would suspend their opinion of his conjectures till they see how they can be supported. For he holds it as ridiculous to alter the text of an author without reason assigned, *as it was dishonourable to publish those alterations without leave obtained.*' And at the next meeting of the committee, a resolution was passed to cancel the letter, a majority of the members having been persuaded or overawed to concur in reprinting the sheet for that purpose.

Thus Hanmer's letter would have been wholly unknown to the public, but for its insertion in the pamphlet which Nichols afterwards published, in a fit of resentment at Warburton about the matter. The pamphlet is entitled 'The Castrated Letter of Sir Thomas Hanmer, in the Sixth Volume of the "Biographia Britannica," wherein is discovered the first Rise of the present Bishop of Gloucester's Quarrel with that Baronet, about his edition of Shakspeare's Plays. To which is prefixed an Account of the Extraordinary Means used to suppress this remarkable Letter. By a Proprietor of that Work. London, 1763. Price 1s.' It has no name of its author on the title-page, but the name of Philip Nichols is given at length within. If we inquire what this Philip Nichols had been, or what he had done, before he became a writer in the 'Biographia Britannica,' we may gain some information from a manuscript note in the copy of the pamphlet in the British Museum, which is called 'The Second Edition, corrected and augmented,' and in which is written 'William Cole, 1763,' showing that it belonged to the well-known Reverend William Cole, the friend of Horace Walpole.* The note is in the same hand as the name and date: 'Philip Nichols, LL.D., and Fellow of Trinity Hall in Cambridge, where he was brought by Sir Nathaniel Lloyd, the master, by a lapse from Oxford. He was in priest's orders, and expelled the University for stealing books out of his own and other libraries in the University.' Such had been Philip Nichols's character; but, as has been said, no charge was ever brought, either by Warburton or any one else, against the truth of his narrative respecting Hanmer's Shakspeare.

* Nichols's Lit. Illustr. vol. viii. p. 578.

When the sixth volume of the 'Biographia Britannica' came out, Nichols went to Warburton, to ask his permission to replace the letter. Warburton received him roughly: 'Whoever,' said he, 'shall print that letter, if I can take any advantage against him, I will.' 'Your lordship,' retorted Nichols, 'is in a passion,' and came away. On January 11, 1763, he wrote a letter to Warburton, an incoherent kind of thing, of which it is difficult to tell the object, except it were a feint of begging Warburton's pardon. 'I became,' he says in it, 'a proprietor in the "Biographia Britannica," with a design to make the best restitution I could for the great injuries done to the University of Cambridge, and some colleges there, besides other private persons. The story is too black in itself, and too grievous for me to relate. My lord of Bristol, to whom I am not unknown, and who was then a Fellow of one of the injured societies, can inform you of the particulars; and I am not anxious to have anything concealed. The shame attending it may be a means of bettering my repentance, which is the greatest work I have to do.' He signs himself 'Your Lordship's most obedient humble servant, Philip Nichols, a poor penitent thief.' To this letter Warburton made no reply.

About the same time, the gentleman who had communicated Sir Thomas Hanmer's letter complained, in the shop of one of the proprietors, in Nichols's hearing, 'of the affront put upon his kindness, and the injury done by the castration, to the memory of Dr. Joseph Smith, in suppressing a testimony of confidence shown to him by a gentleman of such distinguished worth and honour as Sir Thomas Hanmer.' Nichols observed to the gentleman that he had protested against the suppression, and had not laid aside all thoughts of publishing the letter. The gentleman expressed himself well pleased, and, 'assuring Nichols of such assistance as he could give,' made him promise that it should be published. Warburton's answer to Sir Thomas Hanmer, which is given in the second edition of Nichols's pamphlet, seems to have been sent to the 'St. James's Chronicle' after the appearance of the first edition of the pamphlet, of which I know not whether a copy is extant.

In this pamphlet it is stated that, at one of the meetings of the committee, a report was mentioned that Hanmer, before consigning his Shakspeare to the University of Oxford, had offered to sell it for 100*l.* to Tonson, who had declined the purchase. Nichols spoke on the subject to Tonson, who said that the fact was 'imperfectly related,' as Sir Thomas had asked the money, not for his own use, but for that of 'a necessitous friend,' and that he had refused only because Sir Thomas insisted on 'a pompous expensive edition, in quarto.'

This offer to Tonson had been made as early as 1739, in which year Warburton sent a letter to Hanmer, but took the precaution to submit it previously to the inspection of Bishop Sherlock. From Sherlock's answer to Warburton we find that rumour had magnified the one hundred pounds into two hundred:

'May 10, 1739.

'REVEREND SIR,—I am very sorry, and surprised too, at the account you give me relating to a new edition of "Shakspeare;" and the more sorry as I have in some measure been the occasion of it.

'I have no objection to your sending the letter to Sir Thomas. You do not mention to him that he was to have for a friend £200; and perhaps you may as well keep that to yourself, unless it shall be necessary in the course of the correspondence to own your knowledge of it. I can't tell what friend has deserved better in this respect than yourself, and therefore can say nothing to it; but I should have expected that your interest should have been remembered in a treaty of this kind. . . . .

'I inclose the copy of the letter you intend for Sir Thomas, which may save you the trouble of transcribing another.

'I am, Sir,
'Your very humble servant,
'THO. SARUM.' *

Warburton also consulted his great episcopal friend, Dr. Hare, on the subject. Hare replies:

'Sir Thomas Hanmer's proceeding with respect to Shakspeare is very extraordinary. I doubt the friend for whom he wanted the £200 was his own dear self. I think you do very well to get your own papers out of his hands. It is a pity they have been so long in them, since it is probable he has squeezed what he could out of them, which is most ungenerous treatment. I hope you will find leisure to give the world a "Shakspeare" yourself, which the sooner it is made known the better. That will mortify Sir Thomas, and perhaps drive him at last into some agreement with you; since, otherwise, if you come after him, his edition will either not come out, or not sell, which he could very ill bear, especially as he has so good an opinion of his work.' †

Such were the observations of Sherlock and Hare, but we must understand that they took their notions of the matter, in all probability, wholly on Warburton's representation. The general opinion has always been in favour of Hanmer. 'The honour and veracity of Hanmer,' says Disraeli, 'must prevail over the "liveliness" of Warburton, for Hurd lauds his "*lively* preface" to his "Shakspeare."' Sir Henry Bunbury, Hanmer's biographer, expresses his conviction that Warburton's posthumous charges, published fifteen years after Hanmer's death, were 'false and calumnious.' 'Sir Thomas Hanmer,' says Whitaker,‡ one of those most willing to advocate War-

* Kilvert's Selections from Warburton's Papers, p. 84.

† Kilvert, ib. p. 121.

‡ Quart. Rev. vol. vii. p. 391.

burton, 'was a man of probity and honour, had long been Speaker of the House of Commons, and died with unimpeached integrity in a dignified retirement,' and is not to be 'traduced to posterity as a wretched pilferer from Warburton's critical portfolio,' though such might have been his fortune, had not his letter to Dr. Smith been brought to light.

> Strict on the right he kept his steadfast eye,
> With temperate zeal and wise anxiety;
> Nor e'er from Virtue's path was lured aside,
> To plück the flowers of pleasure or of pride.

Hanmer, like Theobald, was unable to answer when Warburton accused the one of having 'sequestered notes,' and the other of having 'trafficked with his papers without his knowledge;' and he had taken care to get out of Hanmer's hands all the letters that he had addressed to him on the subject, so that there might be no written testimony producible against him. 'Dead men,' as the Greek proverb says, 'do not bite,' and Warburton might calumniate Hanmer with equal exultation and security.

CHAPTER XVIII.

SHAKSPEARE.

MERITS OF WARBURTON'S NOTES ON SHAKSPEARE — HE AFFECTS TO THINK LIGHTLY OF THEM — HIS MOTIVES FOR PUBLISHING THEM — HURD'S PRAISE — JOHNSON'S ESTIMATE OF WARBURTON'S ANNOTATIONS — DISSATISFACTION OF WARBURTON WITH JOHNSON — MALONE'S JUST ESTIMATE OF WARBURTON'S EDITION — ATTACKS UPON WARBURTON — EDWARDS, AUTHOR OF THE 'CANONS OF CRITICISM;' ORIGIN OF THE HOSTILITY BETWEEN HIM AND WARBURTON — WARBURTON'S UNGENTLEMANLY SARCASMS ON EDWARDS IN THE NOTES ON THE 'DUNCIAD' — EDWARDS'S RETORTS — SPECIMENS OF EDWARDS'S CRITICISMS — HURD'S INJUDICIOUS PRAISE — HEATH'S 'REVISAL OF SHAKSPEARE'S TEXT'— ZACHARY GREY — SPECIMENS OF WARBURTON'S BEST EMENDATIONS.

THE merits and defects of Warburton's notes on Shakspeare were understood from the first glances cast on them by men of learning and judgment, on the day of their publication. Warburton himself affected to make light of them, and to declare that he would never have given them to the world but for the ill desert of Theobald and Hanmer, and the earnest wishes of Pope. 'Such as they are,' he says, 'they were among my younger amusements, when, many years ago, I used to turn over these sort of writers to unbend myself from more serious applications; and what certainly the public at this time of day had never been troubled with but for the conduct of the two last editors, and the persuasions of dear Mr. Pope, whose memory and name

Semper acerbum,
Semper honoratum (sic Dî voluistis) habebo.

He was desirous I should give a new edition of this poet, as he thought it might contribute to put a stop to the prevailing folly of altering the text of celebrated authors without talents or judgment. And he was willing that his edition should be melted down into mine, as it would, he said, afford him (so great is the modesty of an ingenuous temper) a fit opportunity of confessing his mistakes.* In memory of our friendship, I have, therefore, made it our joint edition.'

But though Warburton refers to Pope's Letters for this persuasion to publish his notes, and this permission to couple them with Pope's own notes, we search in vain for any passage of such purport, in those letters of Pope to Warburton which Warburton afterwards published. If we give him credit, therefore, for veracity on the point, we must give it him, as in the affair with Hanmer, on his own assurance. But the truth seems to be, that a desire of uniting his name more closely with that of Pope, which was sure to keep its place in English literature; a malicious longing, from whatever cause, to vilify the memory of Theobald and Hanmer; and an inclination, which he had always felt, to exhibit his own powers in conjectural criticism, were his great motives to the production of this edition. He sold the copyright to Tonson for five hundred pounds.

Hurd, as might be expected, says all that he can in praise of Warburton. 'Such is the felicity of his genius,' he observes, 'in restoring numberless passages to their integrity, and in explaining others which the author's sublime conceptions, or his licentious expression, had kept out of sight, that this fine edition of "Shakspeare" must ever be highly valued by men of sense and taste; a spirit congenial to that of the author breathing throughout, and easily atoning, with such, for the little mistakes and

* 'See his Letters to me.'

inadvertencies discoverable in it.' * A character of the edition more exactly opposed to its true desert could hardly have been given; and the greater is the 'sense and taste' of its readers, the less acceptable will it be to them.

But the noble and judicious criticism on it by Johnson, who was anxious to praise it as highly as it would bear, yet to condemn in it all that was evidently censurable, has done more to support it in the eyes of the world, and to induce 'men of sense' to regard it with all the favour of which it can be thought deserving, than anything that has been said concerning it. Johnson, in his 'Remarks on Macbeth,' published in 1745, complimented Warburton with the title of 'learned,' and Warburton, in return, spoke of the 'Remarks,' in his Preface to 'Shakspeare,' as the production of 'a man of parts and genius,' and honourably distinguished from anything of the kind that had recently appeared; praise for which Johnson, who was then but emerging into notice, was ready to express his acknowledgments. 'He praised me, Sir,' said he to Boswell, 'when praise was of value to me.' The character given of Warburton's edition in Johnson's Preface it would be unjust to Warburton to omit.

'Of the last editor it is more difficult to speak [than of Hanmer]. Respect is due to high place, tenderness to living reputation, and veneration to genius and learning; but he cannot be justly offended at that liberty of which he has himself so frequently given an example, nor very solicitous what is thought of notes which he ought never to have considered as part of his serious employments, and which, I suppose, since the ardour of composition is remitted, he no longer numbers among his happy effusions.

'The original and predominant error of his commentary is acquiescence in his first thoughts; that precipitation which is produced by consciousness of quick discernment;

* Hurd's Life of Warburton, p. 46.

and that confidence which presumes to do, by surveying the surface, what labour only can perform by penetrating the bottom. His notes exhibit sometimes perverse interpretations, and sometimes improbable conjectures; he at one time gives the author more profundity of meaning than the sentence admits, and at another discovers absurdities when the sense is clear to every other reader. But his emendations are likewise often happy and just; and his interpretation of obscure passages learned and sagacious.

'Of his notes, I have commonly rejected those, against which the general voice of the public has exclaimed, or which their own incongruity immediately condemns, and which, I suppose, the author himself would desire to be forgotten. Of the rest, to part I have given the highest approbation, by inserting the offered reading in the text; part I have left to the judgment of the reader, as doubtful, though specious; and part I have censured without reserve, but I am sure without bitterness of malice, and I hope without wantonness of insult.'

But this balancing of eulogy and censure, joined with the praise of a note on Hamlet as 'having almost set the critic on a level with his author,' by no means satisfied Warburton, who felt the blame more than the commendation, and who, though he said nothing publicly, growled for the affected contempt in his letters to Hurd and to at least one other of his friends. 'Of this Johnson,' he says to Hurd, 'you and I, I believe, think much alike;' and in the letter in which he made this remark, he inclosed a copy of another, in which he indulges in insulting animadversions on Johnson and his Shakspeare, and from which Hurd, very unwisely, thought fit to print a large extract: 'The remarks he makes in every page on my commentaries are full of insolence and malignant reflections, which, had they not in them as much folly as malignity, I should have had reason to be offended with.

As it is, I think myself obliged to him, in thus setting before the public so many of my notes with his remarks upon them; for though I have no great opinion of that trifling part of the public which pretends to judge of this part of literature in which boys and girls decide, yet I think nobody can be mistaken in this comparison; though I think their thoughts have never yet extended thus far as to reflect, that to discover the corruption in an author's text, and by a happy sagacity to restore it to sense, is no easy task; but when the discovery is made, then to cavil at the conjecture, to propose an equivalent, and defend nonsense, by producing out of the thick darkness it occasions a weak and faint glimmering of sense (which has been the business of this editor throughout), is the easiest, as well as dullest, of all literary efforts.'* This is as unjust a character of Johnson's annotation as could well be given, and the hints for it seem to have been taken from Johnson's own remarks on the vainglorious practices of editors in his Preface, of which noble performance Warburton has not offered, or Hurd has not preserved, one word of commendation.

But the happiest illustration of the merits of Warburton's edition is that which is given by Malone. Dr. Warburton was 'a critic, who (as has been said of Salmasius) seems to have erected his throne on a heap of stones, that he might have them at hand to throw at the heads of all those who passed by. His unbounded license in substituting his own chimerical conceits in the place of the author's genuine text, has been so fully shown by his revisers, that I suppose no critical reader will again open his volumes. An hundred strappadoes, according to an Italian comic writer, would not have induced Petrarch, were he living, to subscribe to the meaning which certain commentators after his death had by their glosses

* Letters from an Eminent Prelate, p. 367.

extorted from his works. It is a curious speculation to consider how many thousand would have been requisite for this editor to have inflicted on our great dramatic poet for the same purpose. The defence which has been made for Dr. Warburton, on this subject, by some of his friends, is singular. 'He well knew,' it has been said, 'that much the greater part of his notes do not throw any light on the poet of whose works he undertook the revision, and that he frequently imputed to Shakspeare a meaning of which he never thought; but the editor's great object was to display his own learning, not to illustrate his author; and this end he obtained; for in spite of all the clamour against him, his work added to his reputation as a scholar.' Be it so, then; but let none of his admirers ever dare to unite his name with that of Shakspeare; and let us at least be allowed to wonder, that the learned editor should have had so little respect for the greatest poet that has appeared since the days of Homer, as to use a commentary on his works merely as 'a stalking-horse, under presentation of which he might shoot his wit.'*

The publication, as was to be expected, excited against him attacks and sarcasms of every kind. 'As the public envy was now at its height,' says Hurd, 'from the rising fortune, as well as fame, of the author, this edition awakened a spirit of criticism which haunted him in every shape of dull ridicule and solemn confutation. Happening to speak of this in a letter written to him in 1749, he replies to me in the following lively manner: "I have, as you say, raised a spirit without designing it; and, while I thought I was only conjecturing, it seems I was conjuring. So that I had no sooner evoked the name of Shakspeare from the rotten monument of his former editions, than a crew of strange devils, and more grotesque

* Malone's Preface to Shakspeare.

than any he laughs at in the old farces, came chattering, mewing, and grinning round about me." The outcry against him was, indeed, pretty much what is here pleasantly described.' *

His three great assailants were Edwards, author of the 'Canons of Criticism;' Heath, the eminent Greek scholar, and reviser of Shakspeare's text; and Zachary Grey, the editor of 'Hudibras.' To whom may be added Upton, in his 'Critical Observations on Shakspeare.'

The attack of Edwards is said to have had its origin not wholly in regard for the text of Shakspeare, but partly in personal animosity or dislike towards Warburton. Thomas Edwards, the son of a country gentleman, who left him a small estate at Pitshanger, in Middlesex, from whence he afterwards removed to Turrick, in Buckinghamshire, was for a while in the army, but afterwards studied the law, as his father and grandfather had done, at Lincoln's Inn, and was called to the bar. An account of him in the 'Gentleman's Magazine,'† copied by Disraeli,‡ says that he was educated at Eton, and became a fellow of King's College, Cambridge, and was allowed to retain his fellowship after he entered the army; a permission which had also been granted to Sir William Draper and Mr. Hare. But the truth is, that he was educated at a private school, and was never a member of either of the Universities.§ It happened, however, that, while he was in the army, he visited Bath, soon after Warburton's marriage to Allen's niece, and was introduced at Prior Park, where he became a frequent guest. The conversation often turned on literary subjects, and Warburton was fond of seizing opportunities of showing his knowledge of Greek, not supposing that the young officer

* Hurd's Life of Warburton, p. 44; Letters from an Eminent Prelate, p. 13.

† Vol. lii. p. 288. ‡ Quarrels of Authors, Art. Warburton.

§ Nichols's Lit. Anecd. vol. ii. p. 199; vol. ix. p. 623.

had any acquaintance with the language; till one day, when a dispute arose in the library about some passage in a Greek author, Edwards took down the book, and explained the passage in a sense quite contrary to that which Warburton had given it. Warburton, however, was not willing to own himself refuted, for

> Ev'n though vanquish'd, he could argue still,

and endeavoured to support his own rendering. But Edwards, knowing himself in the right, showed no inclination to yield, and added to the offence of opposition that of endeavouring to convince Warburton that his misconception of the author arose from having trusted to a French translation. This was unpardonable; Warburton was irritated; and, whatever may have been afterwards said on either side, the two were thenceforward mortal enemies. Disraeli says, but I know not on what authority, that the argument took place in the presence of Allen and his niece. Some doubt, it may be observed, is thrown upon the story by an expression in Edwards's dedication of the later editions of the 'Canons of Criticism' to Warburton. For being called into public notice, he says, 'I am more obliged to you, *whom I do not know*, than to any other person whom I do.' If Warburton and he had met several times at Allen's, why should he have said that he did not know Warburton? Nor, it may be added, is there any allusion in the book to Warburton's imperfect acquaintance with Greek, on which it may be thought that Edwards, if he had had personal conviction of it, would, as an enemy, be disposed to cast some reflection?

But certain it is, that, when Warburton's Shakspeare appeared, Edwards sent to the press, in the same year, a keen satire upon it, under the title of 'A Supplement to Mr. Warburton's Edition of Shakspeare,' of which, before the close of the year, a second edition was published, and which, under the title of 'Canons of Criticism,' reached at least a seventh edition. He had some assistance in the work from Mr. Richard Roderick, a fellow of Magdalen College, Cambridge, and a friend of Bishop Newton, the editor of Milton.*

Edwards continued to make additions, for the further exposure of Warburton, in the successive editions; for which, indeed, Warburton gave him sufficient provocation; for though he made no direct reply to Edwards, he took occasion to express bitter contempt of him, and certainly in the most ungentlemanly and outrageous terms, in his notes on Pope's works, published in 1751. In a note on the 'Essay on Criticism,' † where it is said that envy will pursue merit, and that the great must expect to be annoyed by the inferior, he says, 'Sir Walter Raleigh had Alexander Ross, Chillingworth had his Cheynel, and Locke his EDWARDS; not *fungoso* of Lincoln's Inn. *Mr. Locke's Edwards* was a divine of parts and learning; *this Edwards* is a critic with neither. Yet (as Mr. Pope says of Luke Milbourne) *the fairest of all critics*; for, having written against the editor's remarks on Shakspeare, he *did him justice by printing at the same time his own.*' And in the 'Dunciad,' on the lines

> Her children, first, of more distinguished sort,
> Who study Shakspeare at the Inns of Court,‡

he inserts this note, with the signature Scriblerus: 'Ill would that scholiast discharge his duty, who should neglect to honour those whom Dulness has *distinguished*, or suffer them to lie forgotten, when their rare modesty would have left them nameless. Let us not, therefore, overlook the services which have been done her cause by one Mr. Thomas Edwards, a *gentleman*, as he is pleased to

* Pref. to Canons of Criticism, seventh ed.; Nichols's Lit. Illustr. vol. ii. p. 838.

† Ver. 463.

‡ iv. 567.

call himself, of *Lincoln's Inn*, but, in reality, a gentleman only of the "Dunciad;" or, to speak him better, in the plain language of our honest ancestors to such mushrooms, *a gentleman of the last edition*; who, nobly eluding the solicitude of his careful father, very early retained himself in the cause of Dulness against Shakspeare, and with the wit and wisdom of his ancestor Tom Thimble, in the "Rehearsal," and with the air of good nature and politeness of Caliban, in the "Tempest," hath now happily finished *the dunce's progress* in personal abuse. For a libeller is nothing but a Grub Street critic run to seed. Lamentable is the dulness of these gentlemen of the "Dunciad." This *fungoso* and his friends, who are all gentlemen, have exclaimed much against us for reflecting on his *birth*, in the words *a gentleman of the last edition*, which we hereby declare concerns, not his *birth*, but his *adoption* only, and mean no more than that he is become *a gentleman of the last edition of the "Dunciad."* Since gentlemen, then, are so captious, we think it proper to declare that Mr. Thomas Thimble, who is here said to be Mr. Thomas Edwards's ancestor, is only related to him by the Muse's side.'

Edwards, in a subsequent edition of his book, noticed this annotation as follows, as an illustration to the seventeenth of his canons, 'It will be necessary for the professed critic to have by him a good number of pedantic and abusive expressions, to throw about upon proper occasions.' 'The license of abuse mentioned under this canon,' says he, 'being the professed critic's undoubted privilege, he may call any person whom he dislikes,

> A Gentleman of the "Dunciad,"
> A Mushroom,
> A Gentleman of the last edition,
> A Grub Street critic run to seed, and
> A Libeller;

but I would advise him to be cautious how he uses the last appellation, because he may chance to meet with some people who, not knowing, or not allowing, his privilege, may very uncritically move for an information against him in the Court of King's Bench.

'And if the terms he chooses to employ are so gross that he is ashamed to use them in English, he may call his betters son of a b——, or any other hard name, in Latin, with some success; though his reputation for wit and good manners will not extend quite so far as if the compliment had been made in the vulgar tongue.'

The last paragraph refers to the word CANIS in the lines of Horace, prefixed to Warburton's 'Remarks on Several Occasional Reflections,' of which Edwards's translation is given above.

Edwards also dedicated an edition of his book to Warburton, concluding thus: 'I take this opportunity of thanking you for that civil treatment, so becoming a gentleman and a clergyman, which I have received at your hands, and to offer to your protection a work, *from which, if Shakspeare, or good letters, have received any advantage, and the public any benefit or entertainment, the thanks are due to Mr. Warburton*;' turning Warburton's own words, in his Preface, against himself.

In his Preface, also, to the same edition, he addresses Warburton thus: 'I have read Shakspeare at Lincoln's Inn, and have published my "Canons of Criticism;" and for this I am to be degraded of my gentility. A severe sentence this; I find that reading Shakspeare is a greater crime than high treason. Had I been guilty of the latter, I must have been indicted by my addition, tried by my peers, and should not have lost my blood till I had been attainted; whereas, here the punishment is incurred *ipso facto* without jury or trial.

'I might complain of Mr. Warburton to his Masters of the Bench, for degrading a barrister of their house by his sole authority; but I will only reason coolly with him upon the equity of this new proceeding.

'A gentleman (if I do not mean myself, with Mr. Warburton's leave I may use that word), I say, a gentleman, designed for the severe study of the law, must not presume to read, much less to make any observations on Shakspeare, while a Minister of Christ, a divine of the Church of England, and one who, if either of the Universities would have given him that honour, would have been a Doctor in Divinity, or, as in his Preface he decently expresses it, *of the occult sciences*; he, I say, may leave the care of his living in the country, and his chapel in town, to curates, and spend his heaven-devoted hours in writing obscene and immoral notes on that author, and imputing to him sentiments which he would have been ashamed of.

'Who is Mr. Warburton? What is *his* birth, or whence *his* privilege, that the reputations of men both living and dead, of men in birth, character, station, in every instance of true worthiness, much his superiors, must lie at the mercy of his petulant satire, to be hacked and mangled as his ill-mannered spleen shall prompt him, while it shall be unlawful for anybody, under penalty of degradation, to laugh at the unscholar-like blunders, the crude and far-fetched conceits, the illiberal and indecent reflections, which he has endeavoured, with so much self-sufficiency and arrogance, to put off upon the world as a standard of true criticism?'

It is impossible to open Edwards's book anywhere without lighting on the most ludicrous exposures of Warburton's vagaries. As the volume is not in everyone's hands, a few specimens shall be given. Warburton himself suggested the notion and title of the work, for he 'had intended,' he said in his Preface, 'to have given the reader a body of canons for literal criticism, drawn out in form; as well such as concern the art in general, as those that arise from the nature and circumstances of our author's works in particular; but these uses,' he adds, 'may be well supplied by what is occasionally said upon the subject in the course of the following remarks:' 'He had designed also,' he observes, 'to give "a general alphabetic glossary" of peculiar terms, but as each of these is explained in its proper place, there seemed the less occasion for such an index.' On these hints Edwards spake. He gave a series of canons, deduced from Warburton's practice, and exemplified from his annotations; and subjoined a glossary filled with definitions and explanations of Warburton's own produce.

Of the canons, twenty-five in all, some are very happy pieces of satire:

'A professed critic has a right to declare that his author wrote whatever he thinks he ought to have written, with as much positiveness as if he had been at his elbow.

'When he does not like an expression, and yet cannot mend it, he may abuse his author for it.

'Or he may condemn it as a foolish interpolation.

'As every author is to be corrected into all possible perfection, and of that perfection the professed critic is the sole judge, he may alter any word or phrase, which does not want amendment, or which *will do*, provided he can think of anything which he imagines will do better.

'He may interpret his author so as to make him mean directly contrary to what he says.

'He needs not attend to the low accuracy of orthography or pointing, but may ridicule such trivial criticisms in others.

'Yet, when he pleases to condescend to such work, he may value himself upon it.

'He may explain a difficult passage by words absolutely unintelligible.

'He may contradict himself for the sake of showing his critical skill on both sides of the question.

'He may use the very same reasons for confirming his own observations which he has disallowed in his adversary.

'He may alter any passage of his author without reason and against the copies, and then quote the passage so altered as authority for altering any other.'

The examples of Warburton's audacity, given under each canon, are selected with no less felicity.

In King Lear, Act iii. sc. 3, the fool says:

> I'll speak a prophecy or e'er I go;

a line which would surely be thought, by most critics, sound enough to remain undisturbed; but Warburton, denying that 'or e'er I go' is English, though scores of examples of it may be found, declares that the verse should stand thus:

> I'll speak a proph'cy or two, e'er I go;

a fine specimen of metrical harmony.

In 1 Henry VI., Act iii. sc. 4, editors were content with

> —whoso draws a sword, 't is present death;

but Warburton pronounces that Shakspeare must have written:

> —whoso draws a sword i' th' presence, 't 's death,

'A phrase,' says Edwards, 'which seems to have been penned for Cadmus when in the state of a serpent.'

Othello, Act iii. sc. 7, exclaims:

> Farewell the neighing steed, and the shrill trump,
> The spirit-stirring drum, th' ear-piercing fife;

But Warburton is not satisfied with 'ear-piercing,' alleging that it is not expressive of *effect on the hearers*, which the epithet attached to 'fife' ought to denote, and therefore reads, or rather writes,

> —th' fear-'spersing fife,

which Edwards declares to be such a piece of verse as 'no

poet, nor indeed any man who had half an ear, would have thought of;' and on which Heath remarks: 'Shakspeare certainly wrote his tragedies with a view to their being acted, and, if acted, consequently to their being pronounced. Now I will defy any organs of speech to pronounce Mr. Warburton's emendation.'

In 2 Henry IV., Act. i. sc. 1, we have

— and doth *enlarge* his rising,

that is, 'increase his army,' but Warburton *thinks it probable that Shakspeare wrote*

— doth *enlard* his rising;

that is, 'fatten and encourage' his rising.

In Timon of Athens, Act iv. sc. 3, we find

The sea's a thief, whose liquid surge resolves
The moon into salt tears.

But 'the sea melting the moon into tears,' says Warburton, 'is, I believe, a secret in philosophy which nobody but Shakspeare's deep editors ever dream'd of,' and ''t is more reasonable to believe that Shakspeare may allude to the opinion that the saltness of the sea is caused by several ranges or mounds of rock salt under water,' and 'this I think a sufficient authority for changing *moon* into *mounds*:'

The sea 's a thief, whose liquid surge resolves
The mounds into salt tears.

We read in Julius Cæsar, Act i. sc. 3:

— the complexion of th' element
Is fev'rous;

'But,' says Warburton, 'we find from the preceding relation that it was not *one element only* which was disturbed, but *all*; being told that all the sway of the *earth* shook like a thing infirm; that the *winds* rived the knotty oaks;

that the *ocean* rag'd and foam'd, and that there was a tempest dropping *fire*. So that *all the four elements* appear to be disordered. We should read, therefore:

—the complexion of the *elements*,

which is confirmed by the following line:

Most bloody, fiery, and most terrible;

bloody referring to the *water*, *fiery* to the *air* and *fire*; and *terrible* to the *earthquakes*.' 'This reading, with its explanation, is given,' retorts Edwards, 'as far as I can conjecture, for these reasons: *Bloody* is referred to the *water*, because no mention is made of water in the passage; *fiery* to the *air* and *fire*, because the *air* was on *fire*, and 't is hard if a thing may not refer to itself; and, lastly, as for *terrible* to the *earthquakes*, when Mr. Warburton gives us any reason why *terrible* must refer to *earthquakes* rather than to any other objects of terror (except because *terra* is Latin for the earth), I will promise to take this off his hands again.' 'The passage in the speech of Casca,' he adds, 'to which Warburton refers, has nothing in it that can lead us to imagine anything is there meant except disorders and commotions in the air. "Shakes the earth" evidently relates, not to an *earthquake*, but to the *thunder*; a "tempest dropping fire" is a proof that the air is in disorder, but the element of fire is no more disturbed in this than in any other of its common operations. As for the "rising winds" and the "foaming ocean," they are not spoken of by Casca as circumstances then present, but as things which he had formerly seen.

'It may be thought, perhaps, that the difference between the two readings, "element" and "elements," is not of consequence enough to spend so much time about; but, however trifling may be the difference, Mr. Warburton's reasoning about it is absurd and ridiculous:

— we must not give advantage
To stubborn critics, apt, without a theme,
For depravation.'*

Warburton's comments are, indeed, often equally ludicrous with his alterations of the text. 'Mary Queen of Scots,' he says, 'is called a Mermaid,† to denote her beauty and intemperate lust:'

Ut *turpiter* atrum
Desinat in piscem mulier formosa superne,

'Which,' remarks Edwards, 'those who do not understand Latin will perhaps think is a proof of what our critic asserts, or at least *something to his purpose*.' On the words, 'Friends of my soul,' in King Lear, Warburton remarks, 'A Spanish phrase: *Amigo de mi Alma*:' 'Just with the same acuteness,' replies his antagonist, 'a Spanish critic, meeting with the expression, *Amigo de mi Alma*, might say, An English phrase, *Friends of my soul*.' On Sir John Falstaff's exclamation,‡ 'Here's lime in this sack too; there is nothing but roguery to be found in villainous man!' he observes that lime was generally considered to be a cause of the stone, but that the efficacy of Mrs. Stephens's medicine had refuted that opinion.' In 'Much Ado about Nothing,'§ we have 'past the infinite of thought.' 'Human thought,' exclaims Warburton, 'cannot sure be called *infinite*, with any kind of propriety. I suppose the true reading was *definite*.' On Falstaff's saying, 'If I travel but four foot by the square further on foot,'‖ Warburton has this absurd note:

'The thought is humorous, and alludes to his bulk; insinuating that, his legs being *four foot asunder*, when he advanced *four foot*, this put together made *four foot square*,' which gives occasion to the following animadversion from Edwards:

* Troilus and Cressida, act v. sc. 2.

† Mids. N. D. act ii. sc. 2.

‡ 1 Hen. IV. act ii. sc. 4.

§ Act ii. sc. 3.

‖ 1 Hen. IV. act ii. sc. 2.

'According to this known rule, let us measure the leap of the dancer in the "Winter's Tale," who jumped *twelve foot and a-half by the square*, i.e., twelve foot and a-half forwards, and as much sideways. But whether he did this by jumping in the diagonal, or whether he carried his legs twelve foot and a-half asunder, is not very easily determined.

'For want of attending to this mensuration, a very fine piece of humour also will be lost to the reader in 2 Henry IV., where Falstaff says to Prince John of Lancaster: "I speeded hither with *the extremest inch of possibility;*" insinuating, without question, that on this occasion of the battle he travelled by the *inch square* (for, though *square* be not expressed here, I am persuaded it is understood), and carried his legs not above an inch asunder. An extremely natural posture for a coward in a battle.

'By *the square* in both places it is evident that Shakspeare means nothing more than a common measure, or footrule.'

A not less ridiculous note on the word *square* is given by Warburton on this line in King Lear:

> Which the most precious square of sense possesses.

'By the *square of sense*,' he says, 'we are to understand the *four* nobler senses, viz., the sight, hearing, taste, and smell. For a young lady could not with decency insinuate that she knew of any pleasure which the *fifth* afforded. This is imagined with great propriety and delicacy.'

'I believe,' rejoins Edwards, 'that Shakspeare uses square for the full complement of all the senses; and that this imagined propriety and delicacy Mr. Warburton ought to have the praise of: who seems to have been thinking of the *sixth* sense, instead of the *fifth*, when he wrote the note.'

In the Winter's Tale three swine-herds are mentioned 'that have made themselves all men of hair; they call themselves saltiers,' 'that is,' says Warburton, 'they are "nimble" men, "that leap as if they rebounded." The phrase is taken from tennis-balls, which were stuff'd with hair.' Warburton, observes Edwards, should have fixed his attention, not upon 'men of hair,' but upon 'saltiers,' and changed it to *satyrs*, the men being doubtless *made all over hairy*, perhaps *clad in goats' skins.*

In 'Measure for Measure,' Act. ii. sc. 2, we have 'prayers from preserved souls.' Warburton adds, in perfect confidence, this note: 'The metaphor is taken from fruits, *preserved* in sugar.'

The only passage of Edwards's book of which Warburton took any notice, was one in which he made merry with a blunder; whether Warburton's own, or the printer's, may be doubtful. Pope, in a note on 'Measure for Measure,' observed that the story of it was taken from Cinthio's Novels, 'Dec. 8, Nov. 5,' which, in Warburton's edition, appeared thus: 'December 8, November 5.' 'Whether Warburton,' says Edwards, 'thought the story was so long, that it held for two days, and, not being finished the first, was resumed again at almost a twelve month's distance; or whether he designed to hint that Cinthio wrote his Tale *on the eighth of December*, and Shakspeare his Play *on the fifth of November*, we can only conjecture.' Warburton makes this retort: 'There is a set of still lower creatures than these [the small critics], at the tail of which is one Edwards, who can make shift even on a printer's blunder. The late Editor of "Shakspeare" gave order to the corrector of the press that all Mr. Pope's notes should be printed in their places. In one of these there was mention made, as they say, of some Italian novels (I forget whose) in which *Dec.* and *Nov.* were printed thus contractedly. But the printers of the late edition lengthened them into December and November, and in this condition they are charged upon the Editor by this Edwards. Now, was the man such a dunce as to make his criticism with good faith, he is much to be pitied; was he such a knave as to make it without, he is much more to be pitied.' * Edwards made a rejoinder in his next edition, when, remarking on another blunder in a note on the 'Taming of the Shrew,' where a line of Spenser is quoted as from the 'Fairy Queen, Book xi. chap. 9,' he observes that, unless Mr. Warburton has found Spenser's last six books, supposed to be lost in the Irish Sea, the misquotation must be considered as a mere printer's blunder, for 'though, in an outlandish Italian book, he might take *Decade and Novel for December and November*,' yet in a poet of his own country, whom he has so much studied, he could hardly take 'B. ii. c. 9' for '*Book the eleventh, chapter the ninth.*' But 'as to the *Duncery* or *Knavery*,' he adds, 'of imputing to Mr. Warburton himself this pretended blunder of his printer, we would observe, in the first place, that the very great number of cancelled leaves in his edition of "Shakspeare" led us to think that it was revised with extraordinary care and exactness, and, consequently, that the many blunders in spelling, pointing, and the like, were as certainly *his* as those in reasoning and emending.' †

Akenside, when he addressed, a few years afterwards, an 'Ode to Edwards on Warburton's edition of Pope,' did not forget to notice that of 'Shakspeare,' and to intimate what the great poet must have thought of the Commentary attached to his Works, supposing that, in the Elysian fields, it was brought to his knowledge:

> Then Shakspeare, debonnair and mild,
> Brought that strange comment forth to view,
> 'Conceits more deep,' he said, and smil'd,
> 'Than his own fools or madmen knew;'
> But thank'd a generous friend above,
> Who did, with free adventurous love,
> Such pageants from his tomb remove.

* Warburton's Pope; note on Imit. of Hor. B. ii. ep. 2; vol. iv. p. 226.

† Canons of Criticism, canons viii. and xviii. pp. 129, 192.

Hurd makes a very unhappy attempt in defence of Warburton as a critic. He quotes from the 'Nouvelles de la Republique des Lettres,' June 1684, the following apology of 'an eminent French writer' for Joseph Scaliger:

'Je ne sçais si on ne pourroit pas dire que Scaliger avoit trop d'esprit, et trop de science, pour faire un bon commentaire; car à force d'avoir de l'esprit, il trouvoit dans les auteurs qu'il commentoit, plus de finesse, et plus de génie, qu'ils n'en avoient effectivement; et sa profonde littérature étoit cause qu'il voyoit mille rapports entre les pensées d'un auteur et quelque point rare d'antiquité. De sorte qu'il s'imaginoit que son auteur avoit fait quelque allusion à ce point d'antiquité, et sur ce pied-là il corrigeoit un passage. Si on n'aime mieux s'imaginer que l'envie d'éclaircir un mistère d'érudition, inconnu aux autres critiques, l'engageoit à supposer qu'il se trouvoit dans un tel ou tel passage. Quoiqu'il en soit, les commentaires qui viennent de lui sont pleins de conjectures hardies, ingénieuses, et fort sçavantes, mais il n'est guères apparent que les auteurs ayent songé à tout ce qu'il leur fait dire. On s'éloigne de leur sens aussi bien quand on a beaucoup d'esprit, que quand on n'en a pas.'

Supported by these sentiments, Hurd boldly makes the assertion that 'as to what concerns the emendation of the text, the abler the critic, the more liable he is to some extravagance of conjecture, as we see in the case of Bentley himself; it being dulness, and not judgment, that best secures him from this sort of imputation.' A more extraordinary doctrine, in respect to criticism, was never propounded. It argues that the abler the critic, the more numerous will be his offences against just criticism; that Bentley's errors in criticism were proportioned to his eminence as a critic; and that stupidity is of far more use than judgment in qualifying a critic to excel in his art. The general belief has been the very reverse. It has been commonly thought that the ablest critics have possessed the most judgment; that the proof of Bentley's eminence as a critic lies in something different from his proneness to extravagant conjecture; and that stupidity will secure nobody from guessing foolishly. The most excellent verbal critic, probably, that has ever appeared in the world, was Richard Porson; and the next, perhaps, Gottlob Heyne; but neither of them was raised to critical distinction by want of judgment; nor secured from error by dulness; nor is their ability established by propensity to outrageous conjecture. How little dulness, or want of judgment, has to do with the duty of an editor, Hurd might have learned from Johnson's Preface to 'Shakspeare.'

Heath, whom we have next to mention among Warburton's antagonists, was a far different assailant from Edwards. Edwards was desirous to criticise in sport; Heath was disposed to censure with more of gravity. He was a good scholar, and had employed a portion of the leisure which his occupation as a barrister allowed him, in writing notes on the Greek tragic poets, many of which are extremely judicious, though his remarks on the metres were so far from satisfying Hermann, that he called him, to the great indignation of Dr. Parr, *ineptus metrorum omnium perditor.** He then, irritated at Warburton's audacity as a commentator, took to writing notes on Shakspeare, which, after keeping them six years in his desk, he published, with a dedication to Lord Kames, 'the truest judge and most intelligent admirer of Shakspeare;' calling them 'an imperfect attempt towards rescuing Shakspeare's remains from the licentious innovations of injudicious criticism.' But he came to his task furnished with scarcely sufficient critical aids; for he possessed neither of the folio editions, nor any of the old quartos; nor had he seen Sir Thomas Hanmer's edition;

* Herm. ad Hec. ver. 1002.

yet, by gathering such readings of the older copies as were noticed by Theobald and others, and weighing the remarks of his critical predecessors, he produced a number of very sensible annotations, which seem to have deserved, from succeeding critics, more notice than they have received.

In estimating the performances of some of those who went before him, he allows much praise to Theobald, whose careful collation of original editions enabled him to restore many passages on indisputable authority; a merit in which Pope had some, but not an equal, share. Of Theobald's efforts in conjecture, he says that, though often feeble, they were sometimes not unsuccessful. But of Warburton's 'pompous and solemn pretensions, calculated to raise the highest expectations in the reader, expectations surely never before so miserably defeated by the execution,' he cannot speak with patience. He has 'found occasion,' he says, 'in the course of his reading, to have recourse to critical writers in more than one language, but he has never yet had the fortune to meet with one so peculiarly unhappy. The licentiousness of his criticism overleaps all bounds or restraint, while the slightest glitter of a heated imagination is sufficient to lead him into the most improbable conjectures, which are at the same time constantly enforced by the authoritative and frequently almost oracular manner in which they are delivered.'

By these extracts from the Preface to the 'Revisal,' the reader may judge of the spirit of the work itself, of which, having been so liberal of quotations from Edwards, we shall forbear to encumber our pages with specimens.

Of the hostility between Warburton and Zachary Grey it seems impossible to discover the origin. When Grey was collecting materials for his 'Hudibras,' Warburton, as we have seen, readily supplied him, at the solicitation of Tunstall, with such annotations as he had at hand; though he expressed, at the same time, in a letter to Birch, some want of good feeling towards Grey. Grey 'spoke to Mr. Tunstall,' he says, 'to desire him to get what I had on that author for him; and, purely to oblige the latter, I had transcribed the margin of my book for him, excepting what relates to the history of those times, which Grey, I supposed, was perfectly versed in. You know the man; but I could not deny a friend.'* Why Warburton showed this distrust is nowhere manifested. Grey appears to have been generally regarded as a man of honour and good faith. His proposals for publishing 'Hudibras' are said to have been so well received that he cleared, by the subscription, fifteen hundred pounds. His book was, indeed, ridiculed by the wits, as carrying too much of commentators' lumber. Fielding, in his 'Journey to Lisbon,' alludes to 'the laborious much-read Zachary Grey,' and the 'redundant notes' on his 'Hudibras,' 'the single book extant in which above five hundred authors are quoted, not one of which could be found in the collection of the late Dr. Mead;' but, whatever was said against the commentator, no reflections were cast on the man. But Warburton seems to have conceived, or assumed, dislike to Grey in both characters; and, in his Preface to Shakspeare, passed this sentence on him and his 'Hudibras': 'If the follies of particular men were sufficient to bring any branch of learning into disrepute, I do not know any that would stand in a worse situation than that for which I now apologise,' meaning the art of the commentator; 'for,' he adds, 'I hardly think there ever appeared, in any learned language, so execrable a heap of nonsense, under the name of commentaries, as hath lately been given us on a certain satiric poet, of the last age, by his editor and coadjutor.' The coadjutor meant

* Letter to Birch, Aug. 12, 1741; Nichols's Lit. Ill. vol. ii. p. 124.

is Dr. Joseph Smith, who had incurred Warburton's displeasure by assisting Hanmer also in his edition of Shakspeare.

Alexander Chalmers, in his article on Grey, can only consider Warburton's attack as wanton and unprovoked; and Disraeli, who endeavoured to find a cause for it, could imagine no other than that Warburton, having himself contemplated an edition of Butler, 'sickened' at seeing, when Dr. Grey's appeared, how much he was excelled by Grey in the knowledge requisite for an effective commentary on Butler's great poem.

Whatever was the truth of the matter, Grey did not bear Warburton's haughty censures in silence. He hurled against him three pamphlets: 1. 'Remarks upon a late Edition of Shakspeare, with a long string of Emendations borrowed by the celebrated Editor from the Oxford Edition without Acknowledgment.' 2. 'A Word or two of Advice to William Warburton, a Dealer in Many Words. By a Friend. With an Appendix containing a Taste of William's Spirit of Railing.' 3. 'A Free and Familiar Letter to that great Refiner of Pope and Shakspeare, the Rev. Mr. William Warburton.' Nor, when he published his 'Notes on Shakspeare,' in two volumes, eight years afterwards, did he forget to notice Warburton in his Preface, adverting to his unreasonable abuse of Sir Thomas Hanmer, and calling him 'a *gentleman* whose *slander* stands for nothing with every candid and ingenuous person.'

In the first of his pamphlets he states that Sir Thomas Hanmer frequently complained among his friends that Warburton had puffed off as his own many emendations which he had received from Sir Thomas under promise of secresy. But as Hanmer and Warburton had been in intimate communication about Shakspeare, and Warburton's papers had been in Hanmer's hands, it must always be doubtful which was the greater borrower from the other.

He touches on some of Warburton's emendations. In 'As You Like It,' in the stanza,

Blow, blow, thou winter wind,
Thou art not so unkind
As man's ingratitude;
Thy tooth is not so keen,
Because thou art not seen,
Although thy breath be rude,

Warburton altered 'seen' into *sheen*, to which he gave the sense of '*smiling*, like an ungrateful court servant, who flatters while he wounds, which was a very good reason for giving the winter's wind the preference.' He also adduced three quotations to support his interpretation, but in all these Grey very justly replied that it means *shining, bright.* 'But the reason,' he adds, 'that Warburton would have *sheen* signify what it never did before, is that he knew *shining flattery* would be *shining nonsense*; but that *smiling flattery* would be very good sense.' As for the real sense of the words, 'because thou art not seen,' Grey supposes them to mean, '*because thou art no flatterer*; thou art so far from presenting a deceitful outside, that thou presentest no outside, no appearance at all.'

He, as well as Edwards, made merry with Warburton's note on Grumio's words in the 'Taming of the Shrew,'* *the oats have eaten up the horses.* 'Oats,' says Warburton's explanation, 'is the distemper so called.' 'Mr. Warburton,' says Edwards, 'has discovered one distemper incident to horses which neither Markham, Newcastle, Soleysel, nor Bracken, ever dreamed of.'† 'Mr. Warburton,' says Grey, 'has confused *oats* with *bots*, a disease mentioned in 1 K. Hen. IV., Act ii. sc. 1.'

Ophelia says that 'the owl was a baker's daughter.' 'This was a metamorphosis,' observes Warburton, 'of the common people, arising from the mealy appearance of the

* Act iii. sc. 8. † Canons of Criticism, can. vi. ex. 19.

owl's feathers, and *her guarding the bread from mice.*' 'You mean,' retorts Grey, '*guarding the corn in the barns*, owls being of great use in such places, but not in bakers' shops, as every farmer and baker in the neighbourhood could have informed you.'

But as to alterations in the text, Warburton's 'emendation of emendations,' says Dr. Grey,* 'is the change of *cap* to *cup* in "Coriolanus,"† "Take my cup, Jupiter, and I thank thee; hoo, Marcius coming home!" with this reason and explanation of the correction: "I will offer a libation to thee for thy good news," which was the custom at that time; and there is a pleasantry in his way of expressing it very agreeable to his (Menenius's) convivial character. But the editors, not knowing this use of the *cup*, altered it to *cap*.' Here is abundance of absurdity; the editors are represented as not knowing that a cup was used for libations; and libations are made to be offered by throwing up a cup into the air, or holding it up for Jupiter to take it. Johnson very kindly spares this alteration of Warburton's, by leaving it altogether unnoticed, and merely observing, 'Shakspeare so often mentions throwing up caps in this play, that Menenius may be well enough supposed to throw up his cap in thanks to Jupiter.'

Upton's 'Critical Observations on Shakspeare' are well known. The first edition of them was published before Warburton's 'Shakspeare' appeared. He offended Warburton, he says, by noticing Theobald without alluding to Theobald's coadjutor, the author of 'The Divine Legation.' Warburton vindictively took occasion to speak with contempt of the 'Critical Observations.' Upton retaliated in a Preface to his second edition, in which he exposed many of Warburton's transformations of the text,

* Remarks upon a Late Edition of Shakspeare, &c. † Act ii. sc. 1.

calling them errors 'such as the most inveterate enemy would pity, did not an unusual insolence destroy every degree of pity.' Warburton then prepared a gibbet for Upton in one of his 'established places of execution,' a note in the margin of the 'Dunciad,' sneering at him as 'a renegado critic,' who directed against Pope's commentator all the virulence which the Gildons and Dennises had displayed against Pope; but this note, from some cause, was cancelled before publication, though a reference to it still stands in the Index.*

But it would be unjust to Warburton, after having noticed so many of his unhappy attempts at correction, not to specify one or two of his more fortunate efforts. His palmary emendation, as he himself would perhaps have called it, is that in 'Hamlet,' which Johnson declared to 'set the critic almost on a level with the author.' In the speech of Hamlet, Act ii. sc. 2, which, in the old copies, stands, 'For if the sun breed maggots in a dead dog, being a good kissing carrion—Have you a daughter?' he altered 'a good kissing carrion' into 'a god, kissing carrion,' a reading which has since been universally adopted. His comment on the passage, which Johnson, according to Malone, admired more than the emendation, is able and acute, though the remark about 'mankind, dead in original sin, breeding only corruption and vices,' might well have been excluded from an annotation on Shakspeare. His observation that Hamlet is made to leave what he was saying unfinished, and start aside to the question about Polonius's daughter, lest his talk should seem too consequential for insanity, is extremely happy.

Praise is also due to his suggested alteration of another passage in Hamlet, though succeeding editors have justly

* Index to 'Dunciad,' iv. 237. Letters from an Em. Prelate, p. 42; Nichols's Lit. Ill. vol. ii. p. 849.

thought it too bold to be received into the text. In the lines,

> *King.*—But now, my cousin Hamlet, and my son —
> *Ham.* (Aside).—A little more than kin, and less than kind,

he thought, with great reason, that something was wanting to introduce Hamlet's play upon the words *kin* and *kind*, and give occasion to it. He therefore proposed to read,

> But now, my cousin Hamlet,—*kind* my son,

in the sense of '*Good* my son,' a reading and interpretation for which support may be found, and which would clear the passage of much of its difficulty; for Hamlet's remark *aside*, 'a little more than *kin*,' in the sense of *cousin* (in which Farmer says it is still used in the midland counties), 'and less than *kind*,' in the sense of *child* (which Johnson gives it), would then naturally arise from the king's words.

Nor, perhaps, should the proposed change of *defeat* into *disseat* in 'Othello,' Act i. sc. 3, go without commendation. Roderigo says to Iago, 'Defeat thy favour with a usurp'd hand.' Warburton would read, 'Disseat thy favour,' &c., that is, 'turn thy favour out of its seat; change it for another.' For the word 'disseat' authority is found in 'Macbeth': *

> —this push
> Will cheer me ever, or disseat me now.

But, on the whole, in taking leave of Warburton's commentary on Shakspeare, we must acknowledge that the evil in it so far predominates over the good as amply to justify Quin's remarks to the players in the green room: 'He should have confined himself to his own Bible, and left ours alone.'

Charles Yorke, however, who seems to have lost no

* Act v. sc. 3.

opportunity of telling Warburton how much he esteemed him and his works, delighted him with a high eulogy on his Shakspeare: 'Mr. Allen was so good as to show me the two first volumes of your Shakspeare. I had only time to read over the first volume, which gave me the highest entertainment. It is no great compliment to tell you that there is more genius in a little finger of your commentary than in the loins of the heavy Oxford edition of this poet. I observed that you had, with a pen, in the margin, added new notes, sometimes with great success, and now and then not doubted *cædere vineta tua*. You have, with excellent learning and acumen, pursued the general principles of your commentary in particular instances, and shown that what is principally requisite to the understanding of Shakspeare is expounding his antiquated words and allusions, rather than amending his text, which has too often ended in corrupting it.' * The bestower of this praise appears to have written with sincerity, but, if so, certainly with unlucky partiality, for no edition of Shakspeare has presented so many indications how the text may be corrupted under pretence of amending it.

* Letters from an Eminent Prelate, p. 500.

CHAPTER XIX.

RICHARDSON. TOWNE AND JACKSON. DR. NATHANIEL FORSTER.

'LETTER TO A MEMBER OF PARLIAMENT CONCERNING LIBRARY PROPERTY' — PREFACE TO RICHARDSON'S 'CLARISSA' — ARCHDEACON TOWNE — THE REV. JOHN JACKSON — DR. NATHANIEL FORSTER — HIS PRAISE OF WARBURTON — HIS REMARKS ON THE PASSAGE IN JOSEPHUS RELATING TO JESUS CHRIST — OPINIONS OF CRITICS AS TO THE GENUINENESS OF THE PASSAGE — THIRD EDITION OF THE 'ALLIANCE' DEDICATED TO LORD CHESTERFIELD.

THE same year, 1747, Warburton published a pamphlet, entitled 'A Letter from an Author to a Member of Parliament concerning Literary Property,' showing, contrary to what some were at that time maintaining, that an author has as much a natural right in the produce of his mind as an instrument-maker has in what is called the produce of his hand, and that it could only be ignorance or knavery that would represent the Act of Queen Anne in favour of literary property as the sole foundation of it, instead of an additional support to it.*

He presented Richardson, about the same time, with a preface to his 'Clarissa Harlowe,' pointing out the variety in its characters, and commending the moral tendency of a work by which general readers, while they admire how well the minds of its personages are represented, may doubt whether virtue has been much strengthened. It may be mentioned that Richardson, like many other persons favoured by Warburton, fell at last under his displea-

* Warburton's Works, vol. xii. p. 413.

sure. On one occasion, Mr. and Mrs. Allen, being in London, and having Warburton resident with them, left a card on Richardson, who returned their call, but did not find them at home. A few days afterwards, Richardson, walking with Millar in the Strand, met Warburton, who paid much attention to Millar, but would scarcely notice Richardson. The author of 'Clarissa,' surprised at his incivility, and thinking it must be owing to some fancied neglect, observed that he had returned Mr. Allen's call, but that the servant might possibly have forgotten to mention his coming. 'He answered,' says the novelist, '*with a face all his own, and with a voice and manner equally peculiar to himself*, that they were very often abroad.' Warburton's ground for displeasure, as Richardson with some difficulty discovered, was, that he had inserted in a new edition of 'Clarissa' some reflections on Pope which were not in the first, and had had the insolence to present a copy of the edition to Mrs. Warburton. 'I know nothing,' said Richardson, 'of any new reflections on Pope, but I did indeed present a copy to the lady, intending it as a civility to one whom I knew before she was his.' Edwards, the author of the 'Canons of Criticism,' Richardson's intimate friend, to whom he tells the story, learned that one of the objectionable reflections on Pope was a censure of the sentiment, 'Every woman is at heart a rake.'*

He also wrote, this year, a short Preface to the second edition of Towne's 'Critical Enquiry into the Opinions and Practices of the Ancient Philosophers concerning the Nature of the Soul and a Future State.'

Towne was Archdeacon of Stowe, and Rector of Little Ponton, in Lancashire, in which county Warburton had become acquainted with him. As he agreed with Warburton in his views regarding the principal subjects

* Richardson's Correspondence, by Mrs. Barbauld, vol. i. p. 60.

discussed in 'The Divine Legation,' they readily became friends; and he afterwards read Warburton's writings with such attention that Warburton used to say of him that he understood them better than himself.

Jackson, whom we have had occasion to notice before, had written a treatise in opposition to 'The Divine Legation,' and to the first edition of Towne's book, to show that Warburton was wrong in his assertions that the ancient philosophers disbelieved the existence of the soul after death; that they had esoteric and exoteric doctrines; and that, whenever they affirmed the certainty or probability of a future state of rewards and punishments, they advocated it only as a doctrine of salutary influence on the ignorant multitude. Towne remodelled his book to reply to Jackson, and to add new demonstrations that Warburton was right, as was indeed easily made apparent by quotations from the philosophers. The author wants the force of Warburton, but sometimes affects his manner and phraseology. Adducing some passages which, though urged by Warburton, Jackson had disregarded, he says that 'he chooses to rub his nose with them once more.' Jackson, in one place, had told Towne that he 'grossly misrepresented' some point, and called upon Warburton 'for *his own* sake, for the sake of *truth*, and for the sake of common *justice*, not to make himself responsible for such representation.' 'These, we see,' retorts Towne, 'are well joined. I believe he has pretty much the same regard to *truth* and *justice* that he has to *Mr. Warburton*, and is equally solicitous that none of the three suffer at my hands. But what has an *answerer by profession* to do with any of them, unless to misrepresent them?'

Jackson made some reply, in a pamphlet not worth notice. When he brought out his 'Chronological Antiquities,' in three volumes, containing a dissertation on the Eleusinian Mysteries, Warburton remarked to Hurd, 'You would hardly think that all his account of the Mysteries should be one entire theft from me, a transcript of my account, without one word of acknowledgment.' * This was literally true. 'He certainly,' said a correspondent of Mr. Nichols, 'took all that he has said about hieroglyphics and mysteries from Warburton; but so totally forgot or overlooked it (as was his custom on other occasions), that he vainly thought it all his own.' He was author of thirty-six publications, chiefly pamphlets against Tindal, Middleton, and other writers of free opinions, but was himself condemned of Arianism, as a follower of Dr. Clarke. 'The wretch,' said Warburton, 'has passed his days in the republic of letters just as your vagabonds do in the streets of London, in one unvaried course of *begging*, *railing*, and *stealing*.'

Long afterwards, Warburton and Jackson, who were personally unknown to each other, happened to be together in the shop of Whiston, the bookseller. As Warburton was making his way towards Whiston's back parlour, Jackson, who was at some distance, inquired his name of the shopman, and, on hearing it, observed, 'I thought it was some such conceited fellow.' Warburton, just afterwards, noticing Jackson, asked a similar question, and, receiving a reply, made a remark in almost the very words that had been used by Jackson. †

The intimacy between Warburton and Towne continued till Warburton's death, whom he survived some years. He wrote some other theological pieces, chiefly in support of 'The Divine Legation,' some of which he submitted to Warburton for revision, who said of him that he was 'a reasoning engine, as Voltaire calls Dr. Clarke,' ‡ but 'so little skilled in the art of composition, that, when any of his pieces passed through his hands, he had more trouble

* Letters from an Eminent Prelate, p. 117.

† Nichols's Lit. Anec. vol. ii. p. 527.

‡ Letters from an Eminent Prelate, p. 49.

in reforming the style and method of them than it would have cost him to write the whole afresh in his own manner.' *

In the following year, 1748, Warburton was presented by Dr. Nathaniel Forster, who had recently edited his 'Dialogues of Plato,' and was preparing to publish his Hebrew Bible, without points, with his 'Dissertation on Josephus's Account of Jesus Christ,' a tract in which he bestowed much praise on the author of 'The Divine Legation,' calling him 'learned and ingenious,' and 'a great writer.' Forster had also spoken of Warburton in similar terms in his pamphlet of 'Reflections on the High Antiquity of Egypt,' in which he expressed himself of the same opinion with Warburton in regard to the early prosperity and civilization of that country; observing that there were natural foundations for its rapid progress in power and arts, as the land produced with ease and quickness the several necessaries and conveniences of life; the women, as related by Strabo and Pliny, were extremely prolific; and the Nile, by its fertilising exundations, kept the people together on its banks, so that they would soon form into societies, and, feeling the want of union, would establish a general government; while the natives of such a warm country, not being inclined to activity, would indulge in contemplation and cultivate science, and, when they took to building, and meditated distinction in architecture, would be induced, by the uncertain risings of the river, to erect structures of great strength and magnitude, such as would not easily be overthrown or damaged by extraordinary floods.

Warburton, it may be supposed, was well pleased with the advances of a man of learning who showed such concurrence in his views, accompanied with the incense of praise. As to the passage in Josephus, however, War-

* Letter of Hurd to Balguy, 'Kilvert's Hurd,' p. 178.

burton was opposed, but with soft words, by the writer who now addressed him. The author of 'The Divine Legation' had pronounced, in his decisive style, that the passage was 'a rank forgery, and a very stupid one too;' * but Forster endeavoured, with gentle persuasions, to induce him to alter his opinion, offering him, at the same time, what he conceived to be the true sense of it. Warburton had taken the words, ὁ Χριστὸς οὗτος ἦν, in the vulgar acceptation; 'this was the Christ or Messiah;' an assertion which, he said, would never have been made by so sincere a Jew as Josephus. Forster argued that the words meant nothing more than *hic erat ille* or *iste Christus*, 'this was the much talked of Christ, or the man so well known under the name of Christ,' a sense in which a Jew might very well use them. Τἀληθῆ, in the passage, 'true things,' he proposed to alter into τὰ ἀήθη, 'strange things:' a change which would make the passage still more suitable to Josephus. And the following words, which are commonly translated, 'He appeared to them [his followers] alive again on the third day, as the Divine prophets (θείων προφητῶν, which Forster would fain have altered into τῶν ἰδίων προφητῶν) had foretold these and ten thousand other wonderful things concerning Him,' he rendered, 'He appeared to them to be alive again on the third day, their own preachers having reported both these and numberless other wonderful things concerning Him:' a sense somewhat forced, but giving the passage much more the air of being the genuine production of the Jewish historian.

The sense of the whole passage is given by Whiston and Forster as follows. Whiston renders thus:

'Now there was about this time Jesus, a wise man, if it be lawful to call him a man, for he was a doer of wonderful works, a teacher of such men as receive the truth

* Div. Leg., book ii. § 6.

with pleasure. He drew over to him both many of the Jews and many of the Gentiles. He was [the] Christ; and when Pilate, at the suggestion of the principal men amongst us, had condemned him to the cross, those that loved him at the first did not forsake him, for he appeared to them alive again the third day, as the Divine prophets had foretold these and ten thousand other wonderful things concerning him; and the tribe of Christians, so named from him, are not extinct at this day.'

With Forster's emendations the sense would be thus:

Now there lived about this time Jesus, a wise man, if it be lawful to call him a man, for he was a doer of wonderful works, a teacher of such as receive *strange* [or *new*] *things* with pleasure. He drew over to him both many of the Jews and many of the Gentiles. He was *the well known Christ*; and when Pilate, at the suggestion of the principal men amongst us, had condemned him to the cross, those that loved him at the first did not forsake him, for he appeared to them alive again on the third day, *their own preachers* having foretold these and numberless other wonderful things concerning him, &c.

Forster, indeed, might have taken his notion of the words ὁ Χριστὸς οὗτος ἦν from Whiston, who, in his Dissertation on the passage at the end of his volume, published in 1736, expressly asserts that the phrase, *This was Christ*, or *the Christ*, does not mean that this Jesus was the *true Messiah of the Jews*, but that he was distinguished from all other persons of the same name *by the addition of the name Christ*, or that he was the person whom all the world knew as *Jesus called Christ*; though, in his text, he translates the words, 'This was [the] Christ,' giving the unlearned reader a false notion of the sense in which he himself understood them.

Warburton, in returning thanks for the pamphlet, made the following remarks upon it: 'I have read it over,' he says, 'with great pleasure, and will tell you my sentiments of it with a friendly freedom. I think it one of the most ingenious and chaste pieces of criticism that ever was written. *I think* that ὁ Χριστὸς οὗτος ἦν can admit of no sense but the common one, especially while θείων προφητῶν stand their ground. But how far the liberty of altering the text by conjecture only, without support of manuscripts, is to be indulged, when the question is concerning the genuineness of a whole paragraph, I leave to your consideration. So far *on our side*; then, *on yours*, it must be owned that your very fine emendation τὰ ἀήθη, not only greatly mends the sense, but the expression. It is now *really* elegant, which before, I agree with Faber, was *tristis et putida elegantia*.'

Tanaquil Faber was one of those who most strongly maintained the spuriousness of the paragraph; and there can be, indeed, no doubt that it is an interpolation, from its utter want of connexion with what precedes and follows it, while that which follows it has an evident connexion with that which precedes. If it were omitted, all would proceed in regular course. Dr. Parr, who has a right to be heard on such a subject, maintained that it was a manifest interpolation, but gave his opinion that it was inserted by Josephus himself. There is nothing in the style, indeed, to show that it might not have proceeded from Josephus; and, taken in the sense which Forster, with his emendations, would give it, it might be considered as Josephus's; taken in the common acceptation, it must be regarded as the intrusion of a forger. But Forster's emendations are too bold, and his interpretation recedes too far from the natural sense; so that the paragraph, unsuitable as it is to the character of a Jew, must be rejected as spurious.

As to the antiquity of the passage, it is quoted by Eusebius, in his *Demonstratio Evangelica*, as early as A.D. 324, but there was plenty of time for interpolation between the age of Josephus and that of Eusebius. Gifanius and Osiander, in the sixteenth century, were the first that expressed doubts of its genuineness; and their notions were adopted by Daniel Heinsius, Boxhorn, Salmasius, Gronovius, Freinshemius, Tanaquil Faber, and Lardner. Daubuz wrote a treatise in its favour, and Jacob Bryant supported Daubuz, taking the words ὁ Χριστὸς οὗτος ἦν, however, in the same sense as Forster.

Warburton's objections to the alterations which Forster would have made in the text, though they were less audacious than he himself would have made in 'Shakspeare,' were very just; for if such arbitrary innovations were to be allowed in writings, any passage of an author might be moulded to signify anything.

The only thing that Warburton sent to the press this year was a third edition of the 'Alliance between Church and State,' dedicated to Lord Chesterfield. The Dedication served Edwards for the subject of a joke in a subsequent edition of his 'Canons of Criticism.' * 'The first edition of the "Alliance,"' said he, 'came out without a dedication, but was presented to all the Bishops; and, when nothing came of that, the second one was addressed to both the Universities; and, when nothing came of that, the third was dedicated to a noble earl; and nothing has yet come of that.'

* P. 261.

CHAPTER XX.

HURD. BOLINGBROKE. MALLET.

COMMENCEMENT OF 'JULIAN' — ADVANCES OF HURD TO WARBURTON; INTIMACY FORMED BETWEEN THEM — BOLINGBROKE'S CHARGE AGAINST POPE CONCERNING THE 'IDEA OF A PATRIOT KING' — WARBURTON'S DEFENCE OF POPE — 'EPISTLE TO THE MOST IMPUDENT MAN LIVING;' REPLY TO IT — MALLET'S DISLIKE OF WARBURTON — BISHOP NEWTON'S EDITION OF MILTON — WARBURTON'S OPINION OF LAUDER'S BOOK ON MILTON.

THE next literary effort on which Warburton employed himself was 'Julian, or a Discourse Concerning the Earthquake and Fiery Eruption which Defeated Julian's Attempt to Rebuild the Temple at Jerusalem.' But this treatise was not completed till 1750, and, during its progress, he became acquainted with Hurd, to whom he submitted the sheets of it for revisal before they were given to the public. The connexion of Warburton with Hurd was an important event to both, having great effect on the remainder of their lives.

Of the commencement of their personal intimacy there is no account.* In print, the first advance was made by Hurd, who, at the end of the introduction to his 'Comment on Horace's Art of Poetry,' bestowed on Warburton the following eulogy:

'For the kind of interpretation itself' [that is, the interpretation of a running commentary], 'it must be allowed, of all others, the fittest to throw light upon a difficult and obscure subject, and, above all, to convey an exact idea of

* Kilvert, Life of Hurd, p. 34.

the scope and order of any work. It hath, accordingly, been so considered by several of the foreign, particularly the Italian, critics, who have essayed long since to illustrate in this way the very piece before us. But the success of these foreigners is, I am sensible, a slender recommendation of their method. I choose, therefore, to rest on the single authority of a great author, who, in his edition of our English Horace, the best that was ever given of any classic, hath now retrieved and established the full credit of it. What was the amusement of his pen becomes, indeed, the labour of inferior writers. Yet, on these unequal terms, it can be no discredit to have aimed at some resemblance of one of the best of those merits which shed their united honours on the name of the illustrious friend and commentator of Mr. Pope.'

Warburton had at this time edited only a portion of Pope's works. When he sent forth a complete edition, he took occasion to make an ample public repayment of Hurd's compliment.

In the meantime he acknowledged the favour privately in the following letter, in which he thanks Hurd for a present of the 'Commentary on Horace,' and which appears to have formed the commencement of their correspondence. It is evident that they had not yet met; and that no intimacy had arisen between them:

'Bedford Row, June 1, 1749.

'Rev. Sir,—I received the favour of your edition of "Horace's Art of Poetry," for which I beg leave to make my best acknowledgments.

'You have given very little advantage to the critics, but where you speak of me; and yet my self-love will not suffer me to wish it unsaid, when I consider how much real honour is done to every one whom such an author commends.

'I tell you, with all sincerity, I think the notes one of

the most masterly pieces of criticism that ever was written. I am sure, and I ought to be ashamed to say it, that I should have envied you for it, had I not found you so generous to the commentator of Mr. Pope. As it is, I take a pride in it as my own; a greater than I *can* take in any of my own. I wish it was in my power to make a suitable acknowledgment for my obligations. The best thing I have to offer you is a very unprofitable friendship. Such as it is, you have a right to it. And, if you will make me still more your debtor, you must give me yours. You will always find in mine all the frankness and warmth wherewith I now beg leave to subscribe myself,

'Rev. Sir,

'Your very obliged and most faithful humble servant,

'W. WARBURTON.'

What induced Hurd to seek acquaintance with Warburton, he stated in a letter to him written seven years afterwards.

'For the first years of residence at the University,' said he, 'when I was labouring through the usual courses of logic, mathematics, and philosophy, I heard little of your name and writings; and the little I did hear was not likely to encourage a young man, that was under direction, to enquire farther after either. In the meantime, I grew up into the use of a little common sense; my commerce with the people of the place was enlarged. Still the clamours increased against you, and the appearance of your second volume opened many mouths. I was then Bachelor of Arts; and having no immediate business on my hands, I was led, by a spirit of perverseness, to see what there was in these decried volumes that had given such offence.

'To say the truth, there had been so much apparent bigotry and insolence in the invectives I had heard, though echoed, as was said, from men of note amongst us, that I wished, perhaps out of pure spite, to find them ill-founded. And I doubt I was half-determined in your favour before I knew anything of the merits of the case.

'The effect of all this was, that I took "The Divine Legation" with me down into the country, where I was going to spend the summer of, I think, 1741, with my friends. I there read the three volumes at my leisure, and with the impression I shall never forget. I returned to college the winter following, not so properly your convert, as all over spleen and prejudice against your defamers. From that time, I think, I am to date my friendship with you. There was something in your mind, still more than in the matter of your book, that struck me. In a word, I grew a constant reader of you. I enquired after your other works. I got the "Alliance" into my hands, and met with the "Essay on Portents and Prodigies," which last I liked the better, and still like it, because I understood it was most abused by those who owed you no goodwill. Things were in this train when the "Comment on Pope" appeared. That Comment, and the connexion I chanced then to have with Sir Edward Littleton, made me a poor critic; and in that connexion you found me. I became, on the sudden, your acquaintance; and am now happy in being your friend. You have here a slight sketch of my history: at least of the only part of it which will ever deserve notice.'*

It may seem strange that any strong or lasting attachment should have been formed between men of such dissimilar characters. Warburton was hot, Hurd cool; Warburton impetuous, Hurd calm and sedate; Warburton was free and bold in speech, Hurd cautious and restrained; Warburton was daring, Hurd timid and subtle; Warburton was void of taste in writing, Hurd affected and fastidious; Warburton was a son of energy, Hurd a disciple of art; Warburton struck directly at an object, Hurd endea-

* Letters from an Eminent Prelate, let. xcii.

voured to secure a side blow. But the truth is, that the dissimilarity of their dispositions was one great cause of the strength and endurance of their friendship. Each liked those qualities in the other which he had not in himself. Such, indeed, appears to have been the case in most of those friendships which history has celebrated as most lasting; in the attachments of Damon and Pythias, Orestes and Pylades, Achilles and Patroclus; one of the two seems, as in the connexion between man and woman, to have been ready to submit to the more prominent influence of the other; and Virgil has but adhered to nature in establishing such a connexion between Æneas and Achates. One of the two was adapted by nature *cedere potentis amici—imperiis.* They were not like two rough substances, of which, when brought into contact, the prominences of the one are obstructions to those of the other, but like a rough substance and a smooth, which can be rubbed as closely together as possible without impediment. Hurd, assuredly, entered into the connexion with a determination to be as subservient, even as Sir Pertinax Macsycophant himself, to the superior influence of his friend.

When the intimacy was once commenced, there was no delay on either side to improve it. Warburton wrote his letter of thanks for the 'Horace' on the first of June; on the fourth he received an acknowledgment of it; on the sixth he wrote to Hurd to invite him to call on him in town, or at Prior Park; mentioning, at the same time, his contemplated 'Julian,' and recommending Hurd to write a commentary on 'Horace's Epistle to Augustus,' similar to that which he had written on the 'Art of Poetry.' On the ninth Hurd thanked him for the suggestion; and on the thirteenth Warburton thanked him for his thanks. In August, Warburton sent him some manuscript notes of his own on the 'Epistle to Augustus,' and Hurd agreed to write the proposed commentary.

Henceforward they corresponded frequently, on various literary and other subjects. Towards the end of the year Warburton ventured to ask of Sherlock, the Bishop of London, though he was disposed to quarrel with his Lordship for having suffered some of his dependents to attack 'The Divine Legation,' a preachership at Whitehall for Hurd; a request which the Bishop granted, and Hurd entered on his office in the following May.

In the meantime, while Warburton was preparing to send forth 'Julian,' Bolingbroke published his 'Letters on the Idea of a Patriot King, the Spirit of Patriotism, and the State of Parties,' with an Advertisement said to have been written by Mallet, but in reality by Bolingbroke himself, containing the well-known charge against Pope of having printed an edition of those letters without his Lordship's permission or knowledge. The accusation, as made in the name of Mallet, stated that the original draughts were committed to *a man* to whom the author trusted to keep them secret, or to communicate them only to five or six persons who had been named to him; that the author rested in this confidence for some years, but at length began to suspect that the letters had been communicated to more persons than he desired; a suspicion for which he was repeatedly assured there was no ground. After *the man* was dead, however, he discovered that an edition of fifteen hundred copies had been printed, under the superintendence of *the man*, and left in the hands of the printer, except a few copies which *the man* carried away. On an inspection of the copies, it appeared that *the man* had altered certain passages, omitted others, and made new divisions of the matter, to please his own fancy; and it was also found that fragments of them had even been suffered to make their way into a monthly magazine, which was expecting farther portions of them. The copies in the hands of the printer were burnt under Bolingbroke's eye; but his Lordship found portions of the papers so well known, that, to prevent the tenor of the whole from being misunderstood, he had resolved on allowing the editor to publish them entire.

That this Preface was written by Bolingbroke appears from the manuscript of it preserved among the Bolingbroke papers in the British Museum, which is in the hand of an amanuensis, but with corrections in Bolingbroke's. * The persons to whom copies of the 'Letters' were to be presented were Wyndham, Bathurst, Murray, Marchmont, and Lyttelton. Pope had also shown a copy to Ralph Allen, who admired the performance so much that he offered to print an edition of it at his own expense; and it is not certain, indeed, that the cost of the edition which Pope printed was not defrayed by Allen.

For this virulent attack of Bolingbroke on Pope's memory, in so gross and unbecoming a style, there may have been two motives. Bolingbroke may have been displeased at Pope's corrections in his composition, and may have been indignant, also, that the poet should have bequeathed the copyright and control of his works to Warburton instead of himself, and thus secured comments upon them at variance with the philosophical doctrines that he had been constantly endeavouring to instil into the author and into the world.

Warburton lost no time in defending Pope's conduct, in 'A Letter to the Editor of the "Letters on the Spirit of Patriotism, the Idea of a Patriot King, and the State of Parties," occasioned by the Editor's Advertisement.' This is a spirited and judicious performance, and attributes Pope's act, apparently, to its true motives. Pope could not have meditated plagiarism, or thought of assuming to himself the honour of his friend's work, for the pamphlet told on its titlepage that it was written 'By a Person of Quality,' and the real author was known to the printer.

* Cooke's Life of Bolingbroke, vol. ii. p. 218.

who applied to Bolingbroke to know what he should do with the copies. Nor could he have made lucre his object, for he was not in such circumstances as to be even suspected of desiring to appropriate fifteen hundred copies of an eighteenpenny pamphlet. What, then, was his motive? Evidently 'an excessive and superstitious zeal for Lord Bolingbroke's glory:' to whose divine attributes he paid even a kind of idolatrous homage. 'It was his common subject of complaint,' proceeds Warburton, 'among his other friends, that Lord Bolingbroke was faultily negligent of his glory, even where the good of his country, and the happiness of the world, depended on its being unveiled. . . . And this being an important concern was the reason, I suppose, why his friend chose to prevent the loss of those "Letters," which likewise very well accounts,' adds Warburton, with increased sarcasm, 'for his allaying the extreme splendour of them, so offensive to mere mortals, with that terrestrial mixture of his own.' That there was such 'terrestrial mixture' Warburton does not attempt to deny, but offers some justification for it on the ground that Pope expected Bolingbroke, if his Lordship died before him, to leave his writings to his disposal, and that consequently he might reasonably consider himself 'more than a mere *porte feuille* of his friend's papers,' and retouch them, where he thought them susceptible of improvement. As to printing, Pope might have printed the pamphlet in the hope that he would one day overcome Bolingbroke's pretended modesty, and obtain his consent to publication. Or, if he should be disappointed in this expectation, he would at least have consulted his friend's fame, and preserved what he thought an invaluable composition for the admiration and applause of posterity.

Horace Walpole, it may be observed, though no great friend to Pope, expressed the same opinion in respect to his conduct in this matter as Warburton. 'His printing so many copies,' said he, 'was certainly a compliment.

If one had a mind to defend Pope, should not one ask if anybody ever blamed Virgil's executors for not burning the Æneid, as he ordered them?' * Spence, also, was told by Martha Blount, that she had heard Pope speak of Bolingbroke's work, and could take her oath that he printed it merely from esteem for his Lordship and his abilities.

Bolingbroke, calling the agency of Mallet again into operation, immediately issued a rejoinder, under the striking title of 'A Familiar Epistle to the Most Impudent Man Living:' a title that attracted great notice, and made Orator Henley anxious to show that the pamphlet did not refer to himself.† But the title is the most remarkable part of the production; the abuse which it pours forth is coarse and dull, and its argument amounts to nothing. That it was written by Bolingbroke is now well known; for it exists entire in Bolingbroke's hand.‡ The writer begins by owning himself a great favourer of Lord Bolingbroke, and an abhorrer of the scurrilous libels published against him, particularly of Warburton's, which 'have a peculiar indecency distinguishing them from those of any other man.' 'Arnall, an impudent scribbling attorney,' he proceeds, 'was set up to be his casuist in matters of public morality. You,' he continues, addressing Warburton, 'have been an attorney as well as he, and, being a little more impudent than he was (for Arnall never presumed to conceal his turpitude under the gown and scarf), have set yourself up to be his casuist in matters of private morality.

'You have signalised yourself by affecting to be the bully of Mr. Pope's memory, into whose acquaintance, at the latter end of the poor man's life, you were introduced by your nauseous flattery; and whose admirable writings you are about to publish, with commentaries worthy of

* To Sir H. Mann, May 17, 1749.

† Confusion Worse Confounded, p. 8.

‡ Cooke's Life of Bolingbroke, vol. ii. p. 218.

Scriblerus himself; for we may judge of them beforehand by the specimens we have already seen of your skill in criticism.

'. . . Lord Bolingbroke wants no defence. You deserve no answer. You assume, indeed, certain airs of superiority on every occasion, even on those where you have not the least pretence of equality; but you sustain them by nothing better than hypotheses, sophisms, foul language, and impudence. In this you had some success at first. A vain ostentation of literature, awkwardly dragged in, and absurdly applied, had dazzled many. But the imposition did not last. That which some foretold, even then, has been verified. Your readers have discovered that you can neither quote properly nor argue fairly, and that, when you pretend to demonstrate, you do not so much as define. In short, by continuing to write, you have wrote yourself into the contempt of all those who have either sense or taste. You may now scribble about imaginary "Alliances," "Divine Legations," and dramatic criticisms:

> —— Explain the thing till all men doubt it,
> And write about it, goddess, and about it;

or you may indulge yourself in saucy invectives as much as you please. Contempt will be your security, and you will have no reply to apprehend from any man who would not dispute with a common scold, nor wrestle with a chimney-sweep. You have proved yourself incorrigible, as well as unworthy of correction; and all that some very respectable men of your own order have got by attempting to amend you has been to make you rail the loudest at those you could answer the least.

'In this contempt I found you, and in this I leave you. I write against you, not against the miserable productions of your pen; and I join in this manner with every reasonable man to hoot out of society an animal who is a nuisance to it. But besides this contempt you have often had, and have on the present occasion particularly, another security. You cavil, you cannot argue; to write against what you say, would be to write against nothing, and that would be no easy task.'

Having observed that Pope had made known other writings of Bolingbroke, besides those under consideration, without the author's permission, a breach of trust which Bolingbroke had discovered and forgiven, and having expressed his surprise that Pope should not have opened his heart, and confessed this second breach of trust to Bolingbroke on his death-bed, he adds that, though he would give no formal answer to Warburton's libel, he would, out of charity, give him a little advice. 'I would advise you,' he says, 'to keep within that low sphere to which nature and fortune have confined you. Coax your young wife, flatter her old uncle, and be sure, when any corporative dispute arises at Bath, to inform the heedless public of it, to extol him ridiculously, and to rail at those whom he oppresses, or who presume to support such as are oppressed. If you write on any other subject, which I cannot advise you to do, collect plentifully, affirm dogmatically, but never attempt to reason; for they who can reason agree very unanimously that it is not your talent.'

To this 'Familiar Letter' an answer of a similar kind was returned in 'A Letter to the Lord Viscount Bolingbroke, occasioned by his Treatment of a Deceased Friend:' an effusion by some attributed to Warburton; but who was the real author is unknown. Another pamphlet or two, and sundry paragraphs in newspapers, reflecting on Pope or Warburton, kept the matter before the public for some time longer; and Mallet took occasion to deny, in some of the periodical prints, that he was the author of the 'Familiar Letter.' In reference to this denial, there are, among the Bolingbroke manuscripts in the British Museum, two pieces of writing, one of which appears to be a copy of part of a letter addressed to somebody by Warburton, and the other contains a couple of notes attached to it by Mallet. The first is as follows:

'With regard to Mr. Mallet's declaration, there is only one way to convince me he is not the author of the infamous libel [the "Familiar Epistle"], which is, by taking an opportunity of disavowing it publicly. I think my honour is concerned that it be publicly known I had no hand in the letter to Lord B. [the letter in reply to the "Familiar Letter"], merely on account of the Apollo story, and I shall do it on the first occasion. If Mr. M. does not do the same with regard to this libel, I shall consider him the author of it, and act in consequence of that belief. Sir, I desire you would let Mr. Millar know, and, if he chooses, let him have a transcript of what I here say.'

Mallet's notes are these:

'N.B.—I never took the slightest notice of this impudent silly threatening from Warburton. The writer I had no reason to be afraid of; the man I abhorred. A head filled with paradoxes, unproved and unprovable; a heart overflowing with virulence and the most slanderous malice.

'N.B.—I never wrote a pamphlet, nor a sentence in any pamphlet, concerning this wrong-headed and dogmatical pedant.' *

This denial Mallet might fairly make, for the attacks on Warburton were written, as we have seen, by Bolingbroke. The Apollo story was this: Mallet was one day in company with Warburton, who was supposed to be meditating a Life of Pope. As an anecdote for the book, Mallet told Warburton something that had occurred, he said, during Pope's last illness: I was sitting with him one day, he related, when, coming suddenly out of a reverie, and fixing his eyes steadfastly upon me, he said,

* Nichols's Lit. An. vol. v. p. 651.

'Mr. Mallet, I have had an odd kind of vision. Methought I saw my own head open, and Apollo come out of it; I then saw your head open, and Apollo went into it; after which our heads closed up again.' Warburton listened to the story with a sarcastic smile, and replied, 'Why, sir, if I had an intention of writing your life, this might be a proper anecdote; but I don't see that in Mr. Pope's it will be of any consequence at all.'* This retort would not improve Mallet's feelings towards Warburton.

In the course of this year Bishop Newton published his Milton, for which Warburton had given him leave to use the notes that he had sent, some years before, to be printed in the 'History of the Works of the Learned.' They extended, however, no farther than the first three books, for those on the other books were lost—'a loss,' said the Bishop, 'of which the excellence of those that remain sufficiently evinces the greatness.'† Warburton and Newton were each eager to praise the other. Warburton, in his Preface to Shakspeare,‡ announced that an elegant edition of Milton was soon to be expected from a gentleman of distinguished ability and learning; and Newton, in his Preface to Milton,§ asserted, though with much less truth, that Warburton had proved himself to be the best editor of Shakspeare by a variety of happy conjectures on the most difficult passages.

Of Lauder's book on Milton, which appeared about the same time, and to which Johnson showed such unfortunate favour, Warburton formed a much happier estimate. 'I have just read,' he writes to Hurd,‖ 'the most silly and knavish book I ever saw; one Lauder on Milton's imitations. An observation at the bottom of page forty-four

* A Letter to the Lord Viscount Bolingbroke, &c., p. 14. Disraeli's Quarrels of Authors, Art. on Bolingbroke, Mallet, and Pope.

† Pref. to Milton, p. 32. ‡ Sub fin. § P. 30.

‖ Letters from an Eminent Prelate, Dec. 23, 1749.

and the top of forty-five proves him either one or the other with a vengeance. If there are those things in Masenius, why did he not produce them? They are of more weight to prove his charge than all he says besides. I think he has produced about half-a-dozen particular thoughts that look like imitations.' But he adds a remark that shows he felt, or affected to feel, little respect for Milton: 'In one view the book does not displease me: it is likely enough *to mortify all the silly adorers of Milton, who deserve to be laughed at.*'

The same kind of feeling is also manifested in a letter to Jortin, written about the same time, where he observes, 'Lauder has offered much amusement to the public, and they are obliged to him. What the public wants, or subsists on, is news. Milton was their reigning favourite; yet they took it well, of a man they never heard of before, to tell them the news of Milton's being a thief and a plagiary; had he been proved a —— it had pleased them much better. When this was no longer news, they were equally delighted with another [Dr. Douglas], as much a stranger to them, who entertained them with another piece of news, that Lauder was a plagiary and an impostor; had he proved him to be a Jesuit in disguise, nothing had equalled the satisfaction.'

CHAPTER XXI.

'JULIAN.' MIDDLETON. MATHEMATICS.

PUBLICATION OF 'JULIAN' — OCCASION OF IT — MIDDLETON'S OPINION ON MIRACULOUS POWERS IN THE EARLY DAYS OF THE CHURCH — CHARACTER OF THE APOSTOLIC FATHERS; OF THEIR SUCCESSORS — WARBURTON'S REPLIES TO MIDDLETON — CHARACTER AND OBJECTS OF JULIAN — JULIAN'S ATTEMPT TO REBUILD THE TEMPLE AT JERUSALEM; ITS RESULT — WARBURTON'S ARGUMENTS THAT IT WAS DEFEATED BY A MIRACLE — AUTHORS OPPOSED TO THAT NOTION; BASNAGE, GIBBON, LARDNER — ASSERTIONS OF MOYLE AND JORTIN — WARBURTON'S OPINION ON THE EFFECT OF MATHEMATICAL STUDIES ON THE MIND — OPINIONS OF GIBBON AND OTHERS — CONSIDERATIONS ON THE QUESTION.

IN 1750, 'Julian,' which Thomas Dunham Whitaker, Warburton's friendly critic in the 'Quarterly,' calls 'the gravest, the least eccentric, and the most convincing of his works,' was sent forth into the world.

It was occasioned by Dr. Middleton's 'Free Inquiry into the Miraculous Powers which are supposed to have subsisted in the Christian Church from the Earliest Ages through several successive Centuries.' Middleton's design, in this treatise, was to establish the belief that all the accounts of miracles alleged to have been wrought in the Church, after the days of the apostles, are utterly without foundation. 'If miraculous powers,' he argues, 'continued to be communicated from heaven after the apostolic times, it might have been expected that they would have been possessed by men of zeal and piety who had lived under the apostles, and who had been appointed to succeed them in the government of the Church, and that we should find some account of their manifestation in the writings of the apostolic fathers. But we search in vain in the pages of Barnabas, Clement, Ignatius, Polycarp, and Hermas, for any intimation of the least claim or pretension to the power of working miracles, either as exerted by themselves, or as existing in the Church at large. If they speak of spiritual gifts, they mean only the ordinary gifts and graces of the gospel, as faith, hope, and charity, love of God and of man. Wake, indeed, and Dodwell, would willingly suppose that they were endowed with extraordinary gifts of the Spirit; but, if we examine carefully what they have written, we shall find that they even disclaim, especially Ignatius and Polycarp, any possession of extraordinary powers.

Among their immediate successors, however, we meet with repeated declarations of such wonderful powers existing in the Church. Justin Martyr, who is supposed by most critics to have written his first 'Apology' about A.D. 140, speaks of persons possessed with devils being cured; Irenæus, who wrote a few years later, relates that many sick persons were healed, and many dead raised to life, who lived many years afterwards. Theophilus of Antioch, Tertullian, and Minucius Felix, offer similar testimony to the expulsion of devils; Origen, who wrote at the beginning of the third century, says that things to come were foretold, cures performed, and devils driven away by a word; and his disciple, Gregory Thaumaturgus, exercised such eminent power over devils, that, as Socrates records, he could send them off, not only by addressing them when he was present, but even by a message or a letter from a distance. Arnobius, who wrote at the beginning of the fourth century, declares that Christ sometimes appeared to good and pious men, in a bodily shape, and that soothsayers and magicians were struck dumb at the mention of his name; and both he and his scholar Lactantius tell the same story with their predecessors as to the wonderful power of Christians over demons. In the fathers, as they are called, of subsequent times, we find plenty of similar attestations to the working of miracles.

What, then, are we to believe concerning this question? Are we to suppose that the power of working miracles was withheld from the Church for a time, and afterwards restored to it? Or are we to conclude that the ecclesiastical writers who succeeded the apostolical fathers were weak and credulous persons, who were easily deceived by juggling pretenders, and ready to propagate any wild improbability that folly or imposture brought to their knowledge?

Middleton proceeds to examine what credit is due to the successors of the apostolical fathers; observing that our trust in a writer must depend on the notion which we form of his veracity and his judgment. If we consider him veracious, we shall feel assured that he does not willingly deceive us; if we think him a man of judgment, we shall be persuaded that he was not likely to be deceived himself; but, if we see cause to doubt either of these qualities in him, we can have but little confidence in the truth of what he delivers; for the want of judgment, in many cases, and especially in regard to matters of an extraordinary or miraculous nature, will have as ill an effect on his credibility as the want of veracity. Looking first to Justin Martyr, we find in him innumerable manifestations of want of judgment. Remarking on the *mystery of the cross*, he says, 'Consider all the things in the world, whether they could be administered or have any communication with each other, without this form of the cross. The sea could not be passed unless that trophy called the sail were preserved in the ship; the earth could not be tilled without it; for neither diggers nor artificers could do their work but by instruments of this shape. The form of man, in the erection of his body, the extension of his arms, and the projection of his nose from his forehead, through which inspiration is made, shows nothing else but the figure of the cross, in which sense, also, it is spoken of by the prophet, *Christ the Lord is the breath before our face.*' And in another place he says that, when the Israelites fought with the Amalekites, and Moses held up his hands in support of his countrymen, their success was by no means due to his prayers, but simply to his representation of the figure of a cross. He also says 'that Christ, when he was crucified, fulfilled the symbol of the tree of life in Paradise, and of all other things that were to happen afterwards to the righteous; for Moses was sent with a rod to release his people; with this rod he divided the Red Sea; brought water out of the rock; and, with a piece of wood, made the bitter water sweet; Jacob, also, with sticks, made his uncle Laban's sheep bring forth such lambs as were to be his own again,' &c. 'And so,' says Middleton, 'he goes on to apply all the sticks and pieces of wood in the Old Testament to the cross of Christ.'* Silly and ridiculous as these interpretations may seem, Justin dreams that they were all imparted to him from heaven, and gravely asks the Jews, in his 'Dialogue with Trypho,' whether they thought it possible for him to have acquired so profound a knowledge of the Scriptures if he had not received from the Author of the Scriptures grace to understand them.

Irenæus was of a similar character with Justin Martyr, as is sufficiently shown by his affirmation that Christ must have been at least fifty years old when He died; for, as He came to save all men, of all ages, He must surely be thought to have passed through all stages of life; and by his record of a tradition, which he asserts to have received from Christ himself, that, in the millennium, there

* 'Free Inquiry into the Miraculous Powers' *sub init.* Just. Mart. Apol. i., and Dial. with Trypho.

would grow vineyards, each having ten thousand vines, each vine ten thousand branches, each branch ten thousand shoots, each shoot ten thousand bunches, each bunch ten thousand grapes, and each grape yielding twenty-five measures of wine. Could a man who would crowd his pages with such ridiculous notions, whether the product of his own imagination or that of others, be thought a competent witness to the existence of miraculous powers in the Church?

The later fathers must be held in like estimation with these two, whose statements, indeed, they copy on trust, and to whom they refer as undoubted authorities. It would require volumes to exhibit the strange stories they have told of miraculous manifestations, especially in casting out devils, in healing the sick, in prophesying and seeing visions, in expounding the Scriptures, and in speaking with tongues. Theophilus, Tertullian, St. Jerome, Athenagoras, Chrysostom, Gregory of Nyssa, Cyprian, Dionysius of Alexandria, Athanasius, Epiphanius, and other authors of that class, abound in accounts of such wonders. But all these narratives serve only to show the want of judgment, if not the want of veracity, in those who record them; they are trifling, vain, purposeless; they bear, at least most of them, marks of fraud and imposture; and they are altogether of such a nature that, if we are asked whether we should not believe good and pious men when they relate them, we can only answer, shortly and simply, that they are incredible, and that he who relates them as credible cannot be regarded as a writer of authority.

In opposition to all this censure of the fathers as historians, which Middleton added to that of Daillé, Whitby, and Barbeyrac, who condemn them as injudicious interpreters of Scripture, and unsafe moralists, Warburton is willing to try what he can say in their behalf. He enters on his 'Julian' by observing that, as the fathers were once too much reverenced, so there has been a disposition in later times, too much to undervalue them. Though they have been too credulous, they may be competent witnesses to the state of religion in their own day. We are too apt to judge of ancient authors by a modern standard, when, if we form just notions of them, we should estimate them by the standard of their own times. Growing then very bold, he says, 'To know the true value of the fathers, we should place them by their contemporaries, the Pagan writers of greatest estimation; and, if they suffer in their neighbourhood, e'en let them stay, where most of them already are, with the grocers. But it is a fact none acquainted with antiquity will deny, how great a secret soever modern Divines may make of it, that as *polite scholars* (which is a thing their despisers now most affect to value), the Christian writers have indisputably the advantage, both in eloquence and ethics. And we may venture to say that there are some of them who have successively [successfully?] rivalled the best writers of the higher and purer antiquity. St. Chrysostom has more good sense than Plato; and the critic may find in Lactantius almost as many good words as in Tully. So that if, on the principles of a classical taste, we discard the fathers, we should send along with them the Pagan writers of the same ages; unless the wonderful theology of the latter can atone for (what they both have in common) their false rhetoric and bad reasoning.

'These imperfections, therefore, in both being equal, it is plain they were the faults of the time. For whatever advantages the ancients had over us in the arts of poetry, oratory, and history, it is certain we have over them in the science of reasoning, as far as it concerns the investigation of moral truth.' *

Having thus advocated the literary character of the fathers, setting Chrysostom above Plato, and Lactantius

* Introd. to 'Julian:' Works, vol. viii.

almost on a level with Cicero, he observes that they had no immoral intention to deceive (an assertion which, with regard to most of them, may doubtless be received as true), and proceeds to show that whether there was a general cessation of miracles after the days of the Apostles, or not, there had occurred at least one miracle since that time, of which the reality was not to be disputed. This was wrought to decide a contest between Jehovah and Baal, between Christianity and Paganism, between Jesus and Julian. The temple of Jerusalem, it was prophesied, should be destroyed; and the destruction must be final and irremediable; for, if the temple were rebuilt, and the local worship of the Jews restored, there would be an end to all the pretensions of Christianity.

Julian, detesting his uncle Constantine, detested also the religion that he professed, although, while he was still in an inferior station, he was obliged to conceal his desire to exalt its rival. When he became emperor, he manifested his love of Paganism without disguise. He was fond of Greek literature, the soul of which, he said, was the old theology, and that soul he desired to reinstate in its former position. But, in considering what means to adopt for this purpose, whether force or art, he saw that his predecessors, even when the Christians were fewer, had proved the inutility of force, which would assuredly be of still less effect now that their numbers were increased. He therefore had recourse to art; he encouraged Paganism by laws, and ordered the temples to be opened for sacrifice; he revoked the privileges and honours which his uncle and cousin had granted to the clergy, of whom he degraded and banished some of the more arrogant or rebellious; and he disqualified Christian laymen for bearing office in the state. But the most effective means which he adopted was to prohibit all professors of learning, who were of the Christian religion, from teaching in the public schools, thus detaching the youth from the influence of Christianity, and depriving Christianity of the support of profane literature. He endeavoured, at the same time, by his own writings and by personal addresses, to convince the people of the advantage of reviving the ancient superstition.

But not finding his schemes advance so rapidly as desired, he determined on confounding Jewish and Christian prophecy by rebuilding the temple at Jerusalem. When he conceived this design, he was preparing for his expedition into Persia, but his ardour for its execution would not allow him to wait till he should return. He committed the conduct of the affair, during his absence, to Alypius, a nobleman of high character for probity, learning, and versatility of talent, to whom he was greatly attached. Alypius secured the aid of the governor of Palestine, and took proper measures for the performance of the undertaking. The result is told in the well-known passage of Ammianus Marcellinus, thus translated by Warburton, whom Gibbon transcribes without acknowledgment: 'When Alypius had set himself to the vigorous execution of his charge, in which he had all the assistance that the governor of the province could afford him, horrible balls of fire breaking out near the foundations, with frequent and reiterated attacks, rendered the place from time to time inaccessible to the scorched and blasted workmen; and the victorious element continuing in this manner, obstinately and resolutely bent, as it were, to drive them to a distance, Alypius thought best to give over the enterprise.'

The occurrence is also mentioned in three writers that lived shortly after it took place, Ambrose, Chrysostom, and Gregory Nazianzen. Ambrose, who lived at a great distance from the scene, and Chrysostom, who was in the neighbourhood of it, notice the matter but slightly, merely observing that a fire, bursting from the foundations, destroyed or dispersed the workmen. But Gregory Nazianzen gives a much longer and more circumstantial history of the event. Julian assured the Jews, says he, that the time was come when they should return into their own land, and promised to restore their Temple for them to its ancient dignity and splendour. Of Alypius, and the governor of Palestine, he makes no mention; but speaks of the attempt as being wholly an effort of the Jews, who, under the Emperor's encouragement, engaged in the work of rebuilding with great ardour and resolution. But they were driven from their occupation by a violent wind and a sudden earthquake, and fled for refuge to a neighbouring church, when, as some say, the building refused their admission, the doors being shut by an invisible power, and, 'as is now affirmed and believed by all,' when they attempted to effect an entrance by force, the fire, which burst from the foundations of the Temple, met and stopped them, consuming some, and maiming others. 'But the thing most wonderful and illustrious,' he proceeds, 'was a light, which appeared in the heavens, of a cross within a circle. . . . Nay farther, they who were present and partakers of the miracle, show, to this very day, the sign or figure of the cross which was then marked or impressed upon their garments. For, at that time, as these men, whether such as were of us, or strangers, were showing these marks, or attending to others who showed them, each presently observed the wonder, either on himself or his neighbour, having a radiant mark on his body or on his garment; in which there was something that, in art and elegance, exceeded all painting or embroidery.' *

It is the latter part of this miraculous account of which Warburton labours chiefly to establish the probability. 'The light that was seen in the heavens,' he says, 'of a cross within a circle, will give us very little trouble; for it was neither more nor less than one of those meteoric lights, in a still and clouded sky, which are not

* Greg. Nazianz. orat. iv. adv. Julian. Warburton's Julian, b. ii. c. 3.

unfrequently seen in solar or lunar halos.' It was such a phenomenon as appeared to Constantine the Great, and to Cyril of Jerusalem in the time of Constantius; and appearances of the same kind have been recorded, at various times, by historians of the middle ages, who generally noticed them as miraculous, but, since the revival of learning, naturalists and astronomers have attempted to explain their physical causes. For information on this subject he refers to a treatise of J. A. Fabricius, *Exercitatio Critica, quâ disputatur Crucem, quam in cœlis vidisse se juravit Constantinus Imperator, fuisse phænomenon naturale in halone solari*,* observing that he directs the reader to it with much satisfaction; 'for,' he adds, 'it is not my way to repeat what others have proved before me, or to defraud them of the praises due to their discoveries.'

For the crosses on the garments he proceeds to account in a similar manner. The ecclesiastical historian Socrates, in his relation of the occurrence, says that 'fire,' or lightning, 'which fell from heaven, spoiled all the workmen's tools;' a circumstance which is mentioned by no other narrator of the event. Warburton, however, is pleased to take the lightning on the historian's word, and to make the most of it, 'as being,' he says, 'one of the most constant accompaniments of earthquakes and volcanic eruptions. Lightning has been known to leave the impressions of crosses on the clothes and persons of those whom it has enveloped.' To establish this fact, he produces a passage from Isaac Casaubon's 'Adversaria,' written while Casaubon was in England, and, as his son Meric, who preserved it, conjectures, about the year 1611. It gives an account of a thunderstorm, related to Casaubon by Dr. Lancelot Andrews, then Bishop of Ely, who received it from Dr. John Still, Bishop of Wells. 'In the city of Wells,' says the narrative, as translated by Warburton from Casaubon's

* Vid. Bibl. Græc. tom. vi.

Latin, 'about fifteen years ago, one summer's day, while the people were at Divine service in the cathedral church, they heard, as it thundered, two or three claps above measure dreadful, so that the whole congregation, affected alike, threw themselves on their knees at this terrifying sound. It appeared that lightning fell at the same time, but without harm to any one. So far, then, there was nothing but what was common in the like cases. The wonderful part was this, which afterwards was taken notice of by many, that the marks of a cross were found to have been imprinted on the bodies of those who were then at Divine service in the cathedral. The Bishop of Wells told my Lord of Ely that his wife (a woman of uncommon probity) came to him and informed him, as of a great miracle, that she had then the mark of a cross impressed upon her body; which tale, when the Bishop treated as absurd, his wife exposed the part and gave him ocular proof. He afterwards observed that he had upon himself, on his arm (as I take it), the plainest mark of a ×. Others had it on the shoulder, the breast, the back, or other parts. This account that great man, my Lord of Ely, gave me in such a manner as forbade me even to doubt of its truth.' *

But, lest those who doubt the reality of a miracle at the Temple of Jerusalem, should say that, though fire from heaven might imprint crosses on garments or bodies, it is mentioned only by one writer of a later date, and therefore, however frequently repeated, may never have happened, Warburton is ready with another instance to show that the same crosses may also be imprinted by fire from the earth. He finds, in Boyle's 'Discourse of Some Unheeded Causes of the Insalubrity and Salubrity of the Air,' Father Kircher's account of the eruption of Vesuvius in 1660,

* Ex Advers. Is. Casaub. apud Meric. Casaub. in Tract. intit. 'Of Credulity and Incredulity,' p. 118; Warburton's Julian, book ii. c. 3.

which was followed by the appearance of crosses on the clothes of many of the people in the country. 'These crosses,' says Boyle, 'were seen on linen garments, as shirt-sleeves, women's aprons, that had lain open to the air, and upon the exposed parts of sheets; which is the less to be admired, because, as Kircher fairly guesses, the mineral vapours were, by the texture that belongs to linen (which consists of threads crossing one another, for the most part at or near right angles), easily determined to run along in almost straight lines crossing each other, and consequently to frame spots resembling, some one, and some another, kind of crosses. These were extremely numerous in the several parts of the kingdom of Naples; insomuch that the Jesuit, who sent the relation to Kircher, says that he himself found thirty in one altar-cloth, that fifteen were found upon the smock-sleeve of a woman, and that he reckoned eight in a boy's band; also their colour and magnitude were very unequal, and their figures discrepant, as may appear by many pictures of them drawn by the relator; they would not wash out with simple water, but required soap; their duration was also unequal, some lasting ten or fifteen days, and others longer, before they disappeared.' *

'Thus,' remarks Warburton, 'these Vesuvian crosses, proceeding from terrestrial fire, were impressed only on the garments; the crosses at Wells, proceeding from the lightning, only on persons' bodies; while the Julian crosses appeared on both; and the reader may therefore, if he thinks proper, in regard to the fire at Jerusalem, consider that the crosses on the bodies were caused by the lightning, and the crosses on the garments by the flames from the ground.'

Such are the efforts that Warburton makes to render it probable that the fiery eruption at Jerusalem was a

* Boyle's Works, folio, vol. iv. p. 293.

miracle. But the truth is, that the nearer he allies its effects to those of natural phænomena, the more he detracts from the likelihood that it was miraculous. Nor must all the circumstances from which he argues be considered to have been certainly attendant on the event. The earthquake is mentioned only by Christian writers;* the lightning is mentioned only by one of those writers; and, when these two concomitants are withdrawn, there remains only Ammianus's eruption of horrible balls of fire. This, as some, whom Warburton feels himself obliged to notice, contend, may have been produced by some artificial contrivance of the Christians. 'It is said the Egyptians, from the earliest times, had the secret of making combustible materials in such a manner as to produce the effects of exploded gunpowder,' and 'that Sir William Temple, Lord Herbert of Cherbury, and an abler man than either of them, Sir Thomas Browne, of Norwich, have dropped hints as if some of the greatest wonders, both in sacred and profane antiquity, were the effects of this destructive composition.'† Basnage, whom Warburton attempts to refute, concludes, in his 'History of the Jews,'‡ from the variations and contradictions in the different accounts of the occurrence, that it was not only no miracle, but an affair of much less magnitude and importance than is generally supposed. Gibbon observes that, however satisfactory the statement of Marcellinus may appear, 'a philosopher may still require the original evidence of impartial and intelligent spectators;' and argues from the silence of Jerome, as Basnage argues from that of Cyril, both of whom lived at the time, that 'the story which was celebrated at a distance might be despised on the spot.' Jortin, on the contrary, in his 'Remarks on Ecclesiastical History,'§ declares himself of opinion that a miracle was really

* Julian, book ii. c. 2.
† Julian, book ii. c. 5.
‡ Tom. viii. pp. 157-168.
§ Vol. i. p. 297.

wrought, observing that 'the defeat of Julian's attempt to rebuild the Temple may justly be ascribed to a particular providence.' In this belief he concurs with Walter Moyle, whom he quotes, and who calls the occurrence at Jerusalem *a miracle so fully attested that he does not see with what forehead anyone can question the truth of it.** Lardner,† on the contrary, rejects the whole story of the affair, denying that any attempt was ever made by Julian to rebuild the Temple; for Julian, in his 'Letter to the Community of the Jews,' written when he was about to enter on the Persian war, merely promises that, if he terminated that war successfully, *he would then rebuild the Temple*; but, as he never returned from Persia, he could therefore never have set about rebuilding the Temple. He adds that Ammianus Marcellinus was credulous, and might have taken the account from the Christians without examination; that the history of the pretended miracle is loaded with trifling circumstances inconsistent with the Divine Majesty; and that there are two writers of that period, Jerome and Prudentius, as well as Orosius, who lived about fifty years later, that make no mention of the pretended miracle; nor does Cyril, in his books against Julian, allude at all to any miraculous defeat of the Emperor, though, had such an event occurred, it would have been much to his purpose to make the most of it.

Warburton had intended to divide his 'Discourse' into three parts: the first, to establish the truth of the miracle by human testimony; the second, to answer objections; and the third, to inquire what evidence will justify a reasonable man in giving credit to a miraculous fact. The second part he thought might be 'a little ticklish.'‡ The third part, like the third part of 'The Divine Legation,' was never written. He, indeed, glanced again at the

* Moyle's Works, vol. ii. pp. 100, 289.

† Jewish and Heathen Testimonies, vol. iv. p. 47, seq.

‡ Letter to Doddridge, June 15, 1750.

subject in his 'Sermon on the Resurrection,'* observing that 'a miracle, well attested by human authority, is one of the most legitimate objects of belief.' But the fulness with which he enlarged on the first two heads rendered it quite superfluous for him to say much on the third.

Hurd's revision of Julian may have been of some advantage to its style, which is more temperate and correct than that of some of Warburton's other works. Warburton charged Hurd to be very severe before publication, and very indulgent afterwards.†

He was delighted with the attention that the work received in France. 'It has procured me,' said he, 'the goodwill of the best and greatest man in France,' the Duc de Noailles, 'while there is hardly a nobleman in England knows I have written such a book.'‡ Montesquieu, also, in a letter to Charles Yorke, said, 'When you see Dr. Warburton, pray let him know the satisfaction I propose to myself in making a farther acquaintance with him, and in taking a nearer view of his great talents. His Julian charms me.'§ But the book 'had the fate of the author's other writings,' says Hurd, 'to be censured at home.' The attacks on it, however, were far less numerous than those which had been made on 'The Divine Legation,' and are of too little importance to require notice. Sykes menaced an assault, but did nothing. Philip Nichols, Warburton's bitter foe, declared that he had been anticipated by Dr. John Spencer in proving Julian to have been defeated by a miracle, and said what he could besides against the book. 'Sykes threatened,' said Warburton, in a letter to Balguy, 'to draw his redoubtable pen upon poor Julian; but he left the execution to another. And who do you think that other proves? Somebody or other, by far

* Disc. xxix. Works, vol. x. p. 225.

† Letter to Hurd, Aug. 19, 1749.

‡ Letter to Hurd.

§ Hurd's Life of Warburton, p. 53.

more curious than myself, would unearth this vermin; and he is found to be one Nichols, which your University some time ago prosecuted for stealing their books; or rather should have prosecuted. Have I not reason to blame you for your ill-timed clemency? Had they hanged him, as Justice called upon them to do, my book had been safe. It is true he has not fulfilled the old proverb, but rather contributed to a new one, Save a rogue from the gallows, and—he will endeavour to save his fellow. I had gibbeted up Julian, and he comes by night to cut him down.'

But we must not take leave of 'Julian' before we notice certain remarks on mathematics and mathematicians which the author has inserted in his Introduction. He thought that on the study of the mathematics irreligion was a general attendant. 'The mathematicians,' he says to Hurd, 'declare that what happened at the attempt to rebuild the Temple was a natural event. This tribe of men—I do not mean the inventors and geniuses among them, whom I honour, but the demonstrators of others' inventions, who are ten times duller and prouder than a damn'd poet—have a strange aversion to anything that smacks of religion.'*

There are considered to be, he says, two great instruments or aids for the discovery and establishment of truth—logic and mathematics. As to logic, it is in practice, he asserts, more a trick than a science; that we may apply to the art of syllogism what Butler has observed of the art of rhetoric, that it only teaches us to name the tools which nature had before given us, and of which habit had taught us the use; that all its real virtue consists in the compendious detection of a fallacy; that its true value is now well known, and that it is, therefore, unnecessary to put it lower in general estimation.

'However,' he proceeds, 'what logic hath lost of its

* Letters from an Eminent Prelate, let. xix.

credit, mathematics have gained; and geometry is now supposed to do wonders as well in the system of man as of matter. It must be owned, the real virtue it hath, it had acquired long since; for, by what is left us of antiquity, we see how elegantly it was then handled, and how sublimely it was pursued. But the truth is, all its use, for the purpose in question, besides what hath been already mentioned, seems to be only habituating the mind to think long and closely; and it would be well if this advantage made amends for some inconveniences, as inseparable from its study. It may seem, perhaps, too much a paradox to say that long habit in this science incapacitates the mind for reasoning at large, and especially in the search of moral truth. And yet, I believe, nothing is more certain. The object of geometry is demonstration; its subject admits of it, and is almost the only subject that doth. In this science, whatever is not demonstration, goes for nothing, or is, at least, below the sublime inquirer's regard. Probability, through its almost infinite degrees, from simple doubt up to absolute certainty, is the *terra incognita* of the geometer. And yet here it is that the great business of the human mind, the search and discovery of all the important truths which concern us as reasonable beings, is carried on. And here, too, it is that all its vigour is exerted; for to proportion the assent to the probability accompanying every varying degree of moral evidence, requires the most enlarged and sovereign exercise of reason. But as to excel in the use of anything, the habit must always be in proportion to the difficulty, it seems very unlikely that the geometer (long confined to the routine of demonstration, the easiest exercise of reason, where much less of the vigour than of the attention of mind is required to excel) should form a right judgment on subjects whose truth or falsehood is to be rated on the degrees of moral evidence. I venture to call mathematics the easiest exercise of reason, on the authority of Cicero, who observes that *scarce any man ever set himself upon this study, who did not make what progress in it he pleased.** But, besides acquired inability, prejudice renders the veteran mathematician still less capable of judging of moral evidence. He who hath been so long accustomed to lay together and compare ideas, and hath reaped demonstration, the richest fruit of speculative truth, for his labour, regards all the lower degrees of evidence as in the train only of his mathematical principality; and he commonly ranks them in so arbitrary a manner that the *ratio ultima mathematicorum* is become almost as great a libel upon common sense as other sovereign decisions. I might appeal for the truth of this to those wonderful conclusions which geometers, when condescending to write on history, ethics, or theology, have made from their premises. But the thing is notorious, and it is now no secret that the oldest mathematician in England is the worst reasoner in it. But I would not be mistaken as undervaluing the many useful discoveries made from time to time in moral matters by professed mathematicians. Nor will any one so mistake me, who does not first confound the genius and the geometer; and then conclude that which was the achievement of his wit was the result of his theorems.'†

He had previously aimed a similar blow at Sir Isaac Newton in 'The Divine Legation:'‡ 'What is it to truth, what a courtier judges of a church, a politician of conscience, or a geometer, grown grey in *demonstration*, of *moral evidence*?'

Whether these expressions influenced Gibbon when he delivered his judgment on mathematics, is uncertain; but the thought is very similar in both writers. Gibbon says that mathematics 'harden the mind by the habit of rigid

* De Orat. lib. i. c. 1.

† Introd. to 'Julian,' p. xiv.

‡ B. v. sect. iv. Works, vol. v. p. 134.

demonstration, so destructive to the finer feelings of moral evidence, which must determine the actions and opinions of our lives.' He, therefore, relinquished the study before this effect was produced upon him.

Whoever is of opinion with these two authors, will be inclined to question whether it is right, in any public place for general education, that young men should be called upon to devote three or four of the best years of their lives, at a season the most important for training and forming the mind, to the *almost exclusive* study of the mathematics. They who believe that mathematics have that influence on the mind which Warburton and Gibbon impute to them, will question whether young men intended for the church, or the bar, or the senate, are not injured, rather than benefited, by the devotion of so long a period of time to mathematical studies. It is true that the requisition to study mathematics, to a great extent, in those places of education, may be said to be, though strong, not absolute; the students may give but a comparatively moderate portion of their time to mathematics, and devote the greater portion to other studies; but this, with young men of ambition, who are desirous to attain honours and distinctions in their university before they leave it, is not likely to be the case, as long as those honours and distinctions depend principally, if not wholly, on proficiency in mathematics. Or it may be said that they may allot the time which they are to spend at the university before taking their degrees, to mathematics, and may then relinquish the study altogether, and give themselves up to the other pursuits which they may think more necessary for their career in public life ; but then it must be inquired whether the years which have thus been employed on mathematics have not been in a great degree wasted, and whether the students would not enter on public life with better qualifications, and with a better prospect of success, if they had devoted the time spent in mathematical investigations to studies of a literary nature, to the perusal of the great authors in their own and other languages, and to exercise in composition, in writing, or speaking, in which many young men, after long residence at a university, are lamentably deficient.

It must be granted that mathematics have the virtue which Warburton allows them, the power of habituating the mind to close and patient thought. It is not to be forgotten that Plato deemed geometry of so much importance as a preparative to manly studies, that he wrote on the door of his gymnasium, *let no one ignorant of geometry enter.* But Plato seems to have thought, and it is *for us* to consider, whether we ought not to think also, that mathematical or geometrical training should be received in boyhood, and should then be quitted by those who do not intend to continue mathematicians all their lives, for those other studies, philosophical and literary, which are to fit a young man for his career in civil employments.

It is argued by those who defend the present devotion to mathematical studies at the university, that young men who prove themselves able to pursue long investigations in the higher mathematics, who master large portions of Newton's 'Principia,' or other difficult mathematical works, prove their capacity for accomplishing anything whatever. They may prove their capacity, perhaps, for accomplishing anything whatever in mathematics, but, if they are not to be mere mathematicians *for ever*, it is worthy of consideration whether they might not have proved their capacity better in some other kind of mental exercise.

Those, indeed, who, like Warburton and Gibbon, object to mathematics as a means of cultivating the mind, without having made any great progress in the study themselves, are always liable to the retort, *Damnant quod non intelligunt.* But the question is in reality a question of common sense. If long attention to the mathematics, far from expanding the entire powers of the mind, and extending its views of things in general, tends rather to contract and *incapacitate it for reasoning at large,—for the most extensive and sovereign exercise of reason* (a charge which mathematicians themselves have never been able to refute),—how is it fit that young men, at a most influential period of life, should be confined to the study of that which rather disqualifies than prepares them for what they will have to do in after years? Buonaparte hoped to find that La Place, the greatest of mathematicians, would prove one of the most valuable of ministers, but discovered that his previous studies had unfitted him for the ordinary duties of office, and was obliged to let him conceal his deficiencies in a sinecure.

Sir Benjamin Brodie, after observing that to reason well seems the result of faculties originally implanted in us by nature, expresses great doubts whether mathematics, however they may strengthen the power of attention, tend to improve the judgment on those subjects to which they are not immediately applicable;* and adduces support to his belief from the authority of Dugald Stewart, who had remarked the weakness of judgment in mathematicians, and said that he had never met with a mere mathematician who was not credulous to a fault, not only with respect to human testimony, but also in matters of opinion.† And Charles Butler was so convinced of the incompatibility of mathematical studies with other pursuits, that, though he saw a world of intellectual gratification in them, he soon found it would be his duty, if he was to do anything else, to turn his attention from them altogether.‡

As to the discovery of truth, mathematics, it is evident, can discover no truth but in their own department; and, if

* Psychological Inquiries, dial. i. p. 27.

† D. Stewart's Moral Philosophy, vol. iii. p. 280.

‡ Charles Butler's Reminiscences, vol. i. p. 253.

the study of them *destroys the finer feelings of moral evidence*, it disqualifies for the discovery of truth in most other branches of inquiry.

The sum of what is said in favour of mathematical studies, as a beneficial training for the mind, may be considered as contained in the following words of Dr. Thomas Brown:* 'Those precise definitions which insure to every word the same exact signification in the mind of everyone who hears it pronounced, and that lucid progress, in the development of truth after truth, which gives, even to ordinary powers, almost the same facility of comprehension with the highest genius, are unquestionably of the utmost benefit to the mathematical student while he is prosecuting his particular study, without any contemplation of other advantages to be reaped from them. But there can be no doubt that they are, at the same time, preparing his mind for excellence in other inquiries, of which he has then no conception; that he will ever after be less ready to employ, and be more quicksighted than he could otherwise have been in detecting, vague and indefinite phraseology, and loose and incoherent reasoning.' But if these advantages of the study be counterbalanced by inconveniences; if the mind be hardened and cramped by it; and if it be no due preparation, but rather the contrary, for the ordinary pursuits of public life, it still remains a question whether young men, at an age when,

— as the twig is bent, the tree's inclin'd,

should be kept under mathematical influence at any university for so long a period.

* Philosophy of the Human Mind, lect. v.

CHAPTER XXII.

MIDDLETON. EDITION OF POPE. EVANS'S PROPHECIES.

CHARACTER OF CONYERS MIDDLETON'S WRITINGS — WARBURTON'S THOUGHTS RESPECTING HIM — SIR ROBERT SUTTON'S SON — WARBURTON'S EDITION OF POPE; HURD'S OPINION OF IT — AKENSIDE'S ODE TO EDWARDS — JOHN GILBERT COOPER; WARBURTON'S NOTE ON THE DUNCIAD CONCERNING HIM — REMARKS ON WARBURTON'S NOTES ON POPE — 'NEW BOOK OF THE DUNCIAD' — PROPHECIES OF ARISE EVANS — JORTIN AND WARBURTON — 'CONFUSION WORSE CONFOUNDED' —SECOND EDITION OF 'JULIAN'—HURD VISITS ALLEN — ANECDOTES OF QUIN AND WARBURTON.

DR. MIDDLETON did not live long enough to make any reply to this work of Warburton's, even if he had been as well inclined to do so as he was to repel Church and Dodwell, who were made Doctors of Divinity for attacking him. He was preparing answers against these two adversaries, names now forgotten, when he fell ill, and died in July of this year. His character as an English writer, generally accurate, but not very animated or attractive, is well known. His 'Free Inquiry,' and his 'Letter from Rome,' like his assault on Sherlock's book on Prophecy, are said to have arisen from his resentment at being disappointed of church preferment. He left behind him several memoranda for tracts of an equally unfavourable tendency towards the Christian religion. One of these, which he nearly or quite completed, was a treatise on 'The Inefficacy and Inutility of Prayer,' which was shown to Lord Bolingbroke, who approved it, and was anxious that it should be published; but Middleton's widow retained it in manuscript as long as she lived, and

Dr. Heberden, to whom she bequeathed her papers, put it into the fire.* When a friend condoled with him that he had not been made a bishop, he replied, 'Well, Sir, as they have not thought fit to trust me, I am at liberty to speak my mind.' He professed to have but a moderate desire for the temporal bread of the Church, and to be ready to be satisfied with anything but mere emptiness. His great wish, as he declared to Lord Hervey, in a letter written fifteen years before his death, was to see religion reconciled with reason, or, where that cannot be, to have them brought as near together as possible.† Hurd affects to depreciate him as a theologian, saying that his knowledge of divinity was but slight, and his talents unsuited to excel in that science; but Hurd was little inclined to commend anyone whom Warburton opposed, and might have spoken otherwise of Middleton's knowledge had he been on the other side of the question.

Warburton, writing to Hurd, at the time that Middleton's death was expected, says: 'Had he had, I will not say piety, but greatness of mind enough not to suffer the pretended injuries of some churchmen to prejudice him against religion, I should love him living, and honour him when dead. Good God! that man, for the discourtesies done him by his miserable fellow-creatures, should be content to divest himself of the true viaticum, the comfort, the solace, the asylum from all the evils of human life, is perfectly astonishing.' ‡ And in a letter to Jortin, just after Dr. Middleton died, he says he had heard from Cambridge that he had 'declared he should die with that composure of mind which he thought must be the enjoyment of every man who had been a sincere searcher after truth; expressed some concern that he felt his strength and spirits

* Bishop Newton's Life, by Himself, p. 24.

† Nichols's Lit. An. vol. v. p. 421.

‡ Letters from an Eminent Prelate, p. 54.

decline so fast, that he could not complete some designs he had then in hand [the answers to Church and Dodwell]; and that he imagined he had given the miracles of the early ages such a blow as they would not easily recover.'

'I do not see,' remarks Warburton on this intelligence, 'how the mere discovery of truth affords such pleasure. If this truth be, that the providence of God governs the moral as well as natural world, and that, in compassion to human distresses, He has revealed His will to mankind, by which we are enabled to get the better of them by a restoration to his favour, I can easily conceive the pleasure that, at any period of life, must accompany such a discovery. But if the truth discovered be, that we have no farther share in God than as we partake of his natural government of the universe, or that all there is in his moral government is only the natural, necessary effects of virtue and vice upon human agents here, and that all the pretended revelations of an hereafter were begot by fools and hurried up by knaves; if this, I say, be our boasted discovery, it must, I think, prove a very uncomfortable contemplation, especially in our last hours. But every man has his taste. I only speak for myself. All that I hope and wish is, that the scribblers will let his memory alone; for though (after the approbation of the good and wise) one cannot wish anything better for one's self or one's friend, than to be heartily abused by them in this life, because it is as certain a sign of one's merit as a dog's barking at the moon is of her brightness, yet the veil that death draws over us is so sacred that the throwing dirt there has been esteemed at all times, and by all people, a profanation. If the Romans suffered their slaves to abuse their heroes on the day of triumph, they would have regarded the same ribaldries with horror at their funerals.'

Warburton also recommended, about this time, a son of his old patron, Sir Robert Sutton, to the notice of

Hurd, as the most extraordinary boy that he ever knew. The youth was then going to Cambridge, after having been some time at the head of Westminster School. 'Besides his knowledge of the ancient languages,' said Warburton, 'he speaks and writes Spanish and French with great exactness, understands Italian, and is now learning High Dutch. I believe the acquaintance and friendship of so promising a youth will be a pleasure to you.' Dr. Nicoll, who was then Master of Westminster School, said that he never met with his fellow.* 'But Westminster,' he remarks in a subsequent letter, in which he thanks Hurd for having noticed him, 'has made his mind a little whimsical. He has an insatiable thirst after new languages. Pray check this in him. He wrote me word, the other day, he had a mind to study Arabic. I asked him whether the oratory of the writer of 'Pocock's Life' had won upon him, who, in an earnest address to youth to apply themselves to this charming language, assures them, as the height of their solace and consolation, that it contains twelve millions three hundred and fifty thousand fifty and two words. I told him I consented he should learn the odd *two*, provided he chose those two which signified the *ne plus* of the Latins.

'Were I,' he adds, 'to be the reformer of Westminster School (with the highest reverence be it only whispered), I would order that every boy should have impressed upon his accidence, in great gold letters, as on the back of the horn-book, that oracle of Hobbes, that *words are the counters of wise men, and the money of fools.* †

The young man relinquished the pursuit of words for a different sort of occupation; for Hurd, in 1761, speaks of him, on receiving a visit from him at Thurcaston, as being intent on the study and practice of the law, but preserving the same sweetness of temper, and simplicity of manners,

* Letters from an Eminent Prelate, pp. 52, 62. † Ib. p. 75.

that had distinguished his earlier years. * He succeeded to the title on the death of his father.

In 1751 came forth the complete edition of Pope's Works, with such annotations as Warburton thought proper to attach to them. It is amusing to read Hurd's opinion of this publication. 'He appeared again as a critic and commentator in the noble edition he gave of Mr. Pope's Works. And as here there was no room for emendatory criticism, of all others the easiest to be misapplied or misconstrued, so the public found very little to censure on this occasion. Indeed, the main object of the edition being to do justice to his friend, it was natural for him to exert his whole force upon it; and as none can define so happily of a poet's meaning as the well-exercised critic, if he be at the same time of a congenial spirit with his author, it is no wonder that he made this (what I formerly said of it, and still think it to be) *the best edition that was ever given of any classic.*'

It would not have been easy, in the same number of words, to give more commendation less in conformity with truth. The public soon *found very much to censure on the occasion.* The *main object of the edition* was *not to do justice to Warburton's friend*, but to make a display of Warburton's own powers of writing comments. The critic was so far from being of *a congenial spirit with his author*, that it would hardly be possible to produce two minds less congenial. And the edition itself, so far from being the best that was ever given of a classic, is, in regard to the importance of the annotations, one of the very worst.

One of the most offensive peculiarities in the edition was the liberty that Warburton had taken to insert in the notes, especially those on the 'Dunciad,' sarcasms on anyone that had incurred his dislike. He boldly said that he

* Letters from an Eminent Prelate, p. 324.

made the notes his instruments for chastising his adversaries. 'I once saw,' says Disraeli, 'a great literary curiosity; some proof-sheets of "The Dunciad" of Warburton's edition. I observed that some of the bitterest notes were after-thoughts, written on those proof-sheets after he had prepared the book for the press. One of these additions was his note on Edwards. Thus Pope's book afforded renewed opportunities for all the personal hostilities of this singular genius.'* The edition was not unfairly characterised by Akenside in the following 'Ode to Thomas Edwards, Esq.,' which the poet published, as soon as the work appeared, with Warburton's early letter to Concanen appended:

Believe me, Edwards, to restrain
  The license of a railer's tongue,
Is what but seldom men obtain
  By sense or wit, by prose or song:
A task for more Herculean pow'rs,
Nor suited to the sacred hours
Of leisure in the Muses' bow'rs.

In bow'rs, where laurels wed with palm,
  The Muse, the blameless queen, resides,
Fair Fame attends, and Wisdom calm
  Her eloquence harmonious guides;
While shut for ever from her gate,
Oft trying, still repining, wait
Fierce Envy, and calumnious Hate.

Who then from her delightful bounds
  Would step one moment forth to heed
What impotent and savage sounds
  From their unhappy mouth proceed?
No; rather Spenser's lyre again
Prepare, and let thy pious strain
For Pope's dishonour'd shade complain.

---

* Quarrels of Authors, art. Warburton.

Tell how displeas'd was every bard,
  When lately in th' Elysian grove
They of his Muse's guardian heard,
  His delegate to fame above,
And what with one accord they said
Of Wit in drooping age misled,
And Warburton's officious aid :

How Virgil mourn'd the sordid fate
  To that melodious lyre assign'd,
Beneath a tutor who so late
  With Midas and his rout combin'd,
By spiteful clamour, to confound
That very lyre's enchanting sound,
Though list'ning realms admir'd around :

How Horace own'd he thought the fire
  Of his friend Pope's satiric line
Did farther fuel scarce require
  From such a militant divine:
How Milton scorn'd the sophist vain
Who durst approach his hallow'd strain
With unwash'd hands and lips profane.

Then Shakspeare, debonnair and mild,
  Brought that strange comment forth to view;
'Conceits more deep,' he said, and smil'd,
  'Than his own fools or madmen knew;'
But thank'd a generous friend above,
Who did, with free adventurous love,
Such pageants from his tomb remove.

And if to Pope, in equal need,
  The same kind office thou wouldst pay,
Then, Edwards, all the band decreed
  That future bards with frequent lay
Should call on thy auspicious name,
From each absurd intruder's claim
To keep inviolate their fame.

One person on whom Warburton let loose his vengeance in this edition was John Gilbert Cooper, author of the 'Life of Socrates,' 'Letters on Taste,' and some other light publications; a gentleman of fair classical scholarship, having been educated at Westminster under Dr. Nicoll, and well acquainted with the French and Italian languages, and with the literature of his own country. But he had no great force as a writer, and was pronounced by Burke an insufferable coxcomb. According to Malone, he was one of the 'sentimental benevolists,' who expressed unbounded admiration of virtue, but whose feelings affected only their words, having no influence at all on their practice. He was the man, as related by Boswell, whom Mr. Fitzherbert found under violent apprehension, as it seemed, about his son, who was at a school near London, manifesting such dread lest the boy should be ill or dying, as to appear beyond all reach of consolation. At length he exclaimed to Mr. Fitzherbert, 'I'll write an elegy.' Mr. Fitzherbert, being thus enabled to guess the depth of his emotions, disconcerted him by rejoining, 'Had you not better take a post-chaise, and go and see him?'

He was a little fat man, mixed a good deal in society, and took every opportunity of depreciating Johnson, declaring him 'nothing more than a literary Caliban.' When this was repeated to Johnson, he said, 'Well, then, you must allow that he is a literary Punchinello.' Dr. Warton, one day, dining with Johnson and Burke, said something in Cooper's favour, observing that 'he was at least very well informed, and a good scholar.' 'Yes,' said Johnson, 'it cannot be denied that he has good materials for playing the fool; and he makes abundant use of them.' *

He had made some remarks, in his 'Life of Socrates,' in which he was assisted by Dr. John Jackson, who agreed with him in nothing but in hating Warburton, unfavourable to Warburton's notions about certain of the ancient philosophers, and Warburton retorted, in a note on the 'Essay on Criticism,' on the lines,

> The generous critic fann'd the poet's fire,
> And taught the world with reason to admire,

---

* Prior's Life of Malone, p. 427; Croker's Boswell, vol. vi. p. 289.

in the following note: 'For, as *ignorance*, when joined with *humility*, produces stupid admiration, on which account it is so commonly observed to be the *mother of devotion* and blind homage, so, when joined with vanity (as it always is in bad critics), it gives birth to every iniquity of impudent abuse and slander. See an example (for want of a better) in a late worthless and now forgotten thing called the *Life of Socrates*, where the head of the author (as a man of wit observed on reading the book) has just made a shift to do the office of a *camera obscura*, and represent things in an inverted order, himself *above*, and Sprat, Rollin, Voltaire, and every other author of reputation, *below*.'

To this *abuse* Cooper replied in a very weak pamphlet; and indeed it is to be observed of all the replies to Warburton, with but two or three exceptions, that they were weapons of very little strength or sharpness. He, however, not unhappily, called Warburton's comments on Pope 'an indigested heap of learned and unlearned lumber, huddled together from the motley dregs of desultory reading;' and asked him how the 'Life of Socrates,' if it were a thing forgotten, could serve the world for an example. He also reproached him, very justly, with his 'unprovoked treatment' of Akenside, and with being unable to speak of any opponent without abuse. He likewise noticed, with due reprehension, his malicious perversion of 'his master's commendation' of Foster:

> Let modest Foster, if he will, excel
> Ten Metropolitans in preaching well,*

'a commendation so plain,' observes Cooper, 'that one would imagine it was out of the power of dulness to mistake, or the most prejudiced partiality to dare to misinterpret;' yet Mr. Warburton has endeavoured to turn it into satire. 'This confirms,' says he, in a note on the lines,

* Epilogue to the Latins, dial. i. ver. 131.

'an observation which Mr. Hobbes made long ago, that *there be very few bishops that act a sermon so well as divers presbyterians and fanatic preachers do.*'

Such kind of comment, it must be allowed, was a breach of trust to him who had confided his works to Warburton's care. Yet Hurd could speak of 'such a poet being *improved* by such a critic,' and 'cannot enough rejoice at Warburton's editions of our two great poets.' * Walpole was nearer the truth when he called the edition of Pope 'a ridiculous edition.'† Walpole also declares that Warburton, under annoyance from the 'Canons of Criticism,' cancelled, in passing the edition through the press, above a hundred sheets on which he had written notes ;‡ and Mr. Cunningham, in a remark on the passage, says that this is 'curiously confirmed by papers which he had seen in Mr. Croker's possession.'

Many copies of satirical verses were published on this edition of Pope, which were afterwards collected into a pamphlet, entitled 'Verses occasioned by Mr. Warburton's late edition of Mr. Pope's Works.' The following specimens will show the nature of them :

As on the margin of Thames' silver flood
Stand little necessary piles of wood,
So Pope's fair page appears with notes disgrac'd :
Put down the nuisances, ye men of taste.

Close to the grotto of the Twickenham bard,
Too close, adjoins a tanner's yard :
So verse and prose are to each other tied,
So Warburton and Pope allied.

The frontispiece to the edition, also, in which Warburton's bust is larger and more prominent than Pope's, gave

* Letters from an Eminent Prelate, pp. 144, 214.

† Detached Thoughts, Works, vol. iv. p. 371.

‡ Letter to Geo. Montague, June 13, 1751 ; Cunningham's edition of Walpole's Letters, vol. ii. p. 257.

rise to satirical observations. Blakey, who made the drawing for the engraver, told Burke it was by Warburton's express desire that he made him the principal figure, and Pope only secondary, and caused the light to go upward, contrary to the rules of art, from Warburton to Pope. A gentleman who was present when Burke was speaking on the subject, said it was remarkable, too, that the poet and the commentator are looking in different directions.*

Cooper, before he composed his pamphlet, wrote to Warburton, saying that he thought himself very ill used in the note, and intimating an intention of taking public notice of it. Warburton, it appears, vouchsafed no answer to the letter, but told a friend of Cooper's he was surprised the writer should think himself ill used, for he had never mentioned his name or his publications but with commendation, until he wrote a book in which he treated him *with a scurrility worse than Billingsgate*, when all the revenge he took was *the casual mention of the author of the Life of Socrates, with a slight joke.*

'Scurrility worse than Billingsgate' is too strong a term. Sneers there certainly are in the book, which speaks of 'the renowned Mr. Warburton's great sagacity,' and 'parade of explication' on Virgil, and reproaches him for his ignorance in not knowing that Aristophanes was guiltless of the death of Socrates. But the writer stops short of abuse. He, however, does not hesitate, like Warburton himself, to speak contemptuously of great men. Spinosa and Hobbes he calls 'wretches,' and Sprat's 'History of the Royal Society' 'fustian.'

Another satirical publication on Warburton's Pope, which we may notice here, was entitled 'A New Book of the Dunciad, occasioned by Mr. Warburton's New Edition of the Dunciad, by a Gentleman of one of the Inns of

* Prior's Life of Malone, p. 370.

Court.' It is but a weak imitation of Pope's versification, yet has some lines worthy of notice. The subject is the dethronement of Cibber, and the enthronement of Warburton in his place: 'Great Dunce the Second yields to Dunce the Third.' Dulness is represented lying asleep, and Colley near her, when a jovial throng, in which are Knapton and three other booksellers, bearing Warburton on a chair, burst in and awake them:

> 'Down with King Cibber,' was the general cry,
> 'Down with King Cibber,' all Moorfields reply;
> Huzza, huzza! King Warburton 's our own;
> Be he our king, be his King Colley's throne.

Cibber sneaks off at the din, and Warburton is to be enthroned. He is led to the throne by four audacious forms:

> The first was *Impudence*, with dauntless eye,
> With face of brass, and stare that look'd a lie;
> The second *Pedantry*, whose words profess'd
> All skill, all science, and yet none possess'd;
> The third *Scurrility*, whose envious tongue
> With loud abuse and scandal ever rung;
> The fourth proud *Vanity*, puff'd up with air,
> With glass reflecting each self-virtue clear.

When he is seated, Mason and Hurd place the crown on his head. He makes a speech of thanks, and the poem concludes.

During this year Warburton sent forth a few pages which afterwards brought upon him much ridicule.

Jortin was at this time preparing for the press the first volume of his 'Remarks on Ecclesiastical History,' and, in speaking of fancied prophetic dreams and visions, took occasion to mention, with others, those of a Welshman named Rice, Ap-Rice, or Arise Evans, who wandered from his native mountains to London in the time of Oliver Cromwell, where he made pretences to inspiration, and, setting at nought the power of the Round-heads, uttered predictions in favour of the Royalists. In 1652 he published a small book called 'An Eccho from Heaven,' in which his hallucinations were fully set forth. Desiring to know more of this pseudo-prophet, Jortin applied to Warburton, observing that he had heard some of his friends speak of one prophecy of Evans's 'in terms of astonishment.' Warburton, happening to have Evans's book, sent Jortin an extract from it, 'containing,' he said, 'a prophecy which astonishes all who carefully consider it.' This extract, with Warburton's remarks on it, Jortin too easily consented to attach as an Appendix to his volume. 'By some fatality,' says a writer of that day, 'he was duped to accept of a postscript to the first volume of "Ecclesiastical Remarks," exhibiting the visions of a Welsh prophet, with the commentaries of Warburton upon them.'* 'So much more mischief,' says Dr. Disney, in his 'Life of Jortin,' 'does the ill-judging friendship of some men effect than their resentments can accomplish, that Mr. Jortin has lost more credit by the admission of these few pages of Mr. Warburton's than if this imagined Colossus had replied to every line of the "Remarks," or 'whipped him at the cart's tail in a note to "The Divine Legation," the ordinary place of his literary executions, or pilloried him in the "Dunciad," another engine which, as legal proprietor, he very ingeniously and judiciously applied to the same purpose.'†

Let us see what this extract, which caused so much mischief, was. It was entitled 'A Vision that I had presently after the King's Death:'

'I thought,' says Evans, 'I was in a great Hall, like the Shire Hall in the Castle in Winchester, and there was none there but a judge, that sat upon the bench, and

* Disney's Life of Jortin, p. 88. Lowth's Letter to Warburton, p. 4.

† Collection of Letters and Essays in favour of Public Liberty, vol. iii. p. 263.

myself; and, as I turned to a window north-westward, and looking into the palm of my hand, there appeared to me a face, head, and shoulders, like the Lord Fairfax's, and presently it vanished again; then arose the Lord Cromwell, and he vanished likewise; then arose a young face, and he had a crown upon his head, and he vanished also; and another young face arose with a crown on his head, and he vanished also; and another young face arose with a crown upon his head, and he vanished also; and another young face arose with a crown upon his head, and vanished in like manner. And as I turned the palm of my hand back again to me, and looked, there did appear no more in it. Then I turned to the judge, and said to him, There arose in my hand seven, and five of them had crowns; but when I turned my hand, the blood turned to its veins, and there appeared no more; so I awoke.

'The interpretation of this vision is, that after the Lord Cromwell there shall be KINGS again in ENGLAND, which thing is signified unto us by those who arose after him, who were all crowned; but the generations to come may look for a change of the blood and of the name in the royal seat, after five kings' reigns once passed. 2 Kings x. 30.' [The words of this text are: 'And the Lord said unto Jehu, Because thou hast done well in executing that which is right in mine eyes . . . thy children of the fourth generation shall sit on the throne of Israel.']

Such is Arise Evans's prophetic vision. Warburton, treating it as an inspired prediction, annexes to it this elaborate explanation:

'The restoration of the monarchy is here plainly predicted; together with the crown's passing from the House of Stuart into another family. But the prophet, at first sight, appears to be doubtful about the number of reigns before that event. He reckons up in his hand only *four* successions to the monarchy; yet in his speech to the judge he calls them *five*; in his interpretation he says the change shall be after the reign of *five* kings; and yet referring, in conclusion, to a text in the Second Book of Kings, we are brought back again to the number *four*. But it is this very circumstance which makes the prodigious part of this affair. A good guesser (who, an ancient writer says, is the best prophet) might reasonably conjecture the monarchy, after the subverter of it, Cromwell, was taken off, would be restored; and if it continued in the same family for *four* or *five* generations, that was as much as, in the ceaseless revolutions of human affairs, could be expected. But we shall find there was something more in this matter. The succession of the House of Stuart, during the course of these *four* generations, was disturbed; and that circumstance our prophet has distinctly marked out. The *four* crowned heads he saw in his hand denote Charles II., James II., Queen Mary, and Queen Anne. They are afterwards called *five*; and so they were; for King William III. shared the sovereignty with Queen Mary, and reigned alone after her. But he, being of another family, when the *succession* in the House of Stuart is reckoned up, he could not be numbered; so they must be then called *four*. When the prophet reckons the *reigns*, King William comes in, and then they are called *five*. The key to this explanation is the text he concludes with: "Thy children of the *fourth* generation shall sit on the throne."

'A great and extraordinary genius lately deceased, struck with this wonderful coincidence, hath written with his own hand, in the margin of the page, these words: "*A manifest prophecy*." You know,' he says to Jortin, 'who I mean. But every one must judge for himself, unless (which I had rather) you would give us your own sentiments upon it.' *

* Jortin's Remarks on Eccl. Hist. vol. i. p. 252.

Such a grave and serious comment plainly shows that the expositor must have considered what Evans said as a real prophecy. He adds to it also one of Evans's visions, which is thus given in his book:

'My heart was for London; and, as one Mr. Oliver Thomas preached, Cant. ii. 10, *Arise up, my love, my fair one, and come away*, my heart was allured with it, that I thought it was a hastening of me to London; and at the time in a dream methought I was on Islington Hill, by the Water-house, and London appeared before me as if it had been burnt with fire, and there remained nothing of it but a few stone walls; but I made nothing of this dream.'

Warburton favours this vision with the following annotation:

'Whosoever reflects upon what we are told by Burnet in the "History of his Own Times," vol. i. p. 231, of the condition in which the works were put at the Water-house at Islington, when the fire of London happened, cannot but think Evans's making this the scene of his dream a very unaccountable circumstance. His telling us that he *made nothing of this dream* adds to the credit of his relation.'*

Yet Warburton, in the very letter in which he made these communications to Jortin, admitted that Evans, so far from being an open honest fellow, proved himself a knave by showing 'a spice of what we seldom find wanting in the ingredients of a modern prophet, prevarication.' Warburton produces an instance, but dismisses it with no other animadversion than that it 'contains an uncommon fetch of wit.'

'There are two confessions,' says Evans,† 'subscribed by my hand in the city of London, which, if not now, in

* Jortin's Remarks on Eccl. Hist. vol. i. p. 254.

† Eccho from Heaven, p. 42.

after ages will be considered. The one was made at the Spittle, and subscribed with the *right hand*, in the aforesaid vestry, before Sir Walter Earl; and that is a confession made by the inner man, or new man. The other confession is a confession of the flesh, called the outward man, or old man; and this confession I made before Green [the Recorder], and subscribed with the *left hand*, as the difference in the writing, being compared, will make it appear. I know the Bench and the people thought I recanted, but, alas! they were deceived.'

In regard to what Warburton says of this knave by his own confession, Disraeli * very pertinently remarks that he 'has fixed himself in this dilemma: Either he was a greater impostor than Arise Evans, or he was more credulous than even any follower of the Welsh prophet, if he really had any.'

But though many reflections were cast upon this appendix to Jortin's volume at the time of its publication, it was not till twenty years afterwards that it received a full measure of reprobation, when the Rev. Henry Taylor, the author of 'Ben Mordecai's Apology for becoming a Christian,' and some other minor effusions, published 'Confusion Worse Confounded, Rout on Rout,' an examination of Warburton's comments on Rice or Arise Evans's 'Eccho from Heaven,' by Indignatio. In reference to Warburton's assertion that Evans was a prophet, and his admission that he was also a prevaricating knave, Mr. Taylor observes that what people had hitherto said about Warburton arose from their considering him as they consider other men, 'who can only believe *one* side of a contradiction at a time, whereas his Lordship [Warburton had then become a bishop] frequently believes, or at least defends, *both*. So that it would be no great wonder if he should maintain that Evans was both a real prophet and

* Quarrels of Authors, art. Warburton.

an impostor. It was no more than we find in the *adventure* [a use of the word borrowed from Warburton] of the theocracy, in which he attempts to show that an extraordinary providence over the Jews entirely *ceased* upon their return from captivity, and yet *continued* over them till the time of Christ; that is, it *continued* about five hundred years after it had *ceased.* It was no more than we find in the *achievement* [another Warburtonian term] of the Jewish revelation; which revelation consisted, according to his Lordship, in concealing from the Jews what everybody else knew. It is not so easy a thing, therefore, to confute his Lordship, as may be imagined. For, unless you confute both sides of the question, you do your business only by halves.'

As the reader may wish to see another specimen of this publication, we shall extract the remarks on Evans's divination by lot.

Jortin, having procured a copy of Evans's book, added from it the following passage: 'Being perfectly awake, a voice said to me, "Go to thy book;" whereupon I suddenly started up, and to the table I went, where my Bible lay open, immediately fastening my eye upon Eph. v. 14, being these words: "Awake, thou that sleepest, and arise from the dead," &c.' 'Evans, who was illiterate,' observes Jortin upon these words, 'little thought that he was practising a kind of divination in great request among the Pagans and the ancient Jews and Christians, who had recourse to their *Sortes Homericæ, Virgilianæ, Evangelicæ,* and *Biblicæ.* The same causes produce the same effects, and nothing is more like one enthusiast, Mystic, Cabbalist, or Quietist, than another.'

Upon this reflection Taylor, taking a hint from Hotspur's retort to Glendower, that the frame of the earth would shake in a storm, uninfluenced alike either by his own birth, or the kittening of his mother's cat, says:

'But this being a matter of great importance, already

bolted to the bran in a dialogue between Sir Hugh Evans, a relation, I suppose, of Arise Evans, his Lordship's prophet, and his scholar, Master William Page, I shall give it you as I find it in the MS.

Sir Hugh. — William Page, how many kittens had your mother's cat in her last litter?

William Page.— Five, Sir Hugh.

Sir H. — Take up your Virgil, William — for thou art a good sprank lad— and read me the first line that comes into your eye. [*Aside.*] I want to find out whether the *Sortes Virgilianæ* will give me any light into the fate of these kittens, before I venture to try it upon myself.

Will. P. —'*Tres Notus abreptas in saxa latentia torquet.*' That is,

Three by the winds were dash'd against the rocks.

Sir H. — Try again, William; but shut the book first. There, now open it.

Will. P. — '*Apparent rari nantes in gurgite vasto.*'

In the great stream a few are seen to swim.

Sir H. — Try once more, William; for the number *three* is ominous.

Will. P. — '*Tres Eurus ab alto*
In brevia et syrtes urget.'

Three from the deep are driven by the storm
To perish in the shoals.

Sir H. — There is a good William. [*Aside.*] Now I will examine into the fate of the kittens. [*Aloud.*] Have you saved any of the kittens, William?

Will. P. — Yes, two. I saved one, and my sister, Anne Page, the other.

Sir H. — And what is become of the other three?

Will. P. — They were drowned, Sir Hugh.

Sir H. — Drowned! You amaze me. Drowned? You mean they were knocked on the head.

Will. P. — No, Sir Hugh; they were all three drowned in the great pond.

Sir H. — All *three*, do you say? *Tres Notus abreptas* — prodigious! *Tres Eurus ab alto* — Wonderful coincidence! *Apparent rari nantes* — Who can speak of it but in terms of astonishment? And in the great pond, too — *in gurgite vasto* — a manifest prophecy! It is impossible to resist the evidence of these unhappy sufferers. I'll certainly try my own fortune by the same divination.

'*Triste per augurium Teucrorum pectora ducunt.*'
The dismal augury demands our faith.

O wonderful! wonderful! and most wonderfully wonderful! and yet again wonderful, and out of all whooping!

Here ends the dialogue, and Sir Hugh's soliloquy.'

This year Warburton published a second edition of Julian, which varied in some respects, but not greatly, from the first. 'In Julian,' he wrote to Hurd, towards the end of the preceding year, 'there were some things I would not venture to say on the first appearance of it, as you will see when I send you a copy of the second edition, which is now printing.'* 'Mr. Pope used to tell me,' he says in another letter to Hurd, 'that when he had anything better than ordinary to say, and yet too bold, he always reserved it for a second or third edition, and then nobody took any notice of it.'†

Nichols says that Warburton, after the first edition was printed by Bowyer in 1750, 'called in the impression; why,' he adds, 'is not known; but the fact is curious.'‡ I find no mention of this recall elsewhere. The first edition of Julian was in the hands of the public in 1750.

With regard to Bowyer's connexion with Warburton, it may be noticed here that he printed the earlier portions of Warburton's works, but that Warburton, from some fancied want of correctness in his printing, afterwards put his books into other hands. Bowyer wrote him three long letters of remonstrance on the occasion, which were never sent, but which have since found their way into print, as the writer apparently intended, through Mr. Nichols.§ The matter is of no great interest to the public, but the letters, on the whole, seem to indicate that Bowyer could not have been handsomely treated by

* Letters from an Eminent Prelate, let. xxv. † Ib. let. xxxv.
‡ Nichols's Lit. An. vol. ii. p. 182. § Ib. pp. 384-390.

Warburton. As to the first three volumes of 'The Divine Legation,' Bowyer tells him that he appears to have felt no abatement of reputation from the inaccuracy of the printer, though he was sometimes attacked on the impropriety of his translations. There were letters to Bowyer from Warburton, according to Mr. Nichols, showing that 'The Divine Legation' had 'received no small advantage from Bowyer's corrections.'

This year, also, Warburton was permitted by Allen to give Hurd an invitation to Prior Park, where he was afterwards a frequent visitor, and advanced much in the good graces of Mr. and Mrs. Allen. 'I wish you had seen Mr. Allen,' he says in a letter to Balguy, written shortly afterwards; 'he comes up to the notion of my favourites in Queen Elizabeth's reign; good sense in connexion with the plainest manners—*simplex et nuda veritas.*' At his first dinner with Allen he met Fielding, whom he calls 'a poor, emaciated, worn-out rake, whose gout and infirmities have got the better even of his buffoonery.'* Fielding had vitality enough, however, to last four years after this opinion was passed upon him.

Another prominent character, who was often to be seen at Prior Park about this time, was Quin the actor. Warburton, in his talk with Quin before the company, always addressed him in such a way as to remind him that he was but a player, and, as some accounts say, took opportunities of admonishing him on his luxury and looseness of life. One evening, however, with much apparent civility, he requested Quin, whom he should never see on the stage, to give him a specimen of his acting, in presence of a large number of guests, in Mr. Allen's drawing-room. Quin replied, carelessly, that plays were then almost out of his head, but that he

* Kilvert's Life of Hurd, p. 45.

believed he could repeat a few verses of 'Venice Preserved,' and, standing up, declaimed, *ore rotundo*, the passage in which occur the lines

> 'Honest men
> Are the soft easy cushions on which knaves
> Repose and fatten;

and, as he pronounced the words 'honest men' and 'knaves,' directed his looks so pointedly towards Allen and Warburton, that none of the hearers could mistake the intended application. Warburton never afterwards asked the actor for a specimen of his skill.*

Another occurrence between the Bishop and the player, which took place in the same house, is told by Walpole. 'The saucy priest,' says he, 'was haranguing at Bath in behalf of prerogative. Quin said, "Pray, my Lord, spare me; you are not acquainted with my principles; I am a republican; and perhaps I even think that the execution of Charles I. might be justified." "Aye," said Warburton, "by what law?" Quin replied, "By all the laws that he had left them." The Bishop would have got off upon judgments, and bade the player remember that all the regicides came to violent ends — a lie, but no matter. "I would not advise your Lordship," said Quin, "to make use of that inference; for, if I am not mistaken, that was the case of the twelve apostles." There was great wit *ad hominem* in the latter reply, but I think the former equal to anything I ever heard. It is the sum of the whole controversy couched in eight monosyllables, and comprehends at once the king's guilt and the justice of punishing it. The more one examines it, the finer it proves.'†

* Prior's Life of Malone, p. 345.

† Walpole's Letters, vol. v. p. 14.

CHAPTER XXIII.

BYROM. BOLINGBROKE. CLERICAL ADVANCEMENT.

SERMONS AT LINCOLN'S INN — SIX EPISTLES OF DR. BYROM — WARBURTON MADE A PREBENDARY OF GLOUCESTER BY LORD HARDWICKE — LETTER TO HOGARTH — 'VIEW OF LORD BOLINGBROKE'S PHILOSOPHY' CAUSES OF WARBURTON'S ACRIMONY AGAINST BOLINGBROKE — BOLINGBROKE'S ABUSE OF RELIGION AND DIVINES — STYLE OF WARBURTON'S ANIMADVERSIONS; LORD HARDWICKE'S DISLIKE OF IT — SPECIMENS OF BOLINGBROKE'S MANNER — LETTER TO WARBURTON FROM MONTESQUIEU — WARBURTON MADE A KING'S CHAPLAIN AND A DOCTOR OF DIVINITY — RESIGNS THE LIVING OF FRISBY; HIS ATTENTION TO THAT PARISH — SECOND VOLUME OF SERMONS AT LINCOLN'S INN — DEDICATION OF 'THE DIVINE LEGATION' TO LORD HARDWICKE.

IN the summer of the next year, 1752, Mr. and Mrs. Warburton resided for some time at Weymouth, being dislodged from Prior Park by the Princess Amelia, to whom, as she was recommended, for some indisposition, to try the Bath waters, Ralph Allen lent his house for several weeks. Warburton indulged in bathing, and spoke of himself, in his letters, as 'courting the favours of the sea-nymphs every morning except Sunday.'*

Warburton's only publication in 1752 was the first volume of a course of sermons preached at Lincoln's Inn, 'On the Principles of Natural and Revealed Religion.' A second volume followed in 1754. 'The sermons of Warburton,' remarks Bishop Newton,† 'are not the most valuable of his writings;' and the public has readily

* Letters from an Eminent Prelate, let. xlix.

† Life by Himself, p. 68.

concurred in the Bishop's estimation of them. It would be wrong, however, to withhold what Hurd, though too eager a panegyrist, has said in their favour:

'He had used himself very little to write sermons till he came to Lincoln's Inn. His instructions to his parish had either been delivered without notes, or extracted from the plainest discourses of our best preachers. In his present situation he found it necessary to compose his sermons, and with care; his audience consisting wholly of men of education, and those accustomed to reasoning and enquiry. Here was then a scene in which his learning and knowledge might be produced with good effect; and it was in this kind of discourse that his taste and studies had qualified him to excel. His sermons are, accordingly, all of them of this cast; not slight harangues on ordinary subjects, but close, weighty, methodical discourses, on the most momentous doctrines of natural and revealed religion; opening the grounds of them, and supporting them against objections; expressed in that style of nervous eloquence which was natural to him, and brightened occasionally, but without affectation, by the liveliest strokes of imagination. In short, they were written only for the use of men of parts and learning, and will only be relished by such. They are masterly in their way, but fitter for the closet than the church; I mean those mixed auditories that are usually to be expected in that place.'

Another sermon of his, 'The Office and Operations of the Holy Spirit,' which was afterwards incorporated into the 'Doctrine of Grace,' elicited from the amiable visionary, Dr. John Byrom, distinguished alike for his shorthand and his verses, 'Six Familiar Letters to a Friend' upon the subject of sermons, in which it is intimated that the great duty of a preacher is to propagate, not strife, but peace, and to unite Christians rather than set them at variance; otherwise he does not fulfil the conditions of preaching.

The passage which gave Warburton the greatest offence was this:

> With such a fund of learning, and a skill
> To make it serve what argument he will,
> With choice of words for any chosen theme,
> With an alertness rulingly supreme,
> What, sir, can single persons, or a sect,
> When he is pleased to preach at 'em, expect?
> Just what they meet with in the present case—
> All the dogmatic censure and disgrace
> That a commanding genius can exert
> When it becomes religiously alert;
> With narrow proofs, and consequences wide,
> Sets all opponents of its vote aside;
> The Papists first, and then th' inferior fry,
> Fanatics, vanquish'd with a *who but I?*
> These are the modish epithets that strike
> At true religion and at false alike.

In these expressions the author of the sermon chose to think that the letter-writer had taken unwarrantable liberty. 'Byrom,' he writes to Hurd, 'is very libellous upon me, but I forgive him heartily, for he is not malevolent, but mad.' He, however, admits the merits of Byrom's style. 'He is certainly a man of genius,' he says, 'but plunged deep into the rankest fanaticism. His poetical epistles show him both; which, were it not for some unaccountable negligences in his verse and language, would show us that he has hit upon the right style for familiar didactic epistles in verse.' He gives also his own notion of enthusiasm, in opposition to that of Byrom: 'As to Byrom's notion of enthusiasm, I agree with him in this, that it is foolish to confine the passion to religion, when it spreads through all human life; but I disagree with him in supposing an *intense application* of the mind to any object is enthusiasm. If I were to define it, I would say it is such an irregular exercise of it as makes us give a stronger assent to the conclusion than the premises will warrant; then reason begins to be betrayed, and then enthusiasm properly commences. This shows why enthusiasm is more frequent in religious matters than in any other; for those interests being very momentous, the passions bear the greatest sway, and reason is the least heard.'* The English word 'enthusiasm,' which, in the time of Warburton, was almost wholly confined to religion, is now, and has long been, applied to unreasonable or immoderate ardour or fancies in any study or occupation whatever. Byrom was himself much of an enthusiast. He told Warburton in one of his Epistles that men are not to be condemned as fanatics who believe that miracles may still occasionally appear. He was a friend of Wesley, and a reader of Jacob Behmen; and is the 'Behmenist' in the dedication to the second part of 'The Divine Legation,' who is said to have made the last attack on Warburton, the first having been made by the 'false zealot' Webster.

In the early part of the year 1753, Warburton's intimacy with Charles Yorke led to the offer from his father, Lord Chancellor Hardwicke, of a prebend at Gloucester. Lord Hardwicke told him that it was offered as a mark of regard, and wished that it had been better; though it was the best prebend, as Warburton believed, that he had to give. Dr. Birch, who gave him some instruction about the mode of taking possession, observed that it was so long since he had had any preferment that he must have forgotten all the formalities. 'There was another thing,' said Warburton, 'that he did not dream of, that it is so long since I had occasion to inquire about the formalities, that I am become very indifferent to the things themselves.'† Such was his *nolo episcopari* tone; but he expressed due thankfulness to Lord Hardwicke, assuring him that no favours from such a hand could be unaccept-

* Letters from an Eminent Prelate, let. xxxviii. xl.

† Ib. let. lii. liii.

able; and when, in the following year, he published a new edition of 'The Divine Legation,' he dedicated the first volume of it to Lord Hardwicke, observing that it was the first opportunity he had had of tendering his grateful acknowledgments for so distinguishing a mark of favour.

'Some who were curious in observing coincidences,' says Hurd, 'and meant to do honour both to the patron and client, took notice that the stall, to which Mr. Warburton was preferred, was the same in which the Lord Chancellor Nottingham, that great patron of all the learned churchmen in his time, had placed Dr. Cudworth. Such a similitude was there apprehended to be between the two magistrates, and, still more strikingly, between the two divines, authors of *The Intellectual System* and *The Divine Legation*.' Let it be noticed, however, that, as intellectual workers, the ardent and temerarious Warburton and the calm and cautious Cudworth differed greatly.

About the same time Hogarth the painter was soliciting subscriptions for his 'Analysis of Beauty;' and Warburton addressed to him the following complimentary letter:

'March 28, 1753.

'Dear Sir,—I was pleased to find by the public papers that you have determined to give us your original and masterly thoughts on the great principles of your profession. You owe this to your country, for you are both an honour to your profession, and a shame to that worthless crew professing *virtù* and connoisseurship, to whom all that grovel in the splendid poverty of wealth and taste are the miserable bubbles. I beg you would give me leave to contribute my mite towards this work, and permit the inclosed to entitle me to a subscription for two copies.

'I am, dear sir, with a true sense of your superior talents, your very affectionate humble servant,

'W. WARBURTON.'

His next literary effort was an attack on Lord Bolingbroke's writings, under the title of 'A View of Lord Bolingbroke's Philosophy, in Four Letters to a Friend;' the first two of which came forth in 1754 and the others in 1755. His Lordship had died in 1751, and his philosophical works were published in 1753, under the editorship of Mallet. He had been wont to boast, according to Hurd, of the change that his arguments, when they appeared, would make in metaphysics and theology; but during his life he sent forth little on the subject, contenting himself chiefly, to use Johnson's illustration, with charging his blunderbuss, of which a rascally Scotchman, bribed by a legacy of half a crown, was to pull the trigger after his death. Between Bolingbroke and Warburton, ever since their meeting at Murray's table, there had been deadly hatred,

Ira fuit capitalis, ut ultima divideret mors;

hatred which had possibly commenced, on Bolingbroke's side, when Warburton published his reply to Crousaz; for his Lordship was not likely to forgive the man who was too persuasive to Pope. Before he died, he scattered over his pages abundance of sarcasm against the 'Alliance' and 'The Divine Legation,' and plenty of abuse of their author, whom he called, besides other names, 'a scribbler' and 'a stupid fellow.'* Thus Warburton had sufficient provocation, whatever other motive might animate him, to engage with vigour in a hostile criticism.

How Bolingbroke assailed Moses and the prophets, Jews and Christians, religion and the clergy, is well known. He railed and sneered rather than argued. He is said by Warburton, not unfairly, to have manifested 'the rankness of Lowth without his force, and the malignity of Marvel without his wit.' He protested that Moses

* Bolingbroke's Works, vol. iv. p. 417, 418; Warburton's Works, vol. vii. p. 340, 351; vol. xii. p. 310, 338.

must be regarded with contempt as a philosopher, and with horror as a divine; and that St. Paul was a fanatic, who attempted to supply, by artificial theology, the deficiencies of an obscure and imperfect revelation. He called Cudworth's 'Intellectual System' 'a nonsensical paraphrase of nonsense.' He accused Cumberland of 'talking metaphysical jargon and theological blasphemy.' Abbadie he pronounced to be mad; and declared Selden, Grotius, Cumberland, and Puffendorf to be great writers on natural law, just as he might be called a great traveller who should go from London to Paris by the Cape of Good Hope. He even spoke of Montesquieu's 'Spirit of Laws' as a dishonour to the French genius. He called Clarke 'an audacious and vain sophist, full of presumptuous reasoning and profane absurdities;' and abused Wollaston as 'a learned lunatic,' fit only to be a patient of Doctor Monro. The whole body of divines, he asserts, are either incapable of reasoning, or unprincipled supporters of imposture. Duncan Forbes, though something better than a divine, yet is utterly unworthy of attention, for he belonged to 'an unlearned profession, of which ninety-nine in a hundred at least are pettifoggers, sharpers, brawlers, and cavillers.' The writings of all the fathers of the church consist of nothing but nonsense and artifice. But all these disorders and follies, however much to be pitied, can be no subject of wonder, for our whole world, he says, seems to be 'the Bedlam of every other system of intelligent creatures, with this unlucky circumstance, that they who are most mad govern in things of the greatest moment them who are least so.' Most authors, who make any pretence to philosophical discrimination, find somebody to commend; but Bolingbroke, writing as a philosopher, abuses everybody alike.

Unhappily, Warburton's mode of reasoning very much resembles that of his antagonist. His attacks are desultory, and he presents no chain of continuous argument.

He imputes bad motives rather than overthrows weak assertions. The result is that the 'Letters' are terribly tedious; for the reader finds no connexion in the matter to draw him onwards. The friend to whom he addresses them is Ralph Allen, but it may be deemed a matter of certainty that Ralph Allen's friendship was not strong enough to secure from him a complete perusal of what was laid before him. If any other reader has gone through the mass, it must have been Hurd, who found 'the reasoning and the wit alike irresistible, the strongest and keenest that can be conceived.' Other readers the author has pleased as little as the orators who *latrant, non loquuntur*, pleased Cicero. The language is, in many parts, not merely unstudied, but vulgar and offensive.

The style of the whole was so much disliked by Murray that he wrote him an anonymous letter, expostulating with him on the manner in which he had treated both the subject and his adversary. The writer expressed his concern to hear many deciding who the author of the 'View' must be by his 'scurrility and abuse;' and observed that to however little mercy Lord Bolingbroke was entitled, it might be considered dishonourable to a gentleman and a clergyman to give him the treatment which he deserved, especially after his death. 'Everybody,' he added, 'would have applauded your selecting those instances of his reviling, arrogance, and abuse, had you not followed his example.' Warburton surmised who was the writer of this remonstrance, and replied to it publicly in an 'Apology' prefixed to the 'View.' He could not but be strongly moved, he says, at the sight of 'three or four bulky volumes of redhot impiety,' abounding with 'the lowest malice and most barefaced misrepresentation,' and, in attempting a confutation of them, had put himself in the place of a scavenger, who ought not to be blamed for the stench from the dirt which he is endeavouring to remove. But the best defence of his vehemence is given in the following passage:

'When men are sincere in their mistakes, after a diligent and candid search; when the subject is of small moment, such as the mode of discipline, the measure of conformity, or a distinction in metaphysics; the mistaken, and even the perverse, should be treated with tenderness. But when the avowed end of a writer is the destruction of religion in all its forms; when the means he employs are every trick of prevarication and ill-faith, and every term of scurrility and abuse; when, to use the expression of Cicero, *est inter nos, non de terminis, sed de totâ possessione contentio;* then a practised calmness and an affected management look like betraying the cause we are intrusted to defend; or, what is almost as ill, like defending it in that way only which may turn most to our private advantage; as when, in questions of the greatest moment, we comply with this fashionable indifference, or flatter it into a virtue, when we should have striven to rekindle the dying sparks of religion by a vigorous collision with its professed enemies, *whose faces*, to use the unpolite language of the prophet, *are harder than a rock.*' *

He has one very good passage about Bolingbroke's assaults on Clarke. Bolingbroke argued that, though the natural attributes of God could be proved *à posteriori*, his moral attributes could not, and, as to the arguments for them *à priori*, he pronounced them to be all *jargon*, *nonsense*, *impiety*, and *blasphemy*; 'so that,' remarks Warburton, 'the moral attributes of God are fairly erased at once out of the *intellectual system*; and he [Bolingbroke] had no farther trouble on this head than to decorate Clarke, who was chiefly conversant in the reasoning *à priori*, with a variety of abusive names. As to the reasoning itself, our great man's respect for that is so

* Warburton's Works, vol. xii. p. 79.

profound and so distant, that I defy anyone, unacquainted with metaphysical arguments, even to guess what kind of things they are for which the famous minister of St. James's is so severely handled; for, while the *divine* suffers, the *reasoner*, as we say, always escapes. Now, indeed, you see him seized upon, and ready, as you would think, to be cut up alive, and immolated to the first philosophy, when *a fit of railing* shakes his Lordship, and the storm falls upon the whole body of modern schoolmen; and so the doctor escapes for that time. He is again laid hold on, and everything ready for execution, when *a fit of learning* comes upon his Lordship, and Pythagoras, Plato, Socrates, and the whole band of ancient metaphysicians, pass in review, and each receives a lash as he passes; and so the doctor escapes for the second time. After all these victories without bloodshed, his Lordship, as is fitting, takes his ease, intent only on his future triumphs; in the meantime, amidst such self-applause, his essays end, and the subtile doctor remains unhurt.'*

I hope not to weary the reader, if I quote another passage of a similar nature, which characterises Bolingbroke's show of reasoning very justly:

'When I reflect on what this has cost me, the reading over two or three bulky volumes to get possession of a single argument, which now you think you hold, and then again you lose; which meets you full when you least expect it, and slips away from you the very moment it promises to do most; when, I say, I reflect upon all this, I cannot but lament the hard luck of the English clergy, who (though apparently least fit, as being made parties, certainly least affected, as there is nothing that can impose on a scholar, and a great deal that may mislead the people) are likely to be the men most engaged with his Lordship in this controversy. Time was, when, if a

* Let. ii. Warburton's Works, vol. xii. p. 137.

writer had a disposition to seek objections against religion, though he found them hardly, and urged them heavily, yet he would digest his thoughts and methodise his reasoning; the clergy had then nothing to do but to answer him, if they found themselves able. But since this slovenly custom (as Lord Shaftesbury calls it) has got amongst our free-thinkers, of taking their physic in public, of throwing about their loose and crude indigestions under the name of *fragments*, things which in their very name imply, not so much the want, as the exclusion, of all form, the advocate of religion has had a fine time of it; he must work them into consistence, he must mould them into shape, before he can safely lay hold of them himself, or present them handsomely to the public. But these gentlemen have provided that a clergyman should never be idle. All he had of old to attend, was the saving of the souls of those committed to his care; he must now begin his work a great deal higher; he must first convince his flock that they have souls to be saved.'*

In one particular Warburton is unjust to Bolingbroke. He insinuates that his Lordship ought rightly to be deemed an Atheist, as being one who, in Scripture phrase, is 'without God in the world,' because he maintained that God's moral attributes could not be proved from the state of things in the world. But to charge Bolingbroke with atheism is to go too far; his Lordship admitted that 'we know the physical and moral system of the world to be God's work,'† and that God is the physical and moral governor of it, however unable we are to see by its aid into the nature and attributes of God himself.

The fourth letter is little more than a panegyric on 'The Divine Legation' and the 'Alliance between Church and

* Let. ii. Warburton's Works, vol. xii. p. 151.

† Ib. vol. xii. pp. 123, 133, 134.

State;' a mode of drawing attention to those works which Warburton was always ready to adopt.

A present of the 'View' to Montesquieu, accompanied with Warburton's other works, drew from that eminent writer a letter with which Warburton was highly gratified, and which contains some remarks well worthy of attention:

'I have read some of the writings of my Lord Bolingbroke, and, if I may be allowed to say how I was affected by them, I must say that he writes with much warmth; but it seems to me that he generally directs it *against things*, when he ought to employ it only *in painting things*. But in the posthumous work of which you, Sir, have given me a notion, he appears to me to have prepared for you constant matter of triumph. He that attacks revealed religion, attacks revealed religion only; but he that attacks natural religion, attacks all the religions in the world. If men are taught to think themselves under no obligations from revealed religion, they may still consider that they are under other obligations; but it is most pernicious to persuade them that they are under no restraint at all. It is possible to make attempts on revealed religion, inasmuch as it rests on particular facts, and facts are, in their nature, liable to become matter of dispute; but such is not the case with natural religion, for it is drawn from the nature of man, about which there can be no dispute, and from the inmost sentiments of mankind, which are equally incapable of being disputed.

'I would ask, besides, what motive there can be for attacking revealed religion in England, where it is so thoroughly cleared of all destructive prejudices that it can do no harm, but, on the contrary, may produce numberless good effects. I can understand that, in Spain or Portugal, a man who is going to be burnt, or is afraid of being burnt, because he does not believe certain articles connected, or not connected, with revealed religion, may have good reason to attack it, since he may thus hope to provide for his natural defence; but in England the case is different, for there every man who attacks revealed religion attacks it without prospect of personal advantage, and the assailant, although he should succeed, and even be right in the main, would only do away with a large portion of practical benefit for the sake of establishing a merely speculative truth.

'I was pleased to find, Sir, that you have extended your "Divine Legation." This work, and your "Julian," are very well known in this country, and would be still better known if they were translated. I believe, indeed, that a translation of them is about to be undertaken; but I should be sorry that they should fall into the hands of some of our translators, who disfigure all that they touch, and turn gold into iron.' *

In September 1754, Warburton was appointed one of the King's chaplains in ordinary. 'I see in the "Public Advertiser,"' said Akenside in a letter to Birch, 'that Warburton is made King's chaplain, and enters into waiting immediately. Can you tell me whether this be true? If there be any hazard of finding him at Kensington, I shall not choose to go thither to-day.'†

Thinking that this new dignity required him to take his doctor's degree, he obtained that distinction, of which he had been disappointed at Oxford, from Dr. Herring, Archbishop of Canterbury.

Writing to Hurd respecting his appearance at court in his quality of chaplain, 'You expect, perhaps, I should tell you,' says he, 'of the wonders I met with in this new Elysium. I found but two things to admire, as excellent

* Kilvert, Selections from Warburton's Papers, p. 236; Warburton's Works, vol. xii. p. 73.

† Nichols's Lit. Illustr. vol. ii. p. 656.

in their kinds; the one is the beef-eaters, whose broad faces bespeak such repletion of body and inanition of mind as perfectly fright away those two enemies of man, famine and thought. The other curiosity is our table-decker, of so placid a mien and so entire a taciturnity (both of them improved by the late elopement of his wife) that he is much fitter for the service of a minister of state than of the Gospel. In short, I found him the only reasonable man not to converse with.' *

He continued to hold his prebend at Gloucester, till, in 1755, he was offered one of greater value, five hundred a year, at Durham, through the interest of Murray, now Attorney-General, with Bishop Trevor, 'who,' says Hurd, 'did himself honour by the disposal of his preferments.' 'The Bishop of Durham,' he writes to Hurd, 'concurring with the Attorney-General, has given me the prebend which was lately Mangey's. He had other friends, you may imagine, to oblige; so I have resigned the prebend of Gloucester, and I shall resign another piece of preferment in the country. But the free motive and friendly manner in which this thing was done, you will easily believe, enhances the value of it to me. My friends are solicitors in these matters for me; I myself, at this time of life, extremely little.' Such was the mode in which he spoke of the prebend at Gloucester, when it was offered him. Such depreciations of preferment, which is at the same time accepted, every one must believe to be mere affectation.

Warburton, it may be supposed, could hardly be mistaken in saying that the prebend conferred upon him had been held by Dr. Mangey, editor of 'Philo-Judæus,' and author of several theological tracts, who died in 1754; yet there goes a story that Warburton's immediate predecessor in that stall was Lowth, who held it for a short

* Letters from an Eminent Prelate, Oct. 28, 1754.

time, and that the commencement of the ill-feeling between him and Warburton was a disagreement between their wives about the value of some articles of furniture, which the incomer was to take from the outgoer.*

Another story concerning Warburton as prebend of Durham is, that he was the first who disused copes. The occasion is thus told by the writer of an article on Pope in the 'Quarterly Review: †' 'A friend of ours, many years ago, on being shown, among the curiosities of Durham Cathedral, the splendid vestments formerly worn by the prebendaries, asked how they had come to be disused; when the verger said, "It happened in my time. Did you ever hear of one Dr. Warburton, Sir? A very hot man he was, Sir; we never could please him in putting on his robe. The stiff high collar used to ruffle his great full-bottomed wig; till, one day, he threw the robe off in a great passion, and said he would never wear it again; and he never did; and the other gentlemen soon left off theirs too."'

When he went to Durham, he found in the Episcopal Library a copy of Neal's 'History of the Puritans,' but observed that there was no answer to it, without which he said that the book ought not to remain there. He accordingly took the volumes home with him one day, and filled the margins with what he considered to be 'a full confutation of all the false facts and partial representations.' These remarks were included by Hurd in his edition of Warburton's Works. They afford as much proof that he was 'a hot man' as his impatience about the cope. When Neal speaks of something that 'blew up the liberties' of the sectarians, Warburton exclaims, 'Blew up a fool's head!' and abuses the author for

* Nichols's Lit. Anec. vol. ii. p. 421.

† Vol. xxxii. p. 273. See also Rev. G. Ormsby's Sketches of Durham, p. 129.

going on 'the true Puritan principle, that whatever was Popish was false.' In a note of a page long he declares that King Charles was the real author of 'Icon Basilike,' and that Gauden, getting it into his hands, transcribed it.

Soon after, he dined with the clergy at the Archbishop of York's Palace. In the course of conversation his Grace observed that Mr. Ridley, his chaplain, had undertaken to answer Phillips's 'Life of Cardinal Pole.' Warburton was uncourtly enough to observe that he could have wished his Grace had not left the task to his chaplain, but had undertaken it himself; citing Sarpedon in Homer, who tells Glaucus that those who hold superior rank should perform superior achievements. The company were struck dumb for a while. But when they recovered, somebody asked Warburton why he did not take the matter on himself. Warburton replied that when any service could be done for the Church, he did not stay to be called upon; and jestingly referred them to Neal's 'History of the Puritans,' which they might see, if they would go to the Library at Durham, scribbled all over with his refutations. Good humour was thus restored, and the company separated pleasantly.*

'Lord Clarendon's History' and Lord Orrery's 'Letters on Swift' were similarly annotated by Warburton. The remarks on Clarendon have been published. Of those on Lord Orrery's book, still unprinted, now in Hartlebury Library, the character may be sufficiently understood from what Warburton says of his lordship in writing to Hurd, that the sovereign quality of his style is *galimatias*, and that Hurd could hardly have had patience to read enough of 'those detestable letters on Swift' to discover 'the hundredth part of the offences against common sense and science that may be met with in them.'

The piece of preferment in the country which he speaks

* Letters from an Eminent Prelate, p. 355.

of resigning was Frisby, the small living in Lincolnshire, to which, as has been related, he was presented by the Duke of Newcastle in 1730, and which, having never resided on it, he vacated in 1756.

On the mode in which the affairs of this parish were conducted in his absence, some light is thrown by a letter addressed, in March 1820, by the rector of Frisby of that day, to the 'Gentleman's Magazine,' in which some inquiries had been made by a correspondent as to the fact of Warburton having been incumbent of Frisby. He left the superintendence of all parochial matters, temporal and spiritual, to a Mr. Wright, who was to collect the rents of the glebe, and to take care that a curate of good character should be always resident in the parish. In the possession of this Mr. Wright's daughter were left, at her father's death, several letters from Warburton, which the rector was permitted to inspect; but they were all short and unimportant, relating almost wholly to the collection of rents, and remittances to Knapton, the bookseller. The first was written in 1745 and the last in 1755, and they were nearly all franked by Allen. 'He seems,' says the rector, after perusing these letters, 'to have been more inattentive to the temporalities of his living than I was prepared to expect. He tells his agent, Mr. Wright (on whom he is perpetually bestowing the most lavish encomiums for his fidelity and industry, and who in truth was a very respectable character), that his former agent and tenants had not only withheld the rent of the glebe from him, but that they had actually bought and sold it one amongst another, and that it was only in consequence of their having quarrelled in dividing the spoils that he came to hear of their villany.

'To the spiritual concerns of the parish he seems,' in the opinion of the same rector, 'to have been sufficiently attentive;' for 'he repeatedly enjoins Mr. Wright, to whom he intrusted the important task of finding him a curate whenever one is wanted, to take care that he is of a sober virtuous character, and resident in the parish.'*

On one occasion there had been some interruption in the performance of the duties, and a Mr. Whyte, who appears, however, not to have been one of the parishioners, wrote Warburton a letter of complaint on the subject. Warburton replied thus:

'SIR,—You talk as if you wrote by the direction of I can't tell what gentlemen and clergy. I cannot think that any who bear either of those names would be so impertinent as to concern themselves in a matter which belongs only to me and my parish.

'However, long before your letter came, I wrote to Mr. Wright that I must have a resident curate of good and irreproachable character. And I make no doubt, from his care and integrity, but that he will procure one as soon as possible. You seem to be in a great hurry, but a worthy unexceptionable curate is not to be got at the shortest warning for residence.

'Yours, &c.,

'*To Mr. Whyte.* 'W. WARBURTON.'†

From this correspondence it would appear, rather than otherwise, that Warburton left the examination into the curates' characters and merits wholly to Mr. Wright. There seems, indeed, to be no proof that Warburton ever even visited the parish. Things of this kind are managed somewhat differently in the present day.

About the same time he published a second volume of 'Sermons preached at Lincoln's Inn,' which, when they were afterwards republished in 1766, he dedicated briefly to Lady Mansfield. He also printed, in 1755, 'A Sermon preached before the Duke of Marlborough and the Gover-

* Nichols's Lit. Ill. vol. ii. pp. 59, 845.

† Ib. vol. iv. pp. 731-733.

nors of the Small Pox Hospital, at the Church of St. Andrew, Holborn.' 'This,' he said, in a letter to Hurd, 'was a foolish sermon they bullied me into, but on condition they would not press me to print it. I hate,' he adds, 'to have my name in a dirty newspaper on any account, which has always made me decline these charity jobs, that everybody is fit for, and almost everybody ready for.' They offended him, too, by some glaring advertisement of the Sermon; a proceeding in which proclaimers of charity sermons generally show no great delicacy. It was put forth shortly after he was presented to the stall at Durham. 'The impertinence of the advertisement on this occasion,' he says, 'will make it difficult to draw me into another. I don't like that every cobbler should know I am a prebendary of the same church with Dr. Chapman the great.'*

Another impression of 'The Divine Legation,' also, being now required, he printed a fourth edition of the first part of it, in two volumes, with a dedication to the Earl of Hardwicke.

'As an author,' he said, in his address to the Earl, 'I am not solicitous for the reputation of any literary performance. A work given to the world every reader has a right to censure. If it has merit, it will go down to posterity; if it has none, the sooner it dies and is forgot, the better.

'So far as any censure can show that my poor labours are not calculated to promote *letters* or *learning*, to advance *truth*, or, above all, to serve the cause of *religion*, which I profess as a Christian and a member of the Church of England, I own I have missed my end, and will be the first to join with the censure which condemns them.

'In the mean time, the first book of this work, such as it is, is here humbly commended to your Lordship's

* Letters from an Eminent Prelate, Mar. 31, 1755.

protection. For to whom does it so properly belong to patronise an argument showing the *utility* of religion to society, as to that great magistrate, legislator, and statesman, who is best able to recommend and apply the subject, by his being convinced of the *truth* of religion, and by his giving the most exemplary proof of his belief, in a steady regard to its dictates in his life and actions?

'It is this which makes me presume on your Lordship's protection, not anything extraordinary in the work itself. It is enough for your Lordship to find in those you favour a real zeal for the interests of virtue and religion. The effectual service of those interests depends on so many accidents, respecting both the ability of the writer and the disposition of the reader, that your Lordship's humanity and candour, enlarged, and not, as it often happens, diminished, by your great knowledge of mankind, will always dispose you to estimate merit by a better rule than the success.'

In composing this dedication, he conferred with Murray and Mr. Charles Yorke, who suggested a great portion both of the matter and the language.*

* Letters from an Eminent Prelate, p. 176, note.

CHAPTER XXIV.

'DELICACY OF FRIENDSHIP.' HURD. JORTIN.

HURD'S 'SEVENTH DISSERTATION'—FRIENDSHIP BETWEEN WARBURTON AND JORTIN; THEIR CHARACTERS, BY BISHOP NEWTON—DISRUPTION OF THEIR INTIMACY—HURD'S DEFENCE OF WARBURTON; HIS SATIRICAL REMARKS ON JORTIN; HIS FLATTERY—LOWTH'S OPINION OF HURD'S PUBLICATION; BROWN'S AND GIBBON'S—WARBURTON'S GRATIFICATION—JORTIN FINDS SUPPORTERS; WARBURTON'S ABUSE OF HIM—JORTIN'S INDIRECT ALLUSIONS TO WARBURTON—SENSE OF THE WORD 'PRINCEPS'; JORTIN'S REMARKS ON IT—WARBURTON'S LETTER TO JORTIN—JORTIN'S ANSWER.

BUT this year was most to be noted, in Warburton's life, for Hurd's publication of 'The Delicacy of Friendship, a Seventh Dissertation, addressed to the Author of the Sixth;' meaning Dr. Jortin. An examination into the cause of this publication will require us to give a little more attention to Hurd and Jortin than we have yet bestowed upon them.

Warburton and Jortin had for some years been very good friends. Warburton engaged Jortin, in 1747, to assist him occasionally at Lincoln's Inn chapel, an engagement which lasted, apparently to the satisfaction of both, about three years. When Warburton, in 1751, published a second edition of his 'Julian,' he took occasion to say that the world might soon expect to be gratified with 'the learned Mr. Jortin's curious dissertations on Ecclesiastical Antiquity, composed, like his life, not in the spirit of controversy, nor, what is still worse, of party, but of truth and candour.' Jortin, on his part, seemed equally ready to pay compliments to Warburton. He inserted, at the end of his first volume of 'Remarks on Ecclesiastical History,' Warburton's unlucky notice of Arise Evans, and expressed his sincere obligations to Warburton, and to Bishop Pearce, who had sent him a dissertation on the destruction of Jerusalem, for their willingness to appear as his friends and coadjutors in the work; subjoining these verses:

> Ibit et hoc nostri per sæcula fœdus amoris,
> Doctorumque inter nomina nomen ero:
> Forsan et extinctum non spernet Patria dulcis,
> Forsitan et dicet, Tu quoque noster eras.
> Talibus inferiis placabilis umbra quiescet;
> Lenibunt manes talia dona meos.
> Interea labor ipse levat fastidia vitæ:
> Æterno rectum sub duce pergat iter! *

Having occasion, also, to observe that Horace's ode,

> O navis, referent in mare te novi, &c.,

has been a subject of dispute among the commentators, some contending that it is to be understood literally, and others allegorically; but that, in truth, it has a double sense, the poet addressing himself to a real ship, and yet intending, under that emblem, to dissuade the Romans from engaging again in civil war; he added: 'Mr. Warburton made the same remark, and to him I resign it, as to the first occupier, unless he will let me claim a part of it on the privilege of friendship, and as κοινὰ τὰ τῶν φίλων.'† At this time, therefore, 1751, all was friendly between them.

It may be proper to introduce here Bishop Newton's characters of Warburton and Jortin, for an intimacy with both of whom the Bishop was indebted to his edition of Milton. 'They were really,' says Newton, 'two very extraordinary men; and though their characters

* Remarks on Eccl. Hist. vol. i. p. 249.

† Ib. p. 129.

were much alike in some respects, yet they were very different in others. They were both men of great parts and abilities, both men of uncommon learning and erudition; both able critics, both copious writers. But the one was the more universal, the other perhaps the better Greek and Latin, scholar; the one had the larger comprehension of things, the other the more exact knowledge of words; the one had his learning more like cash, ready at hand, the other had his more like bills in his common-place book; the one was the more rapid and flowing, the other the more terse and correct, writer; the one was the more capable of forming the plan and system of a large work, the other excelled more in little loose detached pieces; the sermons of the one are not the most valuable, those of the other are the most valuable, of all their writings. And in themselves, the one was the more open and communicative, more inviting and engaging in his manner; the other was more close and reserved, more shy and forbidding in his appearance; the one was warmer in his commendation, a more zealous friend, and a more generous enemy; the other was more sparing of his praise, cooler both in friendship and enmity, and rather carping and undermining, than freely judging and censuring. But their little failings will die with them; their superior excellences will live in the mouths and memories of men.' *

Friendship continued, to all appearance, between them till 1755, when Jortin published his 'Six Dissertations on Various Subjects.' In the sixth of these disquisitions, which treated of the 'State of the Dead as described by Homer and Virgil,' Jortin, as we have seen, ventured to express himself of a different opinion from Warburton as to the probability of the descent of Æneas into hell, in the sixth book of the Æneid, being a representation of

* Bp. Newton's Life by Himself, p. 67.

an initiation into the Eleusinian Mysteries. But this dissent was signified, as Johnson said of his censures of Warburton's notes on Shakspeare, 'without bitterness of malice, or wantonness of insult.' It was indicated, indeed, so modestly and mildly, that the most irascible could hardly have been thought likely to take offence. 'That the subterraneous adventures of Æneas,' he says, 'were intended by Virgil to represent the initiation of his hero, is an elegant conjecture, which hath been laid before the public, and set forth to the best advantage by a learned friend.' The sixth book of the Æneid, he remarks in another place, is certainly obscure, and presents 'a field open for criticism,' in which 'all of us, who attempt to explain and illustrate Virgil, have reason to hope that we may make some discoveries, and to fear that we may fall into some mistakes; and this should induce us to conjecture with freedom, to propose with diffidence, and to dissent with civility. Ἀγαθὴ δ' ἔρις ἥδε βροτοῖσι.' These are the only remarks that he makes in allusion to Warburton; and it may be thought that they might have been received with calmness. But Warburton could read no objection to his own theories without resentment. Whether he intimated his displeasure to Hurd or not, is nowhere told; but it is probable that Hurd had some hint how Warburton felt. Whatever was the case, Hurd chose to appear in the field as the defender of Warburton, by putting forth a pamphlet entitled 'On the Delicacy of Friendship; a Seventh Dissertation addressed to the Author of the Sixth;' a production printed, indeed, without the writer's name, but with little care for concealment of the authorship.

The 'Dissertation' is a tolerably successful attempt at delicate irony or elegant sneering. The writer's great object is to make it apparent that Jortin's friendship for Warburton, or gratitude to him, which he would willingly have shown, was neutralised by the sense of duty that he felt to oppose Warburton's conjecture. He commences thus:

'Rev. Sir,—As great an admirer as I must profess myself of your writings, I little expected any of them would give me the pleasure that I have just now received from the last of your Six Dissertations on Different Subjects.

'The other five have doubtless their distinct merits. But in this, methinks, I see an assemblage, a very constellation, as it were, of all your virtues, all that can recommend the scholar, or endear the friend. This last, give me leave to say, is so unusual a part of a learned man's character, and appears with so peculiar a lustre in this discourse, that the public will not be displeased to have it set before them in full view, and recommended to general imitation.'

All these praises, it will easily be seen, are to be understood ironically. Hurd then adverts to the great commendations which learned men have bestowed upon each other, and sarcastically praises Jortin for his seasonable endeavour to put a stop to such extravagant flatteries, for his resolute efforts to overcome the inducements which he must have felt to give way to the common weakness, and for setting a precedent of the most heroic magnanimity and self-denial. 'I observe it to your honour,' he proceeds, 'you have ventured on the same ground, in this famous Dissertation, which hath been trodden by the most noted, at least, of our present writers. But this is not enough. It will be of moment to consider a little more particularly the character of the person whom you choose to follow, or rather emulate.' He then bestows, as the effusions of a 'warm friend' of Warburton's, with whom he had lately been conversing, the most extravagant encomiums on Warburton's literary and moral character, calling him 'a writer whose genius and learning have so far subdued envy itself, that every man of sense now esteems him the ornament, and every good man the blessing, of these times;' adding, besides, particular commendations of 'his love of letters and of virtue;' of 'his veneration of great and good men;' of 'his readiness to give their due to all men of real desert whose principles he opposes;' of his 'ingenuous openness and candour, the characteristics of a truly great mind,' displayed to such a degree 'that they whom he opposes cannot be angry, and they whom he censures are not misused.' The reader might well suppose that Hurd, in such encomiums, meant to satirise Warburton as well as Jortin; but such is not the case; he expected Warburton to receive the praises of this 'warm friend' as the offspring of pure sincerity of heart.

'It seems pretty well agreed,' proceeds the author of the 'Seventh Dissertation,' 'that this learned person, though so great a divine, is a very competent judge, and no mean proficient, in classical criticism. There are many specimens of his talents in this way dispersed through the large and miscellaneous work of "The Divine Legation." But the greatest effort of his genius, they say, is seen in the explanation of the sixth book of the "Æneis." And with all its defects, I can easily perceive you were so struck with it, that it was with the utmost reluctance you found yourself obliged, by the regard which every honest critic owes to truth, and by the superior delicacy of your purpose, to censure and expose it.

'Another man, I can easily imagine, would have said to himself, before he entered on this task, "This fine commentary, which sets the most finished part of the 'Æneis,' and indeed the whole poem, in so new and so advantageous a light, though not an essential in it, is yet a considerable ornament of so justly admired a work. The author, too, is my particular friend; a man the farthest of all others from any disposition to lessen the reputation of those he loves. The subject has been well nigh exhausted by him; and the remarks I have to offer on his scheme are not, in truth, of that consequence as to make it a point of duty for me to lay aside the usual regards of friendship on their account. And though he hath greatness of mind enough not to resent this liberty, his impatient and ill-judging friends will be likely to take offence at it. The public itself, as little biased as it seems to be in his favour, may be even scandalised at an attempt of this nature, to which no important interests of religion or learning seem to oblige me."

'After this manner, I say, a common man would have been apt to reason with himself. But you, Sir, understand the rights of literary freedom, and the offices of sacred friendship, at another rate. The one authorises us to deliver our sentiments on any point of literature without reserve; and the other will not suffer you to dishonour the man you love, or require you to sully the purity of your own virtue, by a vicious and vulgar complaisance.'

'This person,' he also observes, 'you have the pleasure to call your friend. Report says, too, that he has more than a common right to this title; that he has won it by many services done to yourself. How doth the consciousness of all this fire you! and what pains do I see you take to restrain that impatient gratitude which would relieve itself by breaking forth in the praises of such a friend!'

Hurd then commends Jortin, with continued irony, first, for writing on the same subject with his friend, since this is to tell him delicately that public attention has been fixed on it; secondly, for expressing dissent from him, since this is to intimate delicately that his work is of importance enough to be opposed; thirdly, for glancing at his arguments without naming him, since this is a delicate display of literary address; fourthly, for objecting to his principles without refuting his reasonings, since such tenderness can belong only to the delicacy of true friendship; fifthly, for suggesting what he thought better reasonings than his, since this is a delicate indication of readiness to support him; sixthly, for quoting from him with qualified approbation, since this is a delicate avoidance of fulsome flattery; seventhly, for insinuating compliments which can hardly give satisfaction to their object, since by such delicate faintness they will be rendered more welcome to the ears of others; and eighthly, for praising the unsubstantial rather than the substantial, for this is a delicate mode of showing anxiety not to commend without discrimination.

The piece is then concluded with a Greek quotation, conveying a sneer at Jortin as being a mere grammarian or sophist.

This Dissertation of Hurd's was cleverly attacked in a pamphlet entitled 'Remarks on Dr. Warburton's Account of the Sentiments of the early Jews concerning the Soul,' published in 1757, the writer of which says that if Hurd's paragraphs be *translated out of Attic irony into plain English*, we shall have the following rules prescribing the proper demeanour of all men towards the great sovereign in the republic of letters:

'1. You must not write on the same subject that he does.

'2. You must not write against him.

'3. You must not glance at his arguments even without naming him, or so much as referring to him.

'4. You must not oppose his principles, though you let his arguments quite alone.

'5. If you find his reasonings ever so faulty, you must not presume to furnish him with better of your own, even though you approve and are desirous to support his conclusions.

'6. You must not pretend to help forward any of his arguments that happen to fall lame, and may seem to require your needful support.

'7. When you design him a compliment, you must express it in full form, and with all the circumstance of panegyrical approbation, without impertinently qualifying your civilities by assigning a reason why you think he deserves them; as this might possibly be taken for a hint that you know something of the matter he is writing about as well as himself.

'8. You must never call any of his discoveries by the name of conjectures, though you allow them their full proportion of elegance, learning, &c.; for you ought to know that this capital genius never proposed anything to the judgment of the public (though ever so new and uncommon) with diffidence, in his life.'

The general feeling of the public, with regard to the author of the 'Delicacy of Friendship,' and the object of his satire, was, even at the time of its publication, when Warburton and Hurd were alive and commanded a certain degree of influence, manifested strongly in favour of Jortin; and it has increased largely in the same direction since their deaths. The author of that Dissertation, wrote Lowth to Warburton, pretends, I suppose, to be your friend; 'what your opinion of him is, I cannot tell; but I think you owe him little thanks for his pains. He has at least shown more zeal than discretion in the undertaking, and more malevolent wit than good sense or honest intention in the performance; the manifest tendency of which is to sow strife and foment discord; and its natural effect, if it has any, must be to lessen the number of those who wish well to you and your designs.'* Brown, the author of the 'Essays on the Characteristics,' alluding to Hurd's publication in a letter to a friend, says, 'Whoever the author be, though I honour his zeal for his friend, yet had I been of the council before it was published, I would have whispered this one criticism in his ear: "I think," my friend, "you are in danger of hurting Dr. W. as well as yourself, by the intemperance of your

* Lowth's Letter to Warburton, 1756.

zeal. For though . . . [Jortin] has certainly offended, yet you so far overrate his offence, and your consequential accusations rise so far beyond it, that the offence, which, if more gently touched, would have seemed considerable in the eyes of the world, will, by these aggravations, apparently groundless, sink into nothing in the opinion of mankind."'* Gibbon† called the Dissertation 'base and malignant.' Even Mr. Kilvert, who never censures Hurd but with reluctance, admits that 'no candid judge can do otherwise than regret that so severe an attack should have been made on a man of Jortin's talent and character on such slight provocation.'‡

But Warburton himself was highly delighted. Nothing could exceed his gratification. 'Just now,' he writes to Hurd, 'Mr. Allen has shown me a pamphlet, which, he says, was sent him by the post; though I had seen the title, without knowing what to make of it, in the newspapers. I have read it, and you may judge with what sentiments. Though I have no *data* to judge from what quarter it comes, yet I am as sure of the author as if I had seen it written; for I know but of one man from whose heart or whose pen so fine a piece of irony could come. Therefore, if I be mistaken, do not undeceive me; for the pleasure of thinking from whence it comes to me is as great as the gift. In the meantime, I say to everybody else (even to Mr. Allen, who, however, on the first reading told me that the keen softness, the politeness, and the delicacy, he thought, could come but from one hand), what I say to you, that I have had no *data* to judge of the author; that I saw it first by accident after the publication; and that I am sure Mr. Jortin will do me the justice to think I had no hand in it, because I am sure he does not think I am able; in which he is not out.

* Brown's Letter to Lowth, 1766; Tracts by Warburton and a Warburtonian, p. 200.

† Misc. Works, vol. i. p. 209.

‡ Life of Hurd, p. 54.

'I will be frank with you; next to the pleasure of seeing myself so finely praised, is the satisfaction I take in seeing Jortin mortified. I know to what degree it will do it. He deserves to be mortified on this occasion; it will do him good; and this is the worst I wish him. There was but one thing that I, in good earnest, resented for its baseness, and grieved at for its meanness. It is where, speaking of Libanius (I think in the "Sixth Dissertation," I am sure it is in one of the six), he evidently insinuates that Julian was murdered by some Christians amongst his own soldiers. You know I have a large note in my "Julian" to refute this calumny; and at the conclusion of it it is that I refer the determination to Jortin in the compliment that the author of the "Seventh Dissertation" makes so fine a use of. And this is the determination that this amiable-minded man thinks fit to make upon the occasion.'*

The compliment to Jortin, it may be remarked, was omitted in the subsequent editions of 'Julian,' and the 'long note' is left, without any reference to the author of the 'Six Dissertations,' to prove, chiefly from the narrative of Ammianus Marcellinus, that Julian was killed by a dart, one of a large shower hurled against the Romans from a body of retreating Persians. Jortin himself, too, it may be added, had given, in his 'Remarks on Ecclesiastical History,'† published in 1752, three years before the 'Six Dissertations,' a similar account of Julian's fate, observing, that 'as this prince had his good as well as bad qualities, Providence seems to have permitted him to fall in battle and to die an honourable death.'

After the publication of the 'Seventh Dissertation,' Hurd fell in with some friends of Jortin, who took his

* Letters from an Eminent Prelate, Dec. 21, 1755.

† Vol. ii. p. 326.

part, seemingly with some earnestness, against Warburton; and Hurd, perhaps with some misgiving or relenting, immediately communicated to Warburton what he had heard. Warburton at once replied: 'Who they are of Jortin's friends you have met with, I don't know; but they must be dirty fellows indeed who can think I have no reason to complain of his mean, low, and ungrateful conduct towards me; or that the pamphlet, which expresses so much resentment of it, was of my writing. Jortin is himself as vain as he is dirty, to imagine I am obliged to him for holding his hand; and perhaps, if the truth were known, it was to this insolence he must ascribe the "Seventh Dissertation." Nobody has yet written against me but at their own expense; and if *he* be a gainer, I will forgive him. The profusiou of compliment in the "Dissertation" is so great, that he must be very malignant who can suppose I gave it to myself; and, at the same time, so warm, that he must be very dull not to see it came from a generous and zealous friend. Whoever he be, I envy him that he has got the start of me, and that it was not my good fortune to do that for him which he has done for me; that is to say, *give a seasonable reproof to little low envy under the mask of friendship.* And I wish you would take an opportunity to say all this from me, and in my name, to those friends of Dr. Jortin.'*

To Hurd's attack Jortin made no direct reply. He knew himself to be far superior to Warburton, and at least equal to Hurd, in what is called scholarship; he was on a level with them in general knowledge; he had done no injury to Hurd, nor given any offence, justly deserving of resentment, to Warburton; and he had no fear that either of them would inflict any serious damage either on his literary or moral reputation. He was aware, too, that to reply to a calumny is to give it greater circulation, and

* Letters from an Eminent Prelate, Dec. 30, 1755.

that he who vindicates himself from a charge shows that the charge was of weight enough to make some impression. But it was not likely that he would altogether forbear from reference, in his subsequent writings, to the published assault upon him. Mr. Kilvert * supposes that the following passage in one of his sermons, on the text, 'To speak evil of no man,' 'bears indirect but forcible allusion' to the subject:†

'And here one cannot well omit the mention of a fault nearly related to evil-speaking, but more pernicious, and that is evil-writing, or satire, in which the defects, weaknesses, indiscretions, follies, and vices, not of corrupted human nature, but of particular persons, are exposed to public view. If these writers can say for themselves that they keep exactly to truth, yet they exercise an authority to which they have no legal and just claim. But they seldom have even that excuse to plead; they often bestow their censures as interest, partiality, ignorance, spleen, and prejudice direct, and are usually *the most malicious revilers of some, and the most sordid flatterers of others. Thus a person shall presume to pass sentence upon his neighbour's reputation who is not fit to open the cause, and shall set himself up for a judge who has not the qualifications requisite even for an ordinary evidence.*

'*And of this tribe of men the most odious are those who shoot their arrows from the dark; who wear a mask, not out of modesty, but of fear and self-preservation; who themselves write without a name, and abuse innocent persons by name: a crime which deserves other correction than words.*'

But more decided allusions to the matter were subsequently made in the 'Life of Erasmus,' of which the first volume was published in 1758, three years afterwards. We have noticed that the 'Dissertation on the Delicacy

* Life of Hurd, p. 53.

† Serm. xii. vol. iv. p. 238.

of Friendship' was concluded with a Greek quotation, which was recommended to Jortin's attention, but without any indication from what author it was taken. It was intended to throw contempt on Jortin as a mere grammarian. Jortin, in a note on his 'Life of Erasmus,' turned the point of the dart against the author of 'The Divine Legation,' by thus quoting the passage in a note, translating it, and commenting upon it:

'I remember to have met with a passage in a certain writer which is not at all favourable to the grammarians: Ἐμοὶ πρὸς φιλοσόφους ἐστι φιλία· πρὸς μέν τοι σοφιστάς, ἢ γραμματιστάς, ἢ τοιοῦτο γένος ἕτερον ἀνθρώπων κακοδαιμόνων, οὔτε νῦν ἐστι φιλία, μήτε ὕστερόν ποτε γένοιτο.

'*My friendship I bestow upon philosophers; as to sophists, little grammarians, and such sort of scoundrels and cacodæmons, I neither have, nor ever will have, any regard for them.*

'The man abhors grammarians; and grammars, I suppose. But who is the author of this bit of Greek? An extraordinary person, I assure you; a projector, a visionaire, a linguist by inspiration, a crack, a conjurer—in short, Apollonius Tyanensis. He is the man; and the grammarians count it no disgrace to be vilified by a mountebank.'*

It must have amused Jortin to string together these terms, of which the learned reader, whether an enemy or an apparent friend to Warburton, could so easily see the application. 'To be misrepresented as a pedant and a dunce,' he observed in another place, 'is no great matter, for time and truth put folly to flight.'†

The note is attached to the following passage in the text, which is aimed at both Warburton and Pope:

'Erasmus, in the earlier part of his life, carefully studied the Greek and Latin grammars, read lectures upon

* Life of Erasmus, vol. i. p. 604. † Ib. p. 599.

them, and translated Greek books into Latin. This was laying a right foundation for criticism and philology; and it is much to be wished that our young students of promising abilities would, in some measure, follow his example. Be you ever so ingenious and industrious, yet, if you neglect to cultivate and to preserve this humble part of knowledge, you will be perpetually stumbling when you tread on classic ground, when you attempt to explain, to translate, or to correct ancient authors, or to discuss any learned subject, or to compose a few pages of Latin in prose or in verse. Then, beware of blunders, and think not to make amends for them by insulting and ridiculing grammarians, scholiasts, commentators, lexicographers, verbal critics, word-catchers, syllable-mongers, and poachers in Stobæus and Suidas.'

He had also Warburton and Hurd in his thoughts when he tells us that Aleander, after he was exalted to high stations, had *wranglers* under him, whom he would set at Erasmus, though the laws of the Church forbid ecclesiastics *alere canes venaticos.* It would be happy, as he had before observed, 'if wrangling geniuses would copy from the examples of Faber and Erasmus, and consider a little how all men of sense and manners applaud such moderation, and how they abhor and despise those who, having begun to quarrel, perhaps, upon mere baubles, never end their contests and animosities till death comes and puts them to silence.'*

But the allusion to Warburton that touched him most, in the 'Life of Erasmus,' was the correction of a blunder that he had made in regard to the sense of the word *princeps* in a passage of Cicero. Quoting what Cicero† says of Plato, *qui princeps de republicâ conscripsit,* he translated the words, '*who wrote best of a republic,*' with this note: 'I read here, with Turnebus, *qui princeps de*

* Disney's Life of Jortin, p. 223. † De Legg. ii. 6.

republicâ conscripsit. Lambin objects to this reading, because we gather from Aristotle that *Plato was not the first who wrote of a republic*, he supposing *princeps* signified *primus*, whereas it means *optimus*. This was Tully's opinion of Plato, as may be gathered from many other places in his writings. And in this sense Turnebus, without doubt, understood the word; a sense familiar to his author, as in Verr. l. iv. c. 49, *in quâ* [patriâ] *multis virtutibus et beneficiis floruit princeps.* But the word *primus* itself is sometimes used in the sense of *princeps*; as in Virgil,

Prima quod ad Trojam ——'

Here was error enough for Jortin's animadversion, who, coming to the word *princeps* in one of the letters of Erasmus, inserted a note upon it, in which he restores the proper sense to the passage which had been thus misrepresented, and, without naming Warburton, closes his observations with a quotation from Terence, which he recommends to the critic as more decisive of his sense of *primus* than that which he had drawn from Virgil. But it will be proper to give Jortin's note entire, as it will show how determined he was to put the question against Warburton past dispute:

'Egnatius, in the letter above-mentioned (Ep. 1272), amongst other handsome compliments to Erasmus, says, *Tu igitur, qui Germanis tuis* princeps *hanc literarum facem prætulisti.*

'There is nothing particular in this use of the word *princeps* for *first*; but it reminds me to do justice to a passage in Cicero which hath been misinterpreted.

'Here is the passage, De Legibus, ii. 6. *Sed ut vir doctissimus facit Plato, atque idem gravissimus philosophorum omnium, qui* princeps *de republicâ conscripsit, idemque separatim de legibus ejus.*

'Here is the misinterpretation: "*Plato,—who wrote* best *of a republic.*"

'It should have been translated, *who wrote* first *of a republic*; and it can admit no other sense.

'When *princeps* means *best*, it cannot mean the adverb *best* (*optimè*), but the adjective *best* (*optimus*). Come then, try it, and substitute *optimus* in the room of *princeps*.

'*Plato,—qui* optimus *de republicâ conscripsit.*

'This, I think, will not pass for a Ciceronian phrase. Let us throw it aside, and proceed.

'*Plato*, says Cicero, *wrote* first *of a republic*; and he hath said the same in another place of this treatise, as his learned editor Davies observes. *Principem Platonem de republicâ disseruisse, testatur noster infra.* It is in III. 6: *Nam veteres verbo tenus, acutè illi quidem, sed non ad hunc usum popularem atque civilem, de republicâ disserebant. Ab hac familiâ magis ista manârunt Platone* principe.—Pòst Aristoteles, &c.

'Plato, then, according to Cicero, was the first who treated the subject in an *extensive*, *useful*, and *practical* way. Cicero hath also hinted the same thing in another treatise:

'*Atque his libris annumerandi sunt sex de Republicâ, quos tunc scripsimus:—magnus* locus philosophiæque proprius, à *Platone*, Aristotele, Theophrasto, totâque Peripateticorum familiâ tractatus uberrimè.—De Divin. II. 1.

'*Princeps* is he *qui primum capit*, and in its original signification it means the first in time or order; and then, by a very easy metaphor, it means the *chief*, *best*, and *most excellent*.

'In *princeps exiit, rediit, scripsit, invenit, sententiam dixit, verba fecit*, in these and such like expressions, *princeps* means *first*, and not *best*. To many passages collected in Gesner, these may be added: *Sicilia* princeps *se ad amicitiam populi Romani applicuit.*—Cic. de Cl. 171, b. *Is* princeps *ex Latinis hæc tractavit.*—De Orat. 154. *Gorgias* princeps *ex omnibus ausus est, &c.*—Acad. 44.

'These citations I take as I find them in Nizolius, Lucret. I. 94:—

'*Nec miseræ prodesse in tali tempore quibat,*
Quod patrio princeps *donârat nomine regem.*

'Horat. Carm. III. 17:

'*Qui Formiarum mœnia dicitur*
Princeps, *et innantem Maricæ*
Littoribus tenuisse Lirim.

'Lambin knew that *princeps conscripsit* could only mean writing *first*; and therefore he proposed to alter the place, because, said he, Plato did not write first concerning a republic. *Falsum est Platonem* principem, *id est*, primum *de Republicâ scripsisse.* But this was not a sufficient cause for attempting an emendation, as Lambin might have seen, if he had considered the case a little better. Horace says of himself, Carm. III. 30:

'Princeps *Æolium carmen ad Italos*
Deduxisse modos.

He meant that he was the *first.* And yet here it might be objected that, strictly speaking, he was not the first, since Catullus, before him, had composed some Sapphic odes. But either Horace did not recollect it, or he might think that Catullus had not done enough that way to earn the name of a lyric poet.

'The person, whose interpretation of Cicero is here examined, hath also informed us, *ex abundanti*, that as *princeps*, so likewise *primus* is used for *best* or *chief*; which he gravely proves from Virgil, Æn. I. 27:

'*Veterisque memor Saturnia belli,*
Prima *quod ad Trojam pro caris gesserat Argis.*

'There is a passage in Terence which would suit him better: Eunuch. II. 11, 17:

'*Est genus hominum qui esse primos se omnium rerum volunt,*
Nec sunt.

Where *primus* certainly and undeniably means *summus, præcipuus.*'*

Dr. Salter, the Master of the Charterhouse, showed these passages, and some others, which he supposed to point at Warburton, to Archbishop Secker. The archbishop expressed doubts, as to most of them, whether they were really intended against Warburton, but, when they came to the note on *princeps*, he at once admitted that there could be no uncertainty as to its design.†

The following passages may have been among those shown by Dr. Salter to the archbishop:—

'Dorpius, writing against Erasmus, represented himself as a divine, and Erasmus as a grammarian.' For this he received castigation in a letter from Sir Thomas More.

'Qui tam indoctas nænias evulgant libris, miro supercilio objurgant, miro fastu insultant et tantùm non triumphant, rectiùs facturi, si discerent interim Græcæ Latinæque Grammatices rudimenta.'—*Erasmus ad* 1 *Cor.* x. 16.

'Et quoniam per saltum, ut aiunt, Doctor factus est Bedda, redeat ad necessariam Grammaticam et Latinam et Græcam, ex cujus inscitiâ toties gravem calumniam intendit proximo, toties non intelligit auctores qui Latinè scripserunt, ut de Græcis taceam.'—*Erasmus adversus Beddam*, t. IX. c. 398.

Warburton, rendered uneasy by these attacks or innuendos, wrote a letter, expressing his displeasure, to Whiston, Jortin's bookseller, to be shown to Jortin, but, before it was despatched, changed his mind about the mode of communication, and sent it direct to Jortin himself. It was as follows:

'Sept. 30, 1758.

'Mr. Whiston,—I have read over Dr. Jortin's "Life of Erasmus" with great pleasure. If all his readers like it

* Life of Erasmus, vol. i. p. 552.

† Disney's Life of Jortin, p. 221.

as well, as I do not doubt they will, you will find your account in it.

'I perceive myself indebted to him here and there, as particularly in note *d*, p. 552. I have only one difficulty about it, which is (as he thinks me mistaken in the sense of *princeps*) how it happened he did not tell me of it during the time he professed a friendship for me. He will say, perhaps, I should not have had it now, but for the joke at the end of it. As to that, the joke has been so much worn, by its frequent application to many of my betters, that it might have been left at rest.

'However, he will give me leave to requite his kindness, and in that way I should have been contented to receive his, in observing to him, and to him only, that when, at p. 114, he translates the words of Bembus, *apud inferos pœna*, by *the pains of hell*, I think it should have been *the pains of purgatory*, and not of hell; as Bembus's *apud inferos* contained both *a hell and a purgatory*.

'But these are trifles. There is another thing more worth his *attention* (for it can hardly have escaped his *knowledge*), that, from the first moment of my acquaintance with him to the last that he would allow me to call him friend, I had the vanity to be always recommending him to those of the first quality whom I knew; some of whom are yet living, and ready to do me justice in this particular. I will go farther, that from that time to this day, I never wrote a line or a word reflecting on him (unless he so interprets my vindication of Socrates' behaviour at his death), nor did I ever instigate any other to do so, nor was I ever privy to anything so done. I have indeed been foolishly enough officious, formerly, to ridicule some of his slanderers in a public paper. As to his own conduct during the same period, I leave that to his own reflections. It is a pleasure to me, though it should be none to him, that he is the first man of parts that has ever entered himself in the numerous list of writers against me.

'Thus much I thought proper to say, and I hope Dr. Jortin will not be so mean and so vain to imagine I had any other purpose in it than to hold him up a faithful picture of things as in a mirror. I think he has given too much ear to tale-bearers and malevolent people; or perhaps I am mistaken, and he acts by his own disposition. But this is not my concern, but his. This paper is for no one's sight but Dr. Jortin's and yours, unless he wills otherwise. 'I am, &c.,

'W. W.

'P.S.—As this is a letter which requires no answer, I judged it best, on second thoughts, to send it direct to the person who only has any concern in it.'*

Jortin lost no time in replying thus:—

'London, Oct. 3, 1758.

'Reverend Sir,—I had the favour of yours, which gave me a mixture of pain and pleasure,—of pain, for having ever been at variance with you; of pleasure, from some prospect of seeing an end of it, unless I deceive myself.

'You complain; I could complain too; but to what purpose would that serve? To irritate, perhaps, and that is not my present design.

'You say that you never was concerned in the attacks made upon me. I ought to believe you; and I do believe you. But, before you informed me of it, I thought otherwise; and so did many a person besides me.

'Give me leave also to say, that I stand equally clear towards you, in that respect, and that I have never, directly or indirectly, been concerned in any of the pieces which have appeared against you.

'That you recommended me to persons who had it in their power to do me service, I doubt not. Vouchers are needless. Your own word sufficeth with me, and I thank you for it.

* Kilvert's Selections from Warburton's Papers, p. 218.

'As to the passage in Cicero, which I ought in civility to have mentioned to you, if I did not mention it, my memory deceives me egregiously. Surely, unless I am utterly mistaken, I did tell you of it; and you replied that Bishop Hare had once said the same thing to you.

'As to Bembus, you know that our English word *hell*, if not in the vulgar way of speaking, yet in its original sense, hath a lax signification, and may answer well enough to *inferi*. But your version is more accurate than mine; and (unless you should forbid it) I would willingly take occasion to mention it in the next volume, with respect, and with thanks.

'*Sit simultatis depositæ et nunquam resumendæ pignus et monumentum!*

'If I should live to publish the volume, I intend that there shall be nothing in it, or in anything else that comes from me, to give you even the slightest offence.

'I ought to return you thanks for the very candid judgment which you pass upon the account which I have given of Erasmus. It is a more favourable judgment than my own hath been, and will give me a better opinion of the work than I had before.

'I am, Sir, your most humble servant,

'J. JORTIN.'*

Jortin kept his word about *apud inferos pœna*, by inserting Warburton's notion of the sense of those words in an appendix to his second volume. 'I am obliged,' says he, 'to Dr. Warburton, who, since I wrote this note, is Bishop of Gloucester, for having reminded me that it should rather be *the pains of purgatory*. I might plead that our English word *hell* is lax enough to answer to *inferi*, or to all the supposed districts of the infernal regions. But I had rather own that his version is more

* Kilvert's Selections from Warburton's Papers, p. 220.

accurate than mine, and take this opportunity to return him my thanks, and to repay civility with civility.'*

There was, however, no renewal of correspondence between Warburton and Jortin. Jortin had said and done enough. He was no Hurd to offer further obsequiousness, and was henceforth regarded by Warburton as an enemy.

It will scarcely be believed that Hurd, to gratify Warburton, set himself, with perverse subtilty, to excogitate a vindication of Warburton's sense of *princeps*, a sense which, with his scholarship, he must have known to be indefensible. Yet such was the case, as appears from Warburton's answer to a letter which Hurd sent to him on the subject, but which is now lost:

'Your last letter,' says Warburton, 'sets the poor man's criticism in a very ridiculous light, but certainly not a false one. How doubly ridiculous must it be, if it be groundless, which it certainly is, and which you partly hint at. It stands on this grammatical principle, that if one Latin adjective cannot be used adverbially, no other, of what are called the synonymous adjectives, can; which is false in almost any language. I told you he was ashamed of himself. I made him so by writing a letter to his bookseller, to be communicated to him, to show him a true picture of himself, by setting together our different conduct to one another. I said, this required no answer. However, I had one, which showed how glad he was to get out of the scrape.' He then alludes to what he had remarked about *apud inferos pœna*, and adds, 'I did this to intimate to him that his translations were full of mistakes, and that this was a gross one, for a man to undertake the life of Erasmus, while he was ignorant of the nature and application of the bulls of indulgences.' Hurd, however, did not venture on laying his exposure of 'the

* Life of Erasmus, vol. ii. Append. p. 712.

poor man's criticism' before the public, but wisely confined it to his correspondence with Warburton. Nor did he ever remark, what he must have well known, that, if Jortin's translations were 'full of mistakes,' the mistakes would have been far more numerous if the translations had been made by Warburton instead of Jortin.

CHAPTER XXV.

HURD. PARR. TRACTS BY WARBURTON AND A WARBURTONIAN.

HURD'S LIFE AND CHARACTER — HIS RESERVE — VISITED BY WARBURTON — HIS LOVE OF EPISCOPAL DISPLAY — HIS STYLE — HIS CONTEMPTUOUS REMARKS ON OTHER WRITERS, EVEN THE MOST EMINENT — INSTANCE OF HIS PEDANTRY — DR. PARR'S PUBLICATION OF 'TRACTS BY WARBURTON AND A WARBURTONIAN' — REASONS WHICH HE GAVE FOR THE PUBLICATION; OTHER ALLEGED REASONS — HURD'S REMARK ON PARR'S SERMON — NOTICES OF PARR'S PREFACE TO THE 'TRACTS' — THOMAS WARTON'S PRAISE OF IT — BANKRUPTCY OF WARBURTON'S PUBLISHER — HONOURABLE CONDUCT OF WARBURTON.

LET us here give a little more attention to Hurd's character. The son of a farmer and a farmer's wife, plain honest people, he made his way, with some talent and much perseverance, to an honourable station in the world; and, like Pope and Warburton, did not forget to honour his parents in the days of his elevation; a merit in the characters of all the three that cannot be too highly praised. He was the second of three brothers, the eldest of whom became a farmer, and the youngest was in the Birmingham trade. The third was the only one that married; and, as he died in the prime of life, and left a widow, Hurd took care of her, and, when he became master of Hartlebury Castle, received her, though she was a person of no education, as a visitor, and used to lead her up, as Mr. Kilvert records, 'with stately courtesy,' to the head of his table.

But with his attention to his relatives, Hurd's amiability of character ends. Perhaps, indeed, his care for his family may be thought to have proceeded from a sense of duty, rather than from affection or feeling; for certainly, when we look to his literary and ecclesiastical character, we find little to love or like. The 'terse, neat, little, thin man,' as one of his college contemporaries describes him, seems to have been sadly deficient in warmth and cordiality. His temper and disposition will be best estimated from his habits and course of life.

When he was about thirty-seven years old, he succeeded, from his fellowship at Emmanuel College, Cambridge, to the rectory of Thurcaston, a small parish about four miles from Leicester, where he resided for several years. Here, as Mr. Cradock, of Gumley Hall, not far from Thurcaston, a member of the same college with Hurd, tells us, he showed himself 'distant and lofty,' and was 'not at all admired by those who did not estimate him in a literary capacity,' and to whom, indeed, he paid little attention, but kept them off as much as possible. In conversation 'he was always so much upon his guard' that Mr. Cradock did not 'believe that either his friend Lord Mansfield, or even Warburton, ever talked freely or intimately with him.' The only man that Cradock ever met, when he visited Thurcaston, was Mr. Ball, the curate, who never spoke of his position but with dissatisfaction. 'I do not pretend,' said he to Mr. Cradock, 'to be very learned, but I have never been treated with such distance, or rather disdain.' Cradock advised him to bear a while longer with Hurd's stiffness, who, he was sure, had a good opinion of him; but his situation grew daily more and more irksome and dreary, and he was preparing to quit it, when Hurd was appointed, by Warburton's influence, to the preachership of Lincoln's Inn, and, by his frequent absences, allowed his curate greater comfort. It is but just, however, to Hurd, to say that, when he became a bishop, he took the earliest opportunity of securing Mr. Ball an incumbency with a comfortable income.

While Hurd was at Thurcaston, he was more than once visited by Warburton. On one occasion, after Warburton had become a bishop, when he came to stay a week, and had been shut up in dulness for two days, he inquired whether there were no neighbours. 'None that might be perfectly agreeable to your lordship,' was the reply, as Mr. Cradock tells the story. 'What,' says the bishop; 'are all the good houses that I see around me here utterly uninhabited? Let us take our horses, and beat up some of their quarters. I have no doubt but that several will be inclined to be friendly and sociable.' 'I certainly cannot refuse attending on your lordship anywhere.' Accordingly they waited upon five gentlemen, 'whom,' says Mr. Cradock, 'I had the pleasure to know; and they all kindly accepted an invitation to take a family dinner at Thurcaston. When I heard of this at Leicester, I determined to call on Mr. Hurd, who received me with great cordiality. "Why, sir," said I, "there is nothing talked of but your gaiety; it has even reached your friend Dr. Bickham at Loughborough." "I don't doubt it," replied he; "and if you will pass the day with me, I will treat you with the remains of the festival, and give you an account of all particulars. I can assure you I was at first alarmed as to the provision that could be made by my little household; but all the company were disposed to be pleased. The bishop was in the highest spirits; and when the gentlemen took leave of me in the hall, they went so far as to declare that they thought they had never passed a much pleasanter day." "And, as you have been so successful, sir," I ventured to add, "in this first effort, I have no doubt but the experiment will soon be repeated." Mr. Hurd was silent.' He returned to the enjoyment of the quiet which, as he said in one of his letters to Warburton, the 'delightfully bad roads' secured him.

But the most remarkable proof of his concentration of

his thoughts on himself, one of the greatest instances, indeed, of extravagant conceit and self-complacency ever exhibited, is given in a letter to Mr. Cradock, regarding an intended visit to Gumley with a friend, specifying what he should like to eat and drink in his entertainer's house. 'My young friend, we shall not reach you till after breakfast, and then you will give us, as usual, only a nice leg of your mutton and some turnips, a roast fowl, and a plain pudding, or something only of that kind, as I do not eat anything but what is plain. I know you will expect me to drink the University of Cambridge in a bumper of your old hock. . . My young friend tells me he has adopted my tea rules from me. I like none so well as Twining's hyson at seventeen shillings a pound; by choice I never take any other, and indeed I never find it affect my nerves.' Surely he might have left the furnishing of the table to his host, without admonishing him of roast fowl, hock, and the most costly hyson.

He maintained, when he was raised to the bench, the same kind of reserve, and desire to draw attention to himself. Hartlebury church is not above a quarter of a mile from Hartlebury castle, yet that quarter of a mile he always travelled in his episcopal coach, with his servants in full dress liveries.* When he used to go from Worcester to Bristol Hot Wells, he never moved without a train of twelve servants. This state he maintained, as he avowed, not from love of ostentation, but to support the dignity necessary to his position and character. Had there been less liking for stateliness in the man, however, there would have been less of it shown in the bishop.

But if this personal assumption, this perpetual intimation that Hurd was somebody, was manifest in the course of his ordinary life, it is equally, if not more, conspicuous

* Kilvert's Life of Hurd, p. 200.

in his literary productions. He writes as one whose purpose is to be stiffly didactic, little solicitous to please, provided that he may be acknowledged to instruct. His style is such as justly to entitle him to Johnson's designation of 'a word-picker;' he is precise and particular, studied and elaborate, but producing pages rather free from faults than attractive with beauties. His matter and his manner alike give the notion of a writer conceited and self-satisfied. These qualities are still more offensively apparent in the supercilious tone in which he speaks of other writers, as Jortin and Leland, authors at least equal to himself. His letter to Dr. Leland, which we shall have occasion to notice hereafter, he wrote 'out of pure indignation at a coxcomb,'* a designation which he was so ready to apply to others, that others may have felt inclined to consider how far it was applicable to himself. 'Toup,' he says, 'is certainly well skilled in the Greek tongue,' but 'with all this he is a piece of a coxcomb. How is it that there are so many coxcombs, indeed so many, that one hardly meets with anything else?'† This was eminently gratifying to Warburton, to whom it was addressed, and who immediately expresses his concurrence in it: 'What you say of Toup is undoubtedly true. Wherever nature has sown her coxcomb-seeds, whether at court or in the country, they will spring up; and the man in the world, and the man out of the world, who was born with them, will be coxcombs alike, though coxcombs of very different species. However, this maxim is verified in all, which I think I once laid down to you in applying it to ——; that nature never yet put one grain of gratitude or generosity into the composition of a coxcomb.'‡ Encouraged thus, it is

* Kilvert's Life of Hurd, p. 94.

† Letters from an Eminent Prelate, pp. 349, 377.

‡ Ibid. p. 378.

no wonder that Hurd persisted in the use of the term. Alluding to Farmer's 'Essay on the Learning of Shakspeare,' in a letter to Balguy, he says that he 'knows nothing of it but from scraps in the papers;' that he knows nothing of Farmer himself, but 'that he is a young man,' but that he remembers the advice 'to shun all authors,' for 'the prince of coxcombs is the scribbling coxcomb.'* Priestley, as may be expected, is dubbed 'a wretched coxcomb;' this, he says, he knows, though he has not been curious enough to read him.† Another person, of a different stamp, poor Bishop Shipley, is, though a good man, 'a very coxcomb!'‡ And Dr. Chapman is 'an insolent coxcomb.'§

But how does he speak of other men, of somewhat higher rank in literature than these? Mr. Kilvert himself regrets the 'superciliousness' and 'self-complacency' with which he allows himself to speak of many men of eminence. Robertson's 'History of America,' he tells Dr. Balguy, 'may be worth your running over; there is a deal of prate in it, according to the Scotch way of writing history, and indeed everything else.' He has, therefore, 'very little kindness for any Scotch writer, except one or two, and for those only or chiefly because they have the feelings of men. Vanity, parade, false taste, and infidelity, are the portion of the rest.'‖ Of Gibbon he says, in a lordly strain, 'The author of the "History of the Decline," &c., *appears to have possessed a considerable share of sense, ingenuity, and knowledge of his subject, together with great industry*;'⸸ a noble specimen of the cunning of 'damning with faint praise.' Johnson, who had offended Warburton by his Shakspeare, was of course to be decried, and is pronounced to be 'a confident, overweening, dictatorial pedant.'**

* Kilvert's Life of Hurd, p. 100.
† Ib. p. 106.
‡ Ib. p. 115.
§ Ib. p. 45.
‖ Ib. pp. 132, 133.
⸸ Ib. p. 250.
** Ib. p. 254.

βασιλῆας ἀνὰ στόμ' ἔχων ἀγορεύει,
Καί σφιν ὀνείδεα . . προφέρει.

Of pedantry he might have been slow to accuse Johnson, being himself much more of a pedant. Towards the close of his life, Mainwaring, Lady Margaret's professor of divinity, paid him a visit, and speaking, during dinner, of some French people that he had seen passing through Worcester, he called them 'emĭgrants.' Hurd laid down his knife and fork, and exclaimed, 'Have I lived to hear the Lady Margaret's professor of Cambridge say *emĭgrant?*' The company were struck with astonishment, and the professor replied, 'My lord, I am certainly aware that the *i* in the Latin *emīgro* is long, but modern usage ——' 'Nay,' interrupted Hurd, 'if you come to modern usage, I certainly say no more.' Mainwaring, from regard to Hurd's age and infirmities, said also no more.* This is pedantry indeed. But if we grant that the first syllable in *mīgro* is always long, did the bishop always adhere to Latin quantities in his English, and always say senātor, orātor, executor, and always speak of the indicātive, imperātive, infinītive moods? Another anecdote, or another version of the same anecdote, in Johnstone's Memoirs of Parr,† makes the bishop himself call the French fugitives *emīgrants.*

The 'Dissertation on the Delicacy of Friendship,' and the 'Letter to Leland,' with Warburton's early 'Miscellaneous Translations' and 'Inquiry into Prodigies and Miracles,' were republished, as is well known, by Dr. Parr, under the title of 'Tracts by Warburton and a Warburtonian, not admitted into the collections of their respective Works.' Parr had, doubtless, some strong motive for this republication. He himself, in his Dedication of the volume to Hurd, and in his Preface, gives certain reasons for the proceeding; but it is universally

* Cradock's 'Memoirs,' vol. iv.

† P. 324.

supposed that he must have had other reasons of a more private and personal nature.

Let us first see what excuses he offers for reproducing the two tracts of Warburton, which Warburton himself had endeavoured to suppress. 'The author,' he says, 'from unnecessary caution, or ill-directed pride, would probably have wished these performances to be forgotten. But, among readers of candour and discernment, the character of Bishop Warburton cannot suffer any diminution of its lustre from this republication. They who are curious in collecting books, must certainly be anxious to possess all the writings of the eminent prelate. They who mark with philosophic precision the progress of the human understanding, will look up to Warburton with greater reverence and greater astonishment, when they compare the better productions of his pen with the worse. The faults of the one are excused by the imperfections of his earlier education; but the excellencies of the other must be ascribed only to the unwearied activity, the unshackled boldness, the uncommon and almost unparalleled vigour of his native genius.' 'If the bishop,' he adds in a note, 'imposed any prohibition' on the republication of those tracts, 'the right reverend editor has acted an honourable part in holding them back. But no obligation of this sort lies upon those to whom the bishop's commands were not communicated.'

These reasons for bringing again to light such forgotten compositions, which their author himself wished to remain in oblivion, are not very cogent; for the gratification to 'readers of candour and discernment,' or the advantage to the public in general, is surely quite insufficient to justify the liberty taken. The motives for the republication of the two 'Tracts by a Warburtonian,' the 'Delicacy of Friendship,' and the 'Letter to Leland,' are given as follows in the Dedication to Hurd:

After observing that the Tracts have become scarce,

Parr says, 'That scarcity has been shrewdly, or, if you please, my lord, perversely imputed, not so much to the avidity of the purchasers as to the management of the writer. But whatever may have been the cause, the fact is notorious, and therefore, in bringing them back to a tribunal, from which they are supposed to shrink, I shall endeavour to rescue them from the oblivion which sometimes overtakes the best publications, even at the hazard of exposing them to that infamy which is never inflicted but on the worst.*

'The biographer of Philip of Macedon, and the author of "Remarks upon Ecclesiastical History," had a right to expect, from their clerical opponent, a milder and more respectful treatment.† To a compensation of some kind or other they are certainly entitled; and your lordship, I trust, will concur with me in thinking that the republication of the books written against them will more effectually answer this honourable and necessary purpose than a direct argumentative defence, which, as the subjects are not exhausted in Jortin's note on Leland's pamphlet, I once intended to prepare for the press. It will show by the brightest proofs that Leland and Jortin scarcely need any elaborate justification; and that their antagonist, however plausible in his objections, or smart in his raillery, cannot, without the greatest difficulty, be justified by himself or his admirers.'‡

To these reasons for the republication, other remarks in its justification are added in a Preface:

'By the writer of these pamphlets, the characters of two very learned and worthy men were attacked with most unprovoked and unprecedented virulence. The attempt to stifle them is, however, a very obscure and equivocal mark of repentance in the offender. Public

* Tracts by Warb. and a Warburtonian, p. 145.

† Ib. p. 162.

‡ Ib. p. 165.

and deliberate was the insult which he offered to the feelings of those whom he assailed, and therefore no compensation ought to be accepted which falls short of a direct and explicit retractation.*

'Jortin and Leland now repose in the sanctuary of the grave, and are placed beyond the reach of human praise and human censure. Be it so. But there was a time when enemies, such as the unfettered opinions of one, and the shining talents of the other, were sure to provoke, found a momentary gratification even from such charges as the letter-writer ventured to allege. There was a time when those charges might have clogged their professional interests, and certainly did disturb the tranquillity of their minds. Yet, while they were living, no balm was poured into their wounded spirits by the hand that pierced them; and if their characters, after death, remain unimpaired by the rude shocks of controversy, and the secret mines of slander, their triumph is to be ascribed partly to their own strength, and partly to the conscious weakness of their antagonist, rather than to his love of justice or his love of peace. That antagonist, too, is still alive, and still finds his admirers among those, who themselves panting after greatness, are careful to utter only *smooth things* concerning the faults of the great. But his silence has not yet been represented even by his friends as the effect of contrition. His pen has not been employed in any subsequent publication to commend two writers against whom he had formerly brandished such censures as, according to his own estimation and his own wishes, were "aculeate and proper." His example—and this is the worst of all—his example, I say, is at hand to encourage any future adventurer, who may first be disposed to attack the best books and the best men, and afterwards, when the real merits of the dispute,

* Tracts by Warb. and a Warburtonian, p. 175.

or the real character of his opponents, are known, may contrive to let his mischievous cavils quietly sink into oblivion, to skulk, as softly as he can, from detection and disgrace; nay, to set up serious pretensions to candour as a writer, to decency as an ecclesiastic, and to meekness as a Christian.

'This republication has not the smallest tendency to "sow strife" among scholars. But it may prevent, and certainly it is intended to prevent them, from scattering the seeds of discord with wanton cruelty. It may deter, and certainly it is intended to deter them, from indulging any mean expectation that a calumniator can derive security from the very *failure* of his calumnies, or that what he has repeatedly and deliberately done in secret will not, sooner or later, be published openly. It may lessen, and certainly it is intended to lessen, the number of those who speak too well of a man by whom Warburton was most extravagantly flattered, Leland most petulantly insulted, and Jortin most inhumanly vilified.' *

For such strong vituperation of Hurd, we repeat, as for Johnson's vilification of excisemen, it has always been considered that there was some sharp personal stimulant in the breast of Parr. What it was, has been matter of frequent conjecture. He himself, it is believed, never told. 'My reasons,' he says, in a letter to Henry Homer, 'are to be found in Hurd's pamphlets, and I shall give no other. Personal reasons are out of the question.' † Perhaps there may have been more incentives than one. Three or four occurrences are related, from each of which may have arisen in Parr dislike or ill feeling towards Hurd.

One account is, that when Parr went to Hartlebury Castle for institution to the benefice of Hatton, which is

* Tracts by Warb. and a Warburtonian, p. 177.

† Johnstone's Life of Parr, p. 303.

in the diocese of Worcester, Hurd received him coldly, and did not even ask him to stay to lunch.* This want of attention, when we consider the reserve of Hurd's character, appears not at all incredible; and Mr. Kilvert allows its probability. But Mr. Kilvert attempts, at the same time, to apologise for Hurd's conduct, by observing that, though it may well seem inexcusable to have received a man of Parr's standing, a member of his own university and even college, with scant entertainment and courtesy, yet that, as party feelings were then running high, and Parr had placed himself in opposition to the court, Hurd, who had received his appointments from the sovereign, might have thought it reasonable to signify his antagonism to Parr's political views by affording him no very warm reception.

Another story is, that when Parr, on the same occasion, laid his papers before Hurd, Hurd objected to one of the signatures. Parr, glowing with rage, took up the paper, and exclaimed, 'That gentleman's name is as respectable as your own, Dr. Hurd.' How they afterwards settled the matter, the story does not tell.

By Dr. Watkins, in his 'Life of the Duke of York,'† Parr's enmity to Hurd is attributed to his disappointment, through Hurd's influence, of obtaining the post of sub-preceptor to the Princes, which, when Parr applied for it, was given to Dr. Arnald. To something of this kind Parr unmistakably alludes in his Dedication to Hurd. Contrasting Warburton's character with that of Hurd, he says, 'He, my lord, threw a cloud over no man's brighter prospects of prosperity or honour by dark and portentous whispers in the ears of the powerful; he blasted no man's good name by shedding over it the cold and deadly mildews of insinuation.'‡

* Johnstone's Life of Parr, p. 307; Quart. Rev. vol. xxxix. p. 276; Kilvert's Life of Hurd, p. 173.

† P. 39. ‡ Tracts by Warb. and a Warburtonian, p. 156.

Another cause of offence, which may indeed have been one of the greatest, is said to have been Hurd's well-known sneer at Parr's grand sermon on Education. Being asked by somebody how he liked it, Hurd replied he did not much like 'Dr. Parr's long vernacular sermon.'

> He prints a sermon; Hurd, with judging eye,
> Reads, and rejects with critic dignity.*

That there was some foundation for this story is plain from a passage in the Dedication: 'Knowing, my lord, the rooted antipathy which you bear to long epistolary introductions in classical writers, to long vernacular sermons from Dr. Parr, and to long Latin annotations from Philip D'Orville, I will take care, in the language of the Warburtonian school, not to stray beyond the limits of a just and legitimate Dedication.' † 'Parr,' observes Disraeli, 'has furnished posterity with a specimen of the force of his own *vernacular* style, giving a lesson to the wary bishop, who had scarcely wanted one all his life, of the dangers of an unlucky epithet.' Hurd seems to have had some special reason for fixing on the word *vernacular*, but I know not what it was. I can discover none in the sermon.

Some weight may also be due to the fact that Parr was patronised by Lowth, to whom Warburton and his followers were outrageously hostile. Whatever was the true cause, or whatever were the concurring causes, of Parr's displeasure, he certainly applied himself to the display of it with a hearty good will. We have paid almost attention enough, perhaps, to the Doctor's Preface and Dedication, but another specimen or two of their spirit may possibly be allowable. The pieces, like most of Parr's writings, consist of imperfectly connected remarks, and

* Pursuits of Literature, Dial. iii. ver. 187; Disraeli's Quarrels of Authors, 'Quarrels from Personal Motives.' Barker's Parriana, vol. ii. p. 333.

† Tracts by Warb. and a Warburtonian, p. 170.

paragraphs not naturally following each other, and contain a strange mixture of vehement and exaggerated praise and censure.

The following irony is very strong and significant:

'I am not apprehensive of any contradiction, even from your lordship, when I venture to pronounce these Tracts to have been produced by the same understanding, to be marked by the same spirit, and to have been directed to the same end. That understanding, doubtless, was acute; that spirit professes, at least, to be candid; and that end, probably, according to your lordship's estimation, was in the highest degree honourable. It was to deliver two illustrious, but whimsical, hypotheses, from the impertinent and tyrannical intrusions of common sense. It was to unmask the hypocrisy, and to subdue the insolence, of two impotent sciolists, one of whom had presumed to commend your patron without adulation, and the other to confute him without asperity. It was to convince an undiscerning and incredulous public that Warburton was an infallible reasoner, Leland a superficial trifler, and Jortin a most dastardly, a most insidious, and a most malignant calumniator.' *

One of the best paragraphs is that which presents a laboured comparison of Warburton and Hurd as writers:

'He blundered against grammar, and you repined against idiom. He, from defect of taste, contaminated English by Gallicism, and you, from excess of affectation, sometimes disgraced what would have risen to ornamental and dignified writing by a profuse mixture of vulgar or antiquated phraseology. He soared into sublimity without effort, and you, by effort, sunk into a kind of familiarity which, without leading to perspicuity, borders upon meanness. He was great by the energies of nature, and you were little by the misapplication of art. He, to show his

* Tracts by Warb. and a Warburtonian, p. 147.

strength, piled up huge and rugged masses of learning, and you, to show your skill, split and shivered them into what your brother critic calls ψήγματα καὶ ἀραιώματα.* He sometimes reached the force of Longinus, but without his elegance, and you exhibited the intricacies of Aristotle, but without his exactness.†

'To grapple with the unwieldy was among the frolics of Warburton, whilst your lordship toiled in chasing the subtle. He often darkened the subject, and you perplexed it. He, by the boldness and magnitude of his conceptions, overwhelmed our minds with astonishment, and you, by the singularity and nicety of your quibbles, benumbed them with surprise. In him, we find our intellectual powers expanded and invigorated by the full and vivid representation which he *sometimes* holds up, both of common and uncommon objects, while you, my lord, contrive to cramp and to cripple them by all the tedious formalities of minute and scrupulous analysis. He scorned every appearance of soothing the reader into attention, and you failed in almost every attempt to decoy him into conviction. He instructed, even where he did not persuade, and you, by your petulant and contemptuous gibes, disgusted every man of sense, whom you might otherwise have amused by your curious and showy conceits.' ‡

Let us conclude with one of the severest passages:

'Your critical writings, my lord, have by few scholars been more frequently read, or more carefully studied, than by myself. I have "paced it," § like Homer's mules, "with many a weary step," through the heights and the depths, the obliquities and the asperities, the archaisms and the modernisms, the strained analogies and the crooked

* Longin. sect. 10.

† Tracts by Warb. and a Warburtonian, p. 149. ‡ Ib. p. 152.

§ An expression from the Letter to Leland.

anomalies, the rhetorical flourishes and the logical quaintnesses, the colloquial familiarities and the oracular solemnities, of your most elaborate and peerless style. To snatch so many varied graces was not beyond the reach of your lordship's art. But I had learned, from the highest authority, that "the more generally the best models are understood, the greater danger there is of running into that worst of literary faults, affectation."* This, my lord, is one of the reasons which deterred me from every presumptuous attempt to *imitate your diction*; another was, the conscious disparity of my intellectual powers; and a third, not less efficacious than the rest, I shall, with the most painful reluctance, now reveal. Let my sincerity atone for my insensibility, when I confess to you that, often as I have read, and much as I may admire your learned researches, I seldom felt myself glow with that enthusiastic fondness for my original, which is indispensably necessary to successful imitation.'†

Tom Warton was so delighted with these antitheses that he told Dr. Routh, if he were desired to point out some of the finest sentences in English prose, he would quote Parr's Preface and Dedication of the Warburtonian Tracts.‡ And, indeed, with all their faults, their verbosity and *ampullæ*, their stiffness of phrase and strain after effect, it must be acknowledged that they are, on the whole, among the most nervous and energetic, and the most happily polished, of Parr's compositions.

Mr. Kilvert blames Parr for attacking Hurd with such virulence when he was sixty-nine years old, in delicate health, and seeking retirement; and intimates that, had Hurd been nearer the meridian of life, Parr would have added another to the list of sufferers for *meddling with*

* Hurd's Comm. on Hor. A. P. ver. 404.

† Tracts by Warb. and a Warburtonian, p. 166.

‡ Johnstone's Life of Parr, p. 325.

strife not belonging to them. But the truth is, that Hurd was not so far sunk in imbecility as to be unable to answer; for he had strength enough, five years afterwards, to give the world his 'Account of the Life of Warburton,' though much of this may indeed have been written previously. That he had any share, as Dr. Johnstone supposed, in a reply to Parr, which appeared before the close of the year in which the 'Tracts' were published, entitled 'A Letter to the Rev. Dr. Parr, occasioned by his Republication of the Tracts of Warburton,' &c., is not, it appears, true, for he told Dr. Balguy that he had 'no degree of guidance *ab extra* to direct his judgment' as to the authorship of it, and observed that it was 'written with great spirit and vivacity, and with such a turn of humour, as well as glow of friendship, that only one person could write it;' which person he conceived, as Mr. Kilvert observes, to have been Mason the poet. But it is now known to have been written by Dr. Lucas, rector of Ripple, near Tewkesbury, who had married one of Hurd's nieces.*

Before we conclude the record of the year 1755, we ought to notice that, during the course of it, Paul Knapton the publisher, whom Pope had recommended to Warburton, failed. He was generally considered to be the richest bookseller in London; his debts were twenty thousand pounds, and his stock was valued at thirty thousand. Warburton, to whom he owed a large sum, but who thought him an honest man, was his principal creditor, and accordingly had the influence, at a meeting of the creditors, to secure him favourable terms, inducing them to put his affairs, till they could be settled, into the hands of trustees, and to allow him, in the meantime, a handsome maintenance. Warburton said that his great fault was extreme indolence, and that he was to be pitied by everyone in his fall.

* Johnstone's Life of Parr, p. 313; Kilvert's Life of Hurd, p. 171; Barker's Parriana, vol. ii. p. 337.

'I was never more satisfied,' he writes to Hurd, 'in any action of my life, than in my service of Mr. Knapton on this occasion, and the preventing (which I hope I have done) his being torn in pieces. Yet you must not be surprised—I am sure I should not—if you hear (so great is the world's love of truth and of me) that *my* severity to him destroyed his credit, and would have pushed him to extremity. I will assure you you have heard many things of me full as true; which, though at present apocryphal, may, by my never contradicting them, in time become Holy Writ, as the poet says.' *

* Letters from an Eminent Prelate, p. 196.

CHAPTER XXVI.

HUME. DR. JOHN TAYLOR.

WARBURTON'S SON — WARBURTON MADE DEAN OF BRISTOL — ANECDOTE OF HIS 'READING IN' — 'REMARKS ON HUME'S NATURAL HISTORY OF RELIGION' BY WARBURTON AND HURD — HUME'S CHARACTER OF THE 'REMARKS' — WARBURTON'S GROSSNESS OF STYLE — UNFAIRNESS OF HIS REASONING — HIS VISIT TO HURD'S MOTHER — DEDICATION OF THE SECOND PART OF 'THE DIVINE LEGATION' TO LORD MANSFIELD — CORRESPONDENCE WITH THE REV. JOSEPH JANE — ATTACK ON DR. TAYLOR — CAUSES OF IT — WARBURTONIAN PHRASEOLOGY — PASSAGES FROM WARBURTON'S LETTERS.

THE only event of any importance in Warburton's life, during the year 1756, was the birth of a son, the only child he ever had, to whom he gave Mr. Allen's Christian name of Ralph. As the boy grew up, the father became extremely fond of him. Being asked to what profession he should devote him, he said he would determine according to his ability. If he proved himself a lad of good parts, he should make him a lawyer; if but mediocre, he should breed him a physician; but that if he turned out a very dull fellow, he should put him into the Church.* The boy gave such proofs of talent that he was destined for the law, but died in his nineteenth year.

He also printed a sermon, which he preached at Lincoln's Inn on a fast day, on 'Natural and Civil Events,' being 'the Instruments of God's Moral Government,' but which requires no particular notice.

In 1757, by the influence of Allen with Pitt, whom he

* Prior's Life of Malone, p. 445.

had assisted to become Member of Parliament for Bath, and that of Pitt with the Duke of Newcastle, he was promoted to the Deanery of Bristol, an elevation of which he affected to speak with the same indifference as he had previously spoken of his appointment to a prebend. As far back as 1753 the Duke of Newcastle had signified to Allen that he thought of asking the King for the Deanery of Bristol for Warburton, supposing it would be acceptable to both on account of its nearness to Prior Park. But '*if it comes*,' said Warburton, 'as Falstaff says of honour, *it comes unlooked for, and there's an end.*' *

'Last Friday,' he writes to Hurd from Weymouth, September 19, 1757,† 'I came to this place with a purpose to stay a week. The next day an express came to me from Bath, acquainting me with the death of the Dean of Bristol. You know I had a kind of promise of it some time ago from the Duke of Newcastle. What alterations some late transactions, or rather what revolutions they have made, in his Grace's promissory system, I can't tell. But I am very indifferent of obligations from that quarter; so I stay here with much tranquillity and unconcern, instead of posting to his levee.' But nine days afterwards he had the pleasure of hearing that Pitt had procured his nomination to the Deanery.

When he went to read himself in, as it is called, at Bristol, he fixed upon a saint's day for the ceremony; a day on which the rubric orders the Athanasian creed to be read. But this creed, perhaps from inadvertence, he omitted. At this omission some of the leading members of the congregation expressed discontent, and would not be satisfied unless he should go through the ceremony again, including the Athanasian creed, on the following Sunday. With this condition he complied. But, in consequence of this irregularity, it has been questioned

* Letters from an Eminent Prelate, p. 154. † Ib. p. 255.

whether he ever was, in legal strictness, Dean of Bristol. He omitted the creed when it was appointed to be read, and read it at a time when it was not appointed, complying with the directions of the rubric in neither of the services. However, the Bristolians were satisfied, and no one took advantage of the breach of rule to annoy Warburton.*

In the same year was published 'Remarks on Hume's "Natural History of Religion,"' a joint production of Hurd and Warburton, of the rise and progress of which we learn the following particulars from Hurd:

'In 1749,' says Hurd, 'Hume gave the public a hash of his stale notions, served up in the taking form and name of "Essays." These Essays came under Warburton's notice about the time that he was sending "Julian" to the press; and he soon after wrote to a friend at Cambridge, saying, "I am tempted to have a stroke at Hume in parting. He is the author of a little book called "Philosophical Essays," in one part of which he argues against the being of a God, and in another (very needlessly you will say) against the possibility of miracles. He has crowned the liberty of the press. And yet he has a very considerable post under the government. I have a great mind to do justice on his arguments against miracles, which I think might be done in a few words. But does he deserve this notice? Is he known amongst you? Pray answer me these questions; for if his own weight keeps him down, I should be sorry to contribute to his advancement to any place but the pillory.'†

What reply was returned to this application is not known; but Warburton left Hume at that time unmolested. Early in 1757, however, came forth his 'Natural History of Religion,' on which Warburton, as he read it,

* MSS. of the Rev. J. Jones, cited in Nichols's Lit. Anec. vol. v. p. 609.

† Hurd's Life of Warburton, p. 66.

made various remarks in the margin, or, when the margin was too narrow, on scraps of paper which he stuck between the leaves. In this condition the book was shown to Hurd, who chanced, at the time, to meet Warburton in London. Hurd, commending the remarks, advised Warburton to prepare them for publication, a suggestion which he at first affected to slight, but afterwards returned to the subject in a letter:*

'As to Hume, I had laid it aside ever since you were here. I will now, however, finish my skeleton. It will be hardly that. If then you think anything can be made of it, and will give yourself the trouble, we may perhaps between us do a little good, which I dare say we shall both think will be worth a little pains. If I have any force in the first rude beating out the mass, you are best able to give it the elegance of form and splendour of polish. This will answer my purpose, to labour together in a joint work to do a little good. I will tell you fairly, it is no more the thing it should be, than the Dantzic iron at the forge is the gilt and painted ware at Birmingham. It will make no more than a pamphlet; but you shall take your own time, and make it your summer's amusement, if you will. I propose it bear something like this title: "Remarks on Mr. Hume's late Essay called 'The Natural History of Religion,' by a Gentleman of Cambridge, in a Letter to the Rev. Dr. Warburton." I propose the address should be with the dryness and reserve of a stranger, who likes the method of the Letters on Bolingbroke's Philosophy, and follows it here against the same sort of writer, inculcating the same impiety, Naturalism, and employing the same kind of arguments. The address will remove it from me; the author, a gentleman of Cambridge, from you; and the secrecy of printing from us both.'

* Letters from an Eminent Prelate, p. 240.

Seeing Warburton in this disposition about the remarks, Hurd transcribed and put them in order, and, adding the Address and a short Conclusion, sent them to the press. Warburton, when he saw the pamphlet, told Hurd that he should have worked up the portions more into a whole, and expressed his fears that the real author would be suspected. But his apprehensions proved groundless, for the disguise, though very slight, served to keep Warburton's share in the performance concealed. Hume tried to discover the writer, and concluded that it was Hurd; for, happening to employ the same bookseller as Hurd, he learned from him, as Hurd supposes, from whom the manuscript had come. 'He was much hurt,' says Hurd,* 'and no wonder, by so lively an attack upon him, and could not help confessing it in what he calls his "Own Life;" in which he has thought fit to honour me with greater marks of his resentment than any other of the writers against him; nay, the spiteful man goes so far as to upbraid me with being *a follower* (indeed a closer, in this instance, than he apprehended) *of the Warburtonian school.*'

Hurd reprinted the 'Remarks' in his edition of Warburton's Works, but without the 'Address.' The passage in which Hume, 'the spiteful man,' complains of the attack on his book, is this: 'Dr. Hurd wrote a pamphlet against it, with all the illiberal petulance, arrogance, and scurrility, which distinguish the Warburtonian school.'

Hume had, indeed, just cause for thus characterising the pamphlet. It may seem strange that Warburton, when he might have adopted a calm gentlemanly tone towards his adversaries, or those whom he chose to regard as adversaries, should have assailed them all alike, the higher and the lower, the more and the less educated, the liberal philosopher and the narrow-minded bigot,

* Life of Warburton, p. 68.

with the coarsest and most unreasonable railing and abuse. He acts the part of a brutal clown making furious assaults on a gentleman, standing sword in hand, with a bludgeon; or he may be likened, to use a comparison of his own, to a scavenger, scattering that 'theological dirt,' as Bishop Watson calls it, which he himself was unwilling to hurl even on Tom Paine. It may seem strange that Hurd, who was to give the pamphlet against Hume 'elegance of form and splendour of polish,' should have left it full of the most offensive and rude phraseology that can well be conceived, of which a very little trouble would have cleared it. It may appear surprising that Hume should not have been induced, by the character of the style, to attribute it to the general-in-chief rather than the lieutenant; for it is certainly very different in diction from any of Hurd's published compositions.

To Hume's philosophy we need pay no more attention than we paid to Bolingbroke's, the one being as well known as the other; but we may, perhaps, not unreasonably bestow a little attention on the phraseology in which Warburton set himself to batter it. To give a notion of the tone of affected superiority pervading the 'Remarks,' it would be requisite to transcribe whole pages; but some conception of it may be formed from the selection of a few phrases and terms: 'Some time or other he may come to his senses; a few animadversions on the Essay before us may help him forwards.'* 'Our philosopher and his gang, with their pedlar's ware.'† 'Running his usual philosophic courses from knavery to nonsense.' 'An essay devoid of all manly sense, and even plausibility of reasoning.'‡ 'This great philosophic detection of one of the prime master-wheels of superstition labours with immovable nonsense.'§ 'His vanity, perverseness, and

* Warburton's Works, 8vo. vol. xii. p. 341.

† Ib. p. 344.

‡ Ib. p. 252.

§ Ib. p. 353.

love of paradox, make him always think at large, and write at random.'* 'I shall let this passage go unexamined, notwithstanding it looks so asquint both to the right and left.'† 'This wretched man.'‡ 'His last effort is to defend his dogmatical nonsense with scepticism still more nonsensical.'§

Enough of these verbal impugnations. But I cannot dismiss these 'Remarks' without noticing one specimen of fallacious reasoning, in which Warburton was as ready to indulge in dealing with Hume as with Bolingbroke. Hume says:

'After the commission of crimes, there arise remorses and secret horrors, which give no rest to the mind, but make it have recourse to religious rites and ceremonies, as expiations of its offences. Whatever weakens or disorders the internal frame, promotes the interests of superstition; and nothing is more destructive to them than a manly steady virtue, which either preserves us from disastrous melancholy accidents, or teaches us to bear them.'

Upon this passage Warburton thus remarks:

'"*Nothing*," says our philosopher, "*is more destructive to the interests of superstition than a manly steady virtue*," which, in plainer English, is: "None will be so free from superstition as the most hardened rogue." For the fact from which he deduces this proposition is this, that *after the commission of crimes, there arise remorses and secret horrors, which make men have recourse to expiatory rites. These remorses, by weakening and disordering the internal frame, promote superstition.* Now, the contrary state of this *internal frame* can be no other than such as enables us to bear the retrospect of our rogueries *without remorse and horror;* this he calls *a manly steady virtue.*'||

* Warburton's Works, 8vo. vol. xii. p. 363.
† Ib. p. 365. ‡ Ib. p. 370. § Ib. p. 376. || Ib. p. 374.

How unfairly Hume's words are treated, even a child may see.

Warburton flattered himself that he had crushed Hume into insignificance. But his exultation reminds us of Reynolds's portrait of Beattie, who, as the author of the 'Essay on Truth,' and for the gratification of George III., is represented by Sir Joshua as trampling on certain demons of infidelity, with faces greatly resembling those of Hume, Gibbon, and Voltaire. But these authors have not been affected by the aggressions of Beattie; they are still read and regarded; while Beattie, though deservedly honoured as a poet, is, as an antagonist of philosophers, utterly forgotten. Warburton affected contempt of Hume, but how much higher a place in literature does Hume now hold than Warburton!

A more pleasing subject of contemplation presents itself in the account of a journey made by Warburton to Durham, in the course of which he visited some of his relatives, and saw Hurd's mother:

'I had the pleasure,' he writes to Hurd from Durham, 'of finding a sister and a niece well at Broughton, with whom I spent a few days with much satisfaction; for you must know I have a numerous family, perhaps the more endeared to me by their sole dependence on me. It pleased Providence that two of my sisters should marry unhappily, and that a third, on the point of venturing, should escape the hazard, and so engage my care only for herself. I reckon this a lucky year; for I have married a niece to a reputable grocer at York, and have got a commission for a nephew in the regiment of artillery; and this fierce man of war lies at present encamped, much at my expense, at Amersham, near High Wycombe, as he notifies to me, with two field-pieces under his command.'* 'I came through Birmingham,' he says in another letter, 'and then I met with a person whose sight and

* Letters from an Eminent Prelate, p. 247.

good health gave me great pleasure.'* Hurd, from his manner of expressing himself, surmised that he meant his mother, and wrote to inquire. 'It was indeed Mrs. Hurd,' he replied, 'that I was so happy to see at Birmingham. You must give me leave to be a sharer with you in your tenderness to her. But it was by great accident I had this pleasure, and not till after two or three blundering messages of my servant. For as soon as I came into town I sent to your brother; but there being two of the name, I wanted to be certain I was right, so sent again and again. All this time I had not the least conception that Mrs. Hurd lived in Birmingham. But she having the goodness to speak to my man, as soon as she knew from whom he came, I got, at last, to the knowledge of her being with her son; and as soon as I did, I went to wait on her. Every word she spoke showed the goodness of her heart; and her sentiments would have become a duchess, or, to speak more properly, a saint. Mentioning you in the manner I thought fit, she said that if you did your duty, and was of honour to your profession, it was the greatest pleasure she could possibly have in hearing of you. In short, all her notions were generous, affectionate, and pious; and you are worthy of one another.'†

To this Hurd made a very sensible and appropriate acknowledgment, for he thought and felt rightly when his relatives were concerned:

'I write one line to tell you how tenderly affected I am by your goodness to my poor mother. The honour of such a visit was best acknowledged by the language of the heart. And this, I am persuaded, would not be wanting, however she might be unable to express her sense of it in any other manner. Nothing, I know, can exceed her gratitude for your constant favours towards me. And if they make me happy on other accounts,

* Letters from an Eminent Prelate, p. 250. † Ib. p. 250.

think how they rejoice me when I see them contribute, as they do, to make her happy who is so dear to me.

'I must have more than the bias of filial piety in my mind to be mistaken in thinking she is all you so kindly conceive of her. My poor father was just such another: the same simplicity of mind and goodness of heart, with an understanding that dignified both. In a word, my dear Sir (for though I spoke of writing but one line, I could fill my paper on this subject), it has pleased Heaven to bestow upon me two of its choicest blessings, the best of parents and the best of friends. While I live, I must retain the warmest sense of such mercies, and, of course, be more than I can express,' &c.*

In 1758, Warburton published a third edition of the second part, that is, of the fourth, fifth, and sixth books, of 'The Divine Legation,' with a dedication to the Earl of Mansfield. As Hurd thought that this dedication would be read by posterity with attention, and be reckoned among the chief honours of the noble person to whom it is addressed,† we may well see of what it consists. Warburton enlarges in it, as he was fond of doing, on his writings and their objects. He first speaks of the purpose of the 'Alliance between Church and State.' He had lived, he says, to see the time when that had come to pass which lawgivers always seemed to dread, as a certain prognostic of public ruin, the loss of the hold of religion on the minds of the people; a state of things which had its origin in the days of King William and Queen Anne, when, under the design of repressing the encroachments of a popish or half-popish hierarchy, the party in power depressed the Church so effectually, that they deprived her in reality of every power and privilege to which, as a society, she had a right, and kept her gagged and bound as a

* Letters from an Eminent Prelate, p. 252.

† Hurd's Life of Warburton, p. 7.

rebel, whereas true policy required them to go no farther than to prevent her from becoming factious, or being made the tool of faction. In this condition the Church continued, as Warburton represents, till his own day, when, 'to repel the cruel inroads made upon its rights and privileges,' he wrote his 'Alliance,' which, though setting forth only what was evidently intended to be, was considered by many as a Utopian refinement. Some, too, from dread of the mischiefs inflicted on society by fanaticism, had, by a strange mistaken policy, encouraged a clamour against *establishments*, the only means of preventing religion from degenerating into fanaticism. But not deterred by opposition, he proceeded to a second effort, 'The Divine Legation,' an endeavour 'to support religion itself,' which, experiencing a strange reception, 'awaked a thousand black passions and idiot prejudices, the zealots inflaming the bigots,' and many, even of the well-meaning, affixing on the work the charge of being paradoxical, a charge, however, which did not prevent them, or the public at large, from being eager to see the conclusion of it. As to the nature of the performance, he says it was a work of reasoning, one in which nothing is introduced which his course of argument did not sanction, for, if he enlarged on the Grecian Mysteries, it was to show the belief of the ancient lawgivers in the use of religion to society; and, if he expatiated on the Egyptian hieroglyphics, it was 'to vindicate the logical propriety of the prophetic language and sentiment;' and whatever other dissertations were inserted, all had reference to the illustration of the subject. But the little respect which is now paid to religion, is, he fears, a sure indication of approaching ruin to the State; for when Aristophanes began to abuse and ridicule the gods at Athens, the fall of that republic soon followed; and when, in England, 'wretches the most contemptible for their parts and the most infernal for their manners,' are allowed to rail against religion and civil authority, the destruction of our constitution may shortly be expected.

Such was his dark description of the nation's prospects; but happily his predictions, like those of many other prophets of evil, deserved no regard.

One passage in this dedication drew forth a mild and respectful remonstrance from the Rev. Joseph Jane, a student and tutor of Christ Church, Oxford, a man of retired life, and justly respected, as Warburton afterwards discovered, for his learning and piety.* The words which gave occasion to Mr. Jane's expostulation were these: Warburton, alluding to the obligation on the part of the clergy, in the generation succeeding the great depression of the Church, to influence the people in favour of religion, and to reason them into it again, had observed: 'Those whom their profession has dedicated to this service, experience has taught that the talents requisite for pushing their fortune lie very remote from such as enable men to figure in a rational defence of religion; and it is very natural to think that, in general, they will chiefly be disposed to cultivate those qualities on which they see their patrons lay the greatest weight.' Mr. Jane's remarks on this passage exhibit a striking mixture of humility and boldness. He begins by calling Warburton 'a man of vast genius, and, for the age, of prodigious learning,' who may well despise what comes from a humble person who is no scholar, and whom nothing but sincere love of truth would have moved 'to declare his abhorrence,' such is his expression, of one paragraph in the dedication which he 'has been no less surprised than grieved at reading.' He then expresses his fears that Warburton may be wanting in 'that poverty of spirit to which the first beatitude is promised,' for, says he,

'Did you not, in sad truth, *love* and study *the praise of*

* Letters from an Eminent Prelate, p. 275.

men more than the praise of God, when you gave way to all that train of thinking of which this is the close: "Those whom their profession has dedicated to" (the cause of Christ, the Gospel of Salvation, the truth in the love of it, would I say) "this service" (say you, "the reasoning the people into their religion again,") "experience has taught that the talents requisite" (for the work of the ministry I would have expected) "for *pushing their fortune*" (whom are you speaking of, Sir, the ministers of Christ or the servants of sin?) "lie very remote from what enable men to figure" (in heaven, I am sure; yea, or truly, you say well) "in a successful defence of revelation."'

This extract will give a notion of the letter, which proceeds to ask Warburton whether, at the last day, he would rather present himself at the tribunal with the simple ejaculation of Stephen the proto-martyr, or with all his 'popular, admired, singularly ingenious, learned, and inimitable productions,' and concludes with observing that the author of 'The Divine Legation,' if he is at all disposed to think with the writer, will, 'far from making a King's Bench matter of this free-spoken, honest, friendly letter,' thank the person who has ventured thus to address him.

Warburton received the letter apparently in a very friendly spirit. 'He wrote a reply,' says Hurd, 'with wonderful softness and condescension,' expressing himself much edified with the appearance of piety which animated all the parts of Mr. Jane's letter, and declaring that so far from being capable of prosecuting the author of such advice as a libeller, he had, 'of a hundred real libellers, never yet called one to account in a court of justice.' He then alludes to the different occupations of labourers in the religious vineyard, and to his own 'poor endeavours to clear the sacred enclosure of profane men and their profane opinions,' and justifies the remark so offensive to Mr. Jane's sentiments, by the following comment:—

'The general body of the clergy have been, and, I am afraid, always will be, very intent upon pushing their temporal fortunes; a fact so apparent to government, both civil and ecclesiastical, that they have found it necessary to provide rewards and honours for such advances in learning and piety as may best enable the clergy to serve and advance the interests of the Church of Christ. And, as this was the case, I endeavoured, in these obnoxious words, to show that if those rewards and honours be so misemployed, that, instead of giving them to learning and merit, they were diverted upon such as can only promote the interests and flatter the passions of the great, young men, in the entrance into life, seeing how matters were carried, would be tempted rather to cultivate the sordid arts of intrigue and adulation (which I insinuate *to lie very remote* from their duty), rather than the liberal endowments of learning and piety, which I call the qualities *that enable men to figure in a successful defence of revelation.*'

'But,' he adds, towards the conclusion of the letter, 'you have taken it for granted that I despise others, and especially men of your turn and character. Believe me, Sir, I am better employed. *Neminem contemno nisi meipsum.* Here I go on good grounds. I know myself best.'

Mr. Jane was delighted with the reply. He knew not *how to acknowledge the honour which Warburton had done him, and which he had gained to himself*, by 'answering his rude address and warm expostulation so meekly and obligingly,' and lamented that a severe illness disabled him from expressing his feelings as he desired, concluding with assurances to Warburton of his high and affectionate regard. 'The good man entertained ever after,' says Hurd, 'the greatest veneration for Dr. Warburton, and showed his letter on all occasions when he was Bishop of Gloucester, by which time Mr. Jane had been preferred by his college to the rectory of Iron-Acton, in that diocese.'

The good man would perhaps have felt less veneration for Warburton, if he had known with what levity, not to say contempt, he spoke of the letter and its writer in a communication to Hurd. 'One Mr. Jane wrote me an expostulatory letter in the very spirit of Methodism. You will not be surprised that I should give much offence to this rigid piety; but you will never guess what he picked out to declare his *abhorrence* of. It was this passage in the dedication, *Those whom their profession has dedicated to this service, experience has taught*, &c. He is scandalised that a minister of Christ should be supposed busied in *pushing his fortune* but towards the cross, or that he can desire to *figure* anywhere but in heaven. There were the marks of great candour and goodness throughout the letter; and it struck my fancy to try whether I could not soften and humanise a little this atrocious virtue, which I attempted to do in a very long answer.'*

But the great distinction of this edition was not the dedication; there was a preface to it, of which the object was a grand attack on Dr. John Taylor, the learned editor of Demosthenes, author of the 'Elements of Civil Law,' and known to all readers of Boswell as the Dr. Taylor that dined in company with Dr. Johnson, and spoke only one word during the whole evening. The pretext for this onset was that Taylor had expressed an opinion different from that of Warburton respecting the persecutions of the Christians in the time of the Roman emperors. Warburton, in his 'Divine Legation,'† had concurred in the general opinion that the primitive Christians held their assemblies secretly and in the night to avoid molestation from the civil power. Taylor, in his

* Letters from an Eminent Prelate, p. 275; Kilvert's Selections from Warburton's Papers, pp. 164-177.

† Book ii. sect. 6.

'Elements of Civil Law,' denied that such was the right view of the matter, and asserted that they suffered molestation from the civil power because their assemblies were secret and nocturnal. For this contradiction, ostensibly, he was assailed with great virulence in a preface of forty pages, entirely devoted to the refutation of his opinion. But the real cause for the assault is said to have been that Taylor, in some company at Cambridge, had thrown out a remark that Warburton was no scholar. This observation, through the agency of some good-natured friend, reached the ears of Warburton, who is reported to have sent somebody, very injudiciously, to inquire of Taylor whether he had really said those words. Dr. Taylor, as the story is told, answered that he did not remember *ever having said* that Dr. Warburton was no scholar, but that he had certainly *always thought* so.* If this was true, it cannot be doubted that Warburton, who was always anxious for fair opinions of his scholarship, would be highly provoked. Warburton, indeed, had spoken very slightingly of Taylor's scholarship in a letter to Birch: 'I have a very poor opinion both of Markland and Taylor's critical abilities, between friends;'† but this probably had not come to Taylor's knowledge.

As to the argument, Warburton appears to be in the right. None of the ancient writers, he shows, assign the holding of nocturnal assemblies as a cause why the Christians were persecuted; the only reason given for molesting them was, that they refused to offer sacrifice to the gods of Rome, and thus to testify that they were good citizens, and well-wishers to the safety of the empire and the state. Mysterious and nocturnal assemblies, for the celebration of religious rites, as those of the Bona Dea, of Ceres, and of Bacchus, had been universally tolerated throughout the Roman dominions; and why should any objection have

* Nichols's Lit. Anec. vol. v. p. 613. † Ib. vol. ii. p. 96.

been made to the nocturnal meetings of the Christians, merely because they were nocturnal?

But Taylor was not to escape from being pelted with the usual Warburtonian phraseology. He is one of 'a bundle of grammarians' who objects to the account of the Christian persecutions because it 'had never passed through his philologic office,' but 'lay open till our master critic was at leisure to examine it.' He is told that a dissertation which he had added to his book, on a tablet containing a decree about the worshippers of Bacchus, is 'a misapplication of his attention upon an old mouldy brass, and a set of strolling Bacchanals;' and that 'he seems much better fitted, whether as critic or civilian, to manage the intrigues of the Greek and Roman alphabets than to develop the policy of empires or adjust the rights of civil and religious societies.' And happening to say, rather unluckily, 'Antiquity, in its civil capacity, was generally indulgent to all who dissented from the established worship,' Warburton took advantage of the phrase to launch a sarcasm against the Antiquarian Society, a society of which Taylor was a great supporter, but which Warburton hated or despised. 'He speaks of *antiquity in its public capacity*, meaning, I suppose, the civil states of Greece and Rome, though in the mode of ordinary language it would be no inelegant periphrasis for the *New Incorporated Society of Antiquaries*.' *

Hurd had previously attempted a sneer at Taylor, in his address to Jortin 'On the Delicacy of Friendship.' 'There are several ways,' says he, 'of a writer's expressing his devotion to his patron, without observing the ordinary forms of dedication, of which, to note it by the way, one of the latest and best instances I have met with is *A certain thing* prefatory to a learned work, entitled *The Elements of Civil Law*.' This was shot forth to please

* Warburton's Works, vol. iv. pp. 39, 43, 51, 57.

Warburton, of whose disposition towards Taylor Hurd must have been well aware.*

Hurd was also consulted about the new preface before it was sent to the press. Warburton had proposed to omit the old preface, and give the new one in its stead. 'If,' replied Hurd, 'the former is to be only displaced, I have no objection. But if you mean to have it quite out, I cannot easily give my assent. I know that a great part of it was chiefly proper at the time; and Webster you think too insignificant (if, besides, the poor man were not disabused before now) to have this distinction continued to him. Yet, for all this, I shall regret the loss. I think it, in point of writing, one of your masterpieces. . . . . Otherwise this has the advantage greatly in many respects. Taylor is a more creditable dunce than Webster; and the object is not so personal as the other. As to the manner of introducing it, I can trust to your judgment to choose the best. . . . But, by the way, what do you think to do with the Appendix to this volume against Tillard and Sykes? I would not lose them on any account. And why might not Taylor rank with them? After all, keep me but the old preface in some shape or other, and I will have no dispute with you about the place.'†

In another letter Hurd suggested that Warburton might omit the former preface for the present, and leave it to be reprinted as one of his controversial pieces, in a complete collection of his works, which was sure at some time to be made. To this proposal Warburton consented, and said, 'As Cibber supplied the place of Tibbald, so shall Taylor take place of Webster, though (I will tell you my mind sincerely) *I do not think he has nearly so good an understanding as Webster!*'‡ In this way could Warburton speak of one of the first scholars of his country, with

* Tracts by Warb. and a Warburtonian, p. 223.

† Letters from an Eminent Prelate, pp. 213, 216.

‡ Ib. p. 225.

whom few would have thought of bringing Webster, though a fair theologic scribbler of periodicals and pamphlets, into comparison.

Of Warburton's clamour Taylor wisely took no notice. He knew by this time the effect of an assault from the author of 'The Divine Legation,' and resolved that there should be no *mecum certâsse feretur*. A friend of Taylor's, however, rose in his defence, and published anonymously a pamphlet, entitled 'Impartial Remarks on Dr. Warburton's Preface;'* but this was a weak performance, the author having neither learning nor ability to give the least weight to Taylor's side of the argument.

In concluding the account of this year, we may notice two passages in his letters which are perhaps worthy of remark.

One relates to the opinions which he had published on Job. 'Job,' he tells Hurd, 'becomes now as much the subject of dissertations abroad as he has been at home; and I am wrote against on the Continent, both in French and Latin; but with more decency than here at home in Billingsgate and English.'† His assailant in French was Bouiller, who propounded objections against his theory somewhat different from Dr. Grey's, 'with more art,' as Maclaine, the translator of Mosheim, observed, 'but with less modesty.'‡ Maclaine offered to insert any refutation from Warburton in the *Bibliothèque des Sciences;* but Warburton made no effort to vindicate himself. He contented himself with inserting among the notes to 'The Divine Legation' a piece of wit which he had previously used in letters to his friends: 'Job's *life*, by means of the Devil and his false friends, was an exercise of his patience; and his *history*, by means of criticism and his commentators, has since been an exercise of ours. I am

* Nichols's Lit. Anec. vol. v. p. 614.

† Letters from an Eminent Prelate, p. 269.

‡ Kilvert's Selections from Warburton's Papers, p. 250.

far from thinking myself unconcerned in this mischief; for by a foolish attempt to support his name and character, I have been the occasion of bringing down whole bands of hostile critics upon him, who, like the Sabæans and Chaldæans of old, soon reduced him back to his dunghill. Some came armed in Latin, some in English, and some in the language of Billingsgate. Most of them were professedly written against me, but all, in reality, bear hardest upon the good old patriarch. . . . If I scribbled ten pages on his back, my adversaries and his have *made long furrows*, and scribbled ten thousand.' *

The other passage is from a letter to Charles Yorke, who had sent him an account of an excursion that he had made into Nottinghamshire. 'I am glad to understand,' writes Warburton in reply, 'that you have amused yourself agreeably with a ramble into Nottinghamshire. It would have been the greatest pleasure to have chopped upon you at Newark, and I would have done so on the least intimation. I could have led you through delicious walks, and picked off, for your amusement in our rambles, a thousand notions which I hung upon every thorn, as I passed, thirty years ago.' †

Such was Warburton's reflection at the age of sixty. Of the notions hung upon the thorns, thirty years before, he had carried some into effect; more, doubtless, remained still unaccomplished. Of those carried into effect, the result of some, we may suppose, had brought him gratification; others, assuredly, had caused him only trouble and vexation of spirit.

* Div. Leg. 2nd note on b. vi.

† Hurd's Life of Warburton, p. 42.

CHAPTER XXVII.

SERMONS. STERNE. LITERARY AFFAIRS.

WARBURTON MADE BISHOP OF GLOUCESTER; BY WHAT INFLUENCE — DEAN TUCKER — HURD'S OBSERVATIONS ON WARBURTON'S PROMOTION — SERMON BEFORE THE HOUSE OF LORDS ON THE 30TH OF JANUARY; ITS MERITS — REPORT CONCERNING 'TRISTRAM SHANDY' — LETTER FROM STERNE TO GARRICK — LETTERS BETWEEN STERNE AND WARBURTON — SERMON ON THE EUCHARIST; OBSERVATIONS ON IT — WARBURTON'S RELIGIOUS LAXITY — NEW EDITION OF POPE — DR. JOSEPH WARTON — HORACE WALPOLE — RUFFHEAD'S 'LIFE OF POPE' — EPITAPH ON POPE.

ON the twenty-second of December, 1759, in the sixty-second year of his age, the Dean of Bristol was nominated to a vacant seat on the bench of bishops.

It was a lucky moment for Warburton, as far as promotion in the Church was concerned, when he first thought of 'rescuing Pope from the talons of Crousaz.' Pope, filled with gratitude, introduced him to Murray, who procured him the preachership of Lincoln's Inn, and afterwards a prebend at Durham; and to Allen, who, having made Pitt, by his influence, member for the city of Bath, had interest to obtain for the husband of his niece the Deanery of Bristol and the Bishopric of Gloucester.

He was consecrated January 20, 1760, and requested Dr. Newton, Bishop of Bristol, to preach his consecration sermon. In one passage of the sermon Warburton is thus commended: 'When divines, eminent for literature, conspicuous as preachers, illustrious as authors, are advanced to the first stations in the Church, it is not only a security to religion, but an encouragement to learning, and a strong incitement to others to prosecute the same studies, and to excel in the same useful arts.'

While he was Dean of Bristol, Mr. Allen had expended for him a considerable sum in repairing the deanery-house, which was not quite finished when Warburton was promoted; but Allen, who was no niggard of his money, was willing to complete what he had begun, provided a gentleman was appointed likely to do honour to the post. Dr. Squire and Dr. Tucker, well known for his writings on trade, were named as the two expectants, and Allen inquired of Warburton what sort of men they were. Warburton replied that the one made religion his trade, and the other trade his religion. Dr. Squire, who was afterwards Bishop of St. David's, and the patron of Dr. Dodd, was the successful candidate. Dr. Tucker was soon after made Dean of Gloucester; but there never appears to have been any great concord between him and his bishop. Bishop Newton gives the following account of their intercourse: Dr. Tucker 'had strong and lively parts, and, with many of the excellencies, it is no wonder that he had also some of the failings of every great genius. He was, too, an excellent parish priest, and an exemplary dean in keeping his residence and performing his duty, in managing the chapter estates, in living hospitably, in repairing and improving his house, and in adorning and beautifying the church and the churchyard. In these things he merited well, and had many good qualities; but it is to be lamented that he had not the respect for the bishop which was really due to his personal character as well as to his higher station, so that there was not that friendship and harmony between them which ought always to subsist between the bishop and the dean of the same cathedral. They were both men of great virtues, but they were both also men of strong passions. Both were irascible, but the bishop was more placable and forgiving; the dean longer bore resentment.'*

Hurd, though he signifies that a bishopric was but due

* Bishop Newton's Life by Himself, p. 79.

to Warburton's merits, cannot forbear intimating some regret that he was raised to that dignity. Mr. Pitt himself, he states, gloried in Warburton's promotion, as an honour to his administration. 'I remember to have seen a letter of his,' he adds, 'in which he said that *nothing of a private nature, since he had been in office, had given him so much pleasure as his bringing Dr. Warburton upon the bench.* This virtuous self-congratulation,' proceeds Hurd, 'became the minister; and others may be of his mind. But I have sometimes doubted with myself whether the proper scene of abilities like his be not a private station, where, only, great writers have the leisure to do great things.

'But let me not,' he continues, 'be misunderstood, when I say that great men should not be taken from their privacy, I mean great men indeed. The Church is, no doubt, much benefited and adorned by a learned prelacy. The pastoral functions cannot well be discharged by any other. But a genius of the high order here mentioned is given by a gracious Providence, now and then in a course of ages, *to correct*, as Dr. Middleton observed, *the sentiments and manners of mankind.* Such a man as this is lessened by elevation; he is in himself, methinks, too great to be advanced.

'But be this as it may, it must be allowed that religion and learning suffered somewhat by his promotion, as it interrupted those designs which he had formed for the service of both, and would have executed, if his whole time had been at his command. He himself lamented this inconvenience of his public station; and, after all, was not able (such was the root his former habits of study had taken in him) to be so active in it as he wished. He performed the ordinary duties of his office with regularity; but further than this he could not prevail with himself to go.' *

* Hurd's Life of Warburton, p. 70.

On the 30th of January following he was called upon to preach before the House of Lords the customary sermon on that anniversary. His sermon, in Hurd's judgment, was one of the best that he ever wrote, and unquestionably the best that was ever preached on that day. He was extremely well acquainted with the history of the times of Charles I., and told Hurd that there was scarcely a memoir or a pamphlet published between 1640 and 1660 which he had not read. His grandfather had been active in those scenes, and his grandmother, as we have observed, had told him stories of them; and, having been thus early initiated into that portion of our annals, he continued through life so fond of it that he had thoughts occasionally of writing the history of the civil wars.*

The excellence which Hurd found in the sermon, indeed, appears in its merit, not as a sermon, but as a history. The preacher gives a rapid sketch of the fortunes of James I. and his son. James, he says, succeeded to a line of imperious monarchs, who had made great encroachments on the liberty of the subject, and was himself eager to carry their over-exercised prerogative into a system of arbitrary power. He trained his son, who was but too willing to obey, to pursue the same course with himself, and the consequences were fatal; for 'what was only policy in James, became religion in the martyr Charles, and king-craft is made of much more ductile stuff than church bigotry.' Charles, on his accession, was unable to see that the people, having become rich by commerce during a long peace, were less disposed to bear whatever they thought oppression. They sought redress for what they considered grievances, but at length found relief hopeless. Meanwhile Puritanism was struggling for toleration, but Charles, detesting the Puritans as the enemies of prelacy, which he regarded, not like his father,

* Hurd's Life of Warburton, p. 73.

as a mere support to the crown, but as an ordinance of heaven, treated them with such severity as to force many of them to quit their country. Thus the patriots and the Puritans were alike disposed to resist his authority. He attempted to govern without the help of parliaments, but, being forced by circumstances to recur to their aid, he called one, which manifested its willingness to treat with him on a reasonable footing, but which he impatiently dissolved; and the next which he assembled, exasperated by his frequent breaches of faith, resolved on efforts for vengeance, and determining to sit as long as they pleased, continued their remorseless proceedings till they brought destruction on the king, the constitution, and themselves; for 'a swarm of armed enthusiasts, who outwitted the patriots, out-prayed the Puritans, and out-fought the cavaliers, overturned and desolated all before them in their extreme haste to set up the fifth monarchy of King Jesus.'

The character which he draws of the king is one of his best literary efforts:

'The king had many virtues, but all of so unsociable a complexion, as to do him neither service nor credit.

'His *religion*, in which he was sincerely zealous, was overrun with scruples, and the simplicity, if not the purity, of his *morals* was debased by casuistry.

'His *natural affections* (a rare virtue in that high station) were so excessive as to render him a slave to all his kin; and his *social* so moderate as only to enable him to lament, not to preserve, his friends and servants.

'His *knowledge* was extensive, though not exact; and his *courage* clear, though not keen; yet, his modesty far surpassing his magnanimity, his *knowledge* only made him obnoxious to the doubts of his more ignorant ministers, and his *courage* to the irresolution of his less adventurous generals.

'In a word, his princely qualities were neither great

enough, nor bad enough, to succeed in that most difficult of all attempts, the enslaving a free and jealous people.

'The full conviction of this truth made Laud (who was not so despicable a politician as we commonly suppose him), upon seeing his coadjutor Strafford led out to slaughter, lament his fate in these emphatic and indignant words: *He served a prince who knew not how to be, nor to be made, great.'* *

Hurd, immediately on the bishop's consecration, was made his chaplain, and assigned one of the best rooms, called the Abbot's apartment, in the palace at Gloucester, an honour, as he tells Warburton, never to be sufficiently appreciated, for 'the chaplains of other bishops, and even Lambeth chaplains, are usually thrust, with the other lumber of the family, into any blind corner.' †

'I shall be obliged,' he writes to Hurd, in February, 'to print my 30th of January sermon; but don't fancy I shall think it worth while to send you one; buy it, and welcome; you may have it for a groat.' Hurd replies, 'I resolve to have your sermon, though at the expense of sixpence, which your lordship will consider as one argument, amongst others, of the regard with which I am ever, &c.' ‡

In the early part of this year a rumour was spread that Sterne, who had, in the preceding year, published the first two volumes of his 'Tristram Shandy,' and, shortly afterwards, two volumes of sermons, intended to make Bishop Warburton Tristram's tutor; and Garrick, who was then intimate with Sterne, mentioned to him the report, to ascertain whether there was any foundation for it. Sterne sent him the following letter, in true Tristram Shandy style:

'Thursday, 10 o'clock, night.

'Dear Sir,—'T was for all the world like a cut across

* Warburton's Works, vol. x. p. 30; Serm. xix.

† Letters from an Eminent Prelate, p. 302. ‡ Ib. pp. 300, 303.

my finger with a sharp penknife. I saw the blood, gave it a suck, wrapped it up, and thought no more about it. But there is more goes to the healing of a wound than this comes to; a wound (unless it is a wound not worth talking of, but, by-the-bye, mine is) must give you some pain after. Nature will take her own way with it; it must ferment; it must digest. *The story you told me of Tristram's pretended tutor this morning.* My letter by right should have set out with this sentence, and then the simile would not have kept you a moment in suspense. This vile story, I say — though I then saw both how and whom it wounded, I felt little from it at first — or, to speak more honestly (though it ruins my simile), I felt a great deal of pain from it, but affected an air, usual on such accidents, of less feeling than I had. I have now got home to my lodgings since the play (you astonish me in it), and have been unwrapping this self-same wound of mine, and shaking my head over it, this half-hour. What the devil! Is there no one learned blockhead, throughout the many schools of misapplied science in the Christian world, to make a tutor of for my Tristram? *Ex quovis ligno non fit.* Are we so run out of stock, that there is no one lumber-headed, muddle headed, monster headed, pudding-headed chap amongst our doctors? Is there no one single wight, of much reading, no learning, amongst the many children in my mother's nursery, who bid high for this charge, but I must disable my judgment by choosing a Warburton? Vengeance! Have I so little concern for the honour of my hero? Am I a wretch so void of sense, so bereft of feeling for the figure he is to make in story, that I should choose a preceptor to rob him of all the immortality I intended him? Oh! dear Mr. Garrick, malice is ingenious, unless where the excess of it outwits itself. I have two comforts in this stroke of it: the first is, that this one is partly of this kind; and, secondly, that it is one of the number of those which so unfairly brought poor Yorick to his grave. The report might draw blood of the author of "Tristram Shandy," but could not harm such a man as the author of "The Divine Legation." God bless him! though, by-the-bye, and according to the natural course of descents, the blessing should come from him to me. Pray have you no interest, lateral or collateral, to get me introduced to his lordship? Why do you ask? My dear sir, I have no claim to such an honour, but what arises from the honour and respect which, in the progress of my work, will be shown the world I owe so great a man.

'Whilst I am talking of owing, I wish, my dear sir, anybody would tell you how much I am indebted to you. I am determined never to do it myself, or say more upon the subject than this, that I am, yours,

'L. Sterne.'

The two volumes of sermons were soon afterwards dispatched to the bishop with the subjoined letter from York:

'York, June 9, 1760.

'My Lord,—Not knowing where to send two sets of my sermons, I could think of no better expedient than to order them in to Mr. Berenger's hands, who has promised me that he will wait upon your lordship with them the first moment he hears you are in town. The truest and humblest thanks I return to your lordship for the generosity of your protection and advice to me; by making a good use of the one, I will hope to deserve the other. I wish your lordship all the health and happiness in this world, for I am your lordship's most obliged and most grateful servant,

'L. Sterne.'

To what offers of 'protection' allusion is here made, I do not know. As to 'advice,' it appears from the following letter, in which Warburton acknowledges the receipt of the sermons, that he had repeatedly admonished Sterne as to his writings, though Sterne, it seems, had never been introduced to him. 'He shows,' says Mr. Kilvert, 'how clearly he saw the errors of his correspondent, and how judiciously, according to the low standard of the day, he applied himself to correct them.'

'Prior Park, June 15, 1760.

'Rev. Sir,—I have your favour of the 9th instant, and am glad to understand you are got safe home, and employed in your proper studies and amusements. You have it in your power to make that which is an amusement to yourself and others useful to both; at least you should, above all things, beware of its becoming hurtful to either, by any violations of decency and good manners; but I have already taken such repeated liberties of advising you on that head, that to say more would be needless, or perhaps unacceptable.

'Whoever is in any way well received by the public is sure to be annoyed by that pest of the public, profligate scribblers. This is the common lot of successful adventurers. But such have often a worse evil to struggle with; I mean the over-officiousness of their indiscreet friends. There are two odes, as they are called, printed by Dodsley. Whoever was the author, he appears to be a monster of impiety and lewdness. Yet, such is the malignity of the scribblers, some have given them to your friend Hall; and others, which is still more impossible, to yourself; though the first ode has the insolence to place you both in a mean and ridiculous light. But this might arise from a tale, equally groundless and malignant, that you had shown them to your acquaintance in MS. before they were given to the public. Nor was their being printed by Dodsley the likeliest means of discrediting the calumny.

'About this time another, under the mask of friendship, pretended to draw your character, which was first published in a *Female Magazine* (for Dulness, who often has as great a hand as the Devil in deforming God's works of the creation, has made *them*, it seems *male* and *female*), and from thence it was transferred into a *Chronicle*. Pray have you read it, or do you know its author?

'But of all these things I dare say Mr. Garrick, whose prudence is equal to his honesty or his talents, has remonstrated to you with the freedom of a friend. He knows the inconstancy of what is called the public towards all, even the best-intentioned, of those who contribute to its pleasure or amusement. He (as every man of honour and discretion would) has availed himself of the public favour to regulate the taste, and, in his proper station, to reform the manners of the fashionable world; while, by a well-judged economy, he has provided against the temptation of a mean and servile dependency on the follies and vices of the great.

'In a word, be assured there is no one more sincerely wishes your welfare and happiness than, Reverend Sir, &c.,

'W. G.'

Sterne did not leave this letter unanswered:

'Coxwould, June 19, 1760.

'My Lord,—This post brought me the honour of your letter, for which, and for your kind and most friendly advice, I return your lordship all I am able, my best thanks. Be assured, my lord, that willingly and knowingly I will give no offence to any mortal by anything which I think can look like the least violation either of decency or good manners; and yet, with all the caution of a heart void of offence or intention of giving it, I may find it very hard, in writing such a book as "Tristram Shandy," to mutilate everything in it down to the prudish humour of every particular. I will, however, do my best; though laugh, my lord, I will, and as loud as I can too.

'With regard to the "Lyric Odes," all I know of them is this: that the first ode, which places me and the author in a ridiculous light, was sent to me in a cover without a name, which, after striking out some parts, as a whimsical performance, I showed to some acquaintance; and as Mr. Garrick had told me, some time before, he would write me an ode, for a day or two I supposed it came from him. I found afterwards it was sent me from Mr. Hall; for from a nineteen years' total interruption of all correspondence with him, I had forgot his hand, which at last when I recollected, I sent it back. The second ode, which abounds with indecencies, is, I suppose, his too; as they are published together, there can be little doubt. He must answer for them; having nothing myself to answer for with regard to them but my extreme concern, and that a man of such great talents as my acquaintance Mr. Hall is, should give the world so much offence. He has it greatly in his power to make amends; and, if I have any penetration, and can depend upon the many assurances he gives me, your lordship will, I hope, live to see it. He is worth reclaiming, being one of those whom nature has enabled to do much hurt or much good.

'Of all the vile things wrote against me, the letter your lordship mentions in the *Female Magazine* is the most inimicitious, and gave me, for that reason, the most concern; under which I had no better relief than denying the facts, and crying out against the hardship done me by such a contexture of his tacked together, not to serve me, but to overthrow me. Such profligate wretches too often gain their end. Every mortal in town says it was wrote by a Dr. Hill, who wrote the *Inspectors*, and, they tell me, has the property and management of that magazine. Garrick tells me the same story, and with reasons to confirm it. These strokes in the dark, with the many kicks, cuffs, and bastinadoes I openly get on all sides of me, are beginning to make me sick of this foolish humour of mine of sallying forth into this wide and wicked world to redress wrongs, &c., of which I shall repent as sorely as ever Sancho Panza did of his in following his evil genius of a Don Quixote through thick and thin; but as the poor fellow apologised for it, so must I: "It was my ill fortune, and my errantry, and that's all that can be said on't." Otherwise, I wish from my heart I had never set pen to paper, but continued hid in the quiet obscurity in which I had so long lived; I was quiet, for I was below envy, and yet above want; and indeed so very far above it, that the idea of it never once entered my head in writing; and as I am 200*l.* a year further from the danger of it than I was then, I think it never will; for I declare I have all I wish or want in this world, being in my calculation of money, all out, as rich as my friend Garrick, whose goodness of heart and honest cowardice in keeping *so far* out of the way of temptation, I nevertheless esteem and admire.

'The Bishop of Carlisle did me the honour yesterday of a call; of whom I had the satisfaction of inquiring after your lordship's health, and particularly how far the waters had relieved you under the pain and indigestion you complained of. He hoped your lordship was better.

'I wish your lordship all the most grateful man can wish—happiness in this world and in the next.

'I am, my lord, with all esteem and duty,

'Your affectionate servant,

'Lau. Sterne.'

The correspondence terminated with the following rejoinder from the bishop:

'Prior Park, June 26, 1760.

'Rev. Sir,—I have the favour of your obliging letter of the 19th. It gives me real pleasure (and I could not but trouble you with these two or three lines to tell you so) that you are resolved to do justice to your genius, and to borrow no aids to support it, but what are of the party of honour, virtue, and religion.

'You say you will continue to laugh aloud. In good time. But one who was no more than even a man of spirit would wish to laugh in good company, where priests and virgins may be present. . . . .

'Do not expect your friends to pity you for the trash and ribaldry scribbled against you; they will be apter to congratulate you upon it.

'Notwithstanding all your wishes for your former obscurity, which your present chagrin excites, yet a wise man cannot but choose the sunshine before the shade; indeed, he would not wish to dwell in the malignant heat of the dog-days, not for the teasing and momentary annoyance of the numberless tribes of insects abroad at that time, but for the more fatal aspect of the superior bodies.

'I would recommend a maxim to you which Bishop Sherlock formerly told me Dr. Bentley recommended to him, that a man was never writ out of the reputation he had once fairly won, but by himself.

'I am, &c.,

'W. G.' *

When Sterne published his fifth and sixth volumes in 1761, Warburton spoke of him, in a letter to Hurd, thus: 'Sterne has published his fifth and sixth volumes of "Tristram;" they are wrote pretty much like the first and second; but whether they will restore his reputation as a writer with the public, is another question. The fellow himself is an irrecoverable scoundrel.' †

Cradock says, I know not on what authority, that Sterne and Warburton were for a while on fair terms, but

* Kilvert's Selections from Warburton's Papers, pp. 239-246. Nichols's Lit. Anecd. vol. v. pp. 616-618.

† Letters from an Eminent Prelate, p. 335.

afterwards quarrelled, when Sterne threatened *in print* to make Warburton the tutor of 'Tristram.'*

In 1761 he revised and reprinted a sermon on the Eucharist, which he had preached some time before, entitling it 'A Rational Account of the Nature and End of the Sacrament of the Lord's Supper.' Of this discourse it will be necessary to give some, but only a brief, notice. Bishop Hoadly had published a tract, from which Warburton took the title of his sermon, called 'A Plain Account of the Nature and End of the Sacrament of the Lord's Supper;' in which he sought to prove, with very elaborate argument, from the words, 'This do in remembrance of me,' that the celebration of the Eucharist is nothing more than the commemoration of a deceased benefactor; a doctrine controverted by William Law, in a pamphlet demonstrating its 'gross and fundamental errors,' characterising the institution as it is generally understood. The Papists, on the other hand, of whom Warburton singles out Bossuet as the champion, go to the extent of asserting that the bread and wine are really changed into that which Protestants consider them only as representing. Between these extremes, Warburton takes a middle position; maintaining that the ceremony of the Eucharist, like that of the passover, is *a feast upon a sacrifice* — the sacrifice, in the one, having been actually slain, but in the other, at the time when the ordinance was instituted, being yet to be offered. He adds that it was also *a federal rite*, conveying the benefits of Christ's death and passion, and that those who were said to be *guilty of the body and blood of Christ* were such as slighted those benefits, and, by rendering Christ's death ineffectual, aided in effect the purpose of those who put him to death. In setting forth this view of the ceremony he is but a disciple of

* Cradock's Lit. and Misc. Memoirs, vol. iv. p. 204.

Cudworth, who advanced the same doctrine in a 'Discourse concerning the true notion of the Lord's Supper,' and whose tenets on the subject Warburton had embraced twenty years before, when he declared Cudworth's 'Discourse' to be a masterpiece in its kind, expressing the true nature and idea of the sacrament, supported with all the author's learning.*

He gives, in this sermon, a singular example of his occasional odd use of words. Refuting the doctrine of the *real presence* against Bossuet, and asserting that the words used at the time of the institution, *this is my body*, *this is my blood*, are figurative, he adds that such 'figurative use' of them was 'easy, natural, *elegant* and necessary;' and in another place he observes that the 'elements substituted were, in an *elegant* conversion, called by the improper, but very necessary, names of body and blood.'

'As concerning my Discourse,' he observes in a letter to Hurd, 'it is assuredly orthodox. So says the Archbishop of Canterbury; and that I have demolished both Hoadly and Bossuet; for

'Tis the same rope at either end they twist.

The archbishop did not say this, but Mr. Pope. However, the archbishop says, what you are likely enough to say after him, that *the people*, for whom I intend this edition, *are not likely to profit much by it.*'†

Mr. Nichols, dipping into the manuscripts of the Rev. John Jones, whom we have previously noticed as curate to the author of the 'Night Thoughts,' finds it there recorded that Warburton is said to have written his discourse on the Eucharist out of 'mere opposition to a much better treatise,' meaning, I suppose, that of Hoadly. How far this opinion regarding Warburton's book spread I cannot say; but the circulation of it seems not to have

* Letter to Birch, Nichols's Lit. Ill. vol. ii. p. 129.

† Letters from an Eminent Prelate, p. 319.

been great; and the prediction, as to its unprofitableness to the people at large, was verified.

The same Mr. Jones relates that Warburton himself was extremely lax in his attendance on the communion, even when regard to his office and character seemed to require his presence. Of this negligence he gives the following anecdotes:

'A gentleman of eminence in the Church assured me that a daughter of his, being in the same pew with Warburton, then a bishop, in a certain great church in London, both on Good Friday and on the Easter-day next following, on both which days the holy communion was there administered, observed with concern the prelate's leaving the church both times, when that solemn act of worship was coming on, and not joining in it. This was his then parish church.

'A worthy dignitary of the Church observed, with equal concern, the same omission or neglect in the Abbey Church at Bath. The Right Reverend went out, to the surprise of the congregation, when the act of administering the communion came on.

'The same dignitary told me this also from his own certain knowledge, and, probably, many similar observations might be added. This great author upon the sacrament, when he himself administers it, is said to be very precise and particular, drawing on a clean pair of white kid-skin gloves, &c. I almost wonder why his reverend lordship should not rather have his gloves for this office made of lawn.' *

This year also Warburton began to adopt very great strictness as to the rite of confirmation, addressing a letter to the clergy of his diocese, requesting them to adhere exactly to his direction concerning this rite, and to take care that no candidates but such as were duly prepared

* Nichols's Lit. Anecd. vol. v. p. 618.

should receive certificates of admission, which appear then to have been a novelty, at least in that diocese. Before he issued these regulations, he consulted Hurd as to their propriety, who apparently offered no opposition. But he seems to have thought the generality of his clergy likely to prove careless or refractory, for the efficiency of all 'will depend,' he says, 'upon the clergy's observing my direction, an attention to me which I do not expect.' * 'If the clergy did not understand confirmation before,' remarked John Yorke to his brother Charles, 'they won't be greatly edified by his lordship's letter.'†

In the midst of these ecclesiastical employments he did not omit his attention to literary subjects. Dr. Joseph Warton, by some remarks about Pope or his editor, had roused Warburton's ire. What the remark was, is now, I suppose, undiscoverable; it was probably something similar to those which are scattered up and down in Warton's 'Essay and Notes on Pope,' as to the groundlessness and futility of many of Warburton's annotations. The booksellers, contemplating a new edition of 'Pope,' asked his editor whether he wished to introduce any improvements; and Warburton wrote an angry note reflecting on Warton, but, before inserting it, sent it to Hurd for his opinion. 'I have added the enclosed,' he says, 'to the long note in the beginning of the *Rape of the Lock*, in answer to an impertinence of Joseph Warton. When you have perused it, you will send it back.' Hurd argued against its insertion, and Warburton listened. 'Your advice,' he replies, 'will determine me to strike out the note; the reasons you give have sufficient weight.' ‡

His wrath was also excited, about the same period, against Horace Walpole, whom he suspected of intending a sneer at him, in conjunction with Tom Hearne and

* Nichols's Lit. Anec. vol. v. p. 619; Letters from an Eminent Prelate, p. 326. † Harris's Life of Lord Hardwicke, vol. iii. p. 484.

‡ Letters from an Eminent Prelate, pp. 335, 339.

Browne Willis, in his 'Anecdotes of Painting.'* He accordingly wrote to Garrick,† requesting him to sound Walpole on the subject, 'for if,' said he, 'he means me, I shall be *about his pots*, as Bentley said to Lord Halifax of Rowe—I mean the gallipots and washes of his toilet; for I know he has a fribble-tutor at his elbow as sicklied o'er with affectation as himself.' Garrick in consequence spoke to Walpole on the matter, who denied on his honour, both to Garrick and Lord Mansfield, that he had Warburton at all in his thoughts when he was writing; and Warburton, in another letter to Garrick,‡ thanks him for communicating with Walpole, and says: 'His denying such intention on his honour gives me full satisfaction, though neither I nor my friends know what the passage aims at if he has not that intention.'

Walpole's own account of the affair is as follows:

'I had been told [by Garrick] that Bishop Warburton resented something in the chapter of Architecture in my "Anecdotes of Painting," and that he intended to abuse me in the new edition of Mr. Pope's works. . . . As I had not once thought of him in that work, it was not easy to guess at what he was offended. On looking over the chapter, I concluded he had hit some nonsense about the Phœnicians; but having read very few of his works, it was impossible for me to tell where to find it. As I would not disoblige even a coxcomb unprovoked, and know how silly a literary controversy is, in which the world only laughs at both sides, I desired Dr. Charles Lyttelton, Bishop of Carlisle, to ask him if what I had said of the Phœnicians was the rock of offence, and to assure him I had read few of his things, and had no intention of laughing at him. I name Bishop Lyttelton, because if it had not come from one of his own order, all arrogant and absurd as Warburton is, one could scarce believe it possible that

* Vol. i. pp. 106, 107. † Feb. 17, 1762. ‡ April 22, 1762.

he could have pushed vanity and folly to such a height as appeared in his answer. He replied: 'The Phœnicians! No, no. He alluded to my note in the edition of "Pope," in which I have spoken of Gothic architecture; I have exhausted the subject.' I will only remark on this excess of impertinent self-conceit, that if he can *exhaust* subjects in so few lines, it was very unnecessary for him to write so many thousands. After this, I would as soon have a controversy with a peacock, or with an only daughter that her parents think handsome. The fowl, the miss, and the bishop, are alike incorrigible. The first struts naturally; the second is spoiled; reason itself has been of no use to the last.' *

The booksellers were at the same time asking him, or, as he expresses it, teasing him for a Life of Pope; and he was sometimes inclined to comply with their solicitations. For the foundation of Pope's biography, he thought of assembling his scattered anecdotes and critical observations into a body; but such a collection would have necessitated an entire remodelling of the notes on Pope, from which everything of the kind must have been withdrawn. But the proposal was never executed; what he did in that way was merely to assist Ruffhead, whose book, after all the aid that it received, gave ample cause for Johnson's remark that the writer 'knew nothing of Pope and nothing of poetry.' Several passages in the work bear evident marks of Warburton's hand. One of them, a glaring *purpureus pannus*, far above the feebleness of Ruffhead, respecting the purpose of 'The Dunciad,' has been marked by Disraeli: 'The *good purpose* intended by this satire was, to the *herd* in general, of less efficacy than our author hoped; for *scribblers* have not the common sense of *other vermin*, who usually abstain from mischief, when they see

* 'Short Notes of My Own Life;' Walpole's Letters, vol. i. p. lxxiii., Cunningham's edition.

any of their kind *gibbeted* or *nailed up* as terrible examples.' A coarse simile, which Warburton has used elsewhere.

But if he did not write the Life of Pope, he compounded an inscription for a monument to him, which, during this year, seventeen years after Pope's death, *the Bishop of Gloucester* thought proper to attach to the wall of Twickenham Church. The inscription, beneath a medallion portrait of the poet, is this:

Alexandro Pope
M.H.
Gulielmus Episcopus Glocestriensis
Amicitiæ causa fac. cur.
MDCCLXI.

Poeta loquitur:

For one who would not be buried in Westminster Abbey.

Heroes and kings, your distance keep!
In peace let one poor poet sleep,
Who never flatter'd folks like you:
Let Horace blush, and Virgil too.

It manifested sad want of judgment, and of what was due to his friend's memory, to select for his monument these light verses, which their author had written but in jest, and without any expectation that they would ever be placed over his own or any other person's grave. He himself had signified in his will a desire that nothing should be written over him but a single line recording the time of his death, subjoined to the following inscription which he had put up to his parents:

D. O. M.

Alexandro Pope, viro innocuo, probro, pio,
Qui vixit annos LXXV. ob. M DCC XVII.
Et Edithæ conjugi inculpabili, pientissimæ,
Quæ vixit annos XCIII. ob. M DCC XXXIII.
Parentibus bene merentibus Filius fecit.

The line to be added was this:

Et sibi. Obiit An. MDCCXLIX. Ætatis LVI.

The Bishop, for whatever reason, kept his tablet at a distance from that of Pope, the one being on the north wall, and the other on the east.

CHAPTER XXVIII.

'DOCTRINE OF GRACE.' WESLEY AND WHITFIELD.

PUBLICATION OF 'THE DOCTRINE OF GRACE'—MIDDLETON ON THE GIFT OF TONGUES — WARBURTON'S ARGUMENTS IN REPLY TO HIM — INSPIRATION OF THE NEW TESTAMENT — DIFFERENT NOTIONS OF ELOQUENCE — WARBURTON'S OPINIONS OF WESLEY AND WHITFIELD — MODERN FANATICS—WESLEY'S JOURNALS—CHARACTERISTICS OF TRUE WISDOM — ZINZENDORF; LAW; THE BEHMENISTS — REMARKS ON WESLEY'S PROCEEDINGS; EXTRAVAGANT EFFECTS OF HIS PREACHING AND THAT OF HIS FOLLOWERS — WESLEY'S DISREGARD OF PRUDENCE — CONCLUSION OF WARBURTON'S BOOK.

THE year 1762 saw the publication of 'The Doctrine of Grace,' two volumes intended chiefly against John Wesley, whose enthusiasm was then fermenting among the lower classes, but, that Wesley might not have the honour of the whole attack, directed in part against Middleton, who had questioned, or rather denied, the plenary inspiration of the Scriptures. The book was an enlargement or re-composition of a sermon which he had printed on the influence of the Holy Spirit, with a copious infusion of Wesley's records of his experiences.

We must review, however briefly, the whole tract, as we shall have occasion to notice Dr. Leland's answer to the first part of it. The full title is, 'The Doctrine of Grace; or, The Office and Operations of the Holy Spirit Vindicated from the Insults of Infidelity and the Abuses of Fanaticism; with some Thoughts (humbly offered to the consideration of the Established Clergy) regarding the Right Method of defending Religion against the Attacks of either Party.'

Warburton had previously published a sermon on the

text, 'Answer not a fool according to his folly, lest thou also be like to him; Answer a fool according to his folly, lest he be wise in his own conceit;' which sermon he now remodelled for a preface to his new work. It was directed principally on the enthusiastic Wesleyans, who were not to be answered according to their folly, lest the answerer should contaminate himself with the abuses which he would remove; and who were to be answered according to their folly, in order that they might be made to perceive, if possible, the grievous consequences arising from conduct prompted by their vain conceit of superior wisdom.

But the first assault is made upon Middleton. That 'learned person,' as Warburton calls him, had declared that the gift of tongues, on the day of Pentecost, was not a lasting endowment, but a mere temporary sign that the person distinguished by it was a chosen preacher of the Gospel. Had it been a permanent qualification, he considers such a gift from the Divinity must have affected the whole language of the New Testament. Had the gift of tongues been lasting, he argues, 'it would have been employed in the composition of the Gospels and Epistles; but that it was not there employed, appears from the barbarity of the style; since whatever comes from God must be perfect in its kind; so that, in this case, we should be sure to find the purity of Plato and the eloquence of Cicero.'

That the gift of tongues was merely temporary, Warburton stoutly denies, because St. Paul expresses his thankfulness that he *spoke with tongues more than they all*, evidently showing that, while others retained the endowment, he himself, as being the apostle of the Gentiles, enjoyed a greater share of it than any of them; and because, when once the gift was conferred, it became a natural power, and to have withdrawn it from the possessors would have required another miracle.

But, as to the other part of Middleton's argument, which tends to show, from the style of the New Testament, that it *was not inspired*, how far do those who maintain its inspiration suppose that the several writers of it *were inspired*, and what sort of inspiration did they receive? Some kind of assistance was doubtless vouchsafed them, the Spirit having been promised to guide them into all truth. Having received the truth, they were to communicate it by two methods of ministration: they were to impart instruction, by oral addresses, to their contemporaries, and to compose written rules for the direction of the Church in all ages; and if they were divinely fit for uttering instruction of a temporary and occasional nature during their lives, it is improbable that they were left unaided in writing what was to remain permanent after their deaths.

What sort of aid, then, did they experience? How were they inspired? They did not receive *organic inspiration*; the writers were not mere passive organs through which every word was conveyed; for, as Warburton argues, such constant inspiration would, in the first place, have been needless, as the writers would state much from their own knowledge; secondly, if it had been afforded, there must have been the most perfect agreement among the four evangelists, even in the minutest particulars; thirdly, there must then have been similar phraseology throughout all the writings; and, fourthly, every word, we must suppose, would in that case have been preserved pure throughout all ages, unaffected by the blindness and mistakes of transcribers, 'otherwise the Holy Spirit would appear to have laboured in vain.' But the sense in which the inspiration given is to be understood is this: that the writers were so far directed, that no error of importance should proceed from them; that they were enlightened in all particulars which were necessary for the instruction of the Church, and which, from ignorance or incapacity, they would have represented imperfectly, partially, or falsely; and that they were under such influence only, as allowed them the use, and left them to the guidance, of their own faculties, as long as they avoided mistakes, and restrained them only when they were in danger of going wrong.*

Such a notion of inspiration not only agrees with the general nature and aspect of the New Testament, but is supported by the very words of its writers. St. Peter, speaking of the Epistles of St. Paul, expresses himself in very temperate phrase concerning their inspiration: *He hath written to you according to the wisdom given unto him.* And St. Paul himself, on one occasion, speaks with doubt of his own inspiration; he first gives his own judgment, and then adds, *and I think that I have the Spirit of God*; a mode of expression which shows that he could not have been under organic inspiration, about the presence of which he could have been in no uncertainty.

'It may be said,' remarks Warburton, 'that on this moderated idea of inspiration we shall never be able to distinguish which parts were written under the immediate influence of the Spirit, and which were the product of human knowledge only.' But 'what,' he asks, 'if we shall not? Where is the mischief or inconvenience? While all we want to know is, that every sentence of Scripture, which but remotely concerns either faith or practice, is infallibly true, it is of little consequence to us to be instructed how or in what manner that truth came to be secured; whether by direct inspiration, or by that virtual superintendence of the Spirit, which preserved the writers of it from error. Scripture is the rule of Christian conduct; and, if the rule be known to be unerring, this is all that is wanting to effectuate its end.' The mode of the delivery of the truths, he adds, does not affect the origin of the truths themselves.†

After thus settling the question as to the degree in

* Doctrine of Grace, b. i. c. 6, 7.

† Ib. c. 7.

which the New Testament was inspired, he considers that Middleton's remarks on the style, purporting that it cannot be inspired at all, require some further comment. Middleton's words are, 'We should naturally expect to find an inspired language to be such as is worthy of God; that is, pure, clear, noble, and affecting, even beyond the force of common speech; since nothing can come from God but what is perfect in its kind. Now, if we try the apostolic language by this rule, we shall be so far from ascribing it to God, that we shall scarce think it worthy of man; that is, of the liberal and polite; it being utterly rude and barbarous, and abounding with every fault that can possibly deform a language. And though some writers, prompted by a false zeal, have attempted to defend the purity of the Scripture Greek, their labour has been idly employed.' *

These observations, says Warburton, are founded on two propositions which are taken for granted, but of which neither is true: the first, that an inspired language must necessarily be a language of eloquence; the second, that eloquence is something 'congenial and essential to human speech.'

On the first proposition he remarks that, even if the style of the New Testament were such as Middleton describes it, 'utterly rude and barbarous, and abounding with every fault that can possibly deform a language,' this rudeness and barbarity would be so far from proving the language not divinely inspired, that it would be a certain mark of its divine original; since the style of persons who had had the Greek tongue 'miraculously infused into them,' and who 'had not afterwards cultivated their knowledge of the language,' as was the case with these persons, 'on the principles of Grecian eloquence, would be precisely such as we find it in the books of the New

* Middleton's Essay on the Gift of Tongues, Works, vol. ii. p. 91.

Testament.' 'For,' he proceeds, and we must quote his own words for fear of misrepresentation, 'if this only be allowed which no one will contest with me, that a strange language acquired by illiterate men, in the ordinary way, would be full of the idioms of their native tongue, just as the Scripture-Greek is observed to be full of Syriasms and Hebraisms, how can it be pretended, by those who reflect on the nature of language, that a strange language divinely infused into illiterate men, like that at the day of Pentecost, could have any other properties or conditions?'*

As to the second proposition, that 'eloquence is something congenial and essential to human speech,' it supposes, he says, that there is some certain archetype in nature, on which eloquence is to be formed and modelled; and indeed, if such were the case, it might be but reasonable to conclude that when the Author of Nature inspired a display of eloquence, he would adhere in every respect to the archetype. But the supposition that there is any such archetype, or that eloquence is an essential of speech, is fanciful and groundless. The qualities of eloquence are unsettled and arbitrary, dependent on the customs and fashions, tempers and manners, of the various nations of the earth. 'So that that mode of composition, which is a model of *perfect eloquence* to one nation or people, must appear extravagant or mean to another.' And thus in fact it was. Indian and Asiatic eloquence were esteemed hyperbolic, abrupt, and puerile, to the more phlegmatic inhabitants of Rome and Athens. And the western eloquence, in its tone, appeared nerveless and effeminate, frigid or insipid, to the hardy and inflamed imaginations of the East. . . . . But inspired writing, the objectors say, implies the *most perfect eloquence.* What human model then was the Holy Ghost to follow? And a human model, of arbitrary constitution, it must needs be, because

* Doctrine of Grace, b. i. c. 8.

there was no other: or, if there was another, it would never suit the purpose, which was to make impressions on the minds and affections; and this impression such an eloquence only as that which had gained the popular ear could effect. Should therefore the Eastern eloquence be employed? But this would be too inflated or gigantic for the West. Should it be the Western? But this would be too cold and torpid for the East. Or suppose the *generic* eloquence of the more polished nations was to be preferred, which *species* of it was to be employed? The rich exuberance of the Asiatic Greeks, or the dry conciseness of the Spartans? The pure and poignant ease and flowing sweetness of the Asiatic modulation, or the strength and grave severity of the Roman tone? Or should all give way to that African torrent which arose from the fermented mixture of the dregs of Greece and Italy, and soon after overflowed the Church with theological conceits in a sparkling luxuriancy of thought, and a sombrous rankness of expression? Thus various were the specieses! all as much decried by a different genus, and each as much disliked by a different species, as the eloquence of the remotest East and West, by one another.'*

But are there not certain substantial principles of eloquence, common to all? Doubtless there are. Why then should not these have been employed in the apostolic language? Because eloquence was not at all required. Neither was the speaker to make an impression on the hearers by the aid of eloquence; nor were the hearers to expect the speaker's words to be recommended by anything else than their sound sense. It was not the feelings that were to be moved, but the reason that was to be convinced. For this purpose it was the great qualities, not of eloquence, but of language in general, that were needed. Preaching was not to be *with enticing words*. *Clearness*

* Doctrine of Grace, b. i. c. 9.

and *precision* of expression were the only requisites; the only means necessary to convey the sense of the speaker or writer to the mind of the hearer or reader. These are the qualities essential to intelligible language; qualities always the same, and independent on custom or climate. These qualities are found, says Warburton, in an eminent degree, in the writers of the New Testament, so that whatever difficulties, in regard to the understanding of their language, present themselves, arise, not from any rudeness or barbarity in it, but from the sublime or obscure nature of the subjects about which it is employed, or occasionally, perhaps, from conciseness of expression in the writer.

The shrewd Wesley and the weak Whitfield had long been objects of attention to Warburton. He had been a diligent reader of Wesley's journals, and had formed from them no unfair estimation of the writer's character. He had for many years regarded such fanatics as insensible to reason, and to be kept down only by drawing on them the ridicule and contempt of their fellow-creatures.

As early as 1738 he had thus spoken of these enthusiasts in a letter to Des Maizeaux: 'What think you of our new set of fanatics, called the *Methodists*? I have seen Whitfield's Journal, and he appears to me to be as mad as ever George Fox the Quaker was. These are very fit missionaries, you will say, to propagate the faith among infidels. There is another of them, one Wesley, who came over from the same mission. He told a friend of mine that he had lived most deliciously the last summer in Georgia, sleeping under trees, and feeding on boiled maize, sauced with the ashes of oak leaves; that he will return thither, and then will cast off his English dress, and wear a dried skin, like the savages, the better to ingratiate himself with them. It would be well for virtue and religion if this humour would lay hold generally of our over-heated bigots, and send them to cool themselves in the Indian marshes. I fancy that Venn and Webster would make a very entertaining, as well as proper, figure in a couple of bear-skins, and marching in this terror of equipage, like the Pagan priests of Hercules of old:

> Jamque sacerdotes, primusque Potitius, ibant,
> *Pellibus* in morem cincti, *flammasque* ferebant.'*

In a letter to Dr. Birch, also, written in the same year, he says, 'Your sentiments of the Methodists are unquestionably right; and of their original from a discountenanced party. Fanaticism rises from oppression ever. A couple of these Methodists, of whom Wesley was one, travelling into this neighbourhood (that of Brant-Broughton) on foot, took up their lodging with a clergyman of their acquaintance. The master of the house going into their chamber in the morning to salute them, perceived' a certain vessel 'full of blood, and on asking the occasion, was told it was *their method*, when the blood grew rebellious, to draw it off by breathing a vein in this manner; that they had been heated with travel, and thought it proper to cool themselves. If common report may be credited, the men from whom they sprung, as Hicks and Collier, had a more natural way of evacuation.' As to Whitfield, he says, 'The poor man is quite mad. I could not but take notice of some very ridiculous expressions he uses [in his Journal]; as that "the more you do for God, the more you may."'† He had also formed the design of exposing these "idle fanatics," as he calls them, by printing, for the purpose of comparison, passages from George Fox's Journals, Ignatius Loyola, the "Trials and last Behaviour of the Regicides," and the Journals of the modern Methodists, showing how all were set on flame with unreasoning enthusiasm.

This design he now partly executed, but confined his attention chiefly to the Journals of Wesley and the accounts

* Nichols's Lit. Illustr. vol. ii. p. 65.

† Ib. pp. 95, 96.

of Wesley's followers, of remarks on which the second part of 'The Doctrine of Grace' chiefly consists.

We see how the minds of the New Testament writers, according to Warburton, were qualified to compose *a Rule of Faith* for the Church. But a set of modern fanatics, he says, have arisen, who conduct themselves as if no such Rule of Faith were in being, or as if it were so imperfect as to require new inspiration to supply its deficiencies. These men read the history of the dispensations to the first propagators of our holy faith; they look with admiration on the privileges and powers conferred on those chosen instruments; their imagination grows heated; they forget the difference between the present and past economy of things; they seem to feel the impressions they hear of; and they assume the airs, and mimic the authority, of prophets and apostles. . . . Were we to make our estimate of the present state of the religious world from the journals of modern fanatics, we should be tempted still to think ourselves in a land of Pagans, with all their prejudices full blown upon them. For the account they give us of their provincial missions always runs on in such strains as these: '*the name of Jesus is preached up* in this city; *the glad tidings of the Gospel conveyed* to that hamlet; *a new light springs up in a land of darkness;* and *life and immortality is now first offered* to those who *sit in the shadow of death.*' When we hear the obstinate claims of these fanatics to *a primitive abundance of the Spirit*, we feel inclined to examine on what ground those claims rest, and call to mind the text in which we are exhorted *to try the Spirits.* 'Believe not every spirit,' says St. John, 'but try the Spirits, whether they be of God, because many false prophets are gone out into the world.' The test by which we may try them we find in another apostle: '*The wisdom that is from above is first pure, then peaceable, gentle, and easy to be intreated, full of mercy and good fruits, without partiality and without hypocrisy.'*

The first distinction of wisdom from above is *purity*, that is, that it is free from carnal and spiritual pollution. But Methodism, whatever be said of its paternity, which appears to have been from Law's 'Christian Perfection' and 'Serious Call,' books which mightily impressed the soul of Mr. Wesley, cannot boast of very pure education, for its cradle was rocked by Count Zinzendorf, the founder of the Moravians, who, to say nothing of their *hymn-book*, a mass of absurd and filthy nonsense, adopted such profane and impure practices in the consummation of marriage (or, as their ritual calls it, the Marriage Economy), as entitle them to be ranked, not in the number of Christian sects, but with the Turlupins of the thirteenth century, the 'Brothers and Sisters of the Free Spirit,' whose creed was Pantheism, and whose practice was exempt from all restraints of morality and religion.

The Behmenists, indeed, have not gone so far from rectitude and decency, but, though they have expressed an abhorrence of *carnal impurity*, yet their great leader among us, Mr. William Law, has fallen very low into *spiritual impurity*, for he has written a book to recommend Pantheism. Mr. Wesley, though he does not adopt this doctrine, yet is so deeply infected with the folly or *impurity of fanaticism*, as to make a separation between reason and religion, for '*it is a point we chiefly insist upon*,' says he, 'that orthodoxy or *right opinion* is at least *but a very slender part of religion, if any part of it at all.*' The religion of Mr. Wesley is therefore very different from that of the primitive ages, which he professes to emulate, for that was *a reasonable service*, a quality by which it was distinguished from the various forms of Pagan worship, arising from the raptures of their prophets or the superstition of their priests. There is little wonder, then, that such a man, who discards reason from religion, should admit the reality of the miracles said to have been wrought at the tomb of the Abbé Paris, since, in his opinion, errors in faith can offer no impediment to the reception of the highest spiritual gifts. Nor is it wonderful that he should have disciples of such a character as he describes in the following words: 'The more I converse with this people, the more I am amazed. That God has wrought a great work is manifest. And yet the main of them are *not able to give a rational account of the plainest principles of religion.*' He speaks even of his teachers and preachers as 'a handful of raw young men, without name, learning, or *eminent sense*,' though senseless as they were, he says, they prosecuted their work efficiently; nor was defect in understanding confined only to the more illiterate among his followers. 'He had made,' says Warburton, 'a proselyte of Mr. D——, vicar of B——. And to show he was no discredit to his master, he delivers him to us under this character: "He seemed to stagger at nothing, though *as yet his understanding is not opened.*" He then attempts at the cause of this strange phænomenon: "It is plain God begins His work at the *heart*; then the inspiration of the Highest giveth *understanding.*" But this solution, though it be in Scripture language, is neither Scripture doctrine nor history. In the first propagation of religion, God began with the *understanding*, and rational conviction won the *heart.*'*

The next quality distinctive of the wisdom from above is that it be *peaceable.* Christ's advent was with *peace and good-will towards men*, and His legacy, when He departed from the world, was *peace.* But that the propagation of Methodism has occasioned great violations of peace, is shown in the 'journalary history,' as Warburton calls it, of Mr. Wesley's adventures. He who bequeathed peace to the world admonished His followers to be, while

* Doctrine of Grace, b. ii. c. 7.

they were *harmless as doves*, *wise* also, or rather *prudent, as serpents*, and gave an example, as well of *prudence* as of *innocence*, in his life. But Mr. Wesley, as is indeed perfectly consistent in one who has parted *reason from religious opinion*, divorces also *prudence from religious practice*. 'God deliver me,' he says, 'and all that seek Him in sincerity, from what the world calls Christian prudence.' He even calls prudence *the mystery of iniquity, and the offspring of hell.* 'I believe,' he records, 'that it pleased God to bless the first sermon most, because it gave most offence, being indeed an open defiance of *that mystery of iniquity which the world calls prudence*;' and he tells a friend, 'I fear *that offspring of hell, worldly or mystic prudence*, hath drawn you away from the simplicity of the Gospel.' 'The Roman satirist pretended,' says Warburton, following the corrupt reading,

——'nullum numen abest, si sit prudentia,'

Where prudence governs, no God is wanting to keep the world in order. We may say, with more sobriety and truth, that when *imprudence* takes the lead, there needs no *devil* to throw it into confusion. What, for instance, more strongly tends to tumult and disorder than for one who professes to propagate only the plain old religion of the Church of England, to set at nought its established discipline, by invading the province of the parochial minister; by assembling in undue places and at unfit times; by speaking evil of dignities, in scurrilous invectives against the governors and pastors of the National Church?' . . . '*Peace* is the cure of *fanaticism*, as *fanaticism* is the bane of *peace*. Sectaries must either kick or be kicked. They must either persecute, or they must provoke persecution. To be in this turbulent state is living in their proper element.'*

'The next mark of celestial wisdom,' proceeds War-

* Doctrine of Grace, b. ii. c. 9.

burton, 'is its being *gentle and easy to be entreated*; that is, neither a rigid reprover of the indifferent manners of others, nor obstinately tenacious of its own; but, as far as truth and honesty will permit, compliant and even obsequious to all men.' Of Mr. Wesley's *gentleness* we have examples in the titles which he bestows upon his opponents, calling them *the devil's servants* and *the devil's children*. How far he was *easy to be entreated*, we have abundance of indications. The Church of God at Herrnhuth had expressed an opinion that they 'might conform to the world so far as to talk on trifling subjects, and to join in worldly diversions, in order to do good.' Wesley, in a letter to them, objected to such conformity. They replied, 'We believe it much better to discourse out of the newspapers than to chatter about holy things to no purpose.' Wesley rejoined, 'Perhaps so; but what is this to the point? I believe both one and the other to be useless, and, therefore, *an abomination to the Lord*.' 'Nay,' continues Warburton, 'he pushed this matter so far as to come to a solemn resolution *never to laugh*; and, to guard himself against the approaches of this paltry infirmity, *never to speak a tittle of worldly things*. And certainly he who carries this dissociability to this extreme is in no danger of *being easily entreated*. He was now fit company only for the devil (with whom, as we have seen, he had a great deal to transact)—indeed, not for him neither, till the more sociable fiend had a little relaxed his muscles; for the first trick Satan played him, after they grew acquainted, was, as he himself tells us, to make him *burst out into an immoderate fit of laughter*. "I was a little surprised at some," he says, "who were *buffeted of Satan* in an unusual manner by such *a spirit of laughter*. I knew the same thing ten or eleven years ago. Part of Sunday my brother and I then used to spend in walking in the meadows and singing Psalms. But one day, just as we were beginning to sing, he *burst out into a loud laughter*.

I began to be very angry, and presently after *to laugh as loud as he.* We were ready to tear ourselves in pieces, but were forced to go home without singing another line." '*

Warburton concludes his remarks on this head with some very happy similes, illustrating the difference of spirit apparent in St. Paul and Mr. Wesley. 'The genial Spirit of God,' operating in St. Paul, 'could breathe nothing but the balm of *gentleness and ease.* The pestilent heat of fanaticism raises an inflammation and a tumour in the mind, whose symptoms are an obdurate rigour and impatience under the probe. The heaven-struck heart is affected like the purer metals, which easily soften, and run speedily at the touch of the ethereal ray. But the fanatic spirit, self-heated by its own fiery nature, retains the property of its congenial earth, which grows harder and more intractable as it burns.'

St. James's description of celestial wisdom rises, as it proceeds, higher and higher in its characteristics. Its next quality is, that it is *full of mercy and good fruits.* What *mercy*, then, is in Methodism, may be seen by its readiness to fling about judgments, to call down fire from Heaven, and to 'deal damnation round the land' on all that venture to oppose it. Every calamity that falls upon its adversaries is called a divine judgment. 'Mr. S.,' says Mr. Wesley, 'while he was speaking against my brother and me to the Society at Kingswood, was in a moment struck raving mad.' 'I preached at Darlaston,' he says on another occasion, 'late a den of lions; but most of the fiercest of them *God had called away by a train of amazing strokes*; and those that remain are now as lambs.' 'We rode to T., where the minister was slowly recovering from a violent fit of the palsy, with which he was struck *immediately after he had been preaching a violent sermon against the Methodists.*' Of certain persons

* Doctrine of Grace, b. ii. c. 4, 10.

who had raised a riot about him, he says, 'One of the chief of those who came to make the disturbance *had hanged himself.* A second of them had been for some days in strong pain, and had many times sent to desire our prayers. A third came to me himself, and confessed he was hired that night, and made drunk on purpose; but when he came to the door, he *knew not what* was the matter, he *could not stir nor open his mouth.*' 'But here, by ill luck,' observes Warburton, 'the miracle suffers; for drunkenness alone is but too apt to deprive a man of his faculties of speech and local motion.' There are many other instances, extracted from Wesley's journals by Warburton, of similar fanciful judgments, but we have noticed enough. Let us next look to the *good fruits* of Mr. Wesley's proceedings.

'Mr. Wesley's idea of true religion,' exclaims Warburton, 'does not promise much' on this head. 'True religion,' he says, 'does not consist in any or all of these three things, *the living harmless, using the means of grace,* and *doing much good*; a man may do all this and have no true religion at all.' 'St. James,' proceeds the Bishop, 'talks another language. *Pure religion* (and, I suppose, *pure* and *true* differ only in sound) *and undefiled before God and the Father is this, to visit the fatherless and widows in their affliction, and to keep himself unspotted from the world.* Now, what is *visiting the fatherless and widows* but *the doing much good?* And what is *keeping one's self unspotted from the world,* but *using the means of grace?*

'In what a fearful taking, then, must Mr. Wesley's zealots be, who, misled by the Bible, have so long mistaken *true religion!* The least it will do is to drive them to despair. But this is the very state in which their master delights to take them up. And his assurance that *true religion consists in God's dwelling and reigning in the soul,* soon makes way for a happier madness; the jaws of hell begin to close, the gates of heaven to open. But what the overlaboured imagination suffered during the course of this operation requires the hand of a master to describe. I shall give it, therefore, in Mr. J. Wesley's own words; and as these, his spiritual cures (which he reports with the exactness of a Hippocrates or a Sydenham), are all the *good fruits* he pretends to, he will not be displeased to have a few of the choicest of them set in a fair light.

'The condition of his audience, on his first operation upon them, is thus graphically described: "I preached in an open place, two or three miles from Newcastle; the wind was high and extremely sharp; but I saw none go away till I went. Yet I observed none seemed to be much convinced; only *stunned, as if cut in the head.*" This was in order. They were first to be *stunned*; the watchman reason was to be laid asleep, before he could set fire to their imaginations. But he brings them to their senses with a vengeance, the vengeance of the devil. "I felt the *fire of hell already kindled in my breast,*" says one, "and all my body was in as much pain as if I had been in a burning fiery furnace." "I was interrupted," says Mr. Wesley, "by the cries of one who was *pricked at the heart;*" one of those, I suppose, who had before been *cut in the head;* and, having now got possession both of the head and the heart, the game begins: "Another person dropped down. A little boy near him was seized in the same manner. A young man who stood behind fixed his eyes on him, and sunk down himself as one dead, but soon began to roar out and beat himself on the ground, so that six men could scarcely hold him. Meanwhile, many others began to cry out to the Saviour of all that he would come and help them, insomuch that all the house, and indeed all the street for some space, was in an uproar." "Forty or fifty of those who were seeking salvation desired leave to spend the night together in the society room. Before ten I left them, and laid down." For our engineer had so amply provided them with combustibles, and so fitly laid his train, that he knew they would take fire from their own collisions. He was not disappointed. Between two and three in the morning he was awaked, and desired to come down stairs. "I immediately," says he, "heard such a confused noise as if a number of men were all putting to the sword. It increased when I came into the room, and began to pray," &c. Others went distracted, and were tied down raving on their beds. And with this spiritual madness,' pursues Warburton, 'he is so enamoured, that he calls it, when at its height, *a glorious time.*

'But though Mr. J. Wesley does so ably in this new trade of turning fools into madmen, yet his craft's-master is certainly one Mr. Wh—y, of whom Mr. Wesley tells this extraordinary tale: "A poor woman gave an account of what I think ought never to be forgotten." Truly, I think so too. "It was four years, she said, since her son, Peter Shaw, then nineteen or twenty years old, by hearing a sermon of Mr. Wh—y, fell into great uneasiness. She thought he was ill, and would have sent for a physician. But he said, No, no, send for Mr. Wh—y. He was sent for, and came; and, after asking a few questions, told her, *The boy is mad; get a coach, and carry him to Dr. Monro; use my name; I have sent several such to him.*" Who this Mr. Wh—y is, or what he is, I know not. But, we see, he sends his people to Monro with the same unconcern in search of lost brains that one would inquire of Sir J. Fielding for a lost portmanteau.

'Such are the exploits which Mr. J. Wesley calls "blessings from God," and which, therefore, we may well call the *good fruits* of his ministry.' *

* Doctrine of Grace, b. ii. c. 11.

The last qualities specified in *the wisdom from above* are, that it is *without partiality and without hypocrisy.* How partial enthusiasts and fanatics are to themselves, as being children of God, and how hostile to their adversaries, as children of the devil, we have already seen. On enthusiasm a few such just remarks are made by Warburton, concluding with an illustration of the character of Cromwell, that I cannot but subjoin them. 'An enthusiast considers himself as an instrument employed by Providence to attain some great end, for the sake of which he was sent out. This makes him diligent in his work; impatient under any let or obstruction, and attentive to every method for removing it. Persuaded of the necessity of the end, and of the Divine commission entrusted to that instrument, he begins to fancy that such a one, for the obtaining so great a purpose, is dispensed with in breaking, nay, is authorised to break, the common laws of morality; which, in the cant of those times when fanaticism had its full play, was called the *being above ordinances.* In the first application of these means, the people are the dupes of their leader; but the success being frequently far beyond even his own conception, he becomes, in his turn, the dupe of himself, and begins in good earnest to believe that the trick which he played them was indeed not of his own contrivance, but the inspired instigation of heaven. This will explain an obscure passage of Tacitus, where, speaking of this sort of character in his oracular way, he says, *fingunt simul creduntque.* Let me add that this seems to have been much the case with Oliver Cromwell, from his first mounting into the saddle and the pulpit, to his last reveries on his death-bed.' *

Last of all, we come to hypocrisy. Partiality may be regarded as the assumption of too much to ourselves,

* Doctrine of Grace, b. ii. c. 12.

and the recognition of too little in others; hypocrisy endeavours to conceal our partiality by false representations. Mr. Wesley is guilty of hypocrisy by indulgence in evasion and prevarication. He gives an example of evasion when he pretends that a miracle is wrought in his favour, but adds an observation to secure himself from presumption in case the miracle should be doubted. He is going to preach, and, just before he begins, there is a very high wind; but, during all the time he held forth, scarce a breath was felt. He evidently intimates that the lull of the wind ought to be considered miraculous. He praises God for it, and then adds, 'Is it enthusiasm to see God in every benefit which we receive?' * If the occurrence was not miraculous, he trusts he may be pardoned for being so much of an enthusiast as to imagine it was. And the same *salvo* may be applied to the other miracles in which his journal abounds. It would be of great use to him when questioners became too importunate.

He is guilty of hypocrisy when he makes pretences to a spirit of forgiveness, and yet manifests strong malice towards those whom he calls his persecutors. At St. Ives, he and his followers are saluted with stones or pieces of dirt. He exalts this puny attack into a violent persecution; a persecution which 'was owing, in a great measure, to the indefatigable labours of Mr. Hoblin and Mr. Simmons; gentlemen,' he says, 'worthy to be had in everlasting remembrance for their unwearied endeavours to destroy heresy:

> Fortunati ambo! Si quid mea pagina possit,
> Nulla dies unquam memori vos eximet ævo.'

'Here,' says Warburton, 'he tells us without disguise that it is his holy purpose to gibbet up the names of

* Doctrine of Grace, b. ii. c. 12.

these his two persecutors, to everlasting infamy; while, by the most unregenerate malice in the world, he dips his curses in the gall of irony, and, that they may strike the deeper, fletches them with a profane classical parody.

'Yet this is the man who says, "God forbid *that I should rail* at a Turk, infidel, or heretic. I would point out their errors, and, I trust, *in the spirit of meekness*."' And in another place he says, 'If I have any strength at all, it is *in forgiving injuries*.' *

It is also strange that Wesley, who had pronounced discourse out of the newspapers to be *an abomination to the Lord*, and had solemnly resolved *never to speak a tittle of worldly things*, should have allowed himself to recur, for a moment, to the profane studies of his youth, and absolutely astonishing that he should have dwelt on the pagan lines of Virgil long enough to produce a parody, and have recorded that parody in his journal, which was written for the edification of all men. Must not his zealous followers, even if they were too illiterate to understand his jest, have felt inclined to think him a backslider?

Wesley, as we have seen, abhorred worldly prudence, as the mystery of iniquity. But he is not disinclined to have recourse to it, when he thinks it likely to promote an object. He had published a sermon *on free grace*; Whitfield had written a letter in answer to it. Wesley told him it was *imprudent* to publish the letter, as putting weapons into the hands of the enemies of them both, and that, if he felt constrained *to bear his testimony*, as he expressed it, against the sermon, he might have done so without mentioning Wesley's name. He was even so prudent that, though he pronounces a certain Mr. G. to be *absolutely above conviction*, he asked Mr. G. *to meet*

* Doctrine of Grace, b. ii. c. 10.

him half way, offering never to preach publicly against Mr. G. if Mr. G. would promise never to preach against him. 'When prudence would have advised him,' says Warburton, 'not to preach publicly against the body of that clergy to which, he says, he belongs, then is prudence the bane of religion, the mystery of iniquity; but when she prompts him to tempt a brother of the same trade *to meet him half way*, and not *to preach publicly against him*, then is prudence of heavenly birth, and sent for the assistance of the saints; at present, indeed, honourably employed in the charitable errand of inviting Mr. G. *to play the hypocrite with him*, for he declares Mr. G. to be *absolutely above conviction*.'*

Another example of what Warburton calls his hypocrisy affects his character strongly. He professed to desire persecution, as a blessing; but when persecution presented itself, he withdrew from it as an intolerable evil. He had no objection that it should light upon his flock, but wanted heart to meet it himself. Thus when, in Georgia, he had the finest opportunity of submitting to be buffeted, he retired before his assailants, content with merely shaking off the dust of his feet against them. In that country he had made acquaintance with one Mrs. Williamson, to whom he refused the sacrament, on the ground that she had done some wrong to her neighbour. Mrs. Williamson's uncle stood forth in her behalf, and desired Wesley to declare publicly what the wrong was. Mr. Wesley declined, alleging that *many ill consequences* might arise from such declaration. 'What you will not do, then,' said the uncle, 'I will do myself. The wrong is, that she has rejected your proposals of marriage, and married Mr. Williamson.' Mr. Williamson, the husband, prosecuted Wesley for defamation of his wife's character, and the wife made affidavit that Wesley had many times proposed

* Doctrine of Grace, b. ii. c. 12.

marriage to her, and been as frequently rejected. The grand jury declared that he ought to be tried, not only for repelling Mrs. Williamson from the sacrament, but for having spoken and written to her, as it appeared, against her husband's consent. Wesley was perplexed, and consulted his friends *whether God did not call him to return to England*; they were of opinion that *he ought to go, but not yet.* But soon after he was found guilty of the charges against him, and declared an enemy to the public peace. He then consulted his friends again; and they agreed that *the time for his departure was come.* He might have met this trial with the devotion of a martyr; but he prepared to flee, giving notice to the Georgians, however, that he intended *to shake off the dust of his feet against them.* But the magistrates ordered that, before he performed this ceremony, he should find security for his appearance before them. As he paid no regard to this requisition, they put forth a placard, commanding all persons to prevent him from leaving the province. Wesley then saw plainly that the hour for his departure was come; and one evening, as soon as prayer was over—'for prayer,' remarks Warburton, 'must always make a part in his stratagems'—about eight o'clock, when he found the tide favourable, he *shook off the dust of his feet*, and decamped without beat of drum. 'He shook off the dust of his feet,' exclaims Warburton: 'much easier done than shaking off his infamy.'

The book concludes with an address to the clergy, counselling them to avoid bigotry, to favour toleration, to discountenance fanaticism, and to prevent schism, as far as possible, by judicious conciliation and correct example. 'This discourse,' says Hurd, 'will, like Pascal's Letters, and for the same reason — the singular merit of the composition — be read when the sect that gave occasion to it is forgotten; or, rather, the sect will find a sort of immortality in this discourse.' This prophecy is rather too confident; but the book well deserves to be kept in memory, and will not be without its use, if it contribute, in the smallest degree, to diminish the evils arising from irrational enthusiasm.

CHAPTER XXIX.

DR. THOMAS LELAND. WILKES.

WESLEY'S REPLY TO WARBURTON; ITS TEMPERANCE — THE REV. JOHN ANDREWS; LETTERS FROM WARBURTON TO HIM — MR. JOHN PAYNE'S 'LETTER TO A FRIEND ON THE DOCTRINE OF GRACE;' HIS ATTEMPTED DEFENCE OF LAW — DR. LELAND'S ANSWER TO WARBURTON; HIS OBSERVATIONS ON ELOQUENCE — HURD'S UNCOURTEOUS REPLY TO LELAND — A BROKEN ARM — WILKES'S 'ESSAY ON WOMAN' — WARBURTON'S SPEECH ON IT IN THE HOUSE OF LORDS — WILKES'S DUEL — A SECOND SPEECH OF WARBURTON'S — DISPLAYS LITTLE ELOQUENCE.

THE work drew pamphlets, in answer, from both Wesley and Whitfield, as well as from others who thought it required contradiction.

Wesley replied to Warburton with such mildness, and even deference, as was amazing towards one who had so insulted him. To Bishop Lavington, of Exeter, who had censured the proceedings of the Methodists in the same tone, and with as much effect, as Warburton, in 'A Comparison between the Enthusiasm of Methodists and of Papists,' showing that the one sort of Christians were as credulous as the other, he had addressed an answer of much asperity, lamenting, however, the heaviness of the work, which he undertook only from a feeling of its necessity, and observing that it was well said by an ancient, 'God made practical divinity necessary, the Devil controversial.' But to Warburton he adopted a gentler mode of address, even apologising for the plainness of speech which he should use, but maintaining the reasonableness of his own course of action, and affirming that his preaching was supported by the attestation of miracles, especially those of casting out devils and healing the sick, which had been beheld by many competent witnesses, so that there would soon be no ground either for denying or contemning them, or disputing that God might add to their number. He desired, he said, only diligent and fair inquiry, and expressed his readiness to name numbers of persons who would give their testimony to the miracles on oath. He did not pretend to work these miracles himself, but felt certain that he was favoured with them by the grace of God. Let Bishop Warburton but examine, and he would be convinced.* Such was Wesley's excessive credulity and self-delusion, such his persuasion that Providence was ready to wait on every Jack and Tom among his followers.

As to his departure from America, through the affair with Mrs. Wi——, he had recourse, he says, not to 'revelations,' as Warburton states, but to consultations with his friends, whether there were not strong reasons for his going; that the magistrates' senseless declaration that he was an enemy to the peace made him go neither sooner nor later; that he neither languished for persecution nor invited it, though he expected and was ready to submit to it; and that Warburton's charge about 'hiding poltroonery in a bravado' was so 'kind and civil, equally serious and genteel,' that he might be excused from taking notice of what followed.

He concludes his pamphlet thus temperately, not to say servilely:

'I have now finished what I had to say, either concerning myself or on the operations of the Holy Spirit. In doing this, I have used great plainness of speech, and yet, I hope, without rudeness. If anything of that kind has slipped from me, I desire to retract it. I desire, on

* A Letter to the Right Rev. the Lord Bp. of Gloucester, by John Wesley, M.A., 1762. Southey's Life of Wesley, vol. ii. pp. 211, 213.

the one hand, to accept no man's person, and yet, on the other, *to give honour to whom honour is due.*

'If your Lordship should think it worth your while to spend any more words upon me, may I presume to request one thing of your Lordship, *to be more serious.* [Warburton had said, in the Preface to the "Doctrine of Grace," that "to employ buffoonery in the service of religion is to violate the majesty of truth," and that "to examine, *men must be serious.*"] It cannot injure your Lordship's *character* or your *cause.* Truth is great and will prevail. Wishing your Lordship all temporal and spiritual blessings,

'I am, my Lord,

'Your Lordship's dutiful and obedient son and servant,

'JOHN WESLEY.'

Wesley survived Warburton, and, after his death, said, 'He is gone to rest, I well hope, in Abraham's bosom.'*

Whitfield's answer was a poor whining pamphlet of four-and-twenty pages, complaining that Warburton would fain withdraw the Holy Spirit from the Church altogether, and crying 'woe to the Christian world if he succeeded in his unhallowed attempt.'

Another pamphlet proceeded from one John Andrews, LL.B., of St. Mary Hall, Oxford, who, after having visited America, and stayed there for some years, had, on his return to England, obtained, through the interest of the Archbishop of Canterbury, the small living of Stinchcombe, in the Bishop of Gloucester's diocese. He, being favourable to Wesley, and offended at the light tone of certain passages in the 'Doctrine of Grace,' thought fit to publish, in 1763, a heavy pamphlet of two hundred and twenty-four pages, to correct his Lordship's notions on the subject of that treatise. The performance is a dull sermon, rather than anything else, aiming merely pellets of wool against the Bishop's buff jerkin, the only

* Nichols's Lit. Anec. vol. v. p. 234.

severe remark in it being that the part which charges Wesley with hypocrisy is full of 'empty declamation, irreverent wit, and personal invective.' He indeed admonishes the Bishop that there is 'a standard of eloquence founded in reason and nature,' and that, 'if the Scripture-language abounded with every fault that could deform a language,' it would be no more a proof of *its Divine original* than the omission of a future state from the writings of Moses would be a proof of *Moses' Divine legation.* But these are the only forcible passages in so many leaves of feebleness; and it would have been wise in one possessed of so little vigour to forbear from showing a warlike front to Warburton.

Before the publication of this volume, Mr. Andrews had given offence to Warburton by his open attachment to Methodism, or other forms of dissent, for he had even preached for Lady Huntingdon at Bath; and he had received from the Bishop, previously to the assault upon him in print, the following letter:

'Mar. 25, 1763.

'Mr. Andrews,—I have received several complaints of you. Those which concern your own curacy, are on account of your frequent absence, and for not giving your parish service both morning and afternoon on a Sunday. Unless I have satisfaction on these two particulars, more especially the former, I shall revoke your licence by process in my court. I shall insist upon your constant residence in your parish, not so much from the good you are likely to do there, as to prevent the mischief you may do by rambling about in other places.

'Your Bishop and
(though your fanatic conduct has almost made me ashamed to own it) your Patron,
'W. Gloucester.'

Mr. Andrews replied to this letter by saying, as to the

first charge, that he had resided in his parish at least two years and nine months out of three years that he had held the living; and, as to the second, that the Bishop, at an interview with him at Bath, had given him leave, in consideration of the smallness of the income, and of Mr. Andrews's delicate health, to officiate at Stinchcombe only once on a Sunday.

The Bishop immediately rejoined:

'If I indulged you in giving your parish only one service on a Sunday, I hereby revoke the indulgence, and insist on your giving them full service.

'W. GLOUCESTER.'

The diocese of Gloucester was thus rendered too hot for Mr. Andrews. But Archbishop Secker had a liking for him, as a pious well-meaning man, and gave him some preferment in Kent.

Another antagonist, of rather more vigour, but able only to offer a dagger of lath to the Bishop's crab-tree truncheon, was Mr. John Payne, once a bookseller, but afterwards accountant of the Bank of England, who dabbled, with a very little learning, in theology; and, in a volume of five hundred pages, consisting half of sundry discourses of his own, and half of a 'Letter to a Friend' on the 'Doctrine of Grace,' accused the Bishop of unfairness towards Mr. Law, of whom he himself was a profound admirer, declaring that his Lordship had made a vigorous attempt to traduce Law's character, but no attempt at all to refute his arguments. To confute Law's arguments indeed, if arguments they could be called, Warburton was very wise not to attempt; for neither Law himself, nor his followers, would have had sense or modesty to know or admit that they were confuted, but would have persisted to argue under defeat. Law himself had previously written a pamphlet against Warburton: 'A short but sufficient Confutation of Dr.

Warburton's projected Defence of Christianity, in a Letter to Bishop Sherlock,' in which he said that Warburton's hypothesis, in 'The Divine Legation,' was 'a scheme so contrary to Scripture and the truth of things, as no art of words, or stretch of genius, however powerful in paradox, could ever be able to support.' Warburton in return had sneered at his 'ravings' and 'execrable frenzy;'* and indeed all his writings, whatever Johnson thought of his reasoning, whatever Gibbon, to whose father he had been tutor, says of his scholarship and ability, and whatever praise Wesley bestowed on his style, may very well be suffered to sink into forgetfulness.

Dr. Thomas Leland, a fellow of Trinity College, Dublin, was an antagonist of very different standing and attainments, but produced a tame and spiritless examination of Warburton's assertions. He told the Bishop, very properly, that his definition of eloquence, as a compound of the three qualities of purity, elegance, and sublimity, was faulty; for the first quality may be considered as included in the second, and the third is not a necessary constituent of eloquence, since a speaker may be highly eloquent without being sublime. He also showed that elegance was not, as Warburton had asserted, the capricious production of fashion or fancy, but founded on the general sense and reason of mankind, as is evident from an examination of the better sort of writings in all civilised countries. All cultivated nations have thought it fit 'that words should be so ranged and connected as to convey the sentiment with ease and perspicuity, relieving the voice and ear with intervals and pauses duly disposed and varied, so as to adorn and harmonise, without weakening, the composition; that all this should be conducted with a due regard to propriety, without discovering a minute and affected solicitude, or diverting the attention from the

* Warburton's Works, vol. iv. p. 68; vi. 350.

more important parts of eloquence. In these again we find nothing capricious or variable; they are the maxims which have been approved and recommended by all polished ages and nations; they have their foundation in truth and nature, in that love of order and harmony, that aversion to confusion and dissonance, which are congenial and essential to the human mind.'* Nor is the true sublime, as Warburton would have us believe, 'whatever is dignified and ennobled by arbitrary or casual connexions,' but that which the man of just critical judgment will, throughout all time, and under all changes of manners, approve and admire. General principles of rational criticism, therefore, in regard to elegance and sublimity, may evidently be established. The Romans studied and admired the same excellences of speech which had been studied and admired in Greece; and the English, and other modern nations, still study and admire the same excellences; and it therefore follows that fitness and propriety of language cannot be merely local or nominal.

As to the style of the New Testament, it is not to be considered that rudeness and barbarity, as Warburton asserts, is a proof of the Divine inspiration of the Apostolic writings, but only that such rudeness and barbarity afford no proof or presumption that the writers *were not inspired.* We are not to look for exquisite elegance in the Apostolic writers, even supposing that the authors received their language by miraculous infusion; for polish of style is a quality, which, even in the ordinary affairs of human life, is accounted but of inferior value, and often obliged to give way to higher and more essential requisites. Matter, rather than manner, in important subjects, is to be regarded. If Newton had written his Principia, 'not in his own neat Latinity,' but in a style less correct and accurate, what should we think of the man who, though

* Leland's Dissertation, p. 43.

capable of following him through all his stupendous investigations, should yet sit down in wilful ignorance, lest his taste should be shocked with phrases not exactly Ciceronian? Or if we knew that a man could teach us a sure method of growing rich, should we be unwilling to receive his directions because we disliked the language in which they were conveyed? Or would a person reduced by sickness to the point of death, reject the advice of an experienced physician, because his prescriptions were inelegantly expressed? We should be satisfied, in these cases, if the language sufficed to communicate the requisite information; and we may be satisfied, for the same reason, observes Leland, with the language of the Evangelists and Apostles; in which we need desire only clearness and simplicity of statement, earnestness of address, and whatever other properties are essential to the language of mankind in general, constituting 'that real and substantial eloquence which no particularities of diction can impair, which does not depend on a nice conformity to the rules of any language, but can abide the severe test of a Longinus, and must approve itself to all nations, tongues, and ages.' *

Such was the reasoning of Leland, addressed to Warburton in language temperate and not uncourteous. But Hurd thought proper to answer it, on behalf of his master, in a tone of sarcasm and contemptuousness, affecting to know nothing of him but *what he had heard of his writings*; but to be willing to think favourably of a scholar, *who, they say, employs himself in works of learning and taste*, and to feel concern at *the hurt he was likely to do himself by engaging in controversy with a writer of such distinguished eminence as Warburton.* Hurd's pamphlet, which Parr republished, we have occasion to notice elsewhere.

* Leland's Dissertation, pp. 41, 42, 50, 68, 76, 89, 92, 93, 98.

During this year Warburton had a slight illness, causing some alarm at Prior Park; but it passed off without any material consequences.* But in the early part of the following year he had a far more serious affliction; he fell down in the garden, and broke his left arm, which, at his age, was a sad disaster. It was some time before the bone was united; and he complained, for months afterwards, of numbness in his wrist and fingers. 'The surgeon's over care,' he writes to Dr. Attwell in April, 'and my lying in bed too long, with my hand motionless, has deprived me of the use of my wrist. I have applied many things of the same intention with a bullock's paunch,' which Dr. Attwell appears to have recommended him. 'If it does not mend faster very soon,' he adds, 'I shall apply to what the physical people here call their sovereign remedy, the Bath pump.' † In the following September he acquainted the same correspondent that a quarter of a year's pumping had restored all but his thumb and forefinger. It was well, he said, that he was left the use of his sword arm. He also used oils recommended by his friend Dr. Stukeley; and his habitual temperance was of effect in promoting the healing.‡

His wife was also much indisposed in April and May, but, after languishing for weeks under the Bath physicians, and resolving, as a last resource, to go to a German Spa, she recovered in London under the care of Dr. Heberden and Dr. Letherland.§

He appeared, however, in some force in the House of Lords in November, in which month Parliament assembled. Lord Halifax sent him notice that it was desirable he should be present at the opening of the session, and, in

* Kilvert's Life of Hurd, p. 85.

† Kilvert's Selections from Warburton's Papers, pp. 266, 267.

‡ Nichols's Lit. Illustr. vol. ii. pp. 56-58, 143; Letters from an Eminent Prelate, pp. 340-347.

§ Letters from an Eminent Prelate, p. 346.

about a week after he had come to town for the purpose, Lord Sandwich came to him from Lord Halifax, to show him Wilkes's parodies on Pope's 'Universal Prayer,' on the *Veni Creator*, and above all, on Pope's 'Essay on Man,' which was travestied into an *Essay on Woman*, accompanied with 'Notes and a Commentary,' in the form of those on Pope's works, and professedly written 'by Dr. Warburton.' Lord Sandwich desired to know whether he would wish to have Wilkes prosecuted for a breach of privilege. Warburton replied that, though he was diabolically treated, in having his name attached to such lewdness and blasphemy, yet that he so much despised the man, as being infinitely beneath him, that he was hardly inclined to prosecute him *unless the King desired it as for his service.* Lord Sandwich declared that his Majesty desired it greatly; and it was agreed between them that Lord Sandwich should bring the matter before the House on the following day, when Warburton would say what he thought necessary.

The matter was well arranged, and brought forward in a very full house. Lord Sandwich (who was himself, it may be observed, no example of morality, and had participated in the orgies of Medmenham Abbey with the man whom he was now going to assail), entered upon his statement with many expressions of horror. It was necessary, in order to support the charge, that some portions of the 'Essay on Woman' should be read, and Lord Sandwich read such passages as he thought would not be too offensive. While he was reading, Lord Lyttelton rose, and, affecting to be shocked, desired that no more might be read. The House, however, said 'Go on.' Lord Sandwich then finished reading those parts which he had selected, and was then expected to call witnesses to prove Wilkes to be the author. But before the witnesses were brought forward, Warburton stood up, and delivered the following speech. He appears to have written it in full before it was spoken. An exact copy was sent the day after to Ralph Allen.

'My Lords, being made a party to this prosecution, till your Lordships had come to some determination, I thought it most decent to keep silent.

'But now, the duty I owe to this House, and the reverence every honest man owes to his own character, whose just boast it is *nullâ pallescere culpâ*, force me to beg your Lordships' indulgence for a few moments.

'It is with just concern apprehended, I say, that some noble Lords, distinguished for their honour and virtue both in public and private life, have appeared not unwilling, as opportunity offered, to soften the edge of justice on this occasion. Their *arguments* I shall leave with all their weight; their *motives*, I am sure, did not want the due share of generosity and honour. But I apprehend there may be a prejudice which will deserve to be examined. It is founded, I suppose, in a certain suspicion that the pure love of virtue and religion, unmixed with the intrigues and resentments of ministers of state, did not set this prosecution on foot.

'Now, not to insist on so uncandid a suspicion, where the crime is so very enormous, let us for a moment suppose that the prosecution was not quite free from the mixture objected to it; I would beg leave to ask those noble Lords (so well acquainted with the history of ancient and modern times), whether they have ever found, throughout the whole story of mankind, any great and general good obtained, or any enormous evil suppressed, when human passions did not mix themselves with the work of that reformer?

'Was the Great Charter obtained and secured by disinterested patriots, out of pure love to the people's liberties? Your Lordships best know that it was wrested from the Crown by a factious, turbulent, and ambitious baronage, into whose hearts the love of the people never entered, in order to share the sovereign power with their master.

'Was the avarice, the usurpation, and the superstition of the Church of Rome overturned on the virtuous principle, the vindication of the rights of mankind? Do we not all know that that dreadful enchantment, which had for so many ages bound up the intellects of a whole people, was broken and dissolved by the rapine, the pride, and the luxurious passions of a single man?

'To descend from generals to particulars. These latter times have seen, on different occasions, the highest magistrates of justice exemplarily arraigned and punished for gross corruption in the execution of their office; but who is so ignorant as not to know that those salutary prosecutions owed their birth to the displeasure and resentments of favourites and ministers of state?

'Alas! were we to stay for reformation till pure virtue set reformers on work, we must wait for the return of that Platonic vision when Virtue is to appear in all her blaze of charms in person.

'Surely it is enough for us that, in the present case, Virtue's most august, most spotless representative, has directed this offender to be brought to justice.

'If the prosecution has not escaped censure, the prosecutor, we may be sure, would be less covertly attacked. A noble Lord, when this affair was last in agitation, told a story, and seemed to recommend it as worthy to have been followed in the present case. As his Lordship was pleased to represent it, it was this. A tract of Servetus fell into the hands of Dr. Gibson, Bishop of London, and he chose rather to suppress than to prosecute it.

'Let us examine, then, the pretended likeness in the two cases.

'1. Servetus had been dead near two hundred years; so here was no offender to be found. And this is all the likeness under the first head.

'2. Again, Servetus had, unhappily, entertained some theologic tenets which the Church justly terms heresy; and for these he was most cruelly and iniquitously burnt at Geneva. But Servetus was serious, was virtuous, was a scholar. Mr. Wilkes you all know to be a buffoon without wit, and a debauchee without delicacy, and a fine gentleman (as I think they call them) without letters. His performances were suitable to his character and talents. They consisted of the most horrid insults on religion, virtue and humanity, and the most shocking blasphemies against the Almighty; which would have subjected him to the faggot, not only in the little State of Geneva, but in every country on the globe (where a God and Providence is confessed), from Calais to Japan. And this is all the likeness under the third.

'3. Again, none of the followers of Servetus had the insolence to put Dr. Gibson's name to a number of notes supporting their master's impieties; but Mr. Wilkes has taken the liberty to put Dr. Warburton's name to a series of notes which countenance and even outdo the bestiality and blasphemy of his doggrel. And this is all the similitude I can find under the third.

'On the whole, then, I suppose your Lordships will be ready to agree with me that in the case of Servetus, the Bishop of Gloucester would have done as the Bishop of London did, and that in the case of Mr. Wilkes, the Bishop of London would have acted as the Bishop of Gloucester has done.

'To conclude, I have, my Lords, given my name to this prosecution out of a pure sense of my duty to God and the King. In this my private resentments had no share. Yet for this I have been further calumniated and outraged in the most villanous and diabolic manner.

'As to enemies of a better rank (if this prosecution has raised up any such against me), virtue whispers me, *tu contra audentior ito;* and as to the natural movements to revenge and vengeance for the calumnies and villanies of cut-throat libellers, I offer them all up at the sacred shrine of religion.'

When Warburton concluded, Lord Sandwich proceeded to examine the witnesses, and had no difficulty in fixing the authorship on Wilkes, who, it appeared, had sent the manuscript of the parodies to the press, had corrected the proofs, and had observed that the compositions cost him great care and labour. Thirteen copies only had been printed, which Wilkes, who had dispersed them among his friends, endeavoured to recal before Parliament met, and thought that he had succeeded.

It came out, in the course of the examination, that some letters of Wilkes, which were produced to confirm the charge against him, had been seized by a general warrant from the Secretary of State. When they were laid before the House, Lord Temple said that he had as great an abhorrence of the parodies as any Lord in the House (though, according to Warburton, it was generally reported that he had at that moment copies of them in his possession, and had been showing them to others with great delight); but that whatever testimony was brought against the accused ought to be legally obtained, as the liberty of the subject was concerned in the proceeding. He was seconded by Lord Sandys, and answered by Lord Sandwich, the Duke of Bedford, Lord Halifax, and Lord Chancellor Thurlow. Lord Temple still urged his objection, till Lord Mansfield ended the dispute by observing that the acquisition of evidence illegally does not render the evidence itself illegal; for evidence of any kind, in whatever manner brought to light, may be used to further the ends of justice. *The wretch*, therefore, as Warburton calls him, was pronounced guilty by the House of Lords; and the House was proceeding to vote upon the case, when Lord Mansfield, again interposing, said he doubted whether it would be regular to vote till Wilkes had been heard in his defence. Lord Sandwich then said that, from regard to that doubt, he would defer the voting till the following day.

While this affair was in agitation in the House of Lords, the House of Commons, in consequence of a message from the King, were debating whether No. 45 of the 'North Briton,' in which his Majesty had been accused of falsehood in his speech to Parliament, was a seditious libel or not. Martin, the member for Camelford, who had been violently assailed in the 'North Briton,' inveighed bitterly against anonymous slanderers, when Wilkes owned himself the author of the paper, and Martin immediately challenged him to fight on the following morning. When they met, Wilkes was so severely wounded as to be incapable of appearing in Parliament. But, in his absence, the House of Lords voted an address to the King, praying that Wilkes, with his aiders and abetters, might be prosecuted by the Attorney-General for blasphemy; and voted also that the offence against Warburton ought to be punished by the House itself. During the debates in the House of Commons, when No. 45 of the 'North Briton' was voted a seditious libel, a vote in which the House of Lords concurred, Pitt, who had the lawyers against him, declared that the impious man who had occasioned the dispute, and had blasphemed God and the King, ought to be thrust out of the House, stretching out his crutch at the same time in the manner of a man driving a noxious animal from him.*

Warburton also delivered himself to the following effect, a few days afterwards, before the House of Lords:

'My Lords, the life and health which Providence has been graciously pleased to bestow upon me have been all employed (and, I hope, neither unfruitfully nor inglo-

* Kilvert's Selections from Warburton's Papers, pp. 224-232.

riously) in the service of religion; in defending revelation, and the Established Church of this land, against the rude attacks of ribald writers of all denominations, atheists, deists, libertines, free-thinkers, bigots, and fanatics, and, what is the accumulation of all that is execrable in one, political scribblers of all sides and parties, the trumpeters, the incendiaries, of sedition and confusion.

'These services, my Lords, have brought down upon me a fierce and dirty torrent of abuse and slander from all quarters; in which, however, not one opprobrious fact ever imputed to my life (if any such have been imputed) was true, nor one fallacious argument ever imputed to my writings has been proved; so that my usual revenge was silence and contempt.

'This is the first time, my Lords, that I ever applied to public justice for assistance; not for myself or my writings, for while I have the hydra infidelity at my feet, I can well bear with its hisses; nor yet for this reverend bench, though I know how severely they feel for every insult offered to religion; no, my Lords, it is for religion itself, for civil society, yea, even for our common humanity, all most audaciously insulted by this man.

'And how insulted? With the arms of a gentleman and a scholar? With wit or with argument? For these have been too often abused and misapplied in support of religion and impiety. No, my Lords, nor with the arms even of a man, or of one who appears to bear any relation to the human species; but with such arms as the demons of lust and blasphemy might be supposed to use when let loose to blot the fair face of day and nature.

'But I injure these elder sons of perdition by my comparison; for let the most poetical imagination set himself on work to conceive how

Devils with devils damn'd hold converse;

and, when he had put his fancy on the rack, he would

still find himself infinitely short of the horrors of these portentous parodies, which, if suffered to go unpunished, not a hundred acts of national humiliation would be sufficient to expiate and atone; in which there is so foul a mixture of sensuality interlarding his fearful blasphemies, that the hardiest inhabitant of hell would *blush*, as well as *tremble*, to hear repeated.' *

It was expected by many that Warburton, when he got into the House of Lords, would be eager to make frequent displays of eloquence, and be ready to put himself forward on every possible occasion. But these oratorical attempts which we have here noticed, must, if delivered as he wrote them down, have sounded but stiff and tame. 'I have heard of a certain minister,' says Hurd, 'who dreaded Warburton's promotion, and thought he saw a second Atterbury in the new Bishop of Gloucester. But all such were egregiously mistaken. Alas! he had neither talents nor inclination for parliamentary intrigue or parliamentary eloquence. He had other instruments of fame and consideration in his hands, and was infinitely above the vanity of being caught

With the fine notion of a busy man,

as one of our poets well expresses it.' †

The Duke of Cumberland, as Warburton himself relates, came up to him one day, as he was sitting, with some other bishops, on the Episcopal bench. 'My lords,' said the Duke, 'it is observed that you always keep silence, and except you,' addressing Warburton, 'I never heard any of the bishops speak.' 'Sir,' said I (as Warburton records his own words), 'whenever I hear *religion* or the *bench* insulted, your Royal Highness shall hear me speak

* Kilvert's Selections from Warburton's Papers, p. 281.

† Hurd's Life of Warburton, p. 72.

in their vindication.' 'Aye, but why will not your Lordships speak on other occasions?' 'Sir,' replied I, 'haranguing in this assembly is a *trade* like other trades, and generally the bishops come to this bench so far advanced in years as to be too old to learn. Besides, Sir,' said I, 'we have been long accustomed to severe reason and exact method; so that we would be as much at a loss to talk *nonsense* as some others, more habituated, to talk *sense*.' *

Wilkes deserved all that Warburton, and all that anybody else, said against him, except that he was a fine gentleman without letters. He had a considerable portion of classical learning, bnt his mind

> Was never yet with Honour caught,
> Nor on poor Virtue lost one thought.

Let those who are disposed to think more favourably concerning him, read the following character of him by Gibbon, a perfectly impartial observer, who wrote it immediately after dining with him at mess when he was a Colonel of the Buckinghamshire Militia. 'He has inexhaustible spirits, infinite wit and humour, but [is] *a thorough profligate in principle as in practice, his life stained with every vice, and his conversation full of blasphemy and indecency. These morals he glories in; for shame is a weakness he has long since surmounted. He told us himself that in this time of public dissension he was resolved to make his fortune.*'† Such was the demagogue whom the deluded or designing extolled as a patriot!

Among his 'aiders and abetters,' in his attacks upon the King, and other great personages, in the 'North Briton,' was the writer from whom we have borrowed the

* Kilvert's Selections from Warburton's Papers, p. 342.

† Gibbon's Misc. Works, vol. i. p. 144.

preceding couplet, which, we need hardly say, he does not apply to Wilkes, whom, on the contrary, he pronounces to be *honoured through the land*, and *whose chief or only crime was that he loved his country too well.* He even couples his name with that of Algernon Sydney, and says that

> Old Time himself, his scythe thrown by,
> Himself lost in eternity,
> An everlasting crown shall twine,
> To make a Wilkes and Sydney join.*

In moral feelings and practice, Wilkes and Churchill, though Churchill doubtless at times showed himself less black than Wilkes, were, on the whole, well suited to each other, and it is therefore no wonder that, when they once came into contact, they formed that sort of connexion, which, as Cicero says, is between the good called friendship, and between the bad confederacy. Churchill assisted Wilkes in the 'North Briton,' supplying prose, however, of an inferior quality to his verses; and when Wilkes, as he well deserved, was reprobated by Warburton in the House of Lords, Churchill was ready to lift his pen in his defence. To this end he produced the vehement and coarse satire on Warburton in the third book of the 'Duellist,' which I have no intention to transfer from Churchill's pages to these. Churchill was a powerful satirist, but so ready to satirise everybody, and so unwilling to find anything to commend in any body, that his satire has been of little effect; he was a *blustering railer*, prepared, like Boreas, to blow on good or bad indiscriminately. Mr. Martin, a man of unreproached character, is visited by him with as heavy blasts of invective as Lord Sandwich.

Churchill was sadly, though not totally, deficient in that which Leslie the painter has called the first requisite of a poet, *a true perception of moral beauty*, and his verses,

* Duellist, b. i. sub fin.

with the exception of a very few couplets, have fallen deservedly into neglect.

Is this the land that boasts a Milton's fire,
And magic Spenser's wildly warbling lyre?
The land that owns th' omnipotence of song,
Where Shakspeare whirls the throbbing heart along?
The land where Pope, with energy divine,
In one strong blaze bade wit and fancy shine?
And shall a Bufo's most polluted name
Stain the bright tablet of untainted fame?
Shall his disgraceful name with theirs be join'd,
Who wish'd and wrought the welfare of their kind?
His name accursed, who, leagued with Wilkes and hell,
Labour'd to rouse, with rude and murderous yell,
Discord the fiend, to toss rebellion's brand,
To whelm in rage and woe a guiltless land,
To frustrate wisdom's, virtue's noblest plan,
And triumph in the miseries of man!
Drivelling and dull, where crawls the reptile muse
Swoln from the sty, and rankling from the stews,
With envy, spleen, and pestilence replete,
And gorg'd with dust she lick'd from Treason's feet,
Who once, like Satan, raised to heaven her sight,
But turn'd abhorrent from the hated light—
O'er such a muse shall wreaths of glory bloom?
No—shame and execration be her doom.

Walpole, always ready to abuse Warburton, makes merry with the part which he acted on this occasion in the House of Lords, a part 'which,' he says, 'was only ridiculous,' and 'was heightened,' he adds, 'by its being known that Potter, his wife's gallant, had had the chief hand in the composition of the verses.' *

There was indeed a report that Thomas Potter, the profligate member of Parliament, son of the Archbishop of Canterbury, an intimate associate of Wilkes, and a frequent visitor at Prior Park,† had paid extraordinary atten-

* Walpole's Letters, i. 312.

† Notes and Queries, 2nd S. vol. iv. p. 41.

tion to Mrs. Warburton; and scandal went even so far as to insinuate that Ralph Allen Warburton, her only child, was the son, not of the Bishop, but of Potter.* Mr. Cradock, who knew Mrs. Warburton well, and was kindly disposed towards her, admits that 'the public had much to say against her;' for, notwithstanding the good sense which she was allowed to possess, she was sometimes guilty of foolish frivolity, as an instance of which Mr. Cradock relates that she once, in sport, scared away a candidate for ordination, by representing the Bishop as so terrific a person that she herself dared hardly look him in the face. Such playfulness might make people talk. But Mr. Cradock observes, at the same time, that she seemed always to entertain much respect for the Bishop, and 'to feel a peculiar satisfaction,' both during his life and after his death,' in recounting his many excellences.' †

That Potter had some concern in the composition of the 'Essay on Woman,' may be inferred from the line in Churchill's 'Dedication' to the 'Great Gloucester,' in allusion to his speech in the House of Lords,

> And Potter trembles even in his grave.

And there is other evidence, besides Walpole's, to the same purpose. Endeavours have even been made to prove that Potter was the author of the whole, and that Wilkes was guilty only of the printing.‡ But Wilkes himself seems to have shown no anxiety to clear himself of the authorship, and none need be solicitous to do for him what he cared not to do for himself. If the charge of writing the parody was altogether groundless, why did he never deny it? Had he so strong a desire for infamy as to clothe himself with that to which he was not entitled?

* Prior's Life of Malone, p. 445.

† Cradock's Lit. and Misc. Memoirs, vol. i. p. 188; iv. p. 205.

‡ Notes and Queries, 2nd S. vol. iv. pp. 1, 21, 41; v. 77.

CHAPTER XXX.

CONTROVERSY WITH LOWTH.

DEATH OF RALPH ALLEN — HIS BEQUESTS TO WARBURTON — WARBURTON'S FAILING HEALTH — LOWTH'S LECTURES, IN WHICH WARBURTON FANCIES HIMSELF ATTACKED — LOWTH'S OBSERVATIONS — LOWTH'S FATHER; HIS COMMENTARIES — TOWNE'S EXAMINATION OF SHERLOCK'S SERMONS; OCCASIONS A SECOND CORRESPONDENCE BETWEEN WARBURTON AND LOWTH — LOWTH'S LONG LETTER TO WARBURTON; EXTRACTS FROM IT — DIFFERENCE IN EARLY EDUCATION BETWEEN WARBURTON AND LOWTH — WHITAKER — JOHNSON'S REMARKS ON THE CONTROVERSY — HURD'S SUPERCILIOUS MENTION OF LOWTH AND SECKER — CUMBERLAND'S PAMPHLET AGAINST LOWTH.

IN the month of June, 1764, died Warburton's amiable patron, Ralph Allen. This event, said the Honourable Charles Yorke, writing to Warburton shortly afterwards, must cause the greatest grief to us both; 'to myself, who regret a friend, and to your Lordship, who mourns a parent,' for 'such he truly was to all mankind, to all who came within the reach of his care and bounty. In short, he was a rare example of piety and charity; one of those excellent persons who always die too soon for the world. He will be sincerely and universally lamented; and that circumstance I have often thought a pleasing advantage which amiable and benevolent men have over the great and ambitious.' *

The munificence which he had practised in his life he did not omit to observe in his will. He left many handsome legacies to his friends and dependents, and for

* Letters from an Eminent Prelate, p. 508.

purposes of charity. To Warburton and his wife he bequeathed 5,000*l.* each; and the reversion of Prior Park and the lands adjoining, with the estate of Claverton, of about 3,000*l.* a year, to Mrs. Warburton on Mrs. Allen's death. Mrs. Allen survived her husband only two years.

Warburton's health, however, was now becoming such as to detract from the enjoyment of additional wealth. He complains, in a letter to Hurd, of his *usual dizziness*, for which he was going to be bled.

This year also was marked by his great controversy with Lowth, with whom he had had some not very friendly correspondence, in reference to 'The Divine Legation,' several years before.

When Lowth published his *Lectures de Sacrâ Poesi Hebræorum*, Warburton thought that certain remarks in them were aimed, particularly and offensively, against portions of his own work. He accordingly spoke to two of his friends, whom Lowth calls Dr. C. and Mr. S.,* on the subject, and requested them to communicate his opinion to Lowth. This commission they executed, and Lowth replied by a letter, in which he said that he had felt obliged to differ in opinion, especially about the Book of Job, from many writers of great authority, as Grotius, Le Clerc, Bishop Hare, Warburton himself, and others whom it was unnecessary to name; and that the chief points which he maintained, in opposition to them, were, that the Book of Job was the most ancient book extant; that it had no reference to the affairs of the Israelites; and that it was neither allegorical nor properly dramatic. 'You seem to think,' he tells Warburton, 'that I ought to have quoted you, or referred to your book; and a friend of yours charges me with writing against you, and being afraid of you. Your friend is mistaken in both these particulars; and the ground of your complaint I

* Lowth's First Letter to Warburton, Sept. 9, 1756.

cannot possibly comprehend. Why should I single out you, and attack you for opinions which were common to you with twenty other authors of note? Would this have been a mark of respect to you? Would it not rather have argued a busy and litigious spirit in me? There were several living writers of great learning and eminence, who stood just in the same situation, with regard to me, that you did. . . . I have never heard that any of those gentlemen have been offended with me for acting with respect to them just in the same manner as I have done with respect to you.'

After alluding to two or three passages, in which Warburtou thought himself designated, but which were not directed against him more than against others, and observing that his Lectures, and every expression in them, might have stood just as they do now, though Warburton's remarks on Job had never been written, he adds, with a just reflection on Hurd, 'I beg the continuance of that regard and esteem which you have been so kind as to express towards me; I will not tell you how highly I shall prize it; your friend, the author of the "Dissertation on the Delicacy of Friendship," has stopped my mouth, and makes me very cautious of saying anything that may be construed into flattery or fear of you.' He then says that he leaves his opinions, which he is still inclined to retain, but of which he is not so fond as to love disputing for them, to such treatment from Warburton as his own cause and the cause of truth may seem to require: 'As to the manner in which you shall treat them,' he concludes, 'I shall be very little concerned about it. If you use me otherwise than I deserve, your own character will suffer, and not mine. Lay aside all regard to me upon this occasion, but respect yourself and the public.'

This letter, as may perhaps be supposed, had little effect in propitiating Warburton. He persisted in pointing out passages which he says must have been intended against him. One of these is as follows: *Hoc autem ut concedamus, vix erit satis; sunt qui majus quiddam postulare videntur. Loquuntur enim de rerum constitutione, de catastrophe dramatis,* Θεὸν ἀπὸ μηχανῆς *induci dicunt—iisdem certè vocibus utuntur.* 'When I read this,' says Warburton, 'I could no longer doubt that I only was meant, because I speak of all these things; and of *the God from the machine* no one could speak but me; because no one else, in their interpretations of the Book of Job, contended for the thing understood by it. You seem yourself to have been sensible that this needed a softening, by your correction, *iisdem certè vocibus utuntur.*' Lowth, in his reply, refers Warburton to a passage of Calmet's 'Preface sur Job,' in which exactly the same expression is used: 'Il s'est trouvé plusieurs ecrivains qui ont douté de la vérité de l'histoire qu'il contient. Ils traitent de paraboles et d'allégories tout ce qui y est raconté. Ils veulent que Job, &c., soient de noms feints et empruntés; que tout ce récit soit fait à plaisir; une pièce de poësie; non ce qui étoit en effet, mais ce qui pouvoit être.' He then gives an account of the conduct and speeches of the book, and says, 'Dieu entre dans cette dispute, paroit dans un tourbillon, comme l'on dit, *Deus è machinâ.* Quoi de plus semblable que tout cela à une tragédie?' 'And why,' he asks, 'should I not have had Calmet in my thoughts as much as yourself? Or I might, indeed, have been supposed to have my mind on Bishop Hare, who declares that the Book of Job is indisputably a drama, divisible into seven acts, in the last of which God appears to produce *the catastrophe.*'

On this point Warburton said no more. But he had remarked to Lowth, in one passage: 'You tell me you are not afraid of me. All I will say to this is, that whoever injures me may not, in the long run, have reason to applaud his situation. But no man need be afraid of him he has not injured. And I am very ready to believe that it is a consciousness of that, which makes you so brave. For my own part, I am not fond of resenting that as an injury which was never intended.'

To this Lowth replies: 'You guess the true reason of my not being afraid of you, and I will give you the reason why I told you so. After what your friend [Hurd] had published to the world, and what you had said yourself, (for your dread of an explanation was attended with a sort of denunciation of your resentment in case of a refusal, or an unsatisfactory account of myself,) I thought it incumbent on me to tell you explicitly, and to repeat it, that I was not to be frightened. I should not have thought of setting forth my bravery if I had not first been called a coward, and accordingly looked upon as one that was to be awed by menaces.'

But there was another complaint that Lowth had against Warburton. Lowth's father, a learned divine, who published 'Commentaries on the Prophets,' and other theological works, had written also 'Notes on Josephus and the Ecclesiastical Historians,' of which Reading had copied some into his edition. Warburton, fixing on one of these in his 'Julian,' had charged the writer with uncharitableness towards Basnage, in accusing him of wilfully suppressing the well-known passage of Ammianus Marcellinus. Against this charge Lowth strongly remonstrated, and remarked also that, as his father had previously applied the account of the meteoric crosses in Casaubon's 'Adversaria' to the phenomena at the temple, it would have been but just and generous in Warburton to have acknowledged his obligation for the indication of the passage; expressing his expectation, at the same time, that Warburton would supply this omission in a future edition of 'Julian.'

Warburton immediately replied that he had never had the least suspicion that the Lowth who had written the 'Notes on the Ecclesiastical Historians,' was Dr. Lowth's father; that if he had known it, he would have forgiven all that was said in the 'Lectures,' since the injurer of his father's memory assuredly deserved no quarter from him; and that he would erase the note reflecting on his father on the first opportunity: a promise which he kept, for the note is not to be found in the later editions. As to the accusation of having taken a hint from the elder Lowth, without acknowledgment, he said, 'That I may not continue worse in your esteem than I deserve, give me leave to tell you I am no plagiary of your father's observations. By an odd fancy to a strange unequal writer, I had read Meric Casaubon's writings through and through; and I had finished my book of "Julian," and it was half printed off, when Dr. Jortin wrote me word of this note of Mr. L.'s. This is a point of honour in which I am particularly delicate. I will venture to boast that I believe no author was ever more averse to take to himself what belonged to another.' 'To your filial piety,' he adds, 'I am ready to sacrifice every disgust that some parts of your last might be naturally supposed to give me.' He then concludes by expressing his willingness to be in friendship with Lowth, and observes that there was a vacancy among the King's chaplains, of which he should be glad to find Lowth take advantage.

Lowth answered, with much courtesy, that he had been unwilling to say anything in behalf of his father, till he had first defended himself; that in those portions of his 'Lectures' which had given offence to Warburton, he would, though they were written, as he could prove, before 'Julian' was published, soften or alter any expressions that Warburton disapproved; that he had meant to say nothing in his last letter but what Warburton's remarks had fairly occasioned; and that he was going to Durham in the following week, when he hoped to have frequent opportunities of improving the concord now arising between them. Thus ended Lowth and

Warburton's first correspondence about their matters of dispute.*

Things remained quiet between them for a few years, but Towne, in his 'Free and Candid Examination' of Bishop Sherlock's Sermons, had chosen to ask this question, in allusion, apparently, to a passage of Lowth's 'Lectures:' 'Where was idolatry ever punished by the magistrate but under the Jewish economy?' Lowth, in the second edition of his Lectures, published in 1763, did not think it well to leave this inquiry unanswered, and noticed it thus: 'It was punished under the economy of the patriarchs, in the families and under the dominion of Abraham, Melchisedec, and Job. As idolatry spread itself more widely, Abraham was divinely called from Chaldea, that he might become the father of a people, which, set apart from all other nations, might worship the true God, might give an example of pure religion, and bear testimony against the worship of false deities. Was it not, then, the special duty and office of Abraham, exercising the sovereignty in his own family, to inflict punishments on idolatry? Was it not the duty of Melchisedec, Job, and all the chiefs of tribes of that period, who still retained the knowledge and worship of the true God, amidst an almost general defection of the surrounding nations, to take care that their own people did not fall away? Was it not incumbent on them to lay restraint on offenders, and to punish the obstinate and rebellious, and such as spread the contagion of this vice?'

On this passage Warburton, publishing a fourth edition of 'The Divine Legation,' in 1765, took occasion, in an Appendix to the sixth book, to animadvert, not in a friendly or courteous style, but in his usual flippant and contemptuous manner, affecting to consider it 'so plea-

* Warburton's Works, vol. xii. pp. 444—463.

sant an answer, and so little needing the masterly hand of the Examiner to correct, that a few strictures in a cursory note would be more than sufficient to do its business.' He then denies that Lowth had any ground for investing these old patriarchs, or chiefs of tribes, with royal dignity; sneers at him for making them act upon a right of his own fancy; assures him that 'such a set of persecuting patriarchs is nowhere to be found but in a poetical prælection;' and warns him that the Examiner, who had not spared Sherlock, would easily demolish the 'prælections,' if he should feel inclined to take them in hand. Such an insolent tone, especially towards one for whom the writer had recently professed friendship, there was nothing in Lowth's observations to justify; and he accordingly prepared, with sufficient reason, to express his resentment in a pamphlet.

This pamphlet, entitled 'A Letter to the Right Reverend Author of the Divine Legation of Moses Demonstrated,' had such attractions for the public that it went through four editions in the course of about eighteen months.

Lowth begins by declaring himself much indebted to Warburton for honouring him with an Appendix appropriated to him alone; an honour which he had previously bestowed upon no one except Lord Bolingbroke. He had heard, he says, that Warburton considered himself affronted, and 'You expressed your indignation,' he tells him, 'to almost every one whom you met, except to myself, whom you, at the same time, received with fair words and a smooth countenance; insomuch that I was then really persuaded that what I had heard of your resentment was all an idle and groundless report. However, I did not imagine, either that the subject on which we differed was so important in itself, or the person who differed from you so considerable in your estimation, as to merit so formal a process and so solemn a chastisement. I thought you might possibly whip me at the cart's tail, in a note to "The Divine Legation," the ordinary place of your literary executions; or pillory me in the "Dunciad," another engine which, as legal proprietor, you have very ingeniously and judiciously applied to the same purpose; or, perhaps, have ordered me a kind of Bridewell correction by one of your beadles in a pamphlet. I never flattered myself with the expectation of being exhibited on a scaffold, erected on purpose for me, and in so conspicuous a place.

'You complain as if I had attacked you in a certain note of mine. How so, my Lord? My note expressly referred to an anonymous book entitled 'A Free and Candid Examination of the Bishop of London's Sermons,' in which I was several times called to account with a peculiar air of insolence that marks the controversial writings that come from a certain quarter. I answered such of the Candid Examiner's objections as I thought at all worth answering. . . . And pray, my Lord, what is all this to you? You will say, perhaps, "They were my arguments." And pray, what is that to me? They were urged against me by the Candid Examiner; if they had come immediately from you, I would have directed my answer to you. If I had taken the contrary method, and fallen upon you instead of the Candid Examiner, you might then, with some reason, have represented me as a petulant and quarrelsome fellow, who had attacked you "without the least provocation given."'

Warburton, at the end of his second Preface to the second part of 'The Divine Legation,' published in 1758, in which he attacked Dr. Taylor, had said that, wishing to settle accounts with the bigots and others who had signalised themselves against his work, he employed a friend to look over their productions, and see what was worthy of attention in them. 'I applied,' says he, 'to a learned person, who, in consideration of our friendship, hath been prevailed upon to undergo the drudgery of turning over this dirty heap, and marking what he imagined would in the least deserve, or could justify, any notice; for I would not have the reader conceive so miserably of me as to think I was ever disposed to look into them myself. He will find, as he goes along, both in the text and the notes, what was thought least unworthy of an answer.' This scornful announcement, with which Towne, humble follower of Warburton as he was, could hardly have been much delighted, Lowth did not fail to turn to good account. 'After all, you may say,' he continues, 'that this is a mere evasion, and that I must know that, in the present case, to attack the Candid Examiner or you was, in effect, the same thing. Why, really, my Lord, there is some truth in this; I did indeed suppose that there was an intimate union between you and the Candid Examiner. I could not but observe the same cause managed much in the same manner, and much of the same spirit breathing in both. His book came forth at least with your approbation; you clapped upon its head a *prologus galeatus* (for the public was not mistaken, I believe, when it ascribed the Preface to you), and while little Teucer shot at all the leaders of Troy, and had the vain ambition to think of vanquishing the great Hector himself, he skulked behind the shade of the mighty Telamonian shield,

> — with seven thick folds o'ercast
> Of tough bull-hides; of solid brass the last.

I presume, my Lord, that the Candid Examiner is the same person whom your Lordship, in regard to his former services, some time since, preferred to the honourable office of being your literary scavenger; whose patent stands upon record at the end of the second Preface to the second part of "The Divine Legation." I applaud your choice; you could not easily have found a person more expert, not only in raking up dirt, but (which is a still more useful qualification) in throwing it too, than this Candid Gentleman; and it must be supposed that your connexion with him is of the closest nature. Still further, my Lord, I will confess that I think it probable, as from some other marks, so in particular from a notion which very often possesses this writer's imagination, that all authors whatever, while they are writing, think of nobody but you, and whatever opinions they advance or confute, they aim at nothing but "The Divine Legation;" from hence, I say, I think it probable that you had some hand in the book itself. But till you publicly acknowledge all this, and lay in your claim to your share of the performance, I shall still think that any one, who has any matters to settle with the Candid Examiner, is quite at liberty to do it in what manner he thinks proper, without being in the least accountable to your Lordship for so doing.'

In reference to their former correspondence, and its seemingly amicable termination, Lowth expresses himself very effectively:

'You signified to me that you were offended, and called upon me to answer to the charge of having dissented in opinion from you. I did not care to protest against the authoritative manner in which you proceeded, or to question your investiture in the high office of inquisitor-general and supreme judge of the opinions of the learned, which you had long before assumed, and had exercised with a ferocity and a despotism without example in the republic of letters, and hardly to be paralleled among the disciples of Dominic; exacting their opinions to the standard of your infallibility, and prosecuting with implacable hatred every one that presumed to differ from you. I knew that such a protest would lead immediately to what I was willing to avoid. I obeyed your summons; I gave you by letter the account of myself which you demanded; and, with due freedom, but, I hope, with civility and good manners, I asserted my right of thinking for myself, and endeavoured to remove the grounds of your resentment. The debate ran out into some length, but ended in an amicable manner, which was much to my satisfaction. You perhaps may still suppose that I was afraid of you. I will tell you fairly what I was really afraid of: I was afraid that two members of the same ecclesiastical society, engaging in an open quarrel and a hostile altercation, (for such I knew it must be, when you were one of the parties,) upon a difference of opinion, in a point not only of no great importance, but so dubious as to be incapable of being perfectly settled between them, would make a contemptible figure, and exhibit a ridiculous spectacle to the public.'

As to the revival of the controversy, Lowth observes that he was much surprised, after having been civilly dismissed from his Lordship's presence, to find his footman, meaning Towne, at the door, armed with his master's cane, ready to lay it upon his back as he went out; that he wrested the weapon from him, and broke it, when his Lordship, it seems, received an unlucky blow in the scuffle; that it was a general complaint of the members of the Republic of Letters, that they could not go peaceably on their business, along the public road, without being liable to meet, at any time, a sturdy bravo to dispute their passage; that Warburton, in quality of Demonstrator-General of 'The Divine Legation of Moses,' (though Moses's Legation had often been demonstrated before, and might be demonstrated by any young student in five pages better than Warburton had demonstrated it in five volumes,) claimed power as Lord Paramount over all the realms of science, and declared that whoever failed of abject submission to him, or offered only moderate praise, was guilty of *malignant parsimony*, *disrespect*, and *indignity*, crimes for which correction had been publicly inflicted on the offender.

This 'correction' is Hurd's 'Delicacy of Friendship,' from which the terms in italics are taken.

I must extract one passage more, one of the strongest and happiest pieces of satire that it contains. Warburton, mindful of the repulse which he had suffered, when he was the companion of Pope, at Oxford, ventured, in his Appendix, to speak thus disrespectfully of the University, and of one whom it regarded among its greatest ornaments: 'The learned Professor who has been hardily brought up in the keen atmosphere of WHOLESOME SEVERITIES, and early taught to distinguish between *de facto* and *de jure*, thought it needless to inquire into *facts* [in regard to the punishment of idolatry], when he was secure of the *right*.' This unhappy sarcasm brought upon him the following powerful retort, 'in which,' says Whitaker, 'the application of Lord Clarendon's character of an attorney's clerk was one of those lucky hits which are seldom given to the most witty and dexterous of mankind more than once in a life. With what affected scorn, with what inward rage and vexation, such a blow must have been received by Warburton, it requires nothing more than an ordinary intuition into his character to conjecture.'

'Pray, my Lord, what is it to the purpose where I have been brought up? You charge me with principles of intolerance, adding a gentle insinuation also of disaffection to the present royal family and government; you infer these principles, it seems, from the place of my education. Is this a necessary consequence? Is it even a fair conclusion? May not one have had the good sense, or the good fortune, to have avoided, or to have gotten the better of the ordinary prejudices of education?. . . To have made a proper use of the advantages of a good education is a just praise; but to have overcome the disadvantages of a bad one, is a much greater. In short, my Lord, I cannot but think that this inquisition concerning my education is quite beside the purpose. Had I not your Lordship's example to justify me, I should think it a piece of extreme impertinence to enquire where YOU were bred; though one might justly plead in excuse for it a natural curiosity to know where and how such a phenomenon was produced. It is commonly said that your Lordship's education was of that particular kind concerning which it is a remark of that great judge of men and manners, Lord Clarendon, (on whom you have therefore with a wonderful happiness of allusion, justness of application, and elegance of expression, conferred *the unrivalled title of the Chancellor of Human Nature,)** that it particularly disposes them to be proud, insolent, and pragmatical: "Colonel Harrison was the son of a butcher, near Nantwich, in Cheshire, and had been bred up in the place of a clerk, under a lawyer of good account in those parts; which kind of education introduces men into the language and practice of business, and, if it be not resisted by the great ingenuity of the person, inclines young men to more pride than any other kind of breeding, and disposes them to be pragmatical and insolent." † Now, my Lord, as you have in your whole behaviour, and in all your writings, remarkably distinguished yourself by your humility, lenity, meekness, forbearance, candour, humanity, civility, decency, good manners, good temper, moderation with regard to the opinions of others, and a modest diffidence of your own, this unpromising circumstance of your education is so far from being a disgrace to you that it highly redounds to your praise.

'But I am wholly precluded from all claim to such merit. On the contrary, it is well for me if I can acquit myself of a charge that is hard upon me, the burden of

* Critical Inquiry into the Causes of Prodigies and Miracles.

† Lord Clarendon's History, vol. iii. p. 246, 8vo.

being responsible for the great advantages which I enjoyed. For, my Lord, I was educated in the University of Oxford; I enjoyed all the advantages, both public and private, which that famous seat of learning so largely affords. I spent many happy years in that illustrious society, in a well-regulated course of useful discipline and studies, and in the agreeable and improving commerce of gentlemen and scholars; in a society where emulation without envy, ambition without jealousy, contention without animosity, incited industry and awakened genius; where a liberal pursuit of knowledge, and a generous freedom of thought, was raised, encouraged, and put forward, by example, by commendation, and by authority. I breathed the same atmosphere that the Hookers, the Chillingworths, and the Lockes, had breathed before; whose benevolence and humanity were as extensive as their vast genius, and their comprehensive knowledge; who always treated their adversaries with civility and respect; who made candour, moderation, and liberal judgment, as much the rule and law, as the subject, of their discourse; who did not amuse their readers with empty declamations and fine-spun theories of toleration, while they were themselves agitated by a furious inquisitorial spirit, seizing every one they could lay hold on for presuming to dissent from them in matters the most indifferent, and dragging them through the fiery ordeal of abusive controversy. And do you reproach me with my education in this place, and this most respectable body, which I shall always esteem my greatest advantage, and my highest honour? . . .'

To characterise these remarks more fully, we will borrow yet a few more words from Whitaker: 'To the dignity, spirit, indignation, and eloquence of this passage, we know of nothing that can fairly be opposed on the part of Warburton; and it is further memorable as one proof, though not the last, that the venerable and illustrious body, whose insulted honour the writer so nobly defends, has never to despair of finding a son able and willing to inflict ample vengeance on the assailant.'

It was not to be expected that the learning of Lowth would be brought to bear upon Warburton without showing something of Warburton's deficiency in that respect. Speaking of Warburton's opinion that the Book of Job was written by Ezra, he says, 'I will venture to affirm that the critic who gives forth this as his decisive judgment, never read either Job or Ezra; I mean, in the original, and with a competent knowledge of the language. I was very well convinced before that the only interpreter who has made the Book of Job intelligible, [a boast of Warburton's,] had never read Job in Hebrew; and I now suspect that the demonstrator of "The Divine Legation" of Moses never read the Hebrew Pentateuch.* . . . . I will venture to say that he who pretends to set up for a deep and critical expositor of the writers of the Old Testament, and of some of the most difficult of them in particular, with no knowledge, or at best a very superficial knowledge, of Hebrew, though he may amuse common readers with fanciful interpretations and ingenious hypotheses, yet will be esteemed by proper judges as no other than a Quack in Commentatorship, and a Mountebank in Criticism.' †

Warburton had called Lowth 'the contemptuous professor.' Lowth rejoins, 'Yes, my Lord, the professor does avow a perfect contempt for a miserable caviller [Towne], who prostitutes his pen to do the drudgery of an imperious task-master. I see, my Lord, you have intimated your orders to him to take the prælections in hand once more; and may I not hope then for the honour of your Lordship's animadversions? *In good time* — when the Candid Examiner understands Latin a little better, and

* Lowth's Letter to Warburton, p. 74. † Ib. p. 89.

when your Lordship has a competent knowledge of Hebrew. And a little more civility, too, may not be amiss; for if he, who has demolished the Appendix, should take it into his head to examine the book itself, he might possibly make some havoc in *The Divine Legation of Moses Demonstrated.*'

This was no empty boast. Had Lowth desired to write a critique on Warburton's work, his learning and acuteness might easily have exhibited plenty of vulnerable parts in its structure; he might have noted erroneous applications of authorities, unintentionally misconceived or wilfully misrepresented, and have discovered abundance of inexact or sophistical reasoning, which Warburton would have found it difficult to justify. Dr. Johnson's account of the dispute between Lowth and Warburton, as given to George III., is by no means fair. 'Warburton has most general, most scholastic learning,' said he; 'Lowth is the more correct scholar. I do not know which of them calls names best.' 'You do not think, then, Dr. Johnson,' said the King, 'that there was much argument in the case?' Johnson said he did not think there was.* But the truth is, that there is much argument, and of the soundest description, in Lowth's pamphlet, though sometimes diluted and weakened by being thrown into too many words. Another statement of Johnson's, that 'Warburton kept his temper all along, while Lowth was in a passion,' and that 'Warburton drew Lowth on to write some very abusive letters, and then asked his leave to publish them, which he knew Lowth could not refuse after what he had done,'† seems to have arisen from some misconception or groundless rumour. Warburton was in as much of a passion at least as Lowth. Lowth published some of Warburton's letters, together with his own,

* Boswell's Johnson, 1767.

† Ib. 1773.

written in 1756, an act of which Warburton affected to complain. 'The strangest thing of all,' says he, 'is this man's publishing my letters without my leave or knowledge. . . . Is not this universally esteemed dishonourable conduct, to publish a man's letters without his knowledge or consent? The absurdity, too, is amazing, to those who will attend to the chronology of this affair. We were come to a good understanding, and some years afterwards he falls again upon poor Job, and in an insulting manner.'* Lowth, it may be supposed, would have let poor Job alone, had not Warburton encouraged Towne to meddle with Lowth, who, doubtless, thought himself justified in printing Warburton's letters with his own, that the public might understand the quarrel from its origin, and see that it commenced with Warburton. But Warburton himself pretended to find another cause: 'I think I see the reason of the publication of these letters; it was to show how he *defied* me, and what a *high opinion* I had of him.'

'But,' he adds, with assumed contempt, 'he is beneath another thought.' 'His *wit* and his *reasoning*, *God knows, and I also*, (as a certain critic said once in a matter of the like great importance,) are much below the qualities that deserve those names. If he expected an answer, he will certainly find himself disappointed; though I believe I could make as good sport with this *devil of a vice* for the public diversion, as ever was made with him in the old Moralities.'† The majority of the public, however, and especially the more judicious, appear to have been of another opinion, and to have thought that Warburton acted very discreetly in leaving Lowth unmolested, and *boasting in safety what he would have done* if he had thought proper. Lowth's epistle, said Gibbon, was 'printed and published,' and 'his victory was clearly

* Letters from an Eminent Prelate, pp. 369, 371. † Ibid.

established by the silent confession of Warburton and his slaves.'

Hurd's account of the controversy, an account which deserves to be noticed for its caution, is this: 'The dispute was managed, on both sides, with too much heat, but on the part of the Bishop' [Warburton] 'with that superiority of wit and argument, which, to say the truth, in all his controversial writings, he could not well help. For it may, I believe, be as truly said of him as of Carneades, that *he never defended an opinion which he did not prove, nor opposed any which he did not confute.*

'Dr. Lowth, afterwards Bishop of London, was a man of learning and ingenuity, and of many virtues; but his friends did his character no service by affecting to bring his merits, whatever they were, into competition with those of the Bishop of Gloucester. His reputation as a writer was raised chiefly on his Hebrew literature, as displayed in those two works, his Latin Lectures on Hebrew Poetry, and his English Version of the Prophet Isaiah. The former is well and elegantly composed, but in a vein of criticism not above the common. The latter, I think, is chiefly valuable as it shows how little is to be expected from Dr. Kennicott's work, (which yet the learned Bishop pronounces to be *the greatest and most important that has been undertaken and accomplished since the revival of letters*,) and from a new translation of the Bible for public use.

'On the subject of his quarrel with the Bishop of Gloucester I could say a great deal, for I was well acquainted with the grounds and the progress of it. But, besides that I purposely avoid entering into details of this sort, I know of no good end that is likely to be answered by exposing to public censure the weaknesses of such men.' *

The reader will observe the whole tone of this passage,

* Hurd's Life of Warburton, p. 79.

and the sarcastic touch on Lowth's *merits, whatever they were.* Whitaker, though a stout champion for Warburton, is nevertheless indignant at this mention of his opponent. 'Of Bishop Lowth, the dignified, the spirited, the only equal antagonist of Warburton,' Hurd 'permits himself to speak in such terms of measured approbation, and comparative though disguised contempt! . . . . The reserve on the part of the good Bishop, it must be confessed, was discreet and charitable; but as he is careful to premise that while "the dispute was managed on both sides with too much heat," but on the part of Warburton "with that superiority of wit and argument *which he could not help*," (meaning, as we suppose, that he earnestly endeavoured to appear inferior,) we shall beg leave to hint a suspicion that it was not *the weaknesses of two great men*, but the strength of Lowth and the petulance of Warburton which the biographer of the latter shrank from exposing.' *

The Monthly Reviewers, it may be worth while to add, were delighted with Lowth's pamphlet. 'When a person of gentle and amiable manners, of unblemished character, and eminent abilities, is calumniated and treated in the most injurious manner by a haughty and overbearing Colossus, it must give pleasure to every generous mind to see such a person vindicating himself with manly freedom, resenting the insult with proper spirit, attacking the imperious aggressor in his turn, and taking ample vengeance for the injury done him. Such is the pleasure which every impartial reader, every true republican in literature, will receive from the perusal of the letter now before us.'†

Another prelate, we may here observe, of whom Hurd allows himself to speak with the same superciliousness as of Lowth, was Archbishop Secker, who had made objec-

* Quarterly Review, vol. vii. p. 386.

† Monthly Review, vol. xxxiii. p. 388.

tions to certain passages in 'The Divine Legation,' and against whom, in consequence, Warburton directed some of his notes. 'Dr. Secker,' says Hurd, 'was a wise man, an edifying preacher, and an exemplary bishop. But the course of his life and studies had not qualified him to decide on such a work as that of "The Divine Legation." Even in the narrow walk of literature he most affected, that of criticising the Hebrew text, it does not appear that he attained to any great distinction. His chief merit (and surely it was a very great one) lay in explaining clearly and popularly in his sermons the principles delivered by his friend Bishop Butler, in his famous book of the "Analogy;" and in showing the important use of them to religion.'

A remonstrance was addressed to Hurd, on behalf of Lowth and Secker, in a pamphlet published in 1796 by the Rev. Ralph Churton, Archdeacon of Oxford, and another, in 1797, by the Rev. Thomas Wintle, Rector of Brightwell, who had been Fellow of Pembroke College, Oxford. Archdeacon Churton asks, very pertinently, 'If Secker, Hebrew scholar as he was, was unqualified to judge of Warburton's "Divine Legation," how could Hurd, who was no Hebrew scholar, think himself so well qualified to pronounce on the labours of Secker?'

Dr. Secker, according to Hurd, has great merit, except when he approaches 'The Divine Legation,' before which he is disqualified and powerless. Yet his course of study had been directed chiefly to the Hebrew text, a knowledge of which would appear to be one great requisite for judging of such a work as Warburton's. Warburton himself, though he spoke lightly of the Hebrew text from its uncertainty, and thought that no man needed the original who had the Septuagint translation, would yet have been better fitted for his work by a better insight into the Jewish language. Lowth praised many of Secker's criticisms as those of a man of great judgment and perspicacity. Bishop Porteus, also, in his 'Life of Secker,' has vindicated the Archbishop, both as a Hebrew critic and as a general scholar, against the rash depreciation of Bishop Hurd.

The controversy, it may be added, drew forth a pamphlet also from Brown, the author of the 'Estimate,' and another from Towne, on behalf of Warburton; but the only other publication, in connexion with the dispute, that need be noticed, is one of Cumberland's, addressed to Lowth, in vindication of the literary character of his grandfather, Dr. Bentley. Warburton had spoken of 'the incomparable Bentley, as standing in the foremost rank of modern critics.' Lowth rejoined that he might stand in the foremost rank of verbal critics, but that, as to taste and judgment for discerning beauties and excellences in writing, he was merely, in the words of Catullus, *Unus caprimulgus aut fossor*, 'terms that in English,' said Cumberland, 'would have been downright blackguardism.' 'In which of Bentley's labours,' he asked Lowth, 'have you traced the brutal ignorance of *a goatherd*, the clownish stupidity of *a hedger and ditcher?*' Had his Lordship not said, he adds, that he was educated at Oxford, it might have been just matter of doubt in what spot of the globe he had acquired such elegance of phraseology. And did he defend his father against Warburton, and suppose that no relative of Bentley would rise in his defence against himself?

Cumberland, before he wrote his pamphlet, applied to his uncle, Richard Bentley, to undertake the task; but he, 'with a philosophical contempt for the sparring of pens,' declined to have anything to do with the affair, saying to Cumberland at the same time, 'you are unequal to maintain an argument against Lowth.'* Cumberland's

* Cumberland's Memoirs, vol. ii. p. 456; Letter to the Rt. Rev. the Lord Bp. of O——d.

pamphlet, however, had an effect, and Lowth made no attempt to reply; but, when a clergyman of his diocese volunteered to be his champion, refused the offer, acknowledging that Cumberland had reason for retaliation. If Cumberland wrote with more will than power, he *had his quarrel just*, and Lowth might very well forbear to vindicate his disrespectful mention of Bentley.

CHAPTER XXXI.

STUKELEY. BIRCH. BROWN. SERMONS AND CHARGES.

DEATH OF DR. STUKELEY; HIS CHARACTER—DEATHS OF DR. BIRCH AND DR. JOHN BROWN—BROWN'S CHARACTER—DECLINE OF WARBURTON'S POWERS—IMPERFECT CONCLUSION OF 'THE DIVINE LEGATION'—WARBURTON'S DISCONTENT AT THE RECEPTION OF THE WORK—REVIEW OF THE NINTH BOOK—INCONSISTENCIES—THIRD VOLUME OF SERMONS—SERMONS FOR THE SOCIETY FOR THE PROPAGATION OF THE GOSPEL, AND FOR THE LONDON HOSPITAL—WARBURTON'S STYLE OF PREACHING—CHARGE TO THE CLERGY OF GLOUCESTER—INSTANCES OF UNCOURTLINESS—ILLNESS—TOUP'S 'EPISTOLA CRITICA.'

IN the early part of this year, Warburton lost his friend Dr. Stukeley, a man known to the public only as an antiquary, but distinguished in private life, it would seem, by many excellent qualities. He was regularly educated for a physician, and practised physic till he was forty-two, when, partly from ill health, and partly, as he says, to combat the infidel spirit so much prevailing in his time, he went, like Dr. Linacre, the founder of the College of Physicians, into the Church. Warburton had become acquainted with him at Brant-Broughton; and 'there was in him,' he remarked to Hurd, 'such a mixture of simplicity, drollery, absurdity, ingenuity, superstition, and antiquarianism, that he often afforded me that kind of well-seasoned repast which the French call an *ambigu*, I suppose from a compound of things never meant to meet together. I have often heard him laughed at by fools who had neither his sense, his knowledge, nor his honesty, though, it must be confessed, that in him they were all strangely travestied.'* Yet he did not escape an occasional sneer from Warburton; writing to Doddridge, he says that Dr. Robert Taylor had acquainted him that, after having visited Dr. Doddridge at Northampton, he had the pleasure of his company 'contrasted by a very different sort of man, *one Stukeley of Stamford, a Doctor, too, in his way.*' 'Did this worthy antiquary,' asks good Mr. Nichols, 'deserve this unkind reflection, either from Dr. Taylor or Warburton?'†

Stukeley's death was soon followed by that of Dr. Birch, with whom Warburton had maintained a correspondence for more than thirty years, in the early part of which period he had sent him papers on Milton and Shakspeare for his General Dictionary. Many letters of Warburton to Birch are preserved among Birch's manuscripts in the British Museum, most of which have been printed in Nichols's 'Literary Illustrations;' but Birch's replies have perished.

Another friend that he lost about the same time was Dr. John Brown, the author of the tragedies, now little known, of 'Barbarossa' and 'Athelstan,' and of the 'Estimate of the Manners and Principles of the Times,' a book which made a noise in its day, by telling the nation, in an imposing and dictatorial tone, that the nobility were universally corrupted by luxury; and which, being published at a time when the body of the people were discontented at the loss of Minorca, and other disasters of the French war, had the fortune to pass through seven editions in a year. He had brought himself under Warburton's notice, as we have seen, by his 'Essay on Satire,' and, through Warburton, under that of Allen and Lord Hardwicke, who gave him a living in Kent,

* Letters from an Eminent Prelate, p. 358.

† Nichols's Lit. Ill. vol. ii. pp. 827, 845, 851.

which he afterwards resigned for one at Newcastle, and died there, in a fit of melancholy and dejection, by his own hand. He seems to have visited Warburton, in the early period of their acquaintance, very frequently, and to have been always ready to extol him, but afterwards became gloomy and sullen towards him; an effect, apparently, of incipient insanity.* Walpole said that Brown was proud to deify Warburton in the first volume of his 'Estimate,' but that, when 'that trumpery' became successful, Warburton grew jealous of him, and good feeling between them ceased.† When Lowth published his letter to Warburton, he alluded to Brown as one of Warburton's extravagant flatterers; Brown, conceiving that his moral character was assailed by Lowth's remarks, replied; Lowth politely rejoined that no reflection on his moral qualities was intended. He observed, in a letter to a friend, about two years before his death, that he was sorry for having far overpainted Warburton. 'I cannot bring myself,' said he, 'to give up the freedom of my mind to Warburton, and therefore we do not agree; but Dr. Hurd will never quarrel with him.'‡ He was a man of considerable power of imagination, but of not much learning; and, as might be expected from his constitutional infirmity, of no great discretion or judgment.

This year, Warburton obtained the royal licence for his son Ralph, and his posterity, to take the surname of Warburton-Allen.

From this time the life of Warburton offers but few events of any importance. He continued to do something with his pen, giving portions of his writings an occasional revision, and producing a few sermons; but no great work afterwards proceeded from him. He printed, in 1766, a fourth edition of the 'Alliance,'

* Letters from an Eminent Prelate, p. 300.

† Walpole's Letters, Cunningham's edit. vol. ii. p. 135.

‡ Davies's Life of Garrick, vol. i. p. 242.

and a fifth edition of the first and second volumes of 'The Divine Legation,' with a postscript, which we have already noticed, to the 'Dedication to the Free-thinkers,' reflecting on Akenside and Lord Kames; but the completion of the great work seems to have been no longer contemplated. We have seen that, from having had the subject long on his hands, and from some other causes, he had many years ago begun to be weary of it; and that, to stimulate himself for a new volume, he had to set the press prematurely to work, so that he might be forced to supply it with copy.* To such efforts he had now lost the power of exciting himself, and shrunk from the work disheartened and disgusted.

The plan of 'The Divine Legation' required three books in addition to the six already published, in order, as the author said, 'to remove all conceivable objections against the conclusion, and to throw in every collateral light upon the premises.' The seventh and eighth books, however, though materials had been collected for them, he made no attempt to compose. The substance of the ninth book he kept under his hands many years, writing portions of it, as Hurd says, who had an intimate knowledge of the closing part of his life, 'by snatches and with difficulty,' and leaving it at last incomplete, though he printed it, such as it was, a year or two before his death, after which event, it remained unpublished for nine years.

The distaste which he felt for continuing the work was owing, partly, to the ill reception which it had experienced from many of the clergy. But if there was any pretext for Lowth's remark, that a young student in theology would have given a better demonstration of 'The Divine Legation of Moses' in five pages, than Warburton had

* Letter to Doddridge, Feb. 2, 1741.

given in his six books, there is little wonder that some of the clergy should have thought the work unnecessary, and that others should have found other grounds of objection to it. As he expressed dissent from many, it is not strange that many expressed dissent from him. But 'his resentment at the established clergy,' says Hurd, 'for their long and fierce opposition to his favourite work, was the greatest weakness I ever observed in him. When he had given two or three of his principal adversaries, as he did, a complete answer, he should not have suffered the clamour of the rest to divert him from the great design he had projected. But his conduct, in this instance, was not that which might have been expected from his usual magnanimity. When I sometimes expostulated with him upon it, his answer was, "I surely have reason to think myself very ill used" by the clergy. "If, indeed, the published volumes of 'The Divine Legation' be so weak or so mischievous as they suppose, I will not add to the offence given them by adding any more."'*

As we have noticed the contents of the other books, we will now look also for a moment into the ninth. The seventh and eighth, we may first remark, were intended to be a continuance of the argumentation that, as the Jewish religion and polity were unsupported by the doctrine of a future state, they must have been upheld by an extraordinary providence. The ninth has for its subject the nature and genius of the Gospel, and reviews the progress of revelation, and the particulars of the several dispensations; setting them in much the same light in which they are generally regarded, and discoursing of them in a much lower tone than that which is used in the preceding part of the work, though the old spirit is sometimes apparent, and paradox shows itself in it more than once. Man, he says, was made at first mortal, (for 'immor-

* Life of Warburton, p. 81.

tal life was a thing extraneous to our nature, and not put into our original paste or composition,') and was left under the guidance of natural religion; when he was put into Paradise, he was placed under the revealed will of God, and received the free gift of immortality; and when he transgressed God's command in Paradise, he became again mortal, having violated the condition on which immortality was given him, and was expelled from Paradise, lest, by eating of the tree of life, he should thus become immortal again, through his own act. He was then left subject as before to natural religion until the law was given.* As to the origin of sacrifice, it sprung, not from any special monition from Heaven, but from the light of natural reason, Cain and Abel, the first that offered sacrifice, being wholly under the government of natural religion; and 'besides, the defects of language, in its early rudiments, necessarily occasioned this mode of intercourse between man and his Maker.' †

It is no wonder that in what he thus produced there should be some contradictions, or some inconsistencies with the previous part of the work. Towne, the great student of Warburton's writings, has observed that the opinion which he here expresses concerning the origin of sacrifice is at variance with that which he had adopted elsewhere, though where he has given another opinion I have not been able to discover. He says in one passage (as he is generally supposed to have believed) that St. Paul was not the author of the Epistle to the Hebrews, and in a subsequent passage that he was; and he interprets a verse in that Epistle, about Moses and the tabernacle, otherwise than he had understood it before in 'The Divine Legation.' In the first chapter of this ninth book he says the words, 'Man became a living soul,' in the second chapter of

* Div. Leg. book ix. ch. i.; Works, vol. vi. pp. 246, 247, 255, 263.

† Ib. p. 279.

Genesis, intimate the continuance of life after the separation of the soul and body: a sense totally different from that which he had once attributed to them, and which the general argument of 'The Divine Legation' requires.*

He greatly abridged his labour, it may be observed, by interweaving into his book large portions of three sermons which he had already laid before the public. One *On Antichrist*, in which he asserts that St. Peter's 'more sure word of prophecy' refers, not, as has been universally understood, to the prophecies of the Old Testament, but wholly to those of the New, especially those of St. John; and that the Antichrist, or Man of Sin, set forth in those prophecies, is unquestionably the Church of Rome; another *On the Fall of Satan*, in which he maintains, in opposition to Mead, that the demoniacs of the New Testament were persons really possessed with devils; and a third *On the Sacrament of the Lord's Supper*, in which he follows Cudworth, as we have already noticed, in representing the Eucharist as 'a feast upon a sacrifice.'

With these brief remarks on this imperfect ninth book, we may take our leave of it.

In 1767 he published a third volume of Sermons, dedicated, in a very quiet style, to Lady Mansfield. The first and second volumes had been published in 1752 and 1754.

He was also called upon, at times, to preach sermons on public occasions. He preached the Anniversary Sermon for the Society for the Propagation of the Gospel before the Lord Mayor, at St. Mary-le-Bow.

In this sermon he extols the Jesuit missionaries, whose practice was to make the teaching of the arts of civil life preliminary and instrumental to the introduction of religious doctrines, and commends them as an example to all who would propagate the Christian religion with success.

* Towne's Letters to Balguy; Kilvert's Selections from Warburton's Papers, pp. 179-191.

Alluding to the early English settlers in North America, he remarks that they carried over with them 'an ample cargo of religion, sufficient for themselves and their posterity,' and might have been left to their own doings, had they not been too poor to find means for disseminating their stock among their neighbours.

The Lord Mayor, when the sermon was ended, invited Warburton and some other bishops to dinner at the Mansion House. In his prayer before the sermon, Warburton had introduced, without precedent, a petition for the Common Council. Giving an account of the affair to Hurd, he says: 'I preached my Propagation Sermon, and ten or a dozen bishops dined with my Lord Mayor, a plain and (for this year at least) a munificent man. Whether I made them wiser than ordinary at Bow, I cannot tell; I certainly made them merrier than ordinary at the Mansion House, where we were magnificently treated. The Lord Mayor told me that "the Common Council were much obliged to me, for that this was the first time he ever heard them prayed for." I said, "I considered them as a body that much needed the prayers of the Church." But, if he told me in what I abounded, I told him in what I thought he was defective, that "I was greatly disappointed to see no custard at table." He said that they "had been so ridiculed for their custard that none had ventured to make its appearance for many years." I told him "I supposed religion and custard went out of fashion together."' It is to be hoped that Warburton has not here recorded the best thing that he said to make the Mayor and his party *merrier than ordinary*, for this is assuredly one of the dullest of dull clerical jokes that ever was written in a book.

He also preached for the London Hospital before the Duke of York, on the 30th of April 1767; and of his performance on that occasion we have the advantage of a full account from Mr. Cradock. He happened to call one morning on Hurd, he says, at Lincoln's Inn, and learned from him that Warburton was about to preach at St. Lawrence's Church, near Guildhall. 'Then, Sir,' said I, 'I shall certainly attend him.' 'I wish you would,' replied he, 'and bring me an account of all particulars. I believe I know the discourse—it is a favourite one; but I could rather have wished that his Lordship would have substituted some other;' then, hesitating, he added, 'but it is perhaps of little consequence, for he does not always adhere to what is written before him; his rich imagination is ever apt to overflow.' I was introduced into the vestry by a friend, where the Lord Mayor and several of the Governors of the Hospital were waiting for the late Duke of York, who was their president; and in the meantime the Bishop did everything in his power to entertain and alleviate their impatience. He was beyond measure condescending and courteous, and even graciously handed some biscuits and wine on a salver to the curate who was to read the prayers. His Lordship, being in good spirits, once rather exceeded the bounds of decorum, by quoting a comic passage from Shakspeare, in his lawn sleeves, and with all his characteristic humour; but, suddenly recollecting himself, he so aptly turned the inadvertence to his own advantage as to raise the admiration of all the company. Many parts of his discourse were quite sublime, and were given with due solemnity; but a few passages were, as in his celebrated Triennial Charge, quite ludicrous; and when he proceeded so far as to describe some charitable monks who had robbed their own begging boxes, he excited more than a smile from most of the audience. 'Though certainly, Sir,' said I, 'there was much to admire; yet, upon the whole, to speak the truth, I was not sorry that you were absent; for I well know that you would not absolutely have approved.' 'Approved, Sir!' said he; 'I should have agonised!'*

* Memoirs of Joseph Cradock, Esq. vol. iv.

The 'celebrated Triennial Charge' was one delivered to the clergy of Gloucester in the year 1761, which at that time we omitted to notice. Looking into it now, we shall find some passages that must have startled some of those that listened to it. He observes that, in the simplicity of old times, when the clergy first met their bishop, it was thought incumbent on him to give them some intimation how he was lifted into 'so eminent but hazardous a station;' but that this custom had gradually fallen into disuse, as the clergy became less solicitous to know 'from whence their bishop had dropped down among them,' and that these meetings were now intended only as occasions for a diocesan to exhort his clergy to the faithful discharge of their pastoral care. He then addresses himself chiefly to the younger part of his flock, and impresses upon them of how much advantage, in conjunction with integrity of life, is extent of knowledge, for the just fulfilment of their duties, as enabling them to oppose and discourage '*fanaticism*, whether spiritual or literary, *bigotry*, whether religious or civil, and *infidelity*, whether philosophical or immoral.' Too many of his hearers, he feared, 'were apt to mistake the completion of their academic courses for the completion of their theologic studies,' and, 'by a false modesty, to despair of knowing more than they would suffer those august places of education to teach them.' But such notions were not to be entertained; study must be continued; for a churchman who neglects to advance himself in knowledge is sure to fall into contempt; a layman may be found wanting in a learned profession, and meet with nothing but neglect, but a clergyman noted for ignorance will be a common object of derision. Nor should a churchman devote himself to studies extraneous to his profession, since, if he does so, he will not only seem to neglect the interests of the Church, but will find himself, probably, arrive at no great eminence in his foreign pursuits. A lawyer who occupies himself in mathematical investigations will disqualify himself for considering the moral evidence on which the interests of his clients depend; the physician who turns poet must hope for no patients but those of as warm imaginations as his own; and so a churchman, if he busies himself in law, will probably make himself nothing better than 'a tolerable justice of the quorum;' or, if he amuses himself with physic, must expect to be nothing more than 'a village doctor.' One may conjecture whether, when he uttered these exhortations, he thought of his own doings with Shakspeare and Pope.

But the most surprising passage is at the conclusion, to which any abridgment would be injustice. 'The usual time you sojourn in the universities,' he proceeds, continuing to address his younger hearers, 'is very laudably employed in the prosecution of such studies as are to fit you for your degrees;' but 'the greater part of you are turned out into the world before those incomparable establishments have put the last hand to your education, and led you through the more sacred parts of the Temple of Wisdom.

'It is true you no sooner step into the world than you have your wants abundantly supplied. Instructors crowd in upon you from all quarters. And, just as on man's entrance into life, in the famed fable of Cebes, every false species of happiness presents itself before him, each striving who shall first get possession of the new comer; so, on your entry on the ministry, every phantom of false science, raised up at the resistless call of the Sages in St. Paul's Churchyard, open wide their hospitable arms to receive you to their daily, their weekly, and their monthly lectures. What shining collections of polite literature, what mighty volumes of profound criticism, have crowned their generous labours! But in *Scriptural abundance* their unsparing bounty chiefly displays itself; Commentaries, Histories, and even Dictionaries of the Holy Bible, keep rolling down upon you from the same perennial source; while the smaller divinity, like *the flies and lice of Egypt from the dust of the land*, meets you in your dish, and lies hid in all you taste and handle. The artful disguise, too, is no less taking than the plenty. And as Flaminius's host of Chalcis entertained his guest with a magnificent variety of viands, and all from the hog-sty, so the whole of this delicious cookery comes from as dirty a place—I mean a bookseller's garret.

'While you retain any tincture of that noble learning with which you were imbued in those pure fountains of science which you left too soon, you will be in no danger from the delusions of these miserable impostors, οὐκ αἰσθομένων τῆς ἑαυτῶν ἀμαθίας, as Origen elegantly expresses it, when he characterises certain false teachers of the same stamp. In this temper you will be prepared for, and indeed worthy of, better instruction. Whether my mediocrity shall be able to impart it, must be left to time, and to your use of it, to determine. Till then you need not blush to recollect and bear in mind what you once learned at school,

> Virtus est vitium fugere, et sapientia prima
> Stultitiâ caruisse.'

He consulted Hurd, in 1766, about printing one of his Charges, observing that it 'might perhaps excite as much malice and nonsense against him as anything he had ever written;' and begging Hurd, therefore, 'to exert his critical acumen on it with all severity.' I know not whether he means this Charge of 1761, or another of 1764; but he speaks of it as one which he had thrown by from being tired of it, but which, having taken it up again, he had begun to like as a novelty. Hurd, in his reply, said that he had noticed the strong passages, but that his Lordship had said much the same on other occasions, and need hardly attempt, at that time of day, 'to affect the fame of an inoffensive writer.' *

His Charge in 1767, which is preserved by Mr. Kilvert,† is of a very harmless character, consisting chiefly of exhortations to the 'spiritual oculist' to take care that there be no beam in his own eye when he offers to extract the mote from his brother's.

He meditated, about this time, some strictures, in three discourses, on Voltaire's censures of the Jewish law and history, but was persuaded by Hurd to desist from pursuing the design. Hurd affected to make excessively light of Voltaire, and told the Bishop that there would be 'no end of confuting every shallow, though fashionable, scribbler against religion;' that he had done enough in exposing Bolingbroke 'to the just scorn of thinking men;' and that to give a formal answer to Voltaire, a writer so little acquainted with the subject under discussion, 'would be *like breaking a butterfly upon a wheel!*' ‡

In the early part of 1767 he was at Court. 'I brought a bad cold with me to town,' he says, writing to Hurd, 'and this being the first day I ventured out of doors, it was employed, as in duty bound, at Court, it being a levee-day. A buffoon lord in waiting (you may guess whom I mean) was very busy marshalling the circle; and he said to me, without ceremony, "Move forward; you clog up the door-way." I replied, with as little, "*Did nobody clog up the King's door-stead more than I, there would be room for all honest men.*" This brought the man to himself. When the King came up to me, he asked why I did not come to town before. I said I understood there was no business going forward in the

* Letters from an Eminent Prelate, pp. 375, 376.

† Selections from Warburton's Papers, p. 347.

‡ Hurd's Life of Warburton, p. 105.

House in which I could be of service to His Majesty. He replied, he supposed the severe storm of snow would have brought me up. I replied, "I was under cover of a very warm house." You see, by all this, how unfit I am for Courts.' *

The cover of a warm house, as he said in his speech to the King, he seems at this time to have needed. He complains, towards the end of the year, of rheumatism in his shoulder, which was not alleviated without much physical discipline. He had also an inflammation, perhaps from cold, in his left eye, for which, he says, he had had as many remedies proposed as visitors.† He had a disorder, too, of the gall-bladder, with symptoms of the gravel, for which he was desired to drink the Seltzer waters, then just come into fashion.‡ In the following summer he complained again of fever and rheumatism, and was obliged to decline a confirmation, which he had undertaken, for the Bishop of Bath and Wells.§

He may possibly have been somewhat gratified with the honour done him by Toup, who, in 1767, published his *Epistola Critica ad Celeberrimum Virum Gulielmum Episcopum Glocestriensem.* The body of this epistle consists wholly of additions to his emendations on Suidas. His praise of Warburton is extravagant, such as he would never have obtained from Hare. He extols him thus at the beginning:

'Quicquid hujus opusculi est, tibi consecratum esse volumus, præstantissime Warburtone, præsul doctissime; nam et nostra libenter legis, et hæc μυστήρια optimè intelligis; quippe qui utrasque literas, tum sacras, tum profanas, ita conjunxisti, ut uberrimos fructus inde retuleris. Quod omnes nôrunt, qui tua scripta nôrunt; à quibus nunquam profectò nisi doctiores discedimus:

* Letters from an Eminent Prelate, p. 392.

† Ib. p. 406. ‡ Ib. p. 413. § Ib. p. 434.

Τοῖα γὰρ ἄμμιν ἔφηνας, ἅ τ' οὐ πάρος ἄνερες ἴσμεν,
'Αμφί τε ἀθανάτους, ἀμφί τε ἡμιθέους.'

And thus at the conclusion:

'Sed tandem jam desino. Neque enim diutius tua tempora morabor, præsul eruditissime. Perge verò, ut facis, de literis, de ecclesiâ, de republicâ, optimè mereri. Rumpantur Codri, Bavii, Mævii. Adplaudunt omnes boni, et quicquid usquam est gentium eruditorum. Sed nolo nimius esse. Vale, Episcoporum doctissime, et nos Tui observantissimos ama.'

In return, Warburton is said to have done his utmost to serve Toup. He regretted that he had no preferment vacant in his see, for, 'had it been otherwise, he should have been too selfish to invite any of his brethren to share with him in the honour of properly distinguishing such merit as Mr. Toup's.' But he recommended Toup to Archbishop Secker, and to Keppel, Bishop of Exeter, who, in consequence, gave him a prebend at Exeter in 1774, and, two years afterwards, the vicarage of St. Merryn, in Cornwall.*

* Gent. Mag. vol. lv. p. 185.

CHAPTER XXXII.

LECTURE AT LINCOLN'S INN FOUNDED — ENDEAVOURS TO SERVE THOMAS WARTON — LETTER FROM ISAAC HAWKINS BROWNE — VISIT TO HURD, AND LETTERS FROM HIM — REMOVAL FROM PRIOR PARK — DEAN TUCKER — DECLINE OF WARBURTON'S FACULTIES — ASSISTS RUFFHEAD — GIBBON'S 'CRITICAL OBSERVATIONS' PUBLISHED — HURD'S EXTRAVAGANT PRAISE OF WARBURTON — ACCIDENT IN HIS LIBRARY — 'HE WILL WRITE NO MORE' — HIS SOLICITUDE ABOUT HIS SON — HIS SON'S DEATH — HURD'S ACCOUNT OF WARBURTON'S LAST YEARS — HIS DEATH — SILENCE OF THE PUBLIC RESPECTING HIM — DISPOSAL OF HIS LIBRARY — HURD'S EDITION OF HIS WORKS, AND MEMOIR OF THE AUTHOR — DESTRUCTION OF HIS LETTERS, EXCEPT THOSE PUBLISHED BY HURD — SPECIMENS OF WARBURTONIAN CRITICISM.

IN 1768, he set apart the sum of 500*l.* in the four per cent. annuities, for the foundation of a lecture, in the form of a course of sermons, at Lincoln's Inn, for the purpose of 'proving the truth of revealed religion in general, and of the Christian in particular, from the fulfilment of the prophecies in the Old and New Testament, which relate to the Christian Church, and especially to the apostasy of Papal Rome.' The money was given in trust to Lord Mansfield, Sir Eardley Wilmot, and Mr. Charles Yorke. Each lecturer was to hold the lectureship for three years, if he preached four sermons a year, or four years, if only three sermons. He was afterwards inclined to double the endowment, but his friends dissuaded him. Hurd, as might be expected, was appointed the first lecturer, and was succeeded by Bishop Hallifax and Bishop Bagot.

Bishop Newton, and others, considered that the field

for the lecturer was too much circumscribed by the terms of its institution. 'It was objected at the first,' says he, 'that the plan was too narrow; that it should have been extended to the prophecies at large; that, being limited to the prophecies relating to the Christian Church, especially to the apostasy of Papal Rome, the subject must, in the course of some years, be quite exhausted; little or nothing could be added; the same things must be repeated again and again; few lecturers could be found to do credit to the institution like Dr. Hurd. This objection was really so well founded, that, after the third in succession, a fourth lecturer could not easily be procured, and there was a failure, at least for some time.'*

Hurd declares himself of a different opinion. 'The subject is infinitely curious, and of vast extent; for those who have taken it to be too much narrowed by specifying the prophecies concerning Antichrist, seem not to have understood the compass of the controversy, nor the terms of the institution itself. The truth is, there is more danger that lecturers will be wanting to the institution than that it will not afford matter and scope enough for their discussion.' Bishop Newton's opinion has proved to be the better grounded.

The same year he made an effort, by application to the Duke of Grafton, to secure the Professorship of Modern History at Oxford for Thomas Warton, which Gray had held as a sinecure, but which it was now resolved to make an effective appointment. He received a civil refusal from the Duke, and the office was given to a Dr. Vivian by the influence of Lord Abingdon. Warburton, in transmitting the Duke's answer to Warton, observes that things were only going 'in their usual train, to the exclusion of superior merit.' On Vivian's death, in 1770, he made another application, on behalf of Warton, to

* Bishop Newton's Life by Himself, p. 155.

Archbishop Cornwallis; but superior merit was again excluded in favour of a Dr. Nowel, Principal of St. Mary Hall. Warburton was annoyed, and Warton was left to console himself with the consciousness of having deserved the success which neither he nor his friends could command.* Posterity are apt to wonder at the fortune of men so undistinguished over men universally known; but interest and envy have had their influence at all times; and there are many, it must be remembered, who, though not seeking to leave memorials to posterity, have well deserved honour among the learned in their own day.

A present of Isaac Hawkins Browne's works, from his son, drew from Warburton the following acknowledgment:

'Prior Park, Feb. 7, 1768.

'SIR,—I have the honour and favour of receiving from you a very valuable present of your father's works, whose great parts and knowledge, in more arts and sciences than one, few men had the pleasing opportunity of knowing more than I had. His happy vein in poetry made him stand among the foremost of the art in his life-time; and he will be amongst the last that barbarity and ignorance (fast returning upon us) shall be able to obliterate. This mark of your filial piety to so distinguished a person will do you lasting honour, and give much pleasure to the friends of his family, in which number I desire to be reckoned, being,

'Sir, your obliged and obedient humble servant,

'W. GLOUCESTER.'†

He began to be sensible of the declension of his faculties. 'You talk,' said he to Hurd, 'of *your golden age of study long past*. For myself, I can only say I

* Wooll's Life of Dr. Joseph Warton. Nichols's Lit. Anecd. vol. v. p. 655.

† Biog. Brit., Art. 'Hawkins Browne.'

have the same appetite for knowledge and learned converse I ever had; though not the same appetite for writing and printing. It is time to begin to live for myself; I have lived for others longer than they deserved of me.'* But he considered the season at which he was then writing, the months of February and March, to be the 'most unfriendly to the health of mind and body of any throughout the whole year.'†

In the summer of 1769 he paid a visit of a fortnight to Hurd at Thurcaston, who, seeing him in weak health, took occasion, in writing to him shortly after, to advise him not to apply too closely to study. 'I have received,' he replies, 'your kind letter of *advice*, and shall, in the banker's phrase, *accept and honour the contents.*

'You know by experience how difficult it is, when we have once got into a wicked habit of *thinking*, to leave it off. All I can promise is, if that will satisfy you, *to think to no purpose;* and this I know by experience I can do, having done so for many a good day.

'I think you have oft heard me say that my delicious season is the autumn, the season which gives most life and vigour to my mental faculties. The light mists, or, as Milton calls them, the *steams*, that rise from the fields in one of these mornings, give the same *relief* to the views that the blue of the plum (to take my ideas from the season) gives to the appetite. But I now enjoy little of this pleasure, compared to what I formerly had in an autumn morning, when I used, with a book in my hand, to traverse the delightful lanes and hedge-rows round about the town of Newark, the *unthinking* place of my nativity. Besides, my rheumatism now keeps me within in a morning, till the sun has exhaled *the blue of the plum.*'‡

* Letters from an Eminent Prelate, Feb. 24, 1768.

† Ib. Mar. 31.

‡ Ib. Sept. 4, 1769.

In August 1769, he removed from Prior Park, which was let to some nobleman, and fixed his residence at Gloucester, to the great joy of Mrs. Warburton, who, on I know not what account, had taken a dislike to her uncle's house.*

The want of cordiality between Warburton and his Dean, Dr. Tucker, whom, nevertheless, he calls 'good-natured,' has been already mentioned. It was shown at a visit which he made this year to Tucker, in company with the Rev. Edward Sparkes, Head Master of Gloucester Grammar School. 'The Dean,' he says, 'soon took advantage of my being off my guard, and confining him to *trade*, and, before I was aware, was got deep into the Calvinistic *Articles*, which he was resolved to clear of that imputation. A flow of more transcendent nonsense I never heard on the occasion. Mr. Sparkes, who owed him a grudge, . . . would needs contradict him; and this was fair. But he would needs understand him; and here the Dean, who did not understand himself, must needs have the advantage. Sense sometimes, though rarely, produces more sense; but it comes up slowly, and requires weeding. But the harvest of nonsense, on good ground, produces a hundredfold, and springs up immediately. In the course of it, our friend was insulted by asking him whether he had read this divine and that divine; and ended in [Tucker's] fairly telling him that his forte lay in classical learning, but that he was a mere stranger to these profound researches. You may judge how the harmless gravity of our friend must have been disconcerted, and even violated, with this rudeness, which nothing but the irresistible ambition of shining as a divine before his Bishop could have drawn the good-natured Dean into.'†

Warburton's health still continued uncertain, and he

* Letters from an Eminent Prelate, p. 438. † Ib. p. 443.

suspected that the pains which he had thought rheumatism arose from St. Antony's fire, which, he said, fouls the blood and continues long in it.* 'Old age,' he observed, 'is a losing game.'† Dr. Heberden recommended an issue in the right arm.‡

Looking back into some of his writings, he said, 'The retrospect is accompanied with a mortifying conviction that the time is now past when I was able to write with that force. Expect to find in my future writings the marks of intellectual decay.'§

Hurd tried to soothe him with the following answer: 'As to your not writing with the *force* you formerly did, it may very well be, and yet be no subject of mortification; for, besides that you can afford to abate something of your ancient force, and yet have enough left, *force* itself has not, in all periods of life, the same grace. The close of one of these long and bright days [in July] has not the flame and heat of noon, and would be less pleasing if it had. And I know not why it may not be true, in the *critical* as well as *moral sense* of the poet's words,

Lenior et *melior* fis accedente senectâ.

But what I would chiefly say on the subject is this, that, whether with force or without it, I would only wish your future writings to be an amusement to you, and not a labour; and this, I think, is the proper use to be made of your observation, if it be ever so well founded.'‖

He had vigour enough, however, during this year, to give considerable assistance to Ruffhead for his 'Life of Pope.'⸸

When Granger's 'Biographical History of England,'

* Letters from an Eminent Prelate, p. 446.

† Ib. p. 448. ‡ Ib. p. 458. § Ib. p. 451.

‖ Ib. p. 454; Hurd's Life of Warburton, p. 85.

⸸ Nichols's Lit. Anec. vol. v. p. 633.

which appeared this year, was published, Warburton bought it, and told Tom Davies, the publisher, that it was *an odd book*. This, said Davies to Granger, is praise from him; for, if he had not thought it worth reading, he would have called it *a sad book*.*

About the same time came forth Gibbon's 'Critical Observations on the Sixth Book of the Æneid.' Gibbon had received, as he said, no private offence, like Lowth, from 'the dictator and tyrant of the world of literature,' whom his flatterers exalted above Aristotle and Longinus, but he was 'ambitious of breaking a lance against the giant's shield,' and he 'aimed his strokes against his person and his hypothesis.' The Bishop and his party made no reply, and the 'Critical Observations' soon fell into neglect. But Hayley and Heyne praised them, and Hayley thought the acrimony of style, which Heyne rather disapproved, justifiable. 'But I could not forgive myself,' said Gibbon, 'the contemptuous treatment of a man who, with all his faults, was entitled to my esteem; and I can less forgive, in a personal attack, the cowardly concealment of my name and character.' The public, however, have excused Gibbon on this head; and his pamphlet has been considered a complete refutation of Warburton's hypothesis, a refutation 'to which,' as Parr said, 'the greatest name might with propriety have been affixed.'

The exaltation of Warburton above Aristotle and Longinus, to which Gibbon alludes, occurs in a passage of Hurd's 'Dedication' to the Bishop of his 'Commentary on the Epistle to Augustus.' Speaking of those two great critics of antiquity, he says: 'It was not enough, in your enlarged views of things, to restore either of these models [Aristotle or Longinus] to their original splendour. They were both to be revived; or rather a new original plan of criticism to be struck out, which should unite the

* Nichols's Lit. Anec. vol. v. p. 633.

virtues of each of them. This experiment is made on the two greatest of our own poets [Shakspeare and Pope], and by reflecting all the lights of the imagination on the severest reason, everything was effected which the warmest admirer of ancient art could promise himself from such a union. *But you went farther*; by joining to these powers a perfect insight into human nature, and so ennobling the exercise of literary by the justest moral censure, *you have now at length advanced criticism to its full glory*.'

In November he was in danger of dying, as was afterwards the fate of Jacob Bryant, by a fall in his library while reaching down a book. Dr. Balguy was with him, and as they wanted to look at some volume that was on a high shelf, Warburton stepped on the window-seat to get it, but lost his footing and his balance, and fell down backward, striking the side of his head against a candlestick, which cut through his ear. The wound was large, but less troublesome than the bruise, and it was wonderful, he told Hurd, that he escaped so well, for the hurt was within half an inch of being fatal.*

Warburton was not yet a very old man. But his intellects seem to have decayed at about the same age with those of Swift, Marlborough, and Southey. Hurd, who wrote very freely to his wife, and his other friends, concerning him, saw the rapid weakening of his faculties, and assured Mrs. Warburton, in a letter, in the early part of 1771, when he was in his sixty-third year, that *he would write no more*. Mrs. Warburton, aware of her husband's condition, and pleased at Hurd's declaration, communicated his opinion to Warburton, who heard it with composure. 'I received this news,' he tells Hurd in the following June, 'with an approving smile. I was charmed with the tenderness of friendship, which conveyed, in so inoffensive a manner, that fatal secret which

* Letters from an Eminent Prelate, p. 460.

Gil Blas was incapable of doing, as he ought, to his patron, the Archbishop of Granada.'*

He received, about the same time, such pleasure as he might find in the intelligence that 'The Divine Legation' had been translated into Dutch, by Abraham Van der Meersch, with a Dedication to himself.† The 'Doctrine of Grace' had been translated into that language five years before.‡

Horace Walpole, who had been reviling him all his life, and saying that his conversion had not had the good fortune, like that of Lord Lyttelton, to be believed, paid him a visit, as he happened to be at Gloucester, in 1774, and found him very infirm, speaking with much hesitation, and beginning, as was said, to lose his memory. §

The remaining years of Warburton's existence are little better than a blank. We find him sending a short letter, now and then, to Hurd, chiefly about the education of his son, the object in which he now felt more interest than in any other. But he became incapable of continued application either to writing or reading. And his faculties were still more clouded and debilitated by the loss of his son, who died of consumption in 1775, in his twentieth year. He had been intended for the law, and placed at Trinity Hall, Cambridge, under the care of Dr. Hallifax, afterwards Bishop of St. Asaph. Warburton's solicitude for his welfare is apparent throughout his letters. He calls him *half his soul*; he notices how he is growing; how he advances in his reading; and how he hopes to live to see him an honest man. *Dîs aliter visum.* Death is a relentless disappointer of man's expectations.

He had made a will in the life-time of his son, which he lodged in the hands of Hurd, but, after his son's death,

* Letters from an Eminent Prelate, p. 462.

† Gent. Mag. for 1771, p. 266.

‡ Letters from an Eminent Prelate, p. 388.

§ Letter to Cole, Aug. 15, 1774.

made another in favour of his wife, whose interests he especially recommended to Hurd's care in the following document:

'To the Lord Bishop of Lichfield and Coventry, to be opened and delivered to him at my decease.—W. G.

'TO MY DEAR FRIEND, DR. RICHARD HURD, Lord Bishop of Lichfield and Coventry.—I do hereby press and conjure him to take under his particular care and protection my dear wife; and to afford her all his assistance and aid against all persons that may be disposed to injure or bear hard upon her. And this I press him to do, and likewise assist her with his best advice, in memory of, and in return for, the warm and sincere affection I have always borne towards him. This earnest request I enforce under my hand this 8th day of April, 1776.' *

The account of his remaining years we must take from Hurd's 'Memoir;' for nowhere else is there any history of his declining days to be found. 'The death of his son,' he says, 'oppressed him to that degree as to put an end to his literary labours, and even amusements, at once. From that disastrous moment he lived on, indeed, for two or three years; but, when he had settled his affairs, as was proper, upon this great change in his family, he took no concern in the ordinary occurrences of life, and grew so indifferent to everything that even his books and writings seemed thenceforth to be utterly disregarded by him.

'Not that his memory and faculties, though very much impaired, were ever wholly disabled. I saw him so late as October, 1778, when I went into his diocese to confirm for him. On his first meeting, before his family, he expressed his concern that I should take that journey, and put myself to so much trouble on his account. And

* Letters from an Eminent Prelate, p. 491.

afterwards he took occasion to say some pertinent and obliging things, which showed, not only his usual friendliness of temper, but the command he had of his attention. Nor was this all. The evening before I left him, he desired the family to withdraw, and then entered into a confidential discourse with me on some private affairs which he had much at heart, with as much pertinence and good sense as he could have done in any former part of his life. Such was the power he had over his mind, when roused to exert himself by some interesting occasion. But this was an effort which could not be sustained very long. In less than half an hour the family returned, and he relapsed into his usual forgetfulness and inattention.

'In this melancholy state he languished till the summer following, when he expired at the palace in Gloucester, on the 7th of June, 1779, and was buried at his cathedral, at no great distance from the west door, and near to the grave of one of his predecessors, Bishop Benson.'

Cradock mentions a striking circumstance which was reported to have occurred at Warburton's death; but gives it only as a report. About the time that his only son died, he became, as has been stated, almost imbecile, and continued to take little interest in anything for several years, till, just before his death, a momentary revival of intellect took place, and he asked his attendant, in a quiet rational tone, 'Is my son really dead, or not?' The servant hesitated how to reply, when the Bishop repeated the question in a firmer voice. The attendant then answered, 'As your Lordship presses the question, I must say, he is dead.' 'I thought so,' said Warburton, and soon after expired.*

It was observed that few men of such eminence have passed to the tomb with so little notice. The periodicals of the time were totally silent respecting him, with the

* Cradock's Lit. and Misc. Memoirs, vol. iv. p. 205.

exception of a short article in the 'Westminster Magazine,' which was copied, with some enlargement, into the 'Gentleman's Magazine.'

A marble monument was erected to him in Gloucester Cathedral, at the expense of his widow, with the following inscription, written by Hurd, over a medallion portrait:

To the Memory of
WILLIAM WARBURTON, D.D.,
For more than nineteen years Bishop of this See:
A Prelate
Of the most sublime Genius and exquisite Learning,
Both which Talents
He employed, through a long life,
in the support
of what he firmly believed,
the Christian Religion,
and of what he esteemed the best Establishment of it,
the Church of England.
He was born at Newark-upon-Trent,
Dec. 24, 1698;
was consecrated Bishop of Gloucester, Jan. 20, 1760;
Died at his Palace, in this City, June 7, 1779,
and was buried near this place.

Remarks were made on this epitaph by some who read it without any stop after the word 'believed.' Cradock showed a copy of it to Dr. Thurlow, Bishop of Lincoln, who, reading it in that way, said, 'Could your friend find nothing better to say in honour of his former idol, thau that he died in the belief of what he conceived to be Christianity?' Others, to whom Cradock showed the copy, thought the language ambiguous, and could scarcely believe that it was correctly transcribed.*

Warburton's widow, about two years after his death, was married to the Rev. John Stafford Smith, Warburton's chaplain, who, by the presentation of Hurd, became Rector

* Cradock's Lit. and Misc. Memoirs, vol. iv. p. 205.

of Fladbury in Worcestershire, a living of something more than seven hundred a-year. She died in 1796, having survived her husband more than seventeen years.

Of his books he bequeathed the principal part, which were at Gloucester, to be sold for the benefit of the Gloucester Infirmary. Hurd purchased them, and deposited them in the library at Hartlebury Castle. Those that were in Grosvenor Square his wife secured, and, finding that he had scribbled much in them in his later years, when he was nearly imbecile, disposed of such as she did not destroy, to Payne, the bookseller.* Some that were sold in London were characterised as not choice, but an awkward farrago in middling condition.†

He had inherited Pope's copies of the quarto editions of 'Shakspeare,' but had valued them so little as to sell them himself to Payne in 1766, who immediately put them into the sale of Mallet's books, among which they were sold for three guineas.‡

His published works were not collected till 1788, nine years after his death, when a handsome edition, said to exhibit his last corrections and improvements, was printed in seven quarto volumes, at the expense of Mrs. Stafford Smith, under the superintendence of Bishop Hurd. At the same time some pieces, which had not before been published, were put forth, oddly enough, in an octavo form; these pieces being the fragment of the ninth book of 'The Divine Legation;' 'Directions for the Study of Theology,' and 'Short Notes on Neal's History of the Puritans,' with some correspondence of Warburton with Middleton and Lowth. It is observable, that of this edition only two hundred and fifty copies were printed: 'a number which seemed to insinuate,' as Parr remarked, 'either that Warburton's writings were too excellent for

* Nichols's Lit. Anecd., vol. v. p. 640; vol. vi. p. 490; Prior's Life of Malone, p. 344.

† Nichols's Lit. Illustr. vol. vi. p. 352.

‡ Prior, ib.

the gross taste of the public, or that the public had shown some inauspicious symptoms of indifference about Warburton's writings.'* A 'Life of Warburton,' also, or rather 'A Discourse by way of General Preface, containing some Account of the Life, Writings, and Character of Warburton,' was promised, in an advertisement prefixed to the edition, and said to have been prepared, but was delayed, with much complaint from many quarters, till 1794, when two hundred and fifty copies of that also were printed. This 'Life,' or 'Discourse,' was written by Hurd, and was found to be a meagre and unsatisfactory panegyric. The author, but for the importunity of certain readers and critics, would have withheld it till after his death.† Parr exclaimed vehemently against the delay; observing that, if the 'Discourse' were withheld because it contained reflections on surviving opponents of Bishop Warburton, they would surely rather meet attacks, which they might hope to repel, while living, than have their memory subject to charges, of which they knew not the nature, after their deaths; or that, if the piece were kept in hand for the sake of improving it, it might be expected to furnish the English language with a proverbial example of accuracy not less apt than the Smyrna of Cinna and the panegyric of Isocrates.‡

The Works have since been uniformly printed in twelve volumes octavo, to which Mr. Kilvert, in 1841, added a thirteenth, consisting of 'Selections from Warburton's Unpublished Papers.'

In the year 1767, Warburton, acting on a suggestion of Mr. Charles Yorke, began to collect the letters which he had received from correspondents, and arrange them in a book in order of time. 'I could have wished,' he

* Tracts by Warb. and a Warburtonian, p. 187.

† Kilvert's Life of Hurd, p. 147.

‡ Tracts by Warb. and a Warburtonian, pp. 189, 191.

said, 'for some of my answers, but as I never took any copies except when I was afraid of misrepresentations, these were extremely rare.' Hurd approved of the design, and observed to him, 'you cannot interpose too many of your own letters, which will make the most valuable part of the collection.'*

This correspondence was destroyed, it is believed, by Warburton's widow. As for Hurd himself, he took care to preserve all the letters that he received from Warburton, and appears to have kept copies of some of his own to him. All these he thought proper to print during his lifetime, in a quarto volume, and to leave for publication after his death, with the following advertisement:

'These letters give so true a picture of the writer's character, and are, besides, so worthy of him in all respects, (I mean, if the reader can forgive the playfulness of his wit in some instances, and the partiality of his friendship in many more,) that, in honour of his memory, I would have them published after my death, and the profits arising from the sale of them applied to the benefit of the Worcester Infirmary.'

Hurd died in 1808, and the volume was given to the public in 1809. Only two hundred and fifty copies, the same number as of Warburton's works, were printed, and the Messrs. Cadell are said to have purchased them for 400*l.*, which sum was applied as Hurd had desired. A second edition, in octavo, was published the same year. The entire correspondence consisted of two hundred and fifty-seven letters of Warburton, twenty-six of Hurd, and five of the Honourable Charles Yorke to Warburton.

Hurd's great motive, as he believed or alleged, for publishing these letters, is stated in one of his communications to Balguy. 'I am turning over my old correspondence with Dr. Warburton, in which I find frequent and friendly

* Letters from an Eminent Prelate, pp. 397, 398.

mention of you. This, among other reasons, will tempt me to preserve many of his letters, and to give them in due time to this wretched world, if it be only to shame it into a better opinion of that excellent man, by *showing the regard he had to real merit.*'*

To a reader who knew nothing of Hurd's *alleged reasons*, the purpose of the publication might seem to have been of an exactly contrary nature; for, if we except Hurd himself, with Balguy and Towne, two names hardly known to the world in general, we shall find almost all the writers of the day, all the men whose *real merit* the world has acknowledged, abused in these letters, sometimes by Hurd, but mostly by Warburton, as persons whose character, literary or moral, or both, was such as it was a favour to notice even with contempt.

Dr. Johnstone and Mr. Field, in their Memoirs of Parr, have amused themselves with collecting some of the flowers of censure and calumny with which these extraordinary pages abound. They may be compared to the conversations of Ben Jonson with Drummond, in which Ben does not speak well of a single individual. Hurd's liberal use of the word 'coxcomb,' approved by Warburton, we have already noticed. Both the correspondents, but Warburton especially, have plenty of other terms at command of a similarly vituperative character. Warburton's letters afford such specimens of defamation as the following: Young, the author of the 'Night Thoughts,' is 'the finest writer of nonsense of any of this age.'† Rutherforth, the author of the 'Essay on Virtue,' is 'the meanest pedant of the age.'‡ Spence, of the 'Anecdotes,' is 'an extreme poor creature.'§ Smollett is 'a vagabond Scot,' who 'writes nonsense ten thousand strong.'|| Johnson is 'this Johnson,' of whom Warburton and Hurd

* Kilvert's Life of Hurd, p. 147.

† Let. cxxix. ‡ Let. xxii. § Let. xlv. || Let. cxxv.

'think much alike,' and whose remarks on Warburton's Shakspeare are 'full of insolence and malignant reflections,' but 'having in them as much folly as malignity.'[a] Jortin, as might be expected, is reviled in many varieties of phrase; he 'is as vain as he is dirty;' his conduct 'is mean, low, and ungrateful;' his 'heart is full of rancour;' he 'played the hypocrite,' and 'his friends are dirty fellows.'[b] Dean Tucker has 'a flow of transcendent nonsense.'[c] Jackson, author of 'Ancient Chronology,' is 'a wretch' who 'spent his days in the republic of letters in one unvaried course of begging, railing, and stealing.'[d] Demosthenes Taylor 'has less understanding than the dunce Webster.[e] Priestley is 'a wretched fellow,' and Voltaire 'a scoundrel.'[f] Harris, of the 'Hermes,' 'leans now to sense, now to nonsense,' as antiquity inclines him.[g] Garrick's Ode 'is below any of Cibber's; Cibber's nonsense was something like sense; but *this man's* sense, *whenever he deviates into it*, is much more like nonsense.'[h] In addition to these animadversions, we are told, in the same tone of derision, that 'the Bench of Bishops is a wooden bench;[i] that 'the angel of dulness is ready to pour his vial into the Cam;'[j] and that 'the Goths and Vandals, return when they will, cannot hurt Cambridge;'[k] that the Court is 'an earthly pandemonium;'[l] that 'the Church is bestrid by some lumpish minister of state, who turns and winds it at his pleasure;'[m] and that 'the discourses of the whole crew of Scotch metaphysicians are commonly full of moonshine.'[n] Of Hurd's share in the correspondence no more need be said than that he is ever ready to re-echo the sentiments of his leader:

[a] Let. clxxv. [b] Lets. lxxxviii. xc. cxxi. [c] Let. ccxxi.
[d] Let. xlvii. [e] Let. xcv. [f] Let. ccxxxiv.
[g] Let. xxxviii. [h] Let. cxxix. [i] Let. ccviii.
[j] Let. lxix. [k] Let. xlvii. [l] Let. vii.
[m] Let. xlvii. [n] Let. ccxxxi.

Sic iterat voces, et verba cadentia tollit,
Ut credas —
— partes mimum tractare secundas.

Hurd has been more censured for publishing these scurrilities than Warburton for writing them; for Warburton threw them out in the heat of the moment, and addressed them in confidential letters to an intimate friend; but Hurd printed them, with cool and malicious deliberation, in his lifetime, and provided for their publication, by his own express directions, after his death. He adhered to his character for wariness when, having resolved to give these railings of his friend to the world, he determined to withhold them till he himself should be insensible to the indignant clamour which they would be certain to excite.

CHAPTER XXXIII.

CHARACTER OF WARBURTON.

WARBURTON'S PERSONAL APPEARANCE — HIS TEMPERANCE — HIS LITERARY COURAGE — HIS CONVERSATION — DR. CUMING'S ACCOUNT OF HIM — INTERVIEW WITH JOHNSON — HIS WANT OF TASTE IN LITERATURE — PRETENDED COMPARISON OF HIM AND JOHNSON — SPECIMENS OF HIS COARSENESS OF STYLE — HIS VIGOUR OF MIND — HIS IMPERFECT ACQUAINTANCE WITH LANGUAGES — HIS LOVE OF PARADOX — HIS FREEDOM FROM BIGOTRY — HIS GENERAL READING — HIS COMMON-PLACE BOOK — HIS SMART SAYINGS — GENERAL CHARACTER OF HIS WORKS — CONCLUSION.

OF the personal appearance and bodily frame of Warburton, we find little description. Some intimations that he was a man of rather large make appear in his correspondence, but the only definite account of his size and stature is that which is given us by Bishop Newton in his memoirs of his own life: 'He was rather a tall, robust, large-boned man, of a frame that seemed to require a good supply of provisions to support it; but he was sensible, if he had lived as other people do, he must have used a good deal of exercise, and, if he had used a good deal of exercise, it must have interrupted the course of his studies, to which he was so devoted as to deny himself any other indulgence, and so became a singular example, not only of temperance, but even of abstinence, in eating and drinking; and yet his spirits were not lowered or exhausted, but were rather raised and increased, by his lowliving.'* He himself observes that he was 'a slender

* Bp. Newton's Life by Himself, p. 155.

supper-man,' and speaks of himself, when he was only in his fifty-ninth year, as being obliged to old age, like Cato, for having diminished his care for eating and drinking, while it increased his desire for conversation.* His temperance in his earlier years, when he was reading hard at Brant-Broughton, was great, though he is supposed, by his extraordinary application, to have laid the foundation, at that period, of his subsequent giddiness and premature decay of intellect.

In his literary character, he was of a bold and determined English spirit, ready to resist all opponents, and willing to consider the state of authorship as a state of war. If any deduction be made from this part of his character, it must be on account of his conduct towards Pope, in his advances to whom there appears no great magnanimity, and whom he has always been suspected of defending rather from hope of possible advantage than from sincerity of settled opinion.

He appears, from what we find related of him, to have been less dogmatical in his conversation than in his publications. Mr. Malone records that Burke, the first time he saw Warburton in company, sat next to him at dinner without knowing who he was, and that, being much struck with his talk, he at last observed, 'Sir, I think it is impossible I can mistake; you must be the celebrated Dr. Warburton; *aut Erasmus aut Diabolus.*' 'Warburton,' adds Malone, 'though so furious a controversialist in print, was very easy and good-humoured in company, and sometimes entertaining.'†

Hurd's account of him as a companion is this: 'In mixed companies he was extremely entertaining, but less guarded than men of the world usually are, and disposed to take to himself a somewhat larger share of the

* Letters from an Eminent Prelate, p. 246.

† Prior's Life of Malone, p. 370.

conversation than very exact breeding is thought to allow. Yet few, I believe, wished him to be more reserved, or less communicative, than he was: so abundant was the information or entertainment which his ready wit and extensive knowledge afforded them! In private, with his friends, he was natural, easy, unpretending; at once the most agreeable and most useful companion in the world. You saw to the very bottom of his mind on any subject of discourse; and his various literature, penetrating judgment, and quick recollection, made him say the liveliest or the justest things upon it. In short, I was in those moments affected by his conversation pretty much as Cato was by that of Maximus Fabius, and may say, as he does in the Dialogue on Old Age, *I was so fond of his discourse, and listened to it so eagerly, as if I had foreseen, what indeed came to pass, that, when I lost him, I should never again meet with so instructive a companion.*'*

Dr. Kippis says of him, 'The only time I had ever the honour of being in his company, which was an hour and a half in his own study, I found him remarkably condescending in his manner, and admirably instructive and entertaining in his conversation.'†

Charles Yorke, who met him at his first visit to Pope, represents himself as delighted with the opportunities which he had of conversing with him; describing him as a man 'surprisingly communicative, of prodigious memory, and of enchanting fancy.' 'The fluency and correctness of his conversation,' he said, was 'beyond most men;' but, he adds, somewhat satirically, 'I regard him as a genius of so high a rank, that, unable to contain himself within the limits of ordinary capacities, he *spurns the dull earth, and soars above the skies;* or, to

* Life of Warburton, p. 112.

† Kippis's Biog. Brit. vol. v. p. 304.

use an expression of his own concerning Mr. Bayle, 'strikes frequently into the province of paradox.' *

Dr. William Cuming, a physician of Dorchester, writing to Dr. Lettsom, about six years after Warburton's death, describes what he was, in manners and conversation, when he was more than sixty years old, as follows:

'Many years ago I read over the polemical and critical works of the late Dr. Warburton, and, from the perusal, I conceived a most unfavourable opinion of the man; so stiff and conceited in opinion; so dictatorial in his sentiments, treating every one who thought differently from himself with the most sovereign contempt. It is above thirty years ago that Ralph Allen, of Prior Park, first came to pass about three months in the summer annually at Weymouth; his niece, Mrs. Warburton, was always of the party. . . . I had been introduced to Mr. Allen's acquaintance soon after his first arrival, and was always professionally employed in the family. After a few years, the Bishop, whom I had never seen, came to pass a month of the summer with Mr. Allen at Weymouth. I was soon after sent for to attend some one in the family. After having visited my patient, Mrs. Warburton took me by the hand and led me to the dining-room, where we found the Bishop alone. She presented me to him with, "Give me leave, my Lord, to introduce to you a friend of mine, to whom you and I have great obligations for the care he has repeatedly taken of our son." He received me courteously enough, but I own to you I felt an awe and awkward uneasiness. I determined to say but little, and to weigh well what I said. We were left alone; it was an hour to dinner; he soon engaged me on some literary subject, in the course of which he gave me the etymology of some word or phrase in the French

* Harris's Life of Lord Hardwicke, vol. i. p. 477.

language, with a "Do not you think so?" I ventured to dissent, and said that I had always conceived its origin to be so and so. To this he immediately replied, "Upon my word I believe you are in the right; nay, 'tis past a doubt; I wonder it never struck me before." Well, to dinner we went; his Lordship was easy, facetious, and entertaining. My awe of him was pretty well dissipated, and I conversed with ease. Some time after dinner, when he was walking about the room, he came behind me, tapped me on the shoulder, and beckoned me into an adjoining room. As soon as we entered, he shut the door, seated himself in an arm-chair on one side of the fire-place, while he directed me by his hand to one on the opposite side. My fit immediately returned; I expected to be catechised and examined; but it was of short duration. He said he was happy in this opportunity of asking the opinion and advice of a gentleman of my character respecting some complaints he had felt for some time past, and which he found increasing. On this my spirits expanded: I did not fear being a match for his Lordship on a medical subject. He then began to detail to me the complaints and feelings of those persons addicted to constant study and a sedentary life. As I mentioned several circumstances which he had omitted in his catalogue, and which he immediately acknowledged, I gained his confidence. He was sensible I was master of my subject. It is a good political maxim, *Docti sunt doctè tractandi.* I explained to him the *rationale* of his complaints, and showed him the propriety of the diet, exercise, and regimen, which I recommended to him. In short, we parted, to join the company, very well satisfied with each other. I found my disgust and prejudice gradually abate. During several subsequent years, I had repeated opportunities of being in company with him, and never saw a single instance of that fastidiousness and arrogance so conspicuous in his writings. He always received me with great good humour; I conversed with him easily and familiarly. On all subjects he showed an attention and deference to the opinion of others. He had a great fund of anecdote, and told his stories with much humour and facetiousness. This change in my opinion relating to Dr. Warburton, was the effect of my being personally acquainted with him; however, I can never forgive him for defacing the immortal Shakspeare by his many ridiculous and unlettered notes, though he made me a present of that and all his works.'*

Warburton is said by Johnson to have shown much good humour when they once met; for of one meeting only between them have we any account. Somebody asked Johnson whether he had ever been in company with Warburton. 'I never saw him,' said he, 'till one evening about a week ago, at the Bishop of St. Asaph's; at first, he looked surlily at me; but after we had been jostled into conversation, he took me to a window, asked me some questions, and before we parted was so well pleased with me that he patted me.' Patting, and tapping on the shoulder, seem to have been among his habits.†

Dr. Monsey, however, the humorous physician of Chelsea Hospital, who was old enough to have seen Warburton in his best days, used to tell an anecdote of him that shows him in a less favourable light. He once dined at Garrick's with him and Dr. Brown, at the time when Brown was Warburton's obsequious flatterer. After dinner, when they were talking over their wine, Garrick said, on some remark from Monsey, 'Now, Monsey, don't indulge in your usual freedom, but let us be a little serious.' 'Oh!' said Brown, 'you may be sure Dr. Monsey will restrain his humour before Dr. Warburton,

* Nichols's Lit. Ill. vol. ii. p. 839.

† Miss Hawkins: Croker's Johnsoniana, vol. i. p. 134.

as he is afraid of him.' Monsey, astonished at Brown's remark, waited a moment or two, to see whether Warburton would say anything to reprove Brown, or ask why Dr. Monsey should be afraid of him; but as Warburton was silent, Monsey retorted, with his customary freedom of speech, 'No, sir, I am afraid neither of Dr. Warburton nor of his jack-pudding.' A solemn pause followed; neither Warburton nor Brown appear to have replied. Garrick was confused, and saw that to restore good humour was hopeless; and the party in consequence soon separated. Here Warburton appears to little advantage. The story is given as Monsey himself, who disliked Warburton as a writer, and thought lightly of him as a scholar, told it to John Taylor of the 'Sun.'

Another anecdote, which gives a somewhat similar view of Warburton, was related to Taylor by Dr. Wolcot. Wolcot knew a garrulous old woman, a cousin of Allen's, who used to say that people were quite mistaken in supposing Warburton to have been a proud man, for she had often met him at Allen's, in the company of Bishops and other great people, when he talked more with her, and paid her more attention, than any of the high people that were present. Wolcot smiled at the old woman's simplicity, and concluded that it was to show his slight estimation of the great people, that Warburton bestowed his attention on a trifling old gossip.*

Perhaps the following passage from Walpole's letters — whose representations of Warburton, however, are seldom to be received without distrust—may be thought to afford some intimation how the Bishop might at times behave in company: 'The Bishop of Carlisle,' says he, 'told me that, t'other day in the House of Lords, Warburton said to another of the Bench, "I was invited by my Lord Mansfield to dine with that Helvetius; but he

* Taylor's 'Records of My Life,' vol. i. pp. 85, 87; vol. ii. p. 238.

is a professed patron of atheism, a rascal, and a scoundrel, and I would not countenance him; besides, I should have worked him, and that Lord Mansfield would not have liked." No, in good truth; who can like such vulgarism? His French, too, I suppose, is equal to his wit and his piety.'*

For the higher branches of literature he was disqualified by want of taste and want of imagination. Of power to approach the sublime or elegant creations of genius, he has nowhere given the least indication. Nor as to poetry, had he any real judgment. If we form an opinion from his early attempts at translation in verse—for on originality in verse he never ventured—we may believe that no cultivation could have made him even a mediocre poet. There is a most ridiculous passage in 'Hurd's Life of Warburton,' in which it is said that when Mason published his monody on the death of Pope, Warburton regarded it as so sure a presage of his future eminence, and 'so advantageous a picture of his mind,' that, on sight of it, he

'With open arms received one poet more.'

The pages of literature scarcely present anything more ludicrous than the author of Warburton's clumsy verses *patting on the shoulder* the refined elegance of Mason.

In poets, as true genius is but rare,
True taste as seldom is the critic's share;
Both must alike from Heaven derive their light,
These born to judge, as well as those to write.

I recollect having observed, in one of the periodicals of some years past, an affected comparison of Warburton, as an author, with Johnson. The attempt was absurd. Doubtless, some points of resemblance might be found between them, as vigour of thought, warmth of temper,

* Letter to the Earl of Hertford, April 5, 1764.

and love of victory over adversaries; but any general comparison between the author of 'Rasselas' and the author of the 'Doctrine of Grace,' between one whose compositions have refined and modulated our language, and one who knew not what refinement or modulation of language meant, between a writer who avoided all that was inelegant, and a writer whose every phrase was tinged with coarseness, is futile and ridiculous.

Johnson, at his interview with George III., was modest enough to tell the King that he had not read so much as Dr. Warburton. Johnson, however, notwithstanding his bad eyesight, his ill health, and his unsettled life, had roamed over many volumes, and, with his tenacious memory, had retained much of their contents; but he might, perhaps, have cast his eye on fewer pages than Warburton in his calm retirement at Brant-Broughton. We must inquire, however, as Seneca has admonished us, not who has read most, but who has read best. 'No man,' said Selden, 'is the wiser for his learning; learning may administer matter to work in, or objects to work upon, but wisdom and wit are born with a man.' The natural abilities and judgment of Johnson had enabled him to turn his reading to far better account than Warburton could turn his.

Warburton's want, or coarseness, of taste, exhibits itself to his reader everywhere, and sometimes in the most ludicrous manner. Speaking of the Grecian artists having taught the Egyptians to form the statues of their gods in a walking posture, he says that the Egyptians then bound them with chains, imagining that 'they had a strange propensity to show them a fair pair of heels.'* Mentioning Alexander the Great as being supposed the son of Jupiter Ammon, he observes that having had a hint from his mother to that effect, he might have boasted of

* Div. Leg. book ii. sect. 4.

it to the priest as a certainty, 'and so the murder came out.'* The Hebrews, he states, adopted their astronomy from the Greeks, and then 'learned the art of new tricking up their sphere, and making it as fashionable as their neighbours.'† Alluding to himself being censured, and Bishop Bull, with whom he agreed, being approved, in a certain publication, he says, 'This is the very *hocus pocus* of controversy; when the bishop and I have paid in the same coin, that from the bishop's pocket shall be true orthodox sterling, while that from mine comes out clipped, washed, and counterfeit.' In the same page he speaks of the writer 'outfacing the fraud,' and 'patching up the cheat.'‡ He speaks of 'hocus pocus tricks,' too, in a Sermon on the Resurrection; and in one of his Charges adverts to 'a magnificent show of viands, and all from the hog-stye.' Dr. Stebbing is told that he asks questions 'with ignorance excusable only in a savage to his catechist,' that he is one of those who come to the study of religion 'with unpurged heads, stuffed full of systems,' and admonished 'to keep his advice for those whom it concerns.'§ In reflecting on Tillard, he observes that he is doubtless a very good member of the *Society for the Propagation of the Gospel in Foreign Parts*, for, 'finding the Gospel staying at home, he does his best to send it packing.'‖ He is not ashamed to display such grammar as the following: 'Who, when he had dissipated this terror by his martial numbers, they rushed on to the charge.'¶ He calls God's moral government 'the bugbear to impiety.'** And as to the coarse names which he applies to his adversaries, 'whoever dares to write or think without Justice Overdo's warrant, he is a *gentleman of the Dunciad*, *a mushroom*, *a*

* Div. Leg. book ii. sect. 4.

† 'Remarks on Several Occasional Reflections;' pt. i. sect. 4; Works, vol. xi. p. 271.

‡ Ib. p. 306.

§ Ib. pp. 331, 349.

‖ Ib. p. 427.

¶ Div. Leg. book ii. sect. 4.

** Julian, book ii. c. 6.

*gentleman of the last edition, a Grub Street critic, a miserable, lost to shame as a man and as a writer, an idle blunderer, an ass, ridiculously stupid, and intolerably nonsensical.'**

The general character of his style is well expressed by Johnson as being 'copious without selection, and forcible without neatness.' 'He took,' adds the critic, 'the words that presented themselves; his diction is coarse and impure, and his sentences are unmeasured.' What he says of it himself is this: 'I have so imperfect an idea of my subject, and rough-cast my composition so loosely, that my works, if they escape damning, are yet in a state of purgatory, and with so much terrestrial matter about them, that they would take till Plato's great year to purge and purify, had I time, and nothing else to do but attend to them. I believe there are some thousand alterations in the language only in the second edition of Julian; and the first volume of "The Divine Legation," now in the press, is so *transmogrified* that you will hardly know it again. Nor is this the effect of modesty (which would be some comfort), but of pride, and the having more respect for myself than the public; who, to give them their due, are not over delicate:

> Curious, not knowing, not exact, but nice.'

In making so many alterations, it is to be wished that he had expelled more vulgarisms. But such was his want of taste that his changes must often have been no improvements, what he substituted being as inelegant as what he removed.

Yet, with all this rudeness, there is so much of energy in the pages as moves the reader still to follow the writer. 'There was something in your mind,' said Hurd to him, 'still more than in the matter of your book, that struck

* Confusion worse Confounded, p. 10.

me.' Thus it has been with most readers; they have felt that

Mens agitat molem, et magno se corpore miscet.

Johnson did him ample justice in this particular. 'In his "Divine Legation," you are always entertained. He carries you round and round, without carrying you forward to the point, but then you do not wish to be carried forward.' At another time he said, 'Warburton is perhaps the last man who has written with a mind full of reading and reflection.'*

'But his knowledge,' as the same authority reminds us, 'was too multifarious to be always exact, and his pursuits too eager to be always cautious.' He knew indeed a good deal of men, and a good deal of books, but his opinions were often hastily and crudely formed, and rashly and presumptuously expressed,

As who should say, I am Sir Oracle,
And, when I ope my mouth, let no dog bark,

and consequently were often at variance with those of men that thought more carefully and sedately. We have seen much of his offensive daring in his letters; we meet with examples of it in numbers of other places. He who recorded that he had a mean opinion of Blackstone, that he pitied Descartes for being a visionary, and despised Leibnitz for being a cheat, was not likely to meet with universal concurrence in his notions.† In regard to languages, his want of exact knowledge, yet venturesomeness of experiment, is often sadly apparent. He could not be said, indeed, to have just perspicacity or judgment in any language whatever. His deficiency in Hebrew

* Croker's Boswell, vol. viii. p. 17.

† Kilvert, Selections from Warburton's Papers, pp. 262, 332.

exposed him to the ridicule of Lowth for imagining that Ezra could have written 'Job.' His imperfect acquaintance with Greek left him dependent on Latin or French translators, the latter of whom he seems to have preferred. His unskilfulness in the niceties of Latin led him into mistakes to be corrected by Jortin, and suffered him to attempt emendations of Velleius Paterculus which scholars could but regard with amazement.

Upton made merry with his quotation from Homer beginning

δ' ἔνδυνε χιτῶνα
Καλόν——.*

observing that as *νῦν* and *καὶ* begin sentences, so might δέ, for aught that Warburton knew to the contrary. The same critic, too, laughed at his derivation of 'discomfit,' from *disconfictus*, a word of his own making, for *dissolutus* or *disruptus*.†

Of his dependence on translators for the sense of his Greek, a very glaring instance has been noticed by the author of 'Confusion worse Confounded.'‡ Quoting, in a note on Shakspeare, the words of Eteocles from the 'Phœnissæ' of Euripides,

Ἐγὼ γὰρ οὐδέν, μᾶτερ, ἀποκρύψας ἐρῶ·
Ἄστρων ἀνέλθοιμ' ἡλίου πρὸς ἀντολάς,
Καὶ γῆς ἔνερθε, δύνατος ὢν δράσαι τάδε,

he translates them thus: 'I will not, madam, disguise my thoughts. I could scale heaven, I could descend to the very entrails of the earth, if so be that by that price I could obtain a kingdom.' A plain rendering of Brumoy's French in the 'Théâtre des Grecs:'§ '*Je ne déguiserai point ici mes sentimens, Madame: j'escalerois le ciel, et je*

* Note on Jul. Cæs. act iii. sc. 2.

† Note on Macbeth, act i. sc. 2.

‡ P. 53.

§ Tom. ii. p. 406.

descendrois aux entrails de la terre; si à ce prix je pouvois conquérir la plus brillante des couronnes.'

Yet his grasp and penetration of mind often enabled him to form admirable general views of matters in the *minutiæ* of which he was but imperfectly versed. He pronounced with great justice, that the existence of the Septuagint version rendered the nice study of Hebrew in a great degree superfluous, as the Hebrew Bible, without that version, would have been as unintelligible as any cypher without its key, especially since the introduction of the points, which were affixed many years after the language was dead, and forced it to say anything that the inventors of them pleased.* Though he had no taste himself, he had just conceptions of the mode in which the public taste is influenced and corrected. 'Whenever the public taste is right,' said he, 'it is set so by half a dozen people of good understanding, who lead the rest to it. Sometimes they readily follow, sometimes not. But what is the genuine public taste, and properly their own, is the most wretched imaginable.'† He knew but little of mathematics, but he saw that that tribe of men, not indeed the inventors and geniuses among them who were to be honoured, but the mere demonstrators of others' inventions, were dull and often conceited, with little general ability, and minds sadly narrowed by confinement to one study.‡

From his limited insight into the learned languages, it follows that his quotations in them are not always to be trusted. No reader should rely for his notion of the sense or tendency of a passage in any author on the sole representation of Bishop Warburton.

He is said by Disraeli to have delineated his own character in describing that of Bayle. 'He struck into the pursuit of paradox as an exercise for the restless vigour

* Letters from an Eminent Prelate, p. 58.

† Ib. p. 3.

‡ Ib. p. 41.

of his mind,' and, notwithstanding his great qualities, 'had not yet enough of real greatness to overcome the last foible of superior geniuses, the temptation of the honour which the academic exercise of wit is conceived to bring to its possessors.' The Bishop is even said by the same writer to have been actuated by this 'secret principle' in the production of all his works, or in other words, to have written nothing but from the desire of saying something paradoxical, something different from what the world in general thought, regarding the subjects of which he treated. But to assert this is to assert too much. His first work, the 'Alliance between Church and State,' was of a calm and rational character, and stated fairly the only principles on which a union between power civil and ecclesiastical can well be conceived to subsist. Of a similar description was 'Julian,' in which he maintains by specious arguments that an event which many were disposed to consider miraculous, was miraculous in reality. Nor can a character very dissimilar be given to 'The Doctrine of Grace,' or to most of his sermons. His love of paradox is shown principally, therefore, in his 'Divine Legation,' and the controversies on minor points into which he was led by the assailants of it; and, we should add, in the notes on Shakspeare, in which, indeed, propensity to paradox is plentifully exhibited.

Whatever faults he had, he was no bigot. With bigots he professed to be at perpetual war. His mind, certainly, was not of the class in which bigotry fixes itself. It is an excellent observation of Mendelssohn, that it is only the smallest minds into which bigotry enters; for, the larger the circle of a man's mind, the more points will it embrace which he can compare with the points in the minds of others; and the more numerous are the points in which he compares himself with others, the less likely will he be to be bigoted on any single point.

His notions about religion appeared to the French so

extremely liberal, that they asked people who came from England whether he was really in earnest in defence of revelation, forming their notions of the state of religion in Britain chiefly on the representations of Voltaire, who told them that there was only just enough of it left there to distinguish the Tories who had little, from the Whigs who had less. Voltaire even remarked that, supposing Warburton was in the right in 'The Divine Legation,' it was not for a bishop to express his opinions on the right with such freedom, and that, instead of being made a bishop by a minister of state, he ought rather to have been required by the Church to recant and ask pardon.

By many, also, in England, his sincerity was distrusted. Bishop Hoadly, in a conversation with Sherlock, happened to observe that he had received some complimentary letters from Warburton bearing on subjects on which Warburton was then writing. Sherlock rejoined that he also had received letters from the same gentleman to the same purpose. 'Have you preserved them, my Lord?' said Hoadly. 'No,' said Sherlock, 'I have destroyed them.' 'I wish you had not,' returned Hoadly; 'I have preserved those with which he favoured me; and my reason for such caution is, that I have often observed writers of this cast change sides, receding from their first positions and pretences; and I like to amuse myself with their inconsistencies.'* Warburton spoke well, at first, of Hoadly's 'Plain Account of the Eucharist,' but afterwards condemned it severely in his sermon on that subject.

Cradock states that one cause of Warburton's desire to withdraw the 'Enquiry into Prodigies and Miracles' from circulation was, that it was supposed to have the same tendency as Middleton's 'Letter from Rome,' or, in the words of Ben Jonson, was designed to show that 'Nature once known, no prodigies remain.' His friends

* Rev. J. Jones's MSS. cited in Nichols's Lit. An. vol. iii. p. 141.

were at first very anxious to buy up the book, but after a while they 'became indifferent, and indeed the great author himself,' says Cradock, 'almost daily gave instances of not being strictly orthodox.'* The book itself, however, touched only on the miracles in profane history; and those who extended its arguments further did so of themselves, not on any suggestion of Warburton's. There was, however, a report, as is noticed by Parr,† that Warburton had been, and, as some said, continued always to be, inclined or attached to infidelity; but Parr declared that he saw no ground for such a belief. But his light manner of expressing himself on sacred subjects was sufficient to make many suspect his sincerity.

He is said to have expected the bishopric of London, and when he was disappointed of it, took occasion, in a sermon at court, to remark that all preferments were bestowed on the most illiterate and worthless objects, and, as he said this, turned about and stared full at Bishop Terrick, who had been recently appointed to that see.‡

He was considered, by his acquaintance, to have such a knowledge of books as to be able to direct their reading on almost any subject. Not only did Hurd consult him about his studies in divinity, but Lord Lyttelton inquired of him what voyages it would be advantageous to read, and expressed a hope of assistance from him in an account of the ancient History of Ireland.§ He says of himself that he was a great reader of history, but a greater still of romances, as nothing came amiss to a man who consulted his appetite more than his digestion;‖ an indica-

* Cradock's Lit. and Misc. Memoirs, vol. iv. p. 20.

† Tracts by Warburton and a Warburtonian, p. 186.

‡ Gray's Letters; Works, vol. iv. p. 49.

§ Kilvert's Selections from Warburton's Papers, p. 206.

‖ Letters from an Eminent Prelate, p. 387.

tion, it would seem, that Bentley's saying had come to his knowledge.

He speaks of himself to Doddridge as being of 'a melancholy habit,' which, with the distractions of life, often impelled him *to seek refuge from the uneasiness of thought in wild and desultory reading.* But his habitual melancholy, according to Hurd, meant no more than that, as his mind was always at work, the activity of his thoughts often exhausted and depressed his powers, and forced him to look for relief in a change of pursuit, and indulge in occasional desultory reading; which, however, was not without its advantage; for, while it repaired the vigour of his faculties, it stored his mind with variety of matter to decorate and vivify his writings.

Cradock, in a conversation with Mrs. Warburton, observed that Hurd had expressed his wonder how the Bishop acquired the knowledge of all the anecdotes in which he so much abounded. 'I could have readily informed him,' replied Mrs. Warburton; 'for when we passed our winters in London, he would often, after his long and severe studies, send out for a whole basketful of books from the circulating libraries, and at times I have gone into his study and found him laughing, though alone, and now and then he would double down some entertaining passages for my after amusement.'*

He is said to have been fond, when he was in a playful humour, of repeating the speeches of Falstaff in Shakspeare, and to have recited them remarkably well.

He kept a common-place book, in which he occasionally entered such thoughts and reflections as occurred to him. One of these he transcribed in a letter to Hurd: 'In your commerce with the great, if you would have it turn to your advantage, you should endeavour, when the person

* Cradock's Lit. and Misc. Memoirs, vol. i. p. 188.

is of great abilities, to make him satisfied with *you*; when he is of none, to make him satisfied with *himself*.' *

He sometimes thought his sayings in conversation worth recording: 'One day that Mr. Lyttelton, Hooke, and I, dined with Mr. Murray, Hooke entertained us with a number of ridiculous stories of the coxcombical vanity of the Chevalier Ramsay; on which Mr. Lyttelton said, "If such be the man, how came you, Mr. Hooke, to follow him perpetually as his *élève*, to cry up his 'Romance of Cyrus,' and to translate it so finely into English?" "As for that matter," said I, "Mr. Hooke acted with the discernment and fidelity of Sancho Panza, who had discovered his master to be a madman, but could not help admiring him as the wisest madman in the world."' †

He has the credit, however, of having uttered smarter sayings than any that he has registered either in this book or in his letters. When Lord Lyttelton, who had held the office of Chancellor of the Exchequer for a short time, was obliged to retire from incapacity, and was succeeded by Mr. Dowdeswell, Warburton observed to Hawkins Browne that there was a curious contrast between the two ministers; for 'the one could never in his life learn that two and two made four, while the other knew nothing else.' ‡ This is very similar to his sarcasm on Dean Tucker and Dr. Squire. His remark on Mallet's 'Life of Bacon,' and projected 'Life of Marlborough,' is well known, that 'Mallet would perhaps forget that Marlborough was a general, as he had forgotten that Bacon was a philosopher.' He has also been called the author of the saying that 'there are two things for which every man thinks himself competent, managing a small farm, and driving a whiskey.' §

* Kilvert's Selections from Warburton's Papers, p. 334; Letters from an Eminent Prelate, p. 379.

† Kilvert, p. 341.

‡ Prior's Life of Malone, p. 443.

§ Quart. Rev. vol. xxxi.

He has the credit, too, of the famous distinction between orthodoxy and heterodoxy: 'Orthodoxy is my doxy, and heterodoxy is another man's doxy:' a reply which he is said to have made Lord Sandwich, who declared himself puzzled to find the difference between the two doxies.

In the difference between the playfulness of his talk and the severity of his writings, he may be compared with Bentley; a character to whom, it may be suspected, he desired to be thought to bear some resemblance. A similar diversity of character, in authorship and conversation, is recorded of Salmasius by Huet: 'If the temper and manners of this eminent person be estimated from his writings, he may appear arrogant, haughty, and self-sufficient; but in the intercourse of life nothing could be more placid, gentle, and ready to oblige.' *

Pope's saying, that Warburton could see into all the possibilities of things, had doubtless much truth; and his power of viewing a matter on all sides inclined him at times to try the 'academic exercise of wit,' and to sport in the fields of conjecture. He was no Locke, or Bacon, or judicious Hooker, to leave a beneficial influence on all time; he sought to strike with temporary astonishment rather than to profit by permanent instruction, and was content to glare like a transient meteor rather than to shine with the perpetual radiance of a sun. His demonstration of Moses's mission deserved, far more than Huet's *Demonstratio Evangelica*, the censure that it demonstrated nothing but the learning of its author. His 'Divine Legation,' as Gibbon observed, is 'a monument of the vigour and weakness of the human mind.' To prove that the doctrine of a future state, while it prevails in all other polities, was not to be found in that of Moses, was not to prove that the polity of Moses had a Divine foundation; this is indeed asserted or supposed throughout War-

* Huet's Memoirs of Himself, by Aikin, vol. i. p. 195.

burton's volumes, but no reader, probably, has regarded it as demonstrated. His 'Julian' we have just noticed as being similar in character, for gravity and sedateness, to the 'Alliance between Church and State;' yet his mode of treating its argument is such, that many, after reading through the work, may think it merits the sarcasm of Walpole, that it proves the occurrence at Jerusalem a miracle by proving it none. As a scholar, he has secured himself no reverence from scholars; nor as a critic, from critics; nor as a divine, from divines; yet he cannot but command, from all classes of readers and thinkers, some share of attention and regard. As to style, he is

> Horridus in jaculis, et pelle Libystidis ursæ;

yet men of taste are not repelled by his language from giving attention to his matter. If there was much good in which he was deficient, there was also much good in which he abounded. He has gained for himself, with all his faults, a permanent name in literature; and his vigorous pages are still read by many who, though they may care little for the subjects of which he treats, desire to see how a mind of such force and dexterity discusses them.

Note on Page 7.

Warburton's Latin epitaph on his cousin is so characteristic of its author, that it should hardly have been omitted in an account of his life. It is inscribed on a brass plate on the wall of Newark Church:—

Si sit in pretio, hospes,
aut virtus aut doctrina,
siste, et libato cineri vicino
Rev. GULIELMI WARBURTON, A.M.

Joannis superst. sancti senis fil.
ex agro Cestriensi
generosâ stirpe atque antiquissimâ
profecti.

Ore trilingui, ac animo omnis capaci
antiquis literis consignatæ sapientiæ,
plurimum pollebat;
Criticus sine fastu,
sine pertinaciâ Theologus.

Sed apage næuias,
apage vos prostibulas
justitiæ, prudentiæ, castimoniæ, etc.
super omnem tumulum quotidie construpatas,
magnificas voces:
virtutem tam sinceram inimico,
tam absolutam, immo etiam temerario amico,
enarrandam
ausim relinquere.

Hujus amplitudinis, si quæras,
qualis data est merces?
Pudet dicere: sileo.
Si tandem quæras,
qualem merebat illa?
Dicam
Tempora feliciora.

Vix. ann. XLI. Ob. AD. MCCXXIX.

Note on Page 180.

The opinions advanced by Sykes on the Gospel demoniacs were much the same as those which Hugh Farmer afterwards maintained, asserting that the phrase *possessed with a demon or devil* was only a popular expression for *affected with epilepsy or madness*, except that Farmer also supposed the demoniacs, or some of them, might be possessed with souls of those dead men whom the ancients worshipped as demons or heroes. Dr. William Worthington, an amiable man and good scholar, wrote an 'Enquiry' in opposition to Farmer, offering some spirited arguments on what was called the orthodox side of the question. Warburton, in his 'Divine Legation,' as well as in his 'Sermon on the Fall of Satan,' expressed sentiments in agreement with those of Jortin and others, that Christ had cast out devils to show that He was to put an end to Satan's kingdom, who had been allowed, at that period, to manifest his power more than at former times, in order to make his discomfiture and subjugation more evident.

The notion that what men called demoniacal possessions were only natural diseases under that name, was advocated in England as early as 1627 by Joseph Mede, in his 'Clavis Apocalyptica;' and Dr. Richard Mead, who, though he wrote his name differently, was of the same family, stoutly maintained that doctrine in his 'Medica Sacra;' both of whom Warburton labours to refute, desiring that believers should consider the devil to have been allowed his part also in the 'Economy of Grace.' The several disquisitions on this subject, all full of argument, illustrate the old lines on the Scripture,

> 'Hic liber est in quo quærit sua dogmata quisque,
> Invenit et quærens dogmata quisque sua.'

INDEX.

CPSIA information can be obtained
at www.ICGtesting.com
Printed in the USA
LVHW100514120522
718524LV00004B/90

9 783375 004064